Renée Michelle Martel lives a diverse life in two countries alongside her family and her passion for art, books, music, and psychology. She is the sum of decades of countless experiences with different and interesting people across America and Europe.

Renée was born with a probing and headstrong personality that enables her to peel back the layers of life and expose what lies beneath the surface. Her imaginative and chaotic brain creates overlapping stories that are inspired by emotions, history, the birth of new generations, and the passage of time.

Her storytelling is a tribute to what people do to life and what life does to people.

To Pam, the most giving person I know.
To me, the most stubborn person I know.
To Luci, the bravest person I know.
To women who never quit. To women like us.

Renée Michelle Martel

The Antique Wooden Trunk

Book One of the Ancestry Series

AUSTIN MACAULEY PUBLISHERS™

LONDON * CAMBRIDGE * NEW YORK * SHARJAH

A CIP catalogue record for this title is available from the British Library.

ISBN 9781528985215 (Paperback)
ISBN 9781528985222 (ePub e-book)

www.austinmacauley.com

First Published 2022
Austin Macauley Publishers Ltd®
1 Canada Square
Canary Wharf
London
E14 5AA

As a writer, each time I create new characters, scenarios, and chapters, I get to live another life in a different world. Thank you to all of the patient people who tolerated my absence, exhaustion, secrecy, and mood swings, while I spent three years, finishing this book.

You know who you are.

Prologue

Life is made up of a series of short stories.
Buried under the surface of even the most outwardly mundane moments
in time, lay interesting people, intertwining tales, and riveting experiences
that are just waiting for someone
to dig them up and give them a voice.

To believe that life is meant for a single purpose we must believe in fate. Blood ties that bind parents to children and brothers to sisters, can be as rigid as they are everlasting. The bond of choice is a link that casts a guiding light upon the roads we travel. As love entwines with hate, loyalty often falls victim to betrayal. A person's destiny can only be revealed at the end of their journey.

From the moment we are born we begin to form a union with others. We have an enduring need to connect, to belong, and to seek out what lay beyond ourselves and our ancestry.

I have a theory about life and time. I believe that if we could go back in time and make a different choice, our new choice would affect our future. My theory claims that when a new choice is made a new opportunity is born. When this happens, our current life splits into a parallel world, like a detour, enabling our mind to live different lives, in different worlds, at the same time.

I only am certain of three things. Where I have been, the people I've met, and the journeys I have taken. I believe that as humans, our paths come together and then they break apart. We can only hope that eventually, in some way, they will lead us back to each other.

Like life itself, every story has a beginning and an ending. I am a very old person whose life will soon be over. Despite my inevitable death, I am on a journey that is far from over. I am linked to you and you are linked to me. This is my story.

Ruby McEwen
1925

*The distinction between the past, present and future
is only a stubbornly persistent illusion.*

~ Albert Einstein ~

Chapter 1

*The last time I was here, it was to identify your body. They told me you
died suddenly and didn't suffer. Even though I despised you, this was
something I appreciated. After seeing you covered in death, it took only a
split second for my life to change.*

*Before I knew it, I was free to be someone else existing in another place. If
I could, I would turn back the clock and reverse time, but I can't. I wish
had the ability to save lives, but I don't. Even if I did, there is no way in
hell I would have saved yours.*

Amos McEwen, 1898

An elderly woman steps off the elevator carrying a bulky, antique wooden
trunk with a tarnished bronze hinge lock. Her arthritis-crippled hands have
a tight and determined grip on the trunk's forged iron handles. She has
amber tinted skin, the shade of raw hazelnuts. Her pigmented complexion is
speckled with so many age spots, she appears to be of Indonesian descent.
The heavier the trunk becomes, the faster her thin blood pumps through her
frail eighty-eight-year-old body.

The old woman has an acute awareness. Born with an energetically
persuasive character, she sees everything and misses nothing. Despite her
tolerant disposition and open-mindedness, she is easily irritated. Although
she can be critical and unpredictable, she effortlessly accepts what is beyond
her control. Her cropped, pure white hair is the colour of freshly fallen snow.
She has blunt cut bangs that are intentionally clipped, just above her
eyebrows, to hide a visible scar across her forehead. Small, round, black
spectacles are perched delicately on the tip of her nose. A looped, suede cord
is attached to her eyeglasses and dangles securely around the nape of her
dainty neck. The trendy cord keeps her spectacles safe and conveniently
within reach. She has full, burgundy-coloured lips, abnormally few wrinkles,
dark, prominent eyelashes, and observant jade green eyes. Her skin tone and
facial features make her appear to be much younger than the date on her
birth certificate. Although her long legs are slightly crooked because of their
age, they've remained firm and shapely.

Today she's wearing a tie-dyed, knee length turquoise coloured dress. A
matching mosaic patterned scarf, with an ornamental knot, is draped loosely
over her collar. Pine green, ankle-length leggings enhance her unusually
attractive legs. The straps of a weathered straw hat are neatly tied into a
discreet bow under her chin. The wide-brimmed hat hangs over her khaki
trench coat and rests comfortably between her drooping shoulders. Similar
to her legs, she has noticeably long fingers. Her fingers are a sign of a detail-

oriented, uncompromising, and idealistic person. It is a sign she agrees with because she believes in signs.

The jewellery she wears is simple, yet elegant. The only trinkets she owns, and the only trinkets she wears, are one pure silver necklace, four gemstone bracelets, and six matching opal earring studs. Despite that she never married, two golden wedding bands decorate her left hand. Her modest and stylish taste in jewellery adds a perfect finishing touch to her outfit. Even her worn in buckskin biker boots compliment her unique style. The elderly woman owns only boots and only wears boots. At home, she has an impressive collection of different coloured leather boots dating back to the 1950s. When isn't wearing boots, she is barefoot.

Someone seeing this old woman for the first time might be unexpectedly drawn to her in a way they most likely wouldn't understand. She is a wise, intuitive, and resourceful person. She is a woman who naturally absorbs people and life in an obscure way. This is something she is known for and something she is utterly unaware of. Likewise, this is what she will be remembered for long after she is dead and gone.

As a rule, her character is tranquil, versatile, and gutsy. She's a nonconformist, who can be eccentric and inflexible at any given time of any given day. Today, the serene side of her character is being challenged by her intense determination to bring the heavy, ornate wooden trunk to Saint Matthew's Hospital in downtown London. Her grit and willpower are much stronger than the pain she feels with each step she takes. Two nurses and an orderly, seeing her struggling to carry such a hefty trunk, had tried to assist her. Despite her age and discomfort, she stubbornly declined their offers.

With a fake smile and typical snippy tone, she brashly declared, "If I need help, I ask for help."

Six minutes after the elevator doors closed, a white-haired, wilful, and slow-moving woman, with rather large ears, finally reaches the end of a very long corridor on the seventh floor. As she enters room 07.11, she is flushed, perspiring, and out of breath. Despite her discomforts, a capable and self-assured expression disguises the enormous effort it took for her to lug the heavy, brass-embossed trunk from the hospital's main entrance. She'd been entrusted with the wooden trunk six and a half decades ago. Since that day, she had not let anyone else touch it. Not even the past sixty-five years of life had weakened her spitfire personality and lifelong mission to protect the contents of the century old, brass-tacked heirloom. Before this day ended, an iron skeleton key would be inserted into the trunk's sturdy, bronze-hinged lock. Once the key was turned and the trunk was unlocked, its decorative, bevelled cover would be raised. The elderly woman was confident that when it was opened, the history and wisdom of its contents would be reborn and put to proper use.

Of this, she was certain. And Ruby McEwen was rarely wrong.

With a relieving thud, she put the rectangular, leather trimmed trunk down on a nearby table. Rubbing the pain out of her throbbing hands and wrists she let out a deep, exhausted sigh. Then she plopped her tired, aching body into an overused Naugahyde recliner in the corner of the spacious room and began talking to herself.

"Sweet Jesus, I bloody hate fake leather," she swore under her breath. "It makes my rump all sweaty and sticky."

Ruby was agitated and whacked. She pulled her baggy chiffon dress down over her kneecaps and smoothed the crinkles out of it. She'd sewn and dyed the dress herself in 1964. Her quirky clothing styles had made statements back then and they were still making statements today. Now she was hungry, thirsty, clammy, and considerably ruffled. As she concentrated on calming her huffing and puffing, she glanced nervously around the intensive care unit. Her observant eyes danced and darted as she scrutinized each aspect of the room. The British female 'coffin dodger' was a born and bred scrutinizer. It took less than ten seconds for her to conclude that *the room was a germ-free space.* Close by the left wall, with her upper body in a slightly inclined position, she could see Jazz Durant lying immobilized in an ICU bed and attached to various types of state-of-the-art medical machines. An array of wires, intravenous lines, and tubes were running in and out of her nose, mouth, veins, and head. Each of them had a specific purpose, colour, thickness, and length.

Beams of hazy, golden sunlight were shining through a small picture window across from the recliner. Feeling a familiar need to stand in the light, Ruby stood up and limped over to the window. Her heart rate and breathing were almost normal again. As she hobbled across the room, she felt a tad steadier. Despite that the window couldn't be opened, it did provide her with a divine outdoor view. It was a view filled with colourful flower gardens, lush lawns, rows of neatly shaped hedges, and artistically lit marble water fountains. What she could see below her was nothing shy of splendid.

Bravo to the talented person who designed these lively gardens, she thought. The feisty and fashionable lady simply adored flowers, the colours of the great outdoors, stone fountains, and the sound of water.

The smell of disinfection hanging in the room's sterile air was making her nauseous and queasy. Her rubber soled, cognac boots squeaked annoyingly as she walked across the floor's pale yellow linoleum tiles. She noticed that the tiles came to life when they were lit up by the sun's beams. The sunlight made her feel invigorated, vibrant, and youthful. Being a true-blue Brit, like millions of other native Englander's, she positively loathed the fog. Truth be told, she was grateful for the small, curtain less window; otherwise, the claustrophobia she'd battled since she was a girl would have her feeling confined and panicky in no time. The beige recliner, a compact night table, a narrow wardrobe closet, a tray stand, and the patient's bed, were the only pieces of furniture in the room.

Recent events of the day began ricocheting through Ruby's anxiety filled mind. Nonstop drones, peeps, and hums of the life support machines intensified her fretfulness. She sensed the onset of a nasty headache. Even the silence in the halls outside the room had become too loud for her to find any comfort in. She felt disturbingly anxious and jittery. She could clearly see that the patient lying in the bed across from where she stood looked grisly, half-dead, and much too vulnerable. There she laid, motionless and attached to machines that steadily pumped life sustaining oxygen into her water-damaged lungs. The swelling and discolouration on the patient's face distorted her normal appearance. The way the she looked was rightly upsetting the old woman. Not recognizing her only great granddaughter was, for Ruby, even more distressing than the coma she was trapped in. She turned away, repressed her tears, and began nervously pacing around the room. Jazz's enflamed face and eyes, reddish-blue bruises, plaster casts, exposed stitches and gauze bandages, were constant reminders of how damaged and broken her petite body was. Despite all of this, she was hopeful that the child would soon awaken up from the unconscious nothingness that now imprisoned her. Furthermore, she was convinced that the patient had a fiery passion burning inside of her that made her a force to be reckoned with. She was a survivor with scorching desires that uncannily resembled the same appetite for life Ruby had been born with almost ninety years ago. Jazz had inherited her great grandmother's fire and brimstone spirit, both of which she'd need to tap into and use if she were to triumph over what lay ahead of her.

The elderly woman stopped pacing and gazed intently over at the bed. Just a few days ago, the patient had been working the breakfast shift at The Seaside, Ruby's shoreline London diner. Even now, standing in silence, she could vividly hear echoes of Jazz's sharp tongued, brutal, loose-lipped mouth sassing back at her. The antagonistic girl was testing her boss by vulgarly and verbally protesting to another rule Ruby had laid down in an attempt to reel her newest, most rambunctious employee in. The diner owner adamantly and intentionally called her *the child,* proclaiming and promising her that only when she stopped behaving like spoiled little child would she call her by her real name. Having been told this in such a blatant way set an irate trigger off in Jazz. It was a trigger that added fuel to her already hot temper.

After witnessing her sizzling reaction, from that moment on, Ruby began calling her the child. She knew this was belittling, nonetheless, she'd hoped that calling her this would be enough for Jazz to want to earn her name back. She didn't believe in coddling people, no matter their age. A motto she lived by was, 'nothing in life is a given. Life was not a birth right, it is something to be earned'. Looking across the room at the girl on the edge of womanhood, who was lying in a critical care bed, visions of the last time she'd seen her flashed through Ruby's weary and worried brain. It was about five hours ago, when she and Jazz had locked horns over another unforeseen incident at the diner.

We are both such hot-tempered females, she silently admitted.

"Blimey child, shut your bloody big mouth for just five minutes! Either you learn to shut your smartass sassy trap, or you'll be mopping the floor on your hands and knees with a goddamn sponge!"

Ruby had wanted to screech this out after enduring one too many days of Jazz's relentless complaining and persistent sarcasms. However, she didn't. Despite her justifiable anger, she chose to ignore her, rather than become entangled in the hostile and argumentative web Jazz had been spinning since the day she arrived. The elderly great grandmother wondered what had happened to her. What had caused her to become so ungrateful, impolite,

14

and bitterly angry after a mere eighteen years of life? The child's outlandish attitude surely had to be a result of much more than just rampant teenage hormones.

Blaming it on female hormones would be stereotypically easy, but rightly wrong, she'd wisely concluded. She was prudent enough to know that talking to an out-of-control adolescent girl about hormones would lead to nothing but another argument she couldn't win.

Despite her rages and bad-mannered behaviour, Ruby did realize that the youngest living female member of her family had been emotionally dented by her father's abandonment and her mother's selfish, neurotic instabilities. Both parents had routine ways of putting themselves and their own needs ahead of their five children. This was especially true of the child's mother, Ruby's granddaughter, Zofia McEwen Durant. Rather than being a positive role model for her only daughter, Zofia was a train wreck waiting to happen. The elderly woman knew, farther than the shadow of a single doubt, that the child was an absolute work in progress. This was why, for as often as Jazz defied her, she was optimistic that she'd find her way, just as Ruby herself had done a slew of times while navigating through her own demanding and sometimes risky life. The elderly women left the warm glow of the sunbeams and limped back over to the bed. There she stood, looking down at the child through little round spectacles poised on the tip of her nose.

Hearing the rhythmic sounds of the ICU apparatuses, she began recalling the events of the past week. Events that had led them both to this room and to the deplorable situation they were now in. Ruby's perceptive brain began to turn and churn.

Earlier that morning, for the third time, the diner owner was reprimanding Jazz for her rude mouth and endless insolence. Without warning, her newest waitress violently slammed the food tray she was carrying onto a table with a loud, furious bam! Spinning on her heels she turned and glared with hateful vengeance at Ruby. The old woman quickly and easily matched the child's stern glare with a stare of equal intensity. Jazz Durant hadn't been working at The Seaside long enough to know what a tough, old British bitch her boss could be. From day one, she'd made it clearer than crystal that when Jazz was in her diner, Ruby was her paycheck, not her oldest family member. Likewise, during business hours she would be treated exactly the same as each of Ruby's other employees. With the sound of the slamming tray still echoing through every nook and cranny in the diner, yelling and words weren't needed to convey the owner's reaction to such a childish outburst. Their mutual exchange of penetrating scowls and defiant ogles had more than reminded the bold as brass teenager of this.

Although the Londoner thought that the child's reaction was a perfect example of *proof in the British bread-and-butter pudding*, she chose not to comment on it. Experience had taught Ruby that a silent glare and stare was much more effective than a lecture was.

With disgust in her eyes, and force in her arms, Jazz's temper exploded as she brutally threw the handful of silverware she was holding into the busboy's bin! Then she stomped off towards the kitchen, swearing more and more with every step she took. Ruby wasn't the least bit impressed. Shortly after her arrival, she'd witnessed the teens first hysterical fit of anger after informing her that *a Wi-Fi code wasn't needed because she had no internet.*

"Tantrums seemed to be deeply embedded in this child," she stated aloud, as the silverware that missed the busboy's dirty dish bin flew wildly across the room and walloped the diner's original black and white checkered floor.

With a cocky grin, the elderly woman cried out, "At least now, the obnoxious brat knows precisely who her employer is!"

Wiping the grime of the day off her hands and onto her apron, the diner owner winked at Finn McGee, her youngest employee. Finn had somehow managed to hold firmly onto his now trembling bin of dirty tableware. The 13-year-old lad, who was obviously very afraid of the foreign girl's temper, hadn't moved a centimetre. Today was the day that Jazz had angrily declared that she had wench for a boss! Although the child had a point, Ruby ignored her comment rather than agree with it. She couldn't help but see that the last eight days of waitressing and being gracious while wearing a fake and happy expression had worn the juvenile delinquent from California out. To avoid quitting a job she hated, and running away from an employer who she hated even more, Jazz made plans to go swimming with The Seaside's 22-year-old Italian dishwasher, Nico Rossario. Ruby had met Nico two years ago, after he'd nonchalantly sprinted through her diner. He was covered in beach sand and looking for work the day their paths unpredictably crossed.

Nico was the polite and hardworking type who refused to accept handouts of any kind. This had impressed Ruby, so she offered him work and living space in the garret above the diner. He'd done a fine job of restoring the attic while taking care not to disturb Ruby's possessions that had been in storage since before he was born. Nico knew that his employer was an independent authoritarian, therefore he knew his place. For these reasons, he had never once tried to overstep any boundary or break any rule that she'd instilled. Nico respected Ruby's personal space because he sensed that she valued her privacy even more than she valued her diner. His insight was spot on correct. She treasured her solitude and her livelihood. She appreciated him and he appreciated her. This was why she was eager for Jazz to get to know him.

Ruby predicted that Nico would have an undeniably good influence on the immature insurgent from the Sunshine State. She hoped that his responsible and adult like behaviour would encourage the foul-mouthed, ill-mannered child to grow up and get her life in order before returning home to start college in September. Jazz came from everything and Nico came from nothing. Surely, somewhere in between this huge difference, she would find a friend and a measure of maturity she desperately lacked. This was something Ruby had secretly yearned for, too many times to tally, since the child had started working for her.

After the last of the customers left and the breakfast shift ended, she realized that both Jazz and Nico had snuck off without punching out on the time clock, or saying a proper goodbye. The child definitely hadn't earned her trust yet, but Ruby did trust Nico. Her trust in him was reassuring enough to be the only reason why Jazz was allowed to go anywhere with him. *She'll be fine,* the old woman had presumed, when she realized that they'd both already left the building. Despite their age difference, she hoped that Nico would be able to handle her. The elderly British woman had been doing an abnormal amount of hoping since Jazz's arrival. Truth be told, there was another, slightly selfish reason, for allowing her to go on a date with Nico. Ruby was eagerly looking forward to a quiet, ordinary, and uneventful afternoon. She had a long overdue date with her chaise lounge and the small stretch of private beach she owned behind the diner. The latest Harlequin Romance novel she'd started to read, before a temperamental Prima Donna invaded her life, was beckoning her. She'd prided herself on being rightly bold and properly old. She was known for her kind-heartedness and her spunk. When necessary she could be a rash and brash person. Despite her righteous character and resilience, since Jazz stepped off the sidewalk at the bus stop in front of The Seaside, she'd completely worn Ruby out.

When she'd first laid eyes on the youngest female member of her family, she saw an angry and petite, westernized wild child, with choppy, untamed, God-awful purple hair. Jazz relished in, and thrived on, hammering home the first impression her scandalous appearance gave people. She had the most peculiar styled eyebrows Ruby had ever seen and a piercing stud in one nostril. The barbwire-tattooed choker around her neck and the devilish look in her eyes had actually shocked the diner owner, which was unusual because she was rarely shocked by people. Jazz's appearance very nearly had her locking the diner door, calling a taxi, and sending the frightening, dinky, overseas monster back to Heathrow Airport.

"Dear Lord, help me," Ruby had muttered to herself last week, when seeing Zofia's daughter for the first time in nearly fourteen years.

"Your mother should have warned me that Satan's little sister would be spending the summer with me," she mumbled aloud while eyeing the patient in the bed.

Ruby's utter astonishment at how Jazz had looked when she'd opened the diner door was a clear and cruel reminder of the lack of everything between herself and the child's mum Zofia. For going on eleven years, there had been virtually no communication between Ruby and her only granddaughter, which in itself was a damn shame, given that she'd essentially raised her. The elderly woman was the only remaining McEwen blood relative Zofia had left, therefore in Ruby's opinion, this made their estranged relationship a triple shame.

One day, out of the blue, the child rang her great granny up and asked if she could work in England and stay with her for two months. Reacting much too spontaneously and enthusiastically, she'd obliged Zofia's daughter, because she was curious and eager to get to know her great granddaughter again. Jazz had sounded so well-mannered on the phone. She'd just graduated high school and was excited to leave her twisted-up parents behind and start a summer adventure abroad. How could Ruby refuse the child? Besides, given how busy the summer season typically was at The Seaside, and how old she'd become, she needed more help. They'd spent a lot of time together when Jazz was just a wee one, therefore Ruby was enthused for a member of Zofia's family to enter her European world for the first time.

"How could I possibly have known what kind of trouble was looking for a summer job?" she said, with a worrisome sigh.

"Blimey, that was only last Wednesday. What a difference eight days can make," Ruby heard herself telling the teenager in a coma.

The number eight had been following her around since she was a little girl. It was her bad luck number. Something she rightly knew, but was too distraught in the moment to pay any attention to. Looking up at the clock hanging above the door she realized that she was particularly grateful for the time zone that separated London and America. Luckily for her, it was still the middle of the night in California. Knowing that the news of the accident would be shocking, Ruby decided to wait until the child's mother was fully awake before telephoning her. Zofia needed to have at least ten percent of her wits about her so she'd be able to deal with the seriousness of the situation. Otherwise, she'd have a half-cocked flip out and what Ruby told her would fall upon deaf, ignorant ears. Because of her granddaughter's behaviour in the past, she suspected that she'd be rendered mute by Zofia's blaring reaction to the news of the accident.

Truth be told, she wasn't ready to share the child with her mother again. She also believed that Jazz wasn't ready to see her mother either. Coma or not, she still needed to prepare her for her family's unexpected arrival. She suspected that a raging river ran under the bridge that connected the patient to her parents. No doubt, their arrival would turn the child's world even more upside down than it already was. This was something, for valid reasons, she was resolutely prepared to protect the patient she was standing next to from.

Jazz had four brothers. The oldest was nineteen and youngest was already a ten-year-old when a baby sister entered their lives. Ruby predicted that the gap between their ages was why Jazz had become the type of daughter a mother feared the most. She was the only baby, out of the entire Durant litter, who'd grown up to become someone her mother couldn't control or rein in. In fairness to the child's parents, they'd tried to put a leash on Jazz and constrain her, but both of them had failed miserably at doing so. Zofia and Tucker Durant's only daughter had been born a rebel with a free and borderless determination that made her reckless and different. Her willpower had her habitually wandering off in search of adventure and trouble. This was something the child had been doing since she was old enough to crawl. One thing was for sure, whenever Jazz Durant wanted to find trouble, she found it. Likewise, she enjoyed the thrill of the hunt each and every time.

Since the morning she re-entered Ruby's world she'd seen the child's inquisitive side more than once. She had an overabundance of assertiveness and she was gutsy. Ruby suspected that these two traits had tested and terrified her mother and father scads of times over the years. The old woman was extremely gifted for her ability to read people of all ages; therefore, she was certain that the child was seriously guilty of deliberately pushing her parent's past their human limits. Actually, Jazz's bizarre behaviour should have been expected.

Following the trail of four roguish, older brothers had undoubtedly played a role in their only sister's mischievous nature. Ruby reasoned that the child's behaviour started to spiral out of control when Tucker began having an affair with a woman who was only six years older than his teenage daughter was.

The elderly woman was convinced that Jazz's life had derailed the second her father started listening to his penis rather than his brain.

Chapter 2

The day Jazz Durant arrived from America she smelled like booze and looked like crime.

Ruby immediately suspected that her youngest female relative was much more than just an 18-year-old handful of too much for her mother. Her wild appearance and angry attitude quickly confirmed the old woman's suspicions. Ruby understood that the child didn't intentionally choose to be a wilful or malicious daughter. On the contrary, she predicted that Jazz knew from a very young age that she didn't want to be caged or confined by anyone, or by anything.

What other choice did she have than to look for life beyond the borders of her parent's backyard, declare her independence, and demand her freedom? Ruby considered, as she stroked Jazz's purple, bloodied bangs.

She hoped that an ICU nurse would be coming in soon to clean the patient up. Seeing bloody hair still matted to the child's sunburned forehead was making Ruby want to cry, and crying was something she avoided and scarcely did.

The elderly woman's round, black metal eyeglasses had fallen from the tip of her nose and were hanging loosely by their suede cord over her breasts. She was deeply lost in thought and unaware that a hospital volunteer had entered and left the room. The well-trained volunteer was a conscientious young man who'd brought her a blanket, a fresh pot of hot tea, and two vanilla biscuits. Ruby tended to clasp her hands and close her eyes whenever she was deeply contemplating about life. This was why, she surmised, that whoever had come into the room probably assumed that she was praying over an accident victim.

After all, she thought, *how could someone have known that a religious, non-praying sceptic was standing at the bedside of a comatose patient in an intensive care unit?*

A few minutes later, she caught a whiff of tea and sweet biscuits. When it came to tea, she was a proper English lady who could smell Earl Grey in her sleep. Appreciative for the hospital's kind gestures, she sat back down on the recliners Naugahyde seat cover, while taking care that her skirt was completely covering her backside. She then spread a plaid blanket, which now hung from recliners armrest, over her lap and long, shapely legs. After pouring herself a generous cup of tea, she realized that it was too hot to drink. Propping one of the sugary biscuits in her mouth, she leaned back and made a rather loud smacking sound as she chewed the sugary morsels. While chomping, smacking, and swallowing, she stared intently at the brass studded, antique wooden trunk. The elderly woman was scrutinizing again.

This time it was the trunk's turn to be examined. Staring keenly at the historic trunk, she envisioned how it had preserved the lives of the ancestors who had lived before and after her birth. Unexpectedly, but not unpredictably, she felt like she could see straight thought its thick, dark

20

frame and was being pulled inside a type of secretive, story-filled darkness. Riding next to it in the back of a police cruiser, and then lugging it into the hospital and down the ICU's long corridor, had reconnected her to it. The reconnection she now felt had put her in the mood to reminisce about the day her grandmother Bessie had passed it down to her. During that time, the ornate trunk held the stories of three ancestral family generations. Since that day, two more generations of women and men had written and stored their written versions of life in it.

Slowly, she closed her eyes and willed her mind to drift back in time. A modest grin appeared on Ruby's wrinkled face as she remembered how grown up, respected, and important she'd felt, decades ago, when her Grandma Bessie had bestowed her most treasured 1800s heirloom upon her.

Three impressive things for an 11-year-old girl to feel, she proudly recalled as her thoughts drifted farther in reverse.

In her mind, the year was 1936. A much younger version of Ruby McEwen was sitting in front of the fireplace in the parlour of her American grandparent's Montana ranch. She was writing a new story in one of her journals when her grandma Bessie walked in carrying the wooden trunk. Bessie told Ruby to *stop writing, close her notebook, put her pen down, and pay attention.* She then told her that *she had something important to give her.* Ruby promptly did as she was told. Disobeying and defiance were not allowed at the Dutton ranch.

The young girl had never seen the antique trunk before. It resembled a pirate's treasure chest, so she was immediately intrigued by it. Waiting for Bessie to explain what it was, her impatient and callow curiosity was making her antsy. It took all of the budding girl's self-control not to jump off her chair, run over to the trunk and snappishly lift its oblique, arched cover. Nevertheless, she didn't. Ruby had learned, from a very young age, that when Grandma Bessie spoke, people listened. No interrupting or impetuous behaviours would be tolerated; otherwise, she'd feel the whack of metal ladle on her hands or backside. Bessie could see both excitement and restraint yanking on her young, hasty granddaughter. Nevertheless, Ruby did as she was told. She remained in her seat and shifted her focus in an attempt to prove to her grandmother that she was ready to listen. Seeing her earnest effort and her ability to control her impetuosity persuaded her grandma that Ruby, despite her tender age, was ready to become a part of the Dutton female circle. This was the day Bessie entrusted Ruby with the past.

Bessie told her granddaughter in training, "You are now the guardian of the bygone years. You are the living link to the male and female ancestors that came before you, and to those who have yet to be born. Your descendants will influence you as the years pass by. Life stands still for no one Ruby girl. Long after I am dead and gone, you will grow to understand and become observant. Time doesn't move in a straight line. It moves in circles. As time goes by, you will bear witness to what life does to people and to what people do to life."

21

This was the first of several impacting turning points in the elderly woman's early years. This was the moment she knew that she was no longer an impulsive adolescent. She had been given a purpose. On that day, as Grandma Bessie handed her prized possession to her, the girl named Ruby Adeline McEwen was left behind.

Bessie had also encouraged her own daughter, Sadie, to write in journals. Ruby's mother Sadie had grown up on her parent's cattle ranch that spread across nearly 500 acres of the American Great Plains. From the time she was a little girl, the age of five or six, she began writing and drawing. Sadie would spend many laidback hours with her journals and pens. Her journals never left her side. During the summer months, she would sit and create stories and sketches by the shade of the barn. Throughout the cold winters, her parents would find the young Sadie writing and drawing by the heat and light of the parlour fireplace. These were her favourite go-to spots on the family property, and the two places where Ruby's mother had spent her childhood and early adolescence, creating and daydreaming.

An American flag, adorning its thirty-eight stars, hung proudly from a steel pole on the Dutton's front porch railing. Through every hour of every season of every year, it paid tribute to the evolving territories of the developing American nation. Bessie's daughter Sadie had lived a diverse and eventful life; therefore, her journals resembled richly illustrated picture books filled with colourfully animated tales.

Roused by the odour of tea and biscuits swirling under her nostrils, her eyes suddenly popped open. With an achy kind of groan, she leaned over to test the warmth of the tea. Something she customarily did by placing her fingertip over the opening in the teapots spout.

"Bloody hell!" she cussed, as she yanked her hand away and stuck her fingertip into her mouth.

The tea was still piping hot, which she should have known, given that drinking tea had been a daily ritual of hers since she was a three-year-old. Ruby had forgotten that she was a sharp-eyed, quick thinker. Recollecting life was something she not only did with ease, she also did it with the speed of a sprinting Cheetah. Logically, this would explain why she had wandered so fast into the past, and returned to tea that was so hot, the tip of her burned finger throbbed against her tongue.

"Dumb move," she grumbled underneath her breath.

Clasping her hands together again, she glanced at the child's IV saline drip bag that hung next to her heart monitor. The brine solution, being administered to prevent dehydration and nourish Jazz, dripped rhythmically from the bag and into the vein of her right hand. Dark yellow, blue, orange, and green digital scanning lines were still rising, falling, and registering her cardiac rhythms. Relieved that the child was being fed, and that her heart was still beating, the old woman tightened the grasp she had on her sore hands. Grasping her hands together was her way of streamlining her attention whenever she had too much on her mind at the same time.

Because she'd just had thought about Montana, the elderly woman's rootless thoughts craved taking her farther back in time. One of the most influential tales from the past that she'd ever been told was demanding her attention. As her eyes closed, her mind spontaneously drifted in the direction of the past. Her thoughts took her back to a legendary and historical Dutton family event. It was a true story that her emotional grandma had told Ruby, more than nine hundred cycles of the moon ago, on the very day she'd inherited the trunk.

The elderly woman willed her mind to take her through her Grandma Bessie Dutton's vivid rendition of the summer and winter of 1888. Her mind travel would begin with the year Bessie's only daughter, Ruby's mother, Sadie, had been born. With her eyes still closed, Ruby glided farther into the depths of the past and reminisced.

It was a blazing hot summer. For months on end, a pitiless sun scorched the prairies, smelting them down to an infertile and barren wasteland. By late 1887, the homesteaders of the Great Plains were in the throes of a historically sweltering, dry summer. It was the worst drought and the hottest weather many of the immigrants and colonists had ever witnessed. Bessie and Samuel Dutton's family, and their neighbours, whose homestead was a few miles down the dirt road, lived directly in the path of the distressing summer elements. Rivers, ponds, and lakes were at their lowest level in twenty-five years. Lumber and flourmills, operated by water energy, were forced to close and suspend operations. Extremely hot and dehydrating conditions continued into the late autumn months. Many farmers reported that *even if the rain started falling, their corn crops would fall short of what they needed to feed their livestock and survive the rest of the year*. Grass was dying across the plains at a record speed. People, ranches, and livestock suffered from the heat and their hunger for crops and water. It was reported that cornstalks were catching on fire and burning up from the excessively hot temperatures. In due course, wildfires broke out.

As the summer finally ended and autumn began, Bessie was pregnant for Ruby's mum Sadie. Throughout those seasons, Bessie had felt Sadie kicking and moving inside her womb. It was a time when a new life grew inside her full belly, whilst she earnestly tried to fill the empty bellies of her husband and their four hungry, growing boys. As the days turned into weeks, and the weeks into months, most of their starving livestock died. An already dire situation became catastrophic, when in early January, a few days after Sadie's birth, a two-day blizzard hit. The winter storm blanketed vast areas of the Great Plains under two feet of snow. Later, when the event found its way into the history books, the storm of 1888 would come to be known as the 'Schoolhouse or the Schoolchildren's Blizzard'. The storm went on to kill hundreds of people. Many of its victims were innocent children of all ages who were crossing the prairies on their way home from school. Because the extreme weather hit with no warning, people and animals were unprepared, as temperatures fell almost 100°in less than 24 hours.

The plains people, who'd grown accustomed to heavy snows, went on to christen the wind as 'The Culprit'. The hostile winds whipped and thrashed at the snow, as thermometers dropped to minus 50° Fahrenheit. Fortunately,

Sadie's father and oldest brothers had stored enough hay for their livestock during the previous autumn. Their ranches remaining cows, fowl and horses were in the barns when the storm hit. Although their animals survived the winter, they were soon, thereafter, killed by the widespread starvation and dehydration that the preceding summer drought had caused. Fenceless and open ranges meant grazing land was cheap, abundant, and easy to come by. Consequently, for hundreds of miles ranchers owned massive herds of cattle, horses, sheep, and fowl. This was a gigantic curse in the end. Not only did ranchers lose their livestock, almost two hundred and fifty people lost their lives during the winter storm.

A considerable loss of life for the 1800s, Ruby subconsciously reminded herself of, as her mind continued to drift through her grandma Bessie's tale.

By the late spring of 1888, approximately one million animals lay dead and decaying on the sun-baked open plains. Ranchers and homesteaders reported sighting carcasses for as far as the human eye could see. The animal's corpses proceeded to clog up the rivers and underground wells. In turn, rotting cadavers poisoned the drinking water and spawned widespread disease. Because of the natural disaster, hundreds of ranchers went bankrupt. The family's livestock and livelihood had barely survived. Despite, what had briefly felt like a true miracle, the Dutton family lost their twin boys to the storm.

The youngest of the Dutton children had moseyed off unnoticed. Apparently, they were innocently searching for the family cat. Less than thirty minutes later, they were found unconscious and huddled up together in the tool shed. When their pa opened the shed door, the boys were a light, bluish-grey hue of almost frozen. Upon seeing them, Samuel instantly turned his head and puked in the snow. He then wiped spew off his face with his coat sleeve and scooped his young boys up. The twins were wearing only their nightshirts, underwear, and little matching cowboy boots when he'd found them.

With the air outside reaching a record minus 48° Fahrenheit, and nearest doctor five miles away, the pending death of the boys loomed in the house. The twin brothers never regained consciousness. They perished that evening less than three minutes apart. The little boys were in front of the fireplace, lying on their shared bed mattress when they both took their last breaths. The missing cat was curled in between them, asleep and purring, when they passed away. The twin's family was gathered around them, on their knees in vigil, crying and praying for a miracle as the young ones left them.

"My fault, my fault, my fault," Bessie rhythmically chanted. Her sorrowful, hanging head swayed from side to side. She blamed herself for turning her back on her precocious twins while tending to newborn baby Sadie.

Throughout the night, Sadie's father built his sons a sturdy pine casket for two. Early the next morning, Samuel and Bessie dressed their youngest boys, identically, in their Sunday church clothes. They would be buried in their matching pants and suitcoats, white chemises, bowties, and button up leather shoes. A devastated Bessie neatly combed the twin's hair, washed off their little faces, and then kissed her dead lads for the last time. Her guilt-ridden moans echoing throughout the house were louder than the sound of the perilous winter wind outside. She was too dazed to shed tears, and too exhausted from breastfeeding a newborn day and night to feel anything. She and Samuel bound their little ones up in the boy's bedsheets and woollen blankets. Their older brothers laid the twins, together with their cherished Buffalo Bill and Five Little Pigs books into their casket. The Dutton boys were just shy of three years old when they died.

As a sign of respect, their pa and his two remaining sons each took turns nailing the boys pine casket shut. The casket was a mere thirty-six inches long. As they carried the deceased out to the barn, Bessie held baby Sadie's tiny hand out so she could touch the casket as it passed by her. She wanted her newest child to feel the brothers she would never know, as they left her world. Because the winter ground outside was still too icebound for digging a grave, the departed youngsters were stored in the root cellar under a large section of floorboards. Laying them temporarily to rest had taken the Dutton males less than ten minutes. Once the casket was covered with two thick horse blankets, the floorboards were repositioned, and the barn door was securely shut. The next day, the Dutton family proceeded to mourn and carry on with attempting to survive the deadly winter. Despite Samuel's earnestly loving efforts, Bessie did not speak a single word until the last patch of snow melted three months later. A sorrow-filled depression had consumed her throughout the winter and prevented her from bonding with baby Sadie.

As February turned into April, wild balsamroot, daisies, and tiger lilies started to blossom, adding speckles of bright colour colours across the ranch's land. Bessie and Tucker knew that spring had arrived, which meant the ground had thawed. With no remnants of snow to be seen or found, the twins were given a respectable, private burial at the Dutton family cemetery, atop a nearby hill, in full view of the ranch. Each morning at sunrise, Ruby's spiritual grandma Bessie, faithfully lit two candles and placed them on the windowsill in the kitchen. From her kitchen window, she could see the graveyard and the silhouette of the boy's headstones. The twin's small, matching cowboy boots had been given a permanent place next to their memorial candles. The commemorative candles burned each day, from sunup to sundown until the day Bessie died.

The climate of 1887 and 1888 changed the cattle industry and the Dutton family forever. Only Ruby's mother Sadie, a newborn still too young for even a memory, had been spared the tragedy.

Chapter 3

Heart breaking visions of the carcasses of decaying, contaminated livestock, and the disintegrating bodies of two little boys in a pine casket, being stored in a root cellar, spun fitfully through the elderly woman's mind. Her body jolted uncontrollably. With a proper fright, she opened her spooked eyes.

My minds wandering too long again, she thought, *the older I get the more it drifts. Even after eighty-eight years of life, I still don't know if this is a gift or a curse.*

Ruby needed to stretch her legs and shake off the brain fog she was feeling. She hoisted herself up and out of the recliner and took a few unsteady steps towards the child's bed. After affectionately squeezing her shoulder, she used her fingers to comb Jazz's purple, blood dried bangs, off her forehead. Although the child was sufficiently warm, she remained as pale and expressionless as an unpainted factory mannequin. She began to plead with a God she wasn't sure she even believed in, to *let the child wake up so she could scowl, complain, and start being her rebelliously insolent self again.* There simply was too much that she still wanted to teach her. Despite her pleads, she knew it was too soon to ask any kind of God for help, therefore, her begging ended almost before it had begun. *Prayers and cries for help would do no good,* she decided, *the child was in another world now. A coma had claimed her.* The droning of the machines and the soft, cobalt coloured radiance of their digital lights, had become quite soothing for Ruby. For as long as the humming noises sustained and the blueish glows didn't fade to black, she'd know that Jazz was still alive. With this slightly comforting belief, she picked her canvas bag up off the floor and went to use the bathroom. She wanted to freshen up, relief herself, and put on some makeup.

"I need to look my best when the child wakes up," she muttered.

About five minutes later, the old woman returned from the bathroom looking rather refreshed. She had combed her hair and was wearing her favourite shade of lipstick and a touch of blusher. She'd chose not to apply any eye makeup, because she knew from experience that tears were never kind to mascara. Even though she wasn't a person who cried easily, given the circumstances, she wanted to be prepared for an unforeseen bout of weeping. She knew herself well and recognized the signs of being old and emotionally on the ledge of life. With mascara and tears being the last amusing thought spinning through her mind, Ruby was unexpectedly overwhelmed with a new kind of interest. She had an idea churning through her alert mind. With the spunk of a 30-year-old, she pulled the trunk off the table and set it down on the floor next to the recliner. She hadn't rummaged through the brass studded wooden trunk since the late 1960s, when her mother Sadie had passed away.

Back then, after Sadie was buried, Ruby had put her mother's last remaining journals into it for safekeeping. Since that day, she had kept the trunk under lock and key in a cargo annex attached to her diner. It had been almost fifty years ago when she'd purchased the diner, its storage building, and the small stretch of beach behind the property. Throughout those years, she'd occasionally opened it up to add another completed journal to it. Nevertheless, for some unknown reason, she'd never had any real desire to delve into the trunk's contents. Therefore she didn't.

Perhaps life just got in the way, she speculated.

The last time she recalled spending a significant amount of time looking through it was on her birthday. It was in June of 1938, the year she had officially become a teenager. That had been the day, when Ruby added the last of her journals, filled with her juvenile thoughts and memories, to it. Then she lowered its bevelled lid and bid farewell to her childhood.

Today, in the here and now of her life, she still didn't actually know why she had become so disinterested in it over the years. Regardless, knowing why this has happened didn't matter anymore. The child in a coma was still breathing, and the trunk was where it was needed the most. This was all that mattered now.

Ruby was easy going and accepting in this way. She prided herself on never making problems out of insignificant things. The trivial side of life bored her. It always had. As she glanced over at the rebel child lying in an ICU bed whilst caged in oblivion, she knew it was time to open it again and give its contents meaning and purpose. The child needed what it could offer her, in a way that even if she were conscious she wouldn't be able to fathom or remotely understand. She bent forward, laid her hands on the wooden surface, grazed her nose over it, and sniffed. The wood's smooth grain felt fertile to her touch. Although she'd never admit it, she knew that it had aged as well as she had. It smelled like a mature and a sophisticated kind of musty, with a well-earned scent of stale.

Reaching around the back of her neck, Ruby fiddled with the solid silver chain she'd worn for decades. With a single, skilled swoop, she pulled it over her head. Then she reached deep inside her blouse and grasped at what was safely hidden from sight. Carefully, she removed a three-inch long, cast iron skeleton key that was nestled between her sagging, aged breasts. The key was as tarnished and ancient as the lock it was made to fit into was. Ruby remembered her grandma Bessie telling her that, the skeleton key was the master key to the trunk. It was the one and only key that existed. Duplicating or replacing it wasn't possible, because, like its handles, the key had been hand forged.

What a responsibility, she thought for the umpteenth time. *Given my old age, I should seriously consider changing the lock, just in case the key ever goes* missing. *Just my luck, some bloody fool at a mortuary will cremate me with the goddamned key still hanging around my neck.* She knew her death was impending; therefore, she chose to mock it rather than fear it.

"The truth is," she said looking up the child in the bed a few feet away, "I won't always be here to protect this key."

Dismissing her morbid thought as quickly as it had come to her, she detached the key from the chain to give it an inspective stare. She wasn't afraid of the end of life. Not the least bit. In every way imaginable, the elderly woman was still too busy living life to ponder over death. Besides, she was confident that eventually, after her death, she'd be returning to in some way, which was a mindset that enriched her life, and prepared her for the inevitable, in a brave way.

The stiffness in her old, hard-worked fingers made unlocking the wooden trunk and unhinging its bronze clasps rather difficult. After hearing the lock and key simultaneously click, Ruby gently raised the bevelled cover and revealed thirty-seven threadbare, timeworn journals. Each one of journals was as different from the other, as the women and men who'd written in them had once been. Meticulously, she began to rearrange them by taking the top one and placing it on the bottom of a stack she was making. She used the nightstand between the recliner and Jazz's bed to stack the journals on. To preserve their pages, the journals had been bound by different types of cord. Some were held together with twine, leather, wire, and string. Others were bound with washed-out, ravelled cotton strips and satin hair ribbons. The newer journals were not bound with anything. Taking care not to damage them, she took the teapot, biscuits, and teacup off the table and cautiously set them down, out of harm's way. She'd become rather shaky and clumsy in her old age and the last thing she needed was to be spilling Earl Grey over five generations.

I am doing something important, Ruby told herself. *The journals need to be read in the correct order, otherwise the lessons, legends, and life in them won't make sense to Jazz. If this happens, the child will become even more lost in time than she already is.*

Ruby was eager to share the tales and recollections in the journals with the child. She knew that her doing so was a necessity and it was a huge undertaking. The moment she opened the trunk, the elderly woman's personal mission began. Her objective was to connect the child to the journal's folklores, traditions, and wisdom-filled tales of life, before it was too late. She realized that time was of the essence, because time didn't come with a guarantee.

What if the future never arrives for this child, Ruby asked herself?

Then she heard herself say, "I am an exceptionally old, stubborn, and impatient woman. Despite that I have never been struck down by disease, my time to make a difference in this child's life is limited. I have a searching mind. It is sharp and it is curious. Nevertheless, my body is weak and crippled. Death is on my horizon. I have no time to waste."

Hearing herself saying this, Ruby realized that her brain fog had lifted. She was no longer deep in thought and had actually begun talking to the child. She finished putting the journals in the proper order that they had been written in. Then, she bent over and pushed the emptied wooden trunk behind the lounger. Painfully, she proceeded to try standing upright, while every joint in her body harshly reminded her that she was almost nine decades old. With a quick sign of endearment, she stroked Jazz's cheek to reassure her that she was not alone. With an equally quick sign of urgency, she told the child, "I need to pee again."

With this being said and done, the old woman limped off towards the restroom. Once her bladder was empty, Ruby washed her hands, fluffed up her hair, and returned to the room. She then settled back into her seat, reached for the oldest journal, and gently placed it on her lap. It was rather trivial in size and visibly very fragile. The journals pastel green front and back covers were considerably water stained. Its black binding was cracked, splintered and peeling. It was securely fastened with a thinning strand of tightly braided, copper coloured leather cord. The cord had a pea-sized bulge about an inch below its tip. The leather cord had been coiled twice around the journal and tied off with a double slipknot.

She looked over at the child and announced with a peppy eager voice, "The best place to begin is at the beginning."

Ruby warily untied the cord, opened the journal, and removed what appeared to be fragments of unbound pages hidden just under the front cover. Fearful of damaging the brittle pages, she gently took them in her trembling hands.

Steady old girl, she told herself, realizing that she was holding something she had never seen before, something rare, fragile, and much older than she was.

What she held appeared to be a letter of about four pages long. Intrigued, she unfolded the pages and delicately placed them in her lap on top of the journal. The pages had been written in a cursive, script style. For this reason she estimated that they'd most likely been written in the 1800s. Gazing down at the pages, through her little round spectacles, she saw a familiar name.

"Minnie," Ruby gasped aloud, realizing that what she was about to read was a handwritten, documented lore about Minnie, her grandmother Bessie's older sister.

Choking on curiosity, she took an intentional deep, calming breath. Then she picked up the first page and started reading out loud to Jazz.

Chapter 4

To the reader of this paper here. My name be Minnie. It is the year 1862. I be going on 11 years old now.

Let it be known that I not be able to write good. Not yet anyhow. I can read some and remember stuff n make a good story from my mind. That is all up till now. My secret friend Jacob he can read and write really good so he be a helping me. Jacob is the youngest son of my owner Master Ballinger Dutton. Nobody with black skin be a knowing why our master has two different surnames. None of us with black skin dares ask for fear of a whipping. Jacob says he don't know himself why. He just was born with three names is all and as my master his son, he be good 'n well knowing what to ask his pa and what none of his concern be. He says he and his brothers they go by Dutton only.

Jacob says he's going to write down exactly what I say and how I say it. It doesn't matter if I say it not good or I get it wrong. Jacob says once I start talking and telling my real story he going to write them in a proper way so peoples can know what my meanings is. Then once

I can write better, I will do it myself because me having my own voice is how it should be.

Jacob is a smart one. His mammy and pappy taught him and his brothers. He's 'n educated soldier boy who soon will be fighting for his pappy's army. I hope someday I get educated and that Jacob don't be getting himself killed cuz' I be really sweet on him.

Jacob says slaves who can read 'n write in the great United States of America is rare. I be from Africa, so I's know nothing 'bout such matters like Jacob his self does. He says slaves like me 'n the others we not allowed to read or write. If we do and we gets caught, we get a bad whipping or something worse. Some niggers, so we be called, did learn reading and writing on their own and they was not afraid of the whipping post, but they keeps how smart they are a secret just the same. They bleed from the whipping but never tell nothing about how much they know inside their heads. Some of the smartest niggers I know act dumb, so our master doesn't suspect they be learning.

It is like Jacob and me being sweethearts is another big secret. Other niggers they was taught reading 'n writing by their master's wives or by holy mission men wanting to teach the religion from the bible to us slaves. Jacob says I got a big important story to tell people about my little sister Bessie and me. Jacob he is gunna help me tell it because

*he's my sweetheart 'n he wants to be a man that's nothing'
like his pappy. His pappy he be the master of my
plantation and he be a real important General man for
the army. His pappy is a mean man. He be nothing like
Jacob. Jacob he is kind. Jacob is a white rich boy. I be
a poor nigger girl.*

~ Written by J. B. Dutton for Minnie ~

After Ruby finished reading, the last line of what Jacob Ballinger Dutton had written for a then practically illiterate Minnie, she reflected for a few moments on who may have last held and read these historical pages. Who was the last person to cast their eyes upon the words she'd just read? Words filled with such tender, young fear and intimacy. With slightly steadier hands, she caringly rearranged the unbound pages. Then, she attentively put the pages on the nightstand next to the stack of journals. Captivated and anxious to learn more about what happened next to Bessie and Minnie, she enthusiastically carried on with the task at hand. Ruby tucked the fleece hospital blanket snugly around her legs, sat up straight, and opened the front cover of the journal. Despite that, what she saw was ink flecked, and the handwriting was slightly scrawled, the writer had made an eloquent penmanship effort. Instinctively she adjusted her spectacles to have a sharper view and recite what she'd be reading in an appropriate way.

This may take some time, she thought, as she cleared her throat and resumed reading to the child.

*I have been a slave girl in New Orleans going on four
years now. In 1860, slave traders kidnapped my little sister
and me. They tied us up and threw us on a big ship. One
morning the ship I sailed on with little Bessie made
landfall and docked at a Louisiana harbour off the coast
of New Orleans. We was in a place called America after*

32

being at sea for 79 days and nights. Since being sold I learned to read and write. I still keep this part of me a secret because Jacob, he tells me to. Jacob knows about such things, so I listen real good to him.

Now that I can write some, I will tell my story about being a slave girl on a ship. Jacob says my stories need to be told. I still make writing mistakes, but I am educating myself as best as I can so I will get better at writing and get smarter. I now have good ears and wide-open eyes. I hear and see everything that be going on and nearly everything being said at the plantation. My mind it has a strong memory. I can remember stuff without writing it down. Jacob says I am lucky in this way cuz' he forgets most things.

~ Written by Jacob Dutton for Minnie ~

Ruby cautiously placed the yellowed, brittle paper she'd just read from on the top of the stack of journals. She then went to the ICU room's bathroom to relieve herself and splash cool water on her face. She was waning fast and needed to feel more awake before reading more to Jazz. She couldn't help but think about her long since deceased father, Horace. The man was an avid lover of history and would have revelled in sharing the contents of the antique wooden box with her. The elderly woman didn't believe in regrets, nor did she have many of them in her life. Nonetheless, knowing now that the tales recorded in the journals could have been shared with Horace, if she'd delved into them while her pa was still alive, weighed on her conscience.

As she sat back in her lounger and continued reading to her father's great-great granddaughter, the last thought that crossed her mind before she resumed was, *Horace most definitely would have adored Jazz's unbridled personality.*

~1865~

Minnie & Bessie

In 1860 we was stole from our village and sailed on a slave ship from Africa to America. My little sister and I was on a ship built to carry 95 people. Below the deck was 364 sick, starving, and suffocating Negro people of all ages. Older people on that ship told me anyone who survived the journey would be stripped naked, then poked and prodded at. When the ship makes landfall, we will be exhibited and sold to the highest bidder. We have no real future. We just are slaves. Slaves on this ship believe only those that die at sea will be set free. I was penned in by people just a finger's length away from me under the deck.

I was like a pig in a crowded smelly place. Down in the dark, stinking, deep belly of the ship, I stared at bodies. There were rows upon endless rows of black dirty bodies. Some of them was rotting because they was dead from disease. Others were dead from old age. Holding my breath was pointless because the sour stink smell never went away. I knew when I left the ship, I be still remembering the awful smell. On the ship, slave's groans and crying grew so loud I covered my ears and tried to muffle the sounds out by singing. When I sing, I hear my own voice over the groans and crying of the others. This be what I call the rest of them, not me and Bessie. Most nights I sang until my body gave out from exhaustion and I had nothing left to do but hope that I would make it to the next day. I became so used to tears being on my face and neck that it felt not right to stop crying. My crying circle made it all seem normal. Maybe this be why I still cry nearly each day here in America. Stopping my tears would break that circle that back then spun around and about, and I would have no daily ritual to follow. I need something ritual each day to do, or I surely will go dead in my head.

Some days I wonder why my little sister Bessie and I were kept down there in that hot, smelly place. She was just three years old. Real young compared to the rest of us. I was seven. Bessie, the others, and me we were kept hidden as the white man's filthy underwater secret.

When they felt the need to be entertained, their black secrets were divulged. They forced us onto the deck in groups to sing or dance or to do the dirty deed with them. I often carried Bessie onto the deck wrapped in a dirty damp empty potato bag. I tied her up good with a short rope to a railing so she couldn't crawl off or fall overboard. Little Bessie needed fresh air otherwise she would die from the black disease that hung in the air below that deck. Of this, I was always scared. The winter air was refreshing at first but after a spell I could not stop shivering. I didn't want to move. I felt frozen and worried about Bessie still being tied up to the railing. It was so cold that my fingers hurt from frostbite. I worried more about my little sister than the frostbite stinging at my fingers and feet. I had no shoes so my toes they got the frostbite too. We were humiliated and shamed while in our gloomiest place. Our hope and dignity disappeared behind the cracking of whips and the screams of the others. Bloody whipping marks became lifetime mementos of our master's cruelty. I wanted to kill him but if I did, I would surely be executed and my little sister would crawl off and fall overboard. Or she would starve. There wasn't any good in that happening now was there?

On that ship, I used to dream of a rebellion. I would be revolting against the people who captured us and kept us prisoners. Then I would think about who'd be keeping little Bessie alive if I was executed for causing an uprising? So, I behaved and made no trouble. I wasn't forced to do the dirty deed with the white men. I on intention smeared my body and my hair with as much piss and grime as I could so I stank real badly. I needed to look dull, ugly, and sickly. This was the only thing I could think to do to keep the ship's crew from taking a fancy to me and sticking their man thing inside me. The white men wanting to stick their man parts inside us weren't afraid of what was ugly, but they avoided what was sick. So, I looked sick a lot.

One time below deck in the ship's belly, I heard other girls saying how much it hurt when a white man stuck his thing inside them. How they saw blood after his thing was pulled out. This made me more scared. I had little slow growing buds under my dress, but no real breasts to speak of had grown out yet. I didn't need to stuff no rags between my legs to catch any blood cuz' I wasn't a woman yet. My time for this and my breast buds growing out was still a ways off. For this, I was blessed. I looked more like a small smelly black boy than a black girl. Because of this, I had no real worrying about being stuck with anything that would hurt or have me bleeding. Sometimes I would wonder about the others who I had seen thrown overboard or executed. Who will act as our saviour and release us from such a hell fate? There weren't any of those holy mission men on the ship to look after us and save our souls like they tried to do in Africa. Only people that endured this kind of cruelty would stand side us. Even then, we would lose in the end.

Why did this happen to us? Were they punishing us because they had white skin and we had black skin? That's the only real difference I could see between them and us. On that ship, I looked at my skin in a way I never did before we got stolen from Africa. It disgusted me when I saw my arms, legs, and dirty bare feet. They were color of river mud. I know now that there on that ship my skin color was the cause of my pain and it made me angry and afraid all the time. I was angry at my skin and at my parents, and at the white men that controlled this world. I was mad at everything I could think of. If I was not a nigger that is what we were called. I wouldn't have been sitting in that dark hole in the ships belly sweating from the body heat of th3e others in the middle of the winter. I wouldn't have been fed rotted vegetable slop or made to use an overflowing bucket filled with slave piss and shit as a toilet. I wouldn't have become extinct at such a young age. I wouldn't have had to fight off the rats that tried to bite us at night or be a mother to my little sister. If I didn't have a little sister. I could have jumped overboard and been done with that life. This I almost did a few times. Jump overboard. What happened on the ship and since we was stole from Africa is all my fault. If I hadn't wandered off into the woods to look for Bessie chasing her butterfly I wouldn't have been separated from my family. I wouldn't have been there on a ship so terrified and lonely and waiting to arrive at a destination

I knew nothing about. Even though I was one of almost four hundred slaves on the ship the isolation I felt made me miss everyone back home something terrible. Even the people I had grown to hate I began to miss. I just wanted to feel safe. I missed my family and my friends. I could not imagine thinking that they were going through the same things Bessie and I was going through. I wanted to know if they were dead. or did they search for us after we were separated? I never loved my Mammy Abada more than I did on that ship. I prayed hard to see her again. I promised our Grandmamma Ouma Etanna. with all the tears I cried and sadness I had that I would return with Bessie to our tiny hut in our little village. Ouma Etanna was my security blanket in Africa. and I was Bessie's security blanket on the ship. There on that long voyage. I had no blanket and no security.

Everything was so devastating. One day I wasn't sure I could take it any longer. I had been having awful nightmares and I always woke up all sweaty and moaning. During the day. I entertained Bessie as best I could to keep her feeling some kind of happy. At night. bad emotions dripped off my body onto hers while I tried to protect her and kept her warm. After some time at sea she stopped growing. her teeth got the co color yellow. and her hair started falling out. This worried me all the time. so I started feeding her from my share of the food slop pail. After a time went by. I got so skinny my bones stuck out but her cheeks plump again. Her teeth stayed yellow. but she was smiling more. so I started to like my bones.

I had one good dream while I was there on that ship. I dreamed about the coast of Africa. and it was beautiful. I saw our village all lit up by the sun. I could no longer taste blood on my tongue or hear the screaming and wailing of insane elders. or reach out to touch a dead person's cold skin. In my dream there was grass instead of water under the ship's belly. I bent down and kissed the grass because I wasn't feeling sick from the sea tossin' me about anymore. I could swim in the sea instead of throwing up in it. In my dream. it was a different world. My life had gone right. and I had long forgotten 'bout those scarring memories of the voyage. I awoke that night of the dream to see a sickly woman dying of the fever. Her sparkling sky colored eyes had turned dark and grey like rocks. Then her tremors ended meaning she gave into death. I was jealous that she was dead. Death set her free whiles my little sister and I we were still prisoners. On that ship. I asked myself if we would be better off being shot by one of the white men. I was weak and wilting like a dying flower. Back then on that ship I didn't know why I made myself endure the torture. I knew then that my life would never be the same after living that way so why did I even try to survive. I now know it was because I could not live in the world if I gave into wanting to throw my little sister overboard all wrapped up in a soiled potato bag that be tied up with a piece of old rope. If I killed her then I would need to kill myself. Mostly, I was just too afraid to perform such a deed knowing if I did, I would be nothing more than a child who killed a child.

I wondered then, and still wonder today, if there is bravery or courage in performing such acts of desperation? Maybe it was braver to undergo that kind of misery and suffering for so long as my body and mind could take it. I was just a scrawny starving seven years old captured African girl trying to keep her little sister alive long enough to survive the voyage. I pleaded with God that someday Bessie would be released from this hell, even if it were among the dead where she could wander eternally in a field of freedom chasing butterflies. In the end, the slave ship made landfall. Bessie held onto my hand real tight. When we gots' sold I was nothing but an ugly skeleton girl wearing black skin.

Chapter 5

Ruby brought the antique diary to her heart and warmly embraced it like a mother cuddling a baby. She then glanced over at the bed. The patient looked like she was in a deep peaceful sleep, rather than imprisoned by the confines of a coma. Her only great granddaughter's struggle to live had become too overwhelming for her. Uncharacteristically, she began to weep.

"Minnie and you are alike," she said through sniffles, "two enslaved females trying to survive."

Intrigued by the heroism both Minnie and Jazz had shown, Ruby dried tears that she scantly shed. Then she inhaled deeply and felt her lungs fill with new energy. After properly repositioning her spectacles to sharpen her vision, the emotional, snivelling, elderly woman read another passage from Minnie's journal to the unconscious teenager.

She could see that the dated pages were out of order; something she chose to overlook, knowing that the sequence of time didn't exist in a coma patient's world.

Rest in Peace Ida

I been living here with Bessie on this plantation for five years. One of the elders says that my reading and writing is really good now. He says my grammar, spelling, and markings are getting better every week. He says I am the smartest slave girl he ever gave lessons to. I say back to him that it because I been practicing so much. I write so much because I am lonely and I miss my Jacob. I heard yesterday that he is coming home next week. It's been a long time since we have seen each other. I hope I am still his secret sweetheart.

Jacob's still fighting in the American Civil War. I am scared for him all the time. His older brothers, they be twins called Eli and Isaac. They aren't soldiers because of something called the Twenty-Slave Law. Here on the plantation the white people call it the Twenty-Nigger Law. I don't like the word nigger. Hearing it makes me feel like a dirty dog. For me it's a stupid law because it is the reason why my sweetheart is a soldier for nearly three years now and his brothers are free not to fight. Eli and Isaac are spoiled and lazy. They are supposed to be working on this slave plantation where I live. Mostly they just do nothing all day and do the dirty deed with slave girls at night. I hate Eli and Isaac real bad.

Their pa, we call him Master General Ballinger, he goes to the slave market often. He keeps buying new slaves soon as one runs off or dies. He does this because the new law says he has to own twenty slaves for each one of his sons if he wants to keep them out of the war. I heard one of his manservants saying that the General has lots of money. Just not enough money to keep his youngest boy Jacob out of the rich man's war. I don't understand it all yet so I need to keep listening and watching and learning. My life has been hard. Tougher. I have heard many times over because I am a slave living and working on a huge plantation in the Deep South. Slaves working on smaller plantations in places like Virginia or Kentucky or Maryland have it easier because there is less work to do. I have no idea where these places are. Whenever I am dusting my master's study off I take a long peek at the big colorful country map on the wall. It is a map of the great country of America with its different states and territories and thirty-six starred flag. I study my master's map hard each day when I be working in his study. This way I can educate myself about where I am living now. and about other places where I maybe one day will be blessed enough to go to.

Bessie's better off than me because she was born all light skinned and sweet faced. She gets away with lots because of her cuteness. Not like me. I am still dark skinned and plain looking. I have to work harder because I am nothing special to look at. I am not jealous of my little sister. These are just facts of who we are is all.

Being a slave child has made my life dangerous and made me rigid. The little ones, like my sister Bessie, have had it much easier since they was sold. Not much is expected of the younger children until they become about the age of six, or maybe seven, depending on how strong they are or how good they learned to listen. Bessie's is older now so her days of not having to work ended about a year or so ago. She fetches water out of the creek all day long with the other younger slaves. They like this work because they jump in the cool water whenever they can. When they get caught they tell our mistress they all slipped and fell in by accident. At the end of the day they are just a bunch of cute little liars who still haven't gotten a whipping yet.

In the beginning while living here I was always smiling and watching a still then little girl Bessie running around the plantation playing with her little white and black friends. Most days I smiled listening to her squealing all happy-like when she would be swinging on the thick long rope that hangs from Master General and Mistress Ballinger's big elm tree in the front yard. From inside the house and from outside in the fields, when I was picking fresh vegetables, or hanging up the just washed laundry, I could hear her just a giggling and a squealing. In the beginning, I could hear Bessie all over the place. Everywhere I was and everywhere went, I liked this because it reminded me of when we were close by each other on the ship. Only then, she never giggled, nor did she squeal all happy like.

Slaves here working outside in the fields are worked much harder than the ones laboring inside the house. I was a blessed slave girl because I don't have to work in the fields, under a blistering sun from dawn to dark with all the snakes and bugs. I hate snakes and bugs. For the slaves it was hardest if the master or mistress used harsh punishments or split your family apart by selling off one or both of your parents or your brother or sister. I first saw this about two months back when Ida, a house girl slave like me who I worked alongside almost every day, suddenly one day just up and went missing. We were the same age, or so I was told. On that particular day, Ida wasn't answering Annabel, the mistress of the house, when she called out for her real loud. Mistress Annabel began searching like a woman gone wild in the head while looking all over the house for Ida. She even had me running from room to room screaming out "Ida. Ida. and Ida!" Then all unexpected-like Mistress Annabel just yanked open the salon door and there was Ida with Master Ballinger. her husband. They were doing the dirty deed right there on the just scrubbed carpet. The General stumbled and ran out of the house while he was pulling up his britches. He mounted his horse quick as he could and rode off to escape from his wife. Master knew his wife would take all her fury out on Ida. but he just kept riding off the property like a man without a spine. I saw him grinning all the way into the distance looking like he just won a prize. Then Mistress Annabel whipped Ida badly and locked her up in one of the smokehouses. After that. Ida got regular beatings. Each time poor Ida was taken to the whipping post and stripped down. any of us slave girls or women working nearby had to stop our chores and meet up to watch the girl being whipped again. Mistress Annabel yelled. with a threatening voice while swinging the bullwhip herself that we should be warned if she caught us doing what Ida did with our master. we would be worse off than poor Ida was! We were all scared right out of our skin of the Generals wife. Before and after poor Ida was caught doing the dirty deed on the just scrubbed carpet.

Some of the old slave servants tried hard to make a real effort. They begged to our mistress because Ida had stopped screaming and crying. She was eating no more food scraps from our plates that we snuck into the smokehouse by the dark of the night. We slaves were all very worried for her. One elderly manservant, who our mistress was kind to, hinted that Master General Ballinger who was to blame, not poor Ida. Her answer was the same cruel answer all the mistresses used when their husbands did the dirty with slave girls. She said after enough beatings when she was finished with her, she would know what not to do again.

After each whipping, Mistress Annabel stormed off in a flame of fury with poor Ida passed out and still tied naked to the whipping post. We slaves shooed the flies away that were drinking from open wounds on her bloody beaten body. We untied her each time, washed her up real good, and bandaged her oozing, lashed back. Then we clothed her before returning her to the smokehouse. Ida was brave but her body was weak. She died in less than a week from hunger and torture. A heavy silence hung over the plantation after her body was seen being carted off in a wagon behind a cantering horse. We never knew where she was buried or in which river she was dumped. We slaves were too frightened to talk about it and too sad to cry for her.

Four days later, I heard the General's familiar cheerful whistling out on the front lawn. He had returned to the big house. The General was still grinning and acting like nothing happened. I was dusting off the pictures hanging in the entry hallway when I heard him. I had the front doors open to let a nice cool breeze in, so I saw my Master get off his horse, climb the porch stairs and enter the house. Then I heard Mistress Annabel loudly declare that she had sold his whore and bought a new dress!

The General was fuming something awful. He bashed the parlor door shut and stormed past me on his way out of the house again. This time his britches was buckled up real high. Startled by his actions I held my breath and stood still so as not to be heard or seen. I was so scared of me master and his dirty ways. Keeping my eyes down real low. I stared hard at the floor thinking surely the General would be turning his roaming eyes on me now that Mistress Annabel went out and bought herself a new dress.

~ Minnie 1865 ~

Feeling stunned and fatigued, Ruby removed one of her hairpins and put it in the binding of the journal. Cleverly, she assumed that her hairpin would make a bookmark. She was right. Then she carefully replaced the letter and unattached pages beneath the front cover and retied the braided leather cord with a knot on the end. Suddenly, the old woman was emotionally breathless. A frightening chill ran through her when she realized that the leather cord, she'd just secured around the journal was the upper section of a bullwhip. Slave plantation masters and mistresses had used this torturous tool to beat slaves into submission or render punishment for disobediences and crimes. Her heart shuddered. Sympathetically, she rolled the tip of the whip's pea-sized knot between her fingers. Then, respectfully, she placed the journal back on the top of the stack.

She was overcome with emotion. She felt dizzy and bewildered from having just held the most painful, injury causing part of a genuine slave whip in her hands.

"I wonder if Bessie or Minnie were ever beaten with this whip," she heard herself timidly ask.

Her university education had taught Ruby about the European Slave Trade and methods of slave imprisonment and torture. She knew that a bullwhip could be flung in such a way that towards the end of the fling, the tip of the whip exceeded the speed of sound, thereby creating a small sonic boom and an agonizing type of pain. The vision she had of a bullwhip clotted with dark, bloodstained human flesh, was more than she could stomach. She reached over, snatched the plastic vomit bowl hanging from the side of the patient's ICU bed and spit up in it.

After returning from the bathroom, where she'd rinsed the vomit bowl and her mouth out, Ruby sat back down and sipped her now cold Earl Grey tea. It was times like this, when she wished she wasn't able to visualize life in such a vivid way. Seeing with her mind's eye could be as disturbing as it was advantageous. Since, visualizing was something she had little control over, she trusted her mind to be gentle with her whenever she needed it to be. Effectively and swiftly, she pushed the nasty images and her bitter questions out of her forever-searching brain.

The English tea was helping to settle her agitated stomach. Cold tea was something she had never minded drinking. Nonetheless, this time the cold tea and visualizations she'd just had, left her feeling chilly. Ruby ate the second vanilla biscuit, rewrapped the blanket around her shoulders, and leaned back into the lounger. With her body relaxing and warming up, she closed her weary eyes. Recognizing a familiar sign, she knew the past was beckoning her again.

The elderly woman then inhaled deeply, five consecutive times. Without any hesitation, she allowed her mind to drift in reverse. Mental drifting allowed her to go into a secret bubble of time and space, to a place where life on the outside ceased to exist.

Chapter 6

With her eyes still closed, she sashayed deeper into a familiar abyss. Whenever she mentally strayed, she was transformed into her clandestine self; someone she intentionally concealed from others. This act of concealment and mind traveling was something she had been doing her entire life. By hiding it, she protected the secret parts of her true self.

By the time she was an adolescent, Ruby had mastered the ability to mind travel, while simultaneously guiding her mind's flow of energy. She'd used this intimate act of brain control as her very own mental device. It was a device that resembled an abstract brain switch; a switch only she controlled, and only she could turn on and off, at will.

Although Ruby was at ease with drifting deeply into a subliminal state, lately the veracity of each passage had become a trifle too mystifying. This was something she conveniently blamed on aging and her chaotic lifestyle as one of the oldest, most active entrepreneurs in London. For as interesting as her mind drifting addiction was, she realized that it occasionally bordered on the paranormal. This was something that outright intrigued her. Ruby Adeline McEwen was born different, had always been different, and liked being different.

Even as a youngster, she had no fear of the magical side of herself. On the contrary, her dreamlike character continuously fascinated her. Despite that life often baffled her, and she often baffled life, she was filled with curiosity and continuously searched for the meaning behind each new and unusual experience. From the time she was a bright eyed, chubby cheeked, little girl with a head covered in ringlets, she'd learned to use her intuitive capabilities wisely. As she matured, her instinctiveness enabled her to cross over to alternative dimensions; distant places, where she could mindfully dance on the threads of time, while turning her brain switch on and off. This was empowering, especially for a child.

Regardless that her aging brain had forgotten its earliest memories, recollections of the past frequently passed through her dreams and hallucinations. Even today, as she entered a familiar place, occupied by the unknown and swathed in memories, she felt safe. As she travelled through the channels of time, daydreams and images nurtured her mind and fed wisdom to her soul. Despite her deteriorating body, her spirit had remained young, intact, and consumed by inquisitive energy. Ruby's spirit didn't age because she wouldn't allow it to. Since her birth, she'd protected her spirit with her life. This happened naturally and was a behaviour she was completely unaware of. The old woman believed in her inner self and her intuition immensely. She was confident that both would safeguard her, like armour, through time and on the farther side of deaths brim. The eccentric, spiritually roving person, sitting in an ICU recliner, didn't believe in boundaries or limits. As a result, her fearless mind flowed effortlessly, back and forth, to and fro.

Bit by bit, a roguelike grin appeared on Ruby's face. As her eyes quivered and gradually opened, she let out an elusive sigh. The sound of her exhale was comforting and definitive. It signified that she'd left the other side and had returned to the here and now. It was very normal for her elderly, limp body to twitch and shudder as it travelled between spheres. Typically, she tended to jerk and quake when her mind wandering episodes were winding down and ending. She'd kept 'the other Ruby' a secret since she was very young; too afraid that someone would tell her strict, passé parents just how peculiar she really was. If this happened, she'd be severely punished for the sake of saving her from her wayward ways. For that very reason, in 1929 a precocious four-year-old female, with the eyes the colour of green mischief, became a Keeper of Secrets. Growing up, many bad things would happen to the gifted female. Nevertheless, she would be all right, because she was learning to keep what happened a secret. Her secrets would become her clandestine life. A life she would learn to, only occasionally, share or trust others with.

Her heartrate increased, and her breathing intensified, as her mind returned to the intensive care room she was in. It took her a few minutes to regain her focus and feel alert again. She knew she should stay alert because she was mentally drained. For this reason, she'd need to keep her mind from roaming again. Drifting whenever she was tired always ended in disaster, and she currently had had all the disaster she could handle lying in the bed across from her.

Wide-awake and ready for more reality, Ruby eagerly reached into her canvas bag and removed one of her own journals that she'd brought from the diner. As she held the journal, she thought of the many trials and tribulations she had lived through at the hands of her parents, especially her father. She knew, first-hand, that having complicated, problematic parents, was something she and the coma patient had in common. For this reason, in that very moment and from that moment on, she would begin talking aloud with the child. She decided that she'd do this as if Jazz was sitting up in bed, wide-awake and ready to listen to her very wise, worldly great grandmother. Ruby then committed to herself to ignore the child's untamed, God-awful purple hair and the barbwire tattoo choker around her neck while she talked and read to her. Otherwise, the reason Jazz had chosen to create such an obvious attention getting appearance would interfere with her flow of thoughts and words.

Rather than bombard the patient with distressing topics about two parents at the same time, she would begin with talking with her about fathers. She remembered, all too well, how her own father had challenged and influenced her life in ways her mother never could, would, or did. With paternal memories swirling through her brain, she started her first actual conversation with the teenager in a coma.

"Fathers, what can daughters do about our fathers?" she asked the child aloud. "We love them on Monday, and we hate them by Friday. You are not the only baby girl born into this great big world whose father has wronged her. You didn't ask for it, but you got it. All the complaining, rebelling, and running away isn't going to change a thing. His blood and genes are running through you. This makes him a lifelong part of you and you a lifelong part of him. This is just one of the many facts of life that no one and nothing can change," Ruby affirmed.

"Accepting this rather than fighting it will make your life much easier. It's that complicated and it's that simple!" she boisterously declared, resembling a passionate Sunday morning preacher staring at a church full of parishioners, while holding an empty collection basket. Now that she was all fired up, she continued her sermon.

"Let me tell you about my own father. For most of what I can remember, he was almost never at home. When he was home, he was proper British wacky back who stirred up buckets of trouble. Whenever my father tipped the whiskey bottle and took one too many swigs, he turned into mean ole' bastard of a man. It was as if I was born to two fathers instead of just one. At the end of any given day, I adored him and detested him at the same time. Despite the never-ending tug of war I was in, between loving him and abhorring him, he was still my father."

The elderly woman caught her breath, calmed her nerves, and continued.

"When we were just wee babies, you and I, if we didn't have a father in our lives, we wouldn't have had a bloody penny to our names or rainbow coloured pots to piss in. Despite his ludicrous bad habits and endless mistakes, in the end, my father did right by me. Likewise, yours will do right by you, if you are forgiving and patient enough to give him the chance to do so. Now you pay attention and heed my words girl. I am going to read things to you that are important. I know you are still in there and can hear me. Forget about your coma, focus and listen. When you are ready to return to this life, follow the sound of my voice and let my words guide you home."

Ruby dabbed beads of nervous perspiration off her forehead with the corner of the blanket and then tucked its warm fleece around her chilled ankles and feet. She'd forgotten how, back then, she'd hand-typed many of her journal entries with the same Remington typewriter she occasionally still used. Seeing how old-fashioned the typed pages appeared immediately put her in a nostalgic mood.

After a few moments of shifting about, she found a more relaxing position. Her little round, black spectacles had slipped down and were now crookedly perched on the tip of her nose. She adjusted them accordingly, opened the journal she was holding and began reading to Jazz.

Chapter 7

Horrible Horace and Al Jolson

I am not a child anymore. Starting today, I won't be calling my parents mother and father. With this being said, when I'm writing my stories, I will be using their real names. They are called Horace and Sadie. They would hate me calling them by their names and I'd get a spanking for being very disrespectful. Because I don't like spankings, I will be writing in secret, just as I do so many other things in my life. In this way, I am the Keeper of Secrets and a rather clever kind of girl. My name is Ruby. It is the year 1936. I am almost eleven and I hate my name. I want to change it to Vivian, so someday, when choices become mine to make, I will be changing it.

How could I know that my first serious lie and disobeying act would be the beginning of years of bending the truth? How can I stop myself from becoming rebellious? I am just a girl with adventure inside her. A girl living in a small, brick house with a fenced in yard who sees strange things and talks to dead people. When my mother Sadie's not paying attention, I sneak over our high backyard fence and run up the steep hill to the nearby cemetery. I am a great climber and can run fast. At the cemetery, I lie on my back in the grass between the tombstones and stare up at clouds. I am always careful not to step on coffins under the ground. Stepping on coffins is bad mannered and not something that the dead people under my shoes would appreciate me doing. I like dead people. Dead people are good listeners. I talk to dead people when there is no one else to talk with. I go to the cemetery because I know Sadie and Horace will never look for me there.

Being the only child means that I am alone a lot. This is why I visit the cemetery and chat with the dead. We talk about all sorts of different things. At times, when I close my eyes while lying in on the respectable side of a tombstone, I can feel myself drifting away. It feels like the clouds are taking me with them as I float far and soar upwards through the sky. Then I see the spirits of dead people in my mind. Talking to dead people, seeing spirits, and visiting the graveyard are my favourite best-kept secrets so far. The older I get the more I adore having my own private world that no one else shares with me. And the more I like secrets.

Graveyards and secrets make me feel different. I like being different. Horace has become a horrible man and one of the angriest people I know. There is force in him and a mean streak that scares me almost all the time. I wonder why the people in our village think of Horace as being a kind and helpful man. I wonder why he becomes a dominant man when he is here at home. I wonder why he acts different with other people than he acts with Sadie and me. I wonder why he has to go to the pubs and drink so much and then come home and act so mean and be so horrible. Sadie says I wonder too much. I need to stop wondering and asking myself questions that I probably will never ever know the answers to. I want to write about life as it now is and not about all the things in my head that I can't explain. From now on, this is what I will be doing. I'll be writing more and asking less.

These days Horace is always mad and his being mad is always because of me. Even if I do nothing wrong. When I am in earshot of him and hear him yelling at someone else, like Sadie, or a villager, it feels like his yelling is meant for me. This isn't easy because mostly I blame myself for it. Sadie sometimes says that Horace has a heart even bigger than his mouth is. I think that she thinks he is a gentle man when on the inside of himself and a rougher man when he's on the outside of himself. Sadie says that I can see him easier from the outside, so this is why I think he is always mad. Maybe Sadie is right. I just don't get grownups yet.

I am not so good at pleasing people or acting the way Horace and Sadie expect me to act. My free personality stops me from being anyone other than who I am. Being me isn't always easy for me, even though I pretend mostly that it is. Just as I pretend like I am okay when other people stare at me too long or judge me. This happens all the time. I hate being judged and stared at because I am still a girl. I will never be okay with other people having wrong opinions of me. Probably this is because I am somewhat shy, which is another secret I keep hidden away.

People think I am the apple of Horace's eye because I am his only child and I'm a daughter, not a son. I think they are right because even though he can be mad a lot, he spoils me. I think because I never had a brother, Horace and Sadie never learned how to like boys. I still don't know very much about my parents. They don't talk about themselves or tell me what they were like when they were my age. So how can I know things about them or other things? I need to start asking my grandparents about Horace and Sadie. My grandparents will want me to know things. They live in London.

I am getting older now. I have become good at hiding the way it really is between Horace and me. I am the keeper of his secrets too. I think maybe that I have become a challenging child for Sadie. She says I think too much for a young girl. Sadie says that I am difficult to point in any direction other than the direction I want to go in. Once I heard Sadie telling my teacher that I am an impulse that is hard to control. Then she said I am just like my father Horace is. Maybe Sadie is right. Maybe I am like Horace. Even though I'm a girl and I don't go to pubs.

I suspect when Sadie goes outdoors to beat the dirty carpets against the house with a thick broom, while the radio is blasting Al Jolson music through the open windows, it's because she is trying to hide the sound of her crying. Sadie cleans like an insane woman whenever she is irritated, or miserable. I can hear Al Jolson music and the sound of her beating up our carpets whenever Horace has been drinking too much again. Mister Al Jolson has been singing a lot in our house this year.

Horace's whiskey drinking makes Sadie lonely and sad. Sadie thinks Horace wants to be with the bottle more than he wants to be with her. Sometimes I think that maybe Sadie would rather be sharing her life with a man like Al Jolson instead of with a man like Horace. I don't know why Horace chooses whiskey over such a pretty woman as

Sadie is. I don't ask anyone about things like this because I am afraid someone will find out about my secrets. Like why Sadie has to cry so much? Why I had to see my father kissing a blonde woman behind grain store last week? I know this to be true because I spied on him when I got bored from waiting for him in his pickup truck. Parents are so confusing, and men can be stupid.

Even though I am not a little girl anymore, I suppose I'm still too young to understand Horace, Sadie, and Al Jolson. I do know that a family like mine makes big messes every week. Our house is small, so it gets all cluttered and dusty. Even so, I know the difference between Sadie cleaning to remove dirt and her cleaning to distract herself from her unhappy life. Some days I feel sorry for Sadie. Even so, I still love Horace.

No matter how angry he gets, he is still my father. I feel stuck in the middle and don't know what to do?
I am clever. So, I have my own ways of distracting myself from my crazy life with these two people who I call my family. When it gets to be too much I wander off and climb up the big hill behind our house. Then I hide and write, or draw, in the journals that Grandma Bessie sends to me. Sadie says I can draw really well for a girl my age

and that I must get this from her. Sadie teaches me to draw whenever she has time. It's nice of her to want to teach me things even though I'd rather be writing in my journals and go exploring so I can find out what is on the other side of our fence. I like learning about new things on my own. Grandma Bessie, she's Sadie's mother, and I wrote letters and then exchanged them. Sometimes I would visit her when I had summer vacation from school. I learned to like words from my grandma and drawing from my mother. Sadie tells me I can also write quite well for my age, and I get this from her mother. I think she is right. Even though she sometimes ignores me, I like it when she thinks I am good at something.

I have another secret. When I grow up, I'm going to be a famous journalist. I am not sure what a journalist is, but being one seems fascinating. I want to be a writer who tells stories about big adventures. Adventures like the ones I'm now reading in my Shirley Temple books. Most days I am a happy and creative almost 11-year-old girl who likes words. A girl who is glad she learned to read, write, and draw pictures before she grows up and needs to beat dirty carpets with a thick broom, while her radio blasts Al Jolson music through open windows.

1936 - Ruby McEwen

Chapter 8

Amused and touched, Ruby folded her journal and delicately placed it on her lap. It had been eons since she'd thought about being a little girl, Al Jolson, her unexplainable parents, and her father kissing a woman behind the grain store.

Even these days, as an elderly woman looking back on her life, she realized that she tended to interpret most of it in a different way than it used to be, or actually was. It wasn't always easy, or enjoyable, being the only daughter of Sadie Dutton and Horace McEwen. Yet, regardless of this undeniable fact, when she was just about the same age as Jazz, things started to change between her and Horace. Lost in thought, Ruby picked her journal back up and started hysterically flipping through its loose pages. The old woman was on a serious seek and find mission.

Please, oh please, let this be the right journal, she pleaded with herself. *I need to read something so bloody important to this child before this day ends. Jazz needs to hear one more tale about fathers, so she will start believing that most fathers are not as bad as the choices they make.*

Feeling a sudden, painless kind of exhilaration, Ruby sat upright on the edge of the recliner with a similar vigour she'd had when she was in her thirties. She'd found what she was looking for and she was excited! Even though it was rather long, it was too symbolic for the teenager not to hear. Besides, she was still proud of it. Self-importance and pride were something Ruby McEwen hardly ever felt. In retrospect, she knew that her passion for writing had been born more than seven decades ago, the week she'd learned to use a typewriter and had written what she was about to share with Jazz. The day had arrived. It was now time for her to pass down her passion for words and life.

With calm enthusiasm, the elderly woman started reading aloud.

The Best Kind of Ignorance is Uninvited.

She couldn't recall how many times they'd leaned against that weathered old fence while gazing out at the scenery in the distance. It had never mattered which one of them arrived at the fence first, after a few minutes, the other one joined alongside. An invitation between them over the years was never needed, even before she'd grown up and he'd grown old. These nearly ceremonial moments of theirs always began with silence, as each of them rejoiced in the spectacular scenery they stood before. Essex County England truly had magnificent views, with its inspiring villages, charming architecture, rolling landscapes, and graceful valleys. Rising hills added rugged, defining contours to its countryside. As deep green tones spanned aimlessly outwards from the borders of its foothills, it was difficult to determine where one valley began and the other one ended.

The sundry, rich countryside was stippled with countless multi-coloured rooftops scattered throughout the small yet expanding communities below. The view portrayed a rural population and the enduring, seasonal development of the Saxon Kingdom region of Britain. It was once a predominately Christian region, that brave settlers had staked their native claims upon, centuries before either of them was born. From where they stood, it looked diversified and stunning; with autumn colours that made the county picturesque and beholding. This was the place they both called home.

There they stood, as so many times before, each of them lost in a private sea of distinct thoughts and individual emotions. Slightly warmed by the early evening sun, and captivated by the dynamic scenery, they began to relax. The valley was ablaze with pulsating tints and lush shades of another Indian summer at its peak. It was the third week in September, and they were standing on the edge of another Global Equinox. It was the second of only two days a year, when the sun would cross the plane of the equator, making the length of night and day, nearly the same, across the earth. He had taught her about the Equinox when she was a child. Since then, she had liked being a part of something people around the world were together a part of on the very same day. This intrigued her and made her feel connected to something that freed her from the confines of her currently dull English existence.

"Mother Nature has outdone herself this year," she proclaimed. Subtly, she turned towards him and said, "There is something mesmerizing in the air. Can you feel it? "His infamous placidity was relentless, so her spirited mind roamed in reverse as she remembered a previous fence side conversation with him, when he'd told her a story about his three times great grandfather Darius. Darius was an adventurous and ambitious young man who, at only 18 years old, had travelled all the way to North America. Legend had it that Darius had somehow managed to pass himself off as a US Citizen. Many years later, as grown man, he became somewhat of a daredevil and a respected entrepreneur. In 1761, together with sixty-five brave and determined visionaries, he chartered a new region of the American Northeast Territory. Thirty years later, almost 180 people had staked claims to the land, asserting their rightful possession of property.

She scoffed at the man standing next to her and his factual memory; questioning why he insisted on speaking about the past with her, when he knew she was only interested in the future. Reminiscing further over that particular fence side chat they'd had, she recalled that he'd gone on to tell her a tale about the American Revolution of 1775. She was studying American history in high school, so with her interest tickled, she had listened intently and hung on his every word. He went on to say, that back then, homesteads being developed in valleys similar to the lowlands of Essex, stood directly in the path of the war. This made it quite dangerous for the colonists who were attempting to live there.

He'd told her if the harsh winters, grizzly bears, smallpox, or the Indians didn't kill the American settlers, the muskets of the revolution eventually did. She remembered him saying that many colonists hesitated before declaring their independence after the war ended, because they'd lost family members and neighbours, which likewise, had made them lose faith in God and Country.

He'd told her how the Declaration of Independence summarized colonial grievances and provided a futuristic vision of an independent American Republic. He talked about bravery, obligation, community, civic duty, and family honour. He went on to tell her that when he was a young man in his early twenties, following in the footsteps of Darius and becoming an American citizen had been a dream of his. However, his dream never came true. His life plan was interrupted when he was commissioned by the British House of Parliament to take part in an expedition into Tibet. Apparently, border issues between Tibet and Northern India needed resolving; therefore, he was summoned to duty. The unendorsed mission he took part in was important. Its purpose was to create diplomatic relations and establish a resolution over serious border disputes between the two regions. He went on to tell her that his partaking in the Tibet Mission and traveling to Asia was one of the most impacting climaxes of his life as a then 21-year-old man. Back then, men called into action didn't question, they obeyed. His tale ended when he told her that, although he never knew exactly why he and his comrades were sent to Tibet, he was nonetheless grateful for the Tibetan Medal of Honor he received from his country and for the opportunity and the once in a lifetime experience.

He was patriotic and intellectual. She was defiant and inexperienced. There she stood, grimacing, while thinking about her inability to control her fantasies of living her life farther than her parent's domestic borders. There he stood, attempting to teach her about the history of countries that she'd never been to. He stood, he hoped, and he prayed, that as time marched on, she'd come to grasp that he was teaching her about so much more than history. That he was rightly instilling integrity, virtue, and righteousness in her. Nevertheless, she was still too young, naïve, and rebellious to appreciate him. This was something that hurt him on occasion, yet, he still tolerated it because he was certain that the passage of time would close the gap that had recently grown between them.

She thought the old man standing next to her was as confusing as he was annoying. Regardless, when they stood side by side leaning against that tattered and worn fence, she felt oddly at ease with him. Typically, she'd begin to talk first, attempting to break the awkwardness that began breeding amongst them in the last year or so. She wasn't sure when, or even why, their relationship began to change, but the changes were making her feel detached when she was away from him and uncomfortable when she was with him.

Characteristically, he was a persuasive and unpredictable man who was unable to manage his frequent verbal impulsiveness. He was notorious for spewing out vindictive words laden with hidden meanings. This was a habit of his that frustrated and infuriated his daughter, especially when he made a scene in public. She cringed with the thought of how many times this had happened. Since she was still an adolescent girl consumed by too many untold emotions, his renowned impulsiveness could be offensive and upsetting. Despite the negative emotional shock waves she would drown in whenever he drank too much and verbally went too far, his rude remarks did force her, at an impressionable age, to reflect upon the consequences and differences between love and hate.

Regardless of their commonly volatile relationship and their vastly different personalities, he was as drawn to her presence as she was to his. He was a conversationalist and a social icon. She was a daring, avid thinker, and a dreamer. Wherever he stood, his feet were embedded with pride upon the ground. Whereas everywhere she went, she drifted poetically with her head in the clouds. Their fiery temperaments often caused them to collide, preventing them from forming a dynamic and tangible bond. A bond they each undeniably yearned for, yet never spoken about. For reasons she'd yet to comprehend, their differences didn't repel her against him. On the contrary, for incomprehensible reasons, they attracted him to her.

She pondered over this often, repeatedly wondering why. Was she interested in his life out of a curious sense of loyalty, or was it because of some basic, vague necessity she was not yet fully aware of? Probably both, she concluded, because life with this man had never been simple. She continued to gaze out over the now familiar scenic countryside, fantasizing again about the day she would be standing somewhere else. The day she'd be anywhere else, but in England, still living with him. There was a time, not too long ago, when Essex, instead of being her home, had become an irritatingly, massive obstacle that was preventing her from living an independent life. Her current life had grown too monotonous to satisfy her inherited adventurous spirit. She knew that her inquisitiveness needed to be set free. Meanwhile, all the old man wanted to do was to tame her and keep her nearby, under his protective wings.

Lost in thought, as she mentally roamed her mind soared. He was accustomed to her slipping away from him in this way, so he continued to gaze out over the scenery he was so in harmony with. Gently he leaned into her. He did realize that lately he'd become an intolerant, and narrow-minded man who had lost all patience with her constant need to vocalize her plans to graduate high school and move away. In that particular moment, standing next to her, he dreamt about the day she would choose not to leave the homestead he'd built and the family he had spun for her. This would be the day he'd been hoping for since she was a just wee lass. This would be the day she'd announce, with conviction that she would never leave home. Shrewdly, he knew that this day of reckoning would certainly never come, and that soon, the unavoidable side of life would take her away from him.

The old man was right. He smirked, considering himself to be slightly weak and delusional. He hated getting old and he loathed expressing his emotions. He lived for being in control and having the upper hand in life. However, deep inside his heart and mind, where his delicate, gentler side coexisted with his most private thoughts, he knew that hoping was futile. His headstrong, independent daughter would one-day move away from him. This was inevitable and just a matter of time. The old man was past the shadow of doubt convinced that once she left, she would never return. Instinctively, he knew that his bold and impatient child was not born to return to anything. Unexpectedly, with an uncommon type of endearment, he tenderly took her hand in his. Feeling his calloused fingers gliding over the grooves between her knuckles, she instinctively nuzzled closer into him. Filled with a sporadic kind of compassion, she nonchalantly laid her head upon his old, sturdy shoulder.

Captured by the pure tranquillity of the moment, the old man with a heavy heart chose to ignore the inevitable for just one more day.

1947 Ruby A. McEwen

Creative Writing - Essex County High School

Ruby had enjoyed reading her high school graduation term paper to the child. What she'd written, seventy-six years ago, had amused her and made her feel young again. Her words were yet another reminder that, it had been much too long since she'd thought about that time in her life. She removed her spectacles, rubbed her weary eyes, shifted herself into a more comfortable position, and reminisced farther.

Graduating high school had taken longer because of World War II and the bombing of London in 1940. She called to mind that only five weeks after she had written the literary piece for her final exam, she should have been moving away from home to further her studies. Nevertheless, Hitler got in her way when England was repeatedly bombed by the Nazi's. Therefore, Ruby, the young high school graduate, postponed her education and aided in post-war relief efforts across Great Britain. Years later, after the dangers and the dust from WWII had settled, she enrolled at the well-established and prestigious University of Dublin, also known as Trinity College. In 1949, Ruby proved her father right, left Essex County, and never returned. As Horace had predicted, his only daughter was not born to return to anything. As time passed, the unsettling gap between them closed.

The elderly woman shut her journal and laid it back on her lap. Then she poured herself another cup of cold Earl Grey, took long laborious drink, and scooched forward in the recliner to be closer to the patient. Bringing her crooked left hand to her forehead, she made a proper sign of the cross over her breasts and between her shoulders. Her spontaneous, holy gesture was an act of endearment that the very old nonbeliever almost never expressed. Then she began to speak.

"There will come a day when you will, like I already have, reach the age of rhyme and reason. The day when you wake up to breathe fresh air and start walking on God's green earth again. On this day, you will need to make some serious decisions. Then you'll need to ask yourself the same question I asked myself when I was about the same age as you now are. Are you going to believe all the things people say and the lies you frequently tell about your parents? Or are you going to start believing in yourself and living a life based on truth?"

Ruby stopped speaking long enough to drink more of her now even colder tea. A few sips later, she spoke again.

"When you choose truth, you will need to tell yourself that your parents made their choices. The choices they made were their choices, not yours. You will need to make your own choices. Your choices will be different from the ones they'd choose for you, because you are different than they are. You are one of a kind. You are unique and irreplaceable. There is absolutely nothing ordinary about you."

She continued talking to the child laboriously, with a steady, conviction filled voice.

"You are bold and freethinking. You have abilities waiting to be discovered and passions waiting to be born. I predict that you will never repeat or return to anything. If you pause long enough to stop chasing life and stop running away from it, life will find you."

Then, she took a deep breath and put her teacup down before continuing.

"I plan to live long enough to see you do something impressive with your life. When you do, your parents are going to be awestricken. Jazz, you have something they never had and something they're never going to have. Once you discover what it is, you will have reached the age of rhyme and reason. I promise you, when this day arrives, you will sparkle like a diamond."

Chapter 9

The ICU was more serene now than it was when the elderly woman had first arrived. Life support machines continued to softly drone and peep in a somewhat surreal way. The rhythmic, beating sound of oxygen being pumped into the patient's blood and lungs uplifted the great grandmother's state of mind and filled her with trust.

The plaster casts on Jazz's arm and leg, her sterile white pillow, and the hygienic bed linens were illuminated by the blueish glow of digital lights from the apparatuses surrounding her bed.

This made the child look even more angelic, Ruby thought.

Intravenous tubes were running into the patient's right hand. Auxiliary tubes were inserted into her mouth. She remained unconscious. The child had an 18cm long, 1 cm deep laceration in her skull that been cleaned and sutured. Ruby was told that the laceration was the reason why a significant amount of her dyed hair had been shaven off.

"At least half that dreadful colour is gone," she whispered under her breath. She could see that the roots of Jazz's hair were a dark auburn colour, although it was too soon to tell for sure. The old woman curiously questioned this, thinking and hoping that Jazz had the same dark, ginger coloured hair she'd herself once had. The silver piercing stud in her nose had been removed to create a germ-free space for the nasal tubes.

Ruby made a mental note to *ask a nurse where the nose stud was so she could polish it and keep it safe until the child woke up.*

The ICU staff and the attending physicians had earlier explained to Ruby that Jazz's lungs were filled with seawater when the ambulance arrived at the scene of the accident. She had stopped breathing and flat lined for approximately three minutes. Therefore, the teenager had been pronounced clinically dead on the shoreline, off a remote island, where the accident had occurred. The medics had resuscitated her twice before transporting her by helicopter to the mainland. Shortly, after arriving at the ICU, a tracheal tube was inserted through her mouth. Oxygen, anaesthetics, and vaporous medicines were being given to her through the different tubes. The conduits would only be removed after the accident victim had regained consciousness and could eat and breathe on her own; or logically speaking, if she died.

Jazz had suffered a brain injury during the accident that had caused her brain to fill with fluid and swell. Her brain was now too swollen, which most likely was the reason she was in a coma. They needed to control Jazz's cranial inflammation immediately. The physicians and neurologists would know more after a Magnetic Resonance Imaging test was performed and the images had been diagnostically studied. An MRI was scheduled for early tomorrow morning. Once the test results were in, the neurologist assigned to Ms. Durant's case would speak to Ruby, his patient's caregiver and next of kin. The specialists had gone on to explain that the patient had a subarachnoid haemorrhage, which meant her brain was bleeding into the thin layer that surrounded it. This thin layer is located just under the inner surface of a person's skull. Although cranial swelling and blood leakage was quite common with a head injury like Jazz's, a very narrow duct had been inserted though her cranium to drain fluid and blood. This procedure would relieve the pressure on her brain and aid with reducing the swelling.

When Ruby asked the physician if the child was in pain, she was told that it was very unusual for a coma to last longer than ten to fourteen days. Comatose patients are entirely unresponsive; therefore, there is no bodily movement. Nor do they react to light or sound. The attending doctor reassured her that a patient in Jazz's condition could not feel pain. When she heard this, Ruby felt her first twinge of relief since the news of the accident had reached her. She was thankful the child wasn't suffering more than necessary. Still, she was rather sceptical that Jazz heard no sounds. Therefore, she would continue to talk with her as much as possible, believing that until she regained consciousness, no one but Jazz could know for sure if she'd heard sounds or not. Ruby knew each patient and each coma was different; therefore, she refused to give into statistics. She was stubborn in this way. The doctor's told the elderly woman that Jazz's vitals were remarkably strong and stable, given extent of her injuries and the trauma's her body was currently enduring. The tending ICU neurologist pointed out, consecutive times, how strong her vitals were, and how they were giving them confidence for a full recovery. Likewise, using a textbook approach, they professionally warned Ruby not to be overly optimistic. *With a substantial brain injury,* they said, *the outcome is never certain until the patient leaves their coma and fully regains consciousness.*

When the physicians and specialists were finished with their examination, Ruby asked them about Nico. Was he also in the hospital? She was told that information on him was either not available or would not being released to her because she was not immediate family. Another thick layer of worry fell hard and wrathfully upon when she heard this. Nico was an illegal immigrant, which was a secret she'd chosen to keep between the two of them since the day she'd met him. One of the specialists assigned to Jazz's case had suggested that Ruby go home and get some rest. The medical team did not anticipate that she'd regain consciousness within the next five to seven hours because she was heavily sedated.

Ruby should take advantage of this and consider her own needs, she was told. As the specialist was leaving his patient's room, the well-intended medical man went on to remind Ruby of her age and her body's need for rest. If she weren't so indebted to him for his care of the child, she'd have swatted him accordingly for his remarks. She hated it whenever anyone pointed out how old she was. However, truth be told, she knew he was right; she was very old and very tired.

Tomorrow she'd begin her search for more information about Nico and the whereabouts of his family. For now, she could only have faith and pray, again, to a God she still wasn't sure she believed in, that her dishwasher and boarder had survived the boat crash? Her life, for as many years as she had left, would be destroyed if the child didn't survive and Nico was injured, deceased, arrested, or deported.

With a heavy, guilt-ridden heart, Ruby attentively stared at the punkish person she'd been given full responsibility for. Despite that she was a nurse's aide before, during, and after World War II, the child's condition and the diagnosis was much too much for her to absorb. The health care system around her had become too modernized, technical, and digital. In addition to this, overnight, her world had become dismal and fickle.

It was almost dark outside. The sun had set in the six hours she'd selfishly spent alone, reminiscing and comforting Jazz. She had taken pleasure in reading and talking with the child and felt confident that she'd put the patient on a path towards recovery. Ruby McEwen, the keeper of the journals and human gateway to the past, had offered Jazz companionship and a way home. Now, her sincerest hope was, that the child would find her way back to life. Moreover, she trusted that the journal's, filled with teachings, wisdom, tales, and experiences, of the people and events that came before both of them, would safeguard the unmanageable American teen, and steer her in the right direction.

"Let the contents of the journals guide you down the proper path," she advised her with a soft whisper.

Ruby was now feeling literally exhausted and hungry. An all too familiar soreness and stiffness in her bones had reappeared. For a third time, she boosted herself up and out of the beige Naugahyde recliner and let out a riled-up sigh as her skin stuck slightly to the fake leather. Then she painfully stood as vertical as an 88-year-old with a crooked spine could stand. She was on the verge of tears again, which she readily ignored. Wiping the fret from her jade coloured eyes, she quietly tiptoed past the patient's bed. The soles of her worn in, cognac leather boots still squeaked with each step she took. Ruby sympathetically kissed Jazz's discoloured, swollen, and bruised cheek before leaving the room on her way to the nurse's station. The room's wide door closed slowly and automatically behind her.

Standing authoritatively in front of the nurse's station, Ruby listed her requests, as politely as her age and fears would allow.

"Have someone sponge bathe and wash the blood off Jazz before I return. She looks disgusting. Have a roll out cot, a pillow, a sandwich, and two blankets brought into her room," she said.

Her calm, yet commanding tone, demanded that the receptionist on duty listen and meet her needs.

"My great granddaughter will not be spending one night alone until she wakes up and leaves her coma behind."

Turning sluggishly on her heels, the elderly woman began limping back down the same long corridor towards the same elevator she'd taken upon her arrival at Saint Matthew's Hospital. Ruby was in search of a telephone. She needed to call overseas speak to the child's mother. Something she was seriously regretting having to do.

How does a person possibly go about ringing someone up, knowing that they are about to ruin a life, she silently asked herself as she hobbled farther along?

Chapter 10

Earlier that day, two police officers had doggedly walked down to the beach behind The Seaside to inform its owner about the accident and to question her. When they arrived, Ruby was sipping on a bottle of ice-cold Coca Cola and reading a new chapter in her Harlequin Romance novel. She was so engrossed in her paperback's steamy storyline and the serenity of being alone that she hadn't heard the constables approaching her.

Both of the officers were reasonably annoyed because apparently, they'd unsuccessfully tried reach her by phone, for two hours, and had better things to do with their time. They went on to inform the elderly woman that a wet and soppy Seaside Diner business card had been found in a wallet at the scene of an accident off the coast. The wallet had a California driver's license in it, belonging to a Ms. Jazz Durant. With fear lodged in her throat, she struggled to breathe and keenly listened.

The waterlogged business card had led them straight to Ruby's address. Jazz's backpack had also been retrieved at the scene. It was discovered bobbing in the North Sea, drenched in salt water and sand. Suspicious illegal drugs were found by a paramedic at the scene of the accident. The recovered drugs were floating in a waterproof Ziploc baggie. The owner of the drugs had not yet been established or questioned.

Despite the seriousness of the accident and the drug implications, the police told Ruby that given the status of the case and the medical gravity of the situation, the drug issue had been temporarily put on hold.

"However," they emphasized, "Make no mistake madam, the matter will be investigated in a few days, after each of the victims are able to give their statements."

Although Ruby was relieved to hear this, she was too distressed and overcome by the news of the accident to be appreciative for any official police gesture. The detective's words, 'each of victims', echoed through her mind, as she wondered how many people had actually been involved? How many others had been hurt? Were there any fatalities?

Her brain questioned, *why Jazz and Nico were on a boat. Where in hell did, they get a boat?*

For as distraught as she was, she was discreet enough not to ask the police officers any questions about Nico Rossario or show them any elderly emotional weakness. The situation was already too tricky, complicated, and risky.

The shocking report of the boating accident had upset her terribly. She was angry and disappointed with herself. If she hadn't chosen to remain longer outdoors reading, she would have been indoors and heard her diner's telephone ringing. Although her intentions had been slightly selfish, they were blameless. After the stride filled morning she'd had, battling with the diner's newest employee, she'd hoped that seeing a magnificent sunset would put a positive spin on a day that the teenage troublemaker from the States had tried to ruin for her. She wasn't sure when, but she'd fallen into a deep sleep, mid-chapter, while listening to the rhythmic sound of the waves washing up on the shore. Since she was a youngster, the sound of water had soothed her, as it drowned out the chaos in her mind. This was the reason why, she explained to the officers, she hadn't heard her telephone when their precinct tried to contact her. The police officers didn't appreciate her excuse for not being available; however, they respected her because she was so old, and rather charming in an eccentrically geriatric way.

Despite her charismatic personality, the officers used every spec of authority they had over her. One constable questioned Ruby in detail, while his partner freely lectured her by saying, "If she was going to be responsible for a teenager, she needed to get with the times and invest in a mobile phone."

Their tactics were the lamest police performance she'd ever seen. So lame in fact, that the elderly woman thought the officers were downright on the near side of comical. Regardless, she knew she deserved some degree of reprimanding, so she swallowed her pride and acted in a more age-appropriate way. Moreover, she'd been taught at a very young age when to laugh and when to obey. Therefore, even though she had no intention whatsoever of following their advice, she nodded agreeably. Ruby had been born without anything digital attached to her life. For this reason she had no internet, and she didn't own a PC, a laptop, or even a tablet. Why in the hell would she need a mobile telephone? She was too old to start making room in her life, or in her grave, for the bloody likes of modern technology! This was a strong conviction that the perceptive diner owner decided to keep to herself in front of the coppers.

Truth be told, she thought the officers did have a proper point. Being accountable for a teenager was indeed something she was not used to anymore. Deep-seated, suppressed, and bleak memories of when she was a single mother raising a daughter on her own was unexpectedly and harshly resurfacing. Between her daunting mental memoirs and the news of the accident, Ruby was more frightened than she dared let on. Since the police officers had found her on the beach, she'd worn a calm, straight-faced mask. Since she was a young girl, she'd been wearing invisible, concealing masks whenever she needed to disguise her anxiety or fear. They were masks only she could see, whenever she caught a glimpse of her face in any reflective surface she passed by.

About twenty minutes after the police had arrived at The Seaside, she'd ridden to the hospital in their cruiser with her arm draped over one of her oldest possessions. Rubbing the surface of the antique wooden trunk on the seat next to her had made her feel safe and grounded. While sitting behind 'nit & wit', she realized that the trunk was giving her courage to face the dire situation she anticipated she was about to be confronted with. She felt a speck of personal pride for thinking to take it out of the diner's annex and bring it with her after being drawn to it in a way she hadn't been for decades.

Hearing the ting of a ceiling bell, her mind left her thoughts behind and returned to what she was doing. Steadily, she stepped off the elevator on the ground floor and exited Saint Matthew's sprawling lobby through the hospital's main entrance. Ruby hadn't planned to leave the child alone in the

ICU, nonetheless, despite her earnest efforts, she wasn't able to find anyone at the hospital willing to let her borrow their cell phone and make an emergency international call. Even her forlorn, babushka expressions, or offering cash for the phone, call wasn't convincing enough. She rightly understood this, knowing that ringing up America from any type of telephone would be expensive. In hindsight, it was better that no one assisted her given that she'd never used a mobile before and hadn't memorized the Durant's home number. Since spending the entire day in the ICU, Ruby had nothing left to give. Despite her apprehensions for leaving Jazz alone on the seventh floor, she was dog-tired and on the verge of surrender. Therefore, she'd sensibly hail a taxi and go home. Once she was back at her diner, she'd call the child's mother before packing an overnight bag and returning to the intensive care unit.

A full moon was casting its golden beauty across the entire city of London. The early evening summer air in Great Britain was typically cool and slightly damp. Standing curbside while waiting for a taxi, she was obliged to the chilly air she now stood in. Spending the past six hours on the top floor of a stale, poorly ventilated and considerably warm hospital, had been very demanding on her body. Being outdoors again, with her straw hat atop her white-haired head while waiting for the cab, was invigorating. Filled with gratitude, she deeply inhaled the fresh evening air. It took only a few minutes for her to feel more alert than she'd felt all day. She was convinced that deeply inhaling fresh air every day, regardless of the weather, is what had kept her alive longer than people from her 1920's generation were meant to live.

When the taxicab punctually arrived, a polite, dark-skinned male driver got out and offered to assist the elderly woman into his cab's back seat. Too fatigued to have a tug of war with the stubborn side of her personality, she graciously accepted his help. The cabbie's tinted skin colour, dark hair, and even darker eyes, reminded her of Nico's striking Italian features. Thinking of Nico had her fighting off uncooperative tears that were welling up in her eyes. Needing to get home more than she needed to cry, she intentionally pushed thoughts of her dishwasher out of her mind and took the cabdriver's supportive arm.

The driver was a gentle and patient man who introduced himself as, 'Deniz with a Z'. He cautiously held Ruby's elbow as she painstakingly positioned herself onto the back seat. After she had properly thanked him, he closed the cab door and promptly took his place behind the steering wheel.

"Where can I take you madam?" he courteously asked.

She gave him her address, buckled her seatbelt, and covered her shoulders and back with the fleece blanket she'd snuck out of the ICU. She then crisscrossed the sides of the blanket forward and over her body and hugged herself with it. The blanket immediately felt like a trusting friend, so she knew she'd never bring it back to the hospital. She was slightly devious and underhanded in this way. Ruby reached over and rolled the window on her side of the taxicab all the way down. She wanted to bask in the cool air as it wafted into the cab's backseat. She hoped that the night air would invigorate her in the same way the sunbeams in the child's ICU room had. It had been a very long day indoors and she now had a serious craving for another Coca

Cola. Since officially opening her diner in 1960, Coca Cola and fresh air were two reliable highpoints of her days. She smirked at herself, realizing that she'd taken a fancy to Coca Cola long before the handsome cabbie in the front seat was even born. The elderly woman was delighting in the cab driver's reflection in his rearview mirror. Finding pleasure in the face of a handsome man was something she'd never grown too old to do. She was a flirt and Mother Nature's girl at heart. Wholeheartedly, she alleged that *'a day spent entirely indoors was an entirely wasted day'*. This was a slogan she'd heard hundreds of times while spending school vacations as a young girl at her grandma Bessie's ranch on the American Great Plains. Some of her finest memories were born and raised on and across the grasslands of Montana.

By the time the taxi parked outside The Seaside she was feeling alive, revived, and wide-awake. Despite that she'd only been away for the latter part of the day, being home again was comforting. She then exited the cab with the driver's assistance, paid the fare, and explicitly instructed him to return in ninety minutes and not one single minute later. If he arrived earlier, he was not to interrupt her. She had things she needed to deal with and did not tolerate interruptions of any kind.

"Just give your horn a few loud toots and hoots and I will come out on my own," she precisely instructed the cabbie.

Deniz nodded in agreement and waved chivalrously as he pulled away from the curb and onto the coastal road adjacent to the diner. Ruby could see that it was an innocent and teasing wave, which made her like the driver straight off. Reaching out to unlock and open the diner door, she saw a bright yellow, handwritten cardboard sign informing her customer's that the diner was closed due to a family emergency. She had completely forgotten about hanging the sign up minutes before the police officers accompanied her and trunk to the hospital. The vivid sign still hung with dignity and purpose next to a white Plexiglas sign with bold red letters. The Plexiglas sign was a permanent addition to the window that Ruby had hung up many years ago.

It read: No Bare Feet • No Internet • No Wi-Fi • No Smoking

Standing outside the diner's entrance, with key in hand, the events of the day began rushing back at her. As she opened the door her freethinking wilful mind strayed back to earlier that morning. She flicked on the overhead lights and entered her place of business and her home base. Turning around to close the door, she felt an insensitive, merciless emotional tidal wave trying to have its bloody squally way with her; causing her to be slightly dizzy and unsteady as she stepped back into her world. Regardless, she instantly sensed her diner's familiar atmosphere embracing her. She felt shielded and confident again.

It had been a very long and uncertain day. Nevertheless, that didn't matter right now. She had returned to her peaceful space; to the place where she could be her true, uninhibited self. The diner looked exactly as it had before the boating accident had crudely disrupted her life and changed everything in the blink of an eye. Ruby put her handbag and straw hat down on the Formica countertop next to the cash register, or the till, as Brits liked to call it. Then, she meticulously glanced around her pride and joy, her income, and her life. A few minutes later, she realized that she'd forgotten to lock the door behind her. After doing so, she walked towards the kitchen to pour herself a large glass of water and fetched a cold bottle of Coke from the walk-in cooler. Seeing her reflection in the long mirror hanging behind the counter, she stared intensely at the earthly image looking back at her. She thought she looked older than she had when she'd woken up that morning.

"As if looking older than almost nine decades is even possible!" she retorted with a laugh.

Ruby's felt her mind on the verge of drifting. Because she was physically drained and her brain had more energy than her body did, her mind kept wandering. Before calling Zofia, the child's mother, she elected to spoil herself with what she referred to as a 'mini dose of self-regard'. She was certain that Eliza's daughter's reaction would be SO over the top that she'd need to be equipped to handle it. After all, mental illness had been drowning in their ancestral pool for generations. Her intuition told her that spending time alone in the hospital today with Jazz and being alone now to regroup after the intensity of the day, were important parts of being ready and able to make such a dreaded phone call. Her intuition was strong and wise. This made listening to it, and then following it, a simple and natural thing to do. Looking up at the clock hanging above the entrance door, the elderly woman was extremely grateful for the time difference that separated England and California. The different time zones had given her the gift of more hours for herself before ringing up America. Her bright green eyes looked through her round black spectacles and zeroed in on her Barcalounger in the far corner of the diner. Her favourite chair was beckoning her. Hearing its cry for attention, she added crushed ice from an automatic ice dispenser to her water glass, filling it to the brim. So many thoughts had been slipping in and out of her mind since paying the cabbie that she'd forgotten all about her hankering desire for a bottle of Coca Cola. Then she hobbled over to her Barcalounger and plopped herself down for a well-deserved rest. Ruby then proceeded to bend over to remove her boots and air out her overheated bare feet with ten crooked toes attached to them.

In spite of her familiar sugar craving, she wasn't thirsty. She intended to use the icy water to keep her brain observant. Staying alert and sharp-eyed would prevent her from mentally traveling too far and for too long. Holding an ice filled glass between her hands and making them colder and colder would keep her mind aware and her body grounded. Likewise, it would keep her awake. She'd devised her mind control technique of hers years back, when she was a teenager living in Essex County and attending middle school.

"Until now, it has worked each time and never let me down," she softly declared, "Why should tonight be any different?"

With her crinkly, nippy hands quickly cooling down, she pushed the soles of her feet firmly into the floor. Then, the barefoot diner owner scrutinized her place of business and gave her mind permission to beckon up the past.

Chapter 11

The Seaside was over sixty years old, and it was timeless. Ruby had decided not to change its name when she purchased it. The popular diner had always been known as The Seaside and changing its long-lived identity didn't feel right or necessary, so its identity was safe with her. Another reason for not changing the name was that the young owner was financially much too frugal to waste money on new, expensive signs and menus. She did consider naming it, Ruby's or Ruby's Place, which she opted not to do given that putting herself or her name in the spotlight was simply not her style.

The original diner has been built out of stable and long-lasting materials. It had a unique and durable style that was ageless. Its 1950s exclusivity included chrome framed, red trimmed Solotone jukeboxes, and gleaming solid brass coat racks fixed to its dining booths. Each of the diner's twelve booths had been designed to seat two to six people comfortably. Customers dining alone were encouraged by Ruby and her staff to take a seat at the diner's elongated counter. The counter was lengthy and accommodated up to twelve people. It had a thick, shiny limestone top with oblique chrome-trimmed, curved corners. Twelve tall and round, red upholstered decorative bar stools, securely bolted to the floor, were located in front of the spacious counter. The stools added a splashy flair to the diner's authenticity.

Not long after she purchased The Seaside, she intentionally introduced a new 'single customer dining rule'. She claimed that customers eating by themselves at a large table often were lonely and wasted the space needed to use for larger groups.

Loneliness and waste had always been things she would not allow at her place of work, in her home, or in life. It didn't take long for the single customer dining policy she'd initiated to be accepted and become as trendy as she was. As the years turned into decades, countless new friendships were born and nurtured between people dining alone. Three short months after she purchased The Seaside, the counter area had become a more popular place to sit than the booths were. The steamy aroma of fresh brewed coffee rolling across its limestone surface was rightly alluring for her patrons. Although her diner hosted an interesting group of regulars, Ruby favoured watching parents with youngsters sitting at the counter. She particularly enjoyed seeing mums dining out with their little daughters. These mothers and daughters reminded her of a time gone by, when her own daughter, Eliza Emilia, was but a wee lass.

The elderly diner owner, still relaxing in her lounge chair, held firmly onto the ice-filled glass between her hands. She knew that her passion for recollecting the past was partly because she was a longstanding member of the senior citizen class of Brits. Born in the 1920s, she was a true and blue British purebred who'd long since passed the eight-decade marker. Because of the purebreds distinguished ages, they each had a profound appreciation for their most recent, their oldest, and their recurring memories. Ruby was one of the fortunate amongst this particular class of Brits. As she aged, her brain remained abnormally strong and sharp, while so many others in her age group were afflicted with dementia and Alzheimer's disease.

Filled with sincerity and gratefulness that she'd been spared such a fate, she tapped once more into her brain and let it take her back to a time she'd appreciated and could remember with ease. She was in the mood to mentally drift. In the mid-1950s, eating out was a rare event in the world she had created for herself and Eliza. Dining out was something they did together, on special occasions, after the threat of WWII had finally departed Britain. Throughout those years, Ruby hoped that while they were out and about, they'd randomly run into her best friend Emilia Doherty. Unfortunately, this never happened. Emilia lived in Northern Ireland at the time, so the chance of an unexpected reunion was rare at best. Back then, it was wishful and unrealistic dreaming on Ruby's part to think that their paths would just one day casually cross.

Eventually and in no time, her little girl became a young woman. As one year rolled off another year, the often hectic life they shared daily was changing. For this reason, Ruby's memories of Emilia, her one, and only best friend slithered into the chaotic side of her London life as a mother raising a child on her own. The last time she'd spoken to her, Emilia was still living in Belfast with her parents and her toddler son. Mia was a farm girl born and raised and she was three years younger than Ruby. Many more months of Sunday's would have to come and go before Emilia would even suspect that Ruby also had become a mother. The post-war 1950s was a turbulent time in Europe. After the war ended, people who'd survived it spent decades rebuilding their lives and restoring whatever they still possessed or could salvage, which for millions of them was next to nothing. With Emilia now occupying the elderly woman's thoughts, her eyes fluttered and closed. Her mind began traveling deeper and farther into the past.

Recognizing that she was about to relive a time that had birthed the first notable highlight of her life, she relaxed and trusted her mind to be kind to her heart. It was the end of 1951 and Emilia Doherty, Mia for short, was in serious trouble. It was the kind of trouble that, even her best friend, Ruby McEwen's superb problem-solving skills couldn't help her with. An unresolvable problem was dividing the friends. After two inseparable years together, their time at the Home for Unwed Mothers in Dublin was suddenly ending. Soon, they would be separated, and they could do absolutely nothing about their predicament. They were powerless to fight the approaching change. Their misfortune had begun twenty-five months earlier and had grown into a force that was mightier than the two of them combined was. At approximately 11:00 pm, on the second day of September, in the year 1949, Emilia Doherty's parents secretly sent their pregnant and unwed, 15-year-old daughter away. Camouflaged by the darkness of the night, Mia was forced to leave the family farm with nothing but the clothes on her back. A buckskin water pack hung around her neck. In her coat pocket were ten shillings. The coins had angry bulls on one side and Celtic harps on the other side. Emilia was strictly instructed to give the money to the carriage coach driver upon her arrival as payment for his services and discretion.

While in route, a real chance for escaping did present itself. Nevertheless, when the driver stopped to take a proper crapper in the woods, Emilia was too scared to run away. She knew the beefy, bearded man, with hair covered knuckles and grimy fingernails, craved a 'hale and hearty' shit because he had boldly professed his 'dung detail' to her. From behind a large pine tree, a mere meter away from Emilia, he hunkered down and pushed Irish poo out of his equally hairy, fat, pimple-covered bum.

"Me missus musta' fed me bad piece of pork for suppa' sees how the shits be a squirtin' out of me poor ole' burnin' arse like sewer water," he revealed, through loud sighs of relief.

Mia cringed, covered her ears, and tried to ignore the vision she had of him squatting and squirting bare-assed behind the tree.

Her trip to Dublin's Home for Unwed Mothers took place when she was in her first trimester and her pregnancy was still physically undetectable. To shield their upstanding Doherty name from disgrace, the girl's parents insisted that both her pregnancy and the inevitable birth be kept hidden. Being ousted from their local Belfast farming and religious communities was a risk they were not willing to take. Not even for their only daughter who was with child. The villagers, churchgoers, and neighbours alike, were told that the very young Emilia Doherty had been sent off to do her part in helping to supplement her family's income. After all, the Irish people knew that times were hard, and money was scarce.

Her parents went on to say that "Being the virtuous girl that she was, she would be working for eighteen months away from home. Her duties would include being a live-in nanny and maid for an affluent couple with four little 'male chisellers' all under the ages of six mind you!"

Her kinfolk declared that "Mia was a born and bred 'Irish culchie' who was proud of her hometown and family roots, so for this reason they knew she would be just fine."

Stacking one lie upon another, her parents stoically told the villagers that the four young lad's very overworked father had himself an addiction for the black liquid called Guinness. Apparently, the man's wife couldn't handle their boisterous, naughty offspring in addition to her daily domestic duties. It was no wonder they'd reached out for help. Hereafter, whilst Mia was in their employ, she'd be teaching the young rascals correct behaviour and she'd tend to the daily household chores. Ireland was still in the clutches of a weak, post-World War II economy. For this reason, Ma and Pa Doherty's decision was admired as a satisfactory choice. The arrangement they made for their daughter was never questioned or examined by anyone. Consequently, two manipulative liars polished and practiced their conniving scheme at their farm during the week and took it with them to church on Sundays.

Folks acquainted with Mia and her parents, who were filled with respect and sympathetic regard, would say, "What a brave and devoted daughter the Doherty's had."

Church folks even doled out compliments like, "Emilia was fortunate to have parents with such generous hearts. An Irish mamaí and dadaí, who out of goodness in their souls were willing to send their only daughter off to a family more in need than they were."

Ma and Pa Doherty's act of kind-heartedness was considered by all to be nothing shy of commendable. Hence, a family lie was born, and a religious swindle was concocted.

"Blasphemy with a capital B!" was Mia's only outspoken reaction, when she was informed about her parent's very tall, deceptive tale.

Her five-word retaliation earned her, in a split-second, a hard, stinging, openhanded slap across the face from her furious father. The slap was followed by her mother forcing her to clench a bar of soap between her teeth for thirty minutes. Emilia's parents were fervent believers in their use of harsh discipline. After about twenty-four minutes, Emilia vomited. Her mother twisted her fingers in the girl's long hair, yanked her daughter's head back, ordered her to clean up her sudsy puke and rinse the bar it off and return it to the soap dish! Slapping and a symbolic soap cleansing, after any behaviour violation their children were guilty of making, were very common occurrences under their roof. These were only a few types of juvenile punishments that Ma and Pa Doherty relied on to send clear disciplinary messages to their Irish offspring. Physical pain was resorted to and used whenever needed. When their hard reprimands didn't impress their misbehaving children enough, off came their father's belt. Depending how many lashes one or both of their children received, they'd sit sorely and act the way they were expected to for the next week to ten days.

The Doherty family secret had been hidden and protected by sending their pregnant daughter away, and by the convenient isolation of their remote farmhouse. Emilia's humiliated, devoutly religious parents, and her older brother, each wanted her to experience a hauntingly painful delivery. Her brother was also born and raised under their parent's curse; accordingly he was rightly more afraid of them than his sister was. Being afraid for blood and having no backbone or mind of his own, he'd always sided with his parents, no matter what they said, thought, or did. Mia was the courageous rebel in the family. Her brother was the cowardly conformist. Since they were kids, for every five punishments their parents doled out, at least four of them had Emilia's name stamped on them. Now that she was pregnant, her family pled to their Dear God, that an oversized, colicky baby would exit her young, petite body in the most excruciating of ways. Her parent's deepest desire was that an enormous, fussy newborn be delivered so that their 'moral less spinster daughter' would, under no circumstances, be spreading her long, agreeable legs again. Nor would she be lusting after unmarried sex for a second time, only to be implanted with more sinfully wicked male seeds.

Since abortion was illegal in Ireland and a mortal sin in the eyes of the Catholic Church, terminating the baby's life was not an option. Even if the opportunity did present itself to them, they would have refused it. Ma and Pa Doherty concluded that the only way to teach their floozy daughter a true lesson was to have her suffer through the pains of a gruelling labour. Thereafter, for all they cared, she could later live out her life with the demure consequences of having a sham of a child, whom they'd denounce, alongside her evil choice, and her immoral ways. If Mia had revealed the name of the boy, or Dear Lord forbid, told them that a nearly 30-year-old man had forcefully impregnated her, the bloke would have been beaten up and hung by his horny balls from the highest beam in the family barn! However, her refusal to name him meant that their decadent daughter would be required to carry the heavy burdens of an unwed sin all on her own; before and after the child entered the world. Little did they know, at the time, that Emilia would go on to prove them extremely wrong? Their fabrications and desires were two ambitions that her heartless parents prayed for each Sunday during mass, as they piously lit their holy votive candles. There they stood. Side by side. A mother and a father, holding their lit tapers in front of a statue of the Blessed Virgin Mary. Dressed in their Sunday best, with heads held high, they demonstrated steady hands as their candle wicks caught the tapers flame and began to flicker. The soft, goldish glow, that radiated upwards and under their sinful chins, added a rather convincing tint to their deception.

Mia's Irish 'dadaí looked rather dashing, wearing his formal satin dickey collar, a black necktie, and his plaid suitcoat. Likewise, her Irish mamaí, playing her part, wore a perky white, starched kerchief that she'd reverently tied under her neck. As a sign of respect and modesty the Roman Catholic Church required all women to wear a head covering whilst inside the House of God. This meant that Mia's mum, like other spiritual women, had a dresser drawer filled with headscarves of various colours. Today, for an obvious reason, she had chosen to wear her purest white kerchief. There he stood. A well-informed and dubious priest, nodding with approval as he heard the chinking and clinking sounds of the Doherty's weekly contribution coins falling into his tin collection can. A sly, fox-like grin graced his face as he held the money canister in front of them. He looked more like a street beggar with a filthy objective than a Man of the Cloth. There they sat. A congregation oblivious to the skeletons Mia's parents were hiding, and the sins they were committing before their very eyes and in the presence of their Beloved God.

There they remained. A compassionate parish, proud of Emilia Doherty for the sacrifice she had made in the name of her family; whilst completely unaware of the atrocious thoughts and dreadful yearnings poisoning her parent's twisted minds and selfish souls. Week after week, as Ma and Pa Doherty stood before Jesus Christ himself, their malevolent thoughts against their ostracized, pregnant daughter lingered on. This sinister religious cycle continued for the next twenty-two months of Sundays, as the Doherty's methodically carried out a clever swindle.

With a venomous kind of devotion and innate skill, Mia's parents became masters at protecting their lies and meticulously acting out their deceitful roles.

Chapter 12

The elderly woman's hands trembled, and her body suddenly jerked. She rustled anxiously in her Barcalounger as her troubled mind erratically continued to drift in reverse.

Shortly after they'd met and a few months into Mia's pregnancy the girls went strolling arm in arm through University of Dublin's botanical gardens. At the time Mia still lived at the Unwed Mothers Home and Ruby lived just off campus with a chubby, spoiled, shedding tomcat.

During their walk, Mia had told Ruby that, "As her belly grew, so did her parent's skill of keeping her pregnancy a dirty, hidden secret."

She went on to ask Ruby, "How could I spite them for it? After all, they are only acting the way decent, honourable Irish Catholic people were expected to act."

Despite Ruby's outwardly astonished reaction at hearing this, Mia continued defending her parents and the Catholic Church.

Something is very wrong with this sick scenario, Ruby silently decided.

"Protecting the reputation of family and church is something Christian's are groomed for the moment Baptism makes us children of God," Mia would claim.

Hearing this was rightly conflicting for the young, blinkered Ruby. In her opinion, Mia's brainwashed religious convictions were appalling. Her friend's words and religious persuasions became something she'd learned to respect yet was never was able to accept or forget. One evening while walking home from the university Ruby wondered, *what would become of Mia's religious beliefs and faith if she ever returned to her parent's strict influences?*

Six months later, and three weeks ahead of schedule, Emilia Doherty gave birth to a premature peewee. He was a fine-looking, lively baby boy. The child bore a striking resemblance to his almost 16-year-old mummy. He had a headful of golden-red curls, a button nose, and two perfectly round, pea-sized dimples. Mia's delivery lasted a mere thirty-six minutes, which she'd shrieked and panted through with angry resolve and lungs of steel. The next day, she scarcely remembered any pain or the sounds of her own screams. Even the merciless nun, who'd flopped the newborn down with a loud wet thud onto his mum's still contracting belly, had gone unnoticed. The tiny baby boy wiggled and waggled like a frog out of water.

"This one has got spunk in his veins," was the only thing the indifferent, rude nun had said to Emilia throughout her labour and the delivery.

When Mia first touched her son, his spiral-shaped umbilical cord was still warm, attached, and pumping nutrient rich blood from her body into his. His elated, teenage mum named him Emmet Mac McEwen Doherty. Emmet was a name that reminded Emilia of her own name. Mac was the first middle name Mia gave him, because she was a teenager and Mia and Mac sounded hands down too cute to dismiss. McEwen, his second middle name, was for honouring his Aunty Ruby's role in his life. The newborn's last name would be Doherty, because this was compulsory according to Irish Surname Law at the time. The only things oversized about the spunky little newborn were his distinctively large ears, which naturally came to be the two things his equally big eared Aunty Ruby cherished the most about him.

Around sundown, on November 22, in the year 1952, the best friend's dilemma began. It had been officially announced that Mia was being forced to leave the Irish Catholic Home for Unwed Mothers. Ruby and Emilia had genuinely shared a glorious two years together in Dublin, caring for and falling in love with baby Emmet and with each other. All awhile, they raised enough Irish shenanigans to have angry nuns regularly chasing them through the facility's corridors. Despite the lifestyle they'd both grown to know and cherish, newly implemented post-war Irish residency policies were more than Mia could compete with. After stalling her departure for many weeks, because she couldn't take Ruby with her, Emilia was told that she had no options left. Her room and Emmet's crib were needed for a new girl about to give birth. A few of the kinder staff members at the unwed mother's facility had hinted that this was nothing more than 'an administrative fabrication'. Regardless, Mia was explicitly told she was to leave the property within twenty-four hours, otherwise baby Emmet would be taken from her, and she'd be arrested as a trespasser by a local law enforcement agency.

Ruby pleaded with the head administrator on Mia's behalf. Sitting across from his desk and his oversized Bible displayed on an oversized easel, she begged numerous times, saying, "It is almost winter. Emilia and Emmet would surely freeze to death outdoors on the streets."

She was brazenly told that, "Neither the weather, nor the seasons of the year, had any influence on the timing or scheduling of anyone's departure. Be it the mother, the child, or both. The shelter had provided for Mia and her son for just shy of two years. Enough kindness had been rendered, enough money had been spent, and enough procrastination had been tolerated! Mia would be given only one opportunity to take Emmet with her. A second chance would not be offered. If she left her child behind, as so many other young, desperate, unwed mothers did, he would be raised at the home as an orphan."

Hearing the word 'procrastination' reminded Ruby of what her hardworking African American grandma Bessie Dutton used to say.

People procrastinate because they are afraid- afraid of failing, of pain and of the unknown. She'd go on to tell Ruby, *not to put off doing, today what needs to be done, because tomorrow may never come.*

"Best be warned," the threat from the administrator continued, "if the Unwed Mothers Home didn't receive her 'fare for care' she'd be obliged to remain at the Home for up to three years paying off her £100 birthing debt, plus lodging and food expenses."

To add fire to the fury, the headmaster went on to say, "If Emilia chose to stay, baby Emmet would be separated from his mother between 7am and 7pm, seven days a week."

Hearing this had Ruby's mind raging with anger. Her mouth opened before she had time to leash her temper.

"In other words, being a poor, destitute 16-year-old mum, Emilia Doherty is a prisoner of the very system that had provided for her in the past two years since her parents discarded her!" She boldly stated to the resolute priest.

Unimpressed by her cheekiness and lack of respect for his institution, he remained unwavering. Her outburst resulted in her being instantly dismissed as a volunteer and banned from the facility for the next sixty days.

"Sod-off," she murmured, unaware of how fortunate she was that he didn't hear her.

Realistic enough to know that she was penniless, unemployed, and unable to survive on her own living on the streets, Emmet's mum made a selfless and responsible decision. Unwilling to accept any of the options that the facility administrator had proposed, Mia bid Ruby a miserable farewell. Emilia then took a leap of faith and returned to her parent's farm in Belfast. Not knowing if they would take her in again, and having no alternative, it was a risk she was obliged to take for the sake of her son. Mia walked and hitchhiked the entire one hundred twenty-two kilometres. Fourteen-month-old baby Emmet was strapped securely to her side with a long, dark green cloth. His mum and Aunty Ruby had torn their bed sheets into wide strips, then hand-sewed the cloth bands together to create a proper baby carrying swaddle. It looked like a papoose that Indian squaws used to carry their young children. Ruby had seen one of these Indian papooses in a picture book at the university library where she was studying Journalism. She and Mia had brilliantly, and in detail, copied the idea. They were both quite proud of their motivated cleverness and the end result.

A few days later, Ruby, who was ready to wave her best friend off, gave Mia an umbrella and a knapsack filled with items she'd been gathering, actually stealing, from the facility's supply room for the past few weeks. She'd anticipated that 'expulsion day' would arrive sooner than Emilia would be ready to receive it. In Ruby's experience with other young unwed mothers who'd bonded with their children, a facility expulsion always took the mum by surprise and left them devastated. She knew all too well that when evictions took place without prior notice, they pushed new mums out of the security they felt as members of their Irish circle of unwed mother. Ruby handed Mia her umbrella. It would shield Emmet and his mum from Ireland's tritely cool and wet late October climate. Autumn days could be warm, yet the nights were cold, damp, and windy, with predictable rain showers. The dark brown canvas knapsack Mia had slung over her shoulder was filled with lightweight food portions, plenty of nappies, water, and boxed milk. Ruby had pinched the items from the university's campus kitchen where she worked. She'd persuaded herself that she was doing charity work on a wee child's behalf, rather than turning into a thief. Her mindset helped her to live guilt-free with her well-intended, yet outright illegal deeds.

Emilia was still breast-feeding, which was something the nuns all deemed scandalous. Each time baby Emmet latched onto one of her nipples, the nuns' nasty reactions fuelled Mia's desire to spite them, which she underhandedly did by breastfeeding her son even longer. *Sweet revenge at its finest*, she'd think, each time a nun scowled at her while Mac suckled. As his mummy's milk dripped off his little chin, the white habits the nuns wore on their heads as a visible sign of their devotion to God and Jesus wilted before Mia's eyes. Aside from Ruby, wilting nun habits would be the only other thing she'd miss seeing each day after she left the holy building. Fortunately, like the heifers on her Pa Doherty's farm, the young mother produced a great quantity of milk. Her maternal good fortune meant feeding baby Emmet along the journey would be the least of her worries. That evening, by the camouflage of a familiar darkness that reminded her of the night her parents sent her away, Emilia Mia Doherty disappeared into the night.

Ruby's last memory of that evening was of baby Emmet cosily wrapped up and fast asleep in his dark green papoose. He was wearing his little orange and blue striped, hooded winter jacket. His mittens were tied securely around his plump wrists. Ruby had cut a small hole in his left-hand mitten so he could still suck his thumb. Mia called him her 'little ciotog' because the boy was as left-handed as left-handed could be. Being able to quickly find and suck his thumb would be calming, whenever their travels became too much for him. When his only aunty saw him for the last time, he was hanging from his mum's back, sleeping soundly and completely unaware of what kind of life he was headed towards. Ruby had briefly caught a glimpse of Mia standing across the campus walkway under the golden radiance of a university street lantern. She thought her best friend from Belfast was one of the prettiest and kindest girls she'd ever met. Bravely and dry-eyed they waved goodbye to each other. Neither of them sheds a single tear. As she watched Mia and Mac dwindle and disappear into the shadows of the darkness, Ruby suspected this would be the last she'd see of either of them.

Of this, she was certain. And Ruby McEwen was rarely wrong.

The tick tock ticking of the diner's large vintage wall clock annoyingly brought her mind back to the here and now. Still sitting in her favourite lounger, she opened her eyes, adjusted her spectacles, and glanced up at the clattering clock. She was relieved to see that she still had plenty of time before the cabdriver would be returning to fetch her. Desiring to dawdle in the olden days with Mia Doherty for a bit longer, she closed her eyes again. With her usual Cheetah-like mental speed, in three blinks of an eye, her brain took her back to the year 1972.

The sound of an elusive sigh meant that the unruffled elderly woman was now calm and mentally drifting again. Within twenty seconds she crossed over and re-entered the past.

Chapter 13

The United Kingdom was experiencing an unusually warm, sun kissed summer. Brits across the island were outside in droves. This meant a record number of customers for The Seaside. The eatery's owner hadn't seen this many people at the English Channel's coastline since her diner had officially re-opened twelve years ago. She was in her 'people-pleasing element' and in a decorously cheery British mood.

Today was proving itself to be yet another frantic workday for Ruby and her staff. She was chatting it up with a one of her regular customers, when Emilia Doherty unexpectedly walked into The Seaside. As all first-time customers did, Emilia waited her turn. She didn't mind waiting because her hope and plan was to surprise her all-time dearest of friends. Hanging in the shadows at the end of the line was the first part of her plan. It had been nearly two decades since the best friends from the 1950s had seen each other. The Dublin farm girl, born and raised, was somewhat apprehensive that she might have changed too much, and Ruby might not recognize her. After all, more than twenty years had passed since their final farewell in Dublin, and time wasn't necessarily kind to aging women. Stealthily, she took her place behind the line of people who were waiting to be seated. This gave Mia a chance to take a gander at the diner's owner in action while anticipating her amazed reaction to their reunion. Fixated on Ruby, Mia loved what she saw. She loved all of it and she loved all of her.

They recognized each other instantly and hugged like the shocked soulmates that they were. Then they proceeded to squeal like two euphoric teenagers. The women were still as free and uninhibited as they'd been the day, they met each other in Ireland. Ruby and Mia had been like two harmonious peas in a pod while living in Dublin; as different as they were alike and in sync. Ruby was dark skinned, tall and sturdy. Mia was fair skinned, many inches shorter and petite. Mia had long, thick, ginger coloured hair flowing down her back, while Ruby had gorgeous shoulder length, auburn hair that accented her dark, prominent features. Ruby's bright green eyes looked like two glass marbles when sunlight shone on them. Mia had nearly identically bright eyes, the colour of a clear blue ocean. Both women had long fingers and full lips that had been generously coloured a dark shade of red at birth. Their looks were as alluring as they were diverse. Despite this, their personalities and life energies were almost identical. Even though at the time they were unaware of it, back in the early 50s, this was what had attracted them to each other the most.

On that day, in 1972, when Emilia entered The Seaside, a new and unforeseen adventure followed her inside. Their elated screeches and hugs were heard and witnessed by everyone in the diner and outside on the beach. When they realized that they both were wearing virtually matching flashy designer jumpsuits, the women roared with laughter. Their one-piece garments were the latest fashion trend being imported straight from Paris.

Ruby's jumpsuit was flowered and calf length. Mia's was plaid and ankle length. Seeing their reflections in the long mirror behind the diner's counter became one of the funniest moments they'd ever shared. They both agreed that they looked like two middle-aged, wannabe Barbie dolls.

Ruby's short order cook immediately left his kitchen and sprinted into the main dining area. He removed his food-stained apron and eagerly began to clap. In less than fifteen seconds everyone in the place, regulars and newcomers alike, were standing and enthusiastically joining in. Rounds of applause, hooting, and hollering that echoed throughout the diner and from the beachside patio definitely took the women by surprise. Their cheeks turned a lovely, blushing, cheery shade of crimson. The ecstatic women simultaneously bowed deeply, the way famous entertainers did when receiving standing ovations. As one final gesture, they waved their handkerchiefs at the crowd of customers. Ruby had a green polka dotted hanky and Mia's was white with red polka dots. When they realized that they even had the same hankies, their happiness could be heard outside to the farthest corner of the parking lot. On that afternoon and in a rare moment like this, The Seaside was enchanted.

After receiving a final round of applause and standing ovation, Ruby introduced Emilia to her staff and patrons, then she decided to close early and take the rest of the day off. She was understaffed because of the amazing summertime weather conditions, so due to this, Mia carried on and helped her out. Her best friend from Ireland worked like an experienced diner employee, clearing the tables, wiping them down, and polishing the red upholstered chrome-trimmed bar stools. While they worked, they yakked, and yakked, and yakked. Even twenty plus years later, neither of them was at a loss for words. Immediately after the last customer and employee departed for the day, Ruby hung up the closed sign. Then the exhilarated women took their excitement out of the diner and down to the shoreline. Under a sunny sky, they walked barefoot and gabbed nonstop along the seashore for almost two hours. Finally, they stopped to take a rest. They'd both agreed that they were thirsty and that they weren't in their twenties anymore. With aching legs and wet, sand covered toes, Mia and Ruby spread a blanket and sat down on it. Sitting closely, side by side, they covered their four cold feet and twenty numbing toes with a large beach towel. After opening a bottle of wine from the picnic basket they'd brought, they heartedly toasted their reunion. Unbeknownst to the other, both women took pleasure in the taste of fine oak flavoured wine. In silence, they sipped Chardonnay and gazed out at the distant skyline.

A few hours earlier, after the hype of their reunion had died down and the diner reclaimed its normal late afternoon pace, Ruby caught herself staring at Mia while she mingled with the staff. Truthfully, Ruby was a touch envious that Mia had remained so attractive. Ruby had never considered herself the eye-catching type. Despite that her father, Horace, and her grandparents had repeatedly told her that she was, she never actually felt physically appealing. It was known that Ruby liked to dress slightly funky; nevertheless, she didn't do this to enhance or improve her looks. She did it for herself. Pampering herself with a bit of makeup and stylish, flashy clothing felt lovely, which is why she did what she did. *To each his own*, was a motto she lived by and lived for.

Seeing Mia again after so many years had Ruby pleased that she had kept up with the newscasts and trends coming out of Great Britain's neighbouring island. Her decision to do this since the mid and late 1950s had helped her to stay updated on Mia's life and homeland. By doing so she'd felt less detached from her friend as the years went by. Ruby was aware that the 60s and 70s had been a liberating time for people everywhere. From London, to France, to San Francisco, the world was changing. She'd learned that despite the emancipating changes globally, Ireland was still a hostile place for women. It was a country where the Catholic Church still had an irrepressible amount of influence and power. She'd also been told that Irish men prided themselves on taking, and having, complete power in the home, in the bedroom, and in business. In her British opinion, *Irish men drank too much, didn't believe in birth control, and impregnated their women as if they were jackrabbits.* After Mia and Emmet were banished from the Catholic Unwed Mother's Home, she'd missed them terribly while continuing her studies at the University of Dublin. Back then, she'd wondered countless times if Mia married and was living a jackrabbit's life? For that reason, Ruby had kept herself updated and knowledgeable about the people and the country of Ireland between 1952 and 1972.

The elderly, white haired woman sitting in her Barcalounger now was feeling too chilled. Exhaustion caused this since she was in her early seventies. She reached down and picked the blanket up off the floor, where it lay like the pile of warm fleece that it was. After situating it over her lap and around her ankles and feet, she settled herself back into a more comfortable position, closed her eyes, and continued recollecting about the day Mia Doherty mysteriously walked back into her life.

On that glorious sun filled summer afternoon the only best friend she'd ever known practically stopped her heart by re-entering her world without warning. Before the sun had set on that same day Mia stole her heart once more, exactly as she'd done between 1950 and 1952. Later that day, after they'd shared a bottle of wine, the women strolled hand in hand along the beach behind the diner. Mia gradually began to open herself up by mentioning the harsher sides of her current life. Ruby knew her probing questions were testing her Irish friend a tad, regardless, she wanted Emilia to tell her more about her return to Belfast and life on her family's farm. Ruby already knew that back in 1949, out of community and religious shame Mia's parents had chosen to spin a lie. That they'd denounced her as their pregnant daughter and sent her off to the Home for Unwed Mothers in Dublin. What Ruby didn't know, was what happened after Mia left Dublin and returned home with baby Emmet.

As they strolled farther down the coastline, the two women were lost in thought, melancholy, and memories. A few moments later Mia rested her hand on Ruby's back. Her hand felt soothing. Ruby had forgotten how much her Irish friend completed her. After a brief moment of stillness Mia resumed telling her version of her life and confinement on a farm in Belfast. She went on to tell Ruby what had transpired and why her parents allowed their daughter and bastard grandson to live on their farm.

"My family lived on that horrible farmstead for many a donkey's years," Mia told Ruby, as her rendition of that time in her life began.

This unforeseeable event all began when Ma and Pa Doherty, dressed in their nightclothes, opened their farmhouse door on a wet, stormy Belfast night. A brutal, tackling Irish rain had been falling for twelve straight hours. Her pa was holding a double-barrelled shotgun that was pointed straight into the face of the person he thought to be an intruder. He was shocked to see his wide-eyed, grungy, very skinny, and fatigued daughter looking down both barrels. In no time flat, he pulled the safety lever on and lowered his shotgun to the floor. Emilia could see that her father was tremendously shaken up by almost shooting the head off his own flesh and blood. Her mother was the first one to spot a likewise, wide-eyed, grungy, curious, and floppy eared baby boy. Emmet had been peeking from around the back of their daughters left shoulder. His ginger coloured curls, bright smile, big blue eyes, and pearly white baby teeth stole his granny's heart instantly. Both mother and child were drenched in rainwater, weather-beaten and beyond haggard. Ma Doherty point blank defied Emilia, as she yanked on the strap around her daughter's belly. Hurriedly and roughly, she untied the makeshift papoose and snatched baby Emmet from his mummy before Mia could retaliate. Mia feared that the boy's grandmamma would claim her son as her own, whilst dictating Mia's life. It would take only forty-eight short and tense hours for her suspicions to be proven right.

Her brother had grown taller since she'd last seen him. He looked like a wishy-washy zombie, standing in the open doorway of his bedroom whilst glaring at his younger sister with the venom of hate in his eyes. Then he hacked up phlegm, spat on the floor, spun on his heels, and slammed the bedroom door behind him. She could hear him effin' and blinden' as he screamed, with a deep Irish twang "feck off siesta!" Nearly three years had passed since she'd seen him. Nonetheless, her brother was still a weak quitter who ran off and hid in his bedroom with the onset of any type of conflict. The banging of the door callously startled a very sleepy and hungry Emmet. He began to wail and cry out for his mummy. What was happening in that Irish house was the finest example of domestic anarchy that Mia suspected existed but had never before seen through the protective eyes of motherhood. Her aged father stood there, still gripping his rifle like a dumb-old, shivering dog. He never spoke a word.

It was doubtlessly evident that her mother was still a matriarch with all the power in and over the family. She was the controlling and dominating parent. Her pa was Mia's mean and revengeful blood relation. Her brother was her parent's idiotic and inexcusable mistake. Realizing, that none of them had changed their ways since she'd been banned from the family was appropriately frightening her. Mia grasped straight away that she was outnumbered and that she and her baby were at risk. She stood there dripping wet, half-starved, and flustered to the bone. Having no other choice, she accepted their grim predicament and adjusted her mindset accordingly.

Respectfully, through fearful stutters, she asked, "Could we spend the night, Pa?"

He agreed after glancing over at his wife and getting her cynical nod of approval. Emilia and her baby Mac went on to spend the night, and each night thereafter until Emmet's fifth birthday.

Even though the Doherty's opened their farmhouse door on that blustery Irish evening, in her parent's eyes Mia had committed a sin against Church and God. As a result, their warped sense of faith never opened up to her again. Two hidden truths had returned to Belfast and were now threatening to divulge their three yearlong secrets. Eventually they'd be exposed for the frauds that they were, unless they thought fast and acted faster. By the end of that week, after hiding their family secret in a barn, they had devised a rightly clever and holy scheme. It was a religious scheme that would help them to avoid the inevitable and save the family name and their reputation with the Roman Catholic Church.

With this being said and done, each Sunday morning, Ma and Pa Doherty virtuously and devoutly took turns carrying their gorgeous little grandson up the church's long aisle towards the altar. They held their heads high and smiled as baby Emmet innocently tried to snatch the Eucharistic host out of the priest's hand whilst they received Holy Communion.

In lieu of the weekly religious efforts they made, and for the sake of 'a Child of God', they were graciously and financially compensated. Their status in the parish was quickly restored. The congregation was swayed into believing that the Doherty's were holier than holy. Their willingness to take a bastard child in off the streets and raise him as their own, was 'a valid testament to their holiness'. As a reward for such Christian kindness, special monthly 'donation masses' were held in young Emmet's honour. Fifty percent of the mass contributions went straight into the Doherty's pockets. The respectable Pastor kept the other fifty percent, in the name of the Good Lord Jesus Christ. The holy scheme that the three of them devised was proving itself to be easy, useful, and profitable. No one, except the preacher and Ma and Pa Doherty ever knew how much money was collected for little Emmet. Nevertheless, each week, the contribution baskets overflowed with monetary offerings of all denominations.

As the months passed, the congregations contributing parishioners remained generous and continued believing that their donations were being offered up for the sake of a poor, abandoned, misbegotten child's future.

Chapter 14

Emmet was a delightful, dazzling, and strong-willed toddler who captured the attention and heartstrings of the congregation, more and more, each time they saw him. Mia's Irish 'slíocht' had become the parish's most charismatic child. Her sons loyally doting grandparents and their priest knew precisely how to cash in on Emilia Doherty's illegitimate heir. Therefore, for forty-nine months of Sundays, they did exactly that.

Emilia, still being an unwed mother, was not welcomed to enter the House of God. Her parents saw to it that within a week of her return, she'd become a renowned sinner who was forbidden to attend weekly Sunday services. Being the disbelieving atheist that she covertly knew she was, this holy fact, and parish rule suited her just fine. Each Sunday morning she remained behind at the farm, ordered to repent by serving out three penances. Three atonements that God, a sly priest, and her guileful parents had duly bestowed upon her. The Doherty's were a fifth generation of Irish agricultural folk. This meant that Mia could expect years of hard labour for the sake of the farm and the repentance of her sinfully demoralized soul.

The elderly woman stirred restlessly in her Barcalounger as she reminisced deeper about Emilia. Her inquisitive mind continued to drift with ease, as it recalled what happened after Mia had suddenly stepped back into her British world in 1972, by spontaneously waltzing into her diner. What she didn't know was, the moment the diner owner saw her again, after twenty years, Mia had turned Ruby's heart inside out.

While she dwelt in the past a bit longer, a shy grin appeared on the face of the mentally drifting old woman as she conjured up more Doherty memories.

For the duration of each of the Sunday church services, Emilia was expected to start her three penances at sunrise. This began with penance number one, which was mucking out the stables where the cattle, horses, pigs, chickens, and calves' shit and pissed all week long. She was not allowed to eat before her atonements began. Ma and Pa Doherty believed food was a reward for hard labour. Therefore, until her work was finished, she would go hungry. In hindsight, she was actually thankful for their extra punishment layer, because each Sunday she'd continually retched from the stable's unbearably nauseating odours. With no food in her empty stomach to puke up, vomiting, if it surfaced, came and went effortlessly. Hence, she was filled with a sly dash of gratefulness. After the stables were finished, she'd continue onto to the second penance. This one involved tending to her mother's vegetable and fruit gardens. This atonement meant harvesting and pruning the plants and vines. After she finished with the gardens, she'd been ordered to pluck the bugs, worms, and beetles off the plants. Then she was to douse them in kerosene, strike a match, and light them on fire. After watching the insects squirm, sizzle and die, she'd was told to collect all their scorched remains and put the singed bug relics into an empty jam jar. This was required to prove to her pa that she'd done what was expected of her. Despite his demands, she would intentionally burn only half of the live beetles, bugs, and worms that she'd picked off the plants. The other half she'd set free in a nearby irrigation ditch. She swore she could see appreciative looks in their beady, little black eyes as they scurried off. This act of insect pardoning was a kind deed that made her feel less hard-hearted like her father was. Pa Doherty was a burly and horrid old man. He had a boulder for a heart and killed anything without batting an eye.

On one unseasonably warm and dry Sunday morning, while granting her weekly quantity of God's innocent pests their freedom, she accidently set the perimeter of the garden on fire. Her mother's prized tomato plants and a handful of cucumbers and pumpkins were a total, crispy loss. When her pa returned from Church and saw the scorched patch of vegetables, she saw the rage in his eyes rise by the second. Seeing Emmet playing in the distance was the only reason she didn't run off and hide until her father had simmered down. She'd do anything to protect her son from the likes of the wicked Doherty seeds that had created the boy's mother. As retribution for her ignorance, her pa lit two long wooden matches and held them under her open hands. Her screams had a sharecropper, who was ploughing his nearby field, stopping his work to take a quick gander at his neighbour's yelping daughter. In no time flat, the normally hesitant and guarded farmer had jumped over the Doherty's fence to see what all the commotion was about. For the better part of two decades he'd had his misgivings about the family who lived within a stone's throw away from his own farm. Despite his reservations, he acted neighbourly, kept his mouth shut, and his eyes wide open since both Doherty children were born. The sharecropper's quick reaction to Mia's shrieking was the only thing that saved her from more severe third-degree burns. As the man approached them, her pa held his daughters burned and branded hands tightly behind her back. He was perceptive enough to know he'd best be hiding his sadistic ways from the alarmed sharecropper who'd just hurdled a fence and was sprinting across the field in their direction.

Pa Doherty chuckled, whilst informing the nosey, gobdaw of a man that, "A big ole' fat green garden snake had frightened the daylight out of his sweet girl."

Emilia was too petrified to cry. On the verge fainting, she confirmed her pa's lie with a convincingly fake and brave smile.

An eerie silence hung in the salty air between the middle-aged females as they gazed out over the English Channel. After ten minutes or so, Ruby reached out and deliberately took Mia's hands in hers. Tenderly, she turned them over. A horrified expression crossed her face as she saw, for the first time, Mia's faded, yet thick, protruding burn scars. She wondered why she hadn't felt them as they strolled the beach hand in hand. The scars were slightly pink in colour, and even after two decades, still clearly visible. She wanted to cry for the torture her best friend had endured without her being there to protect her. However, tears never arrived. Ruby McEwen simply wasn't the crying type. Instead, she delicately opted to kiss the scars on Mia's palms before letting go of her hands. Mia quivered as Ruby's lips grazed her disfigured palms. Then she brushed a single tear away and poured them both another hefty glass of Chardonnay. The Irish woman, for some strange reason she still didn't understand, chose to conceal from Ruby the permanent scars that her parents torment and hate had etched on her soul.

The sensation of a woman's lips on her scars had stirred something unfamiliar within Emilia. She took a large gulp of wine and rested her head on Ruby's shoulder. Sitting on the beach, warmed by a gorgeous sun filled day, both women withheld their affectionate uneasiness from each other. Straightaway, Ruby switched mental gears and pushed an intimidating tingling she felt deep in her stomach aside. As Mia continued to tell her story, Ruby focused raptly on what she was hearing, rather than on what she was feeling. Lovingly, she continued to stroke her best friend's cheek.

Somewhat chilled again and still holding an ice-cold glass the elderly version of Ruby felt an uncommon, weepy wetness rolling down her cheeks. As tears dripped off her chin and landed in her cleavage, she ignored how much they tickled. Tightening her grip, she continued musing over what the dearest person she'd ever known had told her back in 1972, as they sat together on the beach drinking wine and melting into each other's lives.

There was no running water or electricity on their farm, so the Doherty's sanitation was as poor as they were. This meant that there were no modern conveniences like a faucet, bathtub, or an indoor toilet. Part three of Mia's Sunday penance was the removal of more piss and shit. This time it was the humankind. The family's outside toilet was situated nearby the creek on the southern side of the farm. It had a hinged opening called an 'outdoor'. The outdoor was located at the bottom half of the outhouse, behind a two-seater shitter. The outdoor was used for emptying deep pits in the ground that collected human excrement. The two-seater outhouse meant twice the amount of shit and piss for poor Emilia. The only reason farm folks had a two-seater outhouse was because they were too lily-livered to take their pissers and dumpers alone in the dark. Living in Belfast was dangerous in the 1950s. The city's history had been marked by a violent conflict between Irish Catholics and Irish Protestants. In addition to the religious stride, poverty was plaguing the country. Therefore, pickpockets and thieves roamed the land nightly after the sun had set. It was difficult to see a mugger, or to determine anyone's religious denomination, while a person was walking to the shitter through the darkness of night. For this practical reason, folks agreed, it was safer to go to the crapper in pairs than to risk being pounced on alone.

Penance number three was undoubtedly Mia's least favourite one. Something about handling her parents and brother's urine and feces was more demeaning than anything else they'd subjected her to. She was instructed to clean out the putrid, overflowing pits under the outhouse seats each Sunday. She would do this by first scooping out all the urine and toilet paper with a large metal ladle and dumping it into a steel bucket. Then, with a flat-headed shovel, she'd then dig and excavate thick the deposit of shit that

99

had settled to the bottom of the pit. The shit deposit always settled deep and laid under litres of rancid piss. Plainly said and simple done, it was the removal of an almost impenetrable, heavy layer of brownish-green human gunge. The fly covered shit was then carefully shovelled into a separate wider bucket. Doing this was a messy job that required Mia to wear a bandana over her face to filter the stench out of her nostrils. The bandana also kept flies from infesting her mouth. Flies carried diseases. Emilia was more fearful of dying from a disease than she was of her pa's temper. If she died, Emmet would be destined to live the same life that her birth had forced her to live. She wanted more for her son and so goddammit and to hell with her parents, more he would have! Every so often, strands of her waist long, golden red hair would fall out of their pins and ribbons and land straight in the piss and shit filled bucket. She would pinch the hair strands between her fingers and scrape the pee and poo off before securing her hair back up again. There was no way around this.

Per explicit orders from her father, Emilia was to carry each hefty bucketful some three-hundred meters across the field to a manure heap behind the barn. Just because he could, her cruel coward of a brother, would take the wheel off the wheelbarrow and hide it from her before the family went to church. Ma Doherty was too busy being a surrogate mum to Mia's son to notice the wrongdoings her own son. However, Pa Doherty beamed with pride at his boy's slick underhandedness, which only encouraged her brother to devise new weekly 'stick it to me sister' strategies.

Mean fathers breed mean sons, Mia thought, shaking her head in defeat, as more and more the Sunday's passed her sad life by. Despite, that her devout churchgoing family was delighted to know that she was hand carrying heavy buckets filled with their weekly bodily waste to the manure pile, she quickly outsmarted them. Her appetite to spite father was stronger than her fear of his wrath. Seeing the creek a mere thirty-five meters away from the border of the outhouse, she got a clever idea. Because she was secretly an atheist who didn't give a rat's ass if it was a Catholic sin or not, she would dump the shit-filled, overflowing buckets straight into the creek. Mia would then stand on the embankment and vaguely stare out over the water. Like a lifeless ghost, she'd watch lump after lump of human shit with rotted white toilet paper stuck to it, being set free. As the human waste floated serenely into the distance, caressed by the flow of the creeks tranquil current, a severely abused Irish girl questioned how unfair her life was.

Freed shit was on its way to the open ocean, while she was trapped living in hell on earth. In Emilia Doherty's opinion, this was the worst kind of human waste.

Chapter 15

Mia abruptly ended her elaborate rendition of her return to Belfast and stood up. The beach sand she was covered in sprinkled off her reddish-brown skin and speckled onto Ruby. Mia was emotionally drained and tipsy from the wine. She looked down at Ruby with the saddest, most gloom filled eyes the still young British diner owner had ever seen.

Ruby stood up and reached out to her. Hand in hand, they walked to the water's edge. In silence and without forethought the unbridled, sunburned women both stripped down and went for a swim. Their nakedness was over and above stimulating and therapeutic. Emilia didn't mention her parents, the farm, or her brother again. With the passage of time, their reunion glided into a distant past. The time they'd shared in the early 1950s, and again in 1972, gradually became buried under countless layers of life. Nevertheless, their time together was never forgotten. Nor, was it ever replaced, by anything, or anyone more treasured or significant?

Still sitting in her lounger, the elderly woman's ego was toiling with its responsibility for the child and its intentional act of selfishness. With her fleece blanket draped over her body, she hopelessly tried to focus and steer her thoughts back to Mia. Normally, steering her mind was simple and effortless; however, this time doing so was properly challenging her. It was irritating and odd. Her intentional, and slightly self-centred decision to delay calling America, was distracting her ability to stay connected to memories of her Irish soul sister Emilia. It was a noticeable quandary that was rightly upsetting her. For a nanosecond, the now very old version of Ruby was certain that she could hear the faint sound of applauding customers and see vague silhouettes of two giddy women curtseying. She blamed her distressing lapse of clarity on the exhaustion she felt deep in her bones. In that very moment, she decided that the child's mother, her granddaughter, could wait. Zofia Durant would be put 'on hold' long enough for Ruby to bask in a few more of her fondest memories. Besides, she intentionally wanted to delay being falsely accused of not taking proper care of her great granddaughter Jazz. *Bloody hell*, she frustratingly thought, totally regretting having to make such a goddamned phone call.

Inhaling deeply, she ignored her predicament and permitted her mind to glide once more in reverse, cross over into the past, and take her with it.

The day Emilia Doherty and Ruby McEwen were reunited, one of the first things they noticed about each other was how their bodies had undeniably aged, whereas their faces had essentially remained the same. Regardless of their age difference, they had similarities they'd yet to discover. Both women still dyed their hair, which made them look and feel younger than most females over forty-five did. Both Mia and Ruby embraced life with pure passion. The twinkle in their eyes and their energetic personalities were larger than both of the islands that they came from.

In the mid-1950s, while they'd lived in Dublin, aside from when Ruby was attending classes at the university or studying, they had been inseparable. Two decades later, the moment Emilia Doherty casually entered The Seaside diner, an invisible type of magic followed her inside. Mia was the type of person who was extremely prepared for whatever life hurled at her. She had a gift for turning challenges into adventures and defeats into milestones. Ruby had never met anyone like her. Interesting things had started to transpire between the women since Mia's arrival in London yesterday. Compelling, unfamiliar, and sensual feelings were seriously side-tracking them from their normal lives. Impulsively, they ventured into unknown territory, daring to explore new experiences while embracing what little time they had left together. For two days and two nights, they lived through modern and responsive life changing events. In the forty-eight hours they spent together, they defied each other's ethics and lifted each other's spirits to new heights.

The diner owner knew that very shortly after her arrival, Mia would need to leave her London world again and return to her life in Ireland. Mia had reassured Ruby that both she and Emmet had made a fine life for themselves in Belfast. Emmet was now an almost 21-year-old man, who'd honourably become a young husband when his girlfriend told him of their pregnancy. Less than six months after saying 'I do', he became a father of redheaded, dimple-faced triplets. The babies were eighteen months old already. Mia was a nana to one granddaughter and two grandsons. She was, without a doubt, as proud of her three grandbabies as she was of her son Mac. She told Ruby that she always had called him Mac because the name suited his personality more than his birth name, Emmet, did. His wee ones looked exactly like their pappy. The Polaroid she'd taken out of her handbag and shown off had certainly proven her right.

Ruby agreed, saying that, "The triplets looked like Mac did as a baby." She went on to proclaim that, "The baby girl was the spitting image of Mia."

The night before Emilia's return to Ireland, she and Ruby walked back down the sandy knoll behind The Seaside and went for a moonlit stroll along the beach. This time they brought a bottle of Cabernet, a warm loaf of freshly baked French bread, Swiss cheese, and a blanket. They were both subdued and lost in thought as they shared another glorious sunset together. Subtly, Mia reached over and took Ruby's hand in hers.

Then she asked her, "Did you ever have children, or grandchildren?"

Before Ruby could reply, she went on to say, "Since I arrived, we've only been talking about Mac, our Dublin and Belfast experiences, and myself. It feels like there is so much about you that I still know nothing about?"

Emilia was very observant and even more humble. Her 'secretive' friend Ruby was still the private type who just dealt with what life did to her and what she did to life. She seemed to have no real need for sharing her experiences or being pitied or praised for them. Regardless, Mia was born a curious kitten. She was able to purr and probe until she discovered what she was looking for.

"So, tell me," Mia daringly asked, "did you ever fall in love?"

Hearing this, Ruby's mind crashed into her heart so fast it made her brain spin. She was afraid and dazed. She'd been yanked out of her security zone and felt torn between the realities of her life and her privacy. The diner owner, known for being unflappable and in control, was on the verge of panicking.

A persistent and sozzled Mia said, "Come on Ruby, tell me. You know you can tell me anything," she slurred, purred, and coaxed before leaning into Ruby.

Then she began tickling her. Ruby forcefully pushed Mia and her teasing hands away. Mia was instantly sobered up and surprised by the intense abruptness of her friend's reaction. She tried to tickle Ruby again, but her, naïve and playful gesture was met with more force. This time Ruby shoved her so hard that she lost her balance and landed, with a hard smack, on her back in the sand.

Being so brusquely flattened to the ground caused an intuitive light came on in Mia's wine-soaked brain. It was as plain as it was simple; Ruby's private side felt attacked and it wasn't ready to share its complete self with Mia yet.

Meanwhile, Ruby was asking herself, *who did Mia think she was, trying to ruin their time together by insisting that she divulge the details and raw circumstances about her pregnancy and Eliza's troubled life?*

At least this was how it seemed to her. Despite that it was completely innocent, Mia's prying felt like a huge threat that now hung around Ruby's neck. A threat that was choking her air supply off, more and more, each time Mia insisted on tickling her. After so many years, how could Ruby possibly tell Mia, that after she left Dublin with baby Emmet, Ruby had gone through her own unwed pregnancy and birth? How could she begin to tell her that she'd endured similar appalling circumstances at the same Unwed Mother's Home as Mia herself had experienced? The only difference, for Ruby, during that horrific time, was that Emilia Doherty wasn't there to help her through it the way Ruby had been there for her.

Bollocks! Ruby thought, as she bit off a piece of crispy bread and jammed a slice of cheese in her mouth.

"Shit!" She loudly cursed after biting her tongue. Tasting blood in her mouth, she immediately spit the bread and cheese out and then covered the slimy, bloodied gob that had landed next to her foot with beach sand. Her tongue throbbed. She was terrified that she was about to be exposed as 'a hypocrite'. Feeling afraid while in Mia's presence felt strange and intimidating for her. The threat of a serious emotional explosion had lit a fire inside of her. Her past life was a series of sensitive and painful fragments that she still wanted to keep sequestered and buried in times gone by. Despite that she trusted Emilia, she still believed that her skeletons were best kept locked away in eternity's closet.

Bloody hell, she told herself, *the choice to reveal her life was hers and only hers to make, and goddammit she wasn't about to make it!*

"Come on Ruby," Mia, who was sitting upright again, openly teased. She was still unaware of what the woman, who dressed like she did, was thinking or feeling.

"There is so much I don't know about you?" she said.

Ruby winced when she heard this. Then, the Keeper of Secrets took a deep breath, composed herself, and revealed nothing about her life as a mum.

"Come on Ruby," Mia enticed again, after another sip of cabernet. Then, in a most usual way, her uninhibited, passionate side began stroking the woman on the blanket sitting next to her.

Mia pondered, *okay, so she's not the tickling type. Maybe she's more the caressing type.*

With her privacy so unexpectedly threatened, unpredictably, a rattled and panicky Ruby took a huge swig from the nearly half-empty bottle and drained it in one continuous guzzle. Emilia was flabbergasted at the amount of wine she'd swigged. Still unaware of what was happening, and why, her jaw dropped as she stared at her overwrought overcome friend gripping the neck of the bottle. Not knowing what to do, Mia picked up a nearby piece of driftwood and poked at Ruby's toes with it, hoping to lighten up her mood and make her laugh. With a deep red colour of cabernet dripping off her mouth and chin, Ruby began coughing; a sign Mia took as her practically choking on the 14-proof spirits she'd just gulped. To appease herself and to shut her best friend the hell up, Ruby snatched the driftwood away from Emilia and threw it aside. Then, with vengeance, she flung her empty wine glass across the beach. As the alcohol raced to her brain, her head began to swirl, and she staggered slightly. Mia's jaw dropped even farther towards her feet. Impetuously, Ruby leaned over, grabbed Mia by her hair, gnarled it around her long fingers, pulled her in closer, and kissed her long and hard on the lips. Despite that Ruby was rightfully angry at Mia's incessant tickling, her persistence and endless questions, kissing her was an absolute and unplanned act of desperation.

The moisture of Mia's cabernet-soaked lips, still warm on Ruby's mouth made her woozy. Mia Doherty was pleasantly stunned and slightly aroused. With the taste of Ruby's wine kiss lingering deep inside her own mouth, questions and doubts immediately filled the Irish woman's mood and mind. Ruby's own mind was brimming over with a snaking need for answers. Had she, in a hit or miss way, just done something that would shock Mia into stopping with her tickling, teasing, and interfering? Or had she ruined their friendship? Or was she attracted to her in a way that, despite the modern times of the seventies, was still taboo? At the same time, Mia was asking herself, if she had enjoyed the kiss, and did she want Ruby to kiss her again? Truth be told, she already knew the answers to her questions. After swigging so much alcohol and enthusiastically kissing Mia Doherty, the British side of their friendship was convinced that a passionate kiss had just succeeded in shutting the Irish side of their friendship the hell up!

Touché, Ruby thought with a victorious grin.

In the minutes that followed, Ruby tried in vain to pay attention to her own set of doubts and questions, nevertheless, she was too tipsy, and she'd failed herself miserably. Her brain's focus had downright deserted her. Before the middle-aged woman with tinted hazelnut skin, dark hair, and maroon coloured wine stains on her blouse could blink four times, Mia spun around and confidently grabbed Ruby by her shoulders. Then she boldly pulled her startled friend in closer and kissed her back. It was a harder, longer, and more zealous kiss. As Mia's tongue briefly entered her best friend's mouth, the sweet, full-bodied taste of red wine had her swooning. Ruby's equally aroused tongue responded with interest and a slightly messy, yet innocent kind of curiosity. Their aroused bodies heatedly pressed into each other. Then, in a heartbeat, their caressing and kissing ended as spontaneously it had begun.

The women were now lying on their backs, half on and half off the blanket, with their legs outstretched. Nothing more than an empty wine bottle and an arousing, first time experience lay between them. Lost in thought, they held hands as they each steadied their breathing, silently explored their emotions, and stared up at the sky. Despite, that both women knew that they'd positively liked kissing each other, they didn't speak a word. They were still slightly panting and pondering over what had just happened. Emotionally dumbstruck and quite drunk, their hearts beat in unison as they began to unwind from the adrenaline rush, they'd both just felt and enjoyed. The warmth racing through her loins was confusing Ruby to her core. Her head was whirling, and her body trembled. Feeling vulnerable and exposed, she was on the verge of tears.

"Bloody hell, it wasn't supposed to be like this." Ruby concluded with a tone of regret.

"Amazing," Mia said, with a tone of satisfaction.

Mia then rolled onto her side and looked at the woman who had initiated their unexpected exchange of intimacy. Seeing a twinge of tumult and pain in Ruby's eyes, Mia suspected that something else was tormenting her best friend; something much more troubling than being fondled and kissed by an Irish woman on a British beach was. Regardless of her suspicions, Mia knew enough, and cared more than enough, to let it just be what it was meant to be. She'd ignore what had happened and not look for answers, or a recap of the past thirty minutes. With this in mind, she released her friend's hand, stood up, and walked off towards the water. Unfazed by Mia's abruptness, Ruby remained on her back and counted the twilight coloured clouds above.

Brushing reminders and remainders of the beach off her clothes, Mia concluded that whatever Ruby was hiding, or attempting to distract her from, their locking of lips didn't change the fact that Ruby's story was hers to tell; whenever she was willing, ready, and able to tell it. Out of respect for the intimacy they'd just exchanged, Mia decided to give her English friend space and just shut up. Just shy of twenty years had passed since they'd seen each other, and they had only two short days to have fun together. Truth be told, despite that Mia was still basking in an intimate afterglow, she was hopped up to continue telling Ruby about her current life in Belfast. Therefore, as she strolled further, she dismissed the desires she never knew she had, along with her strong urge to kiss the diner owner again and explore their physical attraction even further. About fifteen minutes later, Emilia was back on the blanket relaxing next to Ruby. The lingering tension in the air between them had evaporated. Mia reached over and took Ruby's hand in hers. Because Ruby didn't pull away, Mia felt at home and started sharing more details about her life in Ireland. The English woman, who was now sitting upright, had propped the empty wine bottle between her long legs and dark-skinned feet. The wine and sun had deepened the colour of her tinted skin and burgundy lips.

Dammit, Mia thought looking intently at her, *she has no clue how stunning she is.*

As the Irish woman started to speak, Ruby let go of Mia's hand and began filling the bottle with beach sand. Watching the sand trickle through the neck of the bottle and fall grain by grain into its base reminded her of how miniscule she really was in the grand scheme of things. She continued filling the bottle while Mia shared more of her Irish life.

Since 1970, Emmet and Emilia owned and operated MacaMia's Pub and Bed & Breakfast. Mac Doherty had despised any classroom he had ever spent time in. Since he was a boy, many teachers had failed at trying to inspire him to become educated in the traditional way. Therefore, he opted for opening a business rather than continuing his education after the age of sixteen. Being given a tidy sum of hush money from the priest who had profited from a four year long religious moneymaking scandal had made Mac's decision to leave school an effortless one. As a baby and toddler, Emmet had been used as religious bait. Once the priest's sins had been uncovered, his fear of shame, disgrace, and dismissal from the Catholic Church Diocese enabled Mac to start his life as a pub owner with the hefty payoff he'd received from the church's holy hierarchy. Ruby concluded, after listening to Mia talk for five minutes or so that Emmet had grown to become a student of life just as his mum had. The empty cabernet bottle was almost filled with beach sand by now. Ruby loved Mia irrefutably and thought the name they'd given to their business was symbolically clever. Mia went on to tell her that MacaMia's was a popular Belfast tavern with a spacious, four-room inn above it. The street side tavern was on the ground floor, above a spacious storage cellar. Her inn occupied the top three floors of the building. The pub and bed and breakfast were located in the downtown area. Both were now widely held and profitable money-makers.

Mia invited Ruby to come for a visit anytime, saying, "She and one of her beautiful guestrooms would be waiting for her."

With a hands-off, teasing wink, she reassured Ruby by declaring that "She would only kiss her again if Ruby wanted her to."

The morning Mia flew back to Ireland, the women wept, hugged, made promises, and exchanged their polka dotted handkerchiefs as keepsakes. When Ruby leaned in to give her best friend a goodbye kiss on the cheek Mia turned her face and their lips found each other one last time. Neither of them pulled away or cared what onlookers thought of them. The pockets of their matching pantsuits were filled with new secrets and a lifetime of memories. This would be their second and final farewell since they'd met in Dublin back in 1950. No promises were made. Neither of them wanted to dwell on, or over, what had transpired between them. Nor would they speculate over what the future held. They both knew that, *sometimes, saying goodbye was the only solution to an impossible situation.* As it had been in 1952, this was again one of those times. In the months that followed Mia's return to Belfast, Ruby coped with the loneliness that had crept into her private mind by putting pen to paper. She devoted a sixty-page journal to the forty-eight hours that two women on the wrong side of forty had spent together. Her journal, titled, 1972, remained to this day a collection of the most powerful and rawest writing the then, much younger English woman from Essex County, had ever transcribed.

The elderly woman with ice-cold hands, turned her brain switch off, opened her eyes, and shifted in her seat. The memories she'd just relived slithered, in a flash, into the shadows of her sharp mind. It was in moments like this when she was reminded of just how grateful she was that the past exited her mind the second she flicked her mental switch off.

She heard herself say aloud, "Certain memory snippets are better left where they belong old girl, safely behind you."

Seeing that all the crushed ice in her glass had melted, the old woman drank the remaining cold water. Then she placed the tumbler on the floor next to her recliner. She didn't want to mind travel anymore. She'd had enough of it all for one evening. Recalling the past while being awake was less draining because she was in complete control of her thoughts; whereas, mental drifting steered her, subconsciously, in any direction it desired to take her in. Now and then, meandering through the past would put her on the precarious edge of life. Nowadays, being fully aware of this risk, and after almost nine decades of being alive, she preferred to avoid life's rougher edges.

With this decided, Ruby's now wide-awake and vigilant mind already knew where it would take her next. Whenever she reminisced about Mia's tale of her farmstead experiences, after moving back in with her parents, a disturbing chill ran up and down the elderly woman's crippled spine.

Her hands were now shaking, and her heart was beating faster. She had a strong and healthy old heart; therefore, her heartrate had never worried her or any doctor she'd ever been to. Her mind began to flicker. She was feeling torn between three important things she needed to do. The first was to continue reminiscing about Mia and Emmet, the second was ringing up America to speak to the child's mother, and the third was returning to the intensive care unit. Since the cabdriver Deniz had dropped her off, her mind had been bouncing off every thought and impulse that had crossed its path. This was why her sense of time and priority had now all but vanished. The diner's glass dessert coolers were casting a soft, radiant light on her rumpled face. Being illuminated by the coolers lights, Ruby's pure white hair seemed to glow in the dark. Sitting motionlessly, she started to remember what had occurred in Ireland shortly after Mia's surprise visit to her diner in the early 1970s. Apparently, her mind had stopped flickering, because it easily recollected the incidents of her life during and after Mia's visit to England.

Emilia and Ruby had spent two days and nights together that year. Despite what did and did not happen between them, every so often thereafter, Ruby felt an unnerving and intimidating sensation brewing on the horizon of their friendship. The sensation she had was similar to the one she'd had, the night she waved Emilia and her baby boy off as their journey to her parent's Belfast farm began. Back then, it was a journey that Ruby was positive would lead to nothing but disaster. The diner owner had always had a strong and reliable inner awareness. Since she and Mia had met in 1949, and spent two years together in the early 1950s, she often feared the worse for her Irish friend. She was certain that life in Belfast was about to become more dangerous for Mia, Emmet, and the triplets, than life on the farm with their repulsive relatives had been for five horrendously long years. Although, at the time, Ruby had kept her 'sixth sense premonition' to herself, unfortunately for the Doherty's from Belfast, Ruby McEwen usually got it right, and this time was no different. On 21st of July, in the year 1972, just six days after Mia and Ruby had reunited and given birth to a sensual secret, the Irish Republican Army detonated an estimated twenty-two bombs in Northern Ireland. The majority of them were car bombs. The city of Belfast was hit the hardest. It was reported that one hundred and thirty people were injured. Seven civilians and nine soldiers had been killed. On that harrowingly deadly day, what the Irish people didn't know, was that for the next twenty years nearly ten thousand bombs would be detonated in the name of the IRA's terroristic cause.

The violence changed Ireland forever. The way its citizens trusted their government, took pride in their nationality, and lived on Irish soil, was never the same again.

Chapter 16

Mia, Emmet, and the triplets were in Central Belfast on the day that later came to be known as 'Bloody Friday.' Mac's wife was in Galway attending her mother's funeral at the time. From what Ruby could still recall, survivor's and eyewitnesses had difficulty expressing the true horrors they'd felt and witnessed on that day.

Although Mia's family was not injured, they were deeply traumatized by the violence. Despite that Mac's pub had been closed at the time of the bombings, it suffered severe structural damage. Being located on the second and third floors of the building, Mia's B&B was out of the immediate blast range. Despite her good fortune, the damage to Mac's tavern caused MacaMia's to close its doors for the next six months due to repairs. When Ruby finally was able to reach Mia by phone, nine days had passed since the attacks. Her Irish friend told her what she could remember about that deplorable day. Mia had been cleaning two of her inn's rooms on the second floor in preparation for a guest turnover later that day. The triplets were asleep in their playpen in a vacant bedroom on the third floor. Mia often used a portable playpen as a crib to care for her grandbabies when their mother was away. This conveniently enabled her to be both a nana and an active proprietor at the same time. Emmet was mopping floors downstairs after a profitable night of live music, rowdy musicians, and drunken patrons. The first thing Mia saw, as the bombings started, were hundreds of panic-stricken residents, pedestrians, and staggered shoppers running through the streets seeking safety. After the first bomb exploded, Emmet sprinted up three flights of stairs and gathered his hysterical babies up in his arms. Then he sprinted back down four stairwells, with his mum on his heels.

The family sought shelter in the cellar underneath the pub. The explosions seemed endless and the triplets shrieked through each blast. Their binkies had been left behind upstairs in their playpen. Mia and Emmet's thumbs were used to soothe the wee one's fears as best they could be soothed. Although the strong grips their six tiny hands had on Mia and Mac's arms never weakened, the triplets eventually settled down. As one bomb after the other detonated, Mac and Mia took turns peering outdoors through the cellar's street side window. Plumes of thick, black, blinding smoke rose near and far, blanketing the city streets in fear and ash. Crowds of terror-stricken people stampeded into one other. Despite that they were underground, the Doherty family felt everything but safe. Hours after the last car bomb had exploded, terrified people were still loitering in the streets. They banded together, not knowing where to go.

Ruby recalled Mia telling her, "Children of all ages were screaming up and down the city's boulevards."

The aftermath of the attacks left MacaMia's Pub and Inn surrounded by what looked like, a vast field of broken glass and debris. For the people in the area of the explosions, the car bomb offensive that had detonated twenty-two bombs and lasted eighty-eight minutes, felt like an infinity.

For Mia, this unfamiliar and shockingly gruesome Northern Irish life was hindering her ability to remain in contact with to Ruby. What she didn't know was that at the same time, Ruby was going through a series of her own personal family tragedies. As the weeks passed, their bond remained strong, but their opportunity to remain intertwined was declining. By the end of 1972, the IRA had taken responsibility for 1300 bombs that caused irreparable damage to infrastructures, property, and people. The 1970s had plunged both Mia and Ruby into separate survival modes. Their challenges would last longer than either of them could have even remotely comprehended at the time. In the years that followed, the annihilation, at the hand of the Irish Republican Army, was indescribable. Northern Ireland, where four generations of Doherty's had been born and raised, was perishing and changing at a reckless and fast tempo. For this, and other reasons, the Irish people couldn't keep pace with their anger, their loss of hope, and the threats to their country. Despite the three-decade long destructive changes that WWII, the Vietnam War, and the IRA movement had collectively caused since the two women had first met, Ruby and Mia's friendship endured the hardships and remained unwavering.

The bond that had been born between them at an Unwed Mother's Home in Dublin, during the last year of the 1940s, would and did survive. Flashbacks of the twenty years, before Emilia had just casually stepped back into her life and almost rendered Ruby a heart attack, were now spinning through the elderly woman's mind. Despite that both women had kept in touch as much as they could, slow moving post-war mail and telephone services made corresponding quite the challenge. Especially, for two young female friends, who were used to the luxury of gabbing a night away without interruption. It was a time of rebuilding across Europe; therefore, the Brits from Ruby's generation valued any indulgences they were allowed, or were able to bribe out of a fellow Brit.

When Mia courageously returned to the family farm with her infant son, Ruby was studying journalism and working weekends at a Dublin charity for addicted and homeless people. She was known to be an honest and forthright kind of girl. She was diligent, worked hard for what she had, and didn't cut corners by bribing people. The young Miss McEwen never took the easy way out of anything. She considered herself a capable, compassionate young woman, who liked who she was and what she was doing for others. Despite her slightly overrated self-prophecy, the year after Emilia and Emmet were ousted from the Unwed Mothers Home, she was angry and struggling financially. For these reasons, she became an intentional indulger. The kind-hearted, yet poor student baked one fresh fruit pie a week for a wealthy, very precise old man who owned a telephone. He was a 91-year-old stickler who lived across the street from her Dublin flat. In exchange for her baking skills, she was allowed use his phone to make precisely one, and only one, ten minute phone call every other week. Their deal was that twice a month, upon the delivery of a fresh and warm pie of his choosing, his obliging female neighbour could use his personal house phone.

Their arrangement enabled Ruby to occasionally to check in on Mia and Emmet at the farm in Belfast. From time to time, Emilia's mother, father, or brother would answer the phone. Mia had warned Ruby that her family was well known for being intrusive and listening in on conversations. The staunch Irish called this 'earwigging'. This was why she'd immediately hang up if the voice of anyone, who wasn't Mia, answered the phone. She was too afraid that she'd get her friend into more trouble if one of the 'earwiggers' was eavesdropping in on their private talks.

Despite the 'pie pact' she'd made with a proper, affluent, precise old man across the street, because of the earwigging risk she had only spoken to Mia twice since she left the Unwed Mother's Facility. Regrettably, this was nowhere near enough time for them to stay updated with each other's lives. The then young, struggling Ruby, thought it to be more than slightly unfair that her hoary, nit-picker neighbour received his fresh fruit pies, regardless if she was on his phone for a paltry ten seconds or the full ten minutes. She didn't earn a lot of money and paying for the tart's ingredients wasn't always an easy thing for her to do. In hindsight, their arrangement made them no better, or different, from the next bribing Brit. She and the old man were both as cunning as at least one million other clever, post WWII survivors were. They were all men, women, and children, who schemed, bartered, and bribed each other in an effort to restore the lives that they each were rightly blessed and fortunate to still have. Back then, a freshly baked fruit pie never smelled or tasted so good, and a ten-second, or ten-minute phone call, truly was a gift from God. Ultimately, Hitler's war killed more than four hundred and fifty thousand of Ruby McEwen's fellow Brit's and left piles of dead bodies, destroyed buildings, and German rubble behind for the survivors to clean up. In the end, globally, an estimated seventy-five million people were dead, great cities were reduced to rubble, and families were annihilated and torn apart.

Reflecting upon it now, the elderly woman realized that she'd lived long enough to witness something insightful about the Great War of 1945. A war that, even in today's modern times, was still referred to as Year Zero. Since the war ended, the passing of time had gone on to reveal that decenniums later, humanity had come to recognize something noteworthy. Despite the atrocities and unprecedented hardships the Second World War caused, eventually it accelerated change. As women married servicemen from other nations and moved overseas, countless new blended families were formed. Because a vast majority of disbanded troops had left the United Kingdom to return to their homelands, a lion's share of postwar children was born into fatherless households. Many of these children were likewise fatherless, due war caused deaths. Another layer of hardship the youngest generation at the time experienced was a global increase in divorce rates. Divorce and death forced a great number of families to struggle while they re-adjusted to a cease arms and a world at peace.

Unexpectedly, a vivid vision of her great granddaughter Jazz, lying in an ICU bed, tersely yanked her thoughts back to the here and now. Her abstract brain switch was never useful or needed when images coming from 'the mirror in her mind' appeared to her. Her visions had a willpower that was stronger than her ability to control them. They entered and exited her mind freely or whenever she beckoned them. She was very used to and comfortable with this part of who she was. Ruby urgently had to pee again and reapply her makeup. Deniz the cabdriver would be arriving soon, so she wanted to look presentable. She was hungry, restless, and jittery. She'd already forgotten about her previous thoughts by the time she hoisted herself up out of the recliner and grabbed her makeup case out of her handbag. Since the diner's employee toilet next to the kitchen was closer to where she'd been sitting, logically she moved her stiff body in the shortest and proper direction. After relieving her bladder she skipped the lipstick part of her primping. Her dark burgundy coloured lips hadn't lost their lustre with age so they needed no artificial enhancement. With this being deduced she left the loo. Her overnight bag still needed to be packed and phone call to the child's mother, Zofia, still needed to be made. The call was something she would do straight away, because she now felt slightly invigorated and was ready to tackle such a dreadful task.

"Enough dilly-dallying old girl," she firmly told herself.

Then, she poured a glass of Coca Cola and filled another tall glass with crushed ice. After drinking her Coke and feeling the sugar rushing through her thin blood, she left the kitchen. She was mentally distracted again. Knowing how her brain worked, she knew it was often wise and necessary to keep a glass of what she called 'icy alertness' nearby to ward off another drifting episode. Limping back towards her chair and past the diner's wide, long counter, she glided one of her age spotted hands over all of the red upholstered, chrome-based counter stools. The surface of each stool was still crack free, smooth, and in pristine condition. She'd maintained them exceptionally well over the past sixty years. They were original symbols of her establishment and the first thing customers saw when they entered the diner. This was why she cared for them as if she was caring for The Seaside's reputation. Which in retrospect, she was.

Tapping each of them with her long, crooked fingers, she pondered over how many people had sat on them since they'd been bolted to the floor in 1951. As Eliza grew up, she and Ruby would have conversations about anything and everything 'behind the sun and under the moon'. When she reached the age of twelve or thirteen, the only things she didn't share with her mum were her deepest feelings, her fears, and as anticipated her secrets. She kept the emotional events of her young life extremely hush-hush, especially from her very outgoing and popular mother. Her grandpa, Horace, Ruby's father, knew more about Eliza than her grandma, Sadie, or her own mum did. This trait had made Ruby's daughter a mini version of herself and the next generation's Keeper of Secrets. This was something everyone, except her mum, seemed to be very aware of. It was a birth right, which proved itself a pitiful shame in the end.

"You didn't have many fond memories of that time in Eliza's life old girl," she wisely reminded herself aloud. "Best to embrace what you can while you still can."

It had been a very long time, since she'd heard herself saying her daughter's name aloud. With a tall, ice-filled glass of alertness clenched between her crippled and age-spotted hands, she thought back to when and how her relationship with a diner had begun.

Back in the day, The Seaside was as unique and transparent as it was today. People looking for a quick and delicious meal could see from the outside what they were going to get on the inside. Since the early 1960s, her diner had preserved its charm and allure. Even in this more modern era, The Seaside was one of the few remaining diners with a sleek and basic design. It was one of the elites 'no glitter, no glamour' vintage eateries. It had a high-barrelled roof that was held up by wraparound, chrome-plated metal. Thick, pale green, tinted window glass gave it an authentic appearance.

When the cabdriver, named Deniz with a Z had dropped her off, she'd been consumed with worry about the child in a coma. However, truth be told, she knew Jazz was in adequate and capable medical hands. Knowing that she'd later be spending the night with the child was comforting enough for her to do what she needed to do before returning to the hospital. Realizing what the demands of the next few days would require of her, until at least one of Jazz's parent's arrived, she'd given herself ninety minutes to switch gears and take care of any and all unfinished business at her diner home. The errands she needed to do would take all of ten minutes. This meant she had at least an hour to be efficient while calming her frazzled nerves. Observing an empty and silent diner was something she, as its owner, almost never had the opportunity to do. Ruby repositioned her spectacles and took a long, proper look around her absolute favourite place on the planet.

The Seaside flawlessly symbolized remnants of the post-porcelain and enamel era. The period before Formica was invented and plastic debris in the oceans was first observed. The 1960s was the decade when people began to become increasingly aware of environmental problems. Back then and even today, in the elderly woman's steadfast opinion, the popularity and colossal use of Formica and plastic would in time eventually ruin the elegance of the modern world. Therefore, she'd chosen to preserve her diner's original décor. Despite the cost, its authenticity was worth her money and effort. Little did she know, throughout the 50s and 60s, how spot on her prediction would prove itself to be?

The diner's original main compartment was fashioned with an elongated and shallow design. It had a singular, railroad car shape. Its exterior had been built using sheet metal and burnished chrome-plated panels. In 1970, a modest beach view addition had been constructed in the rear section. The addition was needed to accommodate its increasing patronage. Choosing to remain hospitable and small-sized, Ruby had seen to it that the new space could seat only eight to sixteen customers. Four spaciously sized booths were assembled, and a unisex toilet was installed at the end of the back corridor. The only other major adjustments she'd made to the original 1950s design was when she changed the menu, its interior scheme, and its colour pattern. In 1951, the diner was designed using signature colours of sky and azure blue. In 1960, the proud new, 35-year-old business owner, for a ridiculously obvious reason, changed the interior and trim colours to ruby red. She'd wanted to make the old version of diner into something that would reflect her personality and authenticity. She was intent on building a life and living space for herself and Eliza. In less than two years, after she'd purchased and refashioned it, The Seaside felt like home. Her diner went on to become one of London's oldest, most self-sustaining financial accomplishments.

She left her stool and rotated the dimmer switch that controlled the overhead lights. When she'd arrived from the hospital, she had intentionally dimmed the lights in an attempt to make the diner appear to be closed. The last thing she was in the frame of mind for was small talk with some hungry geezer who was in the mood for french-fries, or a beer. After she adjusted the ceiling lights to a brighter setting, all she desired was to gaze around her finest achievement; the place she had spent two thirds of her life creating, managing, and living in. Since the late 1950s, the interior of the Seaside had boasted a reflective metal and enamel design with unrefined medium dark, wooden booths. It had low embellished timber ceiling beams and classical wall trim. The beams and trim were made from a fine grade of mahogany lumber. Despite that its original black, white, and red checkered floor tiles had worn thin over time, they still served their decorative purpose. The floor was mopped daily and painstakingly buffed once a week. With all the wear and tear it had endured since the diner had been built, it deserved to be cared for and treated with respect. As far as floors went, it was pampered by a useful and long life.

A seemingly endless counter offered fifteen high seats, or bar stools as they later came to be called. The elderly woman cherished their urban style and the pop of colour the stools gave her diner, even on the gloomiest of grey days in London. The sturdy, round, red-topped, 360-degree swivel seats were made of chrome-layered steel. Each stool had feet support rings of various sizes soldered to its base. The footrests had been welded on the frames, at different heights. This was done intentionally, to make them solid enough to support and accommodate the different weights, leg lengths, and foot sizes of her patrons. Depending on where a person sat, at the counter, or at one of the rows of booths situated next to the windows, the diner offered its patrons different views.

From one side of the dining area customers could see a cul-de-sac with tree lined, flower covered hillsides. From the other side of the dining hall they saw a less appealing parking terrain and cars passing by on the main road. As a rule, she'd seat her younger customers on the parking lot side, given that they came for socializing and eating, not for the view. The nicest view from the dining area was of the picturesque coastline, with fishing boats in the distance and seagulls hovering above the English Channel. Most of her regular patrons sat in the same seat's week after week. This meant that tourists and her newest customers often were obligated to sit in the less popular booths. More times than not, they didn't object to this because unlike others, they were usually just passing through the area.

The diner delivered delicious food and a spirited interior design. Its atmosphere and ambiances were more than enough to compensate for the sitting at a booth with a parking lot view. Only on rare occasions was there an empty seat in the place. On the weekends people stood in line at the entrance waiting to be seated. Business was thriving, overhead was low, and profits were high. Since its opening, The Seaside had employed six different grill men, or 'short order cooks' as they later came to be called. Because of its exposed galley design, the grill men could be seen operating a busy, often hectic kitchen. The open galley was why Ruby had trained her kitchen staff to be shipshape. She was adamant about showing her customers a neat, spick span kitchen area. Each of the cooks that she employed over the years had been enthusiastically friendly and amusing chaps. As they flipped the burgers and scrambled the eggs, they sang off tune or whistled a tune, which entertained customers of all ages. Throughout the '60s and '70s the personality and presence of Ruby's short-order cooks was irreplaceable and an enormous part of her diner's charm. Then unpredictably, with the onset of a new decade, this changed.

In 1981, one of Ruby's cooks, a dark-toned man with a thick moustache, one leg shorter than the other, and the devil's blaze in his eyes, was caught stealing from her. His thieving came as a shock because The Seaside's owner was known for being an excellent judge of character. Even so, a very handsome, 47-year-old Greek chap with a distinguished accent and noticeable gimp had tickled a fancy in Ruby. She'd forgotten all about her fancy until he applied for the job. After Mia's return to Ireland, in 1972, she'd convinced herself that her fancy was destined to be forever 'unticklable'. At least half of her female customers over forty could be seen ogling him, blushing, and flirting while their orders were being prepared. Since the cook from Greece had been hired more women patrons were sitting at the counter than ever before. They all wanted a front row seat and a bird's eye view of the most appealing foreign cook the diner owner had ever employed. For nearly two years her cook was something the women seemed to enjoy more than the food they ate. Her profits steadily increased; therefore naively and unfortunately Ruby let her entrepreneur guard down. Petro, the magnanimous, flirtatious Latin grill man had connivingly charmed his way into Ruby's heart, her kitchen, and her cash register.

One afternoon he offered to close up the diner for his overworked, trusting boss, who he kindly told, "Madam Ruby, you appear in need of some time off."

Petro had closed up and cashed out plenty of times before, so Ruby never gave his generous offer a second thought. She readily agreed with his observation and decided to spoil herself by going shopping on Carnaby Street. During the height of the swinging sixties, Carnaby Street had been branded as the beating heart of London's fashion scene. She had a grand time of it all afternoon whilst spending money on herself until sundown. Unfortunately, Petro didn't come into work the next morning and the weekly bank deposit bag in the diner safe was missing. Ruby rightfully suspected that she'd been unjustifiably swindled and robbed. Just shy of £3.700 pounds had vanished.

Early the next morning a Greek chap with a distinct gimp in his gait was apprehended by the police at one of the nearby shipping docks. The thief was boarding a ferry on its way to France. He had a trifling £12 pounds in his pocket. A soiled cook's apron with The Seaside logo embossed on it was found in his duffle bag. He'd denied every accusation made and the money was never recovered. How much he'd stolen from Ruby since she'd hired him was a mystery that she knew would remain unsolved. She blamed herself for allowing his masculinity and his outgoing foreign personality to blind her from seeing a manipulative, underhanded thief lurking beneath his charming surface.

After his apprehension, Ruby burned the uniform and aprons he'd left behind in a fire pit at the beach behind the diner. Petro's timecards and a wool sweater that the police had found while searching his locker went up in flames as well. As the smoke from his dishonesty rose into the air above her head, she bid good riddance to the deceitful, uneven legged man, and to the anger and disappointment she had had in herself for being such a naïve sucker. The 56 year old, flimflammed owner of The Seaside then stepped back from the fire and watched the entire experience burn. The next day she hired a new cook, changed the lock on the safe, and never looked back.

She was laidback in this way. She scarcely dwelt on the past, or things she couldn't control or change. Likewise, she learned from her blunders and never repeated them. This was beyond doubt, a blunder, she'd never make again. Ruby didn't press charges. Her generosity to the burglar wasn't because of her ex-grill man's proclamation of innocence; it was because she wanted to protect her diner's reputation. A reputation that was worth much more than the £3,700 pounds he'd stolen from her.

Three months later, after losing his job, his immigrant visa, and his temporary work permit, Petro was deported. Upon being notified of this, the duped diner owner mentally deleted the entire Greek episode from her life.

Chapter 17

"I'd forgotten all about Peg-a-leg Petro," the elderly woman heard herself saying at the top of her voice. "Pity he had such sticky fingers. He was by far the most fetching, appealing, and finest cook who ever operated my kitchen."

The oldest living member of the Dutton-McEwen family was known for talking to herself. Once someone had gotten to know her, they learned to distinguish the difference between a conversation she was having with them and one she was having with herself. She claimed that 'the reason she talked to herself, was that she was guaranteed someone was listening'. Simply said and simply done was just how she liked it. Numerous other chefs came and went long after Peg-a-leg had freely dipped his greedy paws into Ruby's cashbox. Each of the cooks had walked a now visible groove into the diner's original kitchen floor. The floors permanent indentation trail was never repaired or disdained. On the contrary, it was seen as a symbol that paid tribute to over sixty years of each of their individual diligences and high regard for their craft.

To be assured that customer service was swift and friendly, tips were not accepted at The Seaside. The diner's owner was a true people pleaser; therefore, she trained her staff to be sociable and capable. In her view, *people shouldn't be paid to be nice*. Moreover, *being nice wasn't a choice, it was a requirement*. She'd rather pay her staff and extra pound an hour, than witness their wearing fake smiles for the sake of earning extra tips. This was a conviction of hers that had made The Seaside one of the most popular eateries in the entire city. This wasn't because of the money customers saved on tips, but because of the fantastic service and ambiances they received. If a customer did leave a tip behind, it was fairly split between the staff on duty. Employees caught pocketing tips were unemployed the next day.

She felt chilled again and had begun to shiver. Almost daily she'd forget how old and thin-skinned her body had become. It was rumoured that when a person had a spirit that didn't age, they often overlooked their body. Ruby was a classic example of this type of person. It had been a long, stressful day; her legs were aching, her joints were stiff, and she needed to pee again. The older version of Ruby McEwen urinated a lot. Her bladder had without a doubt aged. She stretched herself out a bit, stood up and limped off in the direction of the toilet. Grinning, she tapped each counter stool as she passed them by. Despite the raw circumstances of the dire situation she was now embedded in, she was happy. Finding bliss in the nooks and crannies of life was a skill that came naturally to her.

After weeing, washing her hands, and fluffing up her cropped hair and blunt cut bangs, she decided to sit back down. On her way back to her recliner, she stopped by the dessert cooler and helped herself to a large piece of strawberry cream pie. She arranged the pastry neatly on a plate, leaned forward and licked at the pie's pinkish frosting. Not realizing how hungry she was, she gulped it down without a fork.

Then, she took inventory of the food that hadn't yet been put into the coolers and walk-in refrigerators and made a mental note to *ring up her kitchen helper, Finn McGee.*

Aside from Nico, he was the only other employee with a diner key. Finn would need sort out the food stock that had been left behind and unattended to when the detectives had rushed her off earlier to Saint Matthew's Hospital. He'd also need to pack up and store all of the fresh food that hadn't been eaten today. She didn't have time to do any of this. She'd known the boy's father since the early 1980s. He and his wife were immigrants from the County Cork region of Ireland. To the Irish, lending a helping hand was as routine as drinking ale was. Finn's family would do whatever was needed for their long time neighbour and son's employer. Likewise they'd ask for nothing in return. Not knowing when the diner could reopen, she wanted to avoid rotted food, a fly infestation, or mice having their way with the kitchen's leftovers. Finn lived within walking distance from his part time job at The Seaside, where he'd been in her employ for the past four years. Therefore, she had complete faith in him. Despite the unexpectedly grim circumstances, she knew her diner would be rightly fine without her for a day or two.

The sugar-addicted old woman with two rather large ears had savoured each strawberry flavoured morsel of her pie. As she sat back down, the pastry's taste reminded her of how much the diner's menu, and its décor reflected the preferences of her customers. The unique simplicity of her style shone through her diner's every niche. She was enjoying being alone in her place of business and her home. This was something that didn't happen often. For this reason she allowed herself the pleasure of reminiscing for a bit longer.

To adapt to new food trends and the changing times a new menu was introduced every five years or so. Since 1960, Ruby had been serving only breakfast and lunch. Being a single mother she'd opted for late afternoons and evenings with her child instead of hosting a dinner service. Pitchers filled with ice water and fresh lemon wedges were available on every table and at the counter. Back in the early 1990s, Ruby ignored a new eatery trend of charging customers for tap water and ice. In her opinion, water was one of the earths most healthy and plentiful elements, therefore, it would be considered a complimentary beverage as long as she owned The Seaside. Although the diner owner never turned away a cup of Earl Grey tea, a steaming mug of strong and hot coffee was her breakfast drink of choice. Her teenage and adult customers tolerated her unusually richly blended, robust coffee very well. Coffee and tea drinkers received one free refill. Either they drank it black or they flavoured their cups to suit their own palates. Cream, sugar, cinnamon containers, honey, and reusable stirring sticks were conveniently positioned at the counter and at each of the booths. Only two short years, after the now very old lady had become a diner owner, The Seaside was thriving faster than her customers placed their orders.

Ruby plopped back down in her lounge chair, licked the remaining strawberry sweetness off her fingertips, and contemplated if Jazz liked the taste of sugar as much as her great grandmother did? For a reason she'd yet to decipher or pay much attention to, she realized that since Jazz's arrival from the States, she'd often seen her younger self in her. Because Eliza had been so very different than Ruby was, finding commonalities in her only child had been a challenge. As she sat in the lounger with the shape of her backside melded into it, she admired the life she'd made for herself and her patrons as her mind churned on with recollections of a time gone by at The Seaside. Over the years, Ruby had insisted that her eatery remain a small and cosy place. As the decades passed, Wi-Fi and the internet globally changed the way people communicated. It was a change she'd wanted absolutely nothing to do with. She obstinately refused to install a broadband connection inside the diner or outdoors nearby her property's stretch of beach.

Even today, nearly four decades later, as the elderly woman sat in her favourite chair, her personal and business convictions about up-to-date, modern technology hadn't changed since the 1980s. The wise and prudent person that she was, passionately believed that *the Internet and Wi-Fi were the beginning of the end of genuine human interaction.*

Ruby was unwavering in her code of ethics and fairness. People from all lifestyles desired a pleasant dining experience, therefore, her objective was to offer them something homey, sociable, and delicious. Her diner would be a place where customers wanted to return to for its exceptionally warm ambiance, not for its high-speed internet connection and free Wi-Fi. Even as early as last week, there had been many protesters to her stringent policies and personal convictions. This was particularly evident after the turn of the century arrived, bringing generations X, Y, and Z with it.

The younger, more digitally addicted generations were the most disappointed and predictable customer's she had. When they realized that their digital devices were not connectable, they'd verbally gripe or stomp off, while acting like tantrums wearing overly priced shoes. Often, they'd openly and crudely lash out at Ruby and her staff. Back then and even as recent as yesterday, she referred to these bad-tempered patrons of hers as, Generation S'ers. In her opinion, they were spoiled, and they were selfish. A few of them took proper stands against her anti-internet policies, by flipping their 'screw you' middle fingers up and then spitting profane words all over her. Their behaviour, if seen, earned them an automatic refusal of service and exit from her diner. Occasionally, some of them apologized and were allowed to place an order, whilst others she never saw again.

Generation S was actually different from other high-tech generations. Her age earned outlook was that despite which type of generation they belonged to, since around 1990, people of all ages had become technologically overindulged. Generation S'ers were like wilful toddlers who had physical outbursts when their androids were not allowed to join them at their tables. When the elderly woman was much younger, she remembered androids being robots that looked like humans. In these modern times, androids were something she couldn't wrap her timeworn brain around. Regardless, she remained steadfast and held her ground; androids would not be allowed to take over her business or her residence. Ruby had become a perceptive proprietor, who prided herself on pleasing and connecting people. Therefore, she refused to let technology and automations disconnect the very people she had worked for years to connect. She took pride in owning and managing a diner that offered her customers, regulars and newcomers alike, a unique and memorable experience. She refused to fall prey to any kind of norm or risk turning her establishment into another mundane eatery that indulged its patrons in digital conveniences. This was not her mentality or style; not at all. She already lived in a fast-paced world and for that reason, when people stepped onto her turf, they would experience life and a meal at a gentler speed. This was a dining quality that she prided herself on and intended to implement until her death. Knowing that the diner would outlive her made her all the more obstinate.

Despite her age, she was the face and the charisma behind The Seaside. She was a hostess who greeted every customer at the door, and she was the person who oversaw every detail of her finest achievement. She was the core and the energy of it all. For these reasons, she was the person who decided if she had a table available for customers or not. Attitude and manners played a large role in whether she sat a person or refused them service. She had swagger and insisted on the giving and receiving of respect. The sharp-minded Brit had owned and operated one of London's most popular dining places for nearly sixty years. She was notoriously bad with numbers, but she never forgot a face or an angry fully extended middle finger. Her goal had always been to run an establishment that was like an old-fashioned watering hole. It would serve as a place where people gathered socially and where even first-time customers communicated with one another. On the other hand, she respected and encouraged those who preferred to dine in silence. As a businesswoman and a born thinker she understood that there were times when a person categorically needed to reflect upon whatever occupied his or her mind. Ruby honestly thought that her greatest gift to her patrons was enabling them to partake in a pleasurable, inexpensive dining experience while quieting their minds or sharing their stories.

Over the years she'd seen the bankruptcy of a number of other small restaurants, diners, pubs, and cafés. This was something that many eatery owners were beginning to blame on a new and popular trend called Free Wi-Fi and Hotspots. Across the city, people eating out were spending more and more time occupying tables, often for hours on end, while fixated on their cell phones, laptops, iPads, and their tablets. In turn, this meant that they spent much less time ordering, eating, socializing, and spending money. Statistics had verified that this was a threatening factor in the recent demise of many small-scaled restaurants. The Seaside was classified as small-scale; therefore, she'd taken matters into her own stubborn and capable hands. In the past sixty-five years, she'd refused to let herself and her livelihood become a statistic of any kind. Ruby McEwen had a reputation for being a decent, sociable, and trendy woman. She was also notorious for being a tough, resilient, and determined business owner who paid zero attention to trends or conformed to anything she didn't believe in. The passage of time and old age hadn't changed this; on the contrary, time and age had solidified who she was.

Trying to relieve the pain in her crooked spine, she shifted about in her lounger. Once she'd settled herself into a more comfortable position, she tucked the blanket tighter around her legs and midriff. Then she patted herself on her back for remaining true to who she was. In that very moment, she realized that she was proud of herself, which was something Ruby Adeline McEwen, on the odd occasion felt, and under no circumstances acknowledged.

Her wilful mind had an unexpected need to drift a tad further in reverse. She easily obliged it by closing her eyes, inhaling deeply, and traveling back to another changing time throughout Great Britain and the United States. Within seconds she had entered the Me-First Decade.

In the late 1980s Londoner's experienced a population boom throughout the city when the 'yuppies' arrived. Yuppies, those self-absorbed young professionals that earned an above average pay, seemed to be sprouting up all over the USA and England. They were keen on cultural attractions, good food, alcohol, and entertainment. Their substantial incomes offered them a limitless number of rewards. The yuppie's sophisticated urban and suburban lifestyles created and influenced a late-twentieth-century cultural phenomenon. In effect, the boom was financing the restaurants, bars, and art districts in and around London's city centre. Their presence and influence changed the quality of life in Britain and metropolises across the USA. Yuppies were bringing people back to the cities. The change was fast and very popular among the majority of Britain and America's habitants. Life, as they had previously known it to be, was changing.

When the 1990s arrived, despite that more and more Londoner's valued a thriving community spirit, many began to realize that they yearned space and tranquillity. In search of their yens, they ventured out into the suburbs for their open spaced parks, entertainment, and restaurants. This increased The Seaside's business threefold within less than a year.

Her Barcalounger was located in the more secluded, back section of the diner; where the now warmer, Ruby was returning to the here and now of her life. She'd needed time for reflecting and unwinding from everything the day had heartlessly dumped in her lap. She felt buried under a stressful weight of the past twenty-four hours, with the police informing her about the accident being the heaviest of her loads. She'd felt her heart skip many a beat when the constables revealed the reason for their unplanned visit earlier today.

"So is life," she heard the accepting side of herself saying aloud. "Carry on Ruby girl. You are very old but the day is still young."

Then, she rubbed the back of her neck, fluffed up her cropped pure white hair and looked scrupulously around her livelihood. Her desire to please, her cleverness, and her unswerving outdated convictions were reasons why the elderly woman's eatery had endured and survived a kaleidoscopic of change. Her diner remained one of the few public eating places in London's outlying coastal area that provided its clientele with three unusual, unique necessities;

no internet, no Wi-Fi, and optional silence. As a result, her customers were unplugging from their demanding lives and congested minds long enough to plug into solitude or a decent conversation. They could be seen taking a break from life while acknowledging and conversing with each other face to face, rather than online.

Ruby, who was still in an observing mood, revelled in her belief that her patrons had learned to care much more about each other than they did about social media and how many stupid, bloody 'likes' they had. Regulars at the iconic diner overlooking the English Channel knew each other by name. They identified with each other, engaged in conversations, and briefly connected their lives while sharing counter or booth space. Despite that her innovative, cyber-free eatery trends were being imitated at a growing number of other cafes, restaurants, and snack bars throughout England; they remained her original ideas and inventively creative, non-artificial concepts. Her digital-free eatery was still popular and offered hundreds of people, each month, healthy alternatives to being online and buried in, and under, portable devices, social media addictions, and their problematic lives. Ce la vie.

She then decided that once she'd rested enough and felt ready, she'd make the overseas phone call she was dreading. Knowing that the child's American mother was still asleep was past the bounds of comforting for her. She didn't want to wake the exaggeratedly emotional and unpredictable Zofia up. Likewise, she wanted to avoid revealing the news of Jazz's accident too soon. Given the events of the past eight hours, Ruby knew it took a brave, strong-willed person to cope with the alarming news of the child's comatose state, not to mention her temporary physical deformities. Seeing her daughter for the first time at Saint Matthew's Hospital would be tenfold as distressing as the phone call would be. Regrettably, strength and resilience were two fortes that Zofia didn't possess. In view of this fact, the timing of Ruby's phone call was crucial.

Once the news of Jazz Durant's perilous situation reached California, the elderly woman's world would drastically change, in an even more radical way than the boating accident had already changed it.

Chapter 18

The New Millennium had arrived, and it was here to stay. Throughout the more modern era, Ruby McEwen, was reputed for her ability to create a social vibe. Even today she was still considered to be an open-minded female, a motivated public pioneer, and a promoter of humane interaction.

Her sincere desire was to leave a meaningful, yet invisible, imprint of herself behind on the country she'd been living in for nearly ninety years. Consequently, she was quite proud to be the bearer of such a reputation. *A considerably honourable thing to feel*, she privately confessed to herself from her Barcalounger, *for an old lady with small round, black metal spectacles perched on the tip of her nose*. Ruby's need to be slightly selfish and spoil herself with 'the gift of more time' had not disappeared. Despite the circumstances, she was feeling oddly cheerful and wanted to embrace her mood for as long as she could. She noticed that all of the ice had melted in the glass she'd been holding. While she'd assumed that she still had plenty of time before the cabbie returned and beeped his horn, she had actually lost track of how late it was while meandering through her past.

Thanks to an extra high armchair feature, she painlessly stood up from her classical styled, wing-backed lounger. Her cushiony, fudge coloured Barcalounger was perfect for compact spaces. This is why she'd positioned it in the farthest, back corner of the diner when construction of its addition was completed. Her recliner was her 'go to place' when she needed to sit for a moment and inhale a healthy amount of relaxation. Out of respect for Ruby and fear of being publicly reprimanded by her, customers and employees never sat in her lounger. It was forbidden and they knew this.

As she aged with each passing year, understandably, her body demanded more maintenance and rest. For this reason, she'd use her recliner to daily observe the people that came, then went, or loitered in her diner world. There she would sit, quite amused whilst enjoying The Seaside's human energy as it buzzed and gyrated around her. Ruby was the kind of person who didn't want to miss a moment of life. Sometimes, her age demanded that she catnap, so she dozed and snoozed at will. Often, she would wake up, not realizing that she'd fallen asleep.

Her Barcalounger had sculptured, wing-shaped, mahogany wood armrests. The original lever that was used to lengthen and raise the footrest had broken off sometime in the early 1990s. Decades later, as a gift for her birthday, her dishwasher Nico had replaced it with a new, handmade handle. He'd fashioned the hand-controlled lever from solid mahogany and mounted it to the chairs adjusting mechanism with a large brass bolt. Nico had chosen mahogany because the wood colour matched the lounger's armrests and the diner's interior décor. A sturdy bolt he'd chosen complemented the brass upholstery studs that held the chairs leather trimmed edges securely in place.

Nico was very thoughtful and handy in this way. He often knew what his employer and her place of business needed even before she knew.

Thinking about Nico was now rightly upsetting her. She knew where Jazz was, but she was clueless as to what had happened to her Italian employee and lodger. She absolutely despised being clueless. Being bollixed made her feel useless. Hobbling back towards the kitchen, she shed a few out of character and suppressed tears. Gazing up at the clock reassured her that she still had enough time for her personal needs before the cabbie returned. Next to the clock hung a framed, black and white photograph of a snow-covered Westminster Abby. Seeing the photo sparked her memory's interest. With her courageously trained mind she quickly dismissed her discerning thoughts of Nico. Tightly clenching the empty glass, she reached over, held it under the ice-cube machine, and brimmed it off. Then she went to the loo again, washed her hands, cleaned her dirty spectacles, and sat back down in her Barcalounger. With the speed of what felt like the blink of her lethargic eyes, she was feeling a degree of cold that reminded her of an event that had taken place more than six decades ago. Her tingling, nearly numb hands had her mind racing swiftly in reverse. She decided that she wouldn't allow her brain to wander this time. This time she would hold on tight to the icy glass and use her reliable mind's control skill to prevent herself from mentally drifting off for too long or too far. Despite that she was too tired for wandering mentally, she was anxious to reminisce about one particular post-World War II winter in the British Isles.

Now relaxed and cocooned in another one of her mental corsets, the elderly woman continued to muse over a specific event from a time gone by. Ruby McEwen was completely at ease with stepping in and out of the past.

Somewhere deep, in a bottomless crevice of her drifting mind, The United Kingdom was in the frozen grip of a nasty winter, unlike one most Brits had ever seen before. In early December, the 26-year-old daughter of Horace and Sadie McEwen had promised her parents that she'd visit them after the hectic holiday season in Ireland had ended. She'd graduated five months previously, after an extremely uncertain senior year at University College in Dublin. She still was volunteering at the Unwed Mother's Home where she'd met her best friend, Mia Doherty, years before. The ambitious girl from Essex also had her first serious boyfriend. Until now, like many other aspects of her life, she'd kept him a secret from her parents. She worked part time at a nearby brasserie to pay for her studio apartment, books, school supplies, living provisions, and kibble for her fat, lazy, spoiled cat. Because she was stubborn, private, and resolute about earning her own life, the student accepted no handouts from her parents or grandparents. Her tenacious personality meant that the intelligent and talented graduate had a busy and demanding life.

She hadn't seen her British family since 1952, when she'd visited her grandparents in London for the last time. Since the challenges that had befallen her in the mid-1950s, it had taken the better part of two years for her emotional wounds to heal. After experiencing a few serious ordeals and making a life changing conclusion, she'd decided to keep the uncertainties that she was still burdened with very secretive. She'd left great happiness and indecision behind in Dublin in an effort to experience a sense of freedom that she'd not had in nearly a year. Only tim9e would tell, if during this visit to Essex County, she'd find the nerve to open up to her parents and divulge what her life in Ireland had become. Ruby had never had an intimate relationship with her parents because the circumstances of their marriage and conflicting goings-on during her childhood years had prevented her from developing any real trust in them. Solving problems and making decisions privately had always been easier than involving them in the details of her life.

The past few years had taken a huge amount of academic diligence, emotional strength, energy, and audacity from her. Throughout that difficult period, every now and then she would wonder, *how she'd gone from being a baby, who at the time was still not damaged or neglected by her parents, Horace and Sadie, to who she now was? How did she get from there to here?*

As her mind probed, despite her never-ending need for answers, her optimistic side enabled her to find appreciation for what she actually did know. She knew that the turbulence of the past twenty-six months was now behind her. She was healthy, somewhat attractive, highly educated, and back on track. Furthermore, she was looking ahead, in love for the first time, and ready to see her family again. Or so she thought.

She'd done an immeasurable amount of maturing since WWII ended. After the wartime delay in graduating high school was over, she left home to pursue her studies in Ireland. She knew that her parent's unstable relationship had left melodramatic scars on her since she was a wee child, therefore now, as the responsible adult she'd become, she was prepared to shield herself from more emotional disfiguring. It was time to make a serious choice; would she remain on the safe and calmer side of the line she'd drawn between herself and them, or would she cross the line and then turn around and erase it? To answer her own question, she'd need to do whatever was necessary, regardless of risk or consequence.

Winter across the British Isles was becoming very intense throughout the days leading up to her trip home. As severe as it was, Ruby reminded herself that it wasn't nearly as deadly and life changing as the Montana winter her grandparents, Bessie and Samuel Dutton, had endured some sixty years ago. Their wretched winter storm tragedy was one of the few stories her foreign mother, Sadie, had ever openly shared about her Dutton family past. Looking back on it now, she realized that the Dutton family folktale, a true story through and through, had left its indelible mark on her.

Before she knew it, she had arrived in Essex and was walking up the front yard path of the only home she'd ever known. As she put her key in the deadbolt to unlock the main door of the common English house where she'd been born and raised, a vision of the winter storm that had besieged the American Midwest in 1887 interrupted her thoughts. Through her mind's eye, she saw the tragic and malicious snowstorm that had claimed the lives of her grandparent's twin boys. She had a ricocheting, free-willed mind that rebounded and echoed off both current events and events from the past. Something her brain was now wilfully doing again as she turned the key in the door further. Despite that the disastrous memory was trying to claim her attention, she redirected her focus to being back in England again for the first time in just under three years. 'Focus' was one thing the visiting student knew she would without question need while spending time with her parents. As the front door opened and she stepped inside, the young woman hoped that the extreme unhappiness and tension between Horace and Sadie was finally over; or at least tolerable.

Great Britain was in the thralls of a winter that was causing severe economic hardships and life-threatening conditions. Ruby had arrived at her family's rural timber and brick home, with its thinning thatched roof, the day before dangerous snowstorm first began. Less than twenty-four hours later extreme weather had caused widespread disruptions across all of England. The effect of the bitter coldness was intensifying remaining post-war fuel and food shortages that still plagued the nation. Ruby remembered vividly, how the scarcities of food and fuel were even more severe in the aftermath of World War II than they'd been for the duration of the war.

It was the year 1955. A spell of dangerous, freezing weather began during the first week of the New Year. What people living in the British Isles didn't know, was that despite a slight thaw towards the end of the month, more snow would begin to fall in the middle of February. The storms notorious first sub-zero winter blast came in around January 21st. Because of her pre-approved extended visit from her work and responsibilities in Dublin, Ruby was still in Essex with her parents at the time Mother Nature dropped a bomb of another kind on Britain. Countless travel complications were occurring across and between the islands, and regardless of her apprehensions the dangerous winter weather prevented her from returning to the newest chapter in her life. It was a reticent chapter that was changing daily and earnestly waiting for her arrival back in Ireland. As snow fell heavily over the Southwestern regions of England, one of the worst winter storms the country had ever witnessed commenced. Temperatures started plummeting at record speeds, reaching an all-time low of -20°. Within two days, it had become so cold, news reports announced that Big Ben had frozen and missed its 9pm chime. Newscasts went on to inform Brits that the Thames River had iced up. Coalmines and factories were closing, with shipping ports already shut down citywide. Thousands of labourers were obliged to stop working and were sent home without pay to tend to their families and livelihoods.

As numerous, larger than normal snowstorms struck, blizzards in the north left parts of the Isles buried under five feet of what some Brits called, 'a frozen solid kismet.' Conditions grew so desperate in remote northern areas that the military organized what was known as Operation Snowdrop. Operation Snowdrop would become a six-day airdrop of supplies to villages and farms stranded by the deep snow and howling bitter cold winds. Hundreds of family homes and granges had been cut off by snowdrifts over thirty-feet high. The low temperatures caused severe frosts and arctic conditions across the entire country. To assist sharecroppers with feeding livestock that were stranded outside in open fields, paddocks, and corrals, The Royal Air Force flew aircrafts and dropped bales of hay and fodder over

British farms, whilst The Royal Navy flew helicopters that dropped domestic provisions, food, and basic medical supplies to other snowbound regions.

Due to an imminent fuel crisis, electricity cuts were a frequent occurrence. The energy cuts propelled a large part of England back into an all too familiar, involuntary darkness that resembled wartime blackouts. Despite that most Brits were accustomed to energy cuts; the blackouts created a merciless type of fear for England's WWII survivors. For the majority of Brits, since Hitler's defeat, the unnerving wartime darkness of air raids was something they'd not yet had enough time to forget. It undermined their ability to leave the brunt of WWII behind them. Post-war traumas were at an all-time high during Ruby's trip home that year. Likewise, other types of unseen and ominous ordeals began that winter and continued long after her return to Ireland.

The wide-eyed elderly woman, still holding onto her ice-filled glass, called to mind all too clearly how the Arctic freeze had brought England another harsh and visible hazard.

Newspapers reported that automobiles driving on slippery, snow-covered roads were repeatedly having all types of accidents. Likewise, pedestrians were being knocked senseless by huge ice spikes that hung off bridges and fell to the streets below. Numerous unfortunate Brits became sidewalk targets because of unpredictable dangers such as this. Ruby's pa, Horace, turned into an intoxicated, domestic bully whenever fuel shortages became a problem he couldn't solve. Britain was already a half million tons short on coal before the winter had begun that year. The British Miners Union had previously consented to employing hundreds of thousands of local and foreign miners after the war. Despite the storm, these fortunate men were able to hold onto their jobs as they continued excavating coal day and night. Regardless of their round the clock efforts, the excavated coal supply couldn't meet coal demands of a nation that was, in fact, freezing to death. On the second night of her visit, an inebriated Horace coaxed Ruby to go outside and into the frigid sub-zero air. He should have known that she still wasn't an even slightly 'coax able' type.

In her rational opinion, going outside was a very stupid and unnecessary thing to do. In the end, she chose to do as she was told for one reason and one reason only; once her father got 'bladdered' his drunkenness would need her protection, otherwise, he'd act stupid and reckless. She'd never liked it when her mother called Horace a drunk. Therefore, with a wee bit of respect for the man who'd put up with the likes of her mother Sadie for the better part of forty years, she referred to him as being 'bladdered', instead of plastered, or drunken. Regardless of her reverential choice of words, she watched as her pa took the last swig of whisky from a nearly empty bottle.

He then blatantly broadcasted, "I just burned our last bucket of coal, and the house is cooling down much too quickly Ruby-girl!"

Sadie was indisputably driving Horace insane with her bloody pissing and moaning about being too damn cold. Ruby's mother was a born and bred hypochondriac. She deathly feared anything from a bug bite to tuberculosis.

Since Ruby had left to study in Ireland, she'd forgotten how much of a complainer her mother truly was. Because her studies began at a slightly older age, in the past five years she'd viewed her parents, more so her mother, through adult eyes, rather than the eyes of a teenager. Sadie was a whiner, and she was lackadaisical. Her laziness was why her daughter had always worked harder than was needed and was determined to accomplish more than women at the time were allowed to or chose to.

"It's time to cut down the old oak tree!" an intoxicated Horace boldly avowed, "I either cut the tree or we'll be burning your mother's furniture by midnight!"

Then he blew his snot filled nose into a dirty hanky, opened the door to the backyard, and enthusiastically demanded, "Ruby-girl, grab your hat, coat, and gloves and meet me outside in two minutes!"

Too dumbfounded for a responsible or sane reaction, the dutiful 'Keeper of Secrets' rolled her eyes and called her father an idiot under her breath. Then, she obediently put on her winter gear and did as she was told.

Chapter 19

Just as if it happened yesterday, the elderly version of the McEwen girl from Essex County, with hands as cold as ice cubes, remembered how bloody pissed off she was when Horace announced his plan to cut the family oak tree down in order to shut Sadie up and keep his complaining, lazy-ass wife warm!

Ruby sat in her lounger shivering as she thought more about that particular winter night. The nerves of steel she'd once had in her youth had turned to putty with age. Nonetheless, she wasn't a coward by any means, however, nowadays, vulnerability tended to challenge her gallant side more often than she ever before could recall. This time, with her eyes open, she rolled the glass back and forth between her palms and long fingers and slipped back in time with ease.

Deep in her sharp mind, she was still in Essex England. She could see herself standing outside, exposed to a nasty blizzard that was blasting her with merciless, bitter cold wind gusts. There she stood, knee deep in snow, in the dark, trembling profusely while waiting in for her intoxicated father. Distinctly, she could see herself on that unusually gruff and hoarfrost night; fearless and possessed by a newfound, bizarre kind of bravery. Horace had just tried to talk her into drinking a gulp of his whiskey to warm her up, which would help her to better endure the harshness of the winter storm.

He exclaimed, "It is weather like this, Ruby-girl that makes me rightly thrilled whiskey doesn't freeze!"

"Come on. Take a swig with your old man," he cajoled.

She shook her head and exasperatedly rolled her eyes once more at him. He knew this meant she was again saying 'hell no' to his whiskey. She never said yes when it came to the bottle. He could see that she'd found her focus and was now ignoring how much of a bloody, goddamned witless moron her father was when he drank! Focused or not, the man was seriously frightening her with his half-brained idea to cut down a nearly five-decade old tree towering over them during the height of a record-breaking blizzard. They barely could stand upright because of the deep snow and ferocious coastal gales. On all sides of their property, especially on the roof, the snow was rising with every passing minute. Snowdrifts were already higher than the windowsills on the ground floor of the house. Ruby was trembling and shrinking from the blustery wind that attempted to blow her off her feet. She tried, but failed, to listen to Horace explaining his strategy 'to act like a professional lumberjack'. Sleet was propelling directly in their faces, which practically blinded their ability to see the big old oak tree. Indoors, Sadie stood atop chair in front of a living room window, casting light from a flashlight onto the snowdrifts in the backyard. The flashlight's beam fell terribly short of being any help at all, but at least she took the initiative to try, Ruby sympathetically concluded. It was as plain as it was simple, her mother was allergic to work. She was perhaps the least resourceful person Ruby had ever known, which was the only reason why her feeble attempt to cast more light onto the tree had earned her a tiny smidgeon of respect from her otherwise critical daughter.

The high, whirling winds were making it virtually impossible for Ruby to hear Horace screaming orders at her. His intuitive and experienced daughter almost went back indoors. Nevertheless, she didn't. She wanted, actually she needed, to protect her inebriated father because since she was a young girl, she'd known no different. Protecting Horace had always come first in the life they shared. She was convinced that chopping down the oak's huge branches and then the entire tree, according to her pa's impetuous plan, was riskier than risky. Despite the potential hazards and sub-zero artic elements, the unyielding male head of the household was insistent on having the fireplace blazing with hot flames throughout the night. Ruby knew exactly what was in her father's mind as he looked up at the huge tree and examined the task before them. She couldn't help wondering if he'd even remotely considered, that what they were about to do, was the least bit dangerous?

Horace wasn't a fool. He knew that his wife would literally beat on him with her bony little fists if he burned even one piece of her favourite furniture. Regardless, despite the threat of another one of Sadie's flare-ups, he felt obliged to keep his best girl Ruby warm. Sadie could freeze her spoiled arse off for all he bloody cared! Only the Good Lord above knew how much he'd missed his daughter since she had grown up, let go of his hand, and left home.

Except for faint rays of light coming from the kitchen windows overlooking their back yard, it was pitch dark. Ruby could smell whisky and gasoline only a few inches away from her face. Taking a deep breath of spunk, she rubbed her stiff, iced up woollen gloves back and forth in an attempt to regain some feeling in her fingertips. The insides of her nostrils were sticking together from the bitter cold air which she had no choice but to inhale. Wanting to shield her face from the winter elements, she pulled her woollen scarf up and covered her nose and mouth. It was a useless effort; the wind pierced the wool within seconds.

Then, for a fleeting moment, she closed her eyes and prayed to a God she didn't think she believed in that tonight she wouldn't fall victim to her drunken father, a rickety old chainsaw, and a huge tree looming over her head like a gigantic death sentence. While quivering and primed to do her part to shield and appease Horace, her irresponsible, tipsy father yanked fast and furiously on the starter cord of his gasoline-powered chain saw. The loud banging sound it made when backfiring startled the living hell out of Ruby! She slipped, stumbled, and toppled onto the frozen winter ground underneath her insulated steel toed boots.

"Drunken old bladdered fool!" she screamed at him as she stood back up.

Her anger fumed! The sputtering and roiling noise of the chainsaw engine immediately muffled out sounds of the gusting wind, her cursing, and her chattering teeth. She bent down and picked up the whiskey bottle Horace had dropped in the snow. With anger and vengeance, she threw it as far into the wintery darkness as she could.

"Bloody fragged sod off old man!" she screeched, purging her lungs of too many whiskeys hating anger filled years. Horace, seeing what she'd done, sternly warned Ruby to keep her eyes wide open, and pay attention! The last thing he wanted to do was accidently kill his best girl in the middle of a storm as severe as this one was! If he heard her damming him, he ignored it. By the time Horace made it to the top of the ladder, Ruby couldn't feel her hands or wrists anymore. The first massive branch came out of nowhere and like a grenade it hit the ground a mere thirty centimetres from where she was standing! The branch's sharp edge grazed her head and took her hat off as its pointy tip hits her feet. The plummeting oak branch left her with a nasty, deep, bleeding laceration across her forehead. Without a hat on her larger than normal ears were exposed to the ruthless winter storm and a drunk for a father. Because of the bitter cold and her fright, the blood dripping down her nose, onto her chin, over her knitted scarf and into the snow, went unnoticed. By now, the piercing winter wind had brutishly penetrated her thick, angora lined leather coat. Her undergarments felt like sheets of ice stuck to her vulnerable skin.

Never before could she recall a time in her life when her hands, on the edge of frostbite, had been so numb. Nor could she remember a time when her mind was so alert and filled with such an intense degree of awareness. This was the night she realized that bitter cold hands could awaken her in a way that kept her mind focused, enabling her to steer her thoughts; a simple tactic that she'd go on to use for many years to come, as she grew into the role of a Master Mind-Traveller.

"Dammit Ruby girl, put your hat and gloves back on and bloody concentrate!" she heard a worried and angry Horace demanding her to do.

The stubborn and bossy man had no idea he'd just injured her. Again, dutifully doing as she was told, she removed her hat from the branch laying across her boots, tucked her gloves into the cuff of her coat, and thought about how much the treasured childhood tree of hers would be missed after it was chopped and gone. It wouldn't take long for her to realize that she was right. After all, the tree had played a role in her life since she'd taken her first breath. Before her birth, the old oak was the only tree on the back lawn behind their house. It stood on the edge of a beautiful, vastly wooded hill that provided a brilliant countryside view from the windows behind their modest home. Just farther than the crest of the densely forested knoll flanking their backyard view, was a cemetery. The cemetery was bordered by a borough. The borough was populated with houses, cars, shops, and one too many pubs for Horace to frequent, which he did.

Unexpectedly, on a warm summer afternoon in 1925, Sadie prematurely went into labour. Ruby was been born in the grass under the oak tree. By the time Horace heard his wife's contraction screams, an infant was peeking its head out of its mother. The newborn's eyes were wide open, as though it yearned to meet and greet the world. Within fifteen seconds, the baby's father slid into a scantily seen, resilient and composed state of self. Seeing the baby lying on the grass in a pool of Sadie's uterine water and blood, he immediately took control of the situation and wrapped his child in a blanket that he'd fetched from the nearby tool-shed. The infant's umbilical cord was still attached to her naval and to her mother. Within about ten seconds after entering her parent's life, on her own, the wee baby girl took her first breath of life. Horace gently held her as she gasped and drew oxygen into her tiny lungs. When the midwife reached them, she finished delivering Horace and Sadie Dutton's first and last daughter. The newborn was lying swaddled on the grass when she'd arrived. Horace had removed his summer jacket and covered his post-delivery, quivering wife with it. He picked his daughter up, gently handed her to the midwife, and then carried on with tending to the frightened and edgy, first time mother's needs. He was sober, tender, engrossed, and stoic throughout the entire event. Horace later learned, from the midwife that his baby girl's gasping was her body reacting to the sudden change in temperature and environment as her lungs filled with air. The complimenting midwife was impressed with his ability to remain calm and concentrate solely on bringing the child safely into the world, while simultaneously tending to the needs of the newborn's mother's. The tale of how baby McEwen was born spread through the region faster that wildfire during a summer drought. The way she'd been born is why people of Essex still, to this day, consider Ruby Adeline McEwen to be Mother Nature's baby first and Sadie and Horace's baby second. Communally, the townspeople agreed that Ruby had been deeply rooted into an earth that had held her before her parents did.

The McEwen's little girl was raised playing in her parent's large backyard with the oak tree growing alongside her. For just shy of twenty turbulent years, both the tree and Ruby withstood many different types of storms. Throughout those years, both tree and child would be tested. Having no siblings had shaped her into a creative, fantasy-rich loner. Therefore, the little girl born under a tree became a hepped up reader who treasured stories. As she grew, her passions for nature, writing, and drawing in her journals, grew together with the time she spent daydreaming. Despite that she was an only child and the 'solitary wolf type', Ruby was never an outsider. On the contrary, from a tender age she was a rare type of physical magnet. She attracted and drew people into her life in the most natural of ways; ways that were equally unintended and unplanned.

The then younger McEwen girl attributed her passion for climbing up high in trees and hanging from their branches to being born under an oak tree. Having no siblings to share life with, while growing up in England, had made her feel, to some extent negligibly isolated at times. In turn, this likewise stimulated her to seek out adventures and make friends. Being an only child suited her because, in hindsight, she never missed what she never had. Be that as it may, it was Sadie and Horace that Ruby grew to miss. As time passed them by their marriage deteriorated. His affection for the pubs and her emotional and mental breakdowns distracted them daily from each other, which side-tracked them from properly parenting her.

Horace was the socializer and the drinker in the family. The combination of these behaviours quickly made women and alcohol two compulsions her pa could not control. Even though Sadie enjoyed a shot of Jameson, or a glass of wine on occasion, she never battled the same addictive hold whiskey had on her husband. Sadie would frequent the taverns just to keep her watchful eyes on his roaming eye. For her, going to the pubs with Horace was never about being a couple or socializing; she went because, despite that she was fervent, needy, and instable, she was adamant about keeping her man in line and her marriage intact. It was quite simple actually. Women loved Horace and Horace loved women. This was a proven fact that kept Sadie on high alert and had her coming in second place to 'his ladies' since they began dating in 1919. Their unstable and self-centred paternal ways had forced Ruby to fend for herself by the time she reached the unpredictable age of twelve. It wasn't the ideal life for an inexperienced, young adolescent, however, over time she'd grow to learn that their choices were teaching her the lasting skills of independence and perseverance. Long before adulthood arrived, to avoid being conflicted by her parent's demons, she mastered the art of keeping herself emotionally intact. Likewise, she avoided any spirits that came in a bottle.

Then the day she'd been waiting for finally came; the day she abruptly pulled her family roots up and out of her parents' ground and fled the only life she'd ever known. Leaving them behind was a defiant, knockback stance; a sign of her refusal to allow another one of Sadie and Horace's domestic storms push her over the edge of anything ever again. Regrettably, her father and her favourite tree couldn't do the same. In her absence, the sad and lonely old man drank more and more while the old oak continued to grow. Both tree and man withstood the crueller side of the outdoor weather and indoor domestic quarrels. Until that particular night in 1955, a daughter returned to her father and the tree was cut down for the sake of keeping a family warm during one of the coldest British winters of the 20th century. Despite the serious fuel shortages that winter, a fire burns consecutively in the McEwen home for forty-five days and forty-six nights. Despite his occasional drunken stupors during that particular visit, Ruby never before recalled Horace being so filled with purpose and so proud of himself.

The Seaside's now elderly owner removed her round, black spectacles and rubbed her forehead while she continued reminiscing about what came to be her last visit to Essex County. Underneath her fingertips, she felt the deformed blemish of a symbolic, scarring birthmark that an old oak tree had left behind before it kept her family from freezing to death.

The winter of 1955 proved to be one of the coldest and hoariest of the Big Freezes that Great Britain experienced between 1947 and 1963. Temperatures reached a record low of -25°C. The severe weather persisted for three weeks in January and returned for another five weeks in February and March. Ruby was back in Ireland studying and tending to her secret life by the time Mother Nature reared her merciless head for a second time that year.

Chapter 20

For most of the elderly woman's younger life her parents were too preoccupied and self-absorbed in their own shitty predicaments to notice the wants and needs of their only child. Their daughter had changed. She'd become a woman right before their eyes and they'd both missed it.

Because of their absence in her daily life, their intelligent, self-assured offspring started increasingly distancing herself from them with each passing week. On deeper levels, they weren't aware of what she struggled with, who she was, or who she was becoming. In great part, they both lived on the surface of life, or so it appeared to their emerging daughter throughout those years. Horace was saddled with his lonely drunken habits and Sadie was likewise burdened with her controversial apathies and instabilities. Despite Ruby's private and independent character traits, the McEwen parents from Essex County were jointly blinded by the effects their negative conducts and selfish needs had on her. During her youth, being a child with no brothers or sisters left her feeling isolated and aching for a sibling. This was one of the first secrets she remembered keeping from her parents back when her pre-teen personality and moralities were developing.

In 1969 her mother Sadie died. Horace passed on much later after reaching a ripe age of ninety. He passed away a very different type of man than Ruby had known him to be when she lived at home. A woman attending Horace's funeral innocently told, the then 50-year-old Ruby, that Sadie experienced two consecutive miscarriages shortly before she'd conceived her. When she'd heard this, the McEwen's now middle-aged, wiser, more compassionate daughter, was finally able to grasp why Sadie was obsessively overprotective of her only living child. She predicted that her mother's intense fear of losing her only living baby had made Sadie a fanatical tyrant. Ruby presumed this most likely was why, and when, Sadie's motherly insecurities peaked, and her emotional instabilities began; thus, her obsessive need to keep her daughter on a restrictively short leash materialized. One lingering regret Ruby would one day take with her to her own grave, was that Sadie never told her about the miscarriages. Ruby believed that she'd surely have taken a different, less opinionated approach with her mother if she'd just known what Sadie had endured.

Throughout the 1920s, as soon as their child took her first steps, the main doors of their Essex house were dead bolted, and a stilted fence was built around their property. The fence and deadbolts would prevent their curious, impish little girl, with dark ginger hair and chubby cheeks, from wandering into the road, drowning in the nearby river, or getting lost in the woodlands that bordered the back yard. At the time, Horace drank away the loss of two babies, plus his wife's post-miscarriage annoying grief and depression. Sadie was 43 years old when Ruby was born. Back in those days having a baby at her age was considered something just shy of a miracle. Six months later, after baby Ruby survived infancy, Sadie methodically persuaded herself that 'a mother was granted only one miracle in life'. Therefore, despite Horace's efforts to plant his seed in her and produce a brother or sister for their only child, Sadie never allowed him to bed her again. Eventually his wife's biological clock stopped ticking, she grew older, and Horace stopped sexually desiring her. As a result, Ruby remained their only child; a girl who'd been born with a uniquely free spirit. She had a life force that her mother was deathly afraid of, and she had a father who tried to keep her close to home and even closer to him. For this reason, their toddler wasn't allowed to venture off alone, hence, the restrictive a deadbolts and enclosed yards. In truth, Sadie's well-intended boundaries backfired. Eventually they only served to stimulate and escalate her daughter's juvenile curiosities and adventurous spirit. Both of which, in turn, had their daughter wandering off the moment she learned how to escape her mother's confines, her father's hovering, and the relentless bedlam her parents created under the roof of the house she was being raised in.

For these reasons, a steel-willed child, named Ruby Adeline, routinely ran away from their arguments, the smell of Horace's whiskey sodden kisses, and Sadie's narcistic, tyrannical style of parenting. For the well-known McEwen lass, life often felt like one never ending rule layered with dictating lectures she was forced to tolerate before and after disobeying. For as hard as she tried, she couldn't control her impulsive needs to evade her parent's restrictive boundaries and explore life. Between the ages of six and ten she'd sneak outside and hike to the top of the hill behind their modest home. Every now and then she'd get caught and punished. Even so, as she grew older and more capable, typically her parents didn't even know she was gone. Horace and Sadie were known by the locals for being tangled up in one catfight after another. Their around-the-clock squabbling was hard on people, especially on three very 'poles apart' McEwen personalities sharing a fenced in house with locked doors and a thatched roof.

Ruby often questioned what happened to the love that had initially attracted her parents to each other. Their intimate disconnection led to her growing up doubting love, because the only type of love she'd ever seen, or known, hurt too much. Therefore, the fledgling McEwen girl grew into a shilly-shallying young woman who sought out adventures whilst mulling over relationships and examining affection while being scared of infatuation. She constantly wondered if falling in love, or being loved, were things to look forward to or things to dread. The sad truth of it was, she never missed Sadie and Horace in the same way her school friends missed their parents when they were separated from them. Later on, in retrospect, she came to learn that how she was raised was actually advantageous for a child born under an oak tree with the sun on her face and sovereignty in her soul.

Throughout those years it didn't matter to her what the weather was on any given day or night; escape was escape, even if it meant freezing at the hand of a harsh Essex winter or sweltering during a summer heatwave. The juvenile version of Ruby wasn't in control of her spontaneity and her impetuous needs, as a result they robotically took her to places she knew Horace and Sadie would never look for her. She was without doubt a clever and precocious girl. The cemetery, just past the edge of the woods bordering their property, was her hiding place of choice. Even after the fence in the backyard was finally taken down and she was given a key to the front door, she continued to sneak off in search of herself, solitude, and peace of mind. On a regular basis she'd find what she searched for while sitting under the dense, green pines and tall, swaying beech trees that lined a ridge located just past a wall of thickets overlooking their property. This was where she felt uninhibited and secluded from the turbulent world she was hiding from at the bottom of the hill. There she'd sit on a tree stump and stare out at the horizon for hours on end. Everywhere she went, she drifted whimsically with her head in the clouds. In the 1930s, dreaming about what her life would someday be like on the other side of County Essex was her saving grace.

The elderly woman who was still sitting composed and content in her lounge chair sighed deeply while she gazed around at 'the other world' she had created for herself. It was a world very unlike the one she'd grown up in. She took a drink of melted ice water and continued thinking about the time she'd spent in Essex, climbing trees, avoiding her parents, spying on boys, and writing in her journals. And so, her self-reflection continued.

By the time the early 1940s arrived she'd become a skilled tree climber. Back in those days, she was sure-footed, fearless, and agile. Climbing trees gave her a sense of power and writing gave her a sense of autonomy. Ruby didn't have the perfect childhood, nor did she have a brother or sister to confide in or to quarrel with. She never had to share anything or defiantly act out in an attempt to gain the attentions of Horace and Sadie, given that there was little attention to be gained. There were no power struggles, between herself and other McEwen children over standing in any kind of family limelight, because there was no limelight to stand in. The only power struggles she was prey to be the daily tiffs between Horace and Sadie. As a young adult, and later as a mother herself, she came to recognize that her parent's intimate relationship never recovered after the loss of their first two children. The harsh reality of her parent's misfortunes was that she paid a sad price for the sake of her dead brothers.

"Not so, unlike my grandmother Bessie," the elderly women heard herself say out loud. "Sadie also paid the price of being raised by a mother mourning the loss of every other member of the original Ballinger Dutton family she was born into."

Even at her ripe age, the meaning if Ruby's life still sporadically fell into place, filled in gaps, and made sense. The old diner owner's spine was now hurting. Even now, decades later, thinking about her mum still tensed her body up to the point of pain. She shifted her position again and tried to dismiss the discomfort in her backbone.

"Basically, I raised myself," she heard herself saying. "It wasn't the ideal childhood, but I have had an interesting life and turned out to be a people prosperous, healthy, and stable old biddy."

Smiling at the pride she seldom felt for herself, the very old version of Ruby continued ruminating about the lass she once was. Now, epochs later, she knew she'd lived long enough to understand that her everyday life habitually reflected her childhood. Growing up the way she had provided her with significant life skills that too many modern-day children of today, unfortunately, were not learning.

The younger Ruby had always been fine with spending large amounts of time by herself. Despite that her customers, and more recently, Finn, Nico and Jazz, had become the older Ruby's extended family, she was still fulfilled and entertained by hard work and socializing with people during the day, then reading books and writing in journals by night. She'd never taken a fancy to television or computers, but she did enjoy going to the movie theatre to see a picture show from time to time. Even now in her eighties, a few times a year she'd indulge herself in simple and satisfying ways. Reading smutty romance novels while drinking a goblet of wine and going incognito to the movies were luxuries she still treasured. She hadn't been a child or become a woman who needed endless stimulation or any type of camaraderie to feel complete. She made her own friends and made her own fun. Above all, she greatly respected the end of each day, because an ending reminded her that another beginning was within her reach. Her favourite time throughout the day was when her world was serenely muted, and her thoughts were set free to ramble. In these moments, she heard little more than the pulsating of her own heart. She was rightly accustomed to making, to taking, and to finding time for herself. Whenever her Seaside Diner world, her staff, and the folks around her made it difficult for her to find seclusion, she'd grow restless and became emotionally lopsided.

She'd grown up to become a relatively laidback and spontaneous person who accepted what life sent her way. Nevertheless, she could bite back with bare teeth and a sharp tongue when necessary. In order to survive an era of two wars, an abundant number of tragedies, and life as an only child, she'd learned to navigate her way with fortitude through perplexing situations. Circumstances that claimed most people long before their time tended to make her stronger and feistier. For as long as she was still breathing, Ruby McEwen refused to be the victim to anyone or to anything. Two years after being entrusted with the antique wooden trunk, a then curious young teenage girl dove into its contents and discovered important intimate family facts and anecdotes Her findings became discoveries that she'd go on to tuck into the recesses of her memory as her life unfolded. Plausibly, at the time, her flush of youth had prevented her from fathoming that she'd live long enough to see nearly a century of people and events come to life and ultimately perish all around her. Even so, in the 1930s, unbeknownst to herself, back then and today, what the teenage Ruby discovered inside the trunk, the patriarch Ruby would repeatedly be reminded of the longer Jazz Durant, remained hospitalized.

In the year 1940, the then budding and rightly troubled daughter of Sadie and Horace McEwen, discovered unmistakable resemblances between her own diaries and her mother's journals. Sadie's memoirs from when she was a girl resembled flamboyantly rich picture books. They were very similar to Ruby's own vividly written and colourfully illustrated diaries from her childhood. Nearly all of their earliest journals were bursting with vibrant drawings and rich, fantasy filled stories. Over the span of two generations

Sadie and Ruby had recorded the events of their lives and created fictitious, illusion laden tales that distanced them both from harsher realities that they were witnessing and weathering. Their journals were filled with expressive tales and fantasies, which satisfied their ever-growing female curiosities. As time passed, and the young girls that Sadie and Ruby once were matured into women, their previously imaginative stories transformed further into more thought-provoking interpretations of real-life experiences.

Bessie Dutton had introduced her daughter, Sadie, to writing in journals when she was still a child. In turn, Sadie had encouraged her own daughter, Ruby, to do the same. Sadie had once told Ruby that her passion for writing in journals was the greatest gift Bessie had passed on to her. Ruby recognized that, despite years of their mother-daughter turmoil, her lifelong passion for writing was the most valuable thing she'd learned from Sadie. For as vastly unalike as these three women, from three spanning generations were, writing and recording life was a similarity they shared. It was the cord that bound them together when fate and circumstances tore them apart.

With her mind returning to the here and now, the elderly woman felt layers of anxiety and worry creeping over her. She knew exactly what the source of her headache and sudden drastic mood change was. She had more fear for her great granddaughter, whom she'd left behind in the ICU, than she'd admitted to herself. On top of this she was filled with apprehension about telephoning the child's mum Zofia. A slight twinge of guilt, for not ringing Zofia up sooner began to weigh heavily on her conscience. For this reason, Ruby gripped the glass tighter, reclaimed her emotional stamina, and reprimanded her doubting self.

"You'll know when the time is right to pick up that receiver," she heard an insightful, inner voice sternly telling her. "Stop doubting yourself old girl. Focus and remember."

Listening to her intuition, with both eyes now wide open, she drank the rest of the melted ice, tightened her grip on the empty glass, and sank deeper into her mind's abyss.

A few years after the winter that had frozen England solid and stopped British life in its tracks was over, the stagnant post-WW2 British economy began to recover. Inventive trades were being developed, imaginative businesses were opening, factories began to thrive again, and London's infrastructure was improving. As jobs returned to the people, the suburbs boomed with growth. In the decade that followed WWII, restaurants, diners, and bars quickly became luring opportunities for a new generation of ambitious entrepreneurs. A then 29-year-old motivated and single mother was keeping an observant eye on a newly opened eatery called The Seaside. The Seaside had been built in 1948 during one of Britain's post-war years of food rationing. At the time, because of government controlled food distributions, its menu was limited and serving sizes were small. Therefore, its then astute male owners relied on its energetic outdoor atmosphere to attract new customers and likewise keep the locals returning weekly. Back then, Ruby was thoroughly impressed with the ingenuity of the diner's male owners. She had a hidden motive, therefore, every chance she had she observed the men, got to know them, and learned from their resourcefulness.

Monthly, often weekly, Ruby witnessed how the sociable owners innovative and exclusive business strategy increased their number of customers both inside, and outdoors at the diners beachside ordering stand. The young, inquisitive, future female businessperson watched and learned as the diner's ambiances yielded the two men one full cashbox after the other. As she observed success unfolding and developing right before her very perceptive eyes, Ruby knew then that someday The Seaside would become a sheer victory. In 1960, The Seaside was unexpectedly put up for sale. It was rumoured that the diner's alleged homosexual owners, both in their mid-seventies, wanted to retire and move to a warmer, less sexually biased country. Regardless of the rumours about the men's sexual preferences, they were both upstanding blokes who were nearly idolized by their customers. Out of respect for the men, gossiping about them was a thing that their patrons did at home, not at the diner or out on the streets. Ruby was one of their most reliable and regular customers. She was someone they knew, liked, and trusted. Therefore, when she returned from tending to a family matter in America, they welcomed her home and offered her first purchase dibs. She accepted their offer without hesitation. Four months later, after the financial details of the procurement were settled, the For Sale sign was taken down, and Ruby McEwen became a diner owner.

Previously, in 1954, post WWII food rationings were lifted. This meant, when she became a business owner and an employer, the British economy was in its sixth global comeback year. Brits had long since resumed enjoying food and spending more of their 'fun money' in the taverns, hotels, restaurants, hostelries, and diners. In the twenty years that passed between 1945 and 1965, Ruby lived through and witnessed, a sensationally unparalleled transformation throughout the cities and villages across Great Britain. There was a histrionic rise in wealth and affluence. The continual rise in prosperity improved living standards, as well as the health, welfare, and educational systems countrywide. Both America and Canada were experiencing a similar lavishness. The economic changes also meant that her parents, Horace and Sadie, would be able to manage their financial debts without needing her assistance any longer. She predicted that such a change would have her father feeling like a productive man again for the first time in the erstwhile seven years, which it rightly did. What was so commonplace in the modern world she now lived in, had, to all intents and purposes, been imagined and created in the 50s and 60s?

These unforeseen and sumptuous changes meant that the future of millions of British children, like Eliza, were finally more promising than before the Nazi's had invaded their land, killed their fellow Brits, bombed their futures, and destroyed their young lives.

Chapter 21

With crinkled hands that trembled from the cold glass she still was clenching, the elderly woman sunk deeper into her lounge chair and fondly began thinking about one particular highlight in her life. She was feeling relaxed and alert. She couldn't recall the last time she'd given herself, what old people globally were calling, 'the gift of time'.

Even with the child lying in an ICU bed, she felt temporarily released from being her guardian. This was a raw, rather innocent realization that she thought to be rightly deserving, in a way others might consider to be twisted. What she hadn't realized, when she'd agreed to employ an American teenager for two months, was what an immense responsibility Jazz would turn out to be. She was positive that the patient was in capable medical hands at the hospital. Nonetheless, to ease her worried mind she decided to call the ICU and check up on her. If she were doing fine, the elderly great grandmother would finish with her diner business, phone America, and then return to the hospital as she'd planned. If the patient had taken a turn for the worse, she'd call Jazz's mother first and then ring up Deniz the cabbie so she could return to Saint Matthew's straightaway.

The call to the ICU took less than five minutes. The receptionist informed her, by saying that there really was no need to hurry and return any sooner mam. The coma patient's heartbeat was steady and strong. She was sustaining and resting comfortably. The now, reassured old woman was thirsty, so she hobbled over to the soda fountain and dispensed herself another tall glass of ice and Coca Cola. Even though the soft drink was invented in 1886, she hadn't had her first glass of the sweet, fizzy, malty flavoured drink until she and Eliza tried it at The Seaside in 1959. One year later, after their first taste of a beverage that would become world-renowned, life changed for her again.

Ruby sat back down, took a long, slow drink of her Coke, and began to slip in and out of the past with ease. This time her mind fleetingly took her back to 1960, a year that had altered a then, much younger Ruby McEwen's life.

Worldwide, it was being reported that a wind of change was blowing through Africa. A transformation signalling the end of Colonial Rule by the European powers was taking place. This meant that Africa was moving in the direction of independence. Even though at the time she didn't know by virtue exactly how, she did know that she had family roots that originated in Africa.

She had been sitting for too long. Shifting her stiff, crooked body into a more relaxed position, she reminded herself that only a few hours ago she'd read journal entries to Jazz that had been written by her slave relatives. While doing so, Ruby had been outright inspired by the legendary folktales transcribed in the 1800s by her African ancestors Bessie and Minnie. Just thinking about this made her eager to return to the ICU and the old-fashioned wooden trunk filled with historical wisdom and five generations of legends and folklore.

With her interest in the trunk once more ignited, she promptly made another mental note *to read more pages from Bessie and Minnie's journals to the child tomorrow.*

For now, with very chilly hands and eight crooked fingers holding firmly onto a slippery ice-filled tumbler, she continued unwinding in the silence of her diner. She still felt modestly indebted to the time zone that separated England and America. Relaxing in her Barcalounger while reminiscing about the past, and observing the life she'd built, was one of her favourite pastimes. It was a pastime passion of sorts that she infrequently made time for. Despite her digital pig-headedness, history, the vintage age, learning new things, and meeting new people were other passions that decorated her life. Of all the heirlooms and possessions that she'd preserved and collected over the years, her favoured diner items were its original antiquated Solotone jukeboxes with built-in speakers. The jukeboxes were mounted on each of the booth's tables, and like diner's owner, the Solotone's had undoubtedly withstood the test of time. Reminiscing over these musical inventions reminded her of how the Fifties had withstood a boom of teenagers like no other decade before it had. Her mind adored reminiscing about the times of yore.

During the 1950s, the legacy of the Second World War forced people to live with remnants of destruction all around them. In the major British cities, predominantly in London, there were vacant bombsites, demolished and unrepaired buildings, temporary prefabricated homes, and shared post-war victory gardens. From what the elderly woman could still recall, or had learned in school, this part of the past all began in September of 1940, when the Lord Mayor of the City of London paged his correspondents across Great Britain to attend a mandatory gathering. His call into action overlapped an increase in Hitler's bombing campaign on the capital's harbours. Plumes of black smoke swirled around the Bank of England as the politicians approached the Mansion House where the Lord Mayor awaited them. As dockside warehouses burned, they heeded an appeal by a key member of the Wartime Cabinet to *"increase the workload of their local food rationing teams."*

One year earlier, on the first day of September, 1939, Hitler had invaded Poland. Two days later, France and Britain declared war on Germany and World War II officially began. In the first week of the Second World War approximately seventy-thousand tons of British freight had been sunk. A large quantity of the lost cargo was food. The unanticipated, immense loss gave birth to the horrendous question of- how was an island of forty-five million people going to find enough food to nourish itself while Britain was being plagued by the Nazi U-boat version of the submarine, or Unterseeboot, as they were called. Three months later, in January of 1940, to ensure that limited nutrient supplies were fairly and squarely distributed, food rationing was enforced countrywide. Ruby was a high school student at the time, who, along with her schoolmates, aided in post-war efforts wherever it was deemed safe enough, and whenever they were called to assist. She used her volunteer status to avoid being confined at home with Horace and Sadie, her bickering, yet rightfully so, war-spooked parents. She remembered all too well how open spaces everywhere, from the villages to city centres, were being transformed into gardening plots.

Families grew domestic gardens on their property, whilst the government offered Public Park gardening space to the general public who'd lost their homes or were living in yard less spaces. Even the lawns outside the Tower of London were turned into vegetable patches. 'How to Dig a Garden and Grow Food' leaflets were part of a massive propaganda campaign targeted at ensuring that Brits could learn how to grow their own food, had enough to eat, and their morale was kept high. Despite the dig and grow efforts, many types of difficult or impossible to grow produce eventually disappeared. Vitamin-rich lemons and bananas could no longer be imported from overseas, which meant there was a tangible hazard that British children would become afflicted by rickets. In no time, onions exported from countries occupied by the German Regime, became such a rarity that they were given as birthday gifts and sweepstake prizes. As a replacement for onions, onion salt was the alternative used across the country for a number of years to come. Parents countrywide desperately sought, bought, and sprinkled onion salt on their children's food, believing it would nourish them despite food shortages and government rations.

Thinking of this reminded Ruby of how throughout the 40s, even her toothbrush tasted like an onion. Still fixated on the past and her parents well intended wartime nutrition efforts, she subtly grinned and gave her mind permission to meander a bit longer though Britain's multi-coloured wartime gardens.

Victory gardens, also known as War Gardens or Food Gardens for Defense, were vegetable, fruit, and herb gardens planted at private residences and public parks. The planting began initially after World War I and continued later after World War II. During the time of war recovery, governments encouraged citizens to plant victory gardens in an effort to supplement their rations and to boost the overall self-esteem of nations that were destroyed and depressed by the atrocities of war. The gardens were used along with Rationing Stamps to significantly reduce demands on the public food supply. Alongside tortuously aiding the war effort, these gardens were also considered a civil self-esteem booster, in that gardeners could feel optimistically empowered by their contribution of labour and rewarded by the produce they'd grown. In turn, this made victory gardens a part of daily life on the home fronts of the United States, Canada, the United Kingdom, Australia, and oddly enough, even Germany.

Even in today's modern Britain, unmanned wartime military bases were still scattered across the countryside. They were reminders of a time when, despite the problems and complications of day-to-day living, people had an immense amount of allegiance to their country. It appeared that then, Londoners who'd survived the war, shared a common purpose in life. Families stayed together through the hard times and people personally knew and relied on their neighbours. It had taken five years, since the 1945 radio broadcast, announcing Hitler's death, for Brits to begin trusting that *life would be okay*. In the mid-1950s, the British people began feeling safe again. Parents would, nine times out of ten, leave their front doors unlocked or hang a house key on a piece of string behind the letterbox when they were out. Youngsters came and went as they pleased. This was the beginning of a new, true sense of autonomy for children, especially true for the nation's teenagers. Virtually everyone who lived during 1950s and '60s, in a post-war UK, had his or her own esteemed memories of that time. Ruby's daughter, Eliza, was definitely one of these children.

The old woman, holding a cold glass of Coca Cola and melting ice cubes simpered. She was alert and delighting in the malty sugar rush speeding through her thin, geriatric blood. She'd never experimented with drugs, but she did bloody adore the rush she got from sweet white granules and caffeine. Smiling dazzlingly at her own memories of that time, her scrutinizing eyes skimmed the interior of her diner. Her gawking paused when she saw an antique sign hanging above one of her floor model jukeboxes. The sign and the jukebox were the only two items that adorned the far corner of the main dining area. Seeing the Friar Court Flats sign instantly reminded her of a triple funeral she'd organized and attended when she was in her twenties. Despite that her twenties were turbulent and challenging years, one of her happiest experiences from that time was the day Friar Court's Flats building manager dismantled the century old sign from the building, and handed it to the eager granddaughter of his former tenants. Ruby later restored it at University of Dublin's Art Centre, where she was a student at the time.

As the elderly woman stared at the plump belly, baldhead, and chubby face of the fat Friar being depicted on the sign, her puckered face lit up. She could still take such pleasure in recollecting the simpler side of her past. The 17th century sign had become one of her most prized possessions. She'd played a key role in one particular McEwen family episode that occurred in the apartment building that the sign dutifully hung off. The Friar's Court sign had been hanging in her diner since 1960. Despite that she wasn't a materialistic person, she did treasure its history and ancestral symbolism.

At that moment, Ruby shifted her gaze to a collection of original, framed retro posters being displayed on one of the nearby walls. The posters took her mind immediately back to a much more innocent time in life. It was a time when she and Eliza were in a good place; when they were actually bonding as females, rather than clashing as mother and daughter. Even today, the colourful and artistic dated posters gave her diner a decorative flare. The prints symbolized what post-World War II life used to be like. The large eared, green eyed old Brit continued to ogle the printed images of Elvis Presley, Chuck Berry, the Beatles, Aretha Franklin, and James Brown. Numerous other reproductions of musical artist's imageries decked the diner wall in a prestigiously respectable way. These iconic images, that were once nothing special, had become tourist and teenage attractions; especially now with LP's making a comeback after two decades. The posters reminded her of the birth of Rock' n' Roll and the hysteria surrounding of a new type of Pop Culture.

She vividly could recall, a never before seen public frenzy, surrounding four young, charismatically fine-looking lads from Liverpool. In her opinion, The Beatles were the Masters of Music. In the mid-1950s and the throughout the 1960s, as Ruby's memory relived those years, the popularity of music was reviving a post-war Britain. Music spread like a remedy that healed the viral effects of a country still in mourning and on the road to recovery. The music and the teenagers of the times were taking over the nation in a way that was then, and still was today, evident throughout the United Kingdom and America.

Back then, young Brits, like Eliza, had more freedom and money to spend than ever before. Ruby's daughter was part of a generation that came of age in the sixties and early seventies. They were an independent, headstrong peer group. She remembered them as being a youthful cluster of adolescents, whom, oddly enough at the time, seemed to want a very different culture. They sought a culture unlike the one they had grown up in, under the same roof, with their parents and grandparents. What Brits labelled as being a 'Hippy Counter-Culture' actually began in the mid-60s. A bohemian underground had always existed with its discreet gay scene and community of eccentric artists. It was an underground culture that, in the more civilized western cultures of today, existed above ground and in plain view. Despite allegations, back in the 'hang loose time' surrounding these non-conformists and their subversive ways, for the most part, they kept their heads down and stayed out of the spotlight and out of trouble. As the 1960s melted into the 1970s, young Brits and Yanks wanted to be more than just the youthful part of the establishment.

Ruby remembered once hearing someone commenting strongly about teenagers, by saying, "not since Viking ships were spotted in the North Sea and the English Channel, had an invasion so gripped the youth of Britain."

The teenage invasion and the Viking invasion, although influential in a similar way, were immeasurably different. Instead of bringing rape, plundering, shields, iron helmets, disgrace and death to Brits, as the Vikings did, the Hippie Movement brought peace, love, music, harmony, orgies, and outlandish, flowery hairdos. Drugs were a prominent and dynamic part of the 60s and 70s scene. However, Europe made much less of an issue about drug-use than America did. This gave the UK the impression that drugs were safer, more acceptable, and less threatening. Time would prove the country's mental make-up to be utterly and rightly wrong. Ruby believed that, even back then, the acceptance of this trend was because Europe had been in the grip of WWII for so long, anything that followed Hitler's carnage was permitted and bearable. Post-war Europeans were afraid of conflict and tired of fighting. So they chose not to.

The American hippies, on the contrary were in the grip of the Vietnam War. The country had been locked in conflict in Vietnam since the mid-1950s. With every year that passed, America's involvement in the war kept increasing. A high majority of its younger citizens were protesting the combat and fleeing the draft. This made them scared, which, back-to-back, turned them hostile against a government that was systematically sending its young men to perish in the jungles of a country they knew nothing about. The 60s

144

and '70s offered a generation of hippies the opportunity to express their strong opinions and radical views worldwide, which they did in various ways. How they dressed, what music they listened to, their sexual openness, drug use, and their expressive dance styles, were all common methods beatniks used to make their statements seen and heard. No adult, or governmental institution was going to dictate to them how they should be leading their lives or for whom they should end their lives.

By the mid-1950s, due to the ten year long, post-war baby boom, more than half of the British population was less than thirty years of age. Her daughter Eliza was one of these Brits. The younger American and European generations were growing up in the midst of a new revolution. It was a time when sexual independence, drug use, and wild music took centre stage in city square's and in living rooms across the globe. Run of the mill teenagers, hippies, and neohippies alike, rebelled after the war era because their parents had remained closed-minded, traditional conformists. In addition, this new generation of 'freethinkers of all ages' had a very strong principle of 'priding themselves on being nothing like their parents'.

Perceptively, Ruby believed that it had always been the role of teens to break free of their parent's and step out of from behind paternalistic shadows and into the light of their own lives. The passage of time hadn't changed how children globally grew up and sought independence from the lives they were born into. When the rebellious behaviours of a wild, purple-haired, pierced teenager arrived and rang her doorbell, the old, reputed owner and empress of The Seaside was reminded of how four decades of new teenage generations hadn't tangibly evolved. The child was a classic clichéd example of how 'the more things changed, the more they stayed the same'.

The elderly woman twirled the cool glass around in her chilled hands and spoke aloud. "How long are young people going to spend interpreting every single opportunity they have, and the choices they make, as a way to prove their parents wrong?" Shrugging her shoulders, she meekly sighed. "It's the one generational curse that time and circumstance still hasn't been able to change."

Chapter 22

Her hands had become so cold they were distracting her from her thoughts and memories. She'd put too much ice in the glass this time. The nipping sensation she felt was sending a frigidness up and down her arthritis-riddled wrists and arms. Her common sense was telling her to put the stupid glass down and stop wandering in and out of the past. Nevertheless, her need to spend a bit more time doing what she loved the most was testing her practicality. Her practicality would eventually lose out to her spontaneity. Her spontaneity was a personality handicap she'd learned to live with. Ce la vie.

A wise, yet demanding inner voice was yelling at her to either finish the goddamn Cola or put the cold glass down and think faster! Even though she was satisfied that she'd given herself permission to mentally dawdle over the past hour or so, she knew time was running out and her taxi would be returning soon. Nevertheless, her mind was still too captivated by its desires and recollections, so she advised it to dredge up the Cheetah spirit that lived within her and to think at a goddamned quicker pace! Although Ruby was very old, she was abnormally sharp minded person who hardly ever missed a beat. With confidence, ease, and the speed she needed, in a flash her trained brain took her back to the 1950s. She was eager to spend more time in the bygone years. After she'd ambled once more through the olden and departed, filled with impacting, bygone events and deceased ancestor's, she'd return to the here and now and ring up the female lunatic in California before returning, spit spot, to the ICU at Saint Matthews Hospital.

With this being decided, thoughts racing through her head immediately went to her convictions and mingled with her strong opinion that the decade of the Fifties had portrayed a kind of innocence. It was a time when a new era of hope had begun, and a period of time layered with the promise of better things to come. In 1954 rationing ended in Britain, which gave way to the inventions and sales of a new wave of electrical appliances. Commercially, for the hospitality and domestic sectors, operations and life quickly became easier. As the years passed by, restaurants and family homes of all kinds were being fully stocked with new and useful appliances. With the surge of new kitchen machines, many families began conveniently eating meals at home. Not since, before the wartime soup kitchens had fed thousands upon thousands of Brits a day, had people been able to eat in their own dining rooms. Restauranteurs across the British Isles asked themselves, would the new appliances eventually make cooking at home so convenient that less people would choose to eat out? At the time, this was the primary concern of eatery owners across the United Kingdom and likewise in the States. Fortunately, for them, it was also a time when the American teenage craze of going to a local café, diner, snack bar, or restaurant, for a quick burger, a milkshake, and the sounds of upbeat Bebop and Hip-hop music were making their way across the Atlantic Ocean to England. When she became a diner entrepreneur, little did Ruby know that interior design, art, and music of the '50s and '60s would prove to be revolutionary, making The Seaside iconic by the 1990s?

When she'd purchased the diner the new appliance buzz was declining, which enabled her, as a single mother raising a pre-schooler, to have faith that she'd made a financially promising business decision. Her parents, Horace and Sadie still lived more than fifty-five miles away in Essex County. By the 1960s, she wasn't sure about the state of their marriage, nor did she give a goddam fragged hoot about it! She'd left the world she was born and raised in behind more than a decade ago. Undeterred by the hardships she'd endured since then, she never returned. Her parents did see their only grandchild on occasion. When this happened, it was on Ruby's terms because she was hell bent on shielding her wee lass from the same bloody domestic crap she'd been exposed to as a child. Therefore, and rightfully so, she unconditionally protected Eliza.

By the time, the original, timber styled, Seaside Diner sign was replaced by a brand-new, larger, metallic retro sign, the popularity of eating out versus eating at home had returned to the British Isles. The commercial outpouring of kitchen conveniences that had once threatened restauranteurs eventually had subsided. As the months turned into years, Ruby saw the 'dining out' trend make a twofold comeback. Her clientele and profits increased at a rate she'd never seen before. In her nearly sixty years as a restaurateur, what she never saw this trend do, was cease to exist. Within a few months, after she'd put a modern spin on the diner, her youngest patrons had won their traditional parents over; convincing them to visit their 'hangout' and see for themselves what all the hype was about. This increased her business nearly too fast for her to keep up with. Her newest clientele raved about their diner experiences, from her casual way with them to the latest Pop music playing at their tables to her funky glimmering counter service. All of this, plus the beachside service and the American style of food, made the newer version of her diner more popular than the original Seaside had ever been. The younger generation craved a seemingly endless amount of the newest fads and different eating experiences. All of which she gave them.

Ruby had a funky chicness to her and a funky diner. Both were considered to be 'far out and cool' with the teens, hippies, and yuppies alike. The diner had an upbeat, yet nonchalant sphere. She was perceptive enough to keep a sufficient amount of its original style to appease her older, longstanding customers. The Seaside's female owner soon became reputed to be as hip and appealing as her diner was. In no time, her younger preteen patrons wanted to introduce their parents to her and share in a different eating out experience with them. Some of them, with parents that feared the changing times, failed miserably at this, while others, with parents eager to see what all the hysteria was about, succeeded easily. Despite the whys and wherefores that people had for going to different types of British restaurants, her clientele steadily continued to grow in numbers.

Repeat local customers and tourists alike were having a splendid time with each other. The mahogany wood panelling, spinning chrome based red counter stools, the jukeboxes, and checkered tile floor gave her place a unique retro charm. The Seaside was where the local and seasonal young

147

people of the 1960s and 1970s went to eat burgers, listen to music, and show off their hot rods outside in a large, very visible parking lot. Its gleaming interior and exterior had a decor that was bold and energetic. As the years rolled by, new generations were born. Time saw to it that post-WWII baby boomers, who'd been responsible for the early success of the diner, became parents. Repeatedly, as time marched on, they could be seen bringing their own young and growing families into the diner. No matter how many generations came and went, and how much the world evolved, her diner world had remained the same. Even today, in an era of metal, punk, emo, and hard-core music, the inviting sweet melodies of '60s and '70s' Pop, R&B, and Soul music could still be heard pulsating through The Seaside's ageless spirit.

Although the Vietnam War had broken out in 1955, by the mid-1960s, Ruby believed then, and even today, despite the grim BBC News flashes covering another war America was involved in, it still was an electrifying and more or less innocent time to be alive. She had witnessed the Second World War in an up-close and personal way, therefore, she knew the difference between the methods of combat used by the Germans and those used by the Vietnamese. The Brits were fortunate because at the time England was not officially sending any combat troops to Vietnam. Nevertheless, if the British Monarchy did choose to get involved and support their American allies, there was a risk that Ruby could be sent to Vietnam.

Granted, the possibility of this happening was slight, it was nevertheless real and needed to be addressed. Because she'd been a nurse's aide in the latter part of the war, she was still a registered Certified Nursing Assistant, so she was, alongside hundreds of other women, placed on standby. It was an unsettling time for the young degreed journalist, single mother, nurse's aide, and entrepreneur. In a rather unanticipated and intimidating way, the Vietnam War had seen to it that her domestic stability and her livelihood both landed in a personally risky region. Although the danger of the probable Vietnam scenario was something to be considered, Ruby didn't let it dictate who she was. Nor would she allow it to define who she'd become. Since she was a wee girl, who'd continuously tried to climb over a tall fence that restricted her from exploring and discovering life, she'd been a diehard optimist. She lived a life beyond borders with enthusiasm and vision.

Given the mild threat of being sent to Vietnam, she and Horace had devised a proper caretaker strategy for her young child. Horace had become her grandparent of choice since Eliza had turned three, because he was the one, she could gauge and trust. By this time, Grandpa Horace had stopped drinking alcohol of any kind and likewise had mended his estranged relationship with his daughter Ruby. Because of this, he was more involved in little Eliza's life than ever before. They were both so similar, it was as if they were two halves of the same person. Their likenesses occasionally shook Ruby to her very core.

In the spring of 1959, Ruby's 102-year-old, African grandmother, Bessie Dutton, died painlessly and peacefully in her sleep. Bessie was Ruby's mother Sadie's mom. Throughout her lifetime, Bessie had lived three very different places; Africa where she was born, on a slave plantation in New Orleans where she'd grown up, and in America where she homesteaded until she passed away. Ruby's pa, Horace, travelled with his girl to Montana, to tend to the details of Bessie's funeral and the burial service. Knowing how much Grandma Bessie had done for his only daughter, he dotingly held Ruby's hand throughout duration of the flight. Transatlantic travel had just begun the previous year, which made their British Airways flight to a funeral both expensive and thrilling. Despite the cost, Horace knew the significance of his best girl attending her grandmother's funeral. The well-intended man had never flown before, so he squinted his eyes closed while getting a bad case of airsickness and retching repeatedly throughout their entire turbulent flight. Never before had Ruby seen her pa more sober or more nauseated. Because she had flying experience, her fearless body was familiar with turbulence, so she slept during the entire night flight. Poor old Horace never let go of her hand or opened his eyes until the planes wheel hit the tarmac in America.

Bessie Dutton's funeral service was held on her ranch's front lawn. Soon thereafter, she was buried at the family plot atop a nearby hill. Since the turn of the century, Grandma Bessie had only one after death wish. She desired to be buried in a similar type of humble, handmade, pine casket that each of the previously deceased Dutton's had been buried in. Folks who knew her as well as Jackson Shepherd, her right -hand man did, attributed her burial request to her desire not to waste hard-earned money on an expensive fancy coffin. Jackson likewise respected that Bessie's wanted to be laid in the ground, in exactly the same way as the first of the previously deceased Dutton's were laid to rest back in the late 1800s. So, with that being acknowledged and respected, exactly one week after she passed onto her next life, Bessie, the African American slave girl, homesteader, and rancher, was buried with the belief in her soul that 'time has no end'. She was laid to rest in full view of her beloved home and ranch. The Dutton family gravesite was simply magnificent.

The first time Ruby saw the view, from the crest of the cemetery's hill, it astounded her. The burial ground was bordered on two sides by expanding fields of wild, rainbow coloured lilies. What appeared to be a million bright white, shining daisies, bordered the graveyard on its third side. Without a care in the world, the wildflowers sashayed and danced innocently, as if they were in mid-air. The flowers appeared to be rootless, swaying, and floating, with nothing holding them down to end their floral pirouetting. The flowers honeyed fragrances blended and swirled as they were lifted upwards and carried away by a warm breeze wafting over the meadows. The fields of florae that encircled the family plot, with their perfumed scents being carried away on the tail of a gentle wind, was simply breath-taking. In a suitably surreal way, florid aromas whirled around the congregation attending the service. It was as though the earth and the air covered the funeralgoers and Bessie's casket, in a perfumed tang of 'life after death'. Ruby stood next to her grandmother's casket and smiled, believing that the sight and smells of these vast fields of flowers were one of the most spectacular portrayals of Mother Nature's talent that she'd ever seen. Bessie Ballinger Dutton would have agreed.

During her service, the Pastor preached the Sacred Word, and a few endearing stories were told by one attendee who was a mere two months older than Bessie was. It was reputed that the man had, despite scorn from villagers, befriended her decades ago as a woman of colour and fellow homesteader. He was a neighbour who was in his mid-nineties and still daily milked his cow and picked wild blackberries in his yards. Ruby and Horace later learned that the man had helped Bessie bury her husband and two oldest sons. Aside from him, her other friends and neighbours attending the service were each well into their seventies and eighties. Bessie's modestly varnished, pine coffin was respectfully and with considerable effort lowered into the earth. Her final resting place was next to each of the previously deceased members of her Dutton family. Her death reunited her with her husband Samuel and their four sons, including their twin boys, who had died during a horrific blizzard in 1888. Bessie had outlived them each by seventy-two years. Her death had made Ruby's mother, Sadie, the last living direct female descendent of the Ballinger Dutton family.

After the burial, before descending the hill and returning to the ranch, each guest laid one long-stemmed rose over the fresh mound of dark, golden-coloured dirt that covered the casket. Each stem had been garlanded with small colourful bows that were made from Bessie's assorted collection of hair ribbons. Ruby had found the ribbons in an old hat box stored in her grandma's bedroom closet. Standing atop the hill, where the Dutton family gravesite was located, Ruby was surrounded by the serenity of sweet melodies coming from fiddles and violins being played by fellow ranchers. After she laid her memorial rose, the ceremony ended and a 'celebration of life' reception began.

It had been Ruby's idea to have the graveside burial end the way it did. The music and flowers honoured Bessie's long, diverse, and meaningful life. Both the funeral and the burial had been intimately tasteful and simple. She was certain that the services were something Sadie's mother would have approved of. The ex-slave, and sister to Minnie, who'd lived to witness more than a century of life, would have praised at the service and the sounds of fiddles and violins swirling around her spirit. Ironically, both her death and her departure had a simplicity to them that her life scarcely and rarely had. People attending the Bessie's funeral service and burial remembered the younger version of Ruby who had attended the Dutton Ranch's annual barbeques when she was just a wee girl. She felt joy while listening to their humorous versions of her hospitable grandmother and her grandpa Samuel.

"Good-ole 'Sammy D' died in his prime before his time," one of the oldest men said.

"Those damn explosives claimed too many young miner's lives," another man retorted in unison.

Ruby never knew her Grandfather Samuel. He was killed long before she was born. Her mother Sadie barely spoke to Ruby about her father, nor did Sadie attend her own mother's funeral. Before making the trip, alone with Horace, Ruby had known better than to even ask Sadie why. Certain family matters were better off left behind in the attic, hiding amongst the cobwebs.

She knew now that she had learned to think in this way because of her deceased grandmother. Bessie had told her frequently that *something's be better left unsaid. A person who goes poking at a rabid dog is surely gunna' get bit.*

As an impressionable girl, this slogan of Bessie's had taught Ruby valuable lessons; like when to open her mouth and when to shut it, who to befriend and who to avoid, and when to search for an answer and when to accept what was, just because it was. One of Bessie's female friends attending her funeral had commented on how much Ruby looked like her grandmother did when she was a younger woman. She'd liked hearing this and had to agree with her, because it was rightly true. Earlier that morning, she'd seen an antique gold framed, colour-dyed tin portrait of Bessie and Samuel hanging in her grandma's bedroom. The resemblance was so uncanny that it was almost eerie. Ruby also thought that Eliza was the spit and image female version of Samuel. Her daughter acted like her grandpa Horace and looked like her great grandpa Samuel. After the last of the guests had departed and the front parlour had been tidied up, Horace and Ruby went outside to enjoy a sunset over the exquisite horizons of the American Great Plains. Standing side by side, they leaned against an old, weathered fence located at the front edge of a paddock next to the stables. The fence, still serving its purpose, corralled four of the ranch's remaining horses, and one very lonely looking cow.

"That lonesome cow standing there, in between those three mares and that majestic stallion, looks to be bored lifeless and out of place," Horace said and Ruby agreed.

While gazing out at the distance and its rich green scenery, she couldn't recall the last time she and Horace had leaned against an old, tattered fence. She wasn't sure when or why their relationship began to change; nonetheless, the changes were making her feel closer to him. Over the years, Horace had learned to tame his verbal impulsiveness and Ruby had learned that there actually was 'no real difference between love and hate'. She now knew that love and hate were rightly the same, just as she and Horace were. The one needed the other to exist. Horace gently took his daughter's hand in his. Captivated by the silence, they continued to embrace impressive views of the seemingly endless grasslands of the American Great Plains. This time, his daughter wasn't fantasizing about the day that she'd be somewhere else. In that moment, standing next to her father, she was as drawn to his presence as he was to hers. Ruby was exactly where she wanted to be, by his side, where Horace had always wanted her to be. With the sun descended over the distant horizon, both father and daughter felt like they were standing on the edge of forever.

As the evening sky darkened, silhouettes of an old man and a young woman leaning against a fence emerged through the evening haze. Hemmed in by vibrantly coloured wildflowers surrounding a gravesite, their image gradually faded into the shadows of another stunning twilight that spanned across the landlocked state of Montana.

Chapter 23

Later that year Ruby inherited a hefty share of the proceeds from the sale of Bessie's ranch and its adjacent 490 acres. A highly competitive farmstead auction was held shortly after the Dutton Estate had been settled. The result of an auction she didn't attend was responsible for her six-figure inheritance. For an unwed mother of a youngster, the public sale of her grandparent's ranch yielded her a generous amount of financial stability. The money Bessie's had left her in her Last Will and Testament and the proceeds from the ranch's auction enabled Ruby to purchase The Seaside and become a financially independent at the age of thirty-five.

The elderly woman was now trembling in her recliner. Her eyes were still wide open. She wasn't blinking and she wasn't cold. Her mind sensed that her brain was about to take her to a part of her past that was still unsettling and unresolved. Despite her shivers and apprehensions, she was calmer than she'd been since a pierced, purple haired, tattooed teenager had arrived and turned her entire world the wrong side up. She leaned over, set the glass down on the floor, pulled the blanket snugly around her shoulders, kept her eyes open, and slid farther back in time.

The Dutton Ranch had a lengthy, pliable, and historical tale attached to it. Aside from Bessie, the farmstead's supervisor knew the most about the homestead. In the days that followed the funeral, before returning to England, Horace and Ruby shared numerous long, leisurely conversations while strolling together across the infinite savannahs of the American Midwest. Horace was in abnormally good shape for a 75-year-old man with an enduring history of whiskey abuse. He had an amazingly sharp memory, which continued to baffle his often-accusatorial daughter. Ruby was well educated as to the dangers and side effects of alcohol. She knew and had witnessed what it did to her father's mind and body. Regardless of his whiskey demons, her pa was an energetic and renowned storyteller at heart. He was a man who could spontaneously talk to people about anything, anyone, or any experience that had ever crossed his path. Horace was known in his hometown as 'a great narrator' who was as brilliant as the stories he told. Despite such a fine reputation, his daughter knew him to be two different types of storytellers.

The first type was a storyteller who drank too much and shrouded behind his humour to hide his deeper emotions. The problem with being this kind of storyteller was that, a few minutes after his first drink kicked in, Horace became uninhibited and amusing. For this reason, his stories made people laugh. The sound of laughter was all it took to embolden him to take his storytelling to the next level. The more people were entertained by him while he spun his stories the happier, he felt about himself. Likewise, the more they cheered him on, with their applauses and chuckling, the more they fuelled his need to feel happy. This led to another story, which in turn, increased his desire to have another drink. Consequently, a vicious, six-decade long storytelling circle was born. As the circle turned, story after story and year after year, Horace's drinking increased. In fairness to the man that she almost never called pa, Ruby understood the rhymes and reason that made him who he was. The three things Horace lived for were to be liked, to tell stories, and to drink whiskey.

Unfortunately, as the whiskey drinking type of storyteller aged, so did his ability to remember his tales, or make them up. As time passed, his memory became vaguer and less reliable. When this happened, Horace became an irate tyrant who'd have another drink to calm his anger. Then he'd spew vindictive words laden with hidden meanings. Eventually, people who listened to his stories couldn't tell where his truths began, and his lies ended. Actually, neither could Horace. Drinking and aging made him dejected, crabby, and unpopular. Therefore, people who knew Ruby's father the longest grew impatient with him, and likewise weary of the man they'd secretly come to call 'Cantankerous Horace'. In due course, they stopped listening to his storytelling, went home and then avoided him. Because people took their attention and laughter with them, Horace became a miserable, abandoned, and often lonely storyteller.

The second type of storyteller was the one that Ruby couldn't get enough of. This storyteller was a sober man who had the ability to bridge the gap between himself and whomever he was telling a tale to. The combination of his passion for history, his intelligence, and his social charms, made whoever listened to his stories feel genuinely inspired. In this way, as one would expect, people were pulled into what Horace was telling them. When he was like this, he left his imprint on others, which was impressive to witness.

The man had a gift. Each time he spoke, with a sober mind, his vibrant stories and renditions of the past came back to life. This type of storyteller wasn't just telling a story, he was creating a feeling. This was when Horace was the most captivating and extremely popular. This was when he enabled the listener to draw their own conclusions from what they'd heard him say. This type of Horace had people engaging in his tales and then passing them onto others. His listeners valued being in his presence because he gave their lives meaning. He connected folks to the life around them, while instilling a sense of honour in them. Despite the wrong choices they were guilty of having made, they felt a sense of decency when they were in his presence. This second kind of storyteller made others feel seen and equal to one another in a very remarkable and entertaining way. As for Ruby, when her father was this second kind of storyteller, he guided her down many different paths in her life. They were cryptic types of paths; where even though the end of one of his stories was in sight, she still had to finish the journey on her own. Which meant she had to listen and learn with a searching mind and an inquisitive soul. Despite the mistakes he'd make and the faults he had; this was the only way Horace knew how to navigate Ruby. Educating such a liberated and independent person without caging her had always challenged him. Open ended stories were the only way he knew how to inspire his free-spirited daughter to discover her own unique life trails, to claim them, and then to make them a part of her own authentic stories, not his stories.

With memories of 'Horace the Storyteller' still lurching in her mind, the elderly woman ran her hands through her pure white, shoulder length hair. Despite that, her hands were still too cold, their coolness was keeping the onset of a throbbing migraine at bay. Ruby picked the glass back up off the floor and clenched it tighter. She removed her spectacles and held the cold glass against her forehead and temples. After a few minutes of slowing her thoughts, she was alert, nearly pain free, and anxious to let her mind take her in reverse again; back to a time when her great granddaughter wasn't injured and lying in an ICU bed. To a time when she still didn't need to ring up the child's parents and tell them what had happened to their teenage daughter after she arrived in London.

The old woman had forty minutes before the taxi returned. She still wasn't ready to make the kind of phone call that never ended well, so she leaned back into her lounge chair, took a deep breath, and summoned up one of her favourite places.

Her mind immediately took her back to the last year of 1950. Back to where she'd just been, in Montana on the afternoon of her grandma Bessie's funeral. She closed her eyes. In a heartbeat, she was on the Great Plains with Horace again.

It was a sporadic and rare time in her life. It was a time when she and her father were harmoniously connected, in an exceptionally unusual way. It was a way she found too unfamiliar to put her trust in. Earlier that week, before Bessie's final farewell, Horace had spent a considerable amount of time consoling the deceased woman's oldest friend and most devoted ranch hand. He was presumed to be an African American ex-slave in his seventies named Jackson Boy Shepherd. No one actually knew his exact age. Jackson called himself, *Shep*, and encouraged other folks to call him this as well. Shep was the nickname he'd smartly given himself after running away with a target that had been placed on his back by a precarious man who'd made a sport out of shooting animals and slaves. Shep's name change occurred on the very day he tasted freedom for the first time in his life. On this day, his actual name, Boy, was officially discarded.

Horace and Shep had worked side-by-side under a blistering sun, for three long and hot days. At night, after the plains cooled down, they worked by the light of the moon. Together the men handcrafted, sanded, and varnished Bessie's personally desired pine casket. They also tended to the barns, groomed the horses, repaired the rain gutters, and paid attention to a lonely old cow named Mildred. The two men spent hour after hour meticulously repairing and polishing a horse-drawn, four-wheeled wagon. Before his sudden demise, Samuel Dutton, the father of Horace's wife Sadie, had used the wagon daily for operating the farmstead and traversing across the ranch's enormous acreage. The wagon had been in storage collecting dirt, soot, idleness, and rust. The last time it was used was when Samuel and the last two remaining Dutton brother's caskets had been put in it before the wagon pulled their coffins up the steep sloping hill, to the family gravesite.

Years back, after burying three of her Dutton men within seven weeks of each other, a distraught and grieving Bessie had commanded that *"the wagon was never, ever, to be used again. It had sorrow seeping out of its wooden pores. It had carried too much death in it to be of any use now."*

For that reason and for the sake of honouring the 'final say' of a grieving mother and wife, the wagon hadn't been used again. Until today. The only remaining pair of the ranch's stallions had pulled a newly polished, buffed, and shining, wagon, carrying Bessie in her freshly made pine casket to the family gravesite. Bessie, wife of Samuel Dutton, had once been a sweet, happy, plump, lightly black skinned Negro child. For her entire adult life, she was known as a full-figured, caring, and most generous woman. She was a substantial, hardworking person who could bake an apple pie and grow a vegetable garden like no other female homesteader in all of the surrounding territories. Her skills in the kitchen kept the palates and bellies of the people she loved and the people she employed very satisfied. Her relationship with the soil and her gardening skills yielded an abundance of fresh vegetables and herbs year after year. Weather permitting of course. Bessie actually could read the atmosphere since she was a young girl. She learned that high humidity often preceded a storm, because her hair got frizzy, the leaves on the trees started curling, and the wood on the barn would swell. These signs had told her that the ranch was in the path of a squall of some sort. Regardless that the squall was still too far away to be seen yet, it was brewing and headed straight for her homestead. Bessie was so connected to her land that she could feel weather approaching long before it arrived.

As a homemaker, planter, and rancher, she used what the sky and heavens sent her way. Therefore, she knew how to be appropriately prepared for what Mother Nature would be delivering, be it during lean times or plentiful times. Since the legendary winter storm of 1888 had plucked her little twin boys out of her protective arms, she'd always remained one-step ahead of the climate. The weather her homestead was gifted with was imperative to what her land and livestock yielded yearly. As she grew into an older woman, her arthritis became her own personal and internal barometer. The more pressure in her body she felt, the more unpredictable the exosphere would become. She used the number of aches and stiffness in her joints to measure and forecast meteorological conditions and changes. Up until she began her ninetieth year on God's Green Earth, she'd kept the ranch's root cellar filled year-round with canned jellies and vegetables. For her, the root cellar was the sun, the sky, the moon, and stars, all sharing one small, dirt-floored space under the barn's floor. It was where she went to feel closer to her deceased sons and to prepare the ranch for every season of every year. This meant planting, harvesting, and canning nine months at a time. Although, she never stopped tending to her daily responsibilities and her ranch hands needs, her age eventually caught up to her ambitious spirit. In due time her body passed its expiration date and she slowed down. Therefore, her fertile and fruitful gardens had decreased in size with the passage of the seasons. Given her life, her death, and her unusual heftiness, the centurion deserved a heartfelt send-off. This meant a large casket built to fit in a spacious hole in the ground and a splendid funeral. All of which Jackson, Horace, and Ruby intended to give to her.

Because of her robustness, out of necessity, Jackson and Horace dug Bessie a wide and deep grave. Out of respect, and in the name of symbolism, they used two iron bladed hand shovels that had been used for the previous five Dutton burials. The men had discovered the rusted, steel shovels under a lap of filthy canvas in the old wagon. Decade old dirt and stones still lay in the wagons worn bed. The men respectively shovelled the same funeral dirt, from the previous Dutton burials, into Bessie's grave. They were both certain that she would have wanted it this way.

The attending Pastor, upon completing the religious part of the burial, sprinkled Holy water over the casket, declaring, "Bessie Dutton's soul has been spiritually cleansed."

He then made, in Ruby's opinion, an ultra-grandiose sign of the cross, indicating that the pearly gates were open, and Heaven was ready to receive her soul. Thereafter, her modest wooden casket, decorated with roses and bows, and filled with all of her buxom goodness, was lowered into the ground by Jackson, Horace, and two much younger, much stronger ranch hands. For the duration of the burial a flock of annoyingly loud vultures hovered and circled in the air above the gravesite. Their bothersome cawing had agitated Ruby something terrible throughout the entire service. Jackson had easily seen her irritation each time he saw her angrily distracted and looking up at the bothersome swarm of birds. This was something she did, in his opinion, about every thirty seconds or so. Ruby's vengeance-filled eyes betrayed her phony composure as she tried to stand still during the ceremony. Jackson and Horace took turns, one shovelful at a time, covering the wide casket with 'earth of the Good Lord'.

Bessie's death, burial, and life experiences connected Horace and Jackson like blood brothers in a matter of days. Ruby recalled watching them from sunup to sundown labouring, jesting, and laughing together. An apparent trust between the two men was growing. Despite that her mother, Sadie, was a half-breed child with a Negro mother and a Caucasian father, Ruby had never before seen Horace befriend a man of colour like he befriended Bessie's foreman. She liked what she saw. The man named Jackson, Shep for short, was good for Horace.

"Those winged scavengers can smell death from ten miles away," Jackson stated, while Ruby and Horace sat with him after the guests had left.

In an attempt to hide from the blistering sun they decided to relax in the shade on a spacious porch behind the ranch's main house. They drank cool, fresh squeezed lemonade and talked about how the day had gone. The three of them were thrilled with each other for what they'd together accomplished for Bessie.

Then, rather flukily Ruby, asked Jackson, "Why don't people didn't just shoot those goddamn bastard buzzards right out of the sky?"

"Mind your tongue girl!" Horace quickly retorted, glaring at his foul-mouthed adult daughter.

A chortling Jackson went on to explain.

"Out here on the open plains ranchers and farmers alike tolerate these black birds because they are our winged messengers from above. Those sharp-eyed, malign looking birds signal us when anything laying on the ground below them is near death or in some cases, already dead. Be it an animal, man, woman, or child."

He went on with further educating the Brits about buzzards.

"Homesteaders living out here in the middle of nowhere have been warned many times over by the vultures that one of their kinfolks or neighbours needs help. Every so often, someone in need is rescued in time because the buzzards have told us exactly where the person is. By swooping in to pick at or remove any dead remains, be it human or animal, these scavengers' tidy-up our land. This bird cleansing, as Plain's people call it, actually helps homesteaders prevent diseases from spreading to their livestock and food supplies. Likewise, maladies are kept from seeping into wells, which in a matter of months deteriorates the quality of our drinking water."

Abruptly and midsentence, Jackson said, "End of story."

Obviously, Shep was done with talking about birds, Horace reckoned.

The wide-eyed, old diner owner, who was still reminiscing about the past, felt elated with the memories of Jackson that were swirling around in her mind. It had been a very long time since she'd thought of the dear man or spent time on the American Great Plains with him. Shifting slightly, in her early 1900s leather lounger, she stretched the kinks out of her long, still shapely and slightly numbing legs. Her oversized ears perked, and her nostrils flared. With her tinted face pointing upwards, she sniffed and listened whilst she felt her spectacles sliding down towards the bridge of her nose. Her mind was having its way with her again; for a second, or two, she swore she heard buzzards cawing and smelled the odour of fresh squeezed lemons.

"Get a grip old girl!" she scolded herself. "Focus and carry on!"

The older version of Ruby was somewhat weird in this way. After mind traveling, she tended to see, hear, and smell things that weren't actually there. They were figments of her astute imagination and a fine-tuned memory. She took this as a sign that her roaming senses were still slightly confused, which was something she was now rightly used to, and therefore, never perturbed by. A quick glance at the diner's retro clock hanging on the wall in front of her told her that she still had a solid thirty minutes before the taxi driver would be announcing his arrival by tooting his horn.

Without hesitation she took a sip and then set the glass back down on the floor. She didn't need its coolness anymore. She was completely alert and in control of her brain as it mentally drifted backwards and took her with it.

The elderly woman had been born different. By the age of fifteen, she was a mastered mind traveller. She kept her exclusiveness private, preferring not to be judged or forced to shield and justify how abstract her ability was. Guiding her mind's flow of energy back and forth between different time spheres is what made her unique and connected her to the people and events that came before her. What the future held didn't interest her. She lived in the moment and for the moment. Actually, she didn't believe in being trapped in the past, despite that she adored roaming in and out of it. Mental drifting and traveling had kept her life stimulating and her paranormal abilities honed. As her body aged her mind became more astute and more curious. Not many people her age could say this about themselves. Ruby McEwen had always been a progressive thinker. As her childhood spun into adulthood she was often infuriated when people around her continuously told her to *stop daydreaming*. She had tried to ignore them, nevertheless, their constant comments had left permanent marks on her. She was different. This she knew and this was fine by her. From her vantage point being different and eccentric made her life a constant type of unanticipated reality. She'd choose the unexpected over the mundane each time. The entire reality of it was, she knew no other way.

Perhaps, she thought, *this is why for as shocked as she was when another eccentric, female troublemaker knocked on her door, she'd taken a real liking to her petite, purple haired, wild looking great granddaughter. It was as if the younger version of herself, excluding the colour purple, had entered her world and brought absolutely nothing mundane with her.* Little did the elderly woman know what was yet to come?

Like Ruby herself, her great granddaughter, Jazz Durant, was offbeat and she dared to be offbeat. This was the part of her that Ruby liked and respected the most. She hoped that fate would give her the opportunity to tell the child how she really felt about her. She then deduced that the rebellious and reckless phase Jazz was now in was the same phase she herself had lived through as a teenager. In the 1940s, she was desperate for even a smidgen of encouraging attention from her parents. Especially from her mother Sadie. Now, it was the child's turn to be seen and heard. Zofia and Tucker Durant's daughter was crying out for their reassurance, affection, and above all else their acceptance.

"Jazz is making a bold statement. Anyone with half a functioning brain should, know this," Ruby concluded aloud as she felt an unexpected need to defend the child in a coma, whilst realizing she still referred to her as 'the child'.

Thinking about Jazz and her parents caused her mind to wander back to her own parents. Her only regret, after their respective deaths, was the layers of unfinished business they'd left behind for her to live on with. This was especially true of her mother Sadie. With the flutter of an eyelid, she flicked her brain switch on and travelled back to where she had just been, moments before she had glanced at the clock.

Effortlessly, Ruby found her focus. Then she faintly sighed and guided her mind backwards, in the direction of a ranch, with a white, wraparound, high arched porch, and a seemingly endless amount of land surrounding it. Within one beat of her drifting heart it was August of 1959. The year temperatures reached a record 111° Fahrenheit across the American Great Plains.

Chapter 24

Jackson stood up from where he was sitting and announced that he was going to the creek for his daily exercise. He needed, what he called, a bodily refreshment. After a swim and cooling off in the creek he'd be going back to his quarters to take a nap before suppertime. Despite that Shep was used to the dry air and was typically very tolerant of the high Mid-west heat, this kind of extreme weather had rendered him a splitting headache.

Given that he didn't ask his houseguests to join him, Ruby and Horace both deduced that Bessie's right-hand man of five decades was in need of time alone. The events of the past fourteen days had taken their toll on the man. They both wished him a brisk dip in the creek and pain free nap. Before waving him off, they all agreed to share a meal together around 7pm. After about five minutes of complete silence, Ruby spoke.

"Is Jackson a conversationalist like you?" she asked her father.

"Indeed he is!" Horace energetically replied, as if he had the answer on the tip of his abstaining tongue. "Would you like to hear a few tales about Jackson and your mother's parents, Samuel and Bessie Dutton?"

"Indeed I would old man." She answered teasingly.

Despite that he hated it when she called him 'old man' he chose to ignore the pet name she'd given him when he turned fifty. Before Horace began his story telling, he reminded her that since their arrival in Montana he'd spent a great amount of time working side-by-side and conversing with Jackson.

"Let me tell you my girl, about the African American brother I never knew I had." The excitement in his voice was a familiar sign that his first tale had begun.

Ruby leaned her perspiring back against the railing of the porch, sipped cold lemonade and watched a very sober man slide into his storyteller role. She was hopeful that she was in for a fantastic afternoon with by far the best narrator she'd ever met.

"Shep my man, as your pa likes to call his new comrade, was for many brutal years an enslaved man working on an Appalachian Plantation. He was the keeper of the plantation's sheep herd. His master, a military man named, General Albert Jackson openly called him *nigger or boy*. His master's humiliation began the day he purchased him at a periodic slave auction where the General was notoriously known for skilfully outbidding other slave traders. Shep was a wee six months old when Master Jackson's lackey ripped him, as a screaming infant, out of his mama's arms. His devastated mammie was whipped into submission after she fought back to rescue her son. Before his newly purchased baby property was bundled up and transported to the Jackson Plantation, a dampened rag was stuffed in his mouth to curtail his wailing. As it came to be, other slaves and his wet nurse were instructed to call him Boy from the day he started living at the plantation. The name

159

identified him for nearly two and a half decades, until the night he ran off his master's property, as a twenty-something imperilled man fleeing for his life."

"I hate the word nigger! Why do you insist on using it when you talk about slaves?" Ruby asked, angrily interrupting a story that had barely begun.

Horace was used to her impulsiveness and outbursts, so he remained calm and patient with her.

"Because nigger is what they were called back then. Nigger was often what they called themselves in the 1700s and 1800s. In those times, when a Negro talked, or wrote about their lives as slaves, nigger was what they were called, so nigger is what they called themselves. Ruby girl, centuries ago, it was all the slaves knew."

He could see that his daughter was still disturbed by the word, so he explained further. While trying to be aware of using such an offensive term, he told her, "The fact of it is, Ruby girl, the history of the word nigger can be traced back to the Latin word Niger, which means Black. I do realize that with the passage of time, ethnic slurs have victimized all racial groups. Nevertheless, in my forthright opinion, no American race of people has endured as many racial nicknames as the Negroes have."

She sat upright as her face softened. He could see that he had her respect and attention now, so he went on.

"Shep told me that during the time he was a slave, a Negro was also called a coon, savage, piccaninny, mammy, and a jigaboo. Despite that no other American racial slur has ever intended such purposeful cruelty; nigger is not a word that I am intentionally using out of disrespect for the slaves or Shep. Really, it isn't. It's a word I just need to use if I am going to authentically tell a story about the history of slaves and their owner's inhumane persecutions," he replied with a tolerant tone. "Does my best girl understand?"

"Yes pa," she immediately mumbled.

He could see that she was lost in thought. This was another part of who she was that her father was quite used to. Horace continued his depiction and presentation of an American time gone by, the way he'd heard it and interpreted it from Shep himself. As he resumed his tale, Ruby reminded herself that her father had once studied Anthropology, consequently, he was more educated on ethnicities and cultures than she was. With this realization engrained in her mind, she began to listen more prudently. Truth be told, she had been hanging off his every word since the moment he referred to Jackson as his 'African American brother.'

"In the late 1800's sheep were the second most plentiful type of livestock on Appalachian Plantations. Slave life, across the fields and in the mountains, meant working sunup to sundown six days a week. Often slaves were given food that wasn't suitable for an animal to consume, regardless, they ate it as a means of pure survival. General Jackson's plantation slaves lived in small shacks with dirt floors, no electricity, no running water, and little or no furniture. He considered himself to be fortunate because life on larger plantations with cruel overseers was oftentimes a much worst fate for a Negro. Eventually, a slave baby named Boy grew into a shrewd lad. With the passing of time he became a strong, surefooted, clever minded, and hardworking young man. From when Boy was a mere seven years old, he learned to feed, shave, and trim the livestock's woollen fleece. By 15 years old he was an overseer on the plantation and responsible for the shearing, castrations, livestock drives, and the overseeing of wool exports. He was also a supervisor, who was in charge of other slaves who also tended, herded, fed, and guarded the plantations numerous herds of sheep. On larger plantations the person who directed the slave's daily work was an administrator and superintendent of sorts. This person was usually a white man, but occasionally an enslaved black man, like Shep, was appointed the position by his master. Some plantations had both a white overseer and a black supervisor. This practice was more common in the Deep South or on plantations where the master was often absent. According to him, his master was gone from the plantation regularly. A fact that gave the slave, called Boy, a taste of free will. When his master was gone, Boy could ease his harsh ways with other slaves, because he wasn't being watched over by their domineering, Master General Albert Jackson.

Ruby continued to dangle off every interesting word Horace spoke.

"Whenever Boy's master sporadically left the plantation, it was to go hunting or to attend a slave auction in an effort to increase his monthly servant stock and his yearly profits. Once or twice a week he left his plantation so he could relieve the uncomfortable, erotic bulge he had in his britches. His protruding, lust filled bulge had a mind of its own. Master Albert tended to his swelling episodes by giving his pent-up sexual needs away to the first willing white woman he came upon."

Ruby began laughing. She'd forgotten how her pa could put an unexpected, humorous twist on any story.

"Mind you not," Horace went on to say, "plantation owners had their pick of any slave girl they wanted to rape or impregnate at any moment of any given day of the week. In spite of this, now and then, a white man hankered after a moral less, fair-skinned woman, with an extra-large bosom and round buttocks. A woman who was nothing like his plantations skinny, overused black girls, or his much too sexually repressed mistress-wife. Sexually willing and exploited women could be found at private, illegal bordello saloons that were visited frequently by white men passing through and men who resided in the area."

Horace went on to tell Ruby that while they were digging Bessie's wide and deep grave, Shep had said, through his yellowed, bloodshot, and pride-filled eyes, that his sheep were more than doubly important to his master than the cattle were. The herds were vital to the Jackson Plantations profits that filled the pockets on either side of Master Albert's recurring and visible carnal urges. The ewes, rams, and lambs were the three life forces that had kept Boy alive and sane while growing up as a nigger slave. Without the livestock, he told me he'd have curled up and died a hundred times over. An intrigued Ruby listened on with intent.

"Those were his exact words," Horace convincingly professed. "The General was a military sharpshooter in the US Army. Any slave caught trying to run off his plantation was shot down dead in their tracks like the animals he considered them to be. General Albert would stand outside on his veranda and discharge his infantry rifle at those *gallant, black, runaway nigger fools,*

161

as he called them. Escaping slaves bolted for their lives, as if they were wild turkeys scattering from the booming sounds of his ammo. Since Boy was old enough to remember, only six, or seven niggers had been shot dead by Master General Jackson. Despite the loss of six or seven black souls, according to typical runaway nigger killing standards at the time, this wasn't many documented dead slaves for one plantation to have."

Horace paused to catch his breath. Because he was aging and his passion for telling a proper tale was still so strong, he'd forget to breathe in a way that would prevent him from becoming winded. Consequently, he'd run short on oxygen while telling his stories. Ruby was used to this side of him. She knew he would need a few minutes to fill his lungs, rest his brain, and regain his composure.

"Take your time Horace," she compassionately said. Then, in silence, she observed the storyteller sitting across from her.

She could see that the old man was trying to calm his beating heart and racing mind. She knew him well. He was priming himself for the second half of his next part of his newest tale. She remembered the first time she'd called him *old man*, or Horace, instead of father or pa. It was the day he celebrated the start of his sixth decade of life. At the time, she was still an adolescent searching for her independence. Rather than being disrespectful, calling him *old man* was a term of endearment and a habit that she still hadn't outgrown.

As Horace clutched clumsily at his glass of lemonade, she saw that his hands were slightly shaking. Ruby knew that this meant that he was still whiskey-free. Despite that he was sober and an expert storyteller, lately his mind was getting as cloudy as his eye was. The passage of time had carved grooves in Horace's furrowed face and transformed it into a roadmap of his life. His skin was as crinkly as piece of bland parchment paper that had aged. Since she resembled him, she rather suspected that her own skin and eyes would one day do the same. Naively, she dismissed her prediction as quickly as it had come to her; believing that turning into an old woman was still a very long way off. The chapters of her father's life were written all over him from head to toes to fingertips. He was a tall, hefty man, with large hands and even larger feet, therefore, he was difficult to construe given that there was six-foot-four-inches and two hundred pounds of him to construe. He still had a full head of pure white curly hair, a cleverly sharp searching mind, and a satisfied personality coiled around his many unpredictably diverse dispositions.

Now and then, he was lost in his recollections of what she referred to as, 'a misplaced love tinged with grief'. He and her mother, Sadie, had shared a bad marriage throughout Ruby's childhood and adolescent years. In the first year after Sadie left him, Ruby saw Horace slips away into loneliness. She predicted that this was why Horace had connected himself so intensely to his granddaughter Eliza. In 1954, when she named her baby girl after his mother, Liza, she created an instant link between Horace the grandpa and Eliza the newborn. This was probably why her child had received such a lavished type of love from him. Nearly daily, Ruby's daughter was showered with a kind of affection from her grandpa that she couldn't recall receiving from him when she herself was a lass. Because of this, the candid side of Ruby's personality

162

could be, on a small and tolerable scale, a tad jealous of her own daughter. Likewise, the grateful side of her was indebted to Horace for how he naturally and without pretence doted on her only child.

Still observing him from the back porch of the Dutton ranch, she realized that she wanted, actually more so needed, to be able to trust him. Recalling his positive involvement in Eliza's life was undeniably giving her a place to start finding faith in her father again.

Who knows, she thought, *perhaps Eliza is one of those threads that bind people? Now, wouldn't that be something,* she hoped, as she tried to imagine such a mischievous child binding anything together, especially someone as exuberant as her grandpa was.

The sober old man with the crumpled face had done nothing biased or dishonourable in his lifetime of mediocrity. Despite that he was a tried-and-true flirt and a womanizer, he'd never been sexually unfaithful to his wife. Not even once. Just after they'd arrived in Montana, he had told his daughter that he attributed his earlier behaviours on the inhibited effects of the whisky. This was something he wasn't proud of but had let go of, because back then, he was a different man.

Horace glanced over at her and sliced the silence between them by saying, "A daughter can blame their father for certain things that have gone wrong in her life, but it's not fair for her to blame him for everything."

Hearing this, Ruby thought, it was as though he could read her mind, fears and regrets. She truly hated him for being able to do this and at the same time appreciated him for doing this. Ruby realized that she also needed to let go of her turbulent past with him and live her life without the effects their past and he had once had on her. Nevertheless, in the reality of how complex their family history was, she needed more time. After about three or four minutes passed, a re-energized Horace transformed back into the crackerjack storyteller that he was. Ruby noticed, as he picked up exactly where he'd left off, that his eye was emitting a bewitching type of eagerness.

Bloody hell, she thought, in a respectful way, *this old man truly adores the spotlight. He is SO not me,* she confirmed with a slow, exasperated roll of her jade green eyes.

"You see Ruby girl, Master Albert Jackson owned the most slaves and had the lowest recorded rate of slave runaways in the entire state. This was a chronicled fact of the times. General Jackson's slaves were his property and his property stayed on his property!" Horace emphasized.

"Why?" she asked, "slaves were famous for their daring escape attempts."

"Frankly," Horace alleged, "this was because once Master Albert's slaves learnt from many a failed attempt that they couldn't outrun his military precision, his sharpshooter's eye, and the bullets from his muskets. For these reasons, they stopped longing for their freedom and stopped fleeing. This was why the General's slaves almost never tried escaping."

"Why?" she asked, "there had to have been more to this than losing their desire for freedom?"

"Because" he answered, "they feared the ammunition from his rifle more than they feared the lashes from his triple knotted bullwhip."

Horace took another long, slow drink from his lemonade filled tin mug, winked at his best girl, and went on with his rendition of the tale he'd heard from the ex-slave, named Jackson

"Bloody goddamned hell, it's hot!" Ruby very unexpectedly and angrily shouted out. Even sitting in the shade, sweat was trickling off her forehead and chin.

"Mind your smutty mouth!" Horace reprimanded. "I raised a respectable young lady, not a lewd mouthed factory worker!"

Despite that, he'd heard it countless times since she'd grown up, he would never get used to his best girl cursing and cussing. Horace came from a generation when women were both timid and dutiful, not outspoken, rebellious females. Glaring at her like a rankled father, he continued with his story.

"With it being established that the keeper of sheep, Boy, was just a baby when he was bought into slavery, there was no actual record of his birth, or his surname. In 1863, President Abraham Lincoln's Emancipation Proclamation, declared that all slaves residing in the southern territories were free. This included the territories that were in rebellion against the Federal Government. The proclamation only applied to states that were active in Civil War rebellion of 1863. This meant that Abe Lincoln's decree didn't include nearly a half a million other slaves who were captive in the slave holding Border Union States. Slaves living and working in these states were later freed by a turn of events and independent state and federal actions. Fortunately, for Shep, the Emancipation Proclamation included the plantation where he resided. During that time, people still called him Boy."

Ruby poured more lemonade into Horace's cup and interrupted him again. This time she used a well-mannered approach and asked him, "Has your newest mate Shep told you about his becoming a free man?"

Horace smiled broadly and said, "Yes, my Negro brother told me about the pinnacles of his life. In fact, he did so in a way that made me feel as if I was experiencing the best parts of Shep's life, right alongside of him!"

He was so excited, almost too excited for the likes of his slightly sceptical daughter. As he continued, Ruby's pa tried to tame his enthusiasm and she tried to trust that he hadn't fallen face first off, the whiskey wagon when she wasn't looking. The combination of whiskey and a storytelling audience, be it one person or ten, had always generated an adrenaline high for Horace. This was why she was becoming more doubtful by the minute. Sometimes, like others who listened to his tales, when it came to Horace, she didn't know 'where the lies ended, and the truths began'. He ignored her changing mood and continued.

"The night his master waved the best, moneymaking sheep keeper he'd ever owned off his land, he was choking on political protest and spattering radical Republican poison out from between his rotting teeth. The drunken General was swinging his infantry rifle above his frenzied head, like an evil-crazed man. The then young slave, standing just within range of Master Albert's politically toxic spit, heard his master screeching, *be off with ya' nigger!* All the scorching vulgarity and cruelty General Albert Jackson had in him, was erupting out the sides of his mouth, rolling off his trimmed beard, and hitting the veranda like drops of boiling, rage-filled rain! *Run nigger run! Run for ya life, for I catch ya' in my aim!*

The slave that had been named Boy, by the man with the musket pointed straight at him, turned tail and bolted like all the slaves before him had. Boy ran as fast as his scraggly, undernourished legs could carry him down a steep and grassy green hill in front of the main house. He was running for his life, carrying no possessions, and wearing nothing but the ragged clothes on his back. As Boy ran, his heart was beating so fast he worried that it would explode, and he'd fall dead in the grass. He had a ghastly fear that he was going to end up the same as one of Master Albert's 'shot dead in their tracks' wild turkeys. What he dreaded even more than this was that his master would not shoot to kill. He'd shoot to wound him, capture him, and then have him tarred and feathered. Unless his profit making, keeper of sheep ignored Abe Lincoln's 'patriotic love for nigga's and stayed on his plantation, his demise was as sure a bet as a sunrise and sunset was. Knowing his Master the way he'd known him his entire life, the sheep keeper suspected that after his capture he'd be forced to pluck his own punishment feathers off a freshly shot dead turkey while Master Albert himself heated up the tar. Still not yet smelling any kind of freedom in the air, a grisly image of his beloved black skin being burned by the boiling tar, and then feathered, got stuck in his head. Choking on his fear of death, Boy kept on running down that steep, grassy hill and into the woods. The petrified Negro lad never looked back."

Ruby was sitting up and weeping now. Horace tenderly put his arm around his best girl and suggested they go inside and have something to eat before he told her more about Shep. He hoped the man had cooled off and was napping serenely in the shaded bunkhouse. After the kind of life he'd lived, the very least that he deserved was a peaceful nap.

They went into the house and made sandwiches and a garden salad. Bessie had a late 17th century armoire in the parlour, filled with tableware that was as old as the cabinet was. Horace assumed it must have come from Bessie's husband Samuel's family plantation. Shep had told him quite a bit about Samuel's background while they'd been buffing and restoring the Dutton's casket-carrying wagon.

He made a mental note to *tell Ruby this story as well.* He was convinced that she would be interested in learning about her grandpa Samuel. He knew his best girl through and through. They shared the same passion for events of the past and ancestral legends. After they'd finished eating a late lunch, Ruby tidied up the dishes and swept the floor. Horace went outdoors to spread a copper coloured, cotton blanket out on the grass under a huge willow tree on the back lawn. It was finally cooling down across the plains and he desired taking his shoes and socks off and stretching out his six-foot-four body. The old man was weary. Twinges of jetlag still tarried in his bones and the result of days of physical labour had cramped up his muscles. He'd selected a sensible spot for the blanket. One with enough distance between the shade of the tree and the hopefully, a still napping ex-slave. This would keep the story he was eager to resume telling out of hearing range of his newest comrade. The last thing Horace wanted was for the man to hear him digging up fragments of his grim past as a slave.

The ranch's brick bunkhouse in the distance was in plain sight of the grassy spot Horace had chosen to spread the blanket. When Jackson woke up, he would see him leaving the bunkhouse and he'd know it was time to end his tale. Ruby's father was deferential and cunning in this way. When she came outside and took her place next to him, he was leaning up against the willow tree. His long legs were outstretched, and he was barefoot. It had been years since Ruby had seen her pa barefoot and looking so uninhibited and healthy. She had forgotten how big Horace's feet were and how disgustingly hairy his knurly toes were. This had her snickering to herself as she sat down next to him. The old man didn't ask her what was so funny. He knew exactly what his only daughter found so amusing, so he reached over, found his intention, and he threw his smelly socks at her; followed by two size twelve shoes. Out of habit, she batted them away as if they were tennis balls.

After being with him in America this past week, Ruby could see that *sobriety agreed with Horace and had added years to his looks in less than eleven months.* With this calming thought, she slid in closer to him. There were too many years that Ruby feared he'd forever lost because of four and a half decades of alcohol abuse and marital misery. She'd never intentionally favoured one parent over the other, nor had she chosen sides whenever their bashing began or after it ended. She was wise enough to know that it took two people to start a relationship and two people to destroy it.

The almost thirty-four-year-old rolled over onto her back and rested her head on Horace's lap. On that particular late afternoon, in 1959, while sitting together on a copper coloured cotton blanket, after burying one of the kindest women both of them had ever known, Horace was the second type of storyteller. Ruby's doubts were disappearing. She could see that he was still clearheaded and unrestricted by the claim whiskey had once had on him for her entire life. Because she honestly couldn't get enough of him when he was sober, she held his large hand, and waited for him to start of the second half of a tale he was clearly eager to finish telling.

Affectionately, he stroked her warm, sunburned cheek and carried on with his story exactly where he had left off. Feeling safe and filled with her typical curiosity, keen to hear more, she cozied up to him.

Chapter 25

"The Emancipation Proclamation of 1863 freed slaves in regions where the US Army was active. President Lincoln's proclamation changed the meaning and tenacity of the Civil War. The war was no longer just about preserving the Union, it was also about freeing enslaved Negroes. Foreign influences like our own Britain and our neighbour France, lost political interest in supporting the U.S. Confederacy." Horace was on a historical roll.

"When the Civil War ended in April of 1865, only about fifteen percent of the slaves had actually been freed. In actual fact, it took the ratification of the Thirteenth Amendment to abolish slavery everywhere in the United States. This meant that all slaves were finally liberated and officially set free. Part of their emancipation required the ex-slaves to register their biological name, date of birth, and other personal identification details." Horace leaned against the tree behind his back and continued.

"At the registry office building, for the better part of nine hours, my man Shep stood outdoors in a long line under a sizzling sun. He wasn't even sure how old he was. Because of the changes in his body and his new ways of thinking about girls, he estimated himself to be maybe 15 or 16 sixteen years old. His not knowing was making him uneasy and skittish as he stood there waiting his turn in line. Acting uneasy and skittish were two things that made a nigger stand out amongst the other niggers."

Ruby cringed, hearing this word twice exiting Horace's mouth again. He saw her reaction but passed over it. He was not a man who rejoiced in repeating himself. Therefore, he left it up to her to recall why he chose to use the word and then to accept his use of it.

"When it finally was Shep's turn, he was asked to state his full name, his date of birth, the country of his birth, what his work was currently doing, and on which plantation he had been employed as a nigger slave. He stood tall and proud in front of the whitest white man he'd ever laid eyes on.

With his shoulders upright and his chin held high, he replied, *Sir, my name be Boy.*

Then guesstimating he said, *I be a seventeen-year long sheep keeper on the plantation of Master General Albert Jackson. I don't know my birthdate or my birthplace. I was sold as a baby with no memory of such facts. I be a just freed nigger slave and I give thanks and the praise of God to a man called Honest Abe!*

Boy was proud of his answer and his proper reference to President Abraham Lincoln. The white clerk behind the table, whose sole duty was to record all the slave's information, rudely sneered and mockingly repeated, "So your name is Boy, you worked on the Jackson Plantation, you be a just-freed nigger now, and you was a shepherd just like Jesus in the Bible?"

Answering in the same order as he was asked, Boy unknowingly responded, *yes sir, I done this, and yes sir I is, but, no sir I is not. There be only one real Jesus. I be a good man all my life, but kind sir, I isn't no Jesus!*

Horace took a drink of his lemonade, wiped the dribble from his chin, and carried on with his rendition of Jackson's story.

"Everyone within earshot, including a few of the clerk's colleagues, roared with laughter. A clueless just freed nigger, who was not trying to be a comic, looked around at the crowd with a naïve, staggered expression. The Official Registry Clerk slammed his clenched fists down on the table so fast and hard he gave Boy, and the other slaves standing in line behind him, a premeditated scare. Then the livid clerk went all bonkers when he saw that his temper had hit the table and spilled his inkwell. His registry feather quill was now laying in the dry Appalachian dirt. The officer started to have an even greater fit of anger. With a familiar protective, kneejerk reaction, Boy jumped backwards out of striking range. He knew first-hand the look of a man about to deliver him a close-fisted blow."

Horace stopped long enough to let out a snorting laugh. His best girl's eyes were wider than he'd ever before seen them. He leashed his own emerging laughter and went on.

With a volume, so loud that all the surrounding Negros could hear, the clerk blared out, *thanks to the man, that half of the Great Country of America is calling Honest Abe, I have been standing out here for the past fifteen days and nights trying to register dumb, ignorant niggers just like you!* The veins on the clerk's neck were prominently sticking out. His inflamed red face looked like it was about to burst and splatter blood all over the petrified, just freed, skinny as a chicken's leg nigger standing before him. The enraged clerk harshly commanded. *Fetch my quill boy! Yes, sir,* he screeched out, *that's it! That's my name! Boy, that's my name!* The laughing, which had all but dwindled from others waiting in line, began all over again. He bent down and picked up the quill that had landed next to his grimy, black feet with their pinkish white soles. Then he humbly blew the dry dirt off the quill's feathers, spat on the barbed tip, wiped his slave saliva off on his sleeve, and then meekly held the feather ink quill out for the clerk to take. *Seems feathers were destined to be part of my road to freedom after all,* he timidly whispered with his head hanging reverently low. Knowing his recent thought about feathers best not heard by the angry clerk, Shep, I mean Boy, kept the rest of his thinking inside his head where it couldn't cause him more trouble."

Sitting across from Horace, who was looked so relaxed in a cross-legged pose, Ruby felt enchanted by his storytelling skill. Her pa carried on with his portrayal of Jackson's past.

"By this time, the Registry Officer's superior was now outside glaring over at the riled-up clerk, whilst trying to determine what all the commotion was about. Upon seeing his superior approaching the table, the clerk, with neck veins still jutting out, calmed himself immediately and regained his composure. With beads of nervous sweat dripping off his brow, the registry clerk dutifully went on with his work. Grumpily, he asked him the same standard registry questions, on the same standard registry form. After getting the same ignorant answers, from an unschooled nigger who persisted to proclaim his praise of Abe Lincoln, the clerk realized he'd wasted too much of his precious time on a stupid slave who called himself Boy.

As thirst parched at the registry clerk's lips, hunger pains clawed at the insides of his tubby belly. The combination of his need for liquids and his growling appetite was agitating the man's extremely impatient and nigger-hating approach with Shep and his ignorant ways. For that reason and that reason alone, without forethought the reluctless clerk decided that he'd just name the dumbass nigger himself. In addition to all the factors causing him to make such an unofficial decision, the flustered clerk needed to get the long line of slaves behind the witless chump standing in front of his registration table moving again. That was his job, and no amount of hunger, thirst, or racist Negro attitude was going to get him out of doing his job!"

Ruby could see that Horace was pleased with his story's rendition.

"So what happened next?" she impatiently asked as she scooched in closer to her pa. Horace carried on effortlessly. The big-footed, burly man had forgotten how much he adored telling a decent story.

"It was then that an overheated, riled clerk made a hasty decision. The slave, who called himself Boy and worked as a 'sheep keeper' on the Jackson Plantation for seventeen years, must be considerably older than he thought he was. Henceforth, on that day, the clerk registered him as a 27-year-old man and named Jackson Boy Shepherd. To this day Jackson still doesn't know his actual date of birth."

Feeling the rush of a thrill going through her, Ruby propped herself up on her elbows in anticipation of how this part of Jackson's life story ended.

"So there you have it!" Horace conclusively bellowed locking eyes with his best girl. Ruby stared back at him with a properly puzzled expression on her face.

"That's it?" she disappointedly asked.

Delighted with his talent for telling a good tale and her inquisitiveness, Horace immediately carried on. The cagey grin on his face never faded.

"An unrecorded number of years after the end of the American Civil War, while making his way westward, a roving African American man roamed around the American Mid-West while minding his own business. Since being confirmed a free man, he'd had many adventures, met many interesting people, and survived too many harrowingly narrow escapes. One early morning, the once young, black keeper of sheep was hungry, dirty, and disoriented. After crisscrossing US territories for many a daring and nerve-racking year, Shep had lost his direction. He was a poor, yet anticipative young man, who was physically weakening by the day. Then, on one particular and unexpected morning, the famished, filthy, vagrant, through the grace of his beloved God, chanced upon a homestead. His birthdate, his name, and his registered status had all changed, but his skin colour had remained the same."

Horace took his cap off, tossed it onto the blanket, and wiped the perspiration from his forehead. The heartless heat of the sun was more than a man who came from the cool climate of the British Isle's was used to. He loudly cleared his throat and spat the slime he coughed up into the grass. Ruby, who was accustomed to his spitting habit, turned her head just in time to avoid seeing what he'd expelled from his innards. He knew she loathed his spew, which was why he'd made an intentionally loud and theatrical kind of sound whenever he spit. Despite how entertaining getting under her skin was, Horace was ready to continue telling his version of Jackson Boy Shepherd's newest adventure.

"The sun had just started to rise over the distant horizon. It was the time of the morning when night and day united. This meant that Shep's eyes hadn't adjusted to sunlight yet. A homesteader in the distance stood stout and steadfast, whilst aiming a Creedmoor rifle at his head. She'd detected him before he even knew he was being watched. She observed him with both of her precise eagle eyes, as he moseyed across one of her nearby potato fields. The underfed and fearful black man was riding bareback on a skinny, overused, silver haired donkey. The donkey was a rightly old and ornery four-legged beast. Because of his belligerent ways, the bad-tempered donkey was being harshly urged to keep trotting forward. A thick rope tied around his neck and a series of fanatic kicks to his ribs from the coloured man straddling the obstinate animal, reminded the donkey of his life's purpose."

Ruby and Horace began to sporadically laugh at the images they each had of the napping Jackson, the proper and orderly man they'd come to know, riding a bareback on a dirty donkey. Ruby then urged her father to tell her more.

"About an hour later, after the black man riding the stinky donkey had taken a long, overdue bath and eaten a generous breakfast, the obliged and recently freed Negro was asked to explain himself. He began by telling a woman who'd just pointed her reliable Creedmoor rifle at his head as the sun rose over the horizon, that he'd found the ole' grey donkey wandering alone on a rugged, rocky trails he was crossing. These trails, he explained, were only a few of the many paths his boots had left their imprints upon since he had bid the US Registration Clerk, and the only life he had ever known, a brave goodbye. He went on to tell the observant homesteader, who was still gripping her weapon under the dining table that his being experienced with large herds of sheep made tending to one skinny, bad-tempered ole' donkey, easier than anything he'd ever done in his life. Only difference, he reckoned, between a sheep and a donkey, was that sheep don't lick people."

"Huh?" Ruby questioned. "How does Jackson go from being lost and having a rifle pointed at him, to a bath and breakfast?"

The wide gap in his story had her doubting Horace's sobriety again. She personally knew how the effects of whiskey drinking tended to make his brain skip around inside his head. She'd seen it and lived it so many times, that the effects of his drinking had robbed her of trusting her pa by the time she was a ten-year-old. The scepticism of being raised by an alcoholic man began churning in her.

"You see," Horace continued, "the smelly ole' donkey had a nasty knack of licking poor ole' Shep while he slept. For as often as the emancipated Negro man smacked the donkey on his snout with a thick tree branch, the crabby beast insisted on licking him with his slimy, rough, mule-like tongue. This, for obvious reasons, prevented the hungry, overtired fella from getting a rightful amount of shuteye."

The image of Jackson being licked by a donkey had Ruby laughing so hard that in no time she forgot about her mistrust in Horace.

170

"Are you two sharing a few laughs about good ole' Shep? Don't you Brits know it's not polite to talk about a bad-mannered donkey, or tell another man's story while he's napping?"

Jackson was rather amused at how he'd rendered a father and daughter speechless faster than they could bat three eyeballs. Obviously, enjoying himself he said, "Let's move this very interesting conversation about this very interesting old black man into the kitchen. You both can help me make a fine pot of thick beef stew and homemade brown bread for supper."

He then gave Ruby a quick, flippant kind of wink and Horace a brawny slap on his back.

"I will take over for Horace and tell you my version of the rest of my story." Jackson concluded.

There they sat, stock-still, a British father and his daughter with identical stunned expressions. Jackson could see that the Brits rightly reckoned that they'd haphazardly been caught in a trap. He was rather enjoying himself, watching them silently squirm like they were stuck in two bowls of figgy pudding. Neither of them had heard Jackson walking towards them and then past the willow tree they were sitting under. Seeing him already climbing the veranda steps, they proceeded to quickly gather their wits, the blanket, the lemonade pitcher, and the drinking glasses from the lawn and porch before going inside. With a relaxed silence, one that at least Jackson was enjoying, they joined him in the kitchen and started preparing dinner. Shep took the lead by delegating the cooking tasks out. He looked refreshed after his invigorating swim and long nap. Once he was sure that they'd both settled into their designated meal preparations, he began sharing more of the legacy of his life. He'd taken a liking to Ruby's father, whom he'd never met before, and felt a familiar fondness for the now older version of Bessie's granddaughter. They had travelled all the way from England to help him give his revered 'Miss Bessie' a respectable send-off and he was beyond grateful for their comradery.

As Jackson stood on a step stool and took a cast-iron stew pan down from the highest pantry shelf, he began to share a portion of his past.

Chapter 26

"It was a long and pitifully hot summer. High temperatures meant the native berries I was accustomed to eating had all dried up along the trail I travelled. Even the wild rabbits and foxes I hunted were scarce. I knew right good and well they'd gone deep underground to avoid the heat. I was feeling a kind of hunger in my gut that I hadn't felt since I was a slave boy eating slop out of a bucket.

A Montana territory homesteader had indeed seen me in the distance crossing the plains, just as I heard Horace correctly telling his doubting daughter." Jackson gave Ruby a receptive wink.

"Let me enlighten you both," Jackson said. "While kicking a lazy donkey in the ribs, I was attempting to keep a fair distance from the homestead I'd just ambled upon; not knowing what would befall me, if I were seen by the likes of a stranger ready to do me harm or steal my only means of transportation. Being a clever man, I kept my head down low and whistled. It was the sweet kind of whistling, mind you both, of a courteous and nonthreatening black man just passing through. You see, I had no actual way of proving that my traveling companion was rightfully mine. The only official papers I had in my pouch were my certificate of freedom and my newly acquired and registered name. Truth be, despite that, the donkey wasn't justly mine and he had a bad stink, I'd come to be very fond of him. For a sensible reason, I'd already dismounted the animal when I saw a rifle staring me down."

Listening to Shep reminded Horace of why they'd connected so easily since he'd arrived at what once was a 10x10 foot, mud-roofed, homesteader's shack. They shared the same gift and passion for telling a worthy, true to life story. As Jackson continued, Horace dismissed his thoughts and gave the man his complete attention.

"At the time, I'd become a true-blue kind of traveling man. After eight years of wandering around I knew better than to wave at strangers. This included the swarthy skirted stranger pointing a long barrelled rifle at me. Back in those times, outsiders greeting someone on an open range of a then undeveloped territory, sent many innocent men to their graves. You see, homesteaders had no way of knowing if a waving outsider was armed and dangerous, or friendly. When the woman with the rifle first laid eyes on me, she was standing alone on a porch in front of a low-roofed house. I had dismounted my whiffy means of transport and was leading the smelly donkey by a neck rope, just in case I needed to run for my life. As I approached the nearby creek, I could see the woman was inspecting me, fierce-like, in a watchful and guarded way."

Fixated on Jackson's story, Ruby stopped peeling potatoes and listened with the kind of focus she'd been born with.

"You see, I'd spotted the creek on the trail a way back, even before I'd spotted farther in the distance what I thought to be remote farm, or maybe a ranch. My four-footed crony was parched and in dire need of some fresh water. I myself was hungrier than a man should be, so I was planning on doing some fishing in the nearby creek. Being a man educated only in the ways of sheep and slaves, aside from grass, I had no idea what a short-tempered, human licking donkey ate. Trouble was, earlier that same day at about the time of sunrise, the burro got himself a bad case of the skits. What was coming out of his backside and hitting the ground, every few hundred feet we travelled, was chunky-like and as green as green can be. Even the dumb ole' Negro man I was at the time knew straight off he'd eaten an unhealthy amount of grass! The poor animal needed something other than long, thick blades of sweet pasture food in his upset donkey gut!"

Ruby was smirking again, thinking about how Jackson had the same talent of creating a fine story from his memories as Horace did. She gave Horace, who was peeling carrots, a quick glance. He looked utterly charmed by Jackson's storytelling. She now, undoubtedly could see why these two men, who'd only known each other since Bessie's passing nine days ago, had grown so close. Jackson, who was cutting fresh beef into bite sized portions before seasoning them, looked over at her and gestured her to kindly get back to her potatoes. Then he carried on with his story.

"The woman, still holding her firearm, called my attention towards the house by ringing a large, triangular, solid iron dinner bell. The bell hung from corner of the porch's tall, angular roof. As of today, that same bell, still hangs from the same hook off the same porch's roof beam. The three-sided bell had a tone that was strong and far-reaching. The first loud clang it made had me obediently, and cautiously, turning my direction of ambling alongside a donkey with diarrhea towards the house."

Simultaneously, Horace and Ruby laughed loudly at the visions they had in their minds. Jackson, ignoring their chuckling at his expense, kept on with his beef stew preparation, and went on with his tale.

"As I stepped onto the front lawn, within killing range of the barrel of her rifle, a kind faced, robust woman was greeting me with a wary wave. She wasn't a very tall woman, maybe five feet five give or take an inch in either direction. What she lacked for in height she made up for in valour and confidence. She stood their firm, and as tall as a short person could stand. She showed no fear of the filthy, traveling, and black as coal stranger approaching. There I was, an outsider with carbon -coloured skin, making his way towards her homestead. She never, not even for a split second, lost her unwavering female composure. When I was close enough to shake her hand, I could see that there was something of a relieving and recognizable similarity between us. She was also a person of colour. I'd happened upon a fellow Negro and most likely, an ex-slave just like myself. Even though she didn't announce the ex-slave part of herself when we first met, a slave gets a quintessential natural feeling around another slave. An exchange of words isn't needed for an understanding between servants, as we are called in these modern times. Upon seeing her skin tone, I started breathing normal like again and felt myself to be a bit safer. You see, I hadn't felt safe before I got

173

emancipated, escaped from being tarred and feathered, got me a real name, and then found a skinny, shit-ridden donkey that was as undernourished as I was, just wandering through no man's land."

Jackson stood up, walked over to the sink, and poured three glasses of ice-cold tap water. He gave a glass to Ruby and Horace and told them how important it was they drink plenty of water with this heat. He then cut a fresh lemon into wedges, put the wedges in a bowl, and slide the bowl across the counter between his houseguests.

Then he proudly told them, "This is the finest, freshest well water from a well I dug, one shovel full at a time, too many years ago to count on two hands."

After putting the beef in a griddle and lighting the flame of the gas grill, he started talking about the past again.

"Back then, she was a lighter shade of black than I was. I tried not to stare. I wanted to hide my nosiness about this young, rather valiant, fine looking woman standing alone on a porch. I asked myself, who she was? Then I started choking on fear-filled misgivings running ramped through my worrisome head. There was a nagging question stuck in my skull distracting me from greeting her in gentleman-like fashion. Where are the men? I heard my suspicious intuition outright asking her."

"Insightful question Shep!" Horace eagerly added with a raised arm sign of praise.

Jackson smiled at him as he kept stirring the spiced beef, paprika, and onions that were frying in the cast iron pan.

"I was Boy, a black man, with a stupid name, but I was no fool!" he proclaimed. "I knew all too well that menfolk in the American Territories, like the Indians they fought off and hunted down, all carried rifles and armaments. Property owners and kinfolk alike were forced to use their firearms to protect what was theirs, especially after the discovery of gold in the Great Plains region. I remember a time when the Great Plains Cavalry protected American settlers, railroaders, wagon trains, businesses, and even gold seekers, from Indian attacks. Plain's people lived in fear day and night. Despite a man's skin colour, if landowners were threatened, they'd shoot a trespasser, or an entire family for good measure, down dead and nonchalantly walk away. After the slaughter, before riding off they'd steal horses and belongings from their lifeless victims. Not one of the murderers and thieves ever looked even slightly shamefaced. Not many guilt-filled eyes were batted in those days. Killings and deaths like these happened all the time out here in these parts."

Jackson stopped talking, went to the icebox, and then filled their empty glasses with cold ginger ale that he'd made himself a few days ago.

"It should be ripe and tasty by now," he said.

Passing by Shep on his way to use the toilet, Horace gave his comrade a solid, robust, manly smack on the back and said, "Nature's calling brother, be right back."

Now that Ruby was alone with Jackson, she asked him, "Did you ever know my mother and her older brothers?"

174

He said he did. Then he suggested they wait courteously for her pa to return before he carried on with his storytelling. Filled with anticipation and new-fangled respect for her father, she agreed with Jackson. Five minutes later, Horace was back in the kitchen enjoying his non-alcoholic beverage and resuming his part of preparing the evening meal. Jackson picked right up where he'd left off.

"So, where were we?" he said tapping on the top of his head. "Oh, yes. A young, self-assured woman of colour could see my noticeable hesitations and fear. She lowered her rifle, lodged it between her apron-covered thighs, and told me I was safe where I stood. She guaranteed that no men would bring any harm to me. I swore then, as I swear to it today, that woman could read my fears, thoughts, and moods quicker than I even knew they were there."

Looking over at Ruby, Shep said, "Then your grandma Bessie pointed to a wash line mounted on a sturdy pole across the lawn and ordered me to hitch up my pitiful looking donkey with grassy shit stuck to his tail. She didn't want any animal crap in her grass or tracked into her clean house. I asked her, was her husband was okay with her having a donkey with dysentery hitched up on his property. The woman with her rifle still just a hand's length away, informed me clearly that, I asked too many questions. I needed to stop yakking and start listening!"

Jackson was in his element now. Ruby and Horace were intrigued. They hung off his story like two curious coats on a rack. They easily coaxed him into telling them more. He went on, picking up where he'd left them dangling.

"I looked up to thank her and saw her wiping tears out of her eyes and off her cheeks. It was buried emotion she was tempting to hide from me. Being a well-mannered man, I pretended as if I hadn't noticed. After I finished harnessing up my donkey, she picked her weapon back up, held her hand out to me, and said I could call her Miss Bessie. I extended her my cleanest, work worn, calloused hand. Despite how dirty even my most dirt-free hand was, she shook it as I introduced myself as Boy, the Keeper of Sheep. She then explicitly, with an authoritative tone, asked to see my traveling documents. She kept an 'in control and ready to fire finger' on her rifle's trigger, which was exactly where I kept both of my 'scared for my life' eyes. After a line-by-line inspection of my registration papers, she returned them to me and received me into her house by saying, nice to meet you Mister Jackson Shepherd. You are welcome here. Boy was your slave's name. Given that you now are a free man, I will call you Jackson. As of this day, the slave named Boy doesn't exist anymore."

"That sounds exactly like something my grandma would do and say," Ruby added, as she put two loaves of hand-made bread in the oven. Jackson gave her another wink and continued.

"I almost started bawling right then and there. Nevertheless, I didn't. I removed my muddy boots, with numerous pathetic holes in them, and wiped my bare, soiled, black feet off on her doormat. Then, I let her pass by me as we walked through the front door. Me, being a poor but polished man, and her being the mistress of the house, this seemed the right thing to do. When I saw that she'd left her Creedmoor outside on the porch, I started letting my guard down. Never, not once in my entire life, had I been allowed to step one foot inside my former masters Jackson Plantation house. What I saw, after closing the door behind me, was by far the freshest, cleanest, and cosiest place I'd ever before seen. It wasn't a spacious house, but it was a welcoming house. Miss Bessie's ability for creating and nurturing something special was as evident on that day as it was on all the days that followed her. After swiftly giving me a large glass of cool wellspring water, she exclaimed, with no disgrace at all, that I stunk something awful!"

By now, Ruby and Horace were rightly sniggering like the pedigreed Brits they both were. The more they learned about Bessie's past life the more their recent memories of her death evaporated from their minds. Jackson went on with his sautéing of the bite sized pieces of beef and onions. Despite their reactions, he remained a composed storyteller.

"Miss Bessie told me that my donkey looked to be in better shape than I did. Imagine that! There stood this short, plump, and kind-hearted woman comparing me, a fetchingly young fella of the same colour as she was, to a damn donkey with grassy poo running out his caboose! Being the shy and smelly man that I was, standing there in her immaculate home, I was duly ashamed. I stood right here, in this very spot, in this very kitchen, when Miss Bessie told me I smelled worse than my donkey did!"

The Brits were really hooting by now, and the normally reserved ex-slave and protector of Miss Bessie and the Dutton Ranch thoroughly valued the sound of their laughter. Jackson wasn't finished yet.

"After I bathed for the first time in my life, in a fancy, deep, oval shaped, zinc bathtub, I dressed myself up really good in a clean outfit. I'd been instructed to select garments and a pair of men's boots without holes in them from the hall closet next to the bathroom. There were enough boots and clothes to choose from Miss Bessie said. I remember feeling all nerved up again, with thoughts of men returning home to find a stranger wearing their attire. I waited for Miss Bessie to call me to come downstairs and sit down in the parlour. Then I stepped into the dining area, graciously doing as I was asked to. Out the large window, I could see my skinny old donkey still tied to the wash line pole. He was eating fresh hay, drinking water from troth, and nibbling on a bucket of big, fat, bright orange carrots. I was appreciative of Miss Bessie's way of not being irritated by caring for a putrid, overused, silver haired donkey with diarrhea. The next thing I saw were three thick and hearty steaming bowls of porridge nourishment next to basket of fine smelling bread and a big pitcher of lemonade. The lemons were still floating in the water, which Miss Bessie taught me, meant that the lemonade was as fresh as lemonade could be."

"She used to tell me the same thing," Ruby interjected, just as quickly as she apologized for interrupting.

Despite that, Horace hadn't actually met Bessie Dutton before, she was nonetheless his ex-wife's mother. What struck him as odd was that Jackson's depictions of Bessie reminded him of his daughter Ruby much more than they reminded him of Bessie's own daughter, his wife Sadie.

I hadn't noticed this before, he thought glancing over at his best girl. He then stood up, walked over to the stove, and added his peeled carrots to the pot of boiling water, as Jackson's saga continued.

"My stomach had been impolitely growling and grumbling something awful since I'd entered her home. My insides were so hungry and had been complaining so loud that I was certain Miss Bessie must have heard them from upstairs under the water inside the bathtub. Before I had time to thank her for her donkey tending skills, her hospitality, or to inquire about the third bowl of nourishment sitting on the table, I heard a sweet, little voice saying, *hello mister*. Following the tiny sound, I turned around to see the most delightful, blue-eyed peewee standing right behind me. She had bright pink and yellow bows in her coiled hair. Her bangs were straight, cut just above her eyebrows. She had dark, curly ringlets that Miss Bessie had decorated with colourful ribbons. The wee one's round, cherub cheeks, sugary smile, and bright sparkling sky-blue eyes, literally took me aback. The little girl captured me instantly with her precocious charms."

Jackson stopped long enough to compose his memory and take a drink of his cold ginger ale. He could see by the familiar look on Ruby's face that she already knew the child he was talking about was her mother, Sadie.

"Never before had I seen a child dressed in the way she was dressed. General Albert Jackson had no children, so in my lifetime, up to that day, I was only used to seeing grubby little, barefooted slave kids wearing rags for clothes. The little girl's innocence and appearance made an on-the-spot impressions on me. The toddler wore a billowing knee length dress with puffy sleeves and delicate pastel lace trimmings at the hem. Her dark brown buttoned up leather waders were as shiny and polished as my masters boots always were before he went to one of his festivities. Miss Bessie had neatly tucked the little one's white bloomers into her stylish boots. The child was holding tiny yellow crocheted gloves in her little hands. The thought of my former Master Albert's ceremonial boots had me quite unexpectedly asking the precious little thing standing next to me if she was going to a party. The child began to giggle. She laid her gloves on the table, took her dress in her hands, and curtsied ever so sweetly. Then, with a slight lisp, she said, my name is Sadie Minnie Dutton and today is Sunday. We are going to church after breakfast. You wanna to come with us mister? My Negro heart melted right there on the floor next to that sweet child wearing her Sunday best outfit. After we finished our porridge and buttered bread, Miss Bessie and little Miss Sadie took me to church with them. For a second time, on that same day, I did something I had never before in my life had ever done. I entered a House of God."

"And you have been going to church ever since," Horace said, putting his arm over Shep's shoulder. "Let us break bread together dear man. I'm starving."

After saying Grace, they each offered up a kind word to the just buried, African woman who'd given an ex-slave a chance and changed Jackson's life the moment she lowered her rifle and took his hand. Once the beef stew and homemade bread had found their way into their rumbling, hungry stomachs, in silence they cleaned up the kitchen. The three of them had agreed that knowing when to stop telling a story took as much talent as knowing how to start telling a story. As the sunset began casting its golden reddish orange luminance across the property, they left the house, went outdoors, and built a bonfire in the huge fire pit. It was chilly outside. Fortunately for all of them the Great Plains region cooled down at night, making its merciless heat waves tolerable. The fresh evening air was a vigorous relief from the high temperatures they'd endured during the funeral events of the day.

After fifteen minutes or so, it was obvious that the heat from the fire was being pulled straight into the frigid night air before it reached their chilled bodies. Realizing this, Horace and Jackson both threw more logs into the fire pit. Golden ginger coloured embers shot upwards as their logs hits the fire. The embers lit up the night sky in a magical way. The men then poked at the fire with long rock solid, iron tipped wooden dowels. Jackson told them how he'd made the fire sticks many years ago from handles that had broken off rakes and spades. Ruby shivered while watching two old men's egos trying to outdo each other with their continuous poking and prodding at the fire. After such a sweltering day, despite that she was sort of chilly, she was grateful to the drastic drop in the temperature outside. Horace walked over to her and draped a blanket around her shoulders and backside. He knew that she cherished the safe feeling of being swathed in a blanket. The expression on her face told him that he was right. Horace adored being right.

While the men threw log after log onto the growing flames, she asked herself what it was about men and an inferno. Despite their efforts the blaze apparently had a mind of its own. It would die down a little and then flare back up again, as if it was deliberately toying with two hard-headed men who tried to control it. Ruby sat back, relaxed, and took delight in seeing two energetic older males, acting like young warriors preparing their encampment before an overnight hunting expedition. Resembling timid predators, the flames licked wildly at the new logs they'd throw into the fire pit. As the flames grew in height, delicate, dwindling sparks flew higher and higher into the cold air above the pit. After about eight logs had been added, a blaze worth taking credit for finally found its confidence and raged. The men then gathered their poking sticks and took their seats. They were slightly winded, yet obviously content with themselves. Tall, rainbow tinted, dancing flames appeared to be celebrating the fire building abilities of Horace and Jackson's swashbuckling overblown egos.

There they each sat, atop three large cowhide covered tree stumps in front of a blazing, first-rate bonfire. Huddled under blankets and sheltered by silence, they watched shadows from the fire flickering off each other and the nearby trees. Countless more embers rose high above them, before disappearing into the blackness of the night. The embers resembled thousands of fireflies playing tag in the dark.

Soon thereafter, the sound of Bessie's right-hand man's voice broke the stillness, as he asked Horace and Ruby, "Would you Brits like to hear more about life on the Great Plains back in the early 1900s?"

In unison, a father and his daughter from England agreeably shook their heads. An intriguing type of curiosity was written all over their faces.

Chapter 27

"After just one week of being at the ranch and eating the way an ole' moke was supposed to eat, my silver-haired donkey was healthy again. Little Miss Sadie had been pestering me for days on end to tell her my donkey's name. I was getting mighty impatient with 'the nuisance with ringlets', so, I went to her momma for advice."

"I wasn't at all used to a pestering youngster following me around like a shadow day in and day out. No matter how cute and sugary your momma was," he said looking over at Ruby.
"I feared I'd lose my ex-slave mind if I couldn't stop her from being so charming and irritating at the same time," Jackson declared, as tactfully as he could.
Ruby was visibly enthralled by his tale.
"Miss Bessie got straight to the point of the matter and calmly told me that the solution to my problem was simple. A man should be a man and name his own damned donkey! And so, to end my dilemma, out of an act of sheer desperation and to appease Miss Sadie, who was as annoying as maple tree gum under my shoes, I manned up and chose a fitting name for my animal."
Horace anticipated what was coming and began to chuckle.
"You see, shortly after the animal started shitting a normal colour of brown again, Miss Bessie informed me that officially a male donkey was called an ass. As I mentioned earlier, my specialty was sheep. So, for logical reasons, I was too inexperienced with the ways of mules, or even horses for that matter. Furthermore, by this time, little Miss Bothersome was really getting on my normally unruffled nerves. Therefore, I solved two problems with one conclusion by deciding that if a male donkey was called an ass, then Ass my donkey would be called. From that day forward, my trustworthy and only means of transportation would be known as the donkey named Ass." Jackson turned and looked at his guests.
Poking aggressively at the fire, as if to hammer home a point, he said, "I named him Ass, not out of disrespect to the animal, but to appease an aggravating child. Once the scraggily donkey had a name, little Miss Sadie befriended old Ass straight away. This gave her a friend to take walks with, feed, and invite to her daily tea parties. The simple act of naming a donkey had in turn gifted me with the right amount of uninterrupted time I needed to earn my room and board as a respectable man should. Despite that I consider myself to be an upright gent, whenever Ass licked little Miss Sadie and sent her off a squealing, I secretly applauded his bad manners as a sign of my gratitude that he'd taken a real liking to the taste of her chubby cheeks and had stopped licking me."
The elderly woman, with hazelnut coloured skin speckled with age spots, let out a deep sigh. Sitting in her Barcalounger and still snuggled up in a

blanket, she rubbed her eyes underneath her spectacles and slowly gazed around her diner. A wide smile crisscrossed her time shrivelled face. Memories of Jackson's story about her mother, as little girl being licked by a dirty, smelly old donkey were amusing her. Back when she was a young girl herself, the old woman couldn't remember a time when she was amused by anything her Mother Sadie had ever done.

Keeping her eyes open, she steered her mind back to her trip to Montana with Horace. Instead of waning away, her smile grew in size. In a matter of seconds, and this time with her senses wide awake, she was back in the year 1959.

Jackson sat back down on his hide-covered stump, looked straight into Ruby's big, bright green eyes, and continued with his tale.

"The day I first met Miss Bessie and your momma Sadie, it was just shy of two months after your grandfather Samuel had tragically died in a mining accident. Miss Bessie went on to tell me that within four months she had buried her husband and both of her remaining sons. When Miss Sadie's older brothers also died in an unfair and tragic manner, your momma was still a toddler. Upon hearing about the Dutton deaths, I understood why the dear woman had a hall closet filled with male attire of all sizes. Boots, shoes, and hats included."

Horace couldn't help but pity the woman who had made his life excessively miserable in the past fifteen years. *Sadie had suffered great losses before the age of five. The wounded heart she had as a child surely must have affected the person she'd become*, he contemplated, with an aberrantly rare touch of compassion for his wife.

Jackson went on to say, "In an effort to save the family's nearly penniless property, the two older Dutton brothers went off to work for the Union Pacific Railroad Company. Throughout those lean times, money and employment were scarce across the Great Plains. Men, women, and even children, did what they had to do to keep their families and livestock alive. A homestead needed to flourish, otherwise every living thing on it, man, and beast alike, eventually died. With the twentieth century nearing, word was spreading across the territories of job opportunities that had opened up in railway branches around the mining districts. Given that the railroad company's office was located in the proximity of the very coalmine that had claimed the life of their father Samuel, the Dutton boys promised to stay together, to stay clear of the mines, and to bring money back home each month. With their ambitious and praiseworthy strategy, the brothers easily persuaded Miss Bessie to let them go off and apply for jobs with Union Pacific Railway. They were motivated, resilient, hardworking, and strongminded young men. Miss Bessie gave them her blessing without hesitation. Mind you, in spite of her approving, before and after they went off, she had a soul filled with fear twenty-four hours a day. Nevertheless, they were all she had left to rely on to earn money and keep the homestead running."

Jackson stood up and stepped closer to the fire pit. Horace remained seated on his stump, knowing enough not to interrupt a fellow storyteller's flow. Ruby was slightly impressed by her pa's instincts. Jackson carried on with his fire poking and his rendition.

"Being the loving mother that she was, Bessie packed each of the brothers a hand sewn travel bag. Their bags carried a five-day supply of dried food, a tin plate, cutlery, a pocketknife, and canned fruit. Given all the creeks and rivers that traversed alongside the trails they'd be taking, they wouldn't thirst for water or crave for fresh fish. This fact gave a slight sense of relief to their momma. Miss Bessie then hung crosses she'd woven from sandy coloured twine around each of their necks. Matching crosses were also hung from each of their horses' saddles. After kissing them on the tops of their handsome heads, she waved them off while standing on the porch of the ranch house. Their almost three-year old sister was clinging to her mama. Little Sadie was sulking and sucking on a piece of liquorice, slightly oblivious to what was happening."

Jackson spun on the heels of his cowboy boots, turned around, and divulged that he needed to relieve himself of all the ginger ale he had put into his body. He then walked off into the night and urinated behind a barn, in the dark, out of the sight of their eyes and the sound of their ears. The man easily could have waited to empty his bladder, but he sought after giving his British houseguests time to absorb his story. He knew by their expressions that he was sharing parts of a mother and wife's life that they'd never heard before. Within ten minutes, he was sitting back down on a cowhide-covered stump, in front of the fire pit and across from his guests. As he continued where he'd left off, the Dutton Ranch foreman broke an oppressive silence from Europe that now circled the flames.

"Seeing her big brothers, riding off farther and farther away from the front porch, suddenly registered with Sadie's young and impressionable mind. She began shrieking something terrible. She then ran off after them, begging them to stay and play with her and her dolls. The poor child had just seen her papa's memorial casket, with nothing in it but his mangled miner's helmet and boots, being lowered into the earth."

"What?" Ruby asked. "Surely she was too young to see such a thing."

"American children, in those times, were not shielded from death as they are in these modern times," Jackson gently informed her.

Ruby nodded with lack of understanding, yet accepting approval, nonetheless.

"Now poor little Miss Sadie was witnessing yet another double Dutton departure of a different kind. Miss Bessie told me all she could do for her sad girl was pick her up and protectively hold her, as her brothers vanished into the distance. To console her child and keep her from running off in the middle of the night searching for them, Miss Sadie slept in her momma's bed for two full weeks. Miss Bessie had once told me that's he'd wondered, many times throughout those horrific weeks, if when Miss Sadie was a newborn, she had sensed that her other two, twin brothers, had perished in a deadly snowstorm during the winter of her birth. Either way, as time passed, eventually Sadie's flare-ups ended and her behaviour settled down. Subsequently Miss Bessie's fears also settled down."

181

Jackson stood up again and turned a few slow burning logs over to reignite them. For a minute or two, he stared intensely at the fiery redness, as if he was in a trance. Then, expressionlessly, he sat back down and went on with his storytelling.

"Miss Bessie never shed a tear, but her poor, young heart was crying something awful on the inside. She was still reeling her broken spirit in from her husband Samuel's death, when her two remaining son's bodies were delivered to her doorstep in wooden railroad crates. She was miserable and scared right out of her mind after losing the homestead's remaining Dutton men. The deaths of her twins, then her husband, and then her older sons, had terminated the entire male side of the Dutton family. Months before her older boy's funeral, their father Samuel had inadvertently and permanently, left their young homesteading family solely in Miss Bessie's care. The very second, he toppled over a dynamite trip wire, blowing himself and six other unsuspecting mineworkers to smithereens, he sealed the fate of his wife, his then living sons, and his only daughter. At the time, the one relief that could be found and held onto by his grieving, widowed wife, was her knowing that her Samuel never felt a thing. As for her two sons, when she opened the timber crates to identify their bodies, it was cruelly obvious to their momma that when they died, the only thing her sons didn't feel was nothing."

Jackson and Ruby could see that Horace was lost in a sea of emotion and thought. They chose to sit in silence, stare at the fire, and give the man who'd married Bessie's only daughter time to collect himself. Hearing Jackson telling them all of this caused an unfamiliar bitter sweetness and a raging anger to crawl up and into Horace's gut. Emotion was wedged tightly in the man's throat. It was obvious that he was on the verge of tears, nevertheless, Horace McEwen didn't cry. The rawness he was feeling was a new sentiment for him. He was a man who hid his feelings away from virtually everyone he knew. He was now overcome with gushes of grief and understanding for his wife. More so, he felt a wretchedness for her, that she had lost so much at such a tender age. Horace was feeling likewise confused by his memories of once being so in love with Sadie. The same woman who had never shared these devastating parts her life with him. They had celebrated an abundance of life together in the early 1920s and throughout the 1930s. He didn't have a lot to offer her when they'd first met, but what he did have and what he came to earn was by the same token hers.

A familiar, threatening mayhem had returned to his mind and was pumping life back into his most private thoughts. He'd been a prisoner to the errors of his marriage and his behaviour's many times over since he and Sadie met. This time he refused to become a hostage to them. He wouldn't allow anyone or anything to make him a convict of his shambolic past. He wouldn't reveal the pain he still felt all these years later. The truth of it was, the pain he now felt, sitting in front of a roaring fire, had been born years before Ruby's birth and long before tonight whilst listening to Shep's story. Years ago, when fate cruelly snatched two baby boys away from him and Sadie, he was changed. That dreadful experience had just about done both of them in, not once, but twice.

Thirteen years later, Sadie had already entered her forties when their baby girl, Ruby, took her first breath. Nine months earlier, with the announcement of Sadie's rare and unexpected conception, everything changed for the second time between the husband and wife. His drinking increased alongside his fears, and her emotional insanities began; both of which triggered the worst in each of them.

After Ruby's birth, people who knew the infant's parents believed that the McEwen's were finally blessed to have a 'miracle baby that had survived.' Despite their positive beliefs and Holy intentions, in Horace's opinion their newborn wasn't the miracle baby everyone thought she was. As far as her father was concerned, she most definitely was not 'a gift from Heaven', or as church folks in their community professed, an 'apology from God for taking her brothers'. In 1925, Horace was still furious with The Almighty when his baby girl was born in the grass under an oak tree. As he swaddled his half-delivered daughter in a blanket, he cursed both God and Jesus Christ. He remembered how her pinkish grey umbilical cord was still pumping blood into her tiny body as he held her. For as much as he tried to deny it, since the moment his only surviving offspring fell out of Sadie's womb and into his fear filled hands, the anger of having previously lost two sons consumed him all over again. It was an anger that he consoled with whiskey, every day, of every week, of every year, until eleven short months ago.

Now here he was, in the year 1959. The man was overcome by too many aching, presumably buried, and forgotten memories that had resurfaced and were trying to devour him. His urge to have a drink had reappeared. Horace swore he could taste Jim Beam bourbon on the tip of his sober, watering tongue. The image he had of the stocked liquor cabinet in Bessie's parlour was tempting his willpower in an unfair and tantalizing way. *It would be so easy to sneak a drink when no one was looking*, he thought. His hands began to tremble.

In an attempt to dismiss his temptations, recollections, and the cruel pain, Horace's alcoholic mind blamed his sudden emotional fury on both Shep and Ruby. It was their fault. He was certain that the endless conversations that they'd been having about the past, since Bessie died, had prompted his addictive urges again. His resentments and accusations shouldn't be feeling like bombshells landing in his lap. Nevertheless, they did. Horace was a proud and stubborn man who was known for blaming his faults on everyone and everything but himself. His wife Sadie, on the other hand, had always blamed his bouts of rude behaviour on whichever whisky bottle he was tipping at the time he misbehaved. The man's alcoholism had made it almost too easy for her to live life as a 'marital martyr' in the eyes of their community.

As for Horace, to admit that he was to blame for his bad behaviours and wrongdoings was something he had never found the courage to do. His recent sobriety was transforming him in a way that was likewise terrifying him. He was now rightly emotional, and he was changing in a tempo that he had no control over. Despite that he'd kept a stiff upper British lip since arriving in America, he didn't recognize himself. In an alarming, unexpected way, Horace's mood drastically altered. Furiously, he stood up and threw the poking stick he was holding to straight into the fire. The he kicked hard at the burning logs and started punching the cowhide-covered stump he'd been sitting on with clenched fists. Jackson could see bolts of anger shooting from the man's eyes. When the stump wasn't enough, he attacked the tree that was closest to Ruby.

With his chest puffed up with rage, Horace brusquely turned towards her and hardheartedly screeched, "In God's name! What kind of daughter doesn't even bother to attend her mother's own funeral? Did something happen between your mother and Bessie that I don't know about?"

Jackson tightly gripped his fire stick and took a protective step in Ruby's direction. He knew the look of a possessed man on the dangerous edge of exploding. Ruby stood up and stood her ground. With a skilled swiftness, she pulled an invisible mask out of mid-air. It was a blank faced mask with a calm and confident expression on it. The mask was a disguise she used to shield herself and conceal her spontaneous reaction to feeling threatened. Her invisible disguise enabled her to keep control, bend the truth, feel confident, and hide behind her fears. She took obscure masks with her wherever she went. They were camouflages she'd been putting on and taking it off since she was old enough to know they existed. In a matter of seconds, her blank faced mask was securely in place. She raised her head, looked up bravely at her tall father, and confidently answered him.

"I have no idea if anything happened between Sadie and Grandma Bessie. Sadie never confided in me while I was growing up," she expressionlessly said and deliberately lied.

Chapter 28

Being sober made it easier for Horace to calm down and regain his composure in a timely manner, which impressed both Ruby and Shep. Sitting again, across from a gorgeous bonfire at the Dutton Ranch, he looked down at his eight bruised and bleeding knuckles. Meekly, he said, "tell me more Shep. I want to hear whatever you remember about the woman I married before I met her."

Jackson methodically lowered his fire stick, stepped over to Horace, and cautiously took his bruising, bloodied fists in his own hands. One by one, he slowly stretched the British man's long fingers and sturdy thumbs out until both of Horace's hands were open and free of tension.

Then he looked deep into his eyes and said, "Sometimes a person needs to die inside before they can heal."

Jackson respectfully asked Ruby if she was okay with hearing more about her mother. Ruby kept staring at the fire and nodded that she was. As soon as she felt safe, she'd take the mask off before the fallout of her lie and the heat of the fire melted it into onto her face. They were each back on their hide-covered stumps when Jackson cleared his throat and continued.

"Even after all these years, at times, what transpired here on the Great Plains feels like it happened yesterday, not seventy-something years ago. When the frequent and volatile quarrels began occurring between Sadie and Miss Bessie, I noticed a considerable change in the energy in the main house and around the ranch. Sadie Dutton, in most people's opinion, was an unruly and stubborn as a mule kind of girl. She had a vulgar mouth, especially for a young woman in the early 1900s."

Horace's grinning reaction to this description of Sadie told Ruby that he knew her mother well, and likewise, he agreed with Shep. The husky Englishman was calmer and had decompressed since physically beating up a tree.

"One tense season, as I still can recall it, was the summer she'd just finished her studies. Like other young women her age, after finishing school she was expected to either marry, or become a teacher or a nurse. In those times an aspiring teacher could attain a two-year rural teaching certificate provided she was a high school graduate, unmarried, and passed aptitude exams in various subjects. The school Sadie had just graduated from provided her with some degree of teacher training during her junior and senior years. Sadie had passed all her exams with ease. She was as intelligent as she was wilful. She'd attended a one-room schoolhouse for most of her young life. After graduating she was ready to do something different than she'd been doing, or been forced to do, as she perceived it, since she was born. She wanted nothing to do with becoming a farm wife or a mother at such a young age. Her diligent Negro momma, Miss Bessie, tried to keep her only remaining and extremely headstrong child nearby the ranch. She attempted twice to marry her off to either one of the neighbour's good-looking, reliable, and eligible white skinned sons. Nonetheless, Sadie had been declaring, since she was a 12-year-old, that she wanted no part of marriage or babies. She wanted to see the world. Her blunt outspokenness was unheard of in those days. The ranch hands, church parishioners, minister, and villagers, who knew her and how she was brought up were sassily shocked over and over again at her brashness. They all avowed that if she'd been raised with a strict father in the house, she would have turned out different. The beautiful, impetuous Dutton girl would have learned obedience and would have been planning a wedding during her last year of school, rather than a cockeyed, daring, slapdash escape."

Jackson stood up, threw a log on the fire, grinned at Ruby, and broke the tension by flicking Horace's hat of his head with the back of his hand. His brotherly gesture made him smile, which knocked an invisible wall of tension down to the ground. It landed next to Horace's hat.

As the history of the event unfolded, Ruby and Horace both learned that Bessie's right-hand man often kept to himself and hid out in the barn during the most turbulent of mother, daughter entanglements. Eventually, as the riffs between Bessie and Sadie reached an all-time high, Jackson knew precisely where his place was and where his place wasn't. Therefore, he kept his mouth shut and he kept his distance. One morning, at daybreak, when he went to fetch fresh eggs from the chicken coop, just as he had done every day for the past thirteen years, he saw Miss Sadie and her horse galloping off into the distance. The only thing she left behind was a thunderous din of hoofs hammering the prairie and a long trail of thick dust. Jackson Boy Shepherd never saw Sadie Minnie Dutton again.

He had sensed that a steel-like rigidity had been fuelling between the mother and daughter months before Miss Sadie fled the ranch where she'd been born and nurtured. He then predicted that a family tempest was approaching, which forever would change the way of life on the ranch. Despite his intuitive ways, he chose not to ask Miss Bessie about any of it. Plain and simple, it wasn't his place to ask. It was his place to do his work and to earn his keep. In all the years that followed, Bessie never mentioned her daughter's departure to him. Not once, after realizing that the girl's belongings and her prize-winning stallion were no longer on the property, had the female homesteader, who was quick with a Creedmoor, spoken about Sadie. Jackson suspected that her feelings of abandonment had returned and were choking off her heart while weighing heavily on her spirit. Sadie's running away opened up deeply planted wounds that resided in Bessie's past. She was the last living Dutton member of her mother's world. Her sudden departure wasn't a death that required a funeral or a burial. On the contrary, it was a desertion and a disappearance that required accepting, forgetting and forgiving; all of which the woman went on to hide in the shadows of her loneliness.

Miss Bessie's pain and anger ran deep. Whenever and if ever she grieved, she did so privately behind closed doors. In public, she was as tolerant, as brave, and as steadfast as she was the day, she rang the ranch's dinner bell and welcomed a filthy ex-slave and a smelly donkey with the runs into her life. Jackson went on to tell Horace and Ruby how years later Miss Bessie received a letter from Sadie. It took months for it to arrive because it was sent by boat and then over land, all the way from Europe. Four red and white British Empire exhibition stamps, with the image of a roaring lion on them, easily told Bessie where her daughter had ended up.

Shep looked at Ruby and said, "Miss Bessie wasn't an educated woman, but it was rumoured that her older sister Minnie was bright as a whip. Now and then she'd brag to him about Minnie's literary skills, and how she'd memorize and bone up on their plantation master's wall maps in the house where she worked as a maid and cook. She told me that her sister had taught her to read and write, and about geography. Minnie used to tell her younger sister that if she was planning on escaping slave life one day, she needed to know where to go and how to communicate verbally and with a quill and ink."

Jackson apologized for getting side-tracked and resumed telling them about Sadie. He looked directly at the father and daughter who were now sitting now side by side, as he carried on.

"The overseas letter from Sadie went on to reveal that your calculating mother and wife had sold her stallion for a sizeable price. Shortly thereafter, she met an Englishman on leave from the war and married him. She was now living far away, in a place called Essex England. She and her new husband were trying to start a family."

For as much as Ruby expected her pa to be crying or frantic, he looked serene and contented as he listened to Shep. The last thing Jackson recalled about that letter was that Bessie finally opened herself up to him. She swore to him, on her life, that one day she would get to know her daughter's husband and children. She vowed that she would move heaven and earth and cross every border to be a grandma to any children Sadie brought into this world. Sadie's letter relit a passionate flame in Miss Bessie. A flame that had been extinguished the morning her life force went missing, along with her last living child, when she saw the hoof prints Sadie's stallion had left behind."

Jackson openly wiped a few tears off his distinguished face with the back of his sleeve and stoked the fire. A motionless Ruby stared deeply at the fire's dwindling flames, coals, and embers. Horace disappeared in thought.

"You both know the rest of the story," the sad and emotionally drained man said. His shoulders had slumped a little and the sharp-eyed Ruby noticed that Jackson looked older than when he began telling his stories. Horace, who was now sitting back on his own stump with his head in his hands, pronounced that he'd had enough for one day and was going inside. He picked up his blanket and walked away from the fire, which was now a pile of red burning cinders and black ash. Horace's eruption of anger and violent reaction was a side of his character that Jackson hadn't witnessed since the man's arrival from England. He knew his friend's soul was troubled, but until now, the man had hidden his deepest pain.

As Horace passed Jackson and the fire pit, Shep warily, yet wisely said, "There comes a moment in our lives when the control we think we have slips through the cracks of our foundation."

Then he turned and faced Horace.

187

"Certain things that a father and his daughter need to discuss are essential to their relationship. Such things are private and none of my business," Shep concluded.

He wasn't sure if his comrade heard him or not. Horace had already walked away. In an attempt to save a very old fire poker, Ruby bent down to fetch the remains of the broken off rake handle that her pa had thrown into the fire pit.

"Let it burn," Jackson told her, "Some memories just need to go up in flames so a person can be done with them."

With that credence being said and heard he took the hand of the subdued single mother and only child standing next to him. Ruby, absorbed in thought, held the calloused hand of a wise, ex-slave, as they followed Horace into the house. Shortly thereafter, they all sat in the parlour and shared a cup of tea before bed. Drinking tea before bed was a ritual of her grandma's that Ruby remembered from when she was a girl. Tonight, that time in her life felt like it was an eternity ago. Jackson had learned from Bessie that a single cup of tea could knowingly reduce anxiety, particularly after a person had suffered through stressful events. In most cases, as he himself had experienced over the years, a cup of tea at bedtime soothed all people of all ages.

Must be this is why Miss Bessie had Sadie drinking so much tea growing up, he silently thought while concealing a private, slightly mischievous smile.

Jackson then laid his large hand on Horace's broad back and said, "Friend, we all, including ole' Shep here, have a past that is filled with often unexplainable reasons for the choices we make and the roads we walk."

He went on to propose that father and daughter take a long walk together tomorrow, down a different road.

"Let it be a road that that neither of you have ever walked on before."

He then recommended that they consider having a frank conversation.

"Candid discussions can reconcile uncertainties and prevent misinterpretations. Appreciating and then accepting how a person perceives their life and the lives of others has a healing power that enables us to resolve unresolved issues," he concluded.

Further than the shadow of any human doubt, the old black man was consumed with dexterous wisdom. After listening to him throughout the evening, both Ruby and Horace could see that Jackson had learned a great deal from working, for so long and so closely, alongside Bessie. Especially Ruby could see that he had her grandmother's common sense and effortlessly gifted way with people. With that being said and understood, Jackson went into the parlour and put on some soft, comforting music. While finishing their chamomile tea, they listened to the sweet sound of the blues. For the last ten minutes, of a very long day, Smokey Wilson and his guitar soothed their weary minds and sensitive souls.

As the music faded into silence, they finished their tea by the chorus-like tones of crickets chirping and the uniform ticking of the parlour's 19th century grandfather clock. They then bid each other goodnight and went to bed. It had been a very hot, long, and emotional day. Not one of them had anything more say or to give.

The next morning was the Sabbath. In the state of Montana, this was a day set aside for rest and worship. Jackson and his pick-up truck were awake, fuelled, and on the road before the roosters had started to crow. He'd left early to attend a sunrise church service with his friends. It was Potluck Picnic Sunday at his parish, so he wouldn't be returning until late afternoon. Being a conscientious man, he'd toyed with his temptation to invite Ruby and Horace to join him but chose not to out of respect for their non-religious ways. To each his own, he concluded; a motto that had served him well since he was a young, agnostic slave boy. Besides, he had another plan up his sleeve for the Brits. After packing his own church picnic basket, Jackson filled another basket for Miss Bessie's favourite relatives from Europe. He left their lunch in plain view on the kitchen table. When they finally woke up and came downstairs for breakfast, they found two tall glasses of fresh squeezed orange juice. Next to the basket was a note from Shep explaining what he was up to and wishing them a beautiful, inspiring walk together.

The Brits had slept in, so they'd gotten a later start than anticipated. After a lazy morning and a light breakfast they groomed the horses and mucked out the stables. Their teamwork was actually a calculated plan that would enable Jackson to take the entire day off after church. Quite unexpectedly, Ruby couldn't resist riding one of Jackson's stallions. It had been years since she'd ridden a horse, nonetheless, she knew that riding a horse was so inbred in her that she had no doubt or dread. Horace, who'd never seen her ride, nervously hoped that his best girl was right. He'd heard years ago that the Dutton Ranch's foreman had taught her how to ride both a horse and a bicycle when she was still a child. Back then, he was too inebriated to store a clear memory in his head. He did know that when she was taught, she was too small to mount the saddle without being hoisted up and onto it or reach the bike pedals without having wooden blocks attached to them.

Now, seeing her sitting straight-backed, with the reins securely positioned in her hands, it was obvious to him that she had a natural sensation for horseback riding. Jackson used to tell her that she felt at one with a horse because she had no fear. This meant horses she rode sensed no fear, so they rewarded her with their trust and gentle temperaments. From the ranch's stables she could set out in any direction she wanted to go. Aside from its paddocks, the property was unrestricted by roads or fences. For nearly hour, while Horace groomed the ranch's second stallion and only mare, Ruby let Jackson's horse take her on a carefree ride. The animal knew the land better than she did, so, with only the steady sound of heavy, pounding hooves on the tundra beneath her, they cantered off and then galloped away. She trusted him to bring her back to the stables without incident or injury. Horace wasn't as trusting.

Despite his fatherly concerns, the horse had a stunning appearance, a willingness to please, and he did whatever she asked of him. Ruby was just as gentle and attentive with him; therefore, he bestowed a superb ride upon her. It was a ride that was fazed by nothing. The wind in her face made her feel cooler and freer than she had felt since leaving her young daughter behind in England with her Grandma Sadie. She'd had serious reservations about traveling so far away without Eliza. Nonetheless, she knew that the child was too young to make the trip. Ruby was still quite unexperienced with motherhood, but beyond her age experienced with trusting her instincts.

Suddenly alarmed, the stallion radically reared and yanked her focus back to where it should have been; on the 1300-pound, muscular animal she was riding. She easily dismissed her thoughts about what was happening back home and turned the horse back in the direction of the ranch. Upon her return, she and Horace rinsed the magnificent animal off with the soft spray of cool water from a garden hose. Then they treated him with a crispy apple and put him out to pasture.

Carrying the picnic basket, Horace picked up their walking pace. The man had always loved a brisk outdoor walk no matter the weather conditions. Slightly envious of the old man's extra-long legs, big feet, and ability to outpace her, Ruby did her best to keep up with him. Truth be told, her legs ached from galloping across the plains on the back of the largest horse she'd ever ridden; a fact she decided not to tell her pa. Even back then, the Keeper of Secrets knew when to reveal and when to remain a mystery. As their journey, on foot and across the Great Plains continued, Horace spoke first.

"Shep told me that with Bessie's husband and sons deceased, he quickly became her right-hand man, and a few years later the ranch foreman and closest ally. Shep was adamant about me believing him when he said that he'd never had any relations with your grandmother. Even though they were both legally free people of colour, she was a widow. He said she was a young, fine-looking widow. It didn't matter that she was a pretty homesteading matriarch whom a man of the same colour could easily fancy, she was a widow, nonetheless. He said that a righteous man of colour respected widows even more than they respected their own kin. I convinced Shep that I had faith in him by telling him that from the moment he first shook my hand, I knew that he was a God-fearing man and a highly regarded fellow. Shep wordlessly told me that he appreciated my trust in him by giving me an out of the blue right and proper man hug. He gave me the kind of tight squeeze that even a grizzly bear couldn't wiggle free from."

Horace laughed at the image he had in his mind of the two men locked in each other's arms. Their brief, robust embrace seemed now rather comical.

Equally out of the blue, Ruby asked Horace, "What did you know about my McEwen grandparents? What do you remember about your parents before I was born?"

She went on to ask him, "Is there more you can tell me about Bessie and Samuel?"

She knew that Horace rarely spoke about his McEwen parents or his grandparents. Nonetheless, she was curious, She hoped that time had healed whatever type of empty anguish the history of Horace's life had left him to grow old with. .

"Let's go over there by that creek and drink those bottles of Coca-Cola that Shep packed for us. We can have a sit down and rest up a spell on those boulders," he suggested, pointing towards the edge of the creek. "It will be dark in a few hours. You have asked some rather big questions, which deserve worthy answers. I have time for one more story before we head back to the ranch. I'll try my best to satisfy your curious brain," he assured her.

They each chose a large bolder, sat down, popped the top off their soft drinks and began quenching their thirst. The open plains were very dry during the summer months. As they gulped the dust out of their throats with the sweet liquid in a bottle, Horace began answering Ruby's questions.

"Let's start with my family. The McEwen ancestor's you never knew."

Chapter 29

"The 1800s was a period when smugglers, rum-runners, and bootleggers roamed the English and Irish Seas. My great grandfather and his son Ezra were two of them. They played a major role in monopolizing the trade of alcohol and spices from India. For years their clever cartelizing prevented contraband shipments from abroad."

After just four sentences, the master storyteller had Ruby's attention in the palm of his oversized, brawny hand.

"The McEwen men formed a three-generation bootlegging clan that lived on an island. The clan was free of taxes and had no trade restrictions boundaries at the time. This was a fact that changed while Ezra, your great grandfather, was becoming one of England's most notorious rum-running bootleggers. He and his father worked side by side with Irishmen who were active in the same illegal trade. With taxes high, and prices even higher, the resourcefulness and merchandise of the rumrunners and bootleggers was hailed by many. As time passed, the illegal traders implemented an inexpensive, tax-free, underground smuggling trade in Great Britain and Ireland. Bankrupt men and fugitives from both countries supported Ezra, his father, and their cohorts."

Completely intrigued, Ruby's eyes glazed over with a gripping type of trepidation.

"A battle soon broke out between the smugglers and elimination men who were hired to assert imperial authority and force tax dodgers to pay what they owed to the King of England. When illicit tax-offenders didn't pay as demanded, they were met with unspeakable endings. Their demises began with torture and ended in executions. Tax offender's family members were also repeatedly victimized. Innocent or not, they were used as bait to lure bootleggers and smugglers into paying what was duly owed to the British Monarchy."

Ruby interrupted by asking, "What about Ezra's wife, and their family? What about your own father?"

Horace took a few deep breaths before answering, "Are you sure you want to know?"

Without hesitation, Ruby replied. "Yes."

Without hesitation, Horace carried on.

"In my opinion, three generations of the McEwen family were cursed. Between 1800 and around 1935, babies and children kept vanishing and dying. Ruby my girl, you come from a long line of remarkably unforgiveable men. As much as we struggle, you and I, and you hate me from time to time, you need to know, and trust, that I am not one of these men."

"I have never hated you Pa," she fibbed.

Spiritedly, he went along with her half-truth, flashed her a fleeting smile, and continued.

"My grandfather, Ezra McEwen, was a second-generation bootlegging drunk who beat his wife and children during the day and pissed his bed at night. He was a bully with a stone-cold heart and a twisted mind. He'd wring the life out of a man for stealing his illegal merchandise, while forcing the thief's wife and young ones to watch. He was born out of hate, stunk like a pig, and lived like a coward. It was implied that he killed a child once because the lad's father couldn't pay his moonshine debt. The local law enforcement knew what he'd done, but even so, they let him hide behind the protection of a posse. The posse was a group of six law enforcement officers who were hired to serve and protect the citizens of the region. They were useless and known for turning twelve blind eyes to his deeds. The posse was either too addicted to the moonshine that the McEwen men's whiskey stills poured free of charge down their throats, or too intimidated by the threats of his wrath."

Ruby had moved over to Horace's bolder and locked arms with him. She wanted him to feel a kindly touch while he told her, for the first time, about his ancestor's sordid past. Regardless of how many years ago the events of his legacy took place; he was born and raised surrounded by the immoral residues of his kin. For the first time in her adult life, her father was starting to make sense to her. Horace went on with telling his tale.

"My father and my grandfather operated our kinfolk's hidden illegal trade. It was a family business that they camouflaged by the thickness of Irish and British colonial forests. The constabularies were too afraid of the felonious ring, which protected the notorious band of kinsmen, to arrest any of them. The men should have been hung dead by their ruthless necks in the village square for all the townspeople to witness. But they never were. Regardless of their publicly ruthless crimes, this never, not even one time, happened. Consequently, for nearly two generations, the McEwen bootlegging cycle continued."

"Sweet Jesus," his best girl softly said, overcome by emotion. Horace squeezed her hand and carried on with purging his past.

"After I was born, and for the better part of thirty years, my grandfather Ezra hung his hat on a hook before entering the Church on Sunday and then he hid the money he'd stolen from the collection canister under his coat when the holy service ended. Practically all of the parishioners knew what he was doing, but no one dared to stop him. Not even the preacher, or the devout sheriff, was courageous enough to stand up to him. They feared him more than they feared God himself, so they didn't interfere with his crimes against the people and the Church. The McEwen moonshine was desired by many, and Ezra's henchmen were feared by everyone."

Horace paused, taking a short dram of time he needed to collect his thoughts before he went on.

"To his advantage and to her regret, Ezra and his wife birthed no daughters. He passed down his seed, his greed, and his blood, onto four sons. Your grandfather Amos was the youngest of the four. Over time, the forbidden trade and addictive whiskey drinking behaviours of the McEwen clan oozed into the blood of seven of his grandsons. I am the youngest of the seven. Scuttlebutt had it that my father Amos had run off one night by the light of a full moon, with his wife, your grandmother, and their sleeping child. I was that child."

Ruby's eyes widened. She bit the inside of her lip and fought off tears while her pa kept sharing his past with her.

"I later learned that they'd bolted with me on the night of my birthday. When Amos's drunken father and brothers had all passed out in front of a fire, my parents escape began. My mother, your grandma Liza, was pregnant at the time. It was presumed that they'd decided to run off before she birthed another McEwen offspring on illegal, crime-ridden ground. They wanted to protect me and my soon to be born sibling from being infected by the moonshine disease, as it was called at the time."

Ruby squeezed his old hand and said, "I had no idea your life was so dangerous when you were a child."

Horace held her hand tighter and went on.

"Although my parents lived in fear until we stepped off a ship a week later in England, we heard that Ezra never searched for us. Most folks rumoured that this was because Amos was alleged to be his bastard baby and he was finally rid of him. You see, his wife had conceived my father when Ezra was locked up behind bars, which was the only time her husband left the property. When he returned home from the jail, she had a visible round belly underneath her long, flowing dress. He'd bribed a judge with a bag full of moonshine money and was set free early, long before Amos was due to be born. Despite his suspicions, the date of her conception was too difficult to pinpoint. Therefore, an agreement was made. If his wife provided him with her nakedness and spread herself for him in a desirable way, whenever his manly longings stirred, no matter how large her belly grew, his suspicions surrounding her pregnancy would be ignored. Your great grandmother held up her end of the bargain, carried my father full term, and then birthed him in the woods. The baby grew up and lived in a shack on his pappy's land until four years after he took a wife, and she gave birth to me. The entire matter was never spoken of again. Until today, that is."

The parched Teller of Tales took another drink from his Coke bottle. He glanced over at his girl and saw that Ruby's focus was intense and hardened.

"Whether the entire folktale has merit or not, your grandparents and I are living testaments. We are tributes to the facts and truths behind how we fled from Ezra's treacherous ways and bootlegging prison, just in time. His remaining spawn kept his pockets lined with enough illegal currency to enable his three-generation moonshine legacy to live on for another ten to twelve years. Eventually, one morning, an old, decrepit, and drunken Ezra was found lifeless and belly up in the river that dissected his woodland. Folks say he'd slipped on the muddy riverbank and drowned. My father Amos returned to identify his body. Not because he would have wanted to save him from death if he could, because he needed to see his pa's corpse to save himself from the threatening blood tie he had to Ezra. His kin buried him on their land somewhere under a tree. By this time, the likes of his sinful soul were not allowed in the Holy ground of the village cemetery. Some year's later whiskey became legal, and folks stopped buying straight from his illegal, overpriced family business. This is what ended this part of your McEwen bequest."

Grasping that the story was being paused, Ruby took her riding boots off and dipped her feet into the creek's cool water. It was bloody hot on the plains this time of day. If they had more time, she'd have taken a swim.

"Continue Horace," she gently urged, "your story is captivating."

"Captivating?" he exclaimed. "When in God's name did, I go from being an inebriated thorn in your arse, to being captivating?"

Truth be told, he liked being captivating. Horace stood up and began pacing around in the dry prairie dirt, as he went on with finishing his family story.

"Legend has it some of Ezra and his kin lived on to carry and spread his DNA somewhere on the West Coast of America. Despite that I don't live in the United States, I assure you that I am not one of these kin. I don't carry his bad seed, or debauched greed in me. Nor did I pass it onto you. Given the McEwen family history, perhaps it was a blessing in disguise that my two sons, your older brothers, died long before they tasted their first drop of whiskey."

Shocked to hear him say this, Ruby spun around on her wet, bare feet. Glaring with vengeance at her father, she yelled, "What the bloody hell Horace!"

Not missing a beat, Horace responded.

"Calm your hot-headed, impulsive temper down Ruby girl and listen! Shut your big mouth and just listen to me! You now know that Sadie and I suffered, for many years after your brothers tragic and unfair deaths. Regardless, I know that our sons died before they'd had a chance to reach an age of enough maturity to reveal if Ezra's seed was passed onto them, or not? What happened to my boys was unspeakable and it was a misfortune. Despite the tragedy, I was terrified for eighteen months while your mother carried those two babies inside her body. I was terrified that his genes had been passed onto both my boys through me. The moment they each entered this world and took their first breaths, my guts exploded from the worry I'd been hiding in it for the better part of two years! In the end, when all was said and done, I learned that there are distinct limits to how much a father can protect his children from the inherited family blood that runs through their veins."

Ruby spoke up, saying, "I had no idea life was so hard for you as a young man Horace. Why did you never speak of it before today?"

She was beginning to understand his meaning and the lifetime of dilemma's he'd endured, in great part, alone. Horace could see that he'd appeased her because her body was now less tense and rigid, and she was swirling her feet around once more in the coolness of the creek. Deciding that the timing was right, he went on with his explanations; after all, she deserved to know how deep, and in which direction, her family roots went.

"Somethings are better left buried in the yesteryears of life Ruby girl," he said. "Like most people, whose paths crossed the path Ezra walked on, Amos despised his own father. Your grandpa and I inherited only one thing from all of the McEwen men who came before us, their addictiveness to the bittersweet whiskey that they once illegally manufactured and sold.

Throughout the first three years of my life, when the foundation of who I was to become was being laid, my playground was a densely wooded yard. It was a plot of land littered with stills that brewed whiskey day and night. This was the same wooded yard that made the hair, skin, and clothing of all the children who played and worked there smelled like malted vapours by the end of the day." Horace could see that he had his daughter's complete and tranquil attention had returned.

"The day your brothers died, I said good riddance to the atrocious examples my grandfather Ezra set for me when I was just a wee lad. Each time, as I lowered my babies' small coffins into the ground, I was consumed by grief and fear. Fear that his hereditary seeds had actually pumped through my blood and caused the death of your brothers. Likewise, I feared that Sadie and I were no different from all the other cursed McEwen's, whose children had died or vanished. Hence, I was determined to raise you without Ezra's hate inside of me. So, for this valid reason, on the day that you were born a baby girl in the backyard, under the old oak tree, I swore, from the second I saw you, to rid myself of his madness and focus on being a decent father."

Horace inhaled, held his breath a bit longer than usual, and then exhaled in a relieving manner. Dawdling through his complex past with his best girl had completely worn him out.

"How did I do?" he teasingly asked her.

She smiled at him and then asked him if her mother Sadie left them because she blamed him for the death of their sons? Horace had suspected over the years that his daughter might have assumed this was the reason why her mother had taken off. He was grateful they were finally talking about it, no matter how long ago it was, or how difficult the topic could be.

"Ruby girl," he said, "as sure as sure can be, your mother left me to escape a life she no longer wanted to live, not, because she blamed me for our lads deaths. We suffered together through that time in our lives. We never got over it and we never will get over it. You and I both know that losing children is not something a parent ever gets over. I believe that only the flames of righteous souls are dowsed in their youth. Not getting over a person's death enables us to remember them. As for your mother Sadie, after thirty years of my flirting with other women and choosing you and whiskey over her, she ran towards the prospects of a better life. There is more to a person than what they show on the outside of themselves Ruby girl. Some people are transparent, whilst others hide their true natures behind a thick, lifelong layer of fright and flakiness. Rest assured now; your mother is already a better grandmother than she was a mother."

She could see he was getting softer and misty eyed.

"Unlike Ezra, I never hurt a child, committed a crime, or stole a thing from anyone. There was a time, long before I met Sadie and we had you, when I needed to execute my own escape. I have tried to be good provider and a moral, truthful, honourable father," he confessed in defense of himself.

Horace defending himself was something unfamiliar to Ruby. Whether he was aware of it or not, he'd earned her complete attention and long overdue respect.

"After being around Ezra and his moonshine gang as a child, my pa Amos saw the emotional impact it was having his family. For survival reasons, he and my mother uprooted me and ran away in search of safety and freedom. Do you believe this?"

She answered, again without reluctance, "Yes, sir, I do. Grandpa Amos and Grandma Liza left their moonshine terrors behind, to runoff and give you a chance at a better life than they'd had."

"Good. I was later told that we fled the night of my third birthday. It was overcast and dark enough to hide out in the shadowy mistiness of the forest. Everyone living at the moonshine camp was either sloshed, asleep, or both. Amos had strapped me to his back and my parents ran as fast their young legs could run. They sprinted through the woods until they came to the river's edge some two miles upstream. Out of pure desperation, they stole a dinghy and rowed while navigating the river throughout the night. Being rocked and soothed by the water's current, I slept through our escape. By early dawn, we'd put plenty of distance behind us and the moonshine camp. As the sun rose fully over the distant ridges, we were safely out of tracking range. Neither our scents nor the trailing skills of Ezra's bloodhounds, or his henchman's muskets could harm us. We'd escaped a horrendous legacy that was ordained to claim us all. My pa left the moonshine life behind because he feared that I was bound to become a bootlegger. Worse, that someday, someone would eventually find our corpses being picked at by buzzards. My father made a decision that, I came to learn later in life, took enormous courage. Just like the courage that your mother Sadie recently showed, with her decision to escape a life with me without leaving you or your child, Eliza, behind. Whether you and I agree with her decision or not, what she chose for, and what she did, took bravery."

Ruby then asked him, "I always thought that people who ran off to avoid difficulties were the week, quitter types. Are you sure that Grandpa Amos never, not even one time, felt like a coward for not standing up to his father Ezra?"

Horace definitively replied, "No. He never felt like a coward, because my girl, cowards don't have courage."

"Well put Horace," she interjected.

He rolled her eyes at her. A gesture she knew meant that she owed him an apology for interrupting him for a second time. Before she could utter one word he was talking again.

"In the end, both your grandpa and I were able to become men without regret or dishonour. We discarded our inherited moonshine life in an effort to start a different life and breed a new generation of descendants who had a chance at a better life than we'd had. Regrettably, we both carried the unforgiving genetic link to alcoholism. For as tough as this gene made life for our families, it nearly destroyed both of us."

Horace walked over to Ruby, who was putting her boots back on. Seeing the blisters on her toes, he reminded her again, as he'd constantly done since she was a girl, that she should wear socks.

He looked straight into her bright green, alert eyes and said, "You are still young Ruby girl. You have more life ahead of you than behind you. On the contrary, I am a soon to be 70-year-old man. I have less life ahead of me than behind me. Let's agree that what we do with our lives from this day forward, and what we did with our lives leading up to this very moment, isn't up to either of us to judge or question. Our choices, and the consequences of our choices, are up to each of us to make and then to live with."

He sounds like a prophet, Ruby thought but didn't say.

"Do you agree?" he rather astutely asked her. Horace waited for a reply as his best girl finished gathering her things. They needed to walk back to the ranch before the sun went down and the blackness of the night blinded them.

"Do you agree?" he repeated.

Instead of answering him, she asked, "What happened to Amos's mother, your grandmother, who was allegedly impregnated while her husband Ezra was in jail?"

Sweet Mother of Jesus! Horace impatiently thought. *Why this child of mine always insists on answering a question with a question will forever be a mystery to me!*

Despite that the old man was overheated, fatigued, talked out, and a trifle vexed, he answered her question.

"She died in childbirth."

Chapter 30

After eating their lunch, they packed the picnic basket back up, scattered breadcrumbs for the birds, and dripped the remaining cola from their bottles onto the dry ground. In no time, a myriad of ants clustered and crept over the wet, sweet, sappy dirt. The old man had taught his girl not to waste anything that could be passed on to humans, animals, plants, or insects. Now, as a young woman, he could see that she'd embraced his lesson. His 'set in stone' child had never been someone who took directions from others easily. Nowadays, as her father, he was grateful that he recognized a part of himself in her.

Horace then held out his hand. She took it and they started walking again.

"Would you like to hear more about your other the other side of who you are, or have I talked enough for one afternoon?" he asked her.

His guarded girl wasn't sure how to answer. She was, as one might reason, concerned that his telling her about his past, for the first time, may turn out to be too distressing for him. His raging outburst at the bonfire last night had shaken her up quite a bit. Nonetheless, because since arriving she'd heard so much about the Ballinger Dutton bloodline that she was linked to, her interest in her family roots had grown. She anticipated that more knowledge about her ancestors from Africa would connect her to them in even deeper way. She knew she shared a degree of African blood, yet despite this, she was rather uneducated about the generations and lineages that came before her.

"Yes, I would," she answered.

Curiosity had always played a role in the choices she made. He smirked at how docile his normally hot-tempered daughter had become since their outing began. With maybe another forty-five minutes of daylight left, they sensibly turned back in the direction of the ranch. After taking a few steps forward, without missing a beat, Horace started his storytelling again. He began exactly where he'd left off. Horace had a knack for keeping a story alive while moving towards its ultimate climax. Ruby liked this about her pa.

"In a way that is still unclear to me, Bessie and Samuel met on a plantation somewhere in one of the deep southern states here in America. I think it was Georgia, or New Orleans. Then again, maybe it was Alabama. I really don't know for sure. What I do know is that Bessie, being a slave, was plantation property and Samuel was the son of the military man who owned Bessie and her older sister Minnie. Despite his birth right Samuel held no inheritance privileges to his father's property; be that of the humankind or the material kind. I don't have all the facts. I do recall being told that he and Bessie had runaway together. She was a young Negro girl, and he was rumoured to be white, entitled, southern purebred. In the late 1800s and early and 1900s, their black and white combination was ethically, legally, and religiously forbidden. Interracial relationships were shunned and outlawed in those times. For a very long time, people considered the comings and goings surrounding Bessie and Samuel to be a myth, because there was no factual documentation of their relationship. The night they ran off to start a secret life together, they both had been digging."

"Digging what?" she asked.

"Sssshhh," he retorted with a symbolic finger over his lips gesture. "Just listen my girl."

"Bessie had just dug a deep hole in the woods and buried her older sister Minnie in an unmarked slave grave, while Samuel was trying to dig himself out from under the weight of a sea of expectations his prominent, dictatorial father had laid upon him. Samuel's pa was an authoritarian who'd had his son's life mapped out for him by the time he was a wee five-year old lad. The fight they had the night Samuel ran away was dangerously explosive. It involved a son being shot at by his own father as he raced away into the obscurity of a dense cornfield that bordered the plantation he'd been born on. Whether Samuel was wounded or not was never actually known. What folks did know be a fact, was that Samuel outran and outlived both his father the U.S. General, and his father the slave owner, who fired buckshot-filled cartridges at his son."

Ruby gasped at the visions spinning through her visually sharp mind. Horace's renditions had her on the edge and filled with anticipation of what happened next.

The old man paused briefly and then added, "Seems Shep wasn't the only young man to be shot at by a military General while running off a plantation."

After a brief lull, he resumed his version of the historical tale.

"The first accurate and documented story I was told, about your Dutton grandparents, was a properly thought provoking one. In the late 1800s, Bessie and Samuel eventually finished building their two-room clapboard, mud-roofed house, which is now the renowned Dutton Ranch, where you spent so many of your summer holidays as a kid. Rumour had it that they'd travelled with a baby, or a small child, that they'd rescued from some ill-fated disaster. The facts of these rumours have never surfaced; so the gossip about this child faded away as the years passed. Their original tiny mud house had only one window, a fireplace with a low chimney, and a loft for storage. The fireplace in Bessie's parlour is actually the original one that Samuel built. He used boulders from the creek that Shep swims in and you just dipped your feet in. Although the initial house was insignificant, leaky, and draftee, it was theirs. For that reason, to them it was more than sufficient. It was home. Later that year a simple structured barn with a root cellar and another loft was built. Samuel and Bessie were mighty thankful and indebted to President Abraham Lincoln; without Abe's assistance they never would have had a life of homesteading or built the Dutton Ranch up from nothing but mud-covered clay beneath their feet."

Horace then went silent and gathered his thoughts.

"Here we goddamn go again!" Ruby crassly snapped at him.

Her reaction was harsh and, in Horace's opinion, *out of the bloody blue!* He stopped walking, dropped her hand, stepped back, and began scrutinizing his daughter. She could see that she'd insulted him with her abrupt, outlandish behaviour and belligerent tone. Like her father, she too had a hot temper that needed to be tamed. Apparently, something he'd just said had caused her blunt reaction. Unfortunately, for both of them, her lasting lack of trust in him had a mind of its own. Before Horace knew it, she'd taken the conversation over. She was clearly heated up by more than the hot plains weather. Before he could react, she started bellowing.

"As your daughter, this is the worst time of day for me! Since I was a little girl, a few hours before the sun set and the moon rose, is the stretch of time I've dreaded the most! Typically, this is when your storytelling changes and turns into anecdotes. Tales that people, I bloody included, believe are fables spiked with fantasy and booze. And if my suspicions are true, the orange juice you drank a few hours ago was spiked with vodka instead of pulp!"

Something in Horace snapped. Her nastiness and accusation had unkindly stabbed and wounded him. Regardless, he remained calm while at the same time refusing to let her rant on and disrespect him.

"Stop yelling at me and stop accusing me Ruby," he said with complete composure. "You can voice your opinions, but you cannot badmouth me in such a nasty way."

He was shaking inside, but he was goddamn certainly not going to let her see that she'd gotten to him. Trying to control the impending disappointment in him, she went on with defiantly challenging him by using a softer tone. Ruby was on verge of tears, but she was goddamn certainly not going to let him see that he'd gotten to her.

"President Abe Lincoln, as sympathetic and generous as he was reputed to be by Negro slaves, was assassinated in 1865. A dead man can't help people build anything!"

In a heartbeat, she lost any self-control she'd attempted to use to calm her rage and be rational. She was all fired up again and adamant about proving this stubborn, most-likely inebriated old man wrong! She suspected that he'd added alcohol to his juice during breakfast, or maybe to his Coca Cola bottle, before their hike began. While Jackson was at church, and she was gone and galloping atop a stallion across the plains, Horace had been alone and unattended for too long. As her suspicions grew, she boldly faced him and started yelling again.

"Admit it! Abe Lincoln never could have helped them build their ranch house! The dates don't line up old man. Get your facts straight! I want a real story, not some fancy spun, alcohol riddled fairy-tale!" She was fuming.

Where in the bloody hell is all her anger unexpectedly coming from? Horace mutely asked himself. He was blindsided, trembling, and feeling rightly attacked by her.

Throughout every age and stage of her life, Ruby McEwen had never been good at controlling her impulsivity. In less thirty seconds, she'd bushwhacked her pa and outright deflated him. All of his passionate storytelling zest leaked out of him like a tire with a steely nail in it. She was too riled up to see the affects her accusations and harsh tone were having on him. She assumed that Horace was moving in the direction of another one of his 80 proof, tall tales, being poured out of a liquor bottle. This was something he always did when he drank. Filled with fear, she glared at him;

certain that his old, rusted habits had crossed the Great Plains and found them both. Ruby had been the victim of Horace's love affair with booze since she was a child. She had a razor sharp and an intolerant ability to dredge up countless bouts of his drunkenness. Likewise, she had a brutally honest way of communicating. This was a 'personality mishmash' of hers, which was not one of her finest qualities. She was known for frequently overreacting, then accusing her pa of being guilty of drinking and carousing with no real motive.

She did realize that Horace has just opened himself up to her by telling her the history and roots of his bootlegging McEwen family clan. What he'd shared had given her more insight into her father's background than she'd ever before had. However, despite his disclosures and admissions, his drinking was a deeply imbedded insecurity and great challenge for her.

Through the heated haze of her anger-filled glare, she saw an obvious injured look in his eyes. Her ranting and raving had prevented her from seeing that he was indeed still sober. Realizing that she'd unfairly and wrongly accused him, guilt overtook her. Fortunately for ole' Horace, the shame she felt rendered her speechless. A heavy silence fell over them. Wrapped in their own emotions and thoughts, neither of them spokes. With different points of view, they continued to walk, now, some six feet apart from each other.

Finally, after twenty minutes or so of silent scrutiny, a teary-eyed Ruby submissively said, "Sorry Pa." Then she asked, "I jumped the bloody gun again, didn't I?"

"Yup, you bloody did," was Horace's reply.

"Ruby girl, listen to me. I need you to hear what I am going to tell you. Then, I need you to remember it even long after I am dead and gone. Are you listening?" Horace directly asked.

"Yes," she obediently answered.

"Doubt, like alcohol abuse, is a disease that contaminates the mind. It creates a mistrust of people's motives and a person's own perceptions," he said. "I stopped drinking for you. Now I need you to stop doubting me, for me."

With his message being sent and received, a slight gleam appeared in his eyes and replaced the painful dent her doubts and accusations had left behind. When it came to Horace, all it took was a sincere apology for him to forgive and then grab hold of the good side of people and life again. Ruby had forgotten that her father had his own internal brain switch. It had been a long time since she'd seen him use it.

This old man is as capable of switching emotional gears as I am of switching my brain on and off, she told herself, grateful that they shared this trait.

Engulfed in silence, they continued walking further on the same trail that paralleled the creek, they listened to it burble and bubble as it flowed above its deep bed and streamed over rocks and branches. The placid rippling and babbling sounds that the water made, as it trickled along, were practically hypnotic. Ruby casually stepped off the path, sat down on a nearby embankment, removed her boots, and dunked her bare feet back into the creek's ice cold, coursing water. Realizing that they'd both just been prey to her bad attitude, she turned around and saw him walking towards her. She wasn't afraid of her father; she was afraid of her ability wound him with words. He knew she'd learned this trait from him, therefore, occasionally needing to forgive her was for Horace the same as forgiving himself. After he took a seat on a bolder next to her, she could see that he was all straight-backed and self-assured again. The look of hurt she'd caused him seemed to have evaporated under the warm dazzle of the onset of another vibrant sunset. His chest was noticeably puffed out, which she knew to be a familiar sign that he'd just inhaled a necessary dose of self-confidence and he had forgiven her. In the past, when it came to his habitual drinking, his best girl had been negatively affected by his alcoholism too many times. Owning his addiction, and its effects on others, meant that he rightfully was able to admit that 'he himself had caused the lack of trust she had in him'.

In that moment, he was stupefied at how effortlessly he was able to dismiss her distrustful judgments and hate-filled words. Horace, the Teller of Tales, didn't intend to waste time proving anything to her. His mind had already switched directions and was traveling towards another impressive story with a riveting climax. The man was a seasoned and a master storyteller. He wasn't financially rich; he was fantasy rich. The man could guide his minds energy to the past and in and out of almost any situation that he landed himself in. This is what made him élite and what connected him to the events and people in his stories. His daughter interpreted his still noticeably puffed out chest as a positive sign. It meant that, this time around, he was tolerating her false accusations of him. They knew each other extremely well. Since she was old enough to find her voice and speak her own mind, they'd both taken turns tolerating each other's outspokenness and individual faults. Despite that they shared numerous akin personality traits and defects, they each had rightly different charismas.

Dipping her bare feet in and out of the cold creek was cooling her hot-tempered side off considerably. Realizing this, she timidly asked him to continue with his story. Despite her recent outbursts, they actually revelled in bantering and hanging out with each other. Given their turbulent father daughter past, adoring being together was a rare treasure neither of them was ready to bury in the ground yet. Feeling the need to apologize again, Ruby told Horace that she had misjudged him. She confessed to him that being a single British mum to young Eliza had distracted her from seeing how hard he had worked on his sobriety. She admitted to herself that she hadn't yet spent enough time with a sober father to trust that her alcoholic father wasn't going to ruin the version of who he'd become. Eleven months, with an alcohol-free Horace, wasn't enough time for her to put an adequate amount of faith in him after a lifetime with an intoxicated Horace. Her confession was honest, endearing, and touching.

He replied by saying, "Let it go child. Human beings profess their own different versions of the truth. This is why they continuously misunderstand and misinterpret each other. Live and learn my girl," he said with fatherly wink.

The old man liked to wink. Winking was his silent sign of approval and affection. She'd forgotten this about him since she'd left home to start a new and different life than the one, they'd shared.

"Now you listen up girl!" he sternly snapped, reclaiming all the attention. "History and Horace like sin and damnation! You just shut that beautiful, high-spirited mouth of yours, stand up, put your boots back on, start walking, and listen to my story!" he demanded. "This time, listen with the kind of respect that, the man that raised you to be upright and proper deserves."

He was teasing his daughter more than reprimanding her. Ruby was very used to his sarcastic humour and immediately began to do what she was told to do; in the proper order she was told to do it. Walking side by side with his girl, he knew that given her perceptive brain, higher education, and fancy degrees, she'd know that what he was about to tell her was based on fact, not on fiction. Nonetheless, Horace liked being in the spotlight, so in the spotlight he would stand. As they walked farther down the trail, he slid, once more, into in his typical 'storyteller' role and resumed his tale exactly where he had left off.

"It was because of America's, not so widely distinguished, President Abraham Lincoln's help, that Bessie and Samuel could acquire the land we have been hiking on. They needed to stake claim to this land first, before they could build their original, tiny, sod-roofed house." Symbolically extending his long arms wide and far, he said, "This is where they staked their claim, right out here in the middle of God's green, lush countryside. Ruby girl, if Abe hadn't signed the Homestead Act, your grandparent's lives would have been very different. Because of his signature, they had an advantage. They were able to claim some of the best land before East Coast migrants with more farming experience eventually arrived. Even though land claims only cost ten dollars at the time, homesteaders had to supply their own farming tools. This proved to be a serious disadvantage to many of the greenhorn migrants."

He stopped and asked her, "Do you know what a greenhorn is?"

Cockily, she answered with the speed of a fledging genius, "Someone who is consider to be a neophyte because they're inexperienced at what they are doing."

Her old man smiled at her level of intelligence and continued with his tale.

"For a decade or so, before Minnie died, young Bessie had worked outside on the plantation's farm where the sisters were housed, trained, castigated, and raised. She became skilled at nearly every aspect of outdoor plantation life. For one year, with a deliberate strategy intact, Samuel and Bessie filched basic tools before they left their respective homes. Some folks would consider this stealing, yet conversely, in those changing times, it was a matter of survival. Therefore, as so many other desperate souls did, they confessed their sins before makeshift crucifixes and kept on thieving in the name of their continued existence. Bessie was nothing more than a slightly plump, black-skinned slave girl, who'd run off in a devious way with a blood-rich, white-skinned Yankee boy. The dashing Samuel defied his father, General Ballinger Dutton, an active member of the Democratic Party who publically supported slavery prior to and during the Civil War. The General had lost his three other sons at the height of the war between the Confederate and Union Armies. He was a dominant plantation owner, who disowned his only remaining son, Sammie, after Samuel had relinquished the family plantation. Before his desertion, being his last surviving heir, Samuel was expected to take over the plantation so that the General could retire in an opulent manner."

Horace's brain had spontaneously and nonchalantly switched gears. It realized that the aging man was side-tracking from his story even before he did. As the years of his life ripened, his minds intellect more easily wandered off and changed its direction at will.

"Let's get back Mr. Lincoln," he said. "Abe, the Great Emancipator of the Slaves, actually aided millions of other pioneers, who never would have had a chance at a decent life without his Homestead Act. This also means that the amazing ranch you are so fond of, where your mother Sadie was born and reared, would never have existed," he concluded.

Ruby's mind, like her pa's, had its own wandering tendencies. She interrupted him and asked, "Do you think the folktales you were told about your third-generation great grandfather Darius are true? Do you remember telling me about him during one of our fence side conversations? I was still in high school at the time. If so, do you think that Darius's traveling to North America and passing himself off as a US Citizen is what made you so interested in America and its history and people?"

"Without a doubt," Horace stated, as he gave her shoulder an embrace of flattery for remembering Darius's legacy. He told her that homesteaders of the 1800s were the same kind of daring and unwavering visionaries that Darius was. With conviction and pride in his voice, he dismissed thoughts of Darius and continued his tale. The tension between them had all but vanished; something they both felt as they continued walking back to the Dutton Ranch.

"Until 1900, The Homestead Act stimulated western migration by providing settlers with access to 160 acres of free public land. In exchange, after the brave, dream-filled homesteaders paid the filing fee, they were required by the government to prove five years of continuous residency on the land they acquired. Once they did this, they received full ownership of the land. The Act allowed men, and even unmarried women, who were American citizens and over the age of twenty-one, to claim their 160 acres of unrestricted public land," he told her.

"Why?" Ruby asked. "160 acres is a titanic amount of free land isn't it?"

"The government's hope," Horace responded, "was that the homesteaders would build houses, farms, and ranches for themselves and their families. The Act would give resolute homesteaders like Bessie and Samuel a fair chance, which eventually it did."

"And it would populate an otherwise remote and undeveloped area of America," Ruby interjected.

"Correct. The government didn't care about the colour of their skin," Horace went on to tell her. "The intention and purpose were to populate the Midwest. It was a simple, ingenious plan. A multitude of homesteaders came to the area to stake a claim, but in comparison, very few stayed. The men, women, and children, of all ages, creed, and colour, who journeyed to claim their share of free land, also faced serious trials and tribulations. Poverty was rampant. Like Samuel and Bessie, who'd ventured off into an unknown area of the country, people yearned for a second chance and a more auspicious life. Their pockets were full of hope and their jackets were lined with promise. In addition to this, the prospect of wealth had many of them, like the two older Dutton brothers, lured by railroad companies broadcasting news of a region that was a rich and auspicious land, filled with milk and honey. Many of them, again like your grandpa Samuel and his sons, met their deaths in search of that Godforsaken bloody milk and honey."

With that being solemnly confirmed, Horace stopped talking.

Ruby's noticed that her pa had begun dragging his feet from weariness. He appeared to be entirely yacked out. Seeing the sun steadily sinking over the horizon, she knew it would be dark in less than ten minutes. She intertwined her arm around her aging father's arm and gently coaxed him to walk on. Cheek by jowl, in complete silence, they made it back to the ranch by the glow of a newly risen moon that lit their path. Ruby was delighted with the perfect weather they'd had. A storm was brewing on the horizon. She could feel it. Less than two hours later, after another fine conversation about the experiences of the day while sharing a meal with Jackson Boy Shepherd, they thanked him for his wisdom and kindness and bid him an affectionate farewell. Jackson had promised the preacher at his Church that he would paint the rectory early in the morning, therefore, he would be gone before they woke up. They both were noticeably disappointed when he told them this.

"Reneging on a promise to a preacher is no different than letting God down," Jackson told them. "Given how I plan on jumping over those Pearly Gates one day, letting God is something ole' Shep knows better than to do."

He told them that he'd arranged for a neighbour's son to drive them to the bus station on time so they wouldn't miss their flight back to Heathrow.

"Taxicabs don't come this far out," he pointed out.

While Ruby tidied up the dishes, Horace fell asleep in the parlour on Bessie's old, dated Victorian couch. She went over to him and removed her pa's favourite cap. He'd worn it all day and all week, except for at Bessie's burial and the dinner table.

"A polite man always removes his hat before burying a soul or breaking bread," he'd affirmed daily to her and Jackson before taking his seat at the dining room table. She noticed that he'd started repeating himself since they'd arrived in the States; something she chose to ignore despite her concern and curiosity as to why.

Although they remained composed and stoic, Horace and Shep would miss each other something terrible. The proof was in the tears they both shed as they said their final farewells. Standing in the doorway of the kitchen, Ruby briefly watched her ageing and sleeping father. Aside from a few outbursts, since they'd arrived at the ranch, she'd felt uncharacteristically charmed and mesmerized by him. It was as though this version of her old man had cast a spell on her in the past ten days. Today had been particularly enchanting for her, because today, Horace had been the second kind of storyteller. Today he was the sort of father that made her want to be with him and never leave him. Today he was type of grandfather that she wanted her little girl to know and to learn from. The sober Horace was a real intellect. His storytelling talent, passions for history, and the people that came before him, had rightly dazzled her over the past few days. Ruby walked over to Bessie's beloved Victorian couch, removed her pa's cap, and kissed him on his balding head. Then she covered him with a thick fleece blanket before dowsing the oil lamps. Both gestures were signs of affection that she seldom showed.

Climbing the stairs on her way to bed, she hesitated and took another glance at Horace. The moon's soft, deep ginger coloured light was casting a faint reddish glow over his face. The moonbeams radiance made Horace look rather Saintly.

Wishful thinking, she light-heartedly thought. For as nice as this trip had been with her father, she knew, beyond the shadow of any Holy doubt, that *Horace McEwen was anything and everything but a Saint.*

Realizing she'd forgotten to blow out the large pillar candles still burning on the kitchen windowsill, she went back down the stairs. Since Bessie's death, Ruby and Jackson had been heedful of their responsibilities for the Dutton family memorial candles. They had taken turns keeping Bessie's seventy-two-year long tradition alive. Jackson would light the candles before gathering the eggs each morning and Ruby, being the last one to go to bed, would blow the candles out each night. Realizing that Shep had spent more time at the ranch with Ruby than he had, Horace tactfully left the intimate ritual to them. For decades, once a month, Bessie and Jackson would wipe down and oil the deceased Dutton twins little leather cowboy boots. The boots had stood on the windowsill next to the candles since the boy's death. Because of the diligent care the boots had received, they still looked exactly as they had on the day the twins died during the infamous winter storm of 1888. Since the day, following the last male Dutton death, each morning, at sunup Bessie had faithfully lit five memorial candles. One for each of her deceased sons and one for her life partner Samuel. Tonight, for the last time, Ruby would blow out each of the five candles, plus an additional sixth one for her grandma.

Ruby was a person who had never needed much sleep. Probably because since she was a girl, she'd been a habitual reader. Nightly, she would read new chapters from her latest novel until the wee hours of the morning. She'd always adored the hours of darkness and the tranquillity the night offered her. The night-time silence had a way of drowning out all the noise that had been deposited in her head throughout the daytime hours. As she stood at the soapstone kitchen sink in front of the window, the young, single mother, was uncharacteristically overcome with sentiment. This was where Grandma Bessie had stood, day in and day out, for almost eighty-five years. Ruby could feel hollow crannies under her feet in the wooden floor, where Bessie's shoes had worn the floorboards down after decades of cooking, doing dishes, and gazing out over her land. The indentations felt welcoming and safe. She shed a few tears, wondering what had occupied her grandmother's mind the last time Bessie had stood where she now stood, staring out the same window into the same dark distance. The Dutton family gravesite, atop the nearby hill, was in full view.

"Why hadn't I noticed this before?" She asked herself aloud as she continued eyeing the darkness beyond the large, rectangular windowpane.

The night sky was sparkling with thousands of brightly lit stars. The location of a full moon was nearby the distant horizon, which made it appear large, incandescent, and carrot-coloured. The luminous, harvest moon was radiant enough for her to distinguish, with ease, the silhouettes of each of the six granite Dutton headstones. Despite that, Ruby wasn't a religious person; the gravesite, under a full moon, was one of Holiest images she'd ever seen. For more years than she could even begin to fathom, this was what her grandmother had cast her eyes upon each night before ending her day.

What an amazing, sanctified sight, Ruby thought, *simply amazing.*

Just as she was serenely pondering over where her mother Sadie, the seventh member of the Dutton family would someday be buried, an abrupt and outrageously loud squawking noise yanked her out of the quiet and hallowed place she was in. A bogus, graveyard buzzard, apparently on a Holy mission to send her one final sacred message, was flying straight towards the kitchen. With a loud thud, it hit the glass and landed, unfazed, on the wide stone windowsill outside, just inches away from the window. Then, a dark brown, featherless, red headed, beady black-eyed turkey buzzard locked eyes with Ruby. There it remained, perched, hissing, and grunting in a stare down with her. The sound it made reminded her of a hungry penned up hog. She almost started to laugh at the ridiculous bird, who'd most likely been a member of the flock that had annoyed throughout the day. Jackson had taught her that vultures were harmless, despite their ugliness and the scary role they play in horror stories and folktales. She knew that they feasted mostly on dead animals and had no reason to attack humans. In spite of this, the dreadful looking intruder had just given her a nasty kind of fright that rendered her breathless.

"Stupid goddam bird," she mumbled as she openhandedly smacked the glass. "Sod bloody off!"

She felt her body quiver as the buzzard, having accomplished what he'd set out to do, flew off into the night. Ruby knew that she'd had enough and needed to end this long, eventful day. Taking a deep breath, she blew six candles out before locking the front door. Climbing the stairs on her way to bed, visions and thoughts of Bessie and Samuel pirouetted through her endlessly searching mind.

Late afternoon, the next day, the McEwen's flew back to London. This time, Ruby's father didn't vomit on the plane and the flight was turbulence-free. Horace never returned to America or saw his *brother of another colour* again.

Chapter 31

The stale burnt sulphur smell, from snuffed out candles, lingered under the elderly woman's wide, fluctuating nostrils. She opened her eyes and looked down at her long, wrinkled fingers. It took her a bit of time to regain her focus, after mentally roaming across the Great Plains of America.

Her hands were folded in her lap and resting on the blanket that kept her legs and feet warm. The glass she'd been holding was now on the floor next to her chair. She found it peculiar that she didn't recall setting the glass down. But then again, she reminded herself that once she opened the gateway to the past, drifting took her wherever she asked it to. She recognized that she'd just taken an important journey. A glass of water, melted ice and diluted cola, was the last thing she should be thinking about. The esoteric scent of extinguished candles reminded her of Bessie and the State of Montana; a place she hadn't visited in almost sixty years. When the old woman sitting in her lounger was still a girl, one of the summertime highlights of visiting the Dutton homestead in America, was helping her grandma prepare food for the ranch's annual summer barbeque. The event was known by folks for as far as the eye could see from beyond the estate's wrap around porch. Once a year, Bessie's supervisor, Mister Shepherd, her friends, ranch hands, the local doctor and priest, her hairdresser, plus half the village, came to eat delicious food and celebrate life in unison. Back then, the then young Ruby would overhear folks say that her grandmother was the finest cook in the county and made the best food they'd ever tasted.

Whenever Ruby heard this, she'd tease the irony of the comment. It was zany and unimaginable for her to believe that her mother, Sadie, had grown up in the same kitchen, alongside the finest cook in all of Beaverhead County. Sadie was an awful cook.

Apparently, being talented in the kitchen had skipped a generation, she thought as she rubbed her stiff hands together.

"Lucky me," she said aloud, as she went on to massage her aching wrists.

Even today, the very old Ruby, who was kneading arthritis pain out of her joints, knew something compelling about herself. As the years passed, and she grew up and into her authentic self, her interest in bringing people together and offering them a healthy meal had grown right alongside her height. Thinking of this had her mind instinctively wandering back towards the love of her life, her diner.

Years before a young, industrious woman purchased The Seaside, it was one of London's original diner's and part of a 1950s restaurant chain that primarily sold hamburgers, french-fries, and milkshakes. The meals, efficiently served on single use paper or plastic plates, arrived at the table within five minutes of ordering it. No silverware was given, or used, if it wasn't needed. Moreover, when it was given, it was the plastic disposable kind. Drinks were served in thick bottles with a straw, and condiments were provided in pre-packaged single serving packets. Despite that these types of convenience food eateries were hugely popular success, Ruby wanted to add more sustenance to her menu and a touch of class to her tables. Likewise, she wanted to offer customers a place to dine out that looked nothing like their own kitchens at home. This mindset inspired her to offer a different type of fast-food experience that would be tinted with a cosy tableside nuance. Therefore, customers were greeted at the door and personally escorted to their seats by the owner. Whether they needed them or not, they were then served cutlery, cloth napkins, ceramic plates, and actual glasses with their meals. Plastic striped straws were still used and given to children and teens because the straws made eating out amusing for her younger patrons.

Ruby was persistent in her belief that no disposable tableware of any kind would be cluttering the garbage bins behind her place of business, which was also her home. The city of London was littered with enough garbage already. Her diner would not add to the current, nearly unmanageable, citywide trash situation. Her belief was that, with the onset and popularity of the disposable era, enough waste was already being generated by mankind. In addition, in her strong opinion, the current global throwaway society was unduly influenced by convenience. Convenience was something she didn't believe in, nor did she want any part of. She refused to have any of the dining features she offered to her customers, adding to the already overflowing garbage pails and finding its way onto the beach, or into the sea behind her establishment. Consequently, after buying The Seaside, she donated its entire supply of remaining stock of disposable ware to a local landfill company. Then she replaced it all with the reusable, washable kind. In this way, the diner owner was very much an activist before her time. She'd always wanted to make a difference for the well-being of people she knew and people she'd never meet. Her most courteous and loyal customers, would tell her that she was as unspoiled and as ageless as The Seaside was. Although, she had a habit of blushing while disregarding any kind of praise, hearing this particular compliment felt rightly uplifting.

Realizing that she was hardly ever alone in her diner after dark, she took a few moments to observe her favourite place on the earth. The place where, since 1960, she'd spent a lifetime earning a living and raising people.

Too many days and nights to tally, she concluded with a pride-filled smirk.

Never forgotten, influential memories of the Swinging Sixties that had once been etched on her life started flooding through into her receptive brain. Back in the early 1960s, she was a tenaciously young, single mother. It was a time when the Vietnam War was escalating, and the Beatles were taking the world by storm. Thinking about being an unwed mother was something she didn't do very often anymore. Thinking about being pregnant not once, but twice, was something the elderly woman did, on rare occasions, when she saw her employee and tenant Nico. Her Italian worker reminded her of what life with a son might have been like, if she hadn't lost her first child some five decades ago.

"Who was now God knowing where?" she heard herself wondering aloud the whereabouts of Nico.

In an effort to force herself not to think about what happened to him during and after the boating accident, Ruby's flicked her brain switch back to when she became a mother. She still could easily recall how dreadful life had been for her before birthing Eliza back in the mid-1950s. She'd been cruelly humiliated as an unwed, expectant, university senior in Ireland. At the time, she'd assumed that telling her parents about her pregnancy, would be the worst humiliation she'd ever have to endure. Although they were shocked when she told them that they were grandparents, more than a year after Eliza's birth, their reactions were trivial compared to the stigma surrounding unmarried mothers in Ireland and England at the time.

Back in the 50s and '60s, no pregnant teenage girl could avoid the shame and dishonour attached to a pregnancy without a marriage certificate. A girl who had gotten herself pregnant twice was considered a double floozy. Subsequently, the young Ruby knew damn well what to tell people about her life and what to hide. An unwed pregnancy was a dreaded scenario that for girls of all ages meant banishment and emotional suffering. According to Roman Catholic Irish standards, the pregnant girls and unmarried mums at the Home for Unwed Mothers, where Mia Doherty and Ruby had first met, were nothing more than depraved outcasts.

According to same Roman Catholic Irish standards, Ruby McEwen was a trustworthy, middleclass British girl who came from a respectable family and was studying at the University of Dublin. When the pregnancy was visible, a panel of her academic superiors considered multiple factors. Because she had continuously demonstrated herself worthy, before the pregnancy was made known, leniency would be deliberated. If her academic performance hadn't been so impeccable, she'd have been immediately dismissed from her studies by means of suspension. Fortunately for her, she had outstanding high grades and an impressionable three-year reputation as a volunteer for various Catholic charities across the city of Dublin. Her diligence, scholastic record, and reliable character enabled her to gain the support of the Dean of Students at the university. Therefore, despite that, her unplanned pregnancy could no longer be hidden, she was deemed worthy of receiving a well-deserved bachelor's degree in Journalism. Religious rehabilitation would begin immediately after the baby was born.

Ruby carried her baby full term and graduated with honours, two days before her daughter was born. In the eyes of the University Disciplinary Counsel, despite her lack of morals, she'd over and over again proven herself worthy of a degree from their prestigious institution. Notwithstanding the scholastically successful side of who she was, the very visibly pregnant student was not allowed to attend the graduation ceremony or receive her numerous collegiate awards with her graduating class. Five days after the ceremony, the Dean of Students hand delivered Ruby's diploma, accolades, and a bouquet of congratulatory flowers to her. The newborn, Eliza Emilia McEwen, received her first and only silver rattle from the dean. The gift wasn't because he was fond of baby's; it was because he was closely acquainted with the young bloke who he suspected had impregnated his prized and praised student from Essex County, England. Accordingly, he felt responsible and mortified as all hell.

Still sitting in her recliner, the old lady with snow-coloured hair, flicked her brain switch again. This time she thought about Nico, her 22-year-old Italian dishwasher and boarder, who her great granddaughter, Jazz Durant, had taken a fancy to the moment they'd been introduced. Occasionally, since Nico Rossario began working at The Seaside, her mind was distracted by her past. Since he'd entered her life, she had begun thinking more about the first time she was pregnant and miscarried a teeny tiny baby boy.

"Sweet Jesus, that was a long time ago," she stated aloud.

Back then, only two people knew what had happened to the very young Miss McEwen, who was attending high school at the time. Two pupils were keeping a gargantuan teenage secret. Knowing the consequences that such an unfathomable secret had attached to it, they swore on their lives to take what they knew and what they'd done, to their graves with them. Even though the much older and unyielding Ruby of today didn't give a bloody crap if the details of her past life were revealed; twenty something years ago her classmate and confidant had already taken their secret to her grave. Out of respect for her classmate's devotion and trust, after her death, the elderly woman chose to never tell anyone what only the two schoolgirls knew. Since she'd met him, Nico had a way of making her wonder what her life would have been like had her first baby lived. Regardless of the gruelling circumstances surrounding the infant's conception, long after her childbearing years were gone, on occasion, she still longed for a son. As her thoughts took her back to 1940, her dozy eyes stared down at two limp, arthritis-inflicted hands situated on her lap.

During each age and stage of her life she had been a curious and passionate person. By the time, she was thirteen, or fourteen she'd already experienced numerous extreme circumstances that had required her to grow up years before her time. On one particular night, laden with such an extremeness, Ruby was emphatically forced to mature too fast. She was a mere 15 years old and trapped in the confines of a secret pregnancy. It was an unforgettable night. It was the night she bit down on a wet rag and watched a very small, stillborn male foetus glide out of her womb and straight into a world besieged by Hitler. Between June 1940 and June 1941, Britain stood alone against the Third Reich, while Ruby stood alone against a series of events that threatened her life, her veracity, a humongous secret, and her human loss. Back then, and for countless years to follow, the life altering experience permanently imprinted itself on her extremely conflicted conscience. It was the night of September 7th, 1940. The night the Blitz, with its strategic Nazi bombing campaign against England first began. It was the night German bombs exploded over her head and made a teenage girl, who wasn't sure she believed in God, grateful that her baby boy didn't live to hear the explosions, or see the day of light. At the time of his delivery, Great Britain was no place for a WWII newborn. Despite this, she recalled easily that her son had been born with a full heard of dark hair. His bushy hair was the only physical remembrance of him she still had. She cut off, and hid, a knotted strand of his thick hair in a mourning locket she'd received from a trusting classmate who'd helped her the night she delivered her baby. During the aftermath of her ordeal, two schoolgirls crept on their hands and knees over the ridge behind the McEwen house. Hidden by the darkness of the night, together they buried the premature newborn in a makeshift, secret grave at the same cemetery Ruby frequented so often as a child and teenager. The then juvenile Ruby never wore the mourning locket. Fear of having its meaning revealed prevented her from doing so. After both of her parents had died, she took it out of hiding and put it in her copper jewellery box, where it still was today, nearly seventy-three years later.

Tears were now welling up in the elderly woman's eyes. Reminiscing over this part of her life was twofold challenging, because it was reminding her of how Nico, the once homeless immigrant, had gradually became a surrogate son to her. Although she'd briefly held the tiny infant, she'd never had the chance to share even one day of life with her newborn baby. Nico, in an abstract way, was giving her this chance. The only lingering regret she still had, over that particular event in her life, was that she never named her son.

Suddenly, she heard herself sternly saying, "Focus old girl! There's no time for reminiscing and weeping about the past. Leave it behind you where it belongs. The child lying in the ICU bed needs you to get your head out of the past, pick up the pace, and get back to her."

She'd never been the crying type. Even so, recently juggling memories of her life, alongside the tragedies of the boating accident, had changed this. Pushing old and unresolved flashbacks out of her mind, she glanced again around her diner in search of a distraction. She immediately realized that what she was looking at was *a type of rare and pure joy.*

In the beginning, when she had first opened her establishment, people referred to it as 'a greasy spoon'. This was a term she quickly came to despise and forbade customers from using. Her diner had charm and it had style. It offered affordable prices and delicious food. Between 1975and 1995, the diner owner gave one free pint of pale ale, or a soft drink to her weekend lunch customers. Her free refill policy had increased her sales, profits, and patronage. Eventually, a 'national anti-drinking and driving campaign' had her liable conscience, along with newly established laws, put an end to a popular twenty-year tradition at The Seaside. Overall, she had made a good life for herself. Her customers, especially the regulars, had become her friends and her extended family. She knew them all by name, and she knew their children and their grandchildren.

For nearly sixty years, generations of customers shared their secrets, dreams, achievements, and failures with her. For as private as she was presumed to be, Ruby was a true people person. She took as great an interest in the people she served as she did the food she served them. She was well known and well liked. Despite making a few adversaries along the way, she was adored my many. After nearly nine decades of being alive, she'd come to believe that in the end, all a person really left behind when their life was over, was their stories.

Leaving the Barcalounger, she hobbled and wobbled through the main area of the diner. Her body felt stiff because she'd been sitting for too long, causing her limbs to protest against her idleness. With a trembling, crooked arm, she reached down to open the small drawer of the diner's wooden telephone stand. She needed to her find her address book and the phone number of Jazz's mother. Since she'd not spoken to her granddaughter Zofia in nearly five years, Ruby rightly hoped that her telephone number hadn't changed. She wasn't at all in the mood for putting any extra effort into locating someone in the United States. Especially someone, who in all probability, wasn't a worthy female role model for the patient trapped in a coma. Despite her concerns, she easily found the telephone number and carried on with the 'task at hand'. It was time.

Dabbing at a few lingering tears with the back of her hand; she took a few more 'in search of strength' deep breaths. Then she picked up the receiver and dialled up America. It was almost 9:15 pm in England.

"I have no idea what the time is in California?" she heard herself saying.

Nervously she listened to the ringtone buzzing off as the overseas number was being connecting. Her heart skipped a beat when she heard the telephone on the other side of the world being answered.

A deep, gregarious, male voice said, "Hello, Thatcher Durant speaking."

Caught slightly off guard, because she'd naively anticipated the child's mother to answer, she warily mumbled, "Hello love. Is Mrs. Durant at home?"

"Yes, madam, she is. Who is calling please?" she heard the polite male voice reply.

"This is her grandmother, Ruby McEwen, from England speaking."

"Hello, grandmother," Thatcher respectfully said. "I recognized your accent right away. I hope you are doing well and surviving life in London with my dodgy little sister. Please hold on one moment while I bring the phone to my mother."

The old Londoner was dumbstruck, rightly stunned, and completely confused.

In less than the speed of single beat of her confused heart, she asked herself, *how in the bloody hell was it possible, that the socially correct and articulate young man, who'd just answered the phone, was related to a scallywag like Jazz?*

Chapter 32

Zofia Durant was a desperately complicated woman. She had a few different personalities that made communicating with her dreadful and infuriating. The injured coma patient's mother enjoyed contradicting and arguing about nothing and everything under the sun. In the past, conversations she'd had with her always left the elderly woman feeling exasperated, tangled up, and lost.

Ruby saw the most noticeable changes in Zofia's behaviour starting to reveal themselves during her pregnancy with Jazz. Likewise, she was convinced that her irrational instabilities had intensified shortly after the child's birth. Zofia didn't suffer from postpartum depression. She suffered from the repercussions of Jazz's father, Tucker, taking a keen interest in younger women while she felt neglected at home with his newborn daughter and four sons. Truth be told, Tucker's taste wasn't just in younger women, it was in much, much younger women. Logically, this seriously threatened his wife and the foundation they'd built a family life on. His womanizing changed who his wife had once been, before he began to wander sexually. The old woman holding the telephone receiver had always understood this. Likewise, she felt a true sense of empathy for her granddaughter back in the late 1990s, when Zofia's domestic world started crumbling and landing cruelly at her feet. Whilst waiting for Jazz's mother to come to the phone, Ruby thought about the numerous times and different ways she'd tried to toughen her up by teaching her to stand straight and tall. Her mind raced with recollections of the efforts she'd made to transform her granddaughter into a woman with 'a backbone made of steel'. There was no forgetting the many times she'd ineffectively attempted to help her become a strong-willed female; the type who would take a 'no tolerance stance' against her adulterous husband. For a few years, between 1991 and 1994, Ruby encouraged her to fight back against Tucker's indiscretions. Despite her reinforcement and guidance, she failed. In the end, Zofia chose to cut all ties with her grandmother and become a victim, not a survivor. Jazz was a mere four year's old at the time.

In her opinion, Zofia never even remotely made an effort to follow her wise advice. On the contrary, her granddaughter became the female casualty of a bad marriage. Consequently, for years, she played the duped wife, devoted mother, and overworked homemaker. After all, being the 'casualty of a cheating husband' gained her the attention she needed to pacify herself and lick the emotional wounds Tucker's infidelities inflicted upon her. At least this was Ruby's opinion of her granddaughter back then. As far as Grandma Ruby was concerned, she often resembled a stunning, toxic cloud that was filled with her own sense of warped superiority. In her younger years, Zofia tested the limits of nearly every person who crossed her jilted path.

Before the boating accident, Jazz had told Ruby that her four older brothers had grown tired of the 'drama queen' that had birthed them. When she'd heard this, Ruby construed that her grandsons had fittingly branded their mother, given her reputation for habitually exaggerating and overreacting too nearly everything. Most of the Durant boys moved away from home at young ages, after feeling trapped between their loyalty for her and the limits of their endurance. Ruby did know that to avoid being trampled upon by their parent's problems and their mother's egotism the lads grew into stable men who could fend for themselves. Their father, Tucker, despite his flaws, had taught his sons to sidestep arguments with their mother, to avoid being sarcastic or critical, and to respect her.

I have to give the man credit, Ruby thought, *he did do right by those boys. As for doing right by his daughter, Jazz will need to attest to this herself, when she wakes up,* she concluded.

For some strange reason, Ruby had begun to refer to Jazz as 'the child' again. This was most likely, she concluded, because certain childish behaviours her great granddaughter displayed, since her arrival in London, reminded her of Jazz's mum. She was dreading speaking with her because Zofia was exceptionally difficult to communicate with. She was constantly on the defensive and had a nasty way of pointing out the faults in situations and people. Given that she was the only female role model in the child's life, she could only imagine in which ways Jazz's mother had negatively affected her daughter. Born Zofia Izzy McEwen, she was Ruby's daughter Eliza's only child. Therefore, despite that Eliza's daughter began from a young age to dismiss the positives in basically everything people did or said, she was Ruby's only remaining McEwen family. Buried deep within one of the elderly woman's iron clad convictions was the credence that 'family never quits on family'. Hence, for the better part of twenty years she tolerated the granddaughter she was still waiting on the line to speak with. In spite of the fact that she was the one who had underhandedly entrusted her grandmother with her complex and defiant teenage daughter, she was Jazz's mother. Ruby planned to be courteous during their phone call, after all, her daughter had been seriously hurt while in England and while in Ruby's care. With that thought in mind, she crisscrossed two of her bony fingers, knowing that she'd need all the luck she could get; otherwise, within seconds, she'd be going ballistic on the phone.

For years, she rightly knew that when it came to family dynamics, in the Durant family, the sons received preferential treatment. They were parentally fostered and praised in supportive ways. Overall, at the time, this was considered to be normal and decent childrearing. Nonetheless, after they birthed a daughter, she remembered seeing for herself, how the baby girl's parents were more actively invested in their boy's upbringings and futures than they were in the nurturing of their last-born child. Thinking back on this now had her questioning where Jazz fit into the Durant family puzzle. Was she the last piece that completed it or the piece that was missing and left a hole in it? Since the Durant's were living links to her daughter Eliza, her mind was constantly searching for the answers to the quandaries that confronted them. Despite that by 1999 she'd been blacklisted from their family, her curiosity and concerns for Eliza's descendants had never ended. She knew it was crucial that she remain very objective in the conversation she was about to have with Zofia. There was a huge chance that she could misinterpret what Ruby was about to tell her. The child's mother had a tendency to yammer on and on. Even though being told that *her daughter was in a coma* was a justifiable reason to yammer nonstop, Ruby knew that she'd need to be cautious, empathetic, assertive, and confident with Jazz's mum. Being patient and maintaining her composure with her could prove to be the 'mother of all virtues'. Right now, she was nervous and still bloody goddamn waiting to talk the child's mother! Knowing that she'd need to remain on the line and not hang up out of anger or frustration, she needed a few virtues on her side. Doing so would only reinforce Zofia's need to be the victim and acquire more attention.

Even more attention, Ruby feared, *than her comatose daughter would be getting from her mother.*

"Hello Ruby, why are you calling me?"

The reminiscing old diner owner heard an all too familiar, unstable and self-centred toned voice asking. Within three seconds, at least five familiar emotional triggers immediately went off inside Ruby. Before she could answer, her granddaughter began to screech, which put the old Brit straightaway on a negative edge of the entire American shebang!

"I hope to hell you don't tell me that you're sending Jazz home early!" She screamed. "I finally have some time for myself without worrying about her twenty-four hours a day! We agreed she would spend the summer with you, and it's only been a week since she left! Why are you calling?" she asked again, through manic screams.

Ruby remained unperturbed and tried to get a word in by saying, "Hi Zofia. I need to tell you something and I need you to remain calm and listen to me. Can you do this?"

Then, Zofia's narcissism flipped and gasped. She did attempt to respond admissibly calmer, but she was still very agitated.

"Tell me what? Please don't tell me anything that is going to ruin the summer plans I have made for myself. I've been through enough with Tucker's betrayals and Jazz's unruly behaviour. Did she tell you that she'd been arrested before she flew to England? Did you know she had been detained by the police just two days before she was scheduled to depart? Can you imagine how hard I have had it raising a juvenile delinquent? I sincerely don't know how I have managed to survive through it all!"

"No. Sorry luv. I..."

She tried again, in vain, to get a word in edgewise, but the looney friggen tune on the other end of the line was ranting and rambling! It was ALL about HER and HER bloody needs! Ruby's intention to remain calm quickly fizzled away the more she heard her saying, I, I, and I. Without realizing it, she'd tuned out her granddaughter, deciding to let the hare-brained woman rant until there was no rant left in her.

I hope she purges all her shit out of her self-absorbed self quickly, Ruby frugally thought, *calling the States from Europe is very expensive.*

As she'd suspected, the purging took too long. A few minutes later, her best intentions were shot down dead by the female zealot's nonstop blabbing on the other end of the phone line.

Before she realized it, she blurted out, "Goddammit Zofia, shut the bloody hell up!"

A bizarre and immediate hush came through the receiver that took her breath away. She closed her eyes, inhaled, found her composure, and said, "There has been an accident. Jazz is in a coma."

The split second the word 'coma' rolled off the tip of her tongue and landed in Zofia's side of the world, she regretted divulging so much so quickly. After her first initial and extremely shocked reaction was over, Zofia began criticizing Ruby for the role she played in the accident. Then she went silent. So silent, that the elderly woman thought they'd been disconnected. Just as Ruby was about to hang up, she began to speak. This time, her tone was empty and shrunken.

She asked, repeatedly, "Is she dead? Is she dead? Is she dead?"

As slowly, briefly and precisely as she could, Ruby went on to explain the state of Jazz's condition to her mother.

"Zofia," she began, "being in a coma means that she is still alive. Now, I need you to listen carefully to me without asking more questions." She paused, then asked, "Are you listening?"

"Yes mam," she obediently replied.

Ruby went on with telling the distraught mother what she knew about the accident, which essentially was not much at all. The child's mother continued to sniffle, but this time she didn't interrupt. This was something Ruby needed and appreciated. Dealing with the mother's hysteria during only one brief phone call had her feeling drained and woozy. She couldn't imagine what life was like for Jazz, or the child's father Tucker for that matter; before and most likely even more so, after he left his wife. *Now you think fair-minded old girl*, Ruby's conscience strictly told her. *Like every coin, there are two sides to every story and every life.* Despite her open-mindedness, she was rightly appalled that Jazz was lying in the ICU, in a coma, and her mother was making herself the victim in all of it. She should have anticipated this with more astuteness, before making the call. While on the phone, Ruby candidly realized that Jazz's mum had been justifiably and hysterically panic-stricken. For this reason, she'd decided to tell her only what she thought she could handle in the moment. Ruby's previous experiences with her daughter Eliza's mental illness enabled her to keep Eliza's offspring in perspective and guide the conversation in a safe and tolerable direction.

Once her granddaughter to stop screaming, "Will she die, will she die will she die?" Ruby went on to explain, as briefly as possible, what had happened. She didn't herself know many of the details yet, so keeping the explanation short was effortless.

To be fair to the child's mother, Ruby could tell that she'd intently listened through her loud sniffles and sobs. She did recognize the effort that the frightened, emotionally instable and shattered woman had made. Even so, soon thereafter, Zofia began to criticize Ruby again, accusing her of being incompetent with Jazz and of holding a grudge against her for what had happened with her ex-husband Tucker. She went on to accuse her old granny of hiding Tucker's affair from her; as if they shared some deep, dark, concealed secret. Ruby was rendered speechless when she heard this. She shook her white-haired head in disbelief. As her spectacles slipped off the tip of her nose, she lost her patience and completely erupted.

"Zofia, you sent your daughter to me! I didn't ask you to put a purple haired, nose pierced, tattooed, rebellious and defiant, teenage girl on airplane and fly her into my world! You did this! Not me!" The elderly woman knew that she'd lost all control. Rightfully so, she was livid and verbally venting. She had tried to remain reasonable and even-handed, but before she knew it, she was spewing her pent-up worry for Jazz all over the child's maternally liable, overwrought mother.

"Now you need to get your bloody shit together woman, hang up, and book a flight! If Thatcher has still there put him back on the goddam telephone! Right now!" she cursed and ordered.

She realized that she'd completely lost her restraint. With a heart beating faster than an 88-year-old heart should beat, she lowered her voice and appeased herself. Then she then switched gears like the 'gear-switching master' that she was and thanked the child's mother for listening to her.

"Please put Thatcher back on the phone," was the last thing she said.

Saying please to Zofia had nearly choked her. She couldn't remember the last time her blood had boiled as fast as it just did. She cleared her throat and took a few deep, pacifying breaths, and waited for Thatcher. Without delay, Ruby heard her slamming the telephone down and screaming for her son. Then, another odd stillness came through the receiver the old woman held in her now trembling hand. For the umpteenth time, her crude behaviour had shot her nerves down dead. Why the woman still needed all of the focus to be on herself was something Ruby couldn't even begin to comprehend. Nor did she have time to comprehend it. The patient needed her now.

The child's nutcase mother would have to stop acting like a victim, take responsibility for daughter, and deal with this emergency, Ruby thought. *Then she'd need to fly to England as soon as possible. There was only one victim in all of this, and it most definitely was not the neurotic, narcissistic, Mrs. Durant.*

A few moments later, Thatcher returned to the phone and spoke to Ruby in a composed, intellectual, and mature way. He apologized for his mother and asked few intelligent medical questions about his younger sister. Then he guaranteed Ruby that Zofia wouldn't be traveling to England alone.

Thatcher told her, "Jazz is a real scrapper. She'll pull though. I am not worried, because I know my little sister in ways no one else does."

Then, Ruby prayed, to a God that she only relied on for emergencies, that her great grandson had her innate knack for being right. She reasoned that Thatcher had probably stepped into the 'man of the house' role after his parent's divorce, or perhaps even years before they'd split. He was already ten years old when Jazz was born. She could tell after their short conversation that the boy she'd once known had grown to become a gifted problem solver and a level-headed communicator. In less than three minutes, she knew that he'd finished law school, completed his Practical Legal training, and passed the California State Bar exam just two weeks ago. He was currently taking his first summer off in six years. He went on to assure Ruby that either he, one of his three brothers, or his father Tucker, would travel with his mother. He would contact each of them and inform them of the situation in England. Ruby cringed when she heard Tucker's name mentioned. Imagining what kind of craziness would be entering her life soon if he showed up with Zofia was generating another one of her nasty migraines. Despite that she had very valid concerns and apprehensions, she wisely left it up to Thatcher to sort out the details. Then she gave him the name of Saint Matthew's Hospital, apologized for not knowing the exact street address, and told him that she needed to get back to Jazz. She didn't want to leave his sister alone any longer. Her great grandson then assured her that the Airport Information Centre at Heathrow would assist them once they arrived in London. Thatcher told her, not to fret, he would Google the hospital. He then asked her how she was, listened to her four-word answer, *I am doing fine*, and genuinely thanked her for everything she was doing for his little sister.

"Give Jazz a kiss from her favourite big brother," was the last thing he said.

Ruby smiled and promptly replied, "Consider it done dear boy."

Even though he didn't actually confirm it, she was convinced that Thatcher would be on the flight with his parents that she'd get on splendidly with him after they were reunited.

With Zofia still muddling up her brain, she asked herself, *how it was possible she distrusted Jazz's mother so deeply, yet could easily, put so much trust in Thatcher*. The logic behind her curiosity reminded her of what her father Horace had told her repeatedly years back, "Doubt is a disease that contaminates the mind, creating a mistrust of people's motives and one's own perceptions."

She'd forgotten what a wise man her father had once been. He was always quoting this or that to deepen the meaning of her life. Thinking about Horace made her realize how fortunate she was, at her ripe age, to have such a sharp memory; a memory that easily connected her to the past, enabling her to witness life, appreciate what it taught her, and be equally aware of life's dangers and rewards. Filled with the kind of sentience that came with old age and experience, she decided that she'd give Zofia a real chance after she arrived. The elderly woman would be more compassionate and patient with her granddaughter. Eliza would have wanted this for her now very adult child. Just as the cliché goes, she would 'kill her with kindnesses. Truth be told, she doubted whether this would make any difference because, despite that she was very old, she wasn't an idiot. Ruby sighed with relief as she hung up the phone. Wondering what the bloody hell Google was, she scurried off to her bedroom to pack an overnight bag. The wrath of Zofia Durant had kept her on the line longer than she'd anticipated and returning to the ICU was all she could think about now. For the time being, until the Durant's arrived, the child was still in her oldest living relative's crooked and capable hands. Which was, in the old Brit's shrewd opinion, the safest place for her to be.

Of this, she was certain. And Ruby McEwen was rarely wrong.

Chapter 33

The elderly woman's home was an efficient two-bedroom, studio apartment. Its pitched roof and elevated ceilings made it appear to be more spacious than it actually was. The studio had a modern styled kitchenette and a commodious bathroom that housed an original, 1920s claw footed bathtub. The tub was an inheritance gift Ruby received from her father after his parents died in 1955.

Four decades later, arthritis claimed her once youthful agility and prevented her from safely climbing in and out of the tub. Rather than allowing her age to prevent her from using something so meaningful, she made a bathtub planter out of it. What she loved the most about her now, 100-year-old plant-filled, indoor Victorian bathtub, was its quirky and colourful aesthetic flair. To this day, the tub continued to remind her of two spirited British McEwen generations and a tragedy gone by. Her cosy living space was located off the backside of her coastal property and had been built as an addition in the mid-1960s. It resembled the apartment she and Eliza had shared in the London for the first nine years of her daughter's life. In 1962, they traded in their concrete terrace in the city centre, for a sandy backyard beach that was just a stone's throw away from their front door. The shoreline was something she and Eliza had taken advantage of every day of every season. Since she paid the mortgage and the property taxes, she'd naturally built the largest bedroom for herself. It was that simple, she'd told the complaining, opinionated preteen who still lived with her back then.

Ruby was a disciplined mother. She believed in openly expressing affection, living by example, and the parental balance of power that existed between compliments and consequences. Therefore, from a young age, she taught her child to be appreciative for whatever was provided for her until she could choose her own path and pay her own way in life. When necessary, which was more often than not, she'd remind her daughter that once she was financially independent, she could quibble and squabble all she wanted to. This mind set of Ruby's was the source of countless confrontations between them before the girl eventually learned to tame her tongue, obey, and live by her mother's rules.

The studio's second bedroom had been empty since 1973, after Eliza graduated high school, left home and moved to Ireland to study Nursing at the University of Dublin. Despite that her mum had never expected her exceedingly wilful daughter to follow in even one of the footsteps she'd left behind, she did study at the same schools Ruby had attended in the '40s and '50s. Neither of them considered the other one to be a friend, which was something they both attributed to the brazen 'sweet and sour' type of bond they'd always shared. For too many years to count, Eliza's vacant bedroom had been serving its purpose as an office and convenient, in-home storage space for Ruby's possessions. A few days before Jazz was expected to arrive, per his employer's explicit instructions, Nico had taken all of her boxed up files and other non-essentials outside to the storage annex. She then tidied up the bedroom and prepared it for the next teenager who needed a place to sleep. That was three weeks ago.

Filled with curiosity, Ruby opened the bedroom door to have a quick peek at where, since her arrival, Jazz Durant had been spending so much time alone, sleeping, or listening to ridiculously loud music. Until this moment, she hadn't had any desire to open the door, nor disrupt the petite troublemaker's privacy. For the old woman, privacy was high on her list of things to be respected and not invaded, which made giving it to the child a completely natural gesture. However, when two boats collided, landing the youngest member of her family in a coma and rendering Nico, her employee, *God knows what*, her opinion about privacy instantly changed.

In lieu of the fact that the police reported their discovery of drugs at the scene of the accident, her intuition knew that before detectives arrived to search her property, she needed to see what Jazz had been up to behind closed doors this past week. She was ruffled and apprehensive. Little by little and inch by inch, she opened the timeworn, creaking bedroom door.

Unanticipated beads of perspiration overcame her and tickled at her upper lip. Her armpits quickly smelled like grilled onions. The nervousness and sweat-filled body odour were both recognizable and instant confirmations of her deep-seated fears and vulnerability. Unsure of what she would find was downright frightening her. For such a, 'normally in control of any situation' type of person, feeling the metal doorknob clutched in her hand, had put her seriously on edge. After the kind of day it had been, her already frazzled nerves couldn't take much more. It took her a few moments before she'd actually mustered up the guts to enter Jazz's room. Once she did, she was utterly flabbergasted. What she saw, was a spare bedroom that was astonishingly neat and orderly. Aside from a few bath towels that had been left dangling off a chair next to Eliza's old school desk, the room was extremely clean and tidy.

"Undeniably neater than when my own teenager still lived at home," she heard herself say. "And even more ship shape than when I used the room for my weekly clerical tasks."

How the space was being so crisply cared for had her immediately questioning, how she could have so visibly misread Jazz? She concluded that someone certainly, in this way, had raised the child appropriately. Never could she have ever imagined that a girl with such a shoddy, peculiar clothing style, reckless behaviour, and slapdash appearance, could be so rightly spit spot orderly. The child had proven Ruby's intuition profoundly wrong, which was something that seldom happened.

"Well, I'll be bloody goddamned!" she heard herself declare.

Regardless of her age, she cursed loudly, and she cursed regularly.

Jazz had travelled to England with only a large backpack, her camera bag, and a standard sized, check-in suitcase. When she entered the old woman's life for the first time in fourteen years, Ruby had no idea what the child had brought with her. Nor, after the shocking debut Jazz had executed since then, did she give a freaking twaddle! Before opening the door, she'd rightly predicted that the bedroom would be a reflection of its occupant; a massive state of disarray with the contents of her belongings scattered everywhere. Like most teenage girls' bedroom's, she anticipated to see heaps of clothes, her most beloved possessions, and strewn makeup cluttering up the space. She'd suspected that the room would be messy and muddled, similar to her great granddaughter's outward style and behaviour. What Ruby was now looking at had proven her stereotypical expectations more than wrong. Given that she'd always accepted her proven ability to read a person and properly gauge them, as being true, she was now, in an atypical way, literally stupefied. She leaned against the doorframe as her searching eyes began skimming the room.

Jazz was using Ruby's oversized, rectangular bulletin board, in the centre of the room's largest wall, as a sort of visual focal point. She'd graphically framed the bulletin board in, by what appeared to be at least one hundred photographs. There were more images than she could count. She was tempted but given that her the taxi would be returning shortly, there was no time for more dilly-dallying or counting pictures. Unaware she was doing so, she moved closer to the wall to have a better look. The collage was classy and diverse. It displayed many different sized, unframed, black and white images. Jazz had signed each of them in a flamboyant way, leaving the viewer with the impression that she was abstract by nature and intimately fulfilled by her photographs. The black and whites caught her eye straightaway. They were defined, inventive, and sharp. They formed the outermost section of an artistic photo-frame that the child had created with them. Assortments of her coloured images formed the innermost section of the collage. They too, had each been signed, *Jazz*. She'd mounted the snapshots in a two-dimensional fashion, using a high and broad, four-sided shape. They extended off each side, past the borders of the bulletin board, and ended just below the ceiling and above the floors moulding. The teenager's talent had given the bedroom an impressive, dramatical, and imaginative flare. The elderly woman had never before seen such a wall décor style as this one was. She was surprised, charmed, and impressed by the teenager's young talent and motivation.

Ruby stepped towards the wall and moved in closer to examine one small piece of white paper that had caught her eye. The paper was the size of a business card and it hung in the centre of the bulletin board. Overshadowed by the photographic images and layout design, initially it hadn't caught her attention. Printed on it were four modish letters that spelled, 'EfiL'. Puzzled by the word, she assumed that it stood for the name of a symbolic place, or person that meant something to Jazz. Having no brain energy left for solving riddles, she made a mental note to *ask about it after the child had exited her coma and Ruby had a chance to explain why she'd gone into her private domain.*

She concluded that Jazz had a profound eye for photography, graphic arts, and layout. She also had an obvious hunger for capturing what she witnessed through her camera's lens. Ruby was positive that the child was hands down delighted with her work, otherwise she wouldn't have signed each photo, travelled across the globe with so many of them, and then created such a dazzling display. She thought it to be somewhat unusual that she hadn't seen Jazz taking any photographs since she'd arrive on this side of their related world. Europe was vastly captivating and different from the relatively young country of America. As a result, for centuries, it had globally attracted photographers and artists from to its shores and borders with ease. As the she turned to scan the room for any potentially damaging evidence connected to the accident, she saw a dark brown polyester camera bag on the bed. It was opened and empty.

Realizing this had her making yet another mental note *to ask the police if Jazz's camera had been found at the accident scene.* Maybe undeveloped film in her camera, if there was any, could provide clues as to what had transpired while she was with Nico.

After seeing the child's creation and talent, she was certain she'd want to use her camera again, after she woke up and left her coma behind. Considering what to do with the camera bag reminded Ruby that she needed to hurry up and pack her overnight bag. She didn't need to look at any clock to know that the cabdriver would be returning at any minute. She took one last admiring glance at the wall-art. She was tempted to close her eyes and let her hands randomly choose a few of the child's photos so she could bring them to the ICU. Despite her well-intended impulse, given that she held the privacy of others in very high regard, she chose not to disturb Jazz's inventiveness. With this mindset, she humbly closed the door and switched directions. Scurrying as fast as her aged, aching body could, she dashed off towards her own bedroom and proceeded to pack her canvas bag. After selecting two outfits and before zipping the bag shut, she added a few bathroom items and a journal she'd been intending to read for months, but still hadn't gotten around to doing.

In the fifty-nine years Ruby had been running her diner, she'd existed alongside a jillion intriguing transformations of how people lived life. She'd learned an immeasurable amount about, and from, the limitless number of stories her customers had shared with her. How they had travelled, lived, loved, and how they'd survived illness, deaths of loved ones, and life in general. As they sprinted their way through the twentieth century, her regular customers had learned to let go of the serious side of their lives and unwind at The Seaside. Before the escalation of enormously large gasoline stations and faceless coffee chains, hungry locals and tourists alike, relied on old-style eating-places like hers to replenish themselves. It didn't matter whether they were on long a journey, lived around the corner or down the block, her customers were as loyal to her as she was to them. She owned one of Britain's last remaining post-WWII seaside cafes. It was a unique place where locals and tourists still could dine on simple, straightforward meals, while spending less than six pounds. For Ruby, being the owner of a diner was never about turning a profit, it was about paying her way through life and pleasing people; something she'd built her character foundation on while under her grandmother, Bessie Dutton's, progressive and protective female wings.

Ruby still hadn't heard the taxi's horn. Although ninety minutes hadn't passed yet, she was growing restless and was eager to get back to the child. She straightened the bright yellow cardboard sign on the window and shut off the ceiling lights before dead bolting the door behind her. Even though The

Seaside had been broken into twice since she'd bought it, she'd never installed an expensive modern alarm system. Nor had she bought a Doberman or Rottweiler, as many people had advised her to do. She refused to live in fear. She'd believed, her entire life, that 'if you don't have too much of anything, then you have little to lose'. Furthermore, she refused to have a barking, smelly, drooling watchdog, stinking up her sweet life.

The breakfast bacon that was fried every morning was more than enough stink for her to cope with, she recalled with a grin. Since she was a child, growing up in Essex County, she'd detested the smell of bacon and loathed the taste of eggs. These were two things, as the five-decade long owner of a popular diner that she wisely kept hidden from her customers. Standing outside on the curb, surrounded by cool night air and waiting for her ride, she noticed that the diner's metallic retro sign, which loomed overhead, was rusted out something dreadful. Despite that the corroding, colourful sign added a twinge of authenticity to The Seaside's vintage ambiance, it now made the exterior of the diner look run down, scruffy, and grungy. Three things she absolutely would not tolerate.

I'll need to have Nico restore it next week. He is handy with fixing things, she scatteredly thought.

Breaking the night-time silence, she heard the taxi pulling up to the curb. She turned to see the driver waving politely at her. With Nico now on her mind, she dismissed the driver's offer to help her and slid, unassisted this time, into the back seat.

"Drive slowly, if you would," she said to the taxi chauffer. "I am a getting older and have spine pain. Every little bump hurts."

The cabbie winked in his rearview mirror at her humour. As he pulled the cab onto the main road, thoughts of three men she cared about, Jackson, Horace, and Nico, mingled together and swirled through her wary mind. With her overnight bag now on her lap and the cab's window still open, Ruby leaned back, closed her eyes, and relaxed. She was looking forward to spending the night at the ICU with the child and hoped for at least six hours of deep, uninterrupted sleep. Tomorrow, she needed to wake up alert and prepared for anything and everything. Tomorrow, her search for Nico and his family would begin. Tomorrow, an emotional female tornado would be arriving from America. With the thought of Zofia's impending arrival in London, she reopened her eyes, rested her elbow slightly on the door's armrest, and stared out the window. Gazing at the night sky above, she hoped that she had enough stamina left in her to survive Eliza's problematic daughter after nearly fifteen years.

A bright, auburn coloured moon stared back at her through contoured remnants of lingering clouds. Tepidly, the weary, age-spotted woman looked up at the heavens, made the sign of the cross, and pleaded with a God she still wasn't sure she believed. "Sweet Jesus, I need your help."

Chapter 34

For as refreshing as the crisp air blowing back in Ruby's face through the cab's window was, it was just as exasperating. Since she was a girl, she hated the feeling of hair tickling her face. For all the challenges in life, which she'd learned to handle or ignore, she'd never quite been able to get this one particular peeve under control. On the flipside, because of the cool evening air, even though her wacked mind was lost and spinning, within a few minutes she felt very alert. The eccentric and elderly Brit was revived and ready for a new venture.

Much too much had happened in the past twelve hours and her quandary was simple; she was too overwhelmed to be able to just sit back, relax, and enjoy the convenience of a comfortable taxi with a dashingly handsome driver. Her predicament was terribly irritating. Before she could strike up a proper British exchange, the cab came to an abrupt, rather startling halt.

"Sorry luv," the cabbie said with an apologetic tone. "It seems we've encountered a traffic jam."

Their faces were now a glowing shade of red from the reflections of the brake lights deflecting off the car that had stopped less than a meter in front of them. She could see that it was obvious they were stuck in traffic behind a seemingly endless row of other most likely, equally annoyed automobilists.

After all, she thought, *the entire world knew how much proper Brits shunned being tardy or inconvenienced.*

"The flashing lights ahead in the distance most likely mean a rather long delay," the cabdriver delicately said, "again, my apologies, madam. Obviously, we are at the scene of an accident. I will do my best to find a shorter route to the hospital."

Deniz the cabbie fiddled with his TomTom then tolerantly sat back waiting to see if his navigation system would reroute them. Being her typical accepting self, Ruby told him not to fret over it. Besides, it had been a boomeranging day. She was exhausted and had no vigour for stressing over something she couldn't change. She asked him if he had a mobile telephone that she could borrow. As one would expect, he did. Then, using all her charms, she put him to work for her. Before he knew it, the cabdriver had Googled the ICU nurses station of Saint Matthew's Hospital in downtown London. Hearing the phone being answered, he immediately handed his cell phone back to her. The elderly woman inquired about Jazz, gave the nurse an update about the traffic situation, and assured her she would be returning as soon as she could. She was on her way. She then handed Deniz his phone, thanked him properly, and went silent. Out of respect for her situation, the cabdriver remained as quiet as she was. After less than a minute, the peppy passenger in the backseat broke the silence. In that moment, her anxiousness was stouter than her feebleness.

"I brought a book with me," she revealed.

Then she asked if she could turn the ceiling light on and read a few pages. "Or will the light be a bother you while you are driving?"

She had impressed herself with her uncharacteristically, end of a long stressful day, politeness.

Smiling in the mirror at her jauntiness, he impishly answered, "Neither the light, nor you dear madam, are a nuisance to me."

"Read away," he reassured her with an approving nod. . "Read aloud if you'd prefer to madam. I myself am a great fan of a decent story and would appreciate the distraction from this traffic delay," he added.

"Brilliant!" she excitedly said.

Ruby had always loved reading stories from books to Eliza, Sadie, and even to Jazz, when they all were little girls. Reading to the child earlier this afternoon, from one of the journals she'd stored in the ornate wooden trunk, had re-lit a long since extinguished spark in her. She desired reading more about Bessie Dutton, her African American and ex-slave grandmother. Promptly she turned on a small, double-bulb light above her hear. Almost in unison, the driver switched on his somewhat brighter overhead to give her even more light to read by. With appreciation, she teasingly gave him a forehead salute.

Back at the diner her mind had been filled with unanswered questions and forgotten answers. She'd just ambled through her past, whilst reminiscing about being in Montana with Horace and Jackson during her grandmother's funeral and burial. She had summoned up deep-rooted memories of the elaborate storytellers that both Jackson and Horace once were. Each man had his own versions of their time with her back then, and likewise with each other. The old woman was now eager to learn more about what life was like in the United States before she was born. This time she'd be hearing it straight from Bessie herself, as she read one of her grandma's most primitive renditions that she'd written in one of her earliest, and now, oldest journals. She knew Bessie had lived a turbulent life in America, and that at different times the country was a perilous place to reside in because its government was radically changing. Bessie had survived a ninety-year lifespan. Throughout it, she'd astutely recorded as much as she could for the sake of her 'yet to be born' ancestors. Bessie Dutton had been Ruby's unshakable, female inspiration. She was eager to share a bit of her long since deceased grandmother's life with the cabbie named Deniz.

Two creasy and crooked fingers reached into her canvas bag and took out the journal she'd taken off her bedroom dresser after packing her overnight bag. Elated with her decision to bring it along, she proceeded to grapple with untangling a sand-coloured piece of twine with two woven leather crosses attached to it. The twine had been diagonally snarled around the journals rawhide cover. She removed the cord with the knotted crosses and put them on the empty seat next to her. Then, she bid a silent reverence to Jackson for telling her about the protective symbols that Bessie had once hung around the necks of her gallant sons. After she buried her two oldest boys, she used the lariats she'd made them to bind and protect perhaps her most private journal. Unexpectedly, Ruby endearingly thought about Shep, who had passed away six years after Bessie died. His death didn't sadden her at the time; it was rather expected, given that he wasn't much younger than Bessie had been at when she passed on. Believing death to be a natural follower of life, she'd never grappled with it.

Annoyed by the mosquitoes buzzing around the cab's overhead lights, she closed the rear window, cleared her throat, blew her nose, and adjusted her little round spectacles. Seeing her prepping herself from the view in his mirror, Deniz rightly anticipated being privy to an interesting tale. With a wide-awake, cheery tone, his elderly passenger began to read.

- By the time 1888 arrived, I was one of the nearly eighteen hundred African Americans who were living in the Territory of Montana. I guessed that roughly thirty-five to forty percent of us were women. This is a presumption because I was never good with numbers. Most homesteading settlers put down their roots in places called Helena, Butte, or Great Falls. I am just one of a lesser group of people. I am fine with admitting to being a homesteader that laid a claim and settled in the Great Plains area of America. Homesteading is tough work and a hard life for me. I am a single woman of color. Homesteading is the only real chance I have to become independent. Being free is important because the first fourteen years of my life, I was nothing more than a piece of plantation property. A rich military man with two surnames bought me when I was a three-year old child. I never owned anything of my own until I became a homesteader. Now I own myself and I own a plot of land. For the first time in my life, I have liberty.

- This new freedom scares me one day and thrills me on the next day. I still look over my shoulder many times in the days and nights. I am sometimes afraid that I am being followed by a master or mistress planning to do me harm. I still fear that a mean dog with sharp teeth and bloody slobber dripping out his mouth will bite me, or another poor Negro that be slower than I am. Being free is new to me. I only feel free when I look at the written record of my land claim. Only my name is on this official paper because I am a not married Negro woman. Samuel Dutton and I have been keeping our loving each other a secret. Just like his brother Jacob and my sister Minnie used to do. His pappy, the US military, General Ballinger, and slave owner, who is an old man by now, is likely having regrets for throwing his last alive son off the family plantation.

- My Samuel is strong and brave, but still fearful of his powerful father. This is why he stopped using his Ballinger plantation family name a long time ago.

228

Samuel expects that his pappy, the General, is still having him tracked and hunted and one day he will find him and force him back home. Samuel talks about these kinds of troubles in his sleep. His pappy is a ruthless and bad man. My Samuel tells me the General be like a bloodhound without a bone. He won't stop chasing down what he wants, 'til he finds it, then sinks his greedy teeth in it. The General don't care if he is pursuing a nigger girl or his own people. To a selfish man like him, we both be nothing more than his property. I am a legally freed woman living in a time when social customs and ethics make it hard for a woman to be independent. My ability to read and write is something of a strong advantage for me. I have my darling passed on sister Minnie and her soldier love Jacob B. Dutton to thank for such skills. I never will be able to express myself in a proper way with fancy words, but I get by just fine. I am educated enough to know what I am reading and writing. Because of these skills, being limited as they might appear to be, there isn't no ill-minded man that can pull the wool over my alert Negro eyes. I am always watching out and ready for danger and discrimination. Discrimination is a big word with a big meaning that Samuel is teaching me to use and to protect myself from.

-I am one of a small handful of unmarried women that I know of in these parts who took the opportunity the Homestead Act offered us. I filed an estate claim last year and so far, I am doing real well for Samuel and me. Once we are legally united, in the eyes of God the Almighty, I will add his name to our claim. Samuel needs this because he is a man of pride and honor with a deep religious background. I hope in the years still to come, that my being a Negro woman who owns property means I can give my skills and time, in a generous way, to the community where I am settling down in. I am not yet sure what this will be, but I am still young and determined, so someday I will know. I have good ideas in my head because I am free.

- Bessie Dutton 1889 -

Absorbed in thought, Ruby stopped reading, rested her head on the back of her seat, and took a couple of deep revitalizing breaths. While the cabdriver had intensely listened to what his elderly customer read, a nagging question had been on the tip of his curious tongue. It was pestering him and demanding a quick answer. He was too intrigued to stay patient long enough for her to start reading again before asking her something.

"Madam, did you know this Negro slave girl, Bessie?" Deniz blurted out.

229

Letting out a loud, exasperating sigh, she harshly snapped back at him, "Bloody hell man! Don't interrupt me!"

Startled by her short temper, he swiftly shut his unintentionally interfering mouth. She was right, he was too impulsive at times. Although she'd finished the passage from the journal, and to some extent appreciated his intrusive mind's prying into her past, the old Brit detested being interrupted by anyone for any reason.

Scolding him, she said, "Now that you've so rudely stolen my concentration I will stop reading for a spell and tell you about Bessie Dutton."

The cabdriver wanted to apologize to her, but this would require interrupting her again and he wasn't a stupid man. Therefore, befittingly, he held his tongue.

"You already have deduced that the woman in the story I just read was once a slave. What you couldn't know, is that she was my African American grandmother. She spent more time with me when I was a child than I did with my own mother."

Ruby caught a glimpse of Deniz's amazed reaction in his rearview mirror. He could see she had a tinted skin tone, but never could have imagined she had an African bloodline.

Her thick British accent certainly overshadowed the Negro lineage in her, he thought but didn't say. The befuddled look on his face instantly pumped new enthusiasm into the stipple skinned elderly woman. She carefully closed Bessie's journal and set it on the seat next to her.

"Now, keep holding your tongue man and just listen!" she glibly demanded.

Gazing down at the Dutton boys protective twine crosses intertwined between her fingers, she began to tell the cabdriver about an America ranch with a legacy embedded deeply in its glacier tilled, clay-rich soil.

Chapter 35

"As you already know, my grandmother Bessie was a slave. She was one of but a handful of unmarried Negro women who successfully staked claim to a plot of land in Montana. She did this by means of President Lincoln's original Homestead Act of 1862. One of the first entries in her journal, which is one of the oldest journals handed down to me, was about the childhood memories of her slave plantation life. She wrote it later in life after she was older and more educated. It is a partial recollection of her youth. Would you like it if I read another excerpt of what she wrote?" Ruby asked the cab driver. "I think it would help you, like it helped me, to understand more about what life for a slave girl was like." She concluded without waiting for his reply.

"Yes, madam, please do," he said, history and people of any kind interest me."

Hearing this, the eager to please side of Ruby's personality thought, *we are going to get along just fine.*

Without hesitation, she picked Bessie's journal back up and started reading from where she'd left off.

Bessie
— 1860 to 1875 —

— My sister Minnie used to tell me that I was perhaps one of a very small number of slave children who was mostly happy in spite of the horrors and cruelties of life around me. My own memories of untroubled childhood days on the plantation, with my little white and black companions still can stir inside me. The great Civil War was raging, which was why neither master nor mistress nor neighbour had time to bestow as much as even a passing thought on me or the other slave kids. For this, we were considered all to be blessed little Negros. The Civil War, that great event in the American history, was something that occurred outside the realm of our young childish interests. Of course, we heard the elders discuss the battles and various events of the great struggle, but it all meant nothing to us. We were just kids being kids.

— On the plantation there were fourteen of us. Ten of us were black nigger children and four of us were white skinned children. Our days were spent roaming about the plantation not knowing or caring what things were going on in the big

world outside the spaces of our young lives. I remember planting and harvest time being the most joyful days for us.

~ Time and again after a harvest the planters would discover cornstalks missing from the ends of the crop rows. They'd blame the crows for the missing corn, calling them slick black thieves. The planters called us little fairy crooks. Whenever our bellies grumbled with the hunger, we stole sweet potatoes, peanuts, and sugar cane. We helped ourselves to mostly anything and became really good at not being caught. We were small and fast and unafraid.

~ The slaves that were not married served the food from the great big house. Once a day, they would send older slave children to bring the food to the workers in the fields. The white kids got educated when we went to the fields. Being a naughty kind of slave child, I followed along behind the older kids. Before we got to the fields, we ate the workers food nearly all up. When the workers returned home, they complained to the housemaster, and we were whipped. I was little so I was not whipped too badly. Just enough to leave plenty of sting on my skin so I would be awake all night in my bed thinking I was no better than the stupid black crows were. Older kids were whipped harder and longer.

~ On Mondays at the time of sunset, the slaves got their allowance of molasses, meat, corn meal, and a kind of flour called dredging's or shorts. Some weeks this allowance would be gone before the next Monday night, in which case the slaves would steal hogs, or eggs and a chicken or two from the master's pens. When they were caught, we'd all be dragged away from whatever we were doing to gather at the whipping–post. Master himself never whipped his slaves. This was left to the overseer. I remember hunger as being a terrible thing. It made slaves do things they might not otherwise do if their bellies were full and their babies didn't cry from the lack of food.

~ We children had no supper cause we didn't work to earn food. We were given only a little piece of bread or a dumpling in the morning. Our dishes consisted of one small wooden bowl and one oyster shell or piece of dried round tree bark we used as our spoons. This one bowl served all ten of us black children. The dogs, the ducks, and the chickens usually licked or pecked at our bowl. We swatted them *away very careful like because we were afraid of them biting us. We learned really fast that hungry ducks and angry chickens can bite as bad as a dog can.*

~ Sometimes we had buttermilk and bread in our food bowl. Other times, we got greens or bones. I learned fast that if I suckled on a bone long enough it started tasting good. Better a bone than nothing between your teeth, the mammies would tell us. I had to be really careful that the dogs didn't sniff the bone out while it was between my teeth. Sometimes a few children had got their faces all bit up fighting over a bone with a starving dog. I needed my face, so I learned early on to stop sucking on bones and just go hungry.

Feeling the need to speak and finish what she'd started, Ruby closed the journal and began to talk. The cabbie remained all ears. He turned around in his seat so he could look into her eyes and give his thought-provoking fare the attention she deserved.

"When my grandma Bessie turned eighteen and became a legal citizen she married, with God as their witness, my grandpa Samuel Dutton. Samuel was, as you already know, a white man who had renounced his birth name, Ballinger, in an effort to find anonymity for himself and safety for his Negro partner Bessie. After a number of years passed, they eventually came to own 650 acres of undeveloped land between the northwest border of Montana and the southeast border of Nebraska. Folks called them 'corner people' because of the location of their property. It took me year of geography lessons before I finally grasped why my African and American relatives were given this nickname."

Caught in a sweet memory, Ruby began to giggle. She had an infectious kind of giggle, which made others want to join in and laugh along, even if they didn't know what was amusing her at the time. Despite this, Deniz deliberately kept a straight, unreadable expression on his face. He'd just learned that she could sum up a man with ease, and now that he was facing her, he rightly knew that he didn't stand a chance. He felt slightly indebted to this fascinating customer of his in the back seat. She had an ability to keep him composed and entertained while they were stuck in traffic. For as much as she hated being interrupted, he equally hated traffic jams.

Given my livelihood, I despise traffic probably more than anything else in life, he concluded, just as he heard an elderly, eloquent voice starting to speak again.

"My grandparent's original homestead, which became a productive and reputed ranch, is where I spent a lot of time while growing up. I am an only child, so their ranch played a major role in giving me structure and teaching me about the practicalities and fundamentals of life. I called it a farmstead because it wasn't just a ranch with horses and livestock; it was also a fully sustainable farm that provided nutrition for its inhabitants and its animals. The Great Plains is the place where I grew up for six weeks at a time. It was the place where I learned about life in an indescribable way. Throughout the summer months, the plains offered me a no-restrictions type of life. It was a life without the confines of my parent's stuffy and complicated British world. I learned things in that American state that shaped me, taught me about bravery, and provided me with a purpose. At the time, I was still too young to spell the word purpose, let alone identify with what it meant. People used to tell me that I was an ambitious and active child. A child whose feet never stopped moving long enough to leave footprints on the ground."

She stopped speaking and sighed deeply.

"What a wonderful way to be remembered!" An eager, deep voice said from the front seat. Deniz flinched as soon as he realized his dumb mistake.

Ignoring his interruption, Ruby carried on telling her story with a pardoning type of expression.

"Even though I was still too green and naïve, back in those days, to comprehend exactly how such a tragedy as The Great Depression would become perhaps the worst economic downturn in the history of the industrialized world, even as a child I did my part. I still have surplus memories of those years and how their intricate effects were influencing and changing America. The 'Great and Depressed America' that I grew up in, part-time, was viewed through the juvenile eyes of my age. For this reason, for me, it was a memorable time; a time like no other time before it on the Great Plains. For many other folks, the era of the Great Depression was too demanding and extremely destructive. Between August of 1929 and March of 1933, the outlooks that millions of people had on life were forever changed. Folks, who previously embraced change and opportunity with hope and confidence, became vindictive and disenchanted. After beginning in the United States, the depression eventually took a global turn. People became apprehensive and suspicious of the impending economical events of strangers, and of neighbours alike. Despair spread among the masses. Like a virus, it killed their faith in their dreams. Like millions of others, my relatives and the farmsteads migrant workers all had it tough. Nonetheless, in contrast, we were also left with more than a few fond recollections of that difficult time."

The old woman could visibly see the puzzled, canvassing look on the cabbie's charismatic and curious face.

"Let me try to explain."

"You need to understand that people living on, and working at, my grandparent's homestead influenced each other and were treated as equals. I used to call them my 'summer earth people'. They lived off the land, therefore, they had no jobs or substantial income to lose when the Great Depression began. Their families and my relatives actually grew closer. Especially, those of them who'd survived the previous drought and deadly influenza epidemic. After the Great Depression, tens of thousands of families fled from the Great Plains. I remember the summers when most of my little farmstead friends and their parents had either died or moved away. I got used to not knowing who would be there when I returned the following year. I learned to appreciate those who were still there to greet me and not to pine after those who were gone when I arrived. Despite the hardships, my grandma Bessie was an amazing visionary. I never knew how she managed it, but despite the circumstances, she kept smiles on our faces and a glimmer of hope in our spirits. Day in and night out, she did so much with so little."

After a minute or two of silence, the cabbie asked, "Can you tell me more madam?"

This was all Ruby needed to hear. Like her pa Horace, and Shep, the Dutton Ranch's supervisor, she was a natural-born storyteller.

"In 1918, before I entered this world, my grandmother Bessie and her foreman Jackson buried three migrant workers and one baby. They had died from a contagious viral infection. Their lifeless bodies were separately enclosed in four thick, durable, sealed grain sacks. Then they were lowered into a group grave. The burial plot was a safe distance from the property, including numerous gorges and moat channels that supplied the homestead with drinking water. Since that day, whenever the news of viral outbreaks reached the ranch, my grandma, being the protector of her ranch family, laid down non-negotiable, strict travel restrictions. To avoid the spread of disease, she enforced the importance of impeccable hygiene. As a precaution, she had men with rifles guarding the perimeters of the homestead's vast acreage. Potential disease carriers were not allowed to travel through, or even step one foot onto her land. Drinking from the creek was also forbidden. The creek water was the main drinking source for the workers. To keep us all safe and healthy, regardless of race, creed, colour, or status, Bessie had everyone drinking the same water, from the same unpolluted wells. Access to the creek was forbidden after she saw dead bodies floating in it from upstream. A makeshift chapel was set up in one of the barns so she and the ranch folks could worship, if they chose to, without sitting in the midst of a germ-infested congregation. The risk was too high to join the group of devout worshipers who prayed on Sunday only to fall down dead by Friday. Grandma Bessie used to say, folks across the plains were dropping dead like flies that landed, and stayed too long, on hot windowsills in the middle of a heat wave."

Ruby stopped talking for a few minutes to catch her breath. Deniz passed her an unopened bottle of cold water and roused her to tell him more. She thanked him with another wink, took a long drink, and continued with her story.

"Daily, my grandma Bessie meticulously delegated the workload, regardless of how big or small it was. She and her right-hand man, Jackson Boy Shepherd, I've already mentioned him, ran the place, side by side and year-round. They did this in any capacity needed and at any time needed. Migrant labourer's children also had age appropriate, explicit chores to do each day. Whenever I stayed at the farmstead I was included as one of them. Depending on our age and the chore, a workday started with the rooster's cock-a-doodle-doos, and ended three times each day; initially with the clanging of the lunch and dinner bell and then again at sunset. The weather influenced every aspect of life on an American farmstead the 1930s and 1940s. A homesteader's garden is what kept country folks and entire families fed."

For a few fleeting moments Ruby paused to catch her breath and drink a bit more water before continuing. Deniz turned back around in his seat, stretched his stiff neck out, and then made eye contact with her again. The elderly woman placed her elbow on the back of the cabbie's seat, cupped her chin in her left hand, focused her gaze on his image in the mirror, and picked up where she'd left off.

"Long before and long after the outbreak of the virus, each year I was thrilled to be included in the circle of children who worked alongside the adults. Our everyday tasks took precedence over playing, education, or squandering our time in the wide, cool creek that ran straight through the property. Chores and duties were superior to swimming or fishing. Children caught being lazy or playing in the creek before their chores were finished were paddled straightaway on their bare bums. This happened to me once. Grandma Bessie bent me over her knee and told me, just before I felt the first wham of the paddle, that *during* the summer months I would to be treated like any other child on the ranch who broke the rules," she tittered at the memory.

"You see, a reprimanding paddle that smacked a wet bottom, versus a dry bottom, hurt twofold over and was more than enough to keep children out of the creek until their work was done. Truth be told, there was more merriment than reprimands during the summertime. Some of the ranch hands let me help them with the daily milking of cows and tending to the chickens. I became attached to any animal of any kind when I was a child. I also grew to learn how to ride, groom, and respect the horses. Partaking in monthly cattle drives was forbidden, no matter how skilled I became with a horse."

She took another drink of cold water, then she ran her hands through her snow-white hair and fluffed up her bangs. Despite that she wasn't out in public and was still shrouded in the reddish glow of the brake lights of a car stuck in traffic in front of the cab; she primped her hair for no other reason than it was a meaningless habit she'd yet to break.

"Have you ever ridden a horse?" Ruby asked, taking her attentive listener by surprise.

The cabbie was starting to delight in how this interesting woman's brain sporadically ricocheted from the past to the present and then back to the past again.

"Yes, madam I have, only one time. I fell off and broke both my arms. My parents sold the horse the next day. Then they bought me a brand-new, symbolic bicycle, on the very day the doctor removed my casts. So, as you perhaps can easily fathom that I avoid horses," Deniz confessed.

Ruby smiled at him in an appreciative way.

At least he tried, she thought, before sneezing twice, leaning back into the headrest, and closing her eyes. Gently caressing the Dutton brothers twine crosses that were still in her hands, she continued with her tale.

"During the plentiful years on the homestead, after I'd reached the age of eight or nine, new breeds of skilled migrant workers were tending to the rooting, harvesting, and grinding of the wheat grain. The migrant women mostly cared for the children, the vegetable gardens, and the ranch's massive potato fields. I remember how we kids learned to make our chores more like a game than work. We'd make music with our gardening tools, and then do a lot of singing and dancing to the beat of whatever rhythm we'd create. Some of us even tried to learn and tell jokes. Most of us failed at being funny, agreeing that adults were better at telling jokes than kids were. I could be seen in two places all summer long. I was either working in the gardens alongside the mothers of my refugee friends, or wearing an apron and doing my part in Bessie's kitchen. My time in Montana with my ranch family gave me a solid foundation to stand and mature upon. My grandma saw to this. She alleged that, 'youngsters only grew up to be strong, motivated, and smart adults by playing hard and by working harder'. She also alleged that 'by reading, praying, observing life, obeying their elders, and appreciating the privilege of an education, children would one day contribute to society from their minds and hearts'. I latched onto all of this, excluding the praying part. Despite this, being on the ranch is where I learned that hard work and diligence were the foundations of life."

The taxi cabdriver waited a few minutes to be certain his customer had finished talking, before asking her another question.

"Madam, did your parents travel with you to Montana? I can't imagine a young girl could make the journey on her own back in those times."

"Very smart of you sir," Ruby replied with an impressed tone.

"Each summer, my father, Horace, remained in England to work. It was my mother's responsibility to travel with me. Sadie was her name. She and my grandmother weren't on speaking terms. So, after we made our way to the States and then the ranch, Sadie would drop me off at the front porch steps before driving off and leaving me behind in a plume of petrol exhaust. She never even got out of the car to kiss me goodbye or greet anyone at the ranch. I was just a kid, so it wasn't until years later that I realized how strange this routine of hers was. Folks used to say that she'd always had a knack for acting selfishly in this way. Once I grew old enough to understand matters of a cheating lady's heart, I suspected that she had a secret lover somewhere, since she'd disappear for weeks at a time. Back then, there were too many secrets in my family."

"Madam is there anything in particular from your past that you still have questions about, or suspect may have happened all those years ago in Montana?" The cabbie openly asked. He felt at ease asking random questions, because this doddering woman, in his opinion, was one of the most 'open-book types' he'd ever met.

"Yes, there is," she quickly said.

This cabdriver asks intriguing questions, she silently thought, as if she'd just read his thoughts.

"Years later, after traces and facts of the Great Depression had gone on to live in the history books, I learned something rightly thought-provoking about that era of misery. It was said that the anticipated poverty and malnutrition of the times would take a mortal toll on the country of America as a whole. When, in fact, during the Great Depression, mortality rates actually fell. I never could quite believe this, especially when I would ride one of the ranch's horses past the gravesite of those poor dead migrant workers and that little baby, whose bodies remained under the ground in four durably sealed, grain sack coffins."

Her voice, now barely audible, was fading off towards some distant place. Deniz, having taken a great interest in American History as a student, looked eagerly in his mirror and opened his mouth. He was ready to share his educated version of why mortality rates actually fell during the Great Depression with the insightful person sitting behind him.

Before he could utter even one remotely intelligent word, he saw that the elderly woman in the back seat had fallen asleep.

Chapter 36

For just under an hour, the cabbie observantly listened while Ruby read and shared her memories. In an effort to respect her age and need for a catnap, he reached up and shut the cab's overhead light off. Stretching himself backwards, he proceeded to also shut off the double bulbed light above his passenger's head.

Darkness and silence draped themselves over the cab in a hospitable and calming way. Deniz's mind was spinning with thoughts of what he'd just heard, and learned, from the old half African-American, half British woman in the back seat, who had started to snore. He was quite certain she had a similar mind spinning effect on most of the people who crossed her path. He was taken back by the fact that out of the nearly fifty thousand taxi and Uber drivers in all of England, he was fortunate enough to be the one who was dispatched to pick this astounding person up. Likewise, he was moved that she'd opened her past up to him, twofold, in one short ride. This customer of his would linger on in his mind, long after she paid the tariff and went on her way in the direction of wherever she was going? Never before had he ever met a person who seemed to be so prepared for whatever life threw at her. This woman was no doubt someone who went through life, turning perplexing situations into an escapades and setbacks into breakthroughs.

Deniz with a Z was, like Ruby, a deep-thinker and a philosophical person. Two-character traits that he'd lost touch with six years ago, after he began driving people around the hectic city and suburbs for eleven hours a day, six days week. Lost in thought, with her words and wisdom jamming up his brain, he heard a loud, interrupting, knuckle-banging thud on his cab window. A London traffic patrol agent was sternly waving his arm and signalling him that traffic was moving again.

The agent then bent down said, with authority, "Put your fog lights on, and move along."

Deniz immediately switched his foggers on and glanced in his rearview mirror. He could see that his customer was stirring in her seat. He softly put his foot on the gas pedal, and then, just as softly, he spoke to her.

"I have good news madam, the collision has been cleared," he murmured with a whispering eagerness. "Please be sure your seatbelt is fastened."

It was too dark to see much of anything. Ruby removed her spectacles, rubbed her dry eyes, and then flicked her overhead light on so she could bind Bessie's journal up again. The cabbie immediately, reached behind his head and in a flash, shut off the light she'd just turned on.

"What the bloody hell!" she exclaimed angrily while whapping at his arm.

"Sorry madam, I have thoroughly valued listening to you read about slaves and tell me about your childhood summers in Montana, but regrettably no lights are allowed to be on inside the cab while I am driving. It

239

is the law. Traffic police officers are lined up and down the road, so I need to obey the law. I cannot afford to pay for a violation ticket."

If they were lucky, he thought, *traffic would soon be detoured around what he could now see was a chain reaction accident.*

Rather than have an old woman tantrum, which she sometimes was guilty of having, she courteously confirmed that her seatbelt was still fastened, apologized for her big mouth, and tenderly held Bessie's journal as the cab picked up speed.

I will rebind it when we exit the highway and are driving under the city's excessively bright streetlights, she told herself.

"Look out your window madam," the driver suggested.

Reading and telling stories about America and her past had distracted Ruby so much that she hadn't noticed the dense fog bank that had rapidly crept in. She wasn't even aware that she'd fallen asleep after Deniz had picked her up in front of her diner and she'd reminisced over this, that, and the other with him. A dark greyish mist was rolling over the thruway and wrapping itself around the cab like an ashen blanket. The United Kingdom had a worldwide reputation for its frequently wet cloudy weather and its notoriously unpredictable fog. Since the beginning of the week an abnormal amount of sunshine had put most Londoner's on alert. Experienced native Brits especially knew that typically the sunshine their country so intensely craved and needed was nine out of ten times being chased by a hazy fog.

"I hope the streets and suburbs are not in such a dire state as the thruway is?" Ruby heard him say.

Looking out the window into the blurred darkness, she felt like her claustrophobia had returned and was sitting beside her in the backseat. For as hard as she tried not to look outside, her curiosity, which nearly always won out, had her rolling the window down again. The expressway looked like a scary horror film. Its creepiness was making her feel nervous and unsettled. Deniz put the heater on, not wanting to force her to roll her window back up. Despite that, her insistence on keeping her window open had invited a foggy dampness into his cab; he chose not to try to recommend anything to her. He surmised that she was a woman who would be very difficult to steer in any direction other than the one she wanted to go in.

It was apparent to him that this old person had obviously had enough for one day. Although the cabbie didn't know what she was coping with at the hospital, he recognized that she was on the edge of something very distressing. He could read people with ease, which was a huge advantage in his line of work.

Unable to see two feet farther than the taxicab was frightening the hell out of Ruby. Sensing her apprehension, a reassuring voice from the front seat said, "I have turned my fog lights on, so no worries luv. I can see the road markings just fine. Besides, the traffic police won't move the rest of the barricades until it is safe for us all to begin driving at a normal speed again."

Although his words were calming, she snapped at him, "Don't treat me like a stupid geriatric female!"

Grinning at another emotional outburst of hers, that had obviously caused her sudden mood swing, he knew that riding the rest of the way in silence would be the wisest choice. Given their situation, her age, and her obvious exhaustion, stillness was all he had to offer her.

Less than three minutes of silence later, Ruby was fast asleep again. Her considerate taxicab driver respectfully kept vigil over her. Twenty minutes later traffic began dispersing and moving forward at normal freeway speed. The fog bank had finally disappeared into the far distance. The considerable long line of cars, and one lone taxicab that had been stuck in traffic for the better part of an hour, were detoured around the accident scene. Even the bright flashing hazard lights of five tow trucks, as they drove past, didn't wake Ruby up. He drove and she snored. As the speed of the traffic excelled, the driver took one more protective peek at her from behind the steering wheel. He could see that that in the dark, her hair was so white, it seemed to have an afterglow. Insulated by her age and presence, his taxi felt oddly safe despite the dangerous fog. Enjoying the sound of nothing, he drove farther down the highway towards their final destination.

"We have arrived luv," Deniz said softly, with a slightly relieved tone.

Due to the accident, he was more than an hour and fifteen minutes behind schedule and losing money with every tick of his cabs meter. Opening her eyes, the elderly woman saw his easy on the eye reflection in the review smiling at her, and she saw that the fog was again surrounding the cab. She felt a little unsteady from having just been in such a deep sleep. Although the well-lit sign, indicating that they were at the main entrance of Saint Matthew's Hospital was hazy, it was still visible. This relieved Ruby. She took a moment to secure Bessie's journal in the same crisscrossed fashion her grandmother had once chosen. The deceased Dutton brothers twine crosses still hung, as they were meant to, from their original sand coloured lariat cords.

Putting the journal in her handbag, she asked, "What time is it?"

"It is nine thirty-five pm madam, my apologies that it is so late. The detour and thick fog made a mockery out of our estimated time of arrival. Would you permit me to walk you to your destination dear lady?" he gallantly asked.

Ruby sniggered at his subtle, yet flirtatious request. She was feeling a tad revived, as if she'd just had a powernap. Coquettishly, like a proper British woman of age, she replied.

"That would be most appreciated kind sir. I am spending the night at the ICU with my great granddaughter Jazz Durant. The ICU is on the seventh floor. You may escort me as far as the elevator and not one step farther," she dictated with a sudden dry, snippy tone.

Deniz the cabdriver was a tolerable and cordial man, so he ignored his elderly customer's habit of swiftly switching gears and dispositions. He concluded that when a person is as old as this woman is, they have earned the right to be moody, bossy, and unpredictable. He took her overnight bag from her lap and ever so gently helped her out of the back seat. He then locked his cab and set the alarm with his digital key.

Deniz held out his arm the way a classy man does when escorting a sophisticated woman to a social event.

Intentionally, using a charming and extra heavy British accent, he said, "At your service madam."

Despite that he was twice her height, they easily intertwined arms, crossed the terrain, and entered the hospital. Six minutes later, two high, double-panelled sliding steel doors automatically open.

Unaccompanied, the elderly woman steps off the elevator. The straw hat she's wearing has slipped down over her cropped, snowy-white bangs. She can barely see beyond its wide brim. Her arthritis-crippled hands have a tight, determined grip on the leather straps of the overnight bag she's carrying. Her knee length, forest green, cotton jacket is hanging loosely from her frail and drooping, shoulders. She has a snugly wrapped, stylish mosaic scarf around her neck. The scarf covers a layer of loose, aged skin that sags from under her jutting chin. Her decorative shawl adds a much-needed pop of colour to her otherwise, washed-out, waxy complexion.

Although her grit and willpower are on seriously the verge of collapsing from fatigue, her determination to walk all the way to the end of the ICU's long corridor is much stronger than the pain she feels with every step she takes.

Chapter 37

Dragging her feet, Ruby shuffled past the nurse's station that was centrally located directly in between twelve of the intensive care unit's patient rooms. Her great granddaughter's room was located at the very end of the corridor. The nurse's station was unmanned.

Odd, she thought, *the staff must be changing shifts.*

As she limped farther in the direction of Jazz's, temporary home, the closer she got to the room, the more she remembered why she had been referring to Jazz as 'the child'.

"None of that is important now," she told herself, hobbling on.

Jazz Durant had been admitted to ICU 07.11. Her room, number eleven, was on the seventh floor, which was a rightly painful distance from the elevator. It was a distance that had the old lady's arthritis-ridden knees and feet throbbing.

"Just my bloody luck," she mumbled through somnolent sighs, as she approached the room's door. Today had been one of those all too familiar days when she'd forgotten her age and ignored her limitations.

She was happy to be back on the seventh floor. Being at The Seaside earlier, raptly musing and drifting, discovering the child's photographic talent, and then calling California, had all been very distracting. The closer she'd gotten to the end of the corridor, the more her anxieties had crept upwards from the depths of her stomach and into her throat. She knew she was in a tug of war with tears that needed to be shed.

All in due time, she thought.

The stamina that she normally would be tapping into by now had ditched her. Three hours had passed since she'd gone home to pack her overnight bag and call America. The extra time she'd spent alone at her diner, plus the traffic jam, had been unforeseen diversions from her worries about Zofia, Tucker, Jazz, and Nico. Not to mention the other accident victims, her diner's maintenance, and the police. Mind traveling had given her the chance to step out of the turbulent present, which was something she never grew tired of or bored with. By mentally drifting she'd reconnect with the past while rekindling intimate relationships and experiences. To this end, she felt oddly joined to countless people and events that had drifted in, and drifted out, of her very diverse life. Nevertheless, that was then, and this was now. She would have been back at the hospital much sooner if the fog and a traffic accident hadn't delayed her return.

"Ce la vie," she heard herself saying, as she opened the door to one of the most worrisome experiences of her now elderly life.

Being at the intensive care unit again and knowing that she planned to be there when the child regained consciousness, made her feel like she was back in control. She didn't want Jazz waking up to a strange hospital staff buzzing around her bed. This would frighten her terribly, which was something Ruby wouldn't tolerate and hoped to prevent. *The child has been through enough, there is no need to ask more from her than she is able to give.* She silently told herself. Earlier that day, one of the ICU's staff had cautioned her that it could be very disturbing for a family member to see someone they care about in a coma. Usually, family members feel scared and helpless. Scared and helpless were two emotions Ruby was undeniably feeling as she stood by the child's bed and stroked her tangled up hair. She was pleased to see that she'd been properly washed. Likewise, the elderly woman was amusingly satisfied to see that the barbwire tattoo was gone from around Jazz's neck. Despite that a few, dull coloured barbs on the wire choker were still slightly visible, the great grandmother was over the moon delighted with the change in the patient's appearance.

"You must have applied a wash-off tattoo choker just to shock people," Ruby muttered under her breath as she stroked the child's cheek.

You little shit! She thought, slightly filled with a misplaced type of pride.

Seeing Jazz lying there so motionless and vulnerable, it felt as if the child had suddenly deserted her. She felt numb and lonely. Without forethought, Ruby began to speak to her, using a strong and persuasive voice.

"You crashed into my life on Monday and then crashed into a boat on Saturday. It's been quite a week for you my talented little American rebel. Listen carefully. I know you can hear me. I am not angry with you. I have crashed into more people and created more chaos than most lifetimes will ever see."

Salty tears began rolling down Ruby's cheeks and dripping off her chin. Despite that she hated without warning bouts of emotion, the tears drippled onto her fully formed cleavage. Of course, they tickled her breasts, which robbed her of any stamina she had left in her after such a day as this one had been.

"The only body parts I inherited from my mother, Sadie, God Bless her cheating soul," she stereotypically remarked to herself, wiping the annoying prickles off with the back of her hand.

Now, being quickly bothered by the thoughts of her deceased mother and the moist interruption between her breasts, she thrust her left hand inside the right side of her brassiere and pulled out Mia's worn handkerchief.

Ahhh, that's better, she thought, as she wiped herself dry and erased all evidence of emotions.

"Hello Mrs. McEwen," Ruby heard an easy-going, cheerful voice out of the blue saying from the doorway. She looked over her shoulder and saw a young, attractive, tall woman with dark brown hair walking towards her.

"Welcome back madam. My name is Olivia Davies. I have been assigned to this room and will be taking care of you and my patient throughout the night," she announced.

The nurse walked over to Ruby, shook her hand, and gave her a proper, cheery British greeting. Ruby could see that she had penetrating blue eyes that resembled two bright sapphires. Her bangs, similar to the old woman's, had been cut just above her exposed and trimmed eyebrows. Her bangs accented the night nurse's intense eyes. Being in the restaurant business meant meeting and greeting people daily. Some of them had familiar faces, whilst others were newcomers whom Ruby had never met before. She seldom paid attention to, or was taken back by, how a person looked. Like a good novel, their storylines were what attracted her to people, not their covers. However, this young woman had, to say the least, a rare type of undeniably stunning cover.

Olivia, oblivious to her beauty and its ability to side-track, went on to say, "I have had an actual bed, rather than a cot, brought into the room. You will be much more comfortable in the bed, which is the same height as your great granddaughter's bed. This way you can easily check on her without having to get out of bed to do so."

"Thank you kindly," a slightly overcome person replied. Seeing her fatigued and dazed expression, the night nurse intentionally slowed the speed of her explanations down.

"There is an extra pillow, a sandwich, an apple, and two fleece blankets for you. A disinfectant soap dispenser is hanging on the wall above the sink. You can find a few basic toiletries, a washcloth, and towel, in the drawer under the sink," she stated, pointing towards the far corner of the now slightly darkened room.

"Madam, please wash your hands each time before you touch Miss Durant. This includes upon entering and leaving her room, coughing or sneezing, or using the toilet. Because you show no signs of having a cold, fever, or allergies, we are allowing you to sleep overnight in the ICU. It is not my intention to disrespect you madam. Although my patient is not fighting an infectious disease, hygiene is imperative throughout the intensive care unit. If her airways become inflamed or congested with mucous, her body could reject the breathing tube," the nurse informed.

"I understand," Ruby attentively said.

"Oh yes, I almost forgot," Olivia quickly added, "I have put two large bottles of spring water and a glass for you on the nightstand next to your bed. Hospital air tends to be quite dry, which may have you feeling congested, thirsty, and even more tired than you already must be. Please be sure to hydrate yourself regularly. To remind yourself of this, consider drinking a glass of water each time after you have used the lavatory. This is important for your own health madam."

Ruby nodded in agreement.

The nurse then suggested she put the antique wooden trunk and Ruby's other personal belongings in the room's narrow, yet functional wall closet. She was concerned that the elderly woman would trip over the trunk unintentionally if she needed the toilet during the night.

"What a beautiful trunk," she, with all sincerity, remarked. "It has a rather historical look to it," she added. What do you store in it madam?"

"My past," was the snappish answer Olivia received. Given the late hour, the night nurse ignored her curiosity, dismissed Ruby's snippiness, and carried on with her work.

"May I hang your jacket up for you?" she asked.

A few moments later, the ICU nurse hung Ruby's summer jacket up, closed the closet door, and set Ruby's overnight bag on the foot of her bed.

"I will leave it up to you to decide whether to lock the closet or not? If you do, take care not to lose the key if you take it with you."

She then put a tender, compassionate hand on her bony shoulder and said, "Before I check your great granddaughter's vitals and you retire for the night, do you have any questions for me?"

Without hesitation, Ruby timorously reacted.

"Yes, I do. I have two questions actually. Can Jazz hear us talking? And do people in comas sleep and wake up like conscious people do?"

"Those are good questions," she complimented. "Just so you know there are coma information packets available in the ICU lounge, which is on the sixth floor, next to the elevator. I will bring one to you later. In the meantime, I do realize that you most likely may need answers in order to fall asleep. Why don't you sit down in the recliner so I can explain a few things to you? Tomorrow, an ICU Patient Caregiver Representative, who is also a Family Counsellor, will schedule a meeting with you and any other family members who would like to attend. At that time, the counsellor will help answer any farther questions you have, or any new ones that arise before they turn into stressors of any sort."

The night nurse held out her arm and helped her sit down in the recliner. She crossed the room, picked up the medical stool next to the child's bed, and put it down in front of Ruby. Taking a seat, she folded her hands, leaned forward, and rested her elbows on her knees. Then she began answering an enormously brave, rightfully worried, great grandmother's questions.

"I am an ICU nurse who has seen hundreds of cataleptic patients in my fifteen-year career. However, I have never myself been even slightly unconscious, or in a coma. Despite this, I have heard, multiple times, from patients who have awoken after a short-term unconscious state that they did recall hearing voices and sounds. Some were clear whilst others muted. Many of them could even vividly recall the dreams and hallucinations they'd had. Recently, one young patient of mine awoke after seven weeks and began incessantly humming to the rhythm of a song he'd heard. The melody was still locked inside his brain. The source of his cerebral beat was the music his sister played in his room each time she visited him."

In spite of her drowsiness, Ruby did her best to remain focused on the nurse's explanation as the she continued speaking.

"Therefore, although I am not a neurologist, I professionally believe that taking time to read, to talk with, and even play music for a coma patient, is very important. Do you agree madam?" Olivia asked.

Ruby was too tired for words. Her simple nod made this clear to the nurse, who continued her explanation, hoping that she could stay awake long enough to listen to her.

"As you yourself now must know, seeing your own relative in a coma is a devastating time. Often, in spite of this, it can be much more traumatic for others than it is for the patient. Family and friends feel powerless to the situation, therefore, what they often naively accept as being true, is that there is no way for them to make a difference for the patient. I myself, many of my colleagues, and our ICU specialists, all believe that the sound of a familiar voice is perhaps the best tool for coma recovery. Hearing a recognizable voice telling a story, or singing a song, has been proven to assist coma patients with recovering their consciousness more rapidly. When this happens, they subsequently start responding at a faster rate to conversations and directions once they regain consciousness," Olivia specified.

"Do ex-coma patients lose their way easily? Is this why they need to have directions?" Ruby interrupted.

"In a sense yes," the nurse answered, "however, I am referring to a different type of directions. I am talking about those people who emerge from a coma and then have to recuperate. Many of them often need to learn to accept, and cope with a brain that is, in varying degrees, different than it was before their coma began. They are often burdened with additional psychological, mental, and physical problems after they return to consciousness. Some patients require help with everyday tasks, like, walking, using a commode, talking, holding utensils while eating, brushing their teeth, and even dressing themselves."

The night nurse compassionately stroked Ruby's arm and continued.

"A family member, like yourself, who reads to and talks with the patient, gains an abstract kind of control over the patient's recovery. Essentially, doing these things with Jazz can give you an opportunity to be part of her treatment," Olivia said. "My advice would be that you keep reading to her and talking with her. Do you believe she knows you are nearby and that she can hear you?" she asked.

"Without a doubt," Ruby confidently replied.

"Then trust in this and let this be enough for now," she suggested.

Looking at her watch she said, "An hour ago, my ICU team made rounds and had shift change consultations. The day staff mentioned that they were impressed with your involvement with Jazz in this way," she concluded with a complimentary pat on Ruby's hand. She then stood up, twisted the cap off the water bottle and filled the drinking glass on the nightstand.

"Here you are madam," she said, recapping the bottle.

"Call me Ruby," she heard her sternly demanding, "I hate being called madam, and it makes me feel like I am as extinct as a bloody dinosaur!"

The night nurse quickly hid her surprised reaction, tried not to smirk, and handed the elderly woman, who was glaring at her, a glass of fresh spring water. Then, Olivia sat back down.

"Now Ruby, let me answer your second question," she began. "You asked me if a coma patient sleeps and can they distinguish between night and day? I don't have a one hundred percent conclusive answer for you, nevertheless, I can explain how, nowadays, more so than ever before, the world of neurological research is nearer to an irrefutable discovery with each passing month."

Her eyes widened with interest.

Where in the name of God does this elderly woman get her thirst for knowledge and strong mental energy? The night nurse silently asked herself. She'd just met her and already felt captivated by Ruby's wise, obsolete spell.

"Have you ever noticed that you tend to feel energized and drowsy around the same time each day?" she asked her.

"I am almost nine decades old. I am drowsy all goddamn day long," Ruby retorted with a teasingly dry tone.

What a ridiculously dumb question for such an intelligent young woman, the elderly woman thought, but didn't say.

"Now, you have made a good point. Let me offer you my apologies and try another approach. Human beings have what is known as a circadian rhythm."

Ruby interrupted her again, "What is that exactly?"

Although she knew what it was, because she'd been a nursing assistant throughout WWII, she was toying with Olivia. She already felt as if she could be herself with the conspicuous night nurse, hence the innocent teasing. Regardless, the elderly woman's interrupting was becoming rather tedious for Olivia. Nonetheless, being a professional, she was aware that this precious, rather cheeky person had heaps to endure in the days and weeks that lay ahead of her. For the sake of this reason, she chose to be tolerant and ignore Ruby's annoying interjections while she explained more to her.

"A circadian is the 24-hour internal clock that runs continuously in the background of the brain. No matter how old a person is, the clock runs," she said, smirking openly. Then she went on to clarify those rhythmic cycles between sleepiness and alertness run at steady intervals. It's also known as your sleep and wake cycle. This cycle is something doctors here at Saint Matthew's Neurology Department consider when diagnosing unconscious patients. They have determined that the time of day when patients are tested is crucial. In addition, creating a healthy sleep and wake environment for patients, one that mimics the light patterns of day and night, may help the patient achieve a normal sleep-wake cycle. Neurologists and sleep-disorder specialists are secure in their beliefs that this may possibly help bring a patient, like your Jazz, with a severe brain injury, closer to consciousness."

Ruby glanced across the darkened room at the child. Her plaster arm and leg casts were covered by a mint green blanket. The green colour clashed terribly with the purple hair on the child's half-shaven head. The sterile white pillow and germ-free bed linens were now even more illuminated by darkness of the room and the blueish hue of numerous digital monitor lights.

The child looks even more angelic, Ruby thought.

She'd forgotten how much of a repetitive thinker and doer she was. Doing and thinking about something just once was not her style. Regardless, it was why she'd often repeat something she'd thought, said, or done. It was now so dark outdoors, and in patient's room, that Ruby hadn't noticed how thick the fog had become. In hindsight, this was a good thing, otherwise, she'd be up most of the evening worried about whatever, and whoever, was flying through the night from the East Coast to England?

Breaking the silence that had ended their conversation, Olivia said, "It is 11pm and time for bed madam. I need to attend to my other patients. Fortunately, it is rather quiet on the ward tonight. It has been a pleasure meeting you Mrs. McEwen. I will check in on you later. If you need anything, please come out to the nurse's station. If Jazz wakes up, I promise you that you will be the first to know. Do try to get some sleep."

With this being said Olivia Davies tenderly shook Ruby's wrinkly hand and bid her goodnight. She watched her as the night nurse walked past the child's bed and gave the big toe on Jazz's right foot a little tweak. She wondered if the nurse had a medical reason for doing this or maybe was looking for a response of some sort.

Probably just a sign of endearment, she concluded.

Ruby liked Olivia Davies. She'd made her feel significant by taking extra time with her and responding to her seemingly never-ending questions. This had made her feel sufficiently important and nurtured. The night nurse had an orthodox way of adding layers of personal touches to her work. It had been a very long time since Ruby had felt so cared for, and even longer since she'd allowed herself to be pampered by someone else. Now she was hungry. She quickly proceeded with eating her sandwich and drinking another glass of water. While doing so, she thought a bit more about herself, who she was and who she had become.

Since she was a wee little lassie growing up in the British region of Essex County, she'd had a stubborn need to solve life on her own and reject help at every turn. She knew she was an optimist, an independent problem solver, and a people pleaser. It was alleged that people pleasers are some of the most pleasurable people anyone could ever know. Nearly everyone who knew her would agree that she fit into this category. As a rule, people pleasers struggle considerably to dole out criticism or negative answers. Despite what others thought of her, she knew that she didn't fit into 'this' category. Ruby wasn't the least bit afraid to speak her mind. For this reason, as a result, she spoke it often. She was reputed to be a woman who knew, before you did, if you needed a favour. Then she would grant it without needing or expecting anything in return.

"Being there for people is a good thing until it becomes a bad thing because I forget to take care of me. Enough psychobabble for one night," she heard herself concluding.

The elderly and beyond exhausted woman was talking to herself again. She left the recliner and went into the bathroom to wash up and brush her teeth. After doing so, she put her favourite ankle length, flannel nightgown on and crossed the room to say goodnight to the child.

"This nightgown is three times older than you are," she said with a faint smile.

After patting the child's cheek, she shambled on bare feet back to the spare bed and laid down. Once she'd punched the pillow into a comfortable shape, she pulled the fleece blanket up and covered herself. The corner of a nearly colourless, red polka dotted handkerchief was sticking out of her brazier that she'd forgotten to remove when she undressed. Drowsily she reached up and grasped it. Then she held it the way a tot holds a stuffed animal at bedtime. With the corner of her once best friend, Mia Doherty's, shabby handkerchief twisted around her kinked fingers, she listened to the rhythmic droning and peeping echoes of high-tech machines that would keep Jazz alive throughout the night. Oddly, their harmonious resonances made her feel safe.

Within five short minutes an elderly woman, with slightly large ears and skin the colour of hazelnuts had conked out and fallen into a deep sleep.

Chapter 38

Whatever may have transpired on the ICU ward and in Jazz Durant's room throughout the night, Ruby slept undisturbed through all of it. She heard nothing and never woke up, not even once to use the toilet. This was a feat that was almost unheard of given the age of her bladder.

Despite her setting a personal sleep record, the elderly woman was now being tersely woken up by someone squeezing her forearm and then nudging her scrawny shoulder. Being so crudely woken up had her still slightly drowsy temper instantly seeing red. Her antique metal alarm clock in her bedroom at home, with its two bells and reliable ringing hammer, was the only thing that had ever been allowed to wake her up each morning. Lord Help anyone who, without permission, interrupted her slumber! They'd be at the mercy of her foul British temper. Even her diner customers and staff had learned not to wake her if her eyes were closed while she was having a sit-down in her Barcalounger, no matter the time of day. Even though she was still half-asleep, she immediately recognized the sound of the soft-spoken voice.

"Good morning madam. How did you sleep?" The nurse's voice delicately asked. She learned in no time to respect this old person, despite her unexpected crotchety attitude and mood swings.

The nurse got no response from the very dedicated lady lying in the spare bed next to the patient. Ruby's nightgown was wide open. A red polka-dotted hankie and two private body parts hung almost entirely out of the lace bra that the she'd been too tired to remove before crawling into bed last night. The nurse continued to speak.

"It is 6:30am madam. The doctors will be making their rounds in thirty minutes, or so. Therefore, I need you to get up. I apologize that it's so early for you. My colleagues need to prepare Miss Durant and her room before morning rounds begin. My shift has ended madam."

Ruby opened her heavy, sleep filled eyes, and saw that Olivia Davies, who looked completely bushed, was attempting to greet her with an alert and bubbly smile. Her piercing, sapphire blue eyes that last night had sparkled, now looked like stagnant pond water. Her bangs hung lifelessly, as if all their follicle energy had been sucked out of them.

She must have had a rough time of it last night, Ruby thought.

Then, with the speed of a bolt of lightning, something in her snapped. Unfairly, she lashed out at Olivia, "Goddammit, I told you to not to call me madam! Bloody hell woman, call me Ruby!"

Seeing the nurse's stunned and rigid reaction shut the rude old woman up instantly. In a fraction of a second, she felt like an ungrateful swank who'd put her foot in it again. Ruby was also reputed for her explosive, foot in the mouth demeanour. The older she got the more frequent one of her bare feet landed between her teeth. She then quickly perked up her voice and apologized with the sincerity the young nurse, who had been so attentive to her needs, genuinely deserved.

"Sorry luv, I guess I've gone and put my foot in it haven't I? How's my great granddaughter doing? Did the child behave throughout the night? How was your nightshift?"

Quickest three question foot removal I've ever seen, a dog-tired nurse jestingly thought.

Ruby sat up in bed, repositioned her handkerchief, tucked her wilted breasts back into their proper places, and buttoned her nightgown up.

"Jazz did really well throughout the night mam. I am not at liberty to give you a detailed overview of her condition. The neurologist assigned to her case, Dr. Vijay Zamier, will do this with you after he examines her. I have brought you a cup of hot Earl Grey and a breakfast scone to help you start your morning. My night was rather frenzied, but it is my job; therefore, no complaints from me," she answered. "I need to get home. My husband has to work, and our wee ones need tending to. School was cancelled, so I am in more of a hurry than I usually am. I wanted to see you before I left for the day."

Olivia handed Ruby the ICU Coma Patient Information packet she'd promised to bring her and wished her a nice day before dashing towards the door.

With one of her white, nursing Croc clogs in the corridor, and the other one still in Jazz's room, the night nurse turned on her heels briefly looked back at Ruby.

Wearing a serious expression, she told her, "The city is dangerously fogged in madam. Ubers are in service, but most taxi companies and all other public transportation services are at a standstill. The underground Metro stations are still open. All above ground transit systems are closed. If you need to go outside be very careful because it will be rightly hazardous. I will see you again later tonight, if you are still here and are still awake. My shift starts at 10 pm. May I ask you why you refer to Miss Durant, at her age, as 'the child'?" Olivia respectfully inquired.

"A brilliant question," Ruby replied and explained. "Excluding Jazz's unfortunate accident and coma, since she arrived from America, she's been a bloody, humungous challenge for me! That petite, irresponsible, angel-like, eighteen-year-old lying over there in that bed, has an impolite and ruthless mouth. Before the accident, I told her that I would refer to her as 'the child', until she stopped behaving like a spoiled little child. My intention was for her to be aware of her credulous, immature behaviour and then to act like the young adult that she is."

Slightly impressed, Olivia said, "Understandable. I appreciate the honest explanation. I myself struggle when my three children often tend to act too hyper or indulged. Now, I really do need to get home and get some sleep. Cheers."

She gave Ruby a quick wave before the door closed behind her. "Enjoy your cuppa," Ruby heard Olivia calling out before her voice faded off down the long corridor.

The elderly woman immediately got out of bed. Her early morning body was its typical stiff and painful self, but it didn't stop her from waddling across the room to greet the child. The patient looked the same as she did seven hours ago before Ruby had fallen asleep. Spontaneously, she began touching the child's nose, then her ears and her hands. She used a familiar, skilled precision while doing so. She was taking care not to shift or disturb any of the respiration and feeding tubes, or the intravenous lines. One slight movement could and would, no doubt, set off an alarm at the nurse's station and get her into all sorts of trouble. Trouble, was something Ruby Adeline McEwen never had to look for in life. It found her all on its own.

She wiped a bit of drool off the patient's chin and hobbled to the end of the bed so she could untuck the blanket and sheet wrapped around Jazz. Then she reached underneath the linens and held her feet for a few moments in her crooked, cool hands. The child's feet were as warm as her nose, ears, and hands were. This was a sincere relief for the elderly woman. Relying on her training and experience as a Nurse's Aide, throughout the 1940s and 50s, she knew that body extremities that were warm to the touch meant that blood circulation was strong. This was a positive sign and a satisfactory way for both of them to start day number two since the accident.

Ruby had a busy schedule ahead of her. After she spoke with the doctor's she planned to start her impending search for her dishwasher Nico and inquire about any other accident victims. She needed to this before Zofia and company arrived from America. Ruby was astute enough to know that the minute they stepped off the Boeing 747 they'd flown in, her time would no longer be hers.

She tucked the child's feet back under the bed coverings and told exclaimed, "Spit spot old girl, and move along, time is a wasting!"

With that being said and done, she scurried off to the bathroom to dress and put on her make-up before tidying the room up. Passing by the nightstand she snatched up the sugar coated, buttery scone and took a big thick bite out of it. The sweet, savoury taste melted, like warm black treacle, over her tongue. The scone's sugar stuck to her teeth was reminding her of how grateful she was that she didn't wear dentures. Now, with sugar in her blood and pep in her step, she carried on with her tasks. Zofia and Tucker's only daughter was in a coma, therefore, she knew all bloody hell would be breaking loose the moment they arrived. Despite this actual family threat, Ruby's optimistic spirit felt enthusiastic and alive. She'd started her day with new, even grittier type of energy. After putting on a touch of lipstick and mascara, she gave her image an approving nod in the bathroom mirror. She rightly liked the person looking back at her. She did realize that when she added a stylish flair to her face and her clothing, people often viewed her as, an antique disguising its age with a youthful appearance. Or so she secretly hoped.

Piss off with their opinions of me, she thought.

She didn't care about opinions. She was unique and age meant nothing to her. For her, age was something people worried too much about and then they died, too young, covered in fusspots. This didn't apply to Ruby. She was different. Long before she was in her twenties, she'd dressed for herself and created her own style. Despite her mother Sadie's endless need to interfere and mold her daughter into a fine young woman, Ruby created her own distinct identity. She was not a self-centred person, nor had she ever feared

252

the aging process. Nevertheless, she did find the pain and stiffness from her chronic rheumatoid arthritis a real goddamn, friggen pity. Although her arthritis didn't make her feel old, it did have physical control over her. It decelerated her, as she defined it. In addition, it made her unpredictably bad-tempered, which was a shame for those standing in her line of fire, or on the other side of one of her nasty moods.

Despite this, her being contradictorily bad-tempered was just another characteristic of hers that either people learned to endure, or they didn't. She couldn't give a British hill of beans what other people thought of her. She was too intent on living life the way she wanted to and not the way others, or society for that matter, expected her to. Ruby was known to be a hot-headed, true humanitarian. She was passionate, genuine, kind, and giving; four traits she'd had since she was very young. These qualities made it possible, and easier, for people to accept her more irritating quirks. She attributed her personality to being raised, in great part, by her grandma Bessie. Bessie was, in the same way, the finest humanitarian the elderly woman had ever known. She was the one female who'd taught her, as a young girl that she couldn't fall down in life if she didn't climb her way through it. The higher she climbed, the harder she'd fall, and the wiser she'd become. Later, as a young woman, Bessie ingrained in Ruby that, when she lost her way she would need to live a counterclockwise life and travel in reverse to find her way back again. The African American grandmother, who prepared her only granddaughter for life, through examples of her diligence and acumen, had died almost sixty-years ago.

"Foolish, that her death was more than half a century ago and I still can't shake her out of my brain," she heard herself saying aloud.

She chalked this up to yesterday and having spent time alone in her diner alongside nearly ninety minutes of recollecting and then, reading from her journals to both Jazz and Deniz the cabdriver. Reading passages from any of the journals tended to open forgotten doors and windows of the past for her. On occasion, this was a calming alternative to mental drifting, mind traveling, or both. Extended periods of doing so tended to leave her slightly confused upon her return to the here and now. Which eventually turned her mind inside out.

Which is normal and familiar. After all, I am old, she would remind herself of whenever she'd pushed herself too far.

Ruby had never been a person whose intention was to satisfy another person, especially a man. Her lifestyle choices were based on who she was and who she wanted to be. She'd never pretended to be, or wanted to be, anyone other than her authentic self; even before she knew who this was. This approach made her life comfortable and simple, even throughout the most turbulent of events she'd witnessed and survived since her birth.

Quite unplanned, she placed Bessie's journal, the one she'd read from in the taxi, back inside the trunk. Given the circumstances, keeping the past together in one place felt like the responsible and proper thing to do. She saw that the trunk was in the closet when she'd fetched her scarf. She'd been so tired when she arrived back at the child's room last night that she'd forgotten all about being told where it was. Staring down at it now, she could see that barely fit inside the compact closet. Its forged iron handles made it bulkier and wider than a normal sized trunk was. She was satisfied that it did fit, because since receiving it decades ago, she'd always kept it under lock and key. Doing so, had given her a needed degree of ancestral security over time, which in this moment, felt like light-years of time. Until she passed the trunk onto the next person in line, someone she herself would deem worthy, she was the trunk's sole guardian. Being 'the Keeper of the Past' was a responsibility she took very seriously.

With Bessie's journal now in the trunk she closed its massive, bevelled lid and secured the ornate bronze hinge lock that had hung off it for over 100 years. After securing the trunk and the closet, she attached both keys to the solid silver polished chain she wore around her neck. Tucking the keys protectively between her breasts, she waddled past the child's bed and gave the first big toe she came to a little tweak.

"Be right back luv," she cheerfully told Jazz. Despite the current calamitous circumstances, Ruby was in an upbeat mood.

"Before this day gets the best of me, I will read more to you," she promised. "There is so much you still don't know about the amazing line of women and men you come from."

Standing in the doorway, she paused and glanced back at the child. Raising her voice an octave or two, she called out, "I'll be only one floor down if you need me. No wagging off while I'm gone, you hear. Open your eyes and come back to Nico and to me."

Her strong belief that Jazz had a thing for Nico gave her hope that hearing his name would have her fighting harder to heal and wake up. She magnanimously believed that the child could hear when she read to her or talked with someone in her ICU room. True or not, this gave Ruby something to grasp a hold of and have faith in. Last night, she'd started to trust that if she spoke louder than normal, Jazz would recognize her voice and follow it back to consciousness. Having nothing to lose, and everything to gain, she'd continue to treat the child as she would if she were not in a coma. Olivia Davies had put her on the proper path towards connecting with a comatose person. The rest of the odyssey was now up to fate. With this conviction spinning through her brain, she left the room.

On her way to the elevator she stopped off briefly at the nurse's station and responsibly told the receptionist on duty where she was going in case anyone needed her. Then she turned around and started her day.

Chapter 39

As she approached the elevator, Ruby could see her reflection in a wide, ceiling high window at the end of the ICU's long corridor. The more often she walked back and forth, between the child's room and the 7th floor elevator, the shorter the distance began to feel.

The closer she moved towards the image of herself in the windowpane, the more satisfied she became. Often times, whenever she saw the version of her mirrored self, she rather liked what she saw. She attributed this to having an accepting nature, a slightly warped sense of self, and an easily elated state of mind. Throughout WWII, she'd learned that life could be cruel. It could shake her and break her, if she let it. Staying one-step ahead of it was her lifelong tactic.

Today, like most days, the elderly woman was happy with her appearance. Regardless of the circumstances that demanded her attention, she customarily took time to groom herself at the beginning of each new day. She'd always thought she owed it to her patrons, and all the more to her self-esteem, to look her best no matter the place or time. Her attire, a light touch of makeup, her youthful attitude and ripened radiance gave her and others the impression that she was energetic and in fine fettle. As The Seaside's owner, she frequently gave too much of herself away to her customers and staff. This was why, giving back to herself had become an essential part of any additional day that she was fortunate enough experience and to live through. The elderly woman's routines and grooming ritual had kept her connected to herself, despite what she encountered on any given day and at any given time. Sure, she indisputably had mood swings, could be unbending and opinionated, and was at times guilty of insensitive remarks; on the other hand, for the most part, she was a balanced, adaptable, wise, and worldly person.

Seeing herself now, so visibly in the reflection of the thick, mirrored glass, she concluded that like all aging people, she looked younger and less scrumpled from a distance, in comparison to when the sun wasn't shining directly in her face. Standing in front of a darkened window next to the elevator, she was persuaded, by her own positive regard, that she looked to be not a day over seventy-five. It didn't matter if her opinion of herself was imaginative, it felt rewarding enough to ignore reality as it stared back at her. There she stood, living in the moment while embracing the view. Despite that others might consider her to be a slightly foolish old biddy, she liked the person she had become. Liking herself and living with integrity and a clear conscience, no matter her age, was all that had ever really mattered to her.

Ruby had slept really well and felt as refreshed as anyone could after spending the night in an intensive care unit. Furthermore, she liked her choice in clothes today. She was wearing a long, stylish, dark red and bronze cardigan. Her open style vest was horizontally striped, from her shoulders to just under her knees. The mid-length vest made her look taller than she actually was. For the past few decades, she'd intentionally tried to look lankier, because she had been shrinking in height since she was in her late sixties. Ruby didn't mind aging, but she regretted that her length was diminishing with each birthday she celebrated. She had always liked being a tall woman. Her height dotingly reminded her of her long-legged father Horace. Her cardigan's light copper tint strikingly complemented her cognac leather boots and dark maroon coloured tunic. She now stood so close to the tall window; it was as if she was looking into a full-length mirror. Scrutinizing her reflection, her first impression of what she saw was that her decorative mosaic scarf clashed dreadfully with the rest of her outfit. Nevertheless, her neck got cold too easily, and she had only the one scarf with her, so she ignored her early morning self-criticism.

As she stood in front of the elevator, waiting for it to arrive, she suddenly realized something; the image of herself that she'd just seen was too sharp and the colour of her clothes were too vibrant for a standard window reflection. Wanting to understand why this was, she removed her spectacles, pressed her nose against the glass, and tried to see outside.

"Where is the daylight?" she heard herself ask, as the elevators bell rang out announcing that its doors had opened.

Not wanting to be caught between two steel doors that would crush her like a skinny paperclip, she quickly entered the elevator and pushed the button with the floor number six on it.

As the elevator began its descent, she noticed a small icon symbol for Starbucks next to the number 6 on the elevator's display panel. A broad, blissful smile appeared on her old face. Ruby was completely bonkers for Starbucks. The American coffee chain had only arrived in the United Kingdom about ten years ago. In her professional opinion, Starbucks was one of the finest USA exports that the Brits had ever allowed onto their island. She was looking forward to a double espresso, or a coffee macchiato, topped with a creamy froth. She'd order a large size, packed with an adequate amount of caffeine to keep her blood pumping until lunchtime.

Even though The Seaside's coffee was excellent and savoured by hundreds of caffeine-addicted patrons every week, the modern, upbeat atmosphere at Starbucks, with its appealing choices, was undoubtedly the best. She was shrewd enough to know that if there were a Starbucks within five kilometres of her establishment, it would destroy her business faster than shit ran through a goose. Regardless of the humourist in her, she rightfully knew that her diner was a true iconic eatery that would suffer financially if a Starbucks opened in the vicinity. With her gratefulness for her diner's rural location churning through her brain, the elevator bell pinged again and announced her stop. As its wide, dense, steel doors automatically opened, a rather fashionable elderly woman wearing a slightly clashing, yet funky looking outfit, stepped out and onto the sixth floor.

After taking about eight, relatively pain-free steps forward, she entered Saint Matthew's spacious and impressive dining area. As she'd anticipated, the line in front of the Starbucks ordering counter was already very long. She could see that it was much longer than the lines at any of the other food vendors. It was still very early in the day. The majority of the people waiting their turn in line were wearing hospital uniforms of various colours and styles.

Perhaps one of these professionals is in the mood to let a very, very, very old person cut the line, she hoped, as she accented her limp with a slightly fake and painful moan with each step she took towards the line.

Being intelligent enough to know that most of the hospital employees would easily spot an over the hill con artist, Ruby planned to walk casually past them, as if she was going to the Starbucks pick-up counter. Then she planned to pretend to be in search of a napkin and sugar for the coffee she'd yet to order. The cunning old charlatan was prepared. If anyone questioned her intentions, she had a logical explanation on the tip of her sly tongue.

Ruby wasn't a cheat, not in any way whatsoever. However, she was a bend the rules type of person. Given her age, she reckoned that she'd earned a free pass for minor obstacles she encountered. Lady Luck was on her side. Just as she was about an arm's length away from the condiment dispensers, a tall, broad built man in green scrubs, with a tray in his hands, spastically spun around and tumbled into her. She fell roughly backwards into two other empty-handed men wearing blue coloured scrubs. They caught her just before her brittle bones hit the floor. Absolutely no drama or acting was involved. Ruby let out a startling, fear-filled cry. All eyes were on her as she toppled and landed smack dab in the dining hall's spotlight. Despite that she hated being in any kind of spotlight, the odour of a slight advantage was in the air just above her nose. It was a scent she needed, so she remained calm. The men, who were actually doctors, put her back in a vertical position as gently as possible. She was then properly dusted off and fussed over by them and a few concerned onlookers.

That was the joy of a hospital, she thought, *everyone wanted to help someone in need, before someone in need knew they needed help.*

A cheeky old woman wearing a flashy outfit had made it to the front of the line in less than one minute. With Lady Luck still on her side she was ready to order. An impatient, pimple faced, Starbucks employee held beverage containers above his head and barked out customers names that had been written on the cups.

"Let's keep the line moving everyone!" he shouted with an excessively stressed-out tone for a chap his age.

The young man wearing green scrubs, who had accidently knocked the elderly woman to the floor, felt like a real schmuck, so he offered to buy her whatever she wanted. Acting shy like, she refused. He relentlessly insisted. Ruby concluded that his kind gesture was the odour of advantage she'd had just smelled. Liking the whiff of another free breakfast, she politely gave into his peace offering by ordering a double espresso, a caramel-filled breakfast scone, and a tall glass of ice water with lemons wedges. Realizing that the only person who knew that she'd already received one free scone today was home dealing with her kids unexpected free day from school, she felt confident that her secret was safe. She was then assisted to a booth with sturdy, sofa-like seats. The cafeteria was overcrowded and literally everyone was talking about the fog. Knowing that the Durant's were flying in from America soon, Ruby wanted to get an update on the current weather conditions over Heathrow airport. Apparently, the fog was so low to the ground, and so dense, that outside it looked to be more like 7pm rather than 7am. The booth she'd been escorted to was next to a modern, large-screen TV that was mounted high on an adjacent wall. As she slid into an empty seat, a particularly tall bloke, wearing a black and white checkered apron and matching cap, was reaching up and manually turning up the televisions volume.

He must be a short order cook, Ruby supposed when she saw his uniform.

Reminding herself that her ears were also going on ninety, she was appreciative of his height and the extra volume. The cafeteria was more crowded now because the BBC News and Weather was about to be broadcasted. Since the table she sat at was closest to the TV, in no time at all it was surrounded by more Brits wanting to hear the latest fog update. She struggled to watch and listen because too many of them had crowded in just as the BBC broadcaster was about to begin his live report. The horde of viewers surrounding her booth was closing in and causing her claustrophobia return. With the space around her rapidly filling she felt confined, jittery, and short of breath. In a flash, Ruby felt herself struggling with claustrophobia; the enclosed sensation was making her feel trapped in a small space clogged with people that were swallowing her up. What was happening was a familiar, sporadic, and persistent struggle that she'd been challenged with since she was an adolescent. Just as she was about to lose control and flee, the special weather report broadcast began and distracted her from the phobia. Her fear dissolved as her focus returned.

She was pleased that a BBC newscast was on and not a CNN news bulletin. The opinionated old Briton detested CNN. She considered American network broadcasters to be overly flashy and dramatic. Not to mentions CNN's unwarranted number of annoying commercials per hour. Hearing the broadcast begin, her opinions disappeared, and her appetite returned. The busy cafeteria quieted instantly as viewers stood still and hung on the male newscasters every word. The fog had captured the attention of all of Great Britain, as well as a myriad of global travellers. She knew that despite Britain's decline as an aviation superpower, London's lead as a top airline hub, over nearly every other city in the world, was still growing.

As the commentator began his in-depth report, the elderly lover of Starbucks sipped on her double espresso. For someone who had just devoured a hearty breakfast less than twenty minutes ago, she took unusually large bites of her sugar coated, caramel breakfast scone.

Chapter 40

A layer of silence covered the dining hall as the BBC newscaster started to deliver a commentary that, it was estimated, millions of Londoners were tuned into at the same time.

"Brits can expect long delays on all roads and at airports today as the UK braces for another weekend of dense fog. The fog has already caused major infrastructure delays, traffic accidents and a number of pedestrian deaths. The murkiness is currently hindering public transportation, including all flights to and from airports across the country. Major airports, Heathrow and Gatwick included, are currently closed to all air traffic. In-coming flights are being rerouted to alternative airport destinations in France, Ireland, The Netherlands, and Germany. Approximately 320,000 outgoing passengers are currently stranded. Emergency services are assisting commuters and travellers in every possible way."

The reporter went on to refer to the hazy, low visibility conditions, as the Copycat Fog. The current fog situation was being compared to the Great Smog of 1952, when an infamous fog trapped London in a deadly cloud of polluted air for five days, choking an estimated twelve-thousand people to death. The elderly woman still remembered the Great Smog in detail. It had claimed the lives of both of her father Horace's parents and his youngest brother. At the time, she was a young university student who was studying in Dublin, oblivious to the catastrophe. Back in 1952, the arrival of the smog marked the first time, since World War II had ended, that she and her fellow Brits were confronted by a threat that resulted in a staggering number of deaths in less than a week.

As soon as she heard the words, Great Smog, she positioned herself firmly in her seat, sat up straight-backed, and placed both of her feet squarely on the floor. Ruby McEwen knew what was coming. Her mind had already begun to race; meaning, within thirty seconds her brain would yank her out of its claustrophobic bubble and fling her back into the year 1952. She'd barely had time to find a comfortable position at the table when she felt her mind altering. Intently she reached forward to grasp her tall glass of ice water with three lemon wedges floating in it. She certainly hadn't anticipated mind traveling this morning. However, considering all the sugar and caffeine she'd ingested in less than one hour, she should have known that a drifting episode would happen. Her mind had a fuel of its own and never needed extra stimulants to activate it. Already knowing where her consciousness would be taking her, she swallowed a gulp of water and held the ice chips in her mouth.

The oldest diner owner in the country knew she needed to get back to the ICU before the Neurologist made his rounds, so she decided that she'd use the freezing cold sensation of the ice in her mouth and between her hands as a way to keep her journey short. Holding the glass firmer, she leaned back deeper into the sofa-seat and let happen what needed to happen. Not fighting her brains need to travel or drift made doing so smoother, rewarding, and much less conflicting. Wanting to maintain a necessary semblance of control, she tightened her grip on the glass, bit down on the ice cubes in her mouth, and kept her eyes fixated on the TV screen.

As she'd predicted, few seconds later her mind took her back to the University of Dublin. It was December 9th, 1952.

Five days ago, the 27-year-old student had waved goodbye to her best friend, Emilia Doherty and Emilia's baby, Emmet. She was emotionally drained and miserable after they'd bid their farewells to each other in the middle of the night. For this reason, the journalism student from Great Britain chose to skip all her classes that week. She'd planned to work at a slow pace on her assignments from home and to sleep in each day. The student earnestly tried to convince herself that she wasn't even a little bit depressed, but she was. Being down in the dumps was something she'd never felt before. Her uncertainties about her emotional stability were the reasons that she was still lying in bed when she was frightfully woken up by a frantic, garish banging on the front door of her studio apartment. Ruby lived alone. Her studio was located just beyond the southern border of the university's campus.

Her only roommate was a stray street cat she'd adopted two days after she moved into her first apartment. She called the stray animal Temple, after Shirley Temple, her favourite childhood writer. The university student, who was guilty of absenteeism, had been bunking off the entire week. Startled awake by whatever the hell was on the other side of her front door, she opened her large green eyes and took a blurry peek at the modern, metal alarm clock she'd received as a high school graduation present. Her Caravel clock was sitting on her nightstand next to her open make-up case and a dirty water glass with long forgotten, green rotting lemons wedges in it.

Knowing that she'd taken a risk by filling her best friend Mia's knapsack to the brim with stolen university contraband, she knew she needed to score more than a few good karma points. Likewise, she knew it was time to start attending classes once more to avoid becoming the centre of the wrong kind of attention. Therefore, yesterday, she'd committed to herself to attend classes at the university again this very afternoon. Today was the day she'd force herself to ignore her unhappiness and find her normal educational groove. She could see that the alarm clock hadn't gone off yet, because the little hammer mechanism that needed to hit the chrome bells on either side of it hadn't moved even a millimetre. Because she'd been expecting the sound of the chrome bells to be ringing, the deafening banging on her door had startled her, which immediately put her in a proper, prissy-missy bitch mood. Even though she knew that her small studio space amplified noises of any kind, the rude fist-thumping sounds had set her on fire with anger! Besides this, she was still filled with less than a week old, melancholic tidbits from the hardest farewell of her life.

All of this, combined with interrupted sleep, had a very impulsive and unpredictable student yanking the door open and raging, "What the bloody hell do you want?"

A shocked, yet unmistakably determined, blonde-haired, blue-eyed wanker puffed his chest up, just as real men of importance did when they were on a mission. Then he pushed his long windblown hair off his forehead and self-assuredly asked, "Are you Ruby McEwen?"

"Bingo!" she cheekily cried out, trying to be more appealing than she already was. Her tone was now deliberately sarcastic.

She knew, in a second or two, that she had an instant problem. The tall blonde male that she'd just blasted, was too friggen good-looking. He had a prominent clef in his chin and Ruby had always had a thing for alluring men with chin clefs.

Seeing that she hadn't even remotely made an impression on him, she changed her answer to a very eager, "Yes, I am."

After scanning her body, as all young blokes did when a stunning young woman opened the door wearing nothing but a nightie, he blushed and slightly stuttered, "Oh, ohh, ohhh, okay. Good to know."

The embarrassed, scarcely dressed Ruby stood there thunderstruck. She fiddled with the ends of her thick, wavy, tawny coloured hair that hung to down her waist. Her long, lean, bare legs and full breasts balanced out her very trim body with its appealing and subtle curves. Standing in front of the clerk, she was still soldering from her irritations. Ruby, like many times before, was oblivious to the effect she had on a man who gawked at her. She had yet to recognize the signs of a fellow being captivated by her female attractiveness, because she had yet to identify with her own femininity. The nightie she wore scarcely covered her. The wide-eyed, blonde clerk was, without doubt, aware of this and he was enjoying every centimetre of its sheerness. After Grady took two steps towards her open door, he delighted in watching her squirm. He intentionally stood closer to her. Her self-consciousness was blushing again.

He was rendered a goner in no time. Ruby had no idea she was such a beauty. Her looks were never commented on at home, or in the rural community where she'd been raised. In all probability, this was because she was almost never in the public eye while growing up under her mother Sadie's watchful eyes. Aside from going to school, she didn't leave her parents backyard. This was why the girl had no idea at all that she was perhaps the loveliest lass in the entire English county of Essex.

Despite her lack of vanity, she was certainly eye-catching and intelligent enough to make an impression. For now, she was admittedly mortified that she'd been so rude to the drop-dead gorgeous fella with a University of Dublin administration office nametag on. Her messy hair was tickling her cheeks, so she tucked it behind her ears.

Hmmm, the clerk thought, as he stared at her lovely face, *this beauty has two flaws.*

Ruby sensed what he was thinking, lost her composure, and blasted him, "If you make one unkind remark about my oversized ears, I will give you a good, hard kicking!"

Blimey, he thought, she's pegged me already.

She untucked her hair, which immediately hid both of her reasonably large embarrassments. Angrily, she grabbed her robe off the bed and covered herself, as all proper young women were expected to do in the 1950s when in the presence of a young man. This put an abrupt end to the clerk giving her another glance over. He hurriedly extended his hand and introduced himself as Grady Walsh.

Then he assertively said, "You need to come with me right now Miss McEwen. The university's dean of students wants to see you straight away. I have been instructed to tell you that it is an emergency."

Seeing a very large, evil looking tomcat with yellow, intense-coloured eyes glaring at him from a windowsill above the kitchenette, Grady stepped backwards and said, "I will wait for you outside. Please hurry or Dean O'Sullivan will have my head on his plate for lunch."

Then he shut the door as fast as he could. Grady Walsh hated cats.

The young Ruby knew that occasionally a situation required her to control her temper, stop flirting, keep her big mouth shut, and just do as she was told. Deciding that this was one of those situations, she fought her itch to be extra charming and got dressed in the speed of a true British whippet. Even though the dean's assistant, Grady, had given her an impulse to apply a bit of makeup, she ignored the urge to 'primp herself for the sake of an irresistible young man'. For some reason she wanted to impress the blonde bloke she'd just met. She'd already melted down him down to a spellbound state, but in her typically naïve, Ruby-fashion, she was oblivious to this. She gave her mute tomcat a friendly petting under his chin and then left her embarrassingly messy studio apartment. The instant the studio door was closed, Temple started purring again. Temple hated men.

Rather pompous-like, Grady was standing just outside her front door, eagerly waiting to carry on with his assignment. She'd almost run into him as she darted out the door.

"Give me some bloody space!" she blared.

"Shut up and follow me!" he blared back, "we really must hurry up."

Ruby was irrefutably worried about what he'd called 'an emergency', but his eye-catching face and muscular physique was an enjoyable distraction from the apprehension she could feel rising from the pit of her stomach.

"Goddammit slow down!" she screamed while running behind the clerk with legs twice as long as hers were.

She's a feisty one, Grady thought, beaming, as he ran even faster.

While they sprinted across the campuses knolls and over its cobblestone paths, she caught a glimpse of the lantern pole she'd stood next to just four nights ago. She kept running and hoping that nothing had happened to Mia and her baby boy. She didn't know what she would do if they were the reason for the dean's urgent request. Ruby had written emergency contact information- her name, and the telephone number of the university on a piece of paper and slipped it deep inside the pocket of Mia's rucksack.

Either something had happened to them, or she was about to be expelled for stealing supplies earlier that week? She concluded.

Fuelled by worry, she put more effort into running faster. With fleeting visions of Mia and Mac now in her mind, her heart raced as it tried to keep pace with her suspicions. She knew that since she was a wee child, whenever her heart raced it was sending her a message. Despite this, she had no time to pay attention to the speed of her heart. She was too busy huffing and puffing behind Grady and his long legs.

Bloody hell, he's goddamn fast, she silently cursed.

Seven nerve-racking minutes later, she sat with cramping leg muscles in front of a massive, dark mahogany desk. Waiting to know what this was all about, she was perspiring, trembling, and psyched up. Grady had instructed her to go in and take a seat before he dismissed himself and closed the office door behind her. She was left alone and curious if she'd ever see this flirtatious blonde guy again. When Dean O'Sullivan entered his office, he was wearing a pinstriped suit and a seriously grave expression. She'd never met him before, so she immediately stood up and extended her hand.

"Sit down," he instructed with professional and utter composure.

Her backside hit the chair before she even realized that she was obeying his command. The dean was a short, light skinned, sharply dressed, and balding man. Ruby assumed that in his prime he must have been a fetching fellow.

Nevertheless, his prime had obviously abandoned him years ago, she guardedly reckoned.

She knew that she shouldn't be having such strong and opinionated ideas about other people, but she was still young, rather socially inexperienced, and a bit impetuous. Trying to be fair to her fallible side, she forgave herself and dismissed her assumptions and self-scolding. The dean then extended his hand and gave her permission to stand up again, which naturally she did. She tried to slouch when she stood up, knowing that her height would have her towering over the small and dumpy dean. It seemed to work, given that they were practically at eye level as they formally greeted each other. After briefly shaking her hand, he immediately commanded the journalism student to sit back down, which she gratefully did because muscle cramps were creeping into her legs after sprinting behind the dapper and cleft chinned whirlwind named Grady Walsh.

Then, the now unexpectedly seething man leaned over his side of the desk. What he lacked for in height, he made up for with pure confidence and positional power. He skipped any informalities and immediately addressed the reason why she'd been summoned.

"Have you heard the news coming out of your country this week?" he sternly asked.

Being an avid lover of books and words, she didn't own a television or a radio. In addition to this, Ruby had been entirely out of touch with life and any off-campus events since she'd been skipping school and hiding her sadness away from the outside world.

Therefore, she cordially and correctly answered, "No sir, I have not heard any news about England this week."

Realizing that she was not being expelled and knowing that Mia and Emmet were traveling to Belfast and not to England, she relaxed and keenly listened. He then demanded and received her full attention. The dean went on to inform her that there had been a severe weather situation over the British Isles in the past five days.

"You need to call your parents straight away." His voice was still stern and composed. "They are in London, waiting by the phone and they need to speak to you immediately."

Ruby's heart descended into her toes and took her ability to breath with it. Although she was dizzy and shaking, she remained unwavering and determined not to let Dean O'Sullivan see her fear.

The dean then pushed a clunky, olive-green, rotary telephone, with its numerical dialling ring across his desk so that it was within her reach.

"Given the disaster and the nature of the situation, you may use my office telephone. I have been instructed to have you call your grandparents house. Your parents are there waiting to receive your call."

Handing her an index card he said, "This is the telephone number in case you don't have it memorized. Keep the call brief. This is a student privilege that the University of Dublin offers in cases of emergency. Do not abuse my kindness young lady."

She quickly interjected by asking, "Disaster. What is the disaster, sir? Are Sadie and Horace in danger?"

He shot back, "Who?"

She knew exactly what he meant and corrected herself in the blink of her jade green eyes.

"My apologies sir. I meant to ask you if my parents are in danger, sir."

He rigidly informed her of an academic code of behaviour.

"I am not at liberty to tell you anything. The University of Dublin has strict protocols in place for extenuating circumstances such as this."

Firmly, he finished his explanation and pushed his sleeve up to look at his fancy man's wristwatch before exiting his office to give her privacy. Ruby knew he'd be timing her phone call. She tried to remain calm, but she was too nervous and afraid. She was grateful for the index card with the telephone number on it. Her overactive and overtired brain felt all higgledy-piggledy and the numbers were scrambling up in her head. She looked at the index card and wasted no time dialling up her grandparent's central London, downtown flat. She was so rattled, that it took her three dialling attempts before the call was eventually connected.

Horace's family lived in a high-rise flat in the Waterloo District, which was a stone's throw away from Big Ben. Hearing the sound of her grandparent's house telephone ringing, the petrified student braced herself for bad news.

Chapter 41

When Ruby's mother, Sadie, picked up the telephone and heard her daughter's voice, she went into a full-blown frenzy. She was coughing, sobbing, rambling, and repeating, "They are dead. They are dead. They're all dead."

Petulantly Ruby asked her, "Who is dead, Sadie?"

Sadie bawled into the phone.

In between coughs she whispered, "Everyone vanished. They are dead. They are gone. Gone. Dead, Stink. All gone."

Ruby wasn't sure if she should put any real merit into Sadie's desperation or not. For all she knew, her grandparent's fish were dead, or their canary had escaped his cage, flown out an open window and vanished on the streets. Because even a dead fish or a missing canary could send her mother into an emotional tailspin, Ruby was immediately sceptical. Scepticism, at her age, was something she was no stranger to, after living with the unhinged woman on the other end of the line for more than twenty years. The year she graduated high school, she'd planned to escape her mother's obsessiveness and absurdity, but Adolf Hitler's German insanity prevented this from happening. It had taken her an additional five years to enrol in a study and begin her post high school education. Those who really knew the McEwen's from Essex County were not the least bit taken back when she chose to study in Ireland, rather than England.

Although she was used to Sadie's ranting, raving, and overreacting to life, since Ruby left home two years ago. She, hadn't missed her British life for even a second, nor had she missed Sadie for that matter. Ruby's earliest memory of her mother's obsessive and dramatic behaviour started the day Sadie fenced in their back yard to prevent her exploring toddler from wandering out of her sight. Then she attached herself to her daughter, the way a leach attaches itself to an unsuspecting victim. Like those horrid little bloodsuckers, Sadie could drain the life out of her daughter in less than an hour. As time passed, the taller Ruby grew the higher the fence became, and the more neurotic her mother became.

Her father Horace did his best to intervene, but Sadie continuously used his whiskey addiction as a spousal self-defense weapon. Time and time again, she'd call him a cheating drunk and then turn all her attention back in the direction of their only child. Once middle school started and Ruby began attending class's fulltime, she was able to shake off her mother's compulsive overprotectiveness, at least during the day. Being rightly clever, she joined as many after school clubs as she could. This meant that during the week, on schooldays, she'd return home just before dinnertime rather than in the early midday as she'd done throughout elementary school. By this time, Ruby was a twelve-year old and her parent's marriage was undeniably in the crapper. Regrettably, for the pre-teen, this had her mother clinging to her even more.

"Focus Ruby," she heard her the sound of her own voice demanding as she listened to Sadie falling apart on the telephone.

Having no time or tolerance for her mother's sob-filled blathering, she remembered that Dean O'Sullivan had explicitly told her that a long-distance phone call was a privilege that shouldn't be taken for granted. She'd had enough, it was time to take control and take action.

She commanded that Sadie put Horace on the line, "And now!"

After overhearing a quick, muffled struggle between her parents, and more coughing, she heard the deep voice of her unglued father.

Using his most cheerful expression, he said, "Hello my girl, I am so happy you called. Have you heard about the fog over here?"

She rattled off questions laden with worry.

"Not really Pa, why are you at your parents apartment? Why are you and Sadie coughing? Are you sick? Has something happened to grandma and grandpa? Are they sick? Is that why you and Sadie are in London? What or who is dying? Did somebody die? Sadie said they're all dead. What does she mean? Horace, tell me who is dead?"

Horace smirked at his daughter's habitual knack of asking a series of nonstop questions whenever she felt confused or on the edge of fear. Wanting to get straight to it, and having no time for important details, he went on to give her as condensed a version of the situation he could muster up. He continued coughing, which Ruby found odd, given that he'd quit smoking on the day she was born. Only once in a blue moon did her pa take ill.

"Shush sweetheart, be still now," he said, interrupting her. "Are you ready to listen to your old man?"

She quietly replied, "Yes, sir I am." Ruby closed her mouth and opened her ears.

Hmmm, she never calls me sir, Horace thought.

His eyes squinted tightly, and a rather puzzled expression appeared on his face.

"I wish I didn't have to tell you this love, but the city has been fogged in by toxic smog for the past five days. It has claimed many lives, including your Grandma Liza, Grandpa Amos, and your Uncle Reggie."

The sound of her gasping was followed by a considerable period of heavy silence before Horace heard her speak.

"All three of them died in one week. What happened to them?" Ruby heard herself feebly asking. She'd braced herself for bad news, but this was an unforeseen, irreparable tragedy.

This must be what being in shock feels like, she numbly thought.

Horace continued. "I need you to listen to me now Ruby girl. No more questions okay. I will give you the details as soon as you arrive. I've tried to order coffins, but the city's funeral homes and mortuaries have all but run out of them. By the time you arrive, I will have finished assembling three improvised coffins from your relative's wooden trundle beds and different table tops in their flat. The caskets will be patched together, but rough and ready. They will easily serve their purposes. It will all be okay. Trust me."

Horace was coughing again, so he stopped his explanation to catch his breath. He didn't want to scare her more than he needed to.

She wanted to cry, but she didn't. Crying was a sign of weakness and forbidden in the world she'd raised herself in. Sadie's loud sobs in the background sounded like a dull, predictable audio cliché that reminded Ruby that there had never been any room for her own emotions in their family. Her mother's tears and dramas had filled every nook and cranny of the family house since Ruby was a newborn. In addition, her father's daily need to tip the whiskey bottle fuelled her mother's emotional depressions and hysteria's. After listening to her father, while hearing her mother's mania-filled noises in the background of their conversation, she was convinced that her grandparent's flat was overflowing with Sadie's narcissism and cloaked in her emotional suffering. Ruby held out hope that Horace would be sober. If he were clearheaded, no matter the size or severity of the situation, together they could properly deal with this tragedy.

Whilst waiting for her pa to stop coughing, the wise beyond her year's student speculated. She ventured that, similar to the aftermath of WWII, the tragedy that had befallen the UK had made it again, a daunting and vulnerable time for the British people. It was a time when even disbelievers, like herself, would begin to pray. Being wise beyond her years made her a bit of an enigma. There were times when, despite her young age, she had the wisdom of someone with an old soul. She could see into things that others normally wouldn't and couldn't see. Nonetheless, the youngest, most devout less member of the McEwen family didn't believe in God, so prayers were the farthest thing from her mind. She had no brothers or sisters, hence, there had been no one else in their house to share the harsher sides of life with. She was alone. Even today, sitting in the dean's office, she was as alone as a person could be. Being an only child meant that she stood unaccompanied and centre stage when it came to her parent's problems, flaws, and broken relationship. Since she was a child, Ruby had intentionally avoided any avoidable circumstances that could have defined her. This was why she'd grown into a young adult, now in her twenties, who despised and dodged any kind of limelight.

Sweet Jesus, will this cycle ever end? She asked herself.

Horace's coughing had stopped. He was back on the line now, ready to explain more. He told her to pay very close attention to what he was about to say. He was speaking to her in a clear-cut, very articulate manner, so she could tell he was sober. This meant, listening to him and taking him seriously would not be difficult. At any rate, trusting him to stay sober was still something, she feared, would be a lifelong work in progress.

"Ruby, please do not interrupt." He earnestly asked of his daughter.

"Yes, Horace, I will not interrupt you," she promised.

"I have spoken in length with Dean O' Sullivan," Horace said. "He is ready to assist you with reserving a flight. The fog has lifted over the British Isles and the skies are finally clear. Visibility has returned and airports have reopened. It may take you a few days to arrive. The severe weather conditions have caused a concerning amount of backed-up air travel. We will try to wait for you before arranging for the bodies to be removed from the flat. This will give you an opportunity to say goodbye to your relatives. Is this something you would want to do?" he asked her.

"Yes, sir," was her considerate and confident two-word reply.

He was appreciating her obedient phone behaviour. In his opinion, his best girl had been born with an overabundance of his complex McEwen genes. This meant she had been slyly adventurous, headstrong, and a downright handful to raise. He continued his explanation.

"You are a natural born citizen of England, so you can easily purchase a paper ticket at the airport. Irish immigrant restrictions don't apply to you. You need to travel with your student visa and identity card. Remember to pack both of them. Without of each of them, you will not be allowed to leave Ireland or enter the UK. Dean O'Sullivan told me that there are virtually no security checks or baggage restrictions. So, if you travel with only one small bag and arrive at the airport at the right time, you should easily be allowed to buy a ticket and board a plane. I have spoken in length with Dean O'Sullivan. Following our instructions should get you here sooner than later. Right now, Ruby girl, this family needs more of sooner and less of later. You know how to get to Waterloo from the airport. Be careful when you are out on the streets. Although, the smog has lifted, it is dangerous out there. Survivors have lost their minds. All across the city Londoner's are doing precarious, crazy, and unforeseeable things."

Ruby noticed that he was repeating himself. She decided not to point this out and give her pa the empathy he deserved. The man had just lost his entire family at the same time to a gruelling and tragic event. Although he was acting stoical, she knew that he had to be hanging off the brink.

"The immediate health risk in London isn't over yet," he went on to say. "There are hundreds, maybe thousands of sick Brits here my girl. People are moving around the city as if they are sleepwalking. The majority of them are in disarray and shock. A state of madness is on every street corner. Keep your eyes wide open. Do you understand me Ruby?" he point blanked asked.

His exhaustion-filled voice was close to being inaudible.

"Yes, Horace, I do," she directly answered, trying to pump a bit of trust and resilience in him. He went on.

"London City and effected counties are trying to get back to normal. Dean O'Sullivan has airfare for you. Be sure you don't miss your flight. The University of Dublin is generously funding your travel costs due to the circumstances. This is a onetime offer. If you miss your flight, we cannot afford to buy you another plane ticket and then pay for three burials."

Ruby could still hear Sadie in the background. Her mother was sobbing and pleading with Horace to give the phone to her so she could talk with her child. Horace was ignoring his wife's yikkering and theatrical begging. He'd started to cough again. This time his coughs sounded more like asphyxiation.

Even though there were things she still didn't comprehend, Ruby felt herself maturing as she listened to Horace's worrisome coughs and explicit instructions. Unexpectedly, and again for the second time that morning, she heard someone dramatically banging. This time it was on the dean's office door. Recalling that Dean O'Sullivan had looked at his watch before leaving his office, this time, despite that the invasive banging was point-blank maddening, she kept a tight leash on her temper.

"Horace, I need to hang up now. If I am not there by tomorrow evening, carry on without me. I will pay my respects to grandma, grandpa, and Uncle Reggie as soon as I can. They should be tended to and buried on time, with or without me there. I'm off now. The time limit on my free phone call has expired. No worries for me, okay. I've lived in Dublin for a few years now and have enough street savvy to be safe. Cheers Horace," she said, ending their conversation.

She was rather anxious to meet her father in London, who needed her to help him deal with three dead people and his verklempt wife. As long as he stayed sober, she was all his. Ruby was hanging the phone up just as the dean re-entered his office. This time he had a slightly empathetic look on his face. Because he'd been informed of the situation the night before, he already had a plan in place for his exchange student from England. She was explicitly told that she had only one hour to pack small carryon bag and to return to his office.

"Pack just the necessities and wear warm clothing," he emphasized, as he took a seat behind his desk. "I will drive you to Dublin Airport and assist you with buying a ticket. The university purser has already issued me the necessary funds.

He'd decided that giving a student fifty pounds in cash for airfare was in his opinion, a very irresponsible and stupid idea. Dean O'Sullivan was neither an irresponsible nor a stupid man. Only after she had a ticket in her hand, he would return to the university. One of his most talented Journalism students, attending his university, would be spending the night at the airport and taking the earliest flight in the morning. Therefore, warm clothing was a necessity. It was expected of her, that she be one of the first passengers in line at the boarding desk when it opened. If she missed her flight, then she was on her own.

Suddenly the dean then stood up. It was a gesture Ruby interpreted as a sign that he was dismissing her. Spontaneously, she also stood up. She wanted to shake his hand and graciously thank him for the use of the telephone and his generosity. Unexpectedly, the undersized, pinstriped man fiercely slapped his hands together. The fury in his eyes and the aggressive way he then slammed his fists into his desktop staggered Ruby to the core.

"I am not finished yet. Sit back down!" he strictly commanded.

She obediently did as she was told. He could see that she was afraid and trembling; regardless, the dominant little man had already ignited his rage of anger.

"You are about to embark upon an experience that will have an effect on you for the rest of your life! It is highly likely that your travels will change you. Despite the legitimacy and urgency of it all, you are about to be absent for at least another week of classes. Do not think for one bloody blind minute Miss McEwen, that I am not aware of your truancy in the past seven days!"

He was really yelling at her now. A very liable Ruby immediately lowered her eyes and started biting her nails. Hot, impatient tears burned behind her eyelids.

"Look at me when I speak to you and stop eating your fingers! Nail biting is for dimwits! Are you a dimwit?" he wanted to know.

"Yes sir. I mean no. I mean no sir, I am not a dimwit," she dutifully answered.

Then she sat on her hands to avoid the nail-biting temptation she'd been born with. When it became obvious to the dean that he was frightening her more than he'd intended to, he lowered his voice, regained his composure and continued his lecture in a calmer way.

"Miss McEwen, I cannot let your truancy go unpunished. Therefore, I expect you to put your instinctive talent with words to proper use while you are in England. In exactly four weeks from today, I expect to see a legible essay on my desk from you. It is to be no less than five thousand words and six pages long. You are a Journalism major at a notable European university. I expect you to write like one. If I deem your submission worthy, I will submit it to an associate of mine. He is the Editor and Chief at the Dublin Gazette, and the owner of a magazine called Ireland Today."

He then asked her, "Are you familiar with these publications?"

"Somewhat, sir, I have seen the Dublin Gazette sir, but not the Irish magazine you mentioned," she said, respectfully looking directly in his eyes.

"So be it. Upon your return, I recommend that you familiarize yourself with these periodicals. If my associate deems your composition to be worthy of publication, it will be considered for print. Let me be very clear. This is a punishment and a gift wrapped up in an opportunity with a strict deadline attached to it."

Ruby held her breath and fought the compulsion to start biting her nails again. His reprimands, punitive tone, and explicit instructions continued.

"Truancy is a serious offense at this institution of higher education. If you do not meet the deadline, you will be expelled on the same day and sent back to Essex County where you came from. A second chance does not come with this offer. Have I made myself clear?" His tone was frightfully calm.

Ruby nodded her head profusely.

"Yes, sir," she said.

After a few moments, she asked the dean if he was finished. Likewise, yet less liberally, he nodded back. His academic lecture was over.

"I will be back within the hour sir. And I will turn in my composition before the deadline," she assured him.

He looked at his fancy wristwatch again and forcefully said, pointing at his office door, "One hour. Now go!"

She hid her dismay, stood up, and bolted out of his office. For a squatty man, he was a powerhouse who made up for his lack of height with an undeniable high level of professionalism and a fiery temperament.

Grady, who was eavesdropping, was painfully smacked by the office door when the beguiling female student flung it open. As she tore past him, he pretended to be filing documents. She had no time for an apology, a sweet hello, flirting, or hemming and hawing for that matter.

She did however find a few extra seconds of her time to mockingly say, "Serves you right!" as she passed him, running backwards down the long hall. Within fifteen seconds, she was out of the building.

Ruby's long legs sprinted back across the university's green, grassy knolls and cobblestone paths, towards her studio rental. Her studio was located just outside the western perimeter of the campus. It also was in perfect view of the Unwed Mother's Home where she'd met Emilia Doherty and volunteered her services. Seeing an opportunity, she took a shortcut that virtually all of the students took when they were running late for classes. The shortcut had her crawling on her belly, and squeezing her lanky body in between nearly impenetrable, thorn rich hedgerows. The campus gardeners had sternly forbidden students from doing this; however, she decided that breaking a rule for the sake of this emergency was worth the risk. Until she reached the other side, Ruby would need to crawl in the dirt, like a soldier exiting a foxhole. Branches and twigs scratched and bloodied her cheeks, hands, and arms up, but the shortcut had saved her at least ten minutes time. Wanting to impress Dean O'Sullivan, and return ahead of schedule, she knew that she'd be going straight through the hedges again on her way back to his office.

As she sped farther across the campus, she made a mental note to *put a week's worth of food and water out for Temple, add extra baking soda and sand to his litter box, and shut the main gas line off before locking her door, sprinting in reverse, and returning to Dean O'Sullivan's office.* All of which she did.

Exactly fifty-two minutes later, eight minutes early, and on time, the wheezing British student of Journalism, brim-full of adrenaline, arrived at the front steps of the University College Dublin administration building. She was out of breath, perspiring, and carrying an overnight bag.

Before she could place one foot on the building's outdoor stairwell, she heard a car horn letting out a long, twanging honk. It sounded like a goose with laryngitis. Ruby spun on her heels and saw a man peering over the steering wheel of a miniature car. The driver, with his face inches away from the car's flat windshield, was Dean O'Sullivan. He was wearing a red and green-crisscrossed derby and oversized, round sunglasses. The way he looked reminded her of a Lilliputian sitting behind the wheel of a midget's car that was part of a circus act.

Controlling her extremely strong urge to burst out laughing, the student with a serious truancy record flashed her free ride to Dublin Airport an obligingly genuine smile.

Chapter 42

At the end of the campus's main drive, the dean steered to the left, onto an L-road, and then he picked up as much speed as his automobile and L-roads in Ireland's allowed. After only a few minutes, he'd decided that Ruby McEwen was strangely excited for a young student on her way to the burial of three family members.

When he questioned her about her giddiness, she told him that, she'd never before seen or ridden in such thing as this car was. He corrected her rather insulting analogy of his prized possession, by informing her that his car was 'not a thing', it was an original Volkswagen Beetle. His only regret, as the owner of a VW, was the cars association to Adolf Hitler. The dean never understood how a man, responsible for a war that killed millions, could have commissioned such a pleasant automobile back in the 1930's. He dismissed his thought immediately, choosing to enjoy the ride rather than revel in the horrid past.

His student couldn't stop giggling, as she bounced up and down in the front seat. Because his VW had no seatbelts, she was tossed around freely with every bump they went over.

"Why are the roads around Dublin so bumpy?" she curiously asked her ride. She deliberately didn't look at him, knowing that his flamboyant derby and poor choice of sunglasses would have her smirking in a way he'd deem disrespectful.

Ruby hoped he was the same kind of conversationalist as her father Horace was. Otherwise, a boring, heavy silence would hang in the car all the way to the airport. She wanted to leave a good impression on him, after the fiery discussion they'd had in his office a little more than an hour ago. Seeing Dean O'Sullivan on the verge of an answer, she was certain that he was a man who enjoyed Irish banter. After a mere three minutes, she was proven right.

Even the younger, inexperienced version of Ruby McEwen was rarely wrong.

As the dean began to speak, she tightly held onto the sturdy, horizontal handle just above the VW's glove compartment. Steadying herself, Ruby turned in her seat, faced the influential man sitting inches away from her, ignored his comical appearance, and gave him her full attention. She adored hearing a good story, especially, when it was being told by someone who had actually lived through the experience.

"Please begin sir," she said with a slight tone of encouragement.

The dean knew that in order to tell her a proper story, he couldn't avoid his distressing thoughts and memories of Hitler. Hence, he cleared his throat, took a deep breath, manned-up, and began talking.

"After WWII, due to military strikes and a lack of repairs, it took years for Dublin's deteriorated streets, boulevards, and thoroughfares to be restored. Many of the remote roads leading to homesteads, farms, and the coastal areas are still not fully passible. Most Brits forget that seven years is a very short time to repair and restore an entire war-ravaged country. Despite that a majority of the groundwork has been completed, people living in the most isolated areas still need to exit taxi's, buses, or their own vehicles, and walk the remainder of the way to their final destinations. Being beholden to have survived Hitler's madness, they trudged on without complaint or resentment. If the native Dubliners, like myself, were infuriated with anyone for destroying Irish cities, infrastructures, and lives in the early 1940s, it was the Third Reich, not the Republic. Major streets and thoroughfares within the country is marked with a T. The T stands for Trunk Road. Less important roads, like the one we are on, that take us to a Trunk Road, are marked with an L. These L-roads are connection roads because they join small villages and major hubs together." Then, he asked her if she understood.

"I think I do, but I don't have a driving license, so I never needed learned about rural and metropolitan transportation substructures or groundworks."

He was so impressed with her inquisitiveness and use of words that he spontaneously stepped out of his dominant role and chose to ignore the fact that she hadn't called him 'Sir'. Although the airport was less than a fifteen kilometer drive, he needed to take one of these T-roads because it connected University College Dublin to major towns and locations. Dublin Airport was just one of these locations. Before he arrived at a T-road, he had to take two smaller L-roads that were in very bad condition. Deep potholes and exposed rocks meant a slow driving speed to protect his car and not increase the degree of road damage. Ruby was thoroughly enjoying her ride in the Beetle; for her, the slower he drove, the longer her newest Irish experience would last.

She'd forgotten all about Horace, Sadie, and her deceased relatives. She was having a grand time of it while listening to him and taking in the sights as they drove through less significant towns and villages. Since her arrival in Ireland two years ago, she'd been very active with her studies, volunteer work, and a part-time job at the university's cafeteria. Shortly after her enrolment she'd volunteered to work in the scullery at an Unwed Mother's Home affiliated with the University. This is where she'd met Emilia and later Mia's baby boy Emmet.

Wanting to push Mia and Mac out of her mind, she intentionally switched her thoughts of them off and asked, "Sir, did you fight in the war?" She hoped she wasn't overstepping a personal or emotionally sensitive line.

In order to answer her, he needed to ignore the emotions that instantaneously threatened his weak heart and clogged his throat. So, he did.

"No, I did not fight directly. I pledged to and believed in a Neutral Ireland. I do recall that the bombings took Irish folks by surprise. Blackouts and curfews were implemented in some areas. Friends of mine and other residents, who lived on the Eastern coastline, reported they sporadically heard the plummeting zooms and clatter of bombs being dropped over your homeland in the beginning of 1940. Nonetheless, for nearly a year, Ireland's lack of bias had essentially respected the fighting supremacies. After the bombings over our land, many Brits concluded that my country, a Neutral

Ireland, was finally suffering the consequences for remaining impartial during the war against the Third Reich."

Triggered by what Dean O'Sullivan had said, Ruby spontaneously spoke out of turn; unaware that she was interrupting him.

"I was living in the strike zone when the city of London was bombed. The sounds of the blasts were thunderous and ear-splitting. It doesn't surprise me at all that the detonations were heard across the Irish Sea. Please continue sir." She said, correcting her rude behaviour with a touch of, just in the nick of time, verbal etiquette.

Surprisingly, for as old-fashioned and odd as he seemed to be, she found him to be a most interesting little man.

"As you wish," he replied.

"After my brother died in the attack on Dublin in 1941, my convictions about a Neutral Ireland changed. My dead brother's first child had been born on Christmas Day that year. We had just celebrated her birth and rung in the New Year when, the next day, the first series of bombs fell over our country. The Republic was very blessed that no one was killed."

Ruby could see that he'd tightened his grip on the steering wheel, given that his protruding knuckles had turned a straining, stressful shade of white. He took a much deeper breath and continued. Knowing first-hand the signs of post-war emotional trauma, she remained very still and attentive.

"Six months later, in late May, another bombing occurred. This time the Nazi's dropped four bombs on North Strand, where my brother and his family lived. My brother was killed instantly."

Ruby quickly asked, "What happened to his baby and wife?"

Apparently, her spontaneity was not in the mood to remain still and attentive. The Dean didn't seem to notice her impulsiveness.

"They were visiting her parents in Limerick at the time, so they survived the attack," he solemnly replied.

"Sweet Jesus," he heard her cynically whisper.

"It took me almost a decade to let go of my fury and to allow myself to enjoy living life again. Being a Dean of Students and helping my sister-in-law raise my niece, have both become my life's work and my redemption."

Ruby waited long enough to be certain she wouldn't interrupt him again before saying, "I don't know much about what happened here in your country. I became a volunteer nurse's aide after the bombing of London. My focus was on my patients and my own survival, not on the internal political struggles between two islands."

She then asked him if he could tell her about how the post-war Irish people now felt about the post-war British people.

"Are there still lingering rivalries or animosities over the Neutrality issue?" she added. She only needed to wait a matter of seconds for his reply.

"I would like continue our conversation, but we are out of time. We have arrived at the airport," he announced.

As the dean parked his Beetle in front of the terminal's main entrance, he immediately changed back into a boringly subdued and serious man. Promptly, he removed his red and green plaid derby hat and sunglasses. He then put his personal belongings his cars glove compartment, straightened his bowtie in the car mirror, and put his everyday eyeglasses back on. The Irish storyteller had disappeared.

"Please gather your things," he told her.

It was as though his VW enabled him to be wanton in a way walking the campus of the University didn't allow, she thought, realizing that she'd never before seen a person change identities as quickly as this man just had.

Ruby exited the Beetle with difficulty because it was so low to the ground and her long legs were sore from just having sprinted three times across the university's campus. She grabbed ahold of the dashboard handle, just under the windshield with her left hand, and tried to push her 1.80 meter length out of the compact car. Seeing deep, blood-crusted scratches on her hand and wrist for the first time, the dean harshly reacted.

"Miss McEwen, let me see your hands," he demanded.

Straightaway, Ruby did as she was told.

"Pull up your sleeves," he demanded of her again.

Again, without delay, she did as she was told.

"What happened to you? Have you been taking the infamous hedge shortcut on the southern side of the campus? You, just like every other student, know that taking this shortcut is forbidden! I have seen similar scratches on student's hands and arms who disobeyed the campus rules."

Oh crap, she thought, *Dean O'Sullivan isn't the foolish little man the entire bloody student body thought he was.*

His tone was threatening again.

"No, sir," she lied out of self-perseverance. "My tomcat, Temple, didn't want me to leave without him."

She's a real cheeky one, she is, he thought, wearing a slight grin. The problem he had with reprimanding this particular student was, he enjoyed her spunk and intelligence too much; something which, as a dean of students, he'd need to be prepensely aware and wary of. For this reason he raised his voice to a deeper pitched dictatorial level.

"You are to wash all the blood off all of the scratches that 'your cat' supposedly inflicted before your parents see you! I do not want them thinking you have been injured while you were in my care! Agreed?"

He knew she was lying, but he also knew what she would be confronted with in London tomorrow morning; therefore, he decided to ignore her deceitfulness for her emotional sake.

"Yes, sir, I agree."

That was way too easy, she thought, closing the door behind her.

Once his passenger was standing curbside and holding her bag, Dean O'Sullivan leaned over and pushed the passenger door lock down with the base of his palm. Volkswagens were notorious for having tight-fitted locks, door fixtures, handles, and knobs that were hard to manoeuvre. Even steering them required considerable upper arm strength. Which was something men tended to favour about the little vehicle, he recalled, as his cars steering wheel locked solidly into position.

For Ruby, it was obvious that the dean really liked his car. Before they'd started talking about the war, he told her that he was one of the first men to own a Volkswagen in Dublin. He had purchased only a few years ago, in 1950. He remembered the day his Beetle arrived. It was packed in a sturdy, steel pin-sealed wooden crate. The car's frame, chassis, and practically all its parts, were in the same crate and needed to be assembled piece-by-piece. The dean had informed her that she was riding in one of the first ten Volkswagens ever built outside Germany.

His father, Mr. O'Sullivan Senior, was a mechanic who worked on the assembly line at a former tram depot where imported cars were being built. This made it possible for him to see his Beetle come to life while it was being assembled. Whenever he drove it, especially when he looked in the rearview mirror and saw his place of employment, dwindling behind him into the distance, he felt a sense of freedom. Touring in his car offered him independence and a type of liberation that he didn't feel while being a dean of students, a surrogate father, and a brother-in-law, plus a WWII survivor.

Seeing his exchange student standing curbside, dreamily gazing over the parking terrain at the one of airports giant hangers, he realized something. With every kilometre they'd driven, he'd become increasingly impressed by her mindset, openness, and verbal clarity. She still needed to domesticate her youthful impulsivity, but he held out leniency for this; trusting that her impulsiveness was the sign of a passionate and gifted brain. For a reason he couldn't quite yet decipher, she had a quality about her that left its mark on him. It had been a very long time since he'd felt so at ease and opened himself up to the past with anyone, especially a student. Perhaps it was because she'd asked the right questions, or because she was a student in need, whose family had been overcome by a British tragedy that was larger than something they, like thousands of other Brits, could resolve on their own.

Was it possible that Miss McEwen, not just his Volkswagen, had brought out the more relaxed and engaging side of his personality? He contemplated.

Either way it didn't matter, he thought, *she is only one of hundreds of students he was responsible for, and he had a job to get back to.*

For that reason, he stopped pondering, finished locking his car doors, and focused on the most pressing matter at hand, who he could see was distracted yet again! Ruby was still absentmindedly lost in the world of daydreaming when the bark of an angry male voice broke the silence and startled her brain back to reality.

"Pay attention young lady and follow me! No more procrastinating, I haven't got all day!"

Seeing the undersized dean stepping onto the curb, she noticed that he'd already transformed and stepped back into his role as the 'proficient leader of students'.

Walking side by side towards the entrance of the airport, it was obvious to her that Dean O'Sullivan had left his carefree charisma behind, in the glovebox of his compact, beige German automobile.

Chapter 43

The distance between the Waterloo Station and her grandparent's residence wasn't very far but took longer Ruby longer than usual because the metropolitan districts were chaotic and overcrowded. The smog had disappeared and the sky was a bright, crystal clear shade of blue. Citywide, occupants were fleeing their polluted homes in search of sunlight and healthier air. Disgusting odours of smoke and death were floating away from the downtown district on the wings of moderate breeze.

Despite the weather change, the heartbreak of the disaster was still evident on the streets and sidewalks of London. Remnants of the airborne, yellow haze that had blanketed the city for nearly five full days continued to pollute buildings like an invisible poison. Everywhere Ruby looked windows and doors were being opened as wide as possible to rid houses, shops, and businesses of the obscure and highly contaminated air. Boulevards were lined with hundreds upon hundreds of sick, grieving, and deceased people. Most of them still wore protective scarfs around their mouths and noses. Nearly everyone had red, puffy, watery, chemically infected eyes. People across the city were in mild shock and convinced that the vapor-filled smog would return and cause another, more fatal crisis. Threat and anxiety had replaced a carcinogenic fog that just six hours earlier, was polluting the air. In the face of all of this, there was a jubilant and ecstatic sentiment in the city, which blended in with toxic leftovers of the past five days. Alongside a residual silence that the tragedy had created in the Waterloo District, out on the streets Ruby did see a random relieved expression, or supportive handshake, being exchanged among the people. Despite the sporadic evidence of a public positivity that was attempting to come back to life, she had to step over a number of dead body's that had yet to be claimed or removed from where they'd fallen. As a sign of respect, the deceased had been covered with a blankets, bedsheets, plastic tarps, and even decorative tablecloths. Mortuary transport vehicles were collecting the corpses as fast as the sheer number of dead bodies could be counted.

By chance, she crossed paths with man in a white uniform using a black marker pen to write on the bare leg of a female corpse. Ruby assumed he was doing this for identification purposes. Stopping to take a closer look, she saw that the woman had been marked in the same way dead soldiers were marked during WWII. With a quick glance, she could see that the uniformed man had written the name of the street the corpse was being collected from on her leg. He'd torn open her opaque nylon stocking to expose her skin before marking her. Somehow, in a surreal sense, given the warped reality that such a colossal catastrophe had created, her ripped-open stocking made the woman's death feel intimate.

Ruby's experience with death, even at her young age, told her that, what the mortuary employee had done would help a surviving family member find one of the UK's latest disaster victims.

It was difficult for her not to stop and ask if she could help people. Even though so many Londoners were in need of assistance, she ignored her humane urges and walked onwards towards others, who she realized, needed her more. She knew her mother, Sadie, would be despondent and her pa, Horace, who had arranged for her travel, was saturated with worry and impatiently waiting for her to arrive safely. Knowing that Sadie was in a state of uselessness, he would need Ruby more than he'd let on when they'd spoken. For that reason, she picked up her pace and walked faster whilst manoeuvring her way through the crowded sidewalks. About ten minutes later, Big Ben chimed, and cathedral bells rang across the city, announcing that it was 12:00 noon. Since leaving the remains of her stomach in a barf bag on the airplane, she felt suddenly rather famished.

Unexpectedly, Ruby thought she'd caught a glimpse of Sir Winston Churchill walking in the distance. Groups of outwardly disillusioned Brits were tagging along behind him. Wearing his signature Homberg hat and walking with his prominent hunched back and cane, the man looked noble, admired, and distinguished. It just has to be him, she decided. She was a young and long-time loyal fan of the Prime Minister. The news buzz she'd heard after her flight landed was that 'the smog had lifted, and it was now time to lift the spirits of Brits.' The newscaster had reported that 'under clear skies, Mr. Churchill had been seen out in public, studying the damage on the streets and consoling the victims of the devastating debacle. He'd even been seen at the local hospitals and mortuaries. Despite, that the man she'd caught a glimpse of, most likely was the Prime Minister, because of her need to pay her respects to her dead relatives, she dismissed her longing to chase after him; opting rather to make a mental note to *tell Horace about seeing Mr. Churchill.*

Horace McEwen adored Winston. She hoped the British people would give the man a chance. After all, he seemed to be being blamed for every controversy that befell the country in recent years.

"Surely the British society won't blame him for the weather?" she heard herself questioning.

Ruby had a longstanding habit of chatting it up with herself; something she attributed to being an only child who'd grown up with imaginary siblings.

"Are you talking to me?" a hoarse female voice with a very strong Waterloo accent asked.

Looking downwards, Ruby followed the sound, turned to answer, and saw a pathetic looking girl around the age of ten or eleven sitting on the sidewalk less than a meter away. On either side of her were two dead bodies swathed in what looked like divan sheets. The sheets were just about the same colour as the sheets she and Mia had torn into strips and used to make a papoose for baby Emmet last week.

"Goddammit, friggen focus Ruby!" she demanded out loud of herself before finding her composure and calmly asking the girl, "Can I help you in some way?

"Thank you kindly, but no, it is too late for any help now. These bodies are already stiff as boards dead."

The croaky youngster on the sidewalk went on to tell Ruby that she was waiting for someone, anyone, from the mortuary or hospital, any mortuary or any hospital, she repeated, to come and fetch her parents. She had the palest skin and the emptiest eyes Ruby had ever seen before. Even the faces she'd witnessed years ago, during WWII relief efforts, didn't compare the grisly appearance of this recently orphaned child.

She is on the threshold of death, Ruby fretfully assumed.

"How long have you been waiting?" she compassionately asked the girl.

The sidewalk the girl was sitting on, and the cloaks covering her parents, were soiled with a dark brown, almost black coloured layer of something Ruby had never laid eyes on before. Even the hem of the girl's dress and the tips of her loose hair ribbons were tarnished with the same colour. The beaten down and whitewashed, yet astute girl, watched as the stranger she'd just met transparently took inventory of what she'd stumbled upon. The perplexed look on Ruby's face was a definite giveaway of the questions in her mind.

"It is leftover soot," the girl told her before being asked.

Then, the lass drew line on the sidewalk, as if she was drawing a line in the sand and held her blackened fingertip up for Ruby to see.

"For almost three full day's, fragments of soot as big as snowflakes fell to the ground. It was as though black snow was falling over the city."

"Blimey! What the bloody hell!" Ruby cried out in disbelieve, "Soot as big as snowflakes!"

Filled with sympathy and without giving it a second thought, she sat down on the death filled street, just in front of the curb, and crossed her lengthy legs. Then she faced the girl, who continued caressing both of her dead parent's bodies with her devoted, ash-covered hands. Ruby noticed that the poor child's fingernails and nostrils were as filthy as the curb she sat on. Although the girl was in distress and deadened, she spoke articulately.

"It was oddly cold for many days before the fog rolled in. People tried to keep warm. Because we Brits hate the cold temps as much as we hate the rain, thousands upon thousands of us piled extra coal into our fireplaces and stoves day and night. This sent a cloud of black, sooty smoke high into the air. The smoke from our houses, shops, and offices, mixed in with the exhaust from the factories and coal-burning power plants. This made the clouds of toxic smoke gigantic."

Wide-eyed and trembling, she paused to collect her wits.

"How do you know, so specifically, that this is what happened? Ruby asked the cast off creature.

"My neighbour is a coalminer," was her direct and listless answer.

The girl's eyes widen even further, as she spread her arms outwards and upwards and said, "It covered the entire city and probably the whole countryside as well."

Bloody hell, Ruby thought, *the goddam city poisoned itself.*

"See what I mean," the frail and pale girl said with her arm still outstretched and pointing to the right.

Ruby looked in the direction the girl pointed in. In the distance she could see three preposterously tall smokestacks looming over the city block where a massive factory stood in the distance. Smoke was still being pumped out of the stacks. Ruby was too shocked to react. Plumes of smouldering ash were still rising like a whitish-grey coloured triangle; straight up and into the sky as if they were bee-lining for Heaven's gates. Without warning, she heard the rumbling sound of a car motor approaching. She swiftly leapt to her feet to get off the street before she was run over. Horace would never forgive her if she gave him another coffin to build and another body to bury.

"How much can you pay?" a boy who appeared to be much too young to be driving shouted through the vehicle's open window. He was wearing a floppy, oversized, button-down black coat. His matching black top hat, which nearly covered his eyes, was clearly much too big for his head. The boy had slowed the hearse he was driving down long enough to make his eager inquiry.

The grieving girl on the sidewalk, who had resumed caressing her dead parents, dejectedly implored, "I have no money."

The young man sped off without hesitation in search of the next curbside victim he'd easily come across. Eventually, someone the boy offered his services to would have enough money to pay for the removal of their dead. Ruby hoped that Horace had enough money to bury their own dead relatives. She'd been doing an incredible amount of hoping since Emilia had left her behind in Dublin six days ago and Dean O'Sullivan had driven her to the airport yesterday. Growing tired of her own pitiful emotions over Mia, she had a deep-seeded hankering to do something worthwhile and make a difference. Given the excessive amount of tragedy she'd just witnessed while walking from the train station, she was certain that as the day unfolded, she'd be needed in a way she'd never before experienced.

"That's the fifth time today someone looking to snatch up dead bodies for a profit has stopped to ask me how much I can pay," the impassive girl said whilst staring upwards at a blinding sun.

Ruby was taken back by the amount of grief-stricken people she'd passed since she'd stepped off the train. Without a moment's hesitation she opened her canvas travel bag and reached deep inside. After a bit of rummaging, she pulled out a small suede, drawstring pouch. She then told the girl to cup both of her hands and hold them out in front of her. The girl confusingly obliged. Ruby then opened the suede pouch and flipped it upside down. The money Dean O'Sullivan had given her for food fell out and into the shivering girl's grime covered hands. Ruby was supposed to eat before the flight, but her fear of flying had killed her appetite before she boarded the plane; therefore, she still had three-shilling coins, two bank notes, and a few sixpence's leftover.

Before the stunned and desolate girl could react, Ruby bent down, gently squeezed her shoulder and said, "Best of everything to you luv."

Then she scurried off, gasping on the smell of soot in her nose and the taste of death in her mouth. About five minutes later, Ruby turned the corner, crossed the road, and stepped onto Friar Court Lane. Her grandparent's residence was only about 150 meters away. Her stomach began to churn and burn. Fear and anxiety had arrived.

"I'll be there in no time," she told herself.

Even though she was tired from the emotional time of it she'd had since Mia's departure, the stress of disaster and death, plus the early flight she'd just taken, adrenaline surged through her body. Being needed always had a way of making her feel exhilarated, especially in the midst of tragedy. Her experiences throughout the Second World War had changed her perspective on life. Despite that she'd had a rough night whilst sleeping on the airport floor atop a stack of old newspapers, she was in a rightly upright mood. At 5:00am when the boarding gate opened, she'd been the second person in line. She reminded herself to tell Dean O'Sullivan about her airport experience. He would want to know, and she would want to brag.

Now, she was hungry and desired a nice hot cuppa before she began helping her family members, the dead ones and the living ones. Knowing that she was, for the first time in a few years, about to become entangled in her mother's lopsided neediness, her mind raced with anticipation. Seeing her grandparent's apartment building across the street, Ruby couldn't help thinking how extremely full Horace's hands must be, with the likes of Sadie and three corpses tainting a small, one-bedroom flat.

She prayed to a Sweet Jesus and the Holy Hail Mary she'd been raised to praise, that Horace hadn't gone berserk yet, or drank himself into a bloody stupor.

Chapter 44

The original Friar Court Flats sign still hung above the main entrance to the four-story apartment building that Ruby had frequently visited while growing up. Although she'd spent summers at her grandma Bessie Dutton's ranch in America, she visited her English grandparents on major holidays like Easter, Christmas, and Boxing Day.

Standing now, almost directly under the familiar sign, she looked up and gawked at it. The sign, which was slightly swaying above her head, had always made her feel like she belonged in the city. She treasured the apartment buildings original, hand-carved symbol. Since she was just a child, seeing it meant that she'd arrived at Granny and Grandpa McEwen's flat. As wee lass, Horace would hoist her up high above his head so she could swat at the sign before they entered the building. It was the first thing they'd traditionally do before going inside the apartment complex and climbing three flights of stairs to greet her grandparents. Likewise, it was the last thing they traditionally did after their visits ended and they descended three flights of stairs before walking to the bus depot on their way back to Essex. Her earliest memories of their visits to London were permanently engraved on her brain. Horace always brought his mother, Liza, fresh cut roses and his father, Amos, a bottle of Jameson whiskey. Reggie, his youngest brother, would receive a popular book or new tool of some sort. Her mother mostly always stayed behind doing whatever it was she did when no one was home. For years, her parents, Horace and Sadie, weren't on speaking terms, which made them polar opposites of her McEwen grandparent's, Amos and Liza. Horace's mum and pa were cheery people who had only one grandchild, therefore, Ruby soon became all the sunshine in their lives. They spoiled her terribly, but not in the customary way. They didn't have many possessions or riches, therefore, beginning when she was still in nappies, they pampered her by doting on her and giving her the gift of their time.

Little Ruby had been allowed to freely explore their London neighbourhood long before she was permitted to explore beyond parents backyard. Given that Sadie had fenced her daughter in until she was nearly 12 years old, if it hadn't been for her grandparents, she would never have learned to become street smart. For the better part of sixteen years they'd insisted that Horace bring her to them alone for visits. Sadie wasn't invited or welcomed. Although they were righteous people, who never openly ridiculed Sadie's parental ways in front of her, they knew that their daughter-in-law's obsessive rearing methods were stifling and emotionally damaging their innocent grandchild. Therefore, they indirectly intervened and made a difference for Ruby as often as they could.

Thinking about all of this was distracting her. She needed to get her lifelong habit of daydreaming under control. She wasn't in London to daydream. A serious purpose was waiting for her inside the old, rather rundown building that now towered over her. A few minutes had already passed since she'd arrived at Friar's Court Flats. Nostalgically, she looked up at again the thick wooden sign with a fat friar on it. Despite that it was soot covered she was delighted that the sign still hung from its original, dinged-up, corroded iron hooks and chains. The timber sign had been handcrafted from a fallen tree in the forest that once bordered the city. It was mounted to the building back in 1840. Although the paint had chipped and the lettering was less distinguishable, the friar's fat round belly, baldhead, and chubby face were still quite prominent. There he was, like the merriest man in all of England, hanging from the same building for almost one hundred and thirteen years. Reminiscing over the sign reminded her how much she revelled in the history of people and things.

One day I really must get my hands on this sign and restore it so it can live on forever, Ruby animatedly thought. Then, she made another one of her incorrigible mental notes to *ask the current proprietor about it.* He'd known her since she was a baby, so she hoped that she'd have a decent chance of one day owning this remnant of the past. Briskly, she was overcome with a mischievous type of childhood bliss. With her deeply scratched hands and scabbing long arms, she jumped up and whapped the sign as hard as she could. As it swung back on forth, the rusty chain made recognizably loud creaking sounds. The smile on her face while she watched the old sign swinging wildly back and forth was nearly as wide as the friar's belly was.

"I swear Ruby girl, one of these days that old sign is going to fall down and knock you out cold!" she heard a man's voice crying out.

Caught off guard, she turned towards the front door, impulsively dropped her bag onto the sidewalk, and called out, "Horace!"

Then she leapt into his arms before he'd had a chance to finish teasing her. He lifted her up and planted a big wet kiss on her forehead. Practically in unison she kissed him on the cheek. Since phoning him from the dean's office and grasping how grim the situation was, she'd been more shaken up and troubled than she'd allowed herself to admit. Truth be told, she'd arrived in London as a bag of roused up nerves. She'd already decided not to tell her pa that when the twin-engine plane she'd flown in had crossed over the sea, and hit patches of turbulence, she'd feared for her life. Nor would she reveal how vomiting into a wax lined paper bag had only made her flight worse. Topping this off, less than fifteen minutes ago she'd encountered a desolate girl on sitting on a sidewalk who was vigilantly safeguarding her dead parents. *I could have been her,* she'd realized, as Dean O'Sullivan's dosh fell into the hands of someone who needed money more than she needed food.

As effected as Ruby was by the harrowing events of the past twelve hours, and the devastation she'd just witnessed since walking from Waterloo Station, she wouldn't be saddling Horace with anything she could handle on her own. He had enough worries already, so accordingly, she kept her mouth shut and lavished him with the type of affection any overwrought and grieving man deserved. It was a rightly hearty greeting that she almost certainly needed more than he did. Her father could see that she'd done a lot of maturing since she had graduated and went off to pursue a higher education in Ireland. The change in his daughter was something Horace recognized as soon as he laid eyes on her. He saw differences in her that surpassed the ones that had been a result of WWII. His daughter was becoming a cultivated and edified woman.

Ruby noticed that he was wheezing. Nevertheless, on the flip side, he smelled like fatigue and sweat, not whiskey. For this reason, his only child was beyond grateful for how bad her father ponged.

"I've missed you Pa," she said, stepping back to give him a proper looking over and supportive smile.

He'd lost some weight, which he needed to lose, but certainly not under these circumstances. In addition, he looked shattered and in poor health, which was rather troublesome for Ruby. His appearance had her feeling indebted to her wisdom, intuition, and decision not to tell him about any of her own predicaments. The man was obviously burdened, and she was in London to lighten his load, not add bricks of her own challenges to it.

With this being decided, she turned on the charm. With a bright faced smile, she endearingly said, "I haven't seen you in almost fifteen full moons Pa."

Hmmm, my best girl hasn't called me pa, or mentioned full moons in years, Horace thought, as he picked up her bag and followed her up the stairs.

"First one to the top!" she spiritedly squealed out.

Then, just as like she'd done so many times before, she sprinted up the stairs taking two steps at a time. It was an unfair race. His daughter had the advantage of inheriting his long legs and her strong body was nearly four decades younger than his was. Since she was about eleven, she'd easily beaten him at any foot race they'd ever had. With this in mind, Horace took his sweet time climbing up the flat's narrow winding staircase to the third floor.

When he finally arrived at the top of the stairwell, he was winded and sweating, dragging his feet and rasping. His haughty daughter sat on the top step and mockingly whistled, as though she'd been waiting for an hour. There she was, sitting all smug-like on the apartment landing in the hallway. He could see that she was overconfident and still too big for her boots. Her arrogance and Pollyannaish female vigour filled the foyer, leaving no space for his out of breath gasps. Seeing her like this again, after what felt like an eternity, reminded Horace of how his best girl had radiated positive energy since she was an infant. Today, despite the horrific circumstances, her enthusiastic stamina was older, unchanged, and greatly needed by her struggling with sobriety and emotionally devastated father. Making it to the last step in front of the landing where she so smugly sat, Horace deliberately, with all his might, flung her heavy travel bag straight at her and knocked her off her beautiful, jaunty arse.

"Take that Blinky!" he cried out with a wink, as she toppled onto her back from the power of his throw.

The man was known for his ability to forcefully hit a target from any distance. He'd called his girl Blinky since she was a wee little lassie, because, in the blink of an eye she could turn something negative, even a catastrophe like the one she was about to encounter, into something upbeat and entertaining.

284

That's my girl, Horace proudly thought, *dammit, it feels liberating to laugh again.*

Ruby was good for her father. She brought out the intuitive and younger man in him. When he was sober, he was just as good for her as she was for him. When he was drunk, she avoided him. His recent sobriety reminded her that she had a man in her life that she could rightly depend on and properly windup. Sadly enough for both of them, when she'd started high school and found her independence, they had grown apart. He knew his boozing and Sadie's phobic ways had taken their toll on Ruby since she was old enough to recognize and feel the emotional wrath of her parent's bad choices. Nevertheless, for now, in this very moment, he couldn't remember the last time they'd been so spontaneous and good-humoured with each other.

Bloody pity, Horace thought as he inserted the key into his parent's apartment door. The old man knew this was about to change.

Chapter 45

The moment Horace opened the door to her grandparents Waterloo flat Ruby was overtaken by a penetrating smell of rotted eggs and bleach. The odour was noticeably stronger than the sulphurous, burnt stench of coal still hanging in the air outdoors and in the Friar Flat's stairwell. The indoor air reeked because the building was putrid and musty, as were so many of the city's structures that had been spared the wrath of Hitler's bombs. Or so she thought.

Her grandparents had lived in this old apartment building since long before she was born. Even though the space inside their home was cramped, it was cosy and functional. The sitting room was where she'd spent most of her time whenever she visited the British side of her lineage. Throughout most of her childhood, this is where she'd played board games, drawn pictures, read books, and written stories. Some of her finest memories were made when her grandfather Amos and her uncle Reggie were both at home during her visits. These two men had a way of livening up her life and including her in whatever mischievous deeds they were up to. As she grew older, listening to the wireless and Reggie's gramophone records replaced her childhood whims and games. Throughout the evening, the entire family sat together around the coal-burning fireplace in the front room laughing and talking. Because Horace and Amos were both fond of a telling a superb story, sitting in silence was something the McEwen's seldom did.

Back then, each morning before breakfast, Ruby's chore was to clean up the sooty mess the coal had left behind in the fireplace after the previous day. Coal was grimy, so she turned into grubby little thing while carrying out her task. She'd didn't mind the grunge on her hands and clothes; being soiled made her feel seen and accomplished. Even at a young age her hardworking character was intact. She'd been born inquisitive and eager to please. Her grandpa preferred coal over wood, so coal it was.

Grandpa Amos knew that coal burned slower than wood, which kept the flat warmer throughout the stonier and damper months of the year. She was allowed to collect the tiny black, burnt-out coal fragments and use them to sketch pictures. In her opinion, this was the best thing about her grandpa's obstinate personality and practical partiality to coal versus wood. Her grandmother, Liza, had a sewing corner in their flat's dining room. It was her private space that was located through an open archway next to the salon; or family room as it used to be called. As her eyes aged, Liza's sewing corner became too dark and dim, making her ability to thread a needle and stitch proper seams annoyingly difficult. In 1920, two years after World War One ended, Horace began earning a good-sized wage, so he bought her a baroque, copper gas lamp with a frosted glass cap. Ruby could now see that the nicest gift he'd ever given his mum still hung from the wall above her darning table. The lamp was only used when Grandma Liza was sewing. By the light of the lamp she would spend hours on end stitching, embroidering, and knitting her family's clothing, the drapes, and all of their household linens. In no time, she began taking on sewing jobs for friends and people in the neighbourhood. This earned her extra pounds each week and made her feel like a financially productive woman. As the decades passed, Mrs. Amos McEwen became known as being a devoted doer and mender. Since the late 1940s, her reputation was most evident when post-WWII garment rationings began, and people were forced to preserve the clothing they already had. It was a grassroots time when frugality still reined in the minds of the masses.

Ruby was now standing next to Eliza's darning table. It was evident that her grandmother had been busy with her craft just before she'd died. The decorative baroque lamp hanging above her sewing table was still lit. Ruby went over to it, turned the gas control lever, and shut the lamp off. Then she hung back a few moments to watch the lamps gas mantle turning a bright orange colour before dwindling out like a firefly at daybreak. She'd always liked watching the gas mantle changing colour. It was a magical type of simplicity for a 1920s child. Despite that, she'd again enjoyed the mantel's glow, as she'd done so many times growing up, this time it told her young adult brain that the apartment's main gas line was still open. Because she was an educated student with a probing awareness, she was seldom frightened of what she encountered or didn't know. Not understanding something stimulated and challenged her searching mind. Despite that she wasn't aware of it yet, during the 40s and 50s, she was a rare breed of female. She would choose, above other options, to figure out life and the way things worked completely on her own. She had a deep-rooted knack for taking chances and researching the how's and why's of life, over being told to do something without knowing the rhymes, reasons, and facts behind the task.

None of that mattered now, because what she did know was that coal and gas fumes could be poisonous and fatal. Worldwide, the combination of hydrogen, methane, carbon monoxide, and Sulphur, were what posed the greatest threat to people living in unventilated spaces. The chemical combination was a highly flammable composition. Occupants of any building with poor aeration ran the risk of carbon monoxide suffocation. The student rightly knew the flat needed to be thoroughly inspected. For this vital reason, she seized the helm and precisely instructed Horace to shut the main gas line off before he did anything else. As her pa walked off towards the utility closet, she continued examining the residence with three dead people in the next room. Her mother Sadie was somewhere in the flat, nevertheless right now, she wasn't even the slightest part of Ruby's priority.

There were two towering picture windows in the front room of the apartment. Both of the window frames began just above the solid oak floor and ended just under a high, white, ornamental plastered ceiling. The windows had deep sills that were still cleverly being used as bookshelves, a place to sit, and indoor plant stands. The lofty windows literally pulled the scope of the city into her grandparent's high-rise home and offered them a splendid metropolitan view. When the Third Reich's bombing of London destroyed some seventy-five percent of the city's infrastructure, including the entire city block directly in front of the Friar Court Flats building, it left the residents of the flat a boundless, panoramic view of a vast city horizon in the distance. As she stood there now, looking out original windows that had survived the war, she relished in the liberated feeling that the infinite view gave her. The view quickly eliminated the feeling of being trapped indoors and separated from the urban outdoor space. Looking out at wide-open, green, tree lined terrain, as opposed to filthy smokestacks in the distance, was rare in the city's downtown districts. After the war, if massive factories with tall flue's had been rebuilt on that particular plot of land, her grandparent's view would have been ruined. Until now almost no new industry had taken over this particular area of the Waterloo District. This was rare, given that so much of London had changed since its annihilation at the hands of the German Regime. Despite the city's current, still undetermined and immeasurable tragedy, at least the two McEwen family survivors had a splendid view to be grateful for. The spacious picture windows could make her grandparents poky living quarters look bright and grandiose. Especially on a day like today, when there wasn't a single cloud in the sky.

She knew that the apartment's open-styled bedchamber also had the same kind of window in it. Unfortunately, it was a rather dismal room that offered the sun very little opportunity to shine its light-filled rays into it. The sleeping quarters spanned the entire width of the flat's back wall, which was located only a few meters adjacent to another high-rise. Of the three windows in the apartment, the bedroom window was the only one that could actually be opened. This was where Horace and Sadie had laid the deceased bodies out. Ruby planned to inspect the safety of that room as well, but not until she was ready to see her dead relatives. She was used to seeing dead bodies, but she'd never before seen the corpse of a deceased family member. She anticipated that this would be quite unpleasant, given that the cadavers would look similar to the bloated, unclaimed bodies she'd just seen and stepped over on the streets below. Looking downwards, towards the sidewalks, she wondered if that poor girl's lifeless parents had been picked up for burial yet.

"Goddammit Ruby, stop being so musing and concentrate!" she heard herself loudly cursing. It was times like this she detested how effortlessly she could become side-tracked.

The coal stove was still burning in the parlour. In lieu of the fact that it had kept that section of the flat warm, seeing the stove's embers had her aptness rightly troubled. The very risky situation they were all still in required her to stop reminiscing, use her knowledge, and take action. To do what she already knew needed to be done, she indisputably needed her unpredictable and strung-out father's cooperation and help.

"Horace did you shut the main gas line off?" she asked with a sombrely demanding tone.

"Yes, I did, about five minutes ago," he responded with confidence in his still raspy voice.

"I need you turn off every gas valve there is in this apartment. Then turn around a recheck them to make sure you haven't overlooked any valves. It is crucial that they are all turned off."

Hearing fear in her voice, he asked her, "Why?"

"You will see soon enough, just get to it. It is important that you are very thorough, time is a wasting."

This time she replied somewhat impatiently. It was a reaction he should have anticipated, knowing how much she disliked repeating herself. Horace went from room to room, as he'd been instructed to do, and shut everything off. This meant that the valves on the stoves, lamps and even the water boilers under the sinks were closed-off. Any appliance that was gas fed was also secured. Overall, this took him about ten minutes to do. Finding the right wrench had taken longer than the actual chore had. Seeing her father perform with real purpose reminded her of how fortunate she was that he was sober. Ruby needed him lucid, because she undeniably couldn't do what needed to be done on her own. He returned and pompously announced that he was finished.

"Are you still sober?"

She had intentionally and insensitively asked him the one thing that she rightly anticipated would anger him. Nonetheless, their situation was critical and his 'attempts at sobriety' had fooled her too many times in times past.

Holding his trembling hands in front of her, as evidence, he said, "Yes, Ruby girl, I am sober."

She knew if his hands trembled that his blood was relatively alcohol free, and he hadn't drank in a few days. As a rule the smell of alcohol on his breath and his whiskey laden, steady hands, had been dead giveaways of his addiction for as long as she could recall. She suspected that his not having a drink in three days wasn't because he didn't crave one or deserve one for that matter. It more likely was because on the first night the fog rolled in, he drank the last drop of liquor in the flat. She knew him, in this way, better than he knew himself. Horace never could have predicted that he wouldn't be able to go to the liquor store the next day to replenish his supply. The fact of the matter was, until greeting Ruby on the street under the swinging Friar Flat's sign, he hadn't been able to leave the building.

She knew that her father's own father, Amos, also had a serious love affair with bottled spirits. Regardless, she was positive that Reginald, Reggie for short, Horace's youngest brother, didn't drink, and died as sober as he was on the day he was born. Both Reginald and Ruby never touched a drop of alcohol. Growing up with alcoholic family members had undeniably seen to this. Ruby could tell by the untidy state of the apartment that Horace had frantically searched in every cabinet, cupboard, and crack and crevice of the place for a hidden stash of whiskey. Her grandma Liza and her mother Sadie were both domestic tyrants when it came to keeping a neat and uncluttered home. She was convinced that this was why Horace hadn't succeeded in finding a bottle. Truth be told, his trembling hands were all she needed to see to know that he was, for the time being, not under the influence.

"I am sober Ruby," he repeated.

"I believe you Horace and I have faith in you."

"Have faith in me for what?"

"Faith that you turned every gas valve off, and we will not be blowing the roof off this building today," she told him.

The next thing Ruby did, even before asking about her mum Sadie, was take a tin container filled with long and sturdy wooden matches from the cupboard in the parlour. She then lit one, blew it out and held it up to the ventilation pipe above the parlour's large built-in corner heater. This was the main exhaust pipe that exited the apartment through the sidewall.

"What are you doing?" Horace asked her.

"I am testing the safety of the stove," she answered. "Come closer and have look."

Horace took a few steps in her direction.

"Because the smoke from the match is coming back into the room, it means there is a backdraft. The breeze outside is making the city air safer, but it is also making being inside this flat very dangerous."

Feeling somewhat uneducated, which he essentially was, he again asked her, "Why?"

Ruby explained, "Carbon monoxide is made when fuels, like gas, oil, coal, and even wood, don't burn in a satisfactory way. When a fire burns in an enclosed room, like this one, the oxygen in the room is gradually used up and replaced with carbon dioxide. Carbon Dioxide is pure poison."

Due to ramifications of the First World War and hardships of the Great Depression, Horace had never completed any type of education. His daughter had always been aware of this. This harsh detail of his life was the single motivating force behind his fatherly conviction that she received fitting educations at legitimate and highly regarded schools. Listening to her now, speaking like a refined chemist, reassured him that she was indeed learning.

Ruby sensed his uneducated shame, therefore she considerately asked him, "Horace, how is it possible that everyone inside the flat choked and died, but you and Sadie didn't take ill or perish from the poisonous air?"

Although he didn't comprehend the scientific facts while listening to his girl explaining how air can become toxic by burning coal, he had reasonably deducted that the reason he and Sadie were alive was a simple and fortunate one. They weren't in the building long enough to die in it. He may not have been an educated man, but he was a logical man who knew the basics. Horace was in no way either intuitively or psychologically prepared to take responsibility for the most recent tragedy that had claimed the lives of his three remaining family members. He had a second-rate, unscrupulous sister, named Cecil, whom Ruby had never met. She had once lived somewhere abroad, in the 'Land of Opportunity'. She'd been presumed dead some twenty years ago. To that end, her family had stopped considering her a part of 'anything McEwen', which included being tallied among the living or the dead. To top this all off, Horace's allegiance to his dead family had been destroyed. His daughter could see that he was buried under a dishonourable kind of regret.

The pungent odour of bereavement in the hallway where they stood was cruelly reminding him of the past few days and nights. In five short days, a harsh series of events had led to an incalculable number of deaths throughout the city district and neighbouring suburbs. Intuition had told him to leave the dead behind and try to save himself and Sadie. Therefore, on the second day of the devastating disaster, he took his wife and left the flat. Ten minutes later he carried, actually picked up and carried, a neurotic and screaming Sadie into an underground Metro tunnel. On that night, the only thing he was grateful for, aside from their surviving the tragedy, was that as soon as they made it to the platform area, the intense silence hanging in the air had shut Sadie up in a blink or two. This was something, in forty years of marriage, he'd never been able to do. The catastrophe that wiped out his entire family in less than twenty-seven hours had claimed thousands of other Brits. At least this was what he remembered hearing coming out of the wireless just before he'd looked out the window and seen his best girl standing on the street below.

Horace Ernest McEwen wanted a shot of whiskey very badly. He pushed the abstract taste of the smooth, malty liquid, and the vision of it washing over his tongue, out of his mind as quickly as it had arrived; he'd rather answer Ruby's questions than give his addiction more than it deserved. He coughed a few times, wiped his spew on a stained hankie he'd pulled out of his trousers, and continued his explanation.

"Besides having the Mother of God and Lady Luck on our sides, there is a logical reason for our survival," he said. "As I told you on the phone, we weren't in the building."

"Ruby girl," he continued, "making the events of the past six days clear to you will take too much too much time. Precious time we don't have."

She listened and he went on.

"Now is not the right time for rhymes, interpretations, and detailed explanations. Time is not on our side. I need to bury the bodies and then have a hard-earned drink of something, of anything stronger than bloody espresso!"

He emphasized his needs and walked off, leaving her standing there holding a half-scorched, extinguished wooden match. She'd forgotten how pragmatic her pa could be when his brain cells weren't drowning in alcohol.

She left him to his sombre thoughts and carried on with inspecting each room in the flat. Her own McEwen family memories had been demanding her attention since she'd slept on the floor at Dublin Airport, puked on the plane, seen Winston Churchill, stepped over dead bodies on the streets below, and whapped a fat friar's wooden belly.

Chapter 46

Ruby had been going to her grandparents flat three to four times a year since she was just a few feet tall. Each time she visited, it had to be for eight consecutive days, not one day less, and not one day longer. Eight was grandma's favourite number and everyone knew that Grandma Liza was an exceptionally superstitious woman, who was known to be tougher and more stubborn than a prowling tigress.

Because of Liza's stalwart personality, from a young age, Ruby had surrendered to her grandma's illogical ways and stopped pleading to stay longer than eight days. By the time she was four she'd learned that no amount of begging could get an inflexible, superstitious, timeworn woman to change her mind. No matter how cute, precocious, and playful the little beggar was. Horace used to say that *he wasn't sure if his mother feared God or the devil more. When a person has qualms with both the devil and God, he would stringently warn, you can better shut your mouth, open your ears, listen, and do exactly as you are told.*

Despite that she was clueless back then, by the time she turned twenty, she'd come to have a deeper understanding of the meaning behind her father's words. Eventually, she stopped trying to compete with the number eight and had learned when to shut up, when to listen, and when to speak.

"Well, most of the time, anyways," she said aloud, knowing Horace would challenge her thinking of herself in this way.

After all, he still was on the receiving end of the brunt of everything she blamed him for. Feeling rather nostalgic, she lit another match to examine the additional seams in the kitchen stove's ventilation pipe. One of them had a definite backdraft, whilst the other was securely taped up with no signs of leakage. Absentmindedly, she took a deep breath and began coughing on the rancid scent of death hanging in the air. Her coughs blew her match out.

"Bollocks!" she annoyingly cursed.

Her mind began to roam, as she attempted to control her nagging cough and went to find Horace.

In the 1930s, when Ruby was very young, all of the windows in her grandparent's flat could be opened and closed. Her grandfather was a man of few words. He was notoriously known for never saying more than was needed to be heard in order to be understood. He was a habitual, seventy-five yearlong pipe smoker. His wife, who made up for his 'lack of words' by gibbering and gabbering nonstop, found the smell of his tobacco to be horrible. Therefore, she had insisted that the apartment windows be opened each day, of each season, of each year. Moreover, regardless of the infamously bad British weather, goddammit the windows would be opened! If he didn't oblige her, he and his pipe would be banned from her home. This threat came to life on many an occasion after Grandpa Amos ingested too much of his beloved 80 proof liquid and forgot to open a window. His wife was a stubborn, uncompromising, strict, and intimidating female. To be candid, she was the type of wife that she had been pushed into becoming, given that in the mid-1800s, she married a third generation, pipe smoking, and whiskey drinking McEwen man. Hence, her hardened ways and her authoritarian 'open window' rule. Open windows meant that little Ruby could, no matter the time of year, smell the city scents during her entire eight-day visit. She had especially liked the aromas of the snack bar, butcher shop, and bakery across the street. Before she was old enough to venture outside on her own, she'd close her eyes and pretend that breakfast, lunch, and dinner, had magically floated upwards, seeped into the apartment, and fed her three delicious meals. This only made her hungry, which in turn had the girl insisting, all day long, that they go to the cafés and shops for a sweet cinnamon bun or tootsie roll pop.

One year, Ruby couldn't remember anymore when it actually happened, Horace caulked two of the three large windows and sealed them permanently shut. He feared for his small, exceedingly curious daughter's safety. Often, little Ruby could be seen three-stories high looking down at the streets below through open windows. The wee one would stand, or sit, in front of the windows and look out at the city for hours at a time. By the time she was a clever and observant, toddler, she already knew how to unlatch and open the windows on her own. For that reason, her protective pappy wasted no time in removing the latches, sealing the windows shut and painting the frames so they'd look polished off and brand new. Horace sustained his protectiveness by installing a window grill on the frame of the flat's third window. He'd hand-constructed the grate at the steel factory where he was employed. After he completed the chore, his parents could easily open their bedroom window, all the way, and ventilate their entire flat without his only child falling to the ground below and dying in a pool of her own blood.

Ruby still could recall how her father had been kind-hearted and attentive to his parents before the WWII broke out, and even more so after it had ended. Back then she came to know that forgiving an enemy was the most unnatural of human emotions when memories were still open, fresh wounds. She also knew how remarkable it was that they had all survived the Bombing of London and had homes that were still intact to return to. Taking a closer look at the sitting room's windows, Ruby could see that the 1930's sealant her pa had used had long since dried up and chipped away. Although the windows in the parlour still couldn't be opened, thin shimmers of sunlight were now shining through the cracks in their frames. There was a three to four centimetre wide chip in the lower corner of one window's thick glass panes. Swiftly, she stuffed a small piece of a blue and green flowered curtain that was hanging over the window, into the crack to seal it off.

No wonder Amos, Liza, and Reggie were poisoned in their own home, she concluded. *Toxic outdoor air had penetrated their home like an invisible and deadly virus.*

Ruby was shrewd enough to know that for days, before they each died, like magic, lethal air had seeped through cracks in window frames and the hole in the glass. Because the fog had prevented the smog from dispersing, the outdoor gases easily penetrated buildings across the entire city. The once solid, outer walls of the Friar Flat's building were less dense now than they had been when the five-story structure was originally built. Ruby could even see extensive, deep, unrepaired cracks in the walls from the 1940s, when the German Blitz invasion damaged the flat and destroyed sixty-something percent of London homes. She remembered learning why the attack was named called the Blitz.

As she continued to inspect the safety of the apartment, her mind wandered in and out of the past and took her with it.

In late 1941, Ruby started volunteering as an active nurse's aide. One afternoon, while stitching up a badly wounded soldier's thigh, he asked her if she knew why the attack on her city was being called the Blitz. She didn't know what had possessed the soldier, struggling with such intense pain, to ask her this while she was tightening and knotting his stitches. He said it was because 'blitz' was the German word for lightning.

Makes perfect sense, given the way the night skies had lit up over England during two years of air raids, she thought, as she ran her fingers up and down the largest wall cracks in her grandparent's parlour.

The splits in the plastered walls had separated her grandmother's now yellowed and peeling flowered wallpaper; wallpaper, that was once visibly vibrant and stylish. The fissures reminded Ruby of how an earthquake could ruthlessly split the landscape. The deeper and wider crevasses were unmistakable reminders of the two years that Nazi Germany dropped thousands of tons of aerial bombs on Britain. That was only eleven short years ago. Her mind was reliving the attack as she licked her finger and slowly traced it over one of the larger openings in the plaster. With break neck speed, Ruby's hand violently jolted. As she fell backwards, her rigid body fell into the wall, slid limply to the floor, and took all of her with it. She'd received a strong electrical shock!

The cafeteria on the sixth floor of Saint Matthew's Hospital was still very quiet considering the number of people that were crowded around its oversized, flat screen television. At least forty of them had gathered and were listening to the BBC's up-to-date weather report about severe fog conditions over the city of London. The expressive, trained voice of the newscaster could easily be heard from every corner in the dining hall. Worried Brits hung on the broadcasters every word. The particularly tall bloke, wearing a black and white checkered apron with a matching cap, was still in the cafeteria. After he'd turned the volume up, he had taken a seat next to a wrinkled, whitehaired, and in his opinion, anciently old lady. She was wearing spectacles and holding a glass of ice water filled with lemon wedges. Since the BBC special broadcast had begun, he'd randomly glanced down at her a couple of times. He had no idea why he'd taken a few glimpses at her. It didn't make sense because he really didn't like old people, or anyone over forty for that matter.

Most of her ice has melted, he thought, looking over at her again. It's *bloody fuckin' strange that she hasn't moved in the past ten minutes.*

If she had moved, he hadn't noticed. Given her obvious old age, he was now a tad worried about her, which again didn't make sense given his rude attitude about age. Uncharacteristically, the tall uniformed bloke leaned over to ask her if she was okay.

"Madam is everything alright?" he whispered, not wanting to disturb other people who were attentively watching the newscast.

"Shit," he said.

The old woman didn't respond. She didn't even flinch.

"Hmmm, can a person die sitting upright?" he asked in a dumbstruck way while looking up at the others sitting at the table.

Being a cook, not a doctor, he'd asked them what he considered to be a rather logical question. He could see that her opened eyes were slightly glazed over and fixated on the television screen. Bending down even farther, to examine her more closely, he could see the tiny, yet clear reflection of the broadcaster on the telly in her black, dilated pupils. Her old eyes were as obscure as the night, which was rightfully spooking him.

At first, he didn't think she could hear him, so he raised his voice an octave or three, and again he asked, "Madam, are you okay?"

Still he got no reaction from her. His patience evaporated.

"Madam are you okay!" he hollered.

Her entire elderly body suddenly jerked! Abruptly, she slammed into his arm with force. Her sudden jolt made him spill his hot cappuccino into his unsuspecting lap, which rightfully scorched his male parts alongside his tolerance!

"Bloody, freaking bollocks your old nutcase!" he screeched. His manners had completely forsaken him.

His favourite breakfast drink was now running off the edge of the table. He jumped up to prevent it from seeping and sopping into his socks and sneakers.

Apparently, his first outburst wasn't satisfying enough, so he bellowed, "Bloody hell old lady! Pay attention!"

He behaved like a real cad; no differently than other attention-seeking junkies did in crowded spaces. His work shift had just begun and the last thing he needed was to be standing on his feet for the next seven hours with cappuccino drenched Nikes. It was a lame excuse but one he blamed his harsh and spoiled reaction on. The bloke was on a proper, verbal, British roll.

"It took me four months' worth of a cafeteria cook's crappy salary to afford these goddamned shoes!" he swore with a scream. Again, "Bloody freaking hell," the cook cursed.

Although his tone was slightly more forgiving, he still was acting like a real inconsiderate ass. The elderly woman, whose entire body had just jolted, was unaware of what had happened. She continued to stare at the TV screen. The tall bloke, now wearing wet cappuccino coloured Nikes, thought that she was trapped in a trance, dead, or sleeping with her eyes open. Unknowingly, the elderly woman blinked three times and then looked up at him. A slightly ambiguous grin crossed her face. She was still holding the ice filled glass between her age-spotted, arthritis ridden fingers, as though nothing peculiar had just taken place.

"What happened?"
A nurse sitting next the tall bloke asked.
"What happened?"
A custodian sitting next to the nurse asked.
"What happened?"
A Star Bucks employee sitting next to the janitor asked.

Chapter 47

"What happened?" Horace asked.

She didn't respond.

"What happened?" he asked again.

She didn't react.

"Ruby girl, what happened!" he hollered at the top of his lungs.

His daughter was still far away when she heard the muffled sound of his familiar voice. She was shaking her head in an attempt to rid herself of the horrific images that her mind had just witnessed. She was on the floor of the flat, leaning into the wall, with her eyes still closed.

Shuddering and monotone-like, she ranted, "Bombs. Bombs. Bombs exploding. Look up. Look out. People hit. Buses. Cross. Crossing street. Fog. Black fog. Dead. Dead people. Blood. More blood. Black snow. Death."

Horace squatted down next to her, moved in closer, and rested his large, calloused hand on her moist forehead. He wondered if her rambling was because she had a fever, or had she been electrocuted. The exposed wires in the apartment were as old as the building was. Then, spasmodically, Ruby forcefully gasped, her eyes suddenly popped open and scared the bloody crap out of him!

Seeing the startled look on his face, like a pro, she scoffed off her unsettledness, reclaimed her focus, and nonchalantly spoke. He could see that, even though she was in her early twenties, she was already a master at controlling her brain.

"No worries Horace. I'm fine. It was just a nasty vision."

He knew that his best girl was trying to return from wherever she'd just been. A few blinks later, after he'd helped her to stand up, it was obvious to him that she was still dazed. Be it so, without hesitation she turned and carried on with her inspection of the damaged flat as if nothing had just happened. Because it had been many years since he'd seen her struggling so hard to return from wherever her mind had taken her, he protectively stood nearby by his daughter.

It was nothing less than a phenomenon that the Friar Court Flats building, and a number of other nearby buildings were still standing given that almost the entire city block had been annihilated during the war, Ruby thought.

Envisioning the residue of the explosion-filled flashbacks that had just crossed her sub consciousness made it within her depth to have such an opinion. She licked her finger for a second time and held it in front of one extra wide crack in the kitchen's exterior wall. She could feel cool, outdoor air coming through the crack. Given the amount of air-born toxins that had been escaping through the open fissures in the walls and the substantial hole she'd discovered in the windowpane, she wasn't at all taken back that the end result was three deaths. If her parents had stayed in the building, her family's death toll would have most definitely climbed. With the added carbon monoxide that had for many days, back drafted into a living space with no ventilation, she knew that her grandparents and uncle never stood a chance as the toxins replaced the level of sustainable oxygen in the flat. Across the city, unaware, exposed victims, fell unconscious and died shortly thereafter, in their sleep, so to speak. Ruby predicted that in a few months, as Londoner's lives returned to normal, Amos, Liza, and Reggie would become statistics of yet another walloping British tragedy.

Thinking about her father's brother Reggie had awoken her vivid memories of another tragic time for the McEwen's and for Great Britain. She propped herself against the wall and let her mind wander farther into the past. Although her eyes were open, both of her arms hung loosely along her sides. Horace, still watching over her, knew exactly what was happening to his daughter. He stepped towards her and stood close enough to catch her in case she lost her balance whilst her mind had its way with her again. He was used to her coming and going in this trancelike way, which was similar to a bad dream lost in a memory; or vice versa. Unfazed, Horace watched her slip away again. He knew she'd be ricocheting in and out of the past, so duly, like a guard dog, he'd wait for her safe return, just as he'd done countless times before since she was a young girl.

As Hitler repeatedly bombed London, her volunteer work as a nurse's aide, before, during, and after the Blitz, caused Ruby to view life very differently. Being supported by the wall and sensing her pa's presence, she contemplated over the fine line between irony and injustice.

Where was the reasoning and justice? It was a mockery. Her relatives had survived years of German obliteration, only to be killed by a dense and deadly smog. For a young idealistic person like herself, this was utterly incomprehensible.

With this query swirling around in her brain, she felt the arrival of uninvited tears. She anticipated that they would be tears wrapped in raw emotions, or sobs that would try to threaten her resilience. Readily, she disregarded her emotional state and reminded herself that there were three dead people in the flat and no room left in this tragedy for her tears. She was coherent again and eager to continue her inspection of the place where her family had died. Or so she'd thought. Then, with strength of character, she put one foot in front of the other and took her wandering thoughts and visions with her. Going from room to room, she probed the apartment for residual threats. Standing in the hallway between the bedroom and the kitchen, she could feel her father's ghostlike presence nearby. Given so, she allowed her young and now fully alert mind to wander back to a time somewhere in between 1940 and 1941.

She was starting her sophomore year at Essex High School. Given the threats of the war, the school was open as often as it could be. Britain's capital and its industrial regions had experienced a multitude of Nazi air attacks against manufacturing targets, townships, and cities. The Germans first goal was to destroy the city, which in great part they succeeded in doing. When the Blitz began, Horace, Sadie and Ruby were living about seventy-five kilometres away from the strike zone. Demographically, County Essex has London on one side of it and a long stretch of coastline on other side.

Ruby had taken a lead pencil from a kitchen drawer and was drawing visible carbon circles around wall cracks that would need repairing. While doing so, she vividly recalled when the Battle of Britain began. Horace could see that she was both alert and lost in thought, so in a quiet, nonobtrusive manner, he stayed close by.

Almost daily, folks in her neighbourhood sporadically heard air raid warnings; nevertheless, no actual bombings were occurring over their hometown. The war movement was happening in the more southern areas of the country. Because of the air raids and bombing uncertainties, her three-person family would frequently spend many hours in their too tiny, four-by-five-meter cellar under the rear side of their house. Horace had secured the cellar with vertical gird beams he'd smuggled out of the steel plant where he worked. *These are desperate times*, Ruby heard him reminding his wife when she accused him of being a drunken war thief. Her pa ignored Sadie's ridiculing sarcasm and carried on with renovating the cellar. Horace was filled with passionate convictions during WWII. He believed in his core that it was a man's job to shield his family, and as God was his witness, Horace McEwen would protect his family with the goddamned steel he'd stolen. His wife could shut the hell up or stay outside and argue with a bloody bomb!

In the 1940s, Horace was a welder, Sadie was a homemaker, and Ruby was fifteen going on sixteen. No matter how risky the war was, she wanted desperately to go to school; therefore, she devised a brilliant plan. The high schooler would graduate a year early and move away from home the day after she received her diploma. She and her book bag had a 'life strategy' that didn't include being stuck in a shelter-cellar with a whiskey-drinking father and an overanxious, obsessive mother. Her parents never ending, ear-splitting bickering was more than she could take on any given day or night while stuck underground with the likes of them. The past few months had been a difficult time for her. The war threatened teenager was feeling weak and worn out. She needed to get away from everything that was ruining her life. Sadie and Horace were at the top on her list of things to leave behind.

Spending so many hours cooped up with them was the only time, in her life, that she ever regretted being an only child. If it weren't for the Abbey Girl's books that she was reading at the time, she'd surely have lost her confined mind. It was a rightly terrible thing it was. Being alive while feeling buried alive, deep beneath the grass, in that square steel hole. Sadie would get especially riled up whenever Ruby had an attack of claustrophobia while they were in Horace's makeshift bomb shelter. Ruby suspected that her extreme fear of confining spaces was the reason why the three of them finally began going to a nearby above ground shelter? On the other hand, perhaps Horace had reconsidered his family's protection plan and feared that they would be buried alive if a bomb landed on their house? Either way, it didn't matter because after the first year of war, he let his girl out of that Godforsaken hole. She'd begun passing the time with her friends and classmates at the public bomb shelter. Life was improving.

The first few nights of The Blitz, very little anti-aircraft retaliation could be heard. Shortly thereafter, there was a great concentration of gunfire for longer periods. When bombs exploded overhead everything changed and nothing was ever the same again. Essex Airfield, home to the British Royal Airforce, was located in close proximity of the McEwen house. Although many of the local residents felt safer with a national military force in their backyards, as the airstrikes continued, the RAF airbases posed an increase in bombardment threats to the region of Essex County. Regardless of the risk and destruction, very few bombs landed near their village. The only actual destruction they'd suffered from the bomb blasts was the loss of co-workers and friends who hadn't been so fortunate. The damaged slates tiles on the roof of their house and numerous shattered windows were overlooked. People in neighbouring counties had endured much more than the village of Essex, or the McEwen's had for that matter.

Horace's youngest brother, Reginald, who everyone called Reggie, played a vital role in WWII. He was an advocate for the constitutional Monarchy. In the name of Her Majesty the Queen, he would perform any duty asked of him. Reginald Hector McEwen was the last born of five children. His mother had birthed one girl and four boys. His oldest brother Horace was well into adulthood when his little brother Reginald entered the world. Similar to Sadie, his mother Liza had also unexpectedly conceived while she was going through her change of life. This was why Reggie had been born only one year and eight months before Ruby came into all of their lives. This made him more of a brother to Ruby than an uncle. Likewise, Ruby was more of a younger sister to Reggie than she was a niece.

When they were children the uncle and niece were two different breeds who were often mistaken for being a brother and sister. They shared an uncanny resemblance, with similar tinted skin tones, dark prominent facial features and full, deep burgundy-coloured lips; all of which they both were gifted with at birth. The type of shared and ruddy features they both had were rather scarce in England, given that the typical native Brit was fair skinned and often blue eyed and freckled, with less prevailing facial features. Even their names, Ruby and Reggie sounded alike. Horace's little brother was teased maliciously as a child. He was called 'the menopause boy' and 'granny-baby' for the better part of his childhood. Horace had already moved away from home years before Reggie was even conceived. He wasn't there to defend his little brother while Reggie was growing up. More importantly, he never was able to teach his kid brother how to defend himself like a red-blooded British male should. Even so, Horace continually told Reginald that the only way to outgrow despicable nicknames was to become someone important. He'd cry out, that'll stick it to those bloody little dastard bastards! Hearing this for the umpteenth time, Reggie would look up at his tall brother with his large and wide, searching eyes, as Horace's powerful dialog continued. Don't use your fists, he'd warn Reggie. Eventually kids become adults, and adults forget who they bullied when they were kids. As that may be, adults never forget someone from their childhood who becomes a legend. Two weeks later, after giving his kid brother one last such pep talk, Reggie

300

turned ten. For his birthday, Horace gave him a colour-illustrated picture book titled, Famous Planes and Famous Flights.

Six years the latter, in September of 1939, the strappingly handsome, almost 16-year-old Reginald McEwen, overheard that trained pilots were urgently needed by the Royal Air Force. Special flying clubs were already enrolling men and searching for more candidates. With the undeniable threat of war on the UK's horizon, time had become an expedient factor in young people's lives. Reginald quit school and enlisted. His parents knew nothing about his plans. He was taller and more mature than his years, therefore, his registered age was never questioned by the RAF. Hence, began his teenage career as a renowned Fighter Pilot during the Second World War. Bizarrely, Reggie survived three years of air battle and returned home. Being a young, post-war veteran, wherever he went, he easily turned the heads of single women. Even betrothed women enjoyed staring at his masculinity and chiseled features.

All the same, he was rightly 'over the border' of being slightly damaged on the inside. Reggie carried around the kind of impairment that couldn't be seen or grasped. Both Amos and Liza's other two sons died heroically during the Blitz. Their only female offspring, Horace's baby sister, Cicely, had moved to America in the mid-1920s after being caught as a willing participant in a hot and steamy sexual fling with a foreigner. As rumour had it, she'd carried on sordidly with a very wealthy and very married man who was on a British holiday. The aristocrat had easily charmed his way into her knickers and her naïve, yearning heart. It was said that the nineteen-year-old spread her aching loins, quenched his erogenous desires, and easily persuaded the tycoon to take her with him to the Land of the Free and the Home of the Brave. Whenever she was within his reach, given the size of his wallet and the uncontrollable bouts of fetishist swelling she caused in his expensive tailored pants, there was little convincing needed. He took his young, erotic plaything with him wherever he went, and she willingly went wherever he took her.

Consequently, gossip about the tale of the Ruby's slutty aunt spread. The rumours were told, and retold, for the better part of the late 1920s and early 1930s. Years later, a then grown-up Ruby, remembered overhearing Horace telling Sadie that his only sister was granted anything her young heart and tight rump desired, if she gave the rich, sleazy bastard her body whenever he wanted it. At the time, according to the Essex County's gossip line, she did just this. Most notably, as the rumour went, Cicely was to keep the scandalous relationship a deeply hidden secret from her lover's wife and kin. The man's threats were bitter and bleak. If the affair was revealed, the ultimate consequences were promised to be much harsher than the harshest degree of bitter and bleak. Regardless of scandal or shame, it was divulged that despite the threats, risks and intimidations, being a wealthy mistress suited the young scarlet perfectly. The year she disappeared, whilst frequenting a local Essex pub, Horace chanced upon a stranger who boasted to be a worldly traveller of sorts. The 'two sheets to the wind' gent told Horace that he'd just returned from America and had seen with his own two eyes, and felt between his own thighs, the popularity of the hot-blooded, alluring, sexually willing western women. Horace was dumbstruck!

301

The man foolishly went on to say, what a time of it I had there! That he still considered himself to be lucky that his trouser snake didn't turn purple and fall off from overuse! The drunken fool then busted a gut with laughter, whilst sliding a hand into his britches and publicly arousing his trouser snake hard enough for all to see. With the smell of whiskey on his breath and a vision of his sister's profane erotic actions raging through his mind, Horace drew his own conclusions. Then he drew his large fists. The taken aback wanker's remarks earned him a black eye, a fat bloody upper lip, and a dislocated shoulder. Apparently, Horace, unaware of his own strength and anger, had wrenched the fella's scrawny masturbating limb just a bit too far behind his back. As the legend went, of the 'family shame' that was being passed around again and again over time, apparently Ruby's kenspeckled, bodacious and promiscuous aunt was infatuated by the adulterous American. She was even more enamoured by the news of the Roaring Twenties coming out of the USA and Canada.

For that reason, as Ruby remembered the reprehensible version of the family disgrace, Horace's sister Cicely left in the middle of the night in the same way her Irish friend Emilia had recently disappeared. As they began new lives, both women had been shielded by an obscurity that the darkness shrouded them in. Up to this very day, for as far as Horace knew, no one ever heard from his sister again. Even today, thirty-two years later, the remaining members of the family still believe that when the young scarlet left England and vanished, they were spared a lifelong scandal. *What is it with Europeans and our knack for disappearing in the dark?* Ruby asked herself. As she circled another crack in the wall, she ruminated a bit more about Mia and Emmet's departure, eight nights and nine days ago. Because Ruby never knew her pa's sister, thoughts of her Aunt Cicely were easily sacked.

Finished with her inspection of the window frame, she sat down on a steel bench in the apartment's narrow hallway. Horace was very subdued. He'd been standing in the kitchen observing her swerving between 'what was over and done and what still needed to be done'. There she sat, consumed by whatever churned through her brain whilst she stared at a wall that was less than three feet in front of her. He couldn't determine if she was being haunted by the past or was being enchanted by it. The hallway was narrow and cluttered with his mother's sewing supplies. His long-legged daughter barely fit between the edge of the bench and the perimeter of the wall she sat across from. After five minutes of waiting for her to stop wasting bloody crucial time because of her mind's hunger for wandering through the past, his old and recently whiskey free patience grew restless. He was irritated with the situation, annoyed with her mental dawdling, and badly craving a drink.

With three foul-smelling, decaying bodies in the next room being prayed over by his psychotic wife, the presumed to be last living McEwen male was on the edge of rage. He approached his daughter and deliberately broke the silence. Despite that delirium tremors had set in because of the absence of alcohol in his blood and brain, Horace McEwen was ready to man up and to take charge.

Chapter 48

"Ruby girl, come back to me. Ruby can you hear me? Come back to me, we have a job to do," she faintly heard Horace say.

He knew from two plus decades of experience that using the right tone with her would bring her back to him quicker. For this reason he put a leash on his temper.

"Ruby girl, come back to me," he repeated.

He'd intentionally interrupted her brains nomadic desire to start drifting again. Hearing his calm voice calling her back, she opened her eyes. He knew better than to just yank her mind out of wherever it took her to when it roved or straggled. Since she was a young girl, he'd recognized that she was different and had a type of psychic gift. She had a way about her that he'd yet to fully understand, nonetheless, he was her pa. For as long as he was alive, being her mind's chaperon and her protector was his life purpose. These were two roles he took very seriously. When he saw that she'd returned to him and was alert again, he gave her hand a familiar, reassuring squeeze. Then he went into the bathroom. No words were exchanged. They understood each other with ease. Since he hadn't been drinking, he was peeing and shitting like a bloody British racehorse.

While Horace was adding a new layer of another kind of stink to her grandparents flat, Ruby suddenly realized she hadn't seen or heard her mother Sadie yet. The strange and sad truth of it was, she hadn't actually thought about her or even desired seeing Sadie. Someone who didn't know her mother might consider this appalling behaviour on Ruby's part. Tragedy or not, Ruby was somewhat selfishly enjoying, what she called, 'the sweet absence of drama'. Even Horace hadn't expressed an interest in his wife since she'd arrived at Friar Court. Sadie, who was camped out in the bedroom keeping vigil over three half-frozen, bloated, squalid corpses, was rather used to being snubbed by her family. Even though she knew they were in the apartment, she chose to stay with the dead rather than engage with the living.

Hearing the toilet flushing, Ruby immediately dismissed thoughts of her mother. Horace opened the door and walked past her towards the living room. He was tired and needed to sit for a spell. Ruby went into the apartment's small bathroom that Horace had just used. She wanted to inspect the water boiler under the sink.

"Bloody hell Horace, I'm gob smacked!" she yelled. "For the love of Jesus, your old arse stinks like a fish out of water during a friggen heatwave!"

Horace could see that 'taming her tongue' was a skill she was still trying to learn, but had yet to master. For as disgusting as the fresh, manly stank that he'd left behind in the bathroom was, at least it was a different odour than the three decomposing bodies in the next room had filled the flat with. Ruby lit two long wooden matches and quickly blew them out. The strong sulfuric smell of a snuffed-out match, was, in her young opinion, the only kind of air freshener a tiny, windowless bathroom needed to fend off the smells of a man like Horace.

"Ahhh, that's better," she said as she saw the match smoke dissipating. "The King would evict you from the country if he knew how much you stunk up a room!"

Laughing at her own humour, she opened the cabinet under the sink and carried on with examining the boiler. Horace left his chair, waltzed back into the bathroom. He sat back down on the off-white ceramic toilet he'd installed for his parents when they'd become too frail to use the tenants communal ground floor loo.

"Ruby Adeline do not be making jokes in front of me about Britain's King!" he scolded her.

Horace, Reginald, and Amos were each lifelong, devoted supporters of the Monarchy. The male McEwen trio shared a patriotism that his young and occasionally naïve daughter had never wholly grasped or committed to.

"It has recently been rumoured that our King George the Sixth is gravely ill. Before this bloody smog fog catastrophe hit our city, word on the street was that the King's daughter Elizabeth is being groomed to become Queen in the event of his expected death."

Horace wouldn't tolerate anyone, even his best girl, speaking ill of the man. The toilet he had installed, some fifteen years ago still didn't have a seat cover on it. His extremely frugal, persistent mother had cyclically told him over the years, that toilet seat covers were a waste of money. If he put bought one and brought it into her home, she'd throw it down the stairwell! He ignored her, bought one anyway, and installed it straightaway. Despite their appreciation of his generosity, the next day, the only part of the new toilet that landed in three clunky pieces on the sidewalk, three stories below, was the seat cover. At the time, while fetching the destroyed toilet seat off the sidewalk, he remembered feeling grateful that he'd securely bolted the privy to the floor. He'd known since he was a lad that his mother had a temper and wore absolutely all of the trousers in the family. Therefore, another toilet seat cover was never purchased, mounted, or used. Ruby thought Horace looked quite ludicrous, sitting on a toilet with his suspenders raised up and properly positioned on his shoulders. He was sneakily watching her, whilst she went on with scrutinizing and analysing her old man. She'd forgotten how lonely her pa was. She knew him well. Despite that the dead bodies in the flat needed tending to, he was content to spend as much time being as alone with her as he could. Oddly enough, he was now watching his best girl stretching her legs, the same way a marathon runner did before a race. He'd never seen her doing this before.

Ruby's muscles were cramping up again.

"Goddammit Grady," she muttered, cursing the blonde university clerk she couldn't forget meeting yesterday.

"Who is Grady?" he asked.

"No one important," she lied.

Realizing that Grady was distracting her, she dismissed her roaming thoughts of him and finished inspecting the loo. Then she sat back down on the steel bench in the hallway.

Take a moment for yourself, she thought.

She took a deep breath and tried to ignore the annoying clinking sounds Horace was making as he twiddled with the toilet's flusher. Because her aching legs were too long, she couldn't fully extend them in the uncommonly narrow hallway. Her muscles were cramping up even more, which made dismissing thoughts of the blonde chap who'd gotten under her skin difficult to ignore. Ruby was inclined to take a deep breath to reel her racing mind in and distract it from her twitching legs. She promptly reminded herself that taking deep breath would be a stupid and risky thing to do. The lingering stench of Horace's booze-free poo, plus three rotting carcasses in one tiny apartment had her breathing shallowly through her mouth to fend off her queasiness. Despite the rancidity of the indoor air, she wasn't ready to see the dead yet.

After she'd arrived at Friar Court Flats nausea had slinked into her stomach the second Horace opened the front door and she entered her grandparent's apartment. Even now, the smells of contaminated flesh continued to penetrate her nostrils and ooze into her throat. It was so overwhelming that she was on the verge of vomiting. Ruby's practical mind and intelligent brain both knew that they needed to do what needed to be done. The bodies must be removed from the flat, and sooner than later. It was a matter of disease control and sanitation. She knew she needed to wheedle Horace into getting on with the significant pending task of tending to the dead. Now, analysing herself, she wondered if she was maybe stalling the inevitable because she was afraid to open the bedroom door and see Sadie and her deceased relatives. Nevertheless, her impassioned mind wasn't finished with its sentimental journey yet.

Bloody hell, she thought as she looked across the hallway. *Come on Ruby girl, focus. There is no more time for conjuring up the past!* She firmly told herself. Despite her mental self-control efforts, her brain switch was offhanded, wilful, and on the young side. Because she and her brain were still in training, neither of them had learned to listen to logic yet. She began to reminisce about the dead people in the next room as she looked at the collage of framed family pictures hanging on wall across from where she was sitting. She'd been in the flat often, yet until today she'd never really given the photographs much attention. Over time, her grandparent's collection of displayed pictures blended in with the wallpaper and went unnoticed. Nevertheless, now, as she sat across from the photographs, the arrays of snapshots were strangely beckoning her. One particular black and white image caught her eye. When she first saw it, she thought it was her Uncle Reggie; at least the man in the picture looked like Reggie did when he was younger. Standing up to inspect the photograph more closely, she was taken back when she realized that the man in the photo was Horace, not Reggie.

Although they looked very similar as callow, dashing men in their primes, she clearly distinguished that the uniform the soldier in the photo was wearing was from WWI not from the Second World War. It had to be Horace before his accident, she concluded. Why don't I remember seeing this picture before?

She remembered a time, while she and Horace were having one of their fence side chats, when her pa mentioned the First World War. He'd told her that his trench combat experiences involved the horrors of mud, gunge, wounded comrades, and sickness. He went on to tell her how the constant threat and noise of the bombardments had made him go mad in his head more than once. How, the heavy artillery, the newest weapons of destruction, and poisonous gas continually threatened his life from a distance.

"How could I have forgotten him telling me this?" she asked herself aloud.

Looking at his wartime snapshot was now reminding her of that stint of time, when they'd leaned together against a weathered, old fence, and gazed out at the rich, green Essex scenery. On that day, Horace had proudly boasted about his hand-to-hand combat skills and how he'd fought with wooden clubs and knives and killed many an enemy during the grisly act of trench raids. He'd told her that when the troops weren't fighting, they were deadlocked in the ditches. That boredom became a very serious mental enemy, in between active combat and being forced into the taciturnity of the trenches and bunkers. From as far back in time as her growing memory could go, after that fence side chat her father never, even once, mentioned being a soldier again.

Ruby had always assumed this was because his WWI battle scars were so visible that talking about them was futile. Her father never dwelled on, or in, the past. He was too busy living life and making people around him either miserable or happy, depending on his mood or level of intoxication. With Horace's wartime story captivating her fantasy-rich mind, the steadfast believer in 'life beyond the grave' was now certain that the dead people in the pictures were sending her messages from their burial places. Because of the smog tragedy, Horace was the only remaining living person in any of the photographs on the wall. Her other family members were the unsuspecting souls who had each just been poisoned by the toxic smoke that the fog had caused. A photograph of her Aunt Cecil was not among the rest. Ruby secretly hoped she'd find one when the apartment was sorted out and emptied after the burials. She was curious to know more about the waggish sibling scapegrace of the McEwen ancestry. The number of family members Ruby had six days ago was cut in half in less than a day.

For years now she'd accepted and even anticipated that her grandparents would soon pass away. Next year, they both would have been entering their nineties. Regardless of the rigid war-ridden, lean years they'd lived through, they'd shared long and fruitful lives together. When Dean O'Sullivan had instructed her to call her father in London, Ruby was rightly prepared to be told that either her Grandma Liza or Grandpa Amos had passed onto to their next life. But, not under any circumstances did she anticipate this kind of passing on. She regretted that she hadn't been able to say a proper goodbye to each of them. As for her Uncle Reggie, she was shocked that he was less than two years older than she was and he had already left her world. What Ruby didn't know, as she scanned the photo's one last time, was that her deep-seeded anger at Reggie's death would arrive years later, and emotionally seize her in a way she'd never before been seized? As she intently stared one last time at the wall photos, the reason for a catastrophe that had exterminated so many people across London was mercilessly unclear to her. Ruby hadn't seen Reggie since she'd before she'd moved to Dublin almost twenty-four months ago. This was now weighing heavily on her conscience. The last time they were together he'd told her many adventurous war stories. His tales about flying from different airfields during the Battle of Britain and the role he played in the combat against the Imperial Japanese Army were impressive.

She knew that her dead uncle was instrumental in defending his country, defeating the Nazi's, and ending WWII. She was also aware that his military service traumatized him beyond repair. After the war ended, Reginald, the youngest male member of the McEwen clan, was not the same teenage boy who'd lied about his age to enlist in a cause that he believed in with his soul. It was renowned that for Horace's youngest brother Reginald, fighting in Hitler's war was his hellish obligation. Whether or not the recruiting officer and enlisting clerk had brainwashed his young, influential mind was never determined. Regardless, Reggie patriotically and openly professed that killing Germans was justified and the only way to end the spread of Nazism. For the duration of the war, and likewise after its widespread, global atrocities ended, her uncle had been outspoken about the financial and human costs of warfare; including the mental torment he was burdened with during and after combat. He'd spoken with his niece a few times about the horror of landing on the war-ravaged island of Iwo Jima. He told her that because the five weeklong Battle of Iwo Jima had destroyed the islands airstrips, there was hardly an open area of terrain large enough for him to land his plane on. From the air, he could see almost thirty-thousand dead bodies decomposing under a scorching sun. He went on to share with her his hidden state of mind and his intense fear of death. He told her that looking down at the massive loss of life on the ground below had him retching in his helmet and pissing in his flying suit.

Back then, she knew that his ability to speak so candidly with her, about things he kept hidden from others, was because they were so close in age. Disregarding that their genders were different and that they looked like twins, her passionate mindset was as young and stalwart as his was. It was a known fact that air raid bomb blasts wreaked havoc on the bodies of fighter pilots. Her uncle was no exception to this wartime circumstance. The pressure from the bombs caused Reggie, alongside hundreds of other subsisted pilots, to become victims of a series of severe lung ailments. Because of this, many of them, including Reginald, became mortally fragile around their military edges. When the war ended, her uncle easily looked ten, maybe twelve years older than she did. Their age similarity was no longer visible, and their paralleled resemblances had all but vanished. Reggie resembled too many other enlisted men, who'd aged at an unbelievably fast speed, once Hitler's German Reich was defeated. Shortly thereafter, he'd attempted, twice within six months, to commit suicide. Horace intervened, rescued him both times, and then insisted that he move in with his parents.

Together with Liza and Amos, Reggie lived out the rest of his days. Ruby thought it to be incomprehensible and ironic that the three of them would all perish together, especially after RAF Pilot, Reginald McEwen had nearly perished, numerous times, in the cockpit of his Bell P39 Airacobra fighter plane.

"Jesus Christ", she conflictingly cursed, "he was so proud of that goddamn plane!"

"Yes, he was!" Horace cried out from the loo. "Such a brave and foolish, patriotic boy he was, enlisting as a nationalistic teenager."

Ruby leaned forward to take a closer look at Reginald, dressed in his uniform whilst posing on the wing of his fighter plane. She was instantly flooded with memories of what they'd done together and what he'd meant to her before, during, and after the war. Growing up as a part of the same generation, her Uncle Reggie was her real-life surrogate brother hero. After WWII ended, he became her real life, offbeat and introverted hero. Becoming a military man had given him a worthy reputation, even before he'd earned his gold pilot wings. Although others viewed Reggie as being damaged war goods as they'd witness one of his uncontrollable fits of rage, Ruby was never afraid of him. Not sure if she believed in God, or even in Heaven, wherever he now was, she hoped her uncle was experiencing the sweetest semblance of a ceasefire that a military man could. Ruby looked through the open bathroom door at her pa, who was elbow deep in the toilet bowl's water whilst fidgeting with the flusher's lever. He was distracted with a new puttering purpose, which was doing him good.

She then turned back around and zeroed in on the World War One picture of the baronial uniformed soldier she called 'her old man'. The swanky famed photograph hung above the one of his youngest brother Reginald. She knew that from 1914 to 1916, her father had served as an infantry soldier during the First World War. While fighting in Belgium, he was seriously wounded and lost the vision in one eye. Actually, he lost the entire eye. An artillery shell that exploded nearby the bunker he was running towards was the cause of his partial blindness. Shrapnel from the bursting mortar missile blew his right eyeball completely out of its socket. For logical reasons, his eyeball was never looked for or recovered. He was rendered fragmentarily blind and left to live on with half his vision, one eyeball, and a macabre type of facial scarring. Horace was certain that his now decomposed eyeball still lay somewhere on that battlefield. The thought of this comforted the man in a way only he understood. He interpreted his partial blindness and missing eyeball as his way of leaving his mark on the frontline of one of the deadliest conflicts in history. Many believed at the time that The Great War, as it was called, set the stage for WWII, just twenty years later.

Two delicate eye surgeries and four months later, his facial wounds healed, and the risk of infection passed. Horace refused to wear an eyepatch. In retrospect, he wore his blindness and malformation as a Badge of Honor. His scars were a tribute to his comrades who were openly killed on the battlefields and buried alive in collapsed trenches. Since the day she took a blurry, newborn peek at the man who'd delivered her under an oak tree, Ruby had never known her father's face to look any different. For this reason, she was one of the few people in Horace's life who'd never been appalled by his looks.

In fairness to her mother, Ruby thought, *Sadie never openly showed repulsion for her husband's misfortune. Horace was a war hero with a unique lust for life when they fell in love and married. His lack of one eye never seemed to matter to his bride. Sadie deserved recognition from her for this.*

If her mum was repelled by his deformity, it was in a way her daughter was never aware of. When Ruby was a teenager, on occasion Horace would secretly wear his eyepatch when he and Sadie were at odds. By then, she was old enough and nifty enough to know that whenever she saw him removing the black patch before entering the house, he'd been drinking and carousing with women at the pubs again. His girl never confronted him with what she suspected; knowing it would create more conflict than it was worth. Besides, if Sadie found out, another daylong spat would be instigated between them. To protect herself from their volatile marriage, she'd keep his eyepatch secret hidden amongst the other secrets of Horace she knew about but didn't speak of.

Although her pa had a valid medical reason not to enlist and fight in World War II, he'd always regretted not doing so. Ruby had known for a very long time that his self-worth was ashamed and humiliated because of his loss of sight. More so, he felt dishonoured to remain a civilian while his adolescent brother Reggie had enlisted on the sly. For all the topics that Horace loved to debate over, and all the stories he was so popular for telling, war, any war, was one he avoided. She knew that his inability to lay claim to having killed Germans was a lifetime pang of conscience that he hid in the recesses of his emotionally saddled soul. Ruby Adeline, the youngest living member the McEwen family clan, was still rather clueless as to the amount of perception and fortitude her resilient brain had. Then, seemingly out of nowhere, she was again overcome by the stench of decaying flesh that surrounded her. The queasiness in her stomach was reminding her of puking on the airplane earlier that morning. Realizing that she was about to chuck up acidy bile that was rising rapidly from her intestines, her mind swiftly found its focus and replaced the aroma of death with more pleasant, abstract scents.

Fortunately, for all of them, her mind was stronger than the repulsive odours of the rigid post-mortem corpses in the next room. She ignored the vomit creeping into her throat and switched gears. Time was of the essence and the three McEwen leftovers in the apartment were running out of it.

Chapter 49

Shortly after he and Sadie returned from the underground metro station and found his entire family dead, Horace had opened the window in his parent's bedroom. This was where he and Sadie had respectively laid their corpses out. It had already been two days since Horace had used a wrench and a hammer to break a thick layer of ice that sealed the window shut from the outside. For this reason, two days and nights of glacial outdoor winter elements now filled the bedroom's indoor space.

Even before the smog had spread itself like a thick woollen blanket over the city, December had proven to be an extraordinarily cold, bone-chilling month in London. Across the metropolis, frigid, unsympathetic air was still trapped inside concrete buildings. This included the Friar Court Flats structure. Since the high-rise had been erected in the 1800s, for the duration of the winter months its residents referred to their homes as 'Friar's Fridge'. Fortunately, for the deceased family members, who'd been temporarily laid to rest on their beds, their bedchamber had remained a constant 1° Celsius. This had kept their bodies from spoiling too rapidly before they could be embalmed and buried. Despite being overwhelmed by grief and fear, tending to the bodies in this way had been a very wise decision on Horace's part. Even so, the ultra-cold, stiff flesh and bones had caused the flat to seriously reek of death. The coal stove continued to burn steadily in the parlour, keeping that part of the living space relatively warm.

Horace, still feeling somewhat uneducated, asked his university student daughter, "How quickly does a body decompose?"

Sensing his need to get a move on and bury his family, she distracted and appeased his urgency by politely blurting out, "I would like to see Sadie and my deceased family members now."

"Are you certain my girl?" he protectively asked, while giving her another sober hug.

"Yes, I am. Death is a part of life Horace. The smell of death has lingered long enough in this apartment," she concluded. "I think we should prepare their bodies, schedule a mortuary service to pick them up and arrange a burial or cremation."

He hated it when she called him Horace. Nonetheless, he followed her lead and knocked on the bedroom door to warn Sadie that they'd be coming in. Entering the bedroom was like stepping into a walk-in freezer. The window was still wide open, and a noticeable layer of frost had changed the colour of the protective grate from steel grey to winter white. As sunbeams reflected off the windows lattice, it made the frost twinkle. As bizarre as it was, the brightness of the sun made the death-filled room look virtually enchanting, as if it had been sprinkled with sequins. Regardless of the amount of demise surrounding her, Ruby was reminded of how she'd adored sunbeams since she was wee girl. Before she looked at her mother or the bloating bodies, she strode over to the window and stood briefly in the sun's rays. In spite of the open window, the stench of death was still too bloody strong. The fresh air coming into the room would at least make it breathing tolerable, as they did what needed to be done, for the sake of the departed. The sound of gagging, a few feet away had Ruby turning around to see Sadie. Her mother was hunched over and upchucking in a bucket. Her untied, tangled, greying hair, hung over the bucket, like an old and dirty cloth mop waiting to be wrung out. Sadie vomited again. She then spit up what looked like a mingled combination of mucous and blood into the bucket.

Looking upwards, she wiped her mouth off with a filthy, wet rag, and slurred, "Hello Ruby." She then put her soiled, trembling index finger over her mouth and said, "Shah, be very quiet, I think Uncle Reggie is still sleeping."

Unprepared for what she saw, Ruby was seriously shocked at how confused, unkempt, and point-blank dingy her mother was. The colour of Sadie's vomit was an immediate concern. The grunge under her fingernails was a clear sign that she hadn't bathed in many days. As she stared out the window, Sadie looked straight through her daughter with glazed over, distress-filled eyes. She looked weak and wore a sadder shade of sad than Ruby had ever before seen.

"Hello Sadie," Ruby replied, "Are you ill?" she asked her.

"No, she isn't," Horace without hesitation replied. "She is easily nauseated. She always has been like this. She'd spat whenever she changed one of your poo-soiled nappies."

"How could I have not known this about my own mother?" Ruby asked him.

Her pa ignored Sadie completely; refusing to allow his distorted wife to make this tragedy about herself. After nearly thirty years of tolerating her, he was done with her self-victimization. Even Ruby's experience with the hollow and empty expressions and conditions of wartime trauma victims didn't prepare her for seeing her mother in this condition. Sadie looked like a lady sentinel, sitting positioned and on guard between her in-laws. Each of them was laid out on their own bed. Someone, she assumed it was Sadie, had thoughtfully covered the bodies with quilts. Even covered, Ruby could see that the bodies were very bloated. She knew this meant bacteria was disintegrating the corpses and releasing the awful smelling gases that were causing them to distend. She also knew that the next stage of the decomposing process was an ugly one. The corpses needed to be embalmed, or burned, before a sickly green ooze of bodily fluids started flowing out of them.

Ruby was grateful that her mother had the insight to cover Amos, Liza, and Reggie's faces. By this stage of the decomposition process, their faces would have caused them all vivid nightmares for the next decade. Respectfully, Sadie had a candle burning on three nightstands at the head of each bed. The large number of burnt-out candle stubs, scattered on the nightstands and floor, were a sign that she'd been affectionately watching over her in-laws for days on end.

Horace stood in front of the closed door, clenched to its frame. He was extremely quiet. Ruby could see that he was in mild shock and fading fast.

She watched as her mother stared out the window and chanted, "I see a streetlight, the fog is lifting. I see a streetlight, the fog is lifting. I see a streetlight, the fog is lifting. I see a ..."

A wet, vomit stained, pastel blue blanket hung off her shoulders. She was hugging her knees into her chest and rocking back and forth. Her sunken, dark rimmed, fatigue filled eyes, seemed to pop outward as sunlight shone on her pale face. Her mother looked spectral, feeble, and fatal. Despite their unstable and blemished past, in that moment, Ruby felt sorry for Sadie, who had started chanting again as she shivered, swayed on the floor, and gaped out the window.

Repetitively she crooned, "I see a streetlight, the fog is lifting I see a streetlight, the fog is lifting I see a streetlight and the fog is lifting."

Horace stood, as if he were a looming, marble statute stuck in a museum's doorway. Ruby shot him a furious and appalled look. Given that her heart was racing, and her nerves were shot to all hell, she remained surprisingly clear-headed and calm. Realizing that Sadie was seeing the sun and not a streetlight, she knew they had to get her out of the death filled bedroom immediately. Sadie needed food, fresh air, fluids, and more sunlight. As her mind rebounded between the expediency and reality of their dire situation, Ruby's anger grew. Even a bloody idiot could see that the woman needed to be reconnected with reality! Otherwise, they'd have three dead bodies and an insane, full-blown, female psychosis to deal with!

Horace was a welder and Ruby was a former nurse's aide and a journalism student. Neither one of them was equipped to handle a Sadie on the cusp of a psychotic meltdown. She concluded that it was time for her to take two things: another deep, re-energizing breath and immediate charge of the situation. With that being decided and done, the irrefutable delegation of tasks began. Before she started flinging orders around, she reminded Horace that the room smelled like decaying dead animals and needed to be tended to before the bodies bloated to the point of skin slippage. Their relatives were already on the threshold of splitting open with all the bacteria in their guts that was releasing unstoppable internal gases. Upon hearing this, he turned around and left the bedroom. His intuitive daughter knew straightaway that the first order of allocating responsibility was to give Horace determination and meaning. Whenever he felt needed, he did what was asked of him with passion and purpose. This was why, the next thing Ruby did, was to haul a repelling Sadie up and off the floor and then force her to walk out into the hallway where Horace stood. She was taken back and concerned by how weak and undercooled her mother was.

"Horace McEwen!" she yelled from the hallway, "When was the last time this woman ate anything!"

Ruby's screams startled her mother into showing a spirited bodily reaction, which gave Ruby hope that she'd, at least physically, come through this tragic ordeal. Then she blatantly, with an authoritative undertone, instructed her father to take his wife to the bathroom, wash her up with warm water, shampoo her hair in the sink, help her dress in clean clothes, give her

312

a glass of water, and bloody feed her! If there was no food in the flat, he was to take her to an open bakery and have a sandwich with her.

"Bring some food back for me," she added to her list of demands, while listening to him cussing her out from the kitchen.

"Spend as little money as you can," she instructed. "We'll need every shilling we have for the unforeseen and unavoidable expenses of three dead people."

"Blinking friggen hell Ruby girl, you take care of Sadie yourself!" Horace loudly shrieked, disputing his daughter's demands that were disguised as instructions.

"I will prepare the bodies and finish assembling the caskets. And stop referring to your dead relatives like they are bloody roadkill!" he roared with all the manly wrath he had in him.

Ruby felt her temper break free and detonate.

"She is YOUR wife and YOUR responsibility, not MINE!" she screeched, locking eyes with her one-eyed, bull-headed father. Never before had she ever felt such a raging anger for him. In that moment she really hated the man.

Because the hate was so intense and she was weakening by the second, she felt poisoned by it. For this reason, with the speed of the fasted transformation she'd ever before experienced, she calmed herself and relied on two things she knew she could rely on; her experience with switching emotional gears and the compassion that resided deep within the kinder side of her personality. Tapping into her private strengths and reserves, she lowered her voice. Ruby knew, without a doubt, that she'd accomplish next to nothing with screaming at the distraught man. Moreover, she needed his help to finish what needed to be done. Getting the right type of cooperation from him meant that she needed to be kinder to him. On top of this, she needed him to remain sober, clearheaded, and more cooperative than his bolshie character had ever been before. Knowing that her grieving and overwhelmed father would soon be out on the streets, she was certain that it was wise to avoid giving Horace any reason to start drinking after he left the building. Ruby immediately put a leash back on her hot temper and tenderly placed her hands on both sides of her father's aging, dismayed face.

Looking deep into his eyes, she softly said, "I know that this has been a very difficult week for you Horace. I can't even imagine how terrified you were, or what it is like to lose both of your parents and only remaining brother while being here alone with Sadie. You must have been at your wits end more than once. However, you are not alone anymore Pa. I am here. I am not going anywhere. I need you and I really need your help."

She could see Horace beginning to perk up, so she continued with her spirited talk. What she didn't know was, his now change of attitude had little to do with her empathetic words; in great part, it was because she'd called him Pa again.

"What can I do Ruby girl?" he obligingly asked, ready to listen.

She always did have him twisted around her slightly long and manipulative pinkie finger.

313

"I need you to take Sadie outdoors and for a walk around the neighbourhood. She is in mild shock and needs to see, for herself, that the fog is gone and there is nothing outside but a bright sun and a blue sky above her head. Check and see if one of the neighbour women can have a cuppa or two with her while you walk to the funeral parlour and arrange for a pickup and three cremations. It will do Sadie good to engage in a regular conversation with another woman who has been through the same hell as she has. People will have a need to share their stories and losses about the events of the past few days. If Sadie opens up and talks about it, even a little bit, this could be very good for her," she said. "Do you understand this pa? Do you realize that I really can't do this on my own?" she asked.

Before he could mentally map out his answer, Ruby said, "Going to the crematorium is the most important thing you can do for your parents and brother right now. They are relying on you Horace. So am I actually. You need to schedule three cremations as quickly as possible."

Ruby could see that now that her father was absorbing what she said and accepting that he had valid reasons to leave the flat; reasons that went far outreached Sadie's needs. He stood tall and gave her his utmost attention. Ruby patted his blubbery cheeks, repositioned his ragged eyepatch, and smiled.

"Thank you for being sober Horace."

For as often as he infuriated her, the man did deserve her gratitude. She could see that the glimmer had returned to her father's bottle green coloured, aging eye.

Horace then confoundedly asked her, "Cremations, what cremations?"

He looked jumpy, puzzled, and on the edge of anger again. Then his eye flickered.

"Bloody and holy hell girl, you want me to give a funeral parlour permission to light our relatives on fire?" He asked her.

He looked outright stupefied, as though he had just been cast into a live nightmare. Horace left his wife's side, walked back into the bedroom and went over to the beds. Ruby's normally resilient and impassive self-shattered into a million pieces as she watched her father caress the stiff, lifeless feet of his parents and only remaining sibling.

"Why would you want to burn them Ruby girl?" he bleakly asked through tears. "We are not Nazi's."

Chapter 50

Horace's voice was pain stricken and his question was a valid one. The man's comparison of his family's cremation to the Nazi acts of burning Jews was justified and understandable.

The Second World War had only ended seven years ago. Seven years was a mediocre amount of time for British survivors to restore their trust and faith in life. Now, adding death to fear, for five hideous days, London had been cloaked in a treacherous mix of fog and smoke; the likes of which Brits had never experienced before, or foreseen. Although there was little time or leeway for remorse of any kind, Ruby felt rightly conflicted since her arrival. She was acclimated to Sadie's phobic ways, but she'd never seen her father's spirit so categorically broken before. With an even more compassion-filled tone, she laid her hand on his shoulder and properly explained the harshness of their situation to Horace.

"Pa, we don't have the money for three in-home embalmment's and three funerals. I am quite certain, after seeing what I just witnessed while walking from Waterloo station that funeral parlours across the city are unable to keep up with the demand for wakes, cemetery burials, or cremations for that matter. As we speak, hundreds upon hundreds of people have already died and hundreds more will still die in hospitals or at home. Time is running out Horace. If you don't get to a crematorium within the next few hours and schedule a pickup, we will have to wait days to do right by them. Are you hearing me Pa?" she asked with newly found, adult like composure.

She knew whenever she courteously called him Pa, she instantly held more than half of his stubbornness in her back pocket.

"What will they do with the ashes after they are burned?" He feebly asked.

"I know from my experience with deceased soldiers that their ashes were put in urns. Do you know what an urn is?" she said, asking him yet another question.

"Hmmm," Horace muttered, "maybe? Do you mean a burial vessel?"

"Yes!" she enthusiastically answered. His face lit up. She liked it when he felt intelligent.

"This type of burial is ancient yet rather new to many people in England. Urns are canisters that hold the ashes of the deceased's remains. The urns are rather small, so they can easily be taken home by living relatives in mourning. Horace, cremation is also relatively new Catholics in the UK. I don't know if taking the urns home is allowed yet by law. But, given how backed up the funeral parlours and crematoriums now are, I don't think it would be too difficult to get permission to do this."

Ruby paused, giving her disarrayed-looking father time to absorb what she was telling him. She was trying to remember that his blood was weaning his brain off the effects of decades of alcohol abuse.

"Or we could just sneak the urns out of the crematorium," she added, knowing how much he liked doing cheeky and sneaky things.

Cremation, ashes, urns, and the deaths of family members was all anomalous for him. In addition to fighting sobriety, Horace had recently been through a traumatic tragedy. She expected that his delirium tremors would be returning soon. She knew that the DT's caused the rapid arrival of confusion because the body was withdrawing from toxins. She'd studied this while training to become a nurse's aide. They usually began three days to four into the withdrawal and lasted for two to three days more days. Horace had a tough time ahead of him, so she knew she needed to stay ahead of his attempt at sobriety and the arrival of the tremors. Likewise, she would know if he began drinking again. She'd grown up witnessing the ricocheting effects of whiskey had on his mind, emotions and body. Not to mention the affects his addiction had, and still had, on Sadie and herself. Nevertheless, right now that didn't concern her. They all needed to do their parts to handle the tragic situation that the killer smog had created for them and this entire region of London.

"Why don't you take a few moments and think this through, while I go and check on Sadie. She's stopped chanting," Ruby said as she left the bedroom and gently closed the door.

Horace deserved and needed a proper amount of time to grieve in silence. It took him about twenty minutes to say his farewells and make his decision. Ruby had Sadie all freshened up by the time he'd reappeared. Her mother was now dressed in her winter coat, hat, scarf, and gloves. Horace's wife, who was still in shock, was waiting by the parlour door for him. She'd been as cooperative as a child trying to earn a piece of candy would be. She'd brushed her teeth, put on a touch of lipstick, and even pinned up her hair. Ruby was taken back by how obliging, her otherwise compulsive, bipolar mother was being. She didn't trust the change in Sadie, but embraced it, nonetheless. What other choice did she have? The timing of the next hour had become imperative. If her mother had another psychiatric breakdown, Ruby wouldn't be able to manage her alongside the threefold demise in the next room.

Sadie had stopped rambling and told Ruby she was hungry. Her daughter took this as an encouraging sign that her mother was exiting her mental prison and was reconnecting to her body. Horace's winter gear was in a chair next to the front door. When he stepped into the parlour, he tried to conceal his swollen, bloodshot eye and tear stained face, but he couldn't.

With unsteady hands, he promptly picked up his tattered, old man derby, and told Sadie to, "Start walking downstairs. I will meet you by the exit door."

Horace knew that the buildings only exit door was locked, meaning she couldn't wander off into the streets without him. Ruby was pleased with his patience for his wife. She could see the satisfied look on Horace's face when he opened the door and ushered her out like a prize he'd just won.

As Sadie began descending the stairs, Horace turned around and asked Ruby, "How am I to pay for three residential cadaver pickups, three cremations, and three urns?"

"Three dead relatives at the same time are indeed expensive, unfair and mind boggling," she sympathetically told him. "You are wise to be considering this."

A promising solution immediately entered her young, inquisitive brain.

"Try not to worry," she told him. "The Uncle Reggie I knew always had a wallet full of banknotes whenever I saw him because he didn't trust banks. He only used the Bank of London to cash in his RAF benefit check each month for a wad of watermarked paper banknotes. How do you think I have been paying for my studio in Dublin each week and my tuition fees each semester?" she asked him with a smile. "Uncle Reggie was very generous to me because he had no children of his own and we literally grew up together. I was his little sister in every way of the meaning, except in the biological way like your sister Cicely was."

Hearing herself saying this had her emotions doing cartwheels, but she didn't shed a tear. She was tough in the face of disaster and not in the least bit afraid of treachery.

"I also know that Grandma Liza hid the money from your father's government pension checks that she cashed in each month. She went to the same bank that your brother frequented. Like Reggie, she had a distained mistrust of the British banking system. Grandma Liza took me along with her to the bank many times over the years. After she converted Grandpa Amos's check, she'd have a pocketbook filled with cash. Then, she'd buy me a lollypop, or an ice cream cone, as a bribe for not telling Grandpa Amos that she'd nicked, what she called, 'her share' of his monthly earnings. Quite often, she'd give me a shilling, as a reward for good behaviour at the bank and for my secrecy."

Still looking down the stairwell after Sadie, Horace began smiling. He had no idea Ruby knew so much about his parents and brother, or that she'd had such a fine relationship with each of them.

"As I grew older, I came to realize that my reward for good behaviour it was really just hush money. Being the recipient of hush money made me feel important when I was a small girl. When we returned home from the candy store, or the ice cream parlour, your ma would dole money out to her husband. He only received the minimum weekly amount he needed to keep him whiskey satisfied, but not whiskey drunk. Over the years, Grandma Liza told me, repeatedly, that she could live with satisfied, but not with drunk. After grandpa got his share, grandma would hide the rest of the money somewhere right under Amos's nose; somewhere too close for him to suspect and too difficult for him to find."

Aces! My daughter hadn't missed a beat in all these years. She knows more about my parents and brother than I do!

The now 'gripped by pride' Horace knew this but didn't praise her for it. The one eyed, huge hearted man had never been big on giving compliments, or saluting a wise mind that was sharper and cleverer than his was. If he had been the complimentary type, he would have been flattering his daughter nonstop since the moment she had leapt in his arms under the Friar Flats

317

sign a few hours ago. Ruby had always fascinated him with her resourcefulness and bravery. She was factually, the polar opposite of her mother.

"Isn't that stealing Ruby girl?" he timidly asked. "I mean it isn't our money we'd be using to embalm, bury, or cremate them. It's theirs."

She knew he was an honest son and brother, but she also knew he wasn't an ignorant, naïve fool. He was quibbling over monetary details and dragging his oversized feet so he didn't have to spend more time than needed with his complex, mourning, and destitute wife. Sadie and Horace were more than polar opposites; they both were equally as combustible as gasoline being poured on an open fire.

Ruby's patience predictably, yet unexpectedly, blew up and spattered all over her father.

"Bloody hell, it's not stealing Horace! Goddammit, they are all dead!" she yelled, a smidgen too loudly.

She had no tolerance left. She was feeling sick and dreadful from the overbearing stench of death in the flat. Horace had forgotten to close the bedroom door after seeing his dead relatives for the last time.

"You should be getting down to Sadie now," Ruby suggested, attempting to muster up a kinder tone. He could see that she'd switched gears again.

Practically pushing him out the door, she said, "I will take care of things here. Remember to eat and go to the crematorium. You need to save money and I need to find money. We can finish their caskets after you find someone for Sadie to visit with so you can return alone."

Horace was now filled with new confidence and tenacity. He grabbed his coat off the chair and then reached under it, telling her that he needed to fetch something. Annoyed with him, she impolitely rolled her eyes as he went into the kitchen. They were still rolling when he returned straightaway.

"Here is a spare key. Lock yourself in, but don't lock yourself out. You'll need to wear your winter coat today if you leave the building. It's sunny brass-monkey weather outside."

Then, he pecked her on the cheek and descended the flight of stairs. Horace was a real exaggerator and a loyal fan of slang.

"Remember, I need you sober!" she reminded him, yelling down the stairwell.

"Yeah, yeah, yeah," he sarcastically bellowed back up at her.

"Dammit to hell!" she cursed, as she turned to re-enter the flat. "Shit. I bloody forgot to tell Horace about seeing Winston Churchill."

She closed the apartment door and locked it. The 'sound of nothing' that instantly blanketed her felt like a type of saving grace that had been gift-wrapped in silence.

For as quiet as it was in the apartment, the rancid smell, her hungry belly, and three rotting corpses in the bedroom, harshly reminded her that time was running out. Ruby was now on a mission. She needed to find money, lots of money, and she needed to find it fast. She would start her search for shillings by removing the back panel from her grandparent's defective

Murphy wireless. They'd been using their large, polished, beach wood box radio as an end table since the late 1930s. A brilliant place for her grandmother to hide a decade's worth of unspent banknotes, she ingeniously decided.

Tucking the apartment's spare key safely inside her bra, she went into the kitchen to search for a screwdriver.

In the year 1952, exactly eight days after her arrival in London, an undergraduate student of journalism returned to the University of Dublin to resume her studies. The next day she began writing a mandatory composition for the university's Dean of Students.

In the year 1953, between December 5th and December 9th, Great Britain honoured the One Year Anniversary of the Great Smog.

A commemorative editorial, paying tribute to London's tragedy appeared in various national Irish and British periodicals. The five-part literary remembrance was titled, Black Snow.

It had been written by Ruby Adeline McEwen.

Chapter 51

With the strong smell of freshly brewed espresso wafting under her nostrils, the elderly woman, with round black spectacles poised on the tip of her nose, turned her head from side to side, let go of her ice filled glass, put her hands in her lap and took a deep breath.

"Ahhhhh," she moaned, savouring the scent of her most favourite aroma in the world. She could feel someone trying to interrupt her moment of basking in the caramelized and nutty, smell of coffee by zealously shaking her arm. The old gammer could hear panicked voices, with loud, troubled tones, asking, "Are you okay madam? Are you okay madam? Madam, are you okay?"

Repeatedly, the voices asked her the same bloody question. Her 'despises of interruption and repetition' were awakening. Exasperated, she stopped relishing in the smell of Starbucks, opened her eyes, and attempted to adjust her eyeglasses. The grasp of a heavy male hand was still fixed to her bony arm.

"My apologies madam," an apprehensive looking, pimply-faced, teenage boy with ginger coloured hair said.

She grabbed him by his upper arm and squeezed with all the might she could muster.

"Bloody hell, you're stronger than my brother is!" the boy exclaimed.

Ruby immediately removed her hand from his arm. In turn he let go of her scraggily arm and asked her if he'd hurt her. After all, it wasn't his intention.

Being triggered by one word, he'd spoken, Ruby screamed out, "Goddammit, stop calling me madam!"

The poor fella jumped back as if he'd been slapped. The elderly woman looked around the table and realized she'd landed herself in the brightest spotlight she'd ever stood in before. Loathing being the centre of attention, she felt rattled and embarrassed. A bug-eyed nurse, whom she'd never seen before was standing across from the booth where she sat and staring at the person who'd just caused a ruckus. She was wearing a blue uniform and she had a stethoscope hanging around her neck. Seeing her reminded the Ruby of Olivia Davies, Jazz's night nurse. In the blink of an eye, the patient upstairs in the intensive care unit entered her now worry-filled mind. She'd lost all track of time and sense of place while leaving the here and now and mentally dallying through the past. Fear crept into her chest and scratched at her throat. On the other side of the table, she recognized the tall bloke who she'd been sitting next to her during the BBC weather broadcast. He was now standing up, about a meter away and safely out of her range of fire. She didn't notice his cappuccino-stained Nikes. Next to the tall bloke, stood was a man with a perplexed expression. He was holding the wooden handle of an old-fashioned, flat headed, straw broom. In no time flat, her rattled, abashed brain woke up. It was angry and filling with vengeance. Ruby was embarrassed and she absolutely despised being stared at.

"Of course I am okay, do I look bloody dead to you people!" she snarled.

Truth be told, she was confused after unintentionally drifting through the past for too long. The older she'd become, the more often feeling dazed made her lose a degree of her self-control over her behaviour, which irritated her even more. The recent combination of too much sugar, caffeine, and mind traveling, was having more and more adverse effects on her emotional resistance. Likewise, she became crabbier when she needed to juggle or manage her zest for sugar, caffeine, and reminiscing.

Sweet Jesus, she laughingly thought, *almost nine decades of life is enough to turn any woman into an occasional bitch.*

Despite the awareness she had of her quirky traits, she calculatingly reeled her bad attitude in. She was earnestly trying to hide her tangled up state of mind from 'the cafeteria spectators' she'd just startled and angered. Given that she was responsible for an eighteen-year-old, purple-haired coma patient in the intensive care unit, she didn't want to be taken away by hospital security.

Make a mental note old girl, she thought, *from now on, only caffeine free beverages and one free sugary cone per day.*

Out of the corner of one of her weary eyes, Ruby saw a familiar face. The ICU receptionist was making her way through the crowded cafeteria. She recognized her instantly. The receptionist looked apprehensive, as she skilfully navigated her way through the dispersing crowd. She was coming straight towards the elderly woman, who was obviously overcome by a dreadful kind of angst.

Had the child woken up or passed away without her great grandmother by her side? She anxiously asked herself.

The receptionist could see anguish written all over her face.

Nearing the front of the table where Ruby was sitting, the receptionist smiled and reassuringly said, "I am sorry to interrupt you Madam, but Doctor Zamier and his assistant, from our Neurology Department, are waiting in Jazz's room. They would like to speak to you immediately. They don't have much time. I was away from my station and regrettably, I was the only one who knew where you were. It has taken us some time to locate you. Would you please come with me straightaway? Try not to worry, Jazz is doing fine."

"Jazz is doing fine!" Ruby sarcastically mocked. "What is so bloody fine about being in a coma?" She was yelling again!

So much for managing my temper, she thought.

"Umm augh, I mean not fine. I mean, augh, given her current state there is no reason to panic mam," the receptionist added with a nervous stutter.

This ornery, old woman makes me so bloody tense, she thought, but professionally kept to herself.

"I don't panic young lady! Moreover, stop bloody calling me madam or mam! My name is Ruby! Ruby friggen Adeline McEwen!"

She'd verbally bitten back like an angry dog. For the third time in less than two minutes, she'd lost every speck of self-control. In the meantime, the nurse, the tall bloke, and the Star Bucks employee, who'd shared a table with her, had each snuck off while Ruby was having a fit. They'd slipped away from the scene of the commotion and returned to their jobs. The clean-cut man wearing green scrubs, who'd accidently toppled into her earlier and knocked her to the floor, was leaving the dining hall. Walking past the booth where Ruby still simmered, he couldn't avoid overhearing what was transpiring between the two women.

Without forethought, he cordially extended his strong, muscular arm and said, "May I escort you back to the ICU, Ruby?"

He knew by now not to call her madam, or mam, as he offered to assist her to the elevator and then back up to the ICU.

"It is on my way." He added.

Again, without forethought, he'd blurted a few fibs out that landed in her lap. It was for a proper cause, he reckoned. He had a particularly dignified face that was framed in with a manly, yet charming smile. She was convinced that any woman, of any age, could not ignore a man like this man; a man who was still holding his arm out for her.

"My name is Doctor Tanner," he said, "You may call me Tristan."

Ruby, being a genuine geriatric flirt, softened her expression and said, "I appreciate the gesture kind Tristan."

Upon witnessing Ruby's coy reply, the ICU receptionist's eyes bowled so far back into their sockets that they nearly disappeared. The green-garbed, striking fellow's manners and charisma reminded Ruby of Deniz, the cabdriver with a Z. Likewise, Tristan Tanner's dark skin and rugged chiselled face reminded her of Nico. She pulled her weak, crippled body into an upright standing position, purposefully abandoned her trash filled food tray, took his hand, and walked as fast as her long, arthritis-stricken legs would allow. Making their way towards the elevator, she held onto his brawny arm every step of the way. The kind of attention she was receiving from him was something she considered 'a well-earned reward' for being a woman at least three times his age. Together with the sceptical and timid receptionist, the three of them took the elevator back up to the seventh floor. When the elevator doors opened, Ruby bid Dr. Tanner, her amiable escort, a kind farewell. Then she deliberately put her temper back on its leash and walked alongside the receptionist, down the long corridor towards the child's room. The young woman was tempted to support Ruby by holding her frail, thin-skinned arm, but by now she knew better than to touch her.

When they reached the room with number 07.11 on the door, the receptionist handed Ruby a folded piece of yellow paper and said, "While you were downstairs, a Mr. Thatcher Durant called for you. This is the message he asked me to give to you."

Ruby had forgotten all about the Durant family traveling from America. The BBC weather report had publicized that all incoming flights were being rerouted due the fog conditions at Heathrow Airport. She'd hoped, for her great grandson, Thatcher, that their flight had been redirected to The Netherlands. She'd heard from tourists visiting her diner that many Americans went to the Dutch city of Amsterdam. After she'd woken up and gone to the cafeteria to hear the news broadcast, she'd briefly thought about the Durant's flying through the night. Nonetheless, given her drifting episode and what had just transpired one floor down, the Durant's had completely slipped her mind. She quickly thanked the receptionist and offered her a sincere apology for her rudeness.

"Blame it on my age," she suggested.

The receptionist wasn't the least bit impressed. Then she tucked Thatcher's message inside her bra, pinched her cheeks so she'd look kind of healthier, and took a deep breath of courage. As a woman nearing ninety, she accepted that looking younger wasn't possible anymore, but looking healthier was. With this belief in mind, she gave her cheeks another quick double pinch. Steady and prepared for whatever waited for her on the other side of the wide, automatic ICU door, Ruby entered the room. Two neurologists and two uniformed detectives stopped talking the second they saw her. They were standing in pairs, on either side of Jazz's bed. A slightly eerie, butch-like silence hanging in the air had muted the droning, peeping, and humming sounds of the life support machines.

With eight intense male eyes staring her down, in less than one beat of her panicky heart, the accurate elderly woman knew she was completely outnumbered.

Chapter 52

"How is she?" Ruby heard the sound of her voice meekly asking the professionally pristine looking, dark-skinned doctor standing at the child's bedside.

Dr. Zamier, turned and gave her a cordial nod of his head. She was relieved to see that he was the same neurologist she'd spoken to the yesterday, the day of the boating accident. A rather gullible and budding medical student, holding a clipboard, was standing wide-eyed next to him. The intern stood poised and straight-backed with pen in hand. He was noticeably eager and ready to start taking notes. He reminded her of a soldier standing at attention while waiting for his orders. Ruby held onto the child's bedframe with one hand and caressed her feet with her other hand. The warm temperature of Jazz's feet and ankles was promising and slightly calming for her great grandmother's nerves.

Before answering her question, Dr. Zamier directly asked both police agents to leave the room and wait in the hallway 'while he gave his patient's caregiver an update over Jazz's condition. Ruby could easily see that he was a man who took charge of people and circumstances. One cooperative officer obliging him stepped straightaway from the side of the bed, and left the room. The second, unduly arrogant, and intolerant looking officer was much less obedient.

"We have been waiting for two days to question our suspect," he defensively blurted out. "Every case we work means planning our investigations, gathering evidence at the crime scene, and interviewing suspects. Then we need to obtain victim and witness statements," he dictated, trying to keep his composure.

Ruby glanced over at the neurologist just in time to see his exasperated, bulging, dark eyes popping out of his professional face. The detective was on an investigative roll.

"We already have another suspect in custody. A suspect who, for some bloody ridiculous reason, is giving us nothing solid to go on! He does however ask, at least ten times a day, about your patient, this young woman in this bed!" he yelled, pointing at Jazz.

The detective then stepped even closer to where Ruby stood. She wasn't intimidated in the least. Dr. Zamier's presence was keeping her stable and grounded. She was more than ready for the likes of such a British imbecile as this detective was. A flickering, yellow light, from another monitor that Ruby hadn't noticed before, reflected off the silver badge the detective wore on his suitcoat. The man and his cocky attitude were clearly unaware that she was, in the face of her age, not a woman who was easily frightened. On the contrary, she was a shrewd, unswerving, old wench when she needed to be. Which was another fact the rude detective was completely ignorant of.

Soon enough, soon enough, she cunningly thought as she locked eyes with his. Using the shortest route, he'd turned his stern, copper focus onto Ruby.

"Can you tell me madam, why an illegal immigrant, who is being paid cash to work at your diner has a need to protect Miss Durant? Why did Mr. Nico Rossario steal a boat from the harbour with an American girl? A girl, from what we have determined, is a wild and irresponsible teenager from California with a juvenile record?"

The detective, trying to be overly intimidating, glared at the elderly woman. He talked much too fast, slightly dribbled spit, and rapidly demanded answers; hence, the drooling. His face reddened while his impatience and threatening anger caused the veins on his neck to protrude. He clearly was attempting to keep a lid on his 'boiling over' annoyance. The man was having a temper tantrum that toddlers worldwide were branded for having. The elderly woman found his behaviour to be droll. Despite her aged analysis of the man, she wisely ignored her impulsiveness and refrained from laughing at him.

"Constable, I have no idea what you are talking about or why you insist on trying to intimidate me. Only your suspects can answer these questions. Sir, I was obviously not on the goddamn, bloody boat!" Ruby yelled back at him.

"Shush," Dr. Zamier commanded, tapping with his pen on the metal chart binder he was holding as he looked austerely at both of them.

The neurology student was eagerly taking notes as fast as he could. Ruby concluded that this detective constable was a rather dumpy and stumpy male, who obviously had an overgrown self-image compensating for his pint size. The detective then took a few steps in her direction. The attentive, Dr. Zamier, seeing a confrontation emerging, casually intervened. He was suspicious as to why the detective's partner had so willingly left his patient's room. This had him wondering if they were acting out a famed, off-coloured, and pre-rehearsed scene of good cop bad cop. Contrarily, he contemplated, perhaps the other detective's partner knew what was coming and had departed before being caught in any verbal crossfire.

"Please lower your voices," Dr. Zamier said, looking again, in the same way, at both of the short-tempered people standing next to his patient's bed.

"Detective, Jazz Durant's condition is private," he stated.

The officer countered with an unmistakable demanding tone, "I need to be called the moment Miss Durant wakes up. This is not a protocoled request; it is an indorsed command."

The neurologist immediately summed up the situation, took charge of the room, and firmly spoke.

"Detective, let me be clear. You have no authority over me, therefore no official right to command anything from myself or my staff. You are not standing on the set of a hospital soap opera. This is real life, not television. On TV programs and in films, viewers are given the impression that someone in a coma wakes up, looks around the room, and is able to think and talk normally only minutes after their consciousness returns. People often think that patients who have regained their awareness have full and vivid memories of what happened before their catatonic state began. However, in real life, the type of life this young coma patient is clinging to, this hardly ever happens."

He was sympathetically patting Jazz's shoulder as he spoke.

"When leaving a coma, patients are confused. Approximately, ninety-five percent of them slowly respond to what's going on, if they respond at all. When my patient wakes up, it will take time for her to recover from her head injury and brain trauma. Her brain is swollen. This is all I will tell you. A swollen and bruised brain needs time to heal."

"How much time are we talking about here Doc?" The detective rudely blurted out, interrupting Dr. Zamier.

"I was about to tell you before you interjected. I am the only one who can, and the only one who will, be determining when she is ready for questioning. I am her primary physician and Mrs. McEwen is her legal guardian until her family arrives from America," he clarified, looking directly at Ruby.

He hoped Ruby sensed his unwavering support. He could see by the expression decorating her age spotted cheeks that she had. He continued.

"Until I determine that my patient is ready for questioning, no police detectives, constables, or investigators of any kind will be allowed in this room," he decisively confirmed.

"What!" The detective reacted angrily.

"Detective, for the last time, I ask you to lower your voice. When I am finished speaking with Mrs. McEwen, a visitor restriction order for this room will be registered with the ICU Director. Authorization will take three minutes at the most," he clarified with the complete authority that he had.

"Is that absolutely necessary?"

The officer sternly probed.

"Constable, your persistent, impolite conduct, and unethical attempts to wake my patient up sooner than is medically safe, are why you and your colleagues are being banned from the ICU," Dr. Zamier conclusively announced.

When the impatient policeman opened his mouth to counteract, Dr. Zamier masterfully extended his arm and put his hand up like a human stop sign, which was properly interpreted as halt and shut the hell up. Both men were now leaning over Jazz's bed and standing their ground. One of them kept his professional composure, while the other one was acting like a spoiled copper who had no choice but to succumb. Jazz laid underneath both of them, oblivious to the male stride that was taking place just above her petite and wounded body.

"Gentlemen, please be quiet," Ruby said with her index finger over her mouth.

She wanted to protect Jazz from the sound of conflict, regardless that she was certain that the child could use some crystal-clear commotion to guide her back to the chaotic world waiting for her on the other side of wherever she now was.

These bloody rhythmic, vibrating sounds filtering through this room, are enough to keep anyone in a coma, she distractedly decided.

Nevertheless, the men's sparring with words and accusations were giving her a headache. She was growing tired of watching two virile egos, driven by macho stubbornness, trying to outdo each other. Despite that, she found it to be rightly ludicrous, it was side-tracking her and wasting precious time. Ruby already knew which ego would win and which one would walk off, dragging its male tail across the room's yellow linoleum floor tiles. This dispute would need to end soon because, she had to pee something terrible. Her old bladder required that the men agree to an immediate truce, otherwise, a puddle of a double Starbuck's expresso would be on the floor in the next thirty-seconds. Forty-five seconds max, if they were very lucky.

"In addition," the human stop sign dynamically said, "I will not tolerate anyone, regardless of their rank, to attempt to rattle this dear old lady in any way. While she is in my hospital, she will be shown a decent degree of due respect from the London Police Department. She is here to nurture and care for a family member. She is not here to accommodate you or your investigation." The detective, apparently not used to being outranked, was rendered speechless. Ruby was enjoying seeing their out of control, amusing, male testosterone battle.

I assumed that only women could catfight, she amusingly thought.

"Only hospital staff and family members will be allowed in this room until I reverse the restriction," Dr. Zamier informed the officer. "Do I make myself clear?"

The neurologist never raised his voice. His conclusive demeanour didn't require an unprofessional flare up. Contrastingly, the detective's face was contorted and irate with anger. Nevertheless, he knew he could do nothing to change a visitor restriction order for a comatose patient at Saint Matthew's Hospital. He'd been down this 'suspect road' before and knew that he'd taken his line of questioning too far. Likewise, the constable also knew it was too late to for him retract what had just transpired; especially his unprofessional impatience and insolence. Dr. Zamier then asked his intern to step out into the corridor and finish explaining the specifics of Saint Matthew's Visitor Restriction Policy to the constable and his partner; whom he assumed was still in the hallway waiting for a ride back to the precinct. The detective hesitated just long enough to reach inside his inside jacket pocket and give the neurologist his police contact card.

Then he sarcastically said, "I expect to hear from you straightaway when my suspect is able to be questioned in an ongoing investigation. Maybe she'll be one of those rare five percent who wakes up to remarkably experience an instant and complete recall."

Doctor Zamier nodded with offended approval. He'd had enough of the man, therefore he held his tongue and responded with a final, short, four-word sentence. "You will be contacted."

At this point, the neurologist would have said and done anything to get this squatty, dribbling man and his pot belly out of his ICU. He was vehement about speaking to Mrs. McEwen, passing his knowledge about Jazz's case onto her, and then finishing his rounds. He'd allowed the detective to deter him from his job for too long.

"Call me straightway and not one minute later." The constable said, bogusly needing to have the last word before admitting that he was being dismissed.

Then, quite unexpectedly, the Neurology Intern, who was still waiting while holding the door open, boldly said, "Detective, time is wasting! Sir, we have patients in need that we are scheduled to examine and rounds to finish! Your cooperation, sir, is expected and appreciated," he finished with a more respectable tone. The detective scowled at the intern's pubescent brashness and turned to offer Ruby his hand. She refused it, which threw him off guard; something of which he was too witless to realize, was exactly her intention.

"Madam, until we meet again at The Seaside, I wish you the best of luck," the puny man said, stepping towards the door.

Ruby replied with a straight face by cheekily saying, "Without a warrant, you are not welcome at my place of business, or my home." He left the room, looking with like a little boy who'd just been reprimanded by his strict granny.

As the door closed behind him, Ruby cried out, "Touché!" and hobbled off to use the loo. A few minutes later, she returned to the child's bedside. Dr. Zamier was reading Jazz's chart that had hung off the foot of the ICU bed since her admission.

"Shall we get started madam?" he asked.

This time Ruby didn't mind being called madam. Not in the very least. Then the elderly woman then asked the same question she'd asked when she'd entered the room after being escorted from the cafeteria one floor down.

"How is she?"

Chapter 53

"Olivia Davies has told me that you have a background that enables you to medically understand what has happened to Jazz. Is she correct?" Dr. Zamier asked.

"Yes, doctor she is," Ruby replied. "However, my brain is much older than it was '40s and '50s."

He smiled at her comment.

"Even so," she continued, "if I don't understand something I am being told, or I don't agree with it, I ask about it. Asking questions comes easy to me Doctor Zamier."

"Understood," he said. "Let's begin. I'll get straight to the point. Knowing now that you can read and comprehend Jazz's vitals, I will skip over that part and explain our designated course of neurological treatment for the next ten days."

Ruby focused and gave him her undivided attention.

"I ordered a medically induced coma for Jazz earlier this morning. The purpose of taking this therapeutic direction is to ensure her neurological protection and to control the current degree of active compression force on her brain. The length of therapeutic inducement that I have scheduled for Miss Durant is mainly due to the degree of cerebral swelling. We are currently treating the swelling and her other injuries, but we need more time. Actually, Jazz needs more time," he intentionally and slowly said, realizing that this was a lot for his patient's guardian to absorb, let alone comprehend.

"Are you familiar with a drug-induced coma?" he asked Ruby.

Her one-word answer was, "No."

Dr. Zamier went on to explain that a drug-induced coma puts a person into a deep state of unconsciousness, which allows the brain to rest and thus decreases its swelling. The decrease in swelling can result in less pressure being put on the brain, which lessens the risk of damaging effects. His team had already overseen the procedure while she was downstairs. They would now be monitoring their patient around the clock until a certain brain wave pattern was reached and recorded. The electroencephalography monitor is being used to follow her brain wave activity. It is undisputed that Jazz's coma began with a brain injury. Her EEG waves had become a tad too erratic, which indicated to my staff that her brain was struggling."

Ruby had begun swaying from left to right while holding onto Jazz's bedrail. Dr. Zamier nonchalantly suggested she sit in the lounge chair. So she did. He continued.

"I want to protect her brain from being over stimulated by internal and external forces while it heals, and the swelling subsides. This is why I ordered an EEG, the drug inducement procedure, and the visitor restriction."

"What are you protecting her brain from?" Ruby asked.

"Her head injury significantly altered the metabolism of her brain. This resulted in an inadequate flow of blood flow to certain cerebral lobes. By inducing her, we are reducing the amount of energy her brain needs to heal. If this is successful, her brain will heal less stressfully and the swelling will go down. A drug-induced coma, as opposed to a customary trauma related coma, is a state of catalepsy that is reversible. My prognosis is that after a significant reduction in swelling, and shortly after the drugs are no longer administered, Jazz's brain will stabilize itself and she will awaken from her unconsciousness.

"How safe is this drug-induced coma she is in?" she asked.

"Good question," the doctor complimented. "A drug-induced coma is actually simple form of sedation. Something you most likely are familiar with."

Ruby nodded in agreement.

"Jazz is receiving a monitored and continuous dose of anaesthetics through her IV. Propofol, pentobarbital, and thiopental are the drugs we use. They have a continuous effect on a patient, keeping them in a sustained state of oblivion that is necessary for healing to begin. According to my daily neurological exam, evaluation, and patient care orders, the ICU team assigned to her case will adjust the dose to reach the desired level of prescribed unconsciousness. In addition to the induced coma therapy, I have ordered ventricular therapy. Later today, a tube will be inserted through Jazz's cranium. The tube will allow trapped cranial fluid to discharge into a drainage system. This procedure in itself is not dangerous for her. It is not necessary for you to be here when the drain is inserted. I'd prefer that only my staff be in the room during the procedure. The drain should accelerate the reduction of swelling. This is ultimately our goal. The ICU team will be monitoring the pressure within her skull every three hours, twenty-four hours a day. Once the pressure is reduced to an acceptable level, we will stop administering the drugs, and I will attempt to wake her up," he concluded.

"Wouldn't that be something," Ruby hopefully said.

"Do you have any more questions madam?" he patiently asked her.

"Yes, just one more," she said. "What are the side effects to medically inducing her?" Ruby asked.

Dr. Zamier replied, "This is difficult to answer. I have ordered these therapies because her situation, although quite threatening, is not grim. Her vitals are registering above the normal ranges. If we were only treating a head wound, I would not have ordered the ventricular therapy. However, her petite body is attempting to heal from numerous other serious injuries, in addition to substantial cerebral and cranial brain traumas. Her broken limbs, deep lacerations, and numerous extensive hematomas, each require a considerable amount of bodily energy to heal. This is energy that her brain requires but won't receive enough of until her other injuries stop needing it. Her wounds, the dispersing of restorative energy, and the brain swelling, are my main reasons for keeping her in her coma. She needs a chance and time to heal."

Dr. Zamier stopped talking while he wrote summaries and recorded stats on his patient's medical chart. Ruby noticed that large bulge on the child's face was slightly decreasing. The puffiness that remained had left a dark, greenish yellow discolouration behind. Her eyes where still swollen shut and her bottom lip was so swollen that it looked like it had wrapped itself around the blue breathing tube inserted through her mouth.

"Although I don't anticipate it, if there are lasting side effects later on," Dr. Zamier said, "it will be extremely difficult to determine if they are the results of the drug-induced coma or the initial brain injury. Saint Matthew's ICU Team is world renowned, Mrs. McEwen. Your great granddaughter is in very capable hands. Our team is precise and mindful. We will be observing and monitoring her twenty-four hours a day for the next ten days. On day eleven, unless she regains consciousness on her own, I will wake her up."

"Thank you kindly, doctor," Ruby said. She had stood up again and was holding Jazz's feet.

He could see this was strenuous for her and she was tiring.

"Have a seat Ruby, we are almost finished." He suggested.

She sat in the lounge chair, draped the blanket over her legs, and watched him pull a stool on wheels in front of where she sat. Ruby listened as this easy-going, tolerant, and compassionate neurologist, began to speak.

"I am a believer in the power of the spontaneous and intuitive mind. When we fall asleep, or go into a coma, the greater part of our consciousness recedes from the surface and plunges into the depths of our subliminal being. Despite this, I am certain there is a life force within the body that persists. You see, a life force can recall and respond to external stimulus. Although Jazz will be in a deeper state of sub consciousness for the next ten days, in a diminutive way she might be partially aware of what is happening in her external world. Her external world currently consists of the bed she is in and the space within these four walls. My advice to you, is to continue talking with her and reading to her. You have impressed my staff with your devotion to Jazz. Music is also allowed if played at a tolerable volume that doesn't interfere with the resonances and reverberations of the monitors. You could consider putting earbuds in her ears if you opt for music. For obvious reasons, I do not allow headsets to put on a patient with a head injury. Sound patterns have proven to be effective for a person in a neurologically immobilized condition."

Dr. Zamier reached over and took her age gnarled hand in his. The elderly woman, who was fading fast, intently looked up at him. In her British point of view, he had a soothing Asian-like face, a spiritual approach, and a New Delhi accent.

Why didn't I notice this before? She asked wordlessly. She was chin wagging with her silent self again. She'd always loved a proper one on one chinwag with herself.

No doubt, you were too distracted old girl, whilst arguing with that pudgy, dodgy, dominant friggen copper. You'll need to be on your toes not to bodge things up when those detectives return. Nico and Jazz are relying on you. Giving and taking her own advice were two other things she quite liked about herself. Even though her sugar rushes were long gone, she realized that the neurologist had put her in a blissful mood again.

As Dr. Zamier began writing on his patient's chart again, Ruby's mind relaxed. The dark-skinned, mild mannered man was an engaging and tranquil person. He wore a cobalt blue neurologist uniform, an indigo blue and green striped tie, and a white overcoat. Astutely, she noticed that his uniform was the same colour as the light emitting from the machine next to the child's bed. He had dubious lips that were the colour of Spanish wine, and thick, black eyebrows. He wore a thinly trimmed moustache and had a slight cleft in his prominent chin. His cleft chin reminded her of Grady Walsh, her first real crush from back in the early 1950's; and of Clark Gable, the once celebrated King of Hollywood, who'd starred in her favourite movie, Gone with the Wind. Gone with the Wind had been the first picture show she'd ever seen. She went to see it with her Uncle Reggie and her father Horace when it was released in the UK in 1940. The old woman was so absorbed in thinking about her first lover and seeing her first talking motion picture that she didn't hear the doctor from India, who was still holding her hand, ask her the same question three times.

"Ruby, have you contacted Jazz's family yet? Her records indicate that she is from America."

"Yes, I have. They are fogged in and most likely stranded in Amsterdam. As soon as the fog lifts and Heathrow Airport reopens, they will arrive."

Hearing herself saying this reminded her to read the message the receptionist had given her from the child's brother Thatcher Durant.

"Now," he decreed, "there certainly are worse cities than Amsterdam to be unpredictably stranded in."

"True, very true," she retorted.

"I have some solid and well-meant advice for you madam. Take the next few days to take care of yourself. Leave the care of our patient in my hands. Permit myself and the hospital's medical professionals to reconnect the neurological pieces of Jazz's condition. I am hopeful that the pieces will all fall into place if everyone who enters this room, for whatever reason, does their part while adhering to my protocols for her treatment strategies and recovery."

Ruby smiled. Despite that she that she barely knew this doctor, she trusted him with Jazz's life and felt a rock solid sense of security when he was nearby.

"Please consider going to your diner and taking care of any unfinished business," he recommended. "I can imagine there are matters there that only you are equipped to tend to."

"You know about my diner?" Her face lit up with surprise.

"Yes, madam, I do. I hear my staff quite often mentioning The Seaside. Apparently, your restaurant has superb food and an unprecedented charm. I've often overheard that its 1950s décor, and beachside dining has earned The Seaside quite a citywide reputation. I consider this, if I may boldly say, to be quite an esteemed achievement for a WWII survivor and a woman who experienced the civil rights movement and the sexual revolution era. My sincere compliments to you madam," he kindly said.

Ruby's age earned, shrivelled face blushed and beamed. Obviously, Dr. Zamier was an intuitive, educated, and gracious man. He'd recognized that her diner was her life. Regardless of the medical circumstances, she missed being there.

"Do consider going home madam. Do you have a mobile telephone?" he asked her.

"No, sir I don't." she whispered back.

"Given that you are the ICU's only contact person for Miss Durant, it would be wise for you to have cell phone in case we need to reach you. You can also use it to call the nurses station to inquire about Jazz's condition from time to time. Nowadays, prepaid telephones with SIM cards are sold on every city corner and even in grocery stores. St. Matthew's visiting hours are between 10am and 7pm. Only you will be allowed in her room before and after visiting hours. Jazz will be fine in our care, even if she is alone. Try to trust this madam. I have given the staff authorization to allow you to remain with her throughout the night, because you are good for my patient," he concluded his plea with a proper, complimenting British chin tip.

She could see that his mannerisms and concentration were changing, which most likely meant he needed to see his next patient. She was right.

"I need to finish my rounds now. Good day to you Ruby McEwen," he said patting her hand and standing up.

She saw him hesitate as he looked at what was on her hand, just under her knuckles.

"Madam, why do you have the number 616 written on your hand?" he demurely asked, as he hung his patients chart back up on the end of the bed, "Wasn't 616 the number that was on the constable detective's police badge?"

Bollocks. Busted again, she thought, looking at him as unknowingly as her overwhelmed and charismatic personality would allow.

"I am searching for someone."

Opening the door, he looked back and with jestingly stern tone said, "Behave yourself out their madam. Doctor's orders."

When he was nearly out of site, she called out his name. He popped his head back inside the room.

Ruby then coyly asked, "Sir, why have you given me so much of your time? Surely, the Chief of Neurology has very little time to spare."

"You remind me of Ratu, my 91-year-old grandmother from Mumbai," he answered.

"In what way am I like her?" she gingerly asked.

As the room's automatic door closed behind him, she faintly heard his answer.

"You're still alive."

Chapter 54

A wrinkled hand, speckled with age and the number 616 written on it, reached inside the old woman's brassiere-and pulled out a crumpled message from the ICU receptionist. With stiff, aching fingers, she unfolded it and let out a slightly unintended whimper. Things are about to change very quickly, she realized, as she stared down at the little yellow post it note.

Ruby knew how densely fogged in the city was even before reading the message, therefore without much doubt, she assumed that she had at least one extra day to sort things out and accomplish what she needed to before the child's family arrived. She read the yellow note and realized her prediction was far beyond right. What she read told her that Thatcher and his parents were, as she'd predicted, in Amsterdam. Their flight was arriving at Heathrow Airport the day after tomorrow at 14:30pm. It was the earliest flight with three available seats that they could arrange. A hotel reservation had been made and they'd be coming straight to hospital before checking in. The mother was struggling. The father was calm. Thatcher was more than ready to arrive and assist.

"Blimey hell and hallelujah!" she cried out, looking over at Jazz. "We have almost three full days before the American cyclone arrives!" she loudly proclaimed.

Then she quickly lowered her voice out of her embarrassment for someone else's misfortune and respect for her surroundings. In her mind, Ruby already had her morning entirely mapped out. She had enough faith in Dr. Zamier and the ICU staff to trust her decision to leave the hospital and take care of a number of her personal affairs until midday. After hoisting herself up and out of the recliner, she walked over to the closet and unlocked it. She wanted to see the trunk. She needed it now because it was filled with journals, and the journals were filled with strength and vigour; two things she believed the child needed to find her way back home. Ruby was rightly optimistic that the contents of the wooden trunk could and would, in great part, return the child to consciousness before her a drug-induced coma ended. She didn't give a diddly about medical statistics; she believed in beating the odds. She turned her head and looked over at Jazz, who was peacefully lying in her ICU bed. She was still motionless with casted limbs and a bandaged-up body connected to tubes. The machines that circled her bed, and others mounted on the wall behind her, continued their humming, droning, bleeping, and peeping. She hoped that wherever this young lady was in this very moment, that she was rebelling against death. She foresaw Jazz navigating her way through past lives and learning more about life, in ways her current life was unable to teach her up to the moment of the boating accident. She hoped that if the child were to wake up in a time that once was, she'd encounter momentous and meaningful things. Things that her parents, her circle of friends, and her current life hadn't exposed her to yet. The elderly woman had spent her life believing in the act of gaining knowledge from what came before her. Likewise, she drew strength off the past and those who existed in it. She knew first-hand the countless unseen powers the bygone held. Likewise, she now knew that Jazz had a vivid photography talent. A talent that could one day open many opportunity-filled doors around the world for her, if she was courageous enough to grab life by the tail and yank on it.

"If I could turn back the clock and reset it to ten days ago, the day the child arrived, would I do it any different? Was there anything I could have done to change the events of the accident and the outcome? On that morning, when I laid eyes upon a girl on my doorstep, with cropped, untamed purple hair, a pierced nose, and a devilish look in her eyes, should I have listened to my urge to call a taxi and send her back to Heathrow? If I had, she wouldn't be lying in an intensive care unit, halfway across the globe, so far from her hometown."

This time Ruby wasn't talking to herself, she was unsure of herself, and this was something that was aberrantly foreign to her. Typically, she was not the kind of person who doubted herself or her decisions. Nevertheless, until this particular moment, she'd had no time for reflecting on the role she may have played in their dire situation. She realized that she needed be mentally prepared for the Durant's arrival from Amsterdam, and she knew that the child's parents, especially her mum, would be questioning, with cynicism, Ruby's ability to care for her daughter. She couldn't help wondering what the hell Zofia could have expected from a woman who was four decades older than she was. Nonetheless, given the seriousness of Jazz's condition, she expected that there would be a stream of inquiries arriving from America with the Durant's. Queries she rightly hoped she could answer, despite that she already knew that most of their questions would have no answers. Not yet anyhow. Their daughter was still trapped in a coma. The answers they needed were trapped somewhere in there with her.

Truth be told, Ruby was feeling edgy and anxious. She hadn't seen the child's mother and father, Zofia and Tucker, in fourteen years. She was aware that a 'strong current of everything turbulent' gushed under their relationship bridge. She was even more aware that she would emotionally drown in their problems if she wasn't very cautious. If this happened, she'd be just like Jazz, who was undeniably hating her life and emotionally sinking when she first arrived at her diner. The child had arrived with a lot more baggage than Ruby had seen in the spare bedroom she was using at the diner. It was heavier baggage of a risky, more damaging kind. Ruby was convinced that the visitor's restriction rule that Dr. Zamier had implemented, would become her calm in the Durant storm. One visitor at a time was what Dr. Zamier's patient needed to shield her from the dangers of her parent's bloody hurly-burlies.

She envisioned that she'd easily find her groove with Thatcher, the youngest of the four Durant boys. He'd left a buoyant impression on her with his first hello and his cordial, organized mannerisms. She also realized that she needed him, for things she knew went selfishly beyond his kid sister's medical condition. If Ruby was to help Nico, she couldn't help him on her own. Thatcher's background and knowledge of the law could prove very beneficial for turning the ideas that were spinning through her intuitive mind, into concrete realties. She certainly had enough money tucked away to pay the ambitious, fledging lawyer for his services and to likewise to assure that Nico's financial needs were met until he became a legal citizen of the UK. How this would all transpire was still a mystery to her. A mystery she'd be, without hesitation, handing over to Thatcher after they got to know each other again.

Ruby tucked the keys hanging from the chain around her neck back in between her breasts. They'd come loose and had fallen out when she'd removed the post-it note. Then she bent her kinked spine down and rested both of her open hands slowly on the top of the trunks threadbare surface. Its wood still felt urbane and fertile to the touch.

She promptly closed her eyes and subtly redirected her concentration. After a few moments she deftly, like a slew of times before, linked herself to, and visualized, the contents of the ornate trunk. This type of connection was a tactic she'd learned from her grandma, Bessie Dutton, back when Ruby was still a very young girl. Over time, this tactic became a ritual which had enabled her to build a lasting kinship with the trunk she'd inherited from Bessie when she was an 11-year-old.

With both of her arthritic ridden hands, now warming above its cover, she felt its vigorous energy. The elderly woman was an avid believer in the power of energy. Any type of energy. Despite that being a diner owner had made her a public figure since the 1960s, her mind and spirit were the most prevailing and enigmatic parts of who she was. This was something, very few people who knew her, were actually aware of. How could they know, given how guarded she still was, and how she concealed her innermost self from others? Beyond the surface of her often modern, hectic, and chaotic life, as the acclaimed and popular owner of The Seaside, she was a no frills, down to earth kind of person.

Doctor Zamier's wise advice had inspired her to take some time with the trunk and to reflect upon herself before leaving the hospital. For this reason, she gave her self-reflection permission to roam and reveal a bit longer.

Ruby had willed herself to live a long and meaningful life whilst overcoming and outliving an immeasurable amount of adversity. She did this by remaining prepared and pragmatic, regardless of the vast number of precarious situations that she'd landed herself in since she was a toddler. She wasn't religious, or at least in her mind she wasn't. She didn't follow any one particular faith. She had different beliefs, convictions, and ideologies about herself, her existence, and the thing mankind called, faith. Most of her life, she'd witnessed a theological and historical link between structured religion and war. Even at her old age, she still didn't agree with, or connect to religious groups using violence in an effort to create peace. Or, in the case of her Irish friend Emilia Doherty, she likewise didn't agree with supposedly religious parents using corporal punishment as a means of controlling and punishing their offspring. She closed her eyes again, and spoke.

"I don't need faith. I am faith. I am faith searching for knowledge and hoping for insight," she heard herself saying aloud.

She'd written this mantra in 1952, the day after she'd helped her parents, Horace and Sadie, cremate three family members in one hour. This was her mantra; a self-professed intonation she lived for and lived by. Throughout her life, she'd followed a simple threefold life discipline. Her discipline was as unpretentious as it was powerful.

When something bad happened, she could either let it define her, strengthen her, or destroy her. The choice was always hers to make and hers to live by.

The warmth from the trunk's ligneous surface coated her hands and wrists. Like so many times before, she felt a type of historical dynamism passing through her. Ruby was not born energy sensitive and intuitive. Life had made her this way.

Opening her bright, alert green eyes, she limped over to the ICU bed and lightly placed one open hand on top of the child's hand. She could feel the stiff, plastic rawness of cool intravenous tubes under her thin-skinned palm. Concentrating on the connecting sensation, she felt the subtle throb of veins that crossed the child's hand. As the feeling travelled upwards towards her wrist and arm, in an unrestrained way she linked herself to Jazz. Skin on skin, their human energies exchanged and blended into one. The child's other hand was in a plaster cast that began just under her shoulder. Her thumb was also fully casted, with only her fingertips entirely exposed. To further deepen their connection, she reached over and lightly pressed her fingertips against Jazz's fingertips. She knew that a subtle, physical touch had strong healing potential. While treating the wounded during WWII, she'd learned that an uplifting, hands on touch, was magical and likewise never lost its mysticism. The touch of compassion, encouragement, and empathy, like a heartfelt handshake, a hug, or even laughter, showed those in need that others cared. Moreover, that she cared. Secondly, she knew that these simple gestures were valuable, pacifying, and therapeutic in every meaning of the word.

Spontaneously, she closed her eyes for the third time in a row and began to plea. She wasn't pleading or praying to a God, or to a religion that even in her late eighties she still wasn't sure she believed in; she was pleading for the child's recovery. Filled with strong motivating perceptions, she spoke to her great granddaughter. For this discerning and mature conversation, she would call her by her name.

"Everything is energy Jazz, literally everything. The force of life lives inside us and around us. There is a sea of energies cocooning all of us. Even though we cannot define or distinguish them with our five human senses, this life force has a profound effect on us. Everything and everyone are connected to everyone and everything. I know you are still in there and can hear me. Keep searching to find your way. Don't be afraid. Let the tales and the people in the journals guide you. Connect yourself to whatever and whoever crosses your path while you're on this solo journey. Listen for the sounds of voices outside yourself. Let the past and the voices show you the way."

Then Ruby went silent. It had been a very long time since she'd contemplated over the parts of herself that could be seen on the outside of who she was. Because she'd lived alone for decades, she wondered if anyone else truly knew how diverse she was. She then subtly withdrew her hands, rubbed them together and tenderly patted child's shoulder. She was now ready to start her day all over again. For a second time that morning, she went into the bathroom to freshen up. The clock hanging above the closet told her it was only 9:40am, still early enough to embrace the feeling of standing on the horizon of another new 88-year-old adventure. Typical of who she was, her silence ended as quickly as it had begun.

"What a lively morning it has been eh? A morning filled with new people, great coffee, free food, aesthetic men, and interesting events," she said, as she entered the ICU room's compact bathroom and saw her image in the mirror.

"Never a dull moment eh, old girl?" she told herself.

Then she turned on the faucet on and reached for the soap dispenser. As the warm tap water mixed with the creamy liquid soap, a sweet white, coconut smelling lather filled her hands.

"Remember to buy a cell phone and a new, extra thick journal. You're going to need both of them in the next ten days," she mockingly said.

The image of a very old person with Indonesian coloured skin, dark prominent eyebrows, hair the colour of freshly fallen snow, looked back at Ruby from the mirror above the sink. She grinned and winked at the aged version of who she'd become. Then she removed her spectacles, washed her face, patted it dry, and began washing her hands. She was in an extra cheerful mood because, in spite of her age, she still liked the person in the mirror. As warm tap water mingled with thick, velvety soapsuds, she watched the number 616 fade from her hand and vanish into the sink's drain.

Today was going to be a good day. Today she would find Nico. Of this, she was certain. And Ruby McEwen was rarely wrong.

Chapter 55

The receptionist at the ICU's Central Nursing Station was again nowhere to be found. Therefore, a slightly annoyed Ruby would need to take the elevator to the ground floor to make her inquiries at St. Matthew's Information Desk. When she finally reached the end of the long corridor, she was asked to wait for a few minutes while the hospital's maintenance crew completed an electrical safety test on the elevator. The now, even more slightly annoyed version of Ruby took a seat on a nearby bench, reminded herself that patience is a virtue, and gave her mind permission to ramble. After all, what else was there to do?

While talking with Dr. Zamier earlier, she'd gotten a better impression of the intricate details of the intensive care unit and its staff's duties. Knowing that Jazz had been medically induced and was being stringently monitored around the clock, she didn't want to waste even one hour of the next two days before the Durant's arrived on the scene. She had a lot to accomplish before time was no longer hers. She intended to read to the child each night, starting just after 7:00pm when visitor's hours ended. She also intended to retire earlier each evening. Even though she was used to being active day-to-day at The Seaside, she felt in every conceivable way that her body and mind needed more sleep. The kind of pace she'd been keeping since Jazz had entered her London life was dangerously demanding for a woman of her age. Much more demanding than greeting customers, supervising employees, and managing the diner's vendors had ever been.

Ruby was confident that she could shine a guiding light on the child's dark comatose path if she started reading to her again. She would begin by reading from the earliest written journals being stored in the wooden trunk. The best place to start any journey is at the beginning, she reminded herself. Tonight, when she returned to the ICU, she'd pick up where she'd left off. She was eager to explore more tales of the life that Minnie and Bessie, her African slave sister relatives had written about back in the 1800s. She was quite curious to learn more about her own grandparents, Bessie and Samuel, as well as her great-aunt Minnie. For an obvious reason, her thoughts gyrated as her mind wandered towards a splashy and popular tourist spot on the other side of the English Channel. Within two blinks of her bright green eyes, she was thinking about an impressive, historical, and diverse metropolis known as Amsterdam. She anticipated that Zofia, Tucker, and Thatcher, being from the liberal state of California, would find the capital of the Netherlands rather intriguing. For a person like Ruby, with an accepting attitude and open-mindedness, Amsterdam's approval of same-sex relationships, the legalization of both soft drugs and prostitution, is what made the Netherlands, in her opinion, a progressive and unique European country. From what she could recall, one of the beauties of Amsterdam was that it had been built around intricate canals, breath-taking architecture, and modern technology. As she knew it to be, it was a city that was vibrant in culture, with a strong presence of healthy living. As for the intricacies of the city's underground criminal world, that left an entirely different European impression on people.

A month or so ago, Dutch tourists visiting The Seaside struck up a conversation with its owner. She'd expressed an interest in where they were from and what life was like in England's neighbouring country. It was easy for her to know that they were from The Netherlands given the foreign language they were speaking. Regardless, the couple conversed easily in English with her and went on to tell Ruby that they were both born and raised, third generation Amsterdammers. They'd told her that for decades after WWII, the war against drugs was not high on Amsterdam's list of priorities. Nevertheless, after the New Millennium arrived, more modern and reoccurring waves of violence were sweeping the city; as was true, they'd added, of the majority of large cities worldwide. Amsterdam was not immune to the changing times and dangers of organized crime. They went on to tell Ruby that local government and law enforcement agencies were earnestly trying to rein in street dealers, and destroy drug labs, because it was evident that dealers and drug lords were dragging normal, run-of-the-mill kids into a dangerous life of addiction and crime. When, the diner tourists realized that they were verbally crapping all over where they lived, they lightened up the conversation. They began sharing a balanced quantity of the positive city attributes Amsterdam had and its characteristics that attract tourists to the city, by the masses, each year.

Given that the Durant's would only be in Amsterdam for a short time, Ruby had no worries that they would be experiencing the less attractive or dangerous sides of being there. Nevertheless, they would need to discover the city themselves and then form their own opinions. She realized that as a family, despite their wonkiness and past indiscretions, they were currently under a lot of duress because of Jazz's accident. For this reason, she hoped that The Netherlands would distract and entertain all three of them. Even for a day. She wondered if they were actually taking advantage of being there by sightseeing and enjoying a few of the Dutch churches, galleries, or museums. She hoped that if they did visit the downtown area, that they'd cruise the canals, visit Dam Square, or stroll through the Red-Light District; a tourist attraction she rightly anticipated that Tucker and Thatcher would find interesting. After all, she contemplated, her great grandson had recently passed the bar exam and he was a 28-year-old man who deserved some experiences that were very different from what America offered him. Still lost in thought and still sitting on the bench nearby the elevator, the elderly woman started recalling the time she travelled to The Netherlands with her daughter, Eliza, and her then 75-year-old father Horace. They'd naturally visited the country's capital in the north and chose to also travel to Maastricht, located in the southern Limburg region of the country. Back then, the Netherlands was reputed as being England's small, structured, and innovative neighbour. It had been a long-time dream of Horace's to visit the Dutch Monarchy, just across the English Channel at the southern tip of the North Sea. Her father had been a loyal supporter of Juliana, Queen of the

Netherlands. Hence, in 1969, a father, a daughter, and a granddaughter took a night ferry between the two countries. Ruby frowned as she remembered how seasick Eliza had been throughout the passage. Her young teenager vomited the night away while her hyperactive, overly excited father kept his daughter Ruby up all night gabbing in between shots of Glen Fiddich.

Horace had proudly told her, "The one thing that a true-blue Englishman who could hold his liquor never did on a ferryboat was puke."

During their Dutch holiday her pa was able to witness a bit of Queen Juliana's 60th birthday celebration. He later, told his best girl Ruby that seeing the queen was one of the golden highlights of his life.

That was a very long time ago, she admitted to herself as her mind dawdled longer in the past.

That was the first and last trip Horace and she had made together, since they travelled to Montana for her Grandma Bessie's funeral in the late 1950s. Decades later, Ruby's only regret about that trip to Holland was that she didn't arrange to have Jackson meet up with them in Amsterdam. Horace and Jackson had kept their male comradery alive since they'd buried Bessie in 1959. The men shared a long distance and paralleled 'bromance' as two trustworthy old cronies. Their kindred connection reminded her of the deep friendship she and her Irish friend, Emilia Doherty had once shared. Sadly enough, Horace died six years after he experienced the Netherlands. On his deathbed, he handed his daughter a package with the name 'Jackson Boy Shepherd' written on it. Years later, when Ruby had found the courage to go through her pa's personal belongings, she discovered the package he'd given her. It was filled with pages, upon pages, of a long goodbye from Horace to Jackson. Essentially, the letter was more of a detailed rendition of their time together than an actual letter. It was Horace's story of their short yet impacting brotherhood. Despite that, they'd kept in touch in the most transfixing of ways, the men were never reunited in person. They were two old chaps, whose paths crossed later in life, yet they'd embraced every moment they shared as true, and proper mates do.

Ruby quickly made a mental note to *find Horace's letter to Jackson, being stored in her diner's annex and reread it after forty-something years.*

Reminiscing about Horace and Jackson had tickled her interest and lit a spark under her curiosity. Jackson passed away before Horace did. Because he was an ex-slave with no birth certificate, no one was ever sure of his exact age. It was rumoured that he was more than 100 years old when he took his last breath and the Good Lord, who welcomed his children of all races and colour, called him home. It took another six years before the news of his death reached Ruby in London. Jackson had left an enamelled, copper strongbox behind for Horace, his British companion. Unfortunately, Horace had already died and never saw the gift from his American comrade. Ruby took charge of the strongbox when the courier delivered it to her at The Seaside. The box was filled with Jackson's private papers, a few memorable trinkets, and his most treasured items. A thick envelope was on the bottom of the strongbox, covered by Jackson's other personal belongings. The envelope was filled with Horace's letters to him. Mixed in with her pa's letters, she found another, smaller envelope of a different kind. It was unsealed, yellowed, creased, and rumpled. Inside the envelope were Jackson's original Name Registration and Certificate of Freedom.

"Focus old girl, focus!" she staunchly told herself aloud. She then dismissed thoughts of the past and she steered her mind in the direction of a more pertinent matter; the ICU family strategy she'd concocted for Jazz's sake.

The old woman had a clever idea for the stranded Durant family. It was an intuitive plan, filled with purpose and intent. A major part of her idea involved a duly amount of support she'd need from Zofia and Tucker. If they played their roles correctly, they would make it possible for her to continue her 'daily quests' outside of the hospital. Likewise, it would separate the child's parents from each other and prevent their animosity from contaminating their daughter's room with odours of their decayed relationship. Her cunning plan would have them both taking turns reading from the journals in the antique wooden trunk. They would need to do this within the twenty-minute visitation intervals ordered by Dr. Zamier. She was confident they would abide by the twenty-minute rule because their daughter's neurologist, not their daughter's incompetent summer employer, had implemented it. When visiting hours ended and they had returned to their hotel, she'd resume reading where they'd left off. After seeing several pictures of Thatcher and Jazz hanging on the photo collage wall the child had made at the diner, Ruby was confident that Thatcher would do his part for his sister without needing to be asked or encouraged. The photographs and his deep concerns for Jazz had already told her that he was a decent kind of brother. If the four of them worked together, to keep the past flowing towards the present, Ruby strongly believed that Jazz had a solid chance of finding her way back to all of them.

If she chooses to come back, she realistically thought.

Either way, she realized that her approach with Zofia and Tucker would require a calculated touch of underhandedness. She knew that they'd always considered her to be an eccentric person, who was not much more than a mishmash of guru and gypsy. Regardless, Ruby had seen their last-born child, who was now lying in an ICU, only a handful of times since Jazz had been born. Oddly enough, recalling how it used to be, Jazz scarcely talked until she was a five-year-old. By this time, Ruby was no longer allowed in the Durant family home. The reason why she was so suddenly ousted back then, and had remained unwanted by them for so long, was still a mystery to her. A mystery that she now realized, had been reborn, when her great granddaughter rang her up after so many years looking for a summer job abroad.

"To each his own," Ruby heard herself saying. Sometimes, especially nowadays, at her ripe age of rhyme and reason, it was easier to immediately let go of unanswered questions for the sake of her sanity. So, once again, she let go.

Despite that she sat on a bench next to the elevator, taunting this 'let it go' mindset of hers, being cast out of the Durant's lives more than a decade ago was still, on occasions like this one, a tad distressing. Now that the family, from the sunny USA state would be entering her world again for the first time since Sadie was in her early twenties, she was a so-so kind of nervous. She'd been so absent in thought that she didn't realize the elevator maintenance check was finished until she heard the dinging of a bell, announcing that its doors would be opening. She readily stepped into the lift and pushed the lobby button. When the steel doors closed and the elevator descended, Ruby switched gears once more, in an effort to prepare herself for the day she still had ahead of her. Thirty seconds later as the steel doors opened, she shed her annoyance like a snake sheds its skin and left it behind on the floor of the elevator. She rightly hoped that someone working at the info desk would be able to assist a very old senior citizen in a very good mood.

A flashy dressed, old, white-haired woman, wearing a glitzy floral knee length jacket, a striped scarf, burnt orange coloured stockings, and leather ankle boots, stepped out of the elevator and into the lobby. The ground floor of Saint Matthew's Hospital was buzzing with people and noisy broadcasts from the ceilings overhead intercom system. Ruby slung her beaded pocketbook over her shoulder, took a deep energizing breath and limped towards the large information counter next to the main entrance. The chinking sound that the metal buckles on her boots made as she walked was adding a significant pep to her step. A few concerned glances, from people in the lobby, gave her the impression that they might think she was tottering along too quickly for her a person of her age who wasn't using a walker. Be it true or not, she planned to take relish in their interpretation of her for as long as she could, given that she knew that within two minutes her nearly nine-decade old joints would be stiff as a board again. London's thick ground fog outside could be easily seen through the hospital's revolving glass foyer doors. Ruby took her rightful place at the end of a rather long line of others waiting for assistance. Although a calculating idea was crossing her occasionally devious and sly brain, she ignored her underhanded notion to scheme her way to the front of yet another long hospital line. Instead, she opted to conduct herself accordingly, just as Dr. Zamier had advised. Contrary to her behaviour upstairs at Star Bucks just a few hours ago, she waited her turn in line like a well-behaved and well-bred English lady. Unfortunately, despite her best effort at waiting her turn, the stupid line was moving at a goddamned snail's pace!

Bloody hell, she silently cursed, as she listened to everyone standing in line talking about the fog. *Obeying rules is so damned boring.* Out of the blue, a young hospital employee came up behind Ruby and gently took her by the arm. Flinching with fright, she reached out a walloped him a good one for sneaking up behind such an old person! In spite of her age, she could still deliver a hard, spur-of-the-moment smack. Once she realized that the employee worked at the information desk and was there to assist her, she calmed down, copiously apologized, and started to conduct herself accordingly again. The employee proceeded to escort her to the information area and then went out of his way to answer, in his digital generation's opinion, her comical questions about a prepaid telephone and a SIM card. He thought it to be quite entertaining that he was actually meeting a person who didn't have a cell phone, or even a clue what a SIM card was. Purely out of respect, he didn't judge, or even grin at the woman in front of his counter.

Because he'd just felt her ability to deliver a hearty blow, he ignored his urge to laugh. Then he wrote the address of a mobile phone store down for her, as well as a second address she'd inquired about. While he Googled both locations, she stood there watching him, amazed at the fifteen second speed of his search. At that point, he called for a taxicab to come and fetch her from the hospital. Although, she'd inquired about an Uber, he explained that there was too much conflict with Uber's nowadays, therefore a taxi would be her most reliable option. Two taxi companies, despite the dangerous driving conditions outside, were open for business and offering citywide service.

"Would a taxi be agreeable with you madam?" he asked.

She willingly agreed and shook his hand, genuinely thanking him for his help. She was not a fool; therefore she knew better than to make a scene by lashing out or barking at him for calling her madam. Ruby buttoned her flowered coat up to its neckline, placed her tatty straw hat properly on her head, and walked lamely towards the exit doors to wait for her taxicab. She was grateful that the exits atrium was made of dense glass because she could wait indoors instead of outside in the damp fog. She despised fog. Its shadowy colour was depressing. Its moisture made her clothes frumpy and turned her hair all curly and unruly. Hair control was her reason for wearing a straw hat, or any kind of hat for that matter. Given Britain's soggy and windy climate, women owned more hats than they did shoes. Ruby was no exception.

As she approached the high automatic-revolving door, she could see that the doors turned much too fast for the likes of her wobbly legs. With one fluent swoop she hit the doors large red speed control button with the palm of her hand. Ruby appreciated it when the door slowed down to a pace that was considerate of her tortoise-like walking speed. As she'd predicted earlier, her joints had become as stiff as a board again. Standing in the vestibule between the revolving doors, she wondered what the possibility was that Deniz might be the driver of the cab dispatched to Saint Matthew's Hospital. She certainly had delighted in her time in his cab last night and his gentleman-like mannerisms.

Lost again in thought, she stared out and into the murky fog. Ruby tried to imagine what the 1952 Londoners had endured, first-hand, during the five days of a deadly fog, which had claimed the lives each remaining member of her father Horace's immediate family. Although she was in the city during the aftermath of the catastrophe, she didn't have to survive it as it happened. She did however have to handle the grim situation and tend to the corpses of her relatives, whose lives were snuffed out by a deadly carbon monoxide suffocation. Having witnessed what she had back then, she suspected now that the infamous fog, which ended so many lives more than five decades ago, made the fog hindering the city today seem like nothing more than a steamed-up locker room. The loud sound of a car horn tooting startled her and snatched her brain out of the haze it was in. Her taxicab had arrived.

"Bollocks and double bollocks," she said, when she saw that the driver was a female. She did realize that the chances of it being Deniz were slim, nonetheless she was disappointed to see a sloppy, gum chewing, cheap looking chick for a driver sitting behind the steering wheel. A plastic engraved name tag attached to the cab's dashboard introduced the cabbie, named Raven, to the old woman in the back seat. Being a fervent fan of the meaning of names, Ruby knew first-hand that Raven stood for a person who characteristically gave up what they wanted so others could have what they needed.

Holy sheep shit! She surprisingly thought. *Someone's parents definitely misnamed their baby. Be nice old girl. Mind your manners.* She sternly told herself.

Wincing from the pain in her spine, the elderly woman pulled the cab door closed. Within ten seconds, the music blaring from the cab's radio was irritating the hell out of her. She felt very uneasy about being driven through such dangerous weather by the likes of a female cabbie who was undeniably haggard and acting too intense; like someone had lit her impatient, fat arse on fire! The driver turned her radio down, blew a large pink bubble with her chewing gum, then flicked it with her fingers and popped it. In the cab's rearview, Ruby could see the cabbie's saliva spattering off the burst bubble. Then the driver slickly sucked the gum, along with the drool it made, back into her wet mouth, glanced back at Ruby in her spit spattered mirror, and started the timer on the cab's meter. Watching her 'paid ride' repeating her bubble blowing and popping a few more times had her witnessing how disgusting someone could make a small, insignificant piece of chewing gum.

It has been ages since I've seen someone smacking on the sweetness of gum, she thought.

The owner of The Seaside had forbidden chewing gum from her establishment in the 1960s, when Bazooka and Chiclet bubble-gum were at a height of popularity in the UK. As the years passed, she'd presumed that what had become a teenage fad would eventually be lost to more modern times and new crazes. Similar to practically everything else in her life, she also had a strong opinion about chewing gum. She'd banned it from her diner's entire terrain because of the mess it left behind on the floors, under all the tables, outside at the beach and in the parking lot. The worst of it was how gobs of gum plugged the drains of the dishwashing sinks. She strongmindedly professed that gum chewing in public places spread germs and was a form of endorsed pollution. The elderly woman laughed at herself, thinking how she was still as strongly blinkered now as she'd been fifty-five ago. Even today, she thought gum chewing to be one of the most tedious things people did. She'd once heard that gum helped reduce the chewer's weight and stress levels. As she sat in the taxi, behind an overweight, tension packed driver who was unable to see even one meter beyond her cab because of the fog, she stopped caring if the weight loss and stress reduction myth about gum chewing carried any merit or not. However, if by chance it was true, she rightfully hoped that the irascible, obese cabbie in the front seat would keep chewing her gum until the taxicab arrived safely at her destination. Ruby then let out a long sigh and silently began thinking about Deniz again. What a bloody difference a cabdriver could make.

She made a mental note to *fetch Deniz's business card she'd left behind at the diner last night.*

Knowing that she and the child's family would need a cab regularly throughout the next ten days, she wanted to give him their business. Truth be told, she wanted to see Deniz again. She wasn't sure why and she didn't care why, she just liked the man. *It is what it is what it is*, she silently reminded herself.

"Where to lady?" the boisterous cabbie abruptly blurted out from the front seat.

Ruby knew in an instant that she wanted to exit this cab as quickly as humanly possible. Therefore, she would shorten the trip considerably by purchasing a prepaid mobile telephone later in the day.

"77 Pope Lane!" she arrogantly blurted back.

Then she watched the cabdriver program her navigation system that was mounted on the cabs dashboard. Smack! Another bubble popped and splattered itself all over the cab's windshield and the cabbie's already grungy face. The smell of sugary saliva spittle filled the cab. The elderly woman in the back seat inhaled through her mouth to avoid the odour, while holding tightly onto the leash she'd put on her sharp and rightfully disgusted temper. As tempting as it was, blasting the driver's rude and crude ass would solve nothing and put a dent in the timing of her ability to do what needed to be done before the day ended. As the taxi pulled away from the curb, Ruby fastened her seatbelt and spontaneously made the sign of the cross. She still wasn't a holy woman, nonetheless, the sign of the cross was a ritual she'd learned to perform as a child before each meal. Even though her family didn't attend any type of church, protecting their souls by using this blessed gesture began when the WWII air raids started over Great Britain. Fear and fury were to blame for her family's nonstop bickering and making the sacred sign whenever they were avoiding death by huddling together in an underground shelter. Thinking about bombs, Hitler, and her complicated parents, instantly put her ricocheting brain in a proper British piss-ass mood!

The cabdriver peered in her from the front seat rear view and interrupted Ruby's intimate thoughts by boldly asking, "Why is an old lady like you going to Precinct 616 on a day like this?"

The old lady going to Precinct 616 answered by brashly bellowing out, "It's a private matter! Goddammit woman spit your damn gum out, keep your friggen eyes on the road, show some bloody respect! And, for the love of God call me madam!"

Chapter 56

The taxicab came to a halt in front of the City of London Police station. The shoddy, plumper than plumb, cabbie pierced the silence in the cab by loudly announcing their arrival at 77 Pope Lane. Then she spat her last wad of bright pink Bazooka out her cab's open window.

Ruby opened her eyes and immediately scolded herself for having been too afraid to roll her passenger window down and have a proper look at the fogged in streets. She wasn't aware that she'd been keeping her eyes squeezed tightly shut. Despite her earnest efforts to feel that she was in safe hands, the stress of the cabbie's rudeness and the dangerous, low visibility outside had given her a slight headache. Still, she did feel somewhat relieved as the cab slowed down and safely parked curbside; hence, she reckoned that the pressure of stress behind her eyes was worth it. Perhaps the combination of mind traveling to and through her deep-rooted memories of London's 1952 Great Smog and drinking too much Starbucks coffee had shaken her up a bit.

Actually, she thought, *it was rightly fathomable that memories of being confined with Horace and Sadie, in a flat with three deceased and decomposing relatives had rattled my buried, but not forgotten fears.*

She did realize that completely blaming an anxiety headache on the cabdriver wasn't fair. After all, logic reminded her of how *the rawness of impacting memories never die.* At times her habit of analysing people and life, coupled with mentally wandering, was more than she could handle. Every so often, it bordered on bigotry.

"Bugger off!" she strictly told her self-examining points of view.

"What did you say?" the cabbie gruffly retorted.

"Nothing," she guardedly replied.

She'd had enough stride for one intense and fuzzy morning. The last thing she needed was to lose her sharp mental edge by becoming too muddled up by the likes of irksome people. After all, she was on a mission to find Nico and hear his version of the boating accident. She had so many unanswered questions for him. Questions that, for legal whys and wherefores, she couldn't just 'let go' of. For this reason, she decided to respect the person who'd just been responsible for her transportation safety. Ruby could be an opinionated and cranky old bitch, but she wasn't as tyrannical as the female ancestor's that came before her had once been.

In fairness to the gimcrack cabbie, she thought, *the woman had driven cautiously, despite that she'd rolled her window down three times to spit her chewing gum and dribble out and onto the street.*

Eyes closed or not, even a blind person would have known what was happening from the front seat of the taxicab. The driver's ill-mannered habits and unkempt appearance were things about her that Ruby knew she needed to accept and ignore; like the gazillion other situations that had been outside of her control since her birth in the 1920s. She used to be very seasoned at doing just this, however aging was robbing her personality of its ability to be compliant. So there she sat, in the back seat of another cab, stuck in between a bedraggled, cheap, and repulsive driver in the front seat and her own efforts at tactfulness. Just thinking about it all again was putting her in a sad and foul mood.

"Sweet Jesus, just bugger off," she repeated with a whisper, in an effort to keep her thoughts from wandering again and not being overheard by the cabbie.

This time her mind obeyed and her thoughts and opinions buggered off straightaway and as pronto as they were told to. She then only paid the driver the fare. Despite that the cabbie had transported her in one piece to her destination she didn't receive a tip. The diner owner was pennywise in this way. Then, following the cabbie's advice, she exited the taxi curbside to avoid being run over by a passing car.

"Good riddance," she said, as the cab vanished into the fog.

She now stood on the sidewalk and looked up at a tall, escalating, brick building about ten feet away from her. The building loomed out of the mist like a rectangular, stone giant. Hanging off both sides of the building, above its double wooden main entrance doors, were two well-lit, dark blue police station signs. Hanging next to the signs were pre-19th century lanterns that had been mounted on decorative steel brackets. Even through the murkiness of the fog, it was easy to see that she was standing in front of an epoch London police station. Ruby held firmly onto the buildings moist and robust brass railing as she arduously moved her stiff legs and hips, one step at a time, up the stations wide, deep marble stairs. Just as she was about to step foot onto the front entrance's landing, one of the thick decoratively carved wooden doors suddenly swung open in her direction. She tightened her grip on the brass rail and did her best to move out of the way. An officer carrying a small crying child wrapped in a blanket was exiting the building.

"Pardon us madam," he said, seeing a very old lady struggling to climb the stairs.

He held the door open for her until she had both feet securely planted on the top step and was able to stand steadily upon the landing. The officer was smartly dressed in a well-defined dark blue uniform. Because of the bright lights inside the entrance hall, as he stepped aside to let her pass him by, his shiny eight-pointed, Brunswick helmet star reflected a goldish colour off the lobby's dark interior wall. She could see that he wore a collar ID number, but he passed her too quickly for her to make it out clearly.

Ruby took the door from him and said, "Good day to you Officer."

He nodded politely, and then descended the stairs holding the pouting child firmly with every step he took.

She could hear the metropolitan constable consoling the wee one by saying, "Everything is okay little man. I'm taking you home to see mummy and daddy. Shush now sweet boy, everything will be okay."

She then watched him reach inside his uniform pocket and pull out a bright red and yellow striped lollipop. He paused for a brief moment on the bottom stair to unwrap it. As he did the child's eyes widened. The lad then wiped his snotty nose on the shoulder of officer's jacket and stared with sweet anticipation at the candy on a stick. The elderly woman enjoyed watching the policeman as he teasingly twirled the lolly around in front of who she presumed to be a lost and scared toddler. The scene reminded her that for as historical, eventful, and chaotically challenging life could be, sometimes it was as simple and harmonious as a lollipop. The child seized the candy and propped it into his mouth. It took only a matter of seconds for the sugary sweetness to stop the lad's whining and whimpering. Before entering the station house, she watched the constable and the boy disappear into the dense, hazy mist. The last thing she could make out, before the fog swallowed them up, was the glow of the lollipop's white stick protruding from the youngster's mouth.

Grinning, the old woman then limped a few more steps and entered the building. Every joint in her body was screaming at her because of the effects weather was having on her rheumatoid arthritis. A heavy timber trimmed door with a solid brass Precinct 616 sign on it closed automatically behind her. Her senses woke up the moment she heard an automated mechanism snap the door shut as she stepped into the brightly lit entryway. The speed at which she went from being lethargic because of the grey misty dimness outside, to feeling alert and energetic under a brightly lit foyer, was downright astounding; and a clear indication that she, like millions of other Brits, needed much more sun than they got.

The station house was bustling with a noisy and frenzied kind of commotion, which immediately roused her wits. The police station's open indoor space was a brilliantly lit, uplifting change from the obscure and dismal outdoors she'd just left behind. Its lively interior colours radiating from each of its lofty walls, gave her a sudden rush of enlivened buoyancy. A rush she hadn't felt in weeks.

I have a notion that today will bring me answers, she utopianly thought. *Bravo old girl,* she proudly applauded herself, as a surge of new energy pulsated through her weary, aged body.

"If Nico is in this building, you will find him!" she assertively said aloud, not giving a hoot if anyone heard her talking to herself or not.

The elderly Brit had a textbook personality combination. She was both sassy and dodgy; the type of disposition that was neither innocent nor outright underhanded. On the contrary, her harmless and dastardly nature was layered with shrewdness and determination. These character traits had opened many doors for her throughout her life. They were doors that less driven or less clever people never tried to open and walk through.

"Hats off to me," she heard herself saying, as she ambled towards the clerk standing behind the precinct's public visitor desk.

"How can I help you today madam?" the chirpy PD clerk with a hurried, yet skilful tone asked.

Ruby was in a rightfully happy mood again, and likewise tickled with herself for finding the city station without a hitch. She'd been crafty enough back at the ICU to write the infuriating constable's precinct number on her hand after seeing it on his badge. Even though she'd always been deplorable at recalling numbers, given her age, her mind was still very instinctual. Be it three digits, or thirty-three digits, the amount or combinations didn't matter. She'd never had even the remotest of knacks for arithmetic. She was a people person, not a calculator or mathematician. This was why she preferred words to numbers. Which in hindsight had suited her just fine since she'd been in grammar school. Words had taken her much farther in life than numbers ever had.

"Come on Ruby, focus," she heard herself mutter again.

She knew all too well that her brain had its way of taking her mind wherever it wanted to whenever it wanted to. For as much as she could control it, its knack for roaming at will was often distracting and inconvenient.

"My name is Darby. How can I help you today madam?" The PD clerk repeated while ignoring an urge to ask her what she'd just mumbled. The clerk loathed mumbling.

Because of what had transpired at the ICU earlier between herself, Dr. Zamier, and a rude detective, she quickly scanned the precinct floor. The stationhouse's workspace spanned out on both sides from behind the front desk. She knew she needed to be very careful not to be seen by either of the constables she'd had a run in with about an hour ago. Especially the cocky one she had stood up to and rightly pissed off.

Darby asked again, "Madam, how can I help you?"

This time her tone revealed that her patience was running thin. Ruby stretched her arm up, rested it on the rather high front desk, and leaned forward on her elbow. She then reached up to pull her straw hat down and over her forehead to conceal her face. In vain, she grasped at nothing but empty space. One failed attempt to grip her hat's brim told her that it wasn't on her head.

"Bloody hell, I forgot my hat in the goddam taxicab!" Ruby exclaimed looking up at the clerk.

The female clerk was clueless as to why this very old senior citizen standing in front of her was flapping her hand and publicly cursing. Silently, Ruby criticized herself for her forgetfulness.

The PD clerk took a deep breath and repeated, with an even more rushed tone, "Madam, for the last time, how can I help you?"

The elderly woman snapped her mind back to what was happening right in front of her and quickly apologized for her inattentiveness and profanity.

"I am looking for Nico Rossario," she said. "Could you tell me if he has been arrested and booked, or if he is here?"

"How do you know this Mr. Nico Rossario?" the clerk asked.

"He is an employee of mine," Ruby answered. "I am the proprietor of The Seaside, on Ocean Grove Lane. Nico Ros..."

The clerk suddenly interrupted her and heartily said, "I thought I recognized you Ruby! My children and I have eaten at your diner a few times. Have a seat over there luv," she said, pointing to a long, crowded metal bench with only a few empty spaces left on it.

It had been a while since she had been so randomly recognized in public as The Seaside's owner. She could feel her cheeks turning a warm, slightly proud blushing colour of crimson red.

The clerk went on to explain, "I will need to make a few inquiries. It could take some time because we are backed up. Due to the weather most of our police force is out on the streets and the precinct is rather shorthanded. There is a restroom to your left if you need to use the toilet while you are waiting mam."

As she listened to the clerk, Ruby wished she could remember the faces of all the people who came in and out of The Seaside, but there simply were too many of them each year. Only her regular customers were etched in her mind, and she'd already outlived most of them. Given the hectic activity inside the station house and the continuous ringing of telephones, she sensed a drawn-out wait on her horizon.

"Can you give me an idea how long I may be waiting," she asked gregariously while wearing a proper forlorn expression.

"Hmmm, no less than an hour and no more than two hours," was the answer she heard. "Sorry mam, it is the best I can do given the circumstances. If your request can wait a day or two, until after the fog lifts, I'd advise you to come back. Myself, or one of my colleagues, will be able to assist you much quicker later in the week," she concluded.

The clerk then motioned the next person waiting in the line to move forward. The elderly woman turned around to see a rather long line that had formed behind her.

Ruby tamely asked, "Have I been dismissed?"

Like a typical Londoner who was finished with whatever was going on, Darby nodded her head instead of giving Ruby a verbal confirmation. Words were not needed. Ruby knew exactly what she meant and what was expected.

Shut your trap old girl, she silently warned herself. *There is no need to go botching up your mission to discover where Nico is. Finding him is much more crucial than articulating another sarcastic rebuttal dangling on the tip of your brash British tongue.*

Then, as instructed, she took a seat on the long bench next to the wall across from the visitor's station. Despite that she dreadfully needed to pee, she wisely disregarded her bladders urgency and claimed her spot before the bench filled with the people who'd also stood in the same line she'd just left. Ruby then opened her glitzy and floral knee length jacket, removed her bright striped scarf, and draped it over her carrot-coloured stockings. With her long fingers she fluffed up her pure white shoulder length hair and cropped bangs. Opening her beaded handbag, she removed her cosmetic case, took out a compact mirror, and gave herself a good look over.

"Bollocks," she cried out, seeing how curly the hair on her hatless head had become in less than ten godamned damp minutes.

She grabbed her favourite shade of lipstick and a blusher and reapplied just the right touch of makeup. Her usual tinted skin tone had somewhat faded with worry and exhaustion since Jazz Durant's arrival. She then gave her face another quick go-over. She wanted to look her best when she found Nico.

Regardless of her age, looking her best had always been important to Ruby McEwen.

Chapter 57

It had been nearly fifty years since Ruby had been inside a police station. This was a fact that she was now appreciative of given the dire and mortal circumstances of her last visit.

Although she'd never seen this particular station before, it resembled the one she'd spent time in back in the late 1960s. She wasn't in the mood to make small talk with the strangers sitting next to her, so the elderly woman just sat and gazed around the interior of Precinct 616. The intriguing main floor was enormous. It had open office spaces where constables, detectives, and the administrative staff did their work. Desks were lined neatly, side-by-side and back-to-back in a square formation around the entire floor. Despite the precinct's tastefully colourful interior, overall, she found it to be rather shabby looking. The lively 'first-look impression' she'd had was now being pitifully overshadowed by a ridiculously large amount of clutter on the stations bureaus and file cabinets. To make it worse, there was a mumbled and jumbled series of wires connecting an overabundance of landline telephones, computers, monitors, and other gadgets. The disarray was crisscrossing the desks and cabinets on its way to electrical sockets fixed to the floor. She had never seen such an amount of electronic litter inside a building before.

Still glancing around the precinct, she noticed that several of the desks were empty while others were occupied by uniformed constables interviewing and nattering with folks from all walks of life. A few of them had been handcuffed, which of course meant they were detainees being booked. There was a rather large, double steel door dissecting the furthest back wall. She expected that it led to holding cells for suspects and detainees. The dark grey security door reminded her of a steel money vault in a bank. She knew from her last visit to a police station that the rows of doors with small windows in them were interview rooms. She assumed that various other rooms were used for more private, legal affairs, or consultations.

In the mid-60's Ruby was interviewed as a non-detained visitor in a similar type of room. Again, not wanting to waste her time obsessing over a time gone by, she intentionally switched mental gears because she knew, in the end, her recollections would eventually return to her. They always did. The antsy, old woman sitting on the crammed bench, still waiting her turn, clashed with an all too familiar, nasty claustrophobic sensation that had begun pinching off her air supply. She fought the urge to stand up and flee. Looking up at the clock hanging above the clerk's desk she saw that only eleven minutes had passed since she'd taken a seat. The bench was almost full and the visitor's section was teeming with people who were each waiting their turns. Feeling as if she was a sardine being squished into tiny, smelly tin can, she struggled to ignore her phobia and an overfull, impatient bladder that was thumping mercilessly on her insides. Nevertheless, she was smart enough to know not to stand up, not to flee, and not to pee. Three obscenely tough and rough looking men, whom resembled hooligans, drug dealers, or pimps, were leaning against the wall across from her. They were scanning the space and staring hatefully at everyone sitting on both sides of her. Their stern expressions were making the oldest living being in the building feel very insecure. In that moment, Ruby decided that even today, people waiting at police stations, just like they'd been back in the 1960-something days of orgies and LSD, were too jittery, mean, or afraid, to give a rat's ass if a nearly ninety-year-old bladder was about to burst! Regardless, fulfilling her need to use the loo wasn't an option; not if it meant losing her seat on the metal bench and standing side by side with the more ragged and jagged side of London's inhabitants.

Thinking about these types of people had her clichédly tightening the grip on her handbag that she had put on her lap after she'd sat down. In an attempt to calm her nerves, she went on to keep her mouth shut and continued observing the precinct. The cheery mood she'd brought into the building with her was waning fast. With a bit of luck she'd soon be receiving information about her employee Nico and be on her way to see him. Wherever he was? To pass the time she looked around and tried to guess what everything she saw meant and what it was used for?

On the far side of the precincts open interior were two maroon coloured swinging doors. Officers, detainees, and visitors went in at out of these doors every few minutes. A complaining, hunched over fella in handcuffs, who'd just conked his head on the doorframe, was swearing something awful and trying to rub his sore noggin with handcuffs on. An officer was roughly jerking him around and trying to shut him up. Ruby assumed that the maroon doors lead to a corridor that led to rooms used for storing evidence, case files, firearms, and most likely, seized possessions. She was certain interrogation rooms with two-way mirrored windows would be back there as well. Precincts used two-ways specifically for observation of criminal suspects and during interrogations and identification line-ups. Somewhere in the building there would be precinct employee lockers. She presumed that storerooms used for stowing police equipment were probably also located behind the double maroon doors.

Realizing that she knew too much about the inside of a police station, she made a mental note to *stop watching her favourite action-packed, detective series on the telly. It was time to switch to the Animal Channel.*

Her tailbone and hips were in a lot of pain after sitting sedentary for so long on the rigid and cold bench. The noise level in the station house was making her brain feel as foggy as the weather outside was. She didn't like being over stimulated by chaos and noise. Before she was even aware of it, her patience had turned into an extremely infuriating pile of putty. Forgetting completely about her need to use the restroom, she looked over at the clerk's desk to see what was going on and to see what time it was again. The line of people was completely gone, but the waiting area was still fully occupied.

Strange, she thought. Shifting the direction of her gaze, Ruby saw two male police constables standing in front of the PD clerk who'd just recognized her as The Seaside's owner. The constables were both leisurely chatting it up with her like they had the day off. The younger constable, who was flirting with the bonnie and dimpled clerk, openly stared at two perky breasts protruding from beneath her tailored uniform. The older, more sophisticated looking MP watched his young officer shilly-shallying with the clerk, as if what his colleague was doing was a daily occurrence. Ruby could tell they were Metropolitan Police officers because of the uniforms and helmets they wore. The shorter MP wore a slightly different uniform than the taller officer had on. Although their uniforms were the same deep blue British military colour, the badges and emblems they wore were noticeably different. The constables were too far off for her to see the details of the silver badges and striped embroidered patches on their uniforms. She wanted to know what their MP rankings were. Metropolitan Police officers were as common and visible on the city streets as London's red double-decker busses were. Looking now at Darby, she saw that her dimples were perfectly round, pronounced, and noticeable from a distance.

Why hadn't I seen her dimples when I talked with her? She asked herself. Despite the reason, the clerk's dimples had Ruby's mind desiring time to reminisce about Emmet, the dimple-faced baby boy of her dearest friend, Mia Doherty, from Belfast.

"Bloody hell, focus old girl!" she reminded herself in the stern way she'd been reminding herself since she was just a girl. "There is no time for dawdling in the days of yore. This isn't the safest place for drifting back in time. Goddammit attention!"

The two people sitting on either side of her long, frail body, were squishing the urine out of her. They both sceptically eyed the strange old, wrinkled lady who was having a chat up with herself. Their burrowing eyes and confused expressions were making Ruby feel rightly uneasy. As she returned their stares, with a penetrating stare of her own, she construed that they'd both appropriately botched up their lives and were ready to botch up hers. She wasn't at all interested in getting into an 'argy-bargy' over nothing worthwhile with them. She hated confrontation of any kind; therefore, she merely chose to ignore them by distracting her mind again. The more she ignored the more they glared. Steering her mind's thoughts and her impulses in the right direction was something she'd been doing since she was a child. At times, her mind took her to places she didn't want to go. When it drifted impetuously, it forced her to mentally cross over into an emotional wilderness. One thing her mind hardly ever did, was get crushed by negativity or unhappiness. She was not the melancholy type. Her engrained and keen personality was too resilient to allow or tolerate gloom and doom. In spite of her idiosyncrasies, she'd been born with a mental advantage. Her mind tended to roam around in circles while it repeatedly reprocessed and reused similar thoughts and information. It was a brain trait of hers which had become particularly active the more she aged. She was an avid thinker, which meant that often, her cognizance sped through life and crashed into things she'd rather have avoided. Whenever this happened, she'd lose her centre and her mental drifting would begin. The abstract, yet simple, ice cubes in a glass technique she'd use to prevent her brain's wandering at the wrong times rarely let her down.

The elderly woman's mind was a complex and wondrous means of private transportation. She had a unique brain that she'd been gifted with at birth. Her mind's power enabled her to travel in and out of the past with ease. She almost never voyaged into the future; a fact she attributed to being so content, present, and actively engaged in 'the here and now' of her life. She was a person intensely interested in the people, events, and experiences that had paved the way for her. Because of her lifelong, practiced ability of consciously navigating her thoughts, she could summon her concentration to return to her no matter where it had wandered off to. In this way, she was her own cognitive steering wheel. She knew her mind had no brake pedal because it never stood still. Even so, she'd mastered controlling and preventing its wilful cravings while cutting down an old oak tree, back in 1955, during one of England's most historical and notorious winter storms. She shuddered just thinking about that horrifically dangerous night.

Despite her unique mental capacities, being forced to balance her frail body on a rock-hard metal bench for too long, the soreness and pain in the bones of her bum was rapidly causing her temper to heat up and rise. She hoped she'd have time to control it before it lashed out and got her into trouble. In an effort to divert her impatient and brewing anger, she turned her attention back to the PD Clerk's desk. The older MP, whom she predicted to be a Deputy Chief Constable, which was the second highest rank in all of the police forces in the UK, looked to be past the age of forty-five. His trimmed hair that jutted out from under his helmet was greying. He appeared to be very professional with a well-trained, strong in character type of appeal. He was quite tall, seemed to be composed, and was hunky and lanky. Just like Nico was. The other constable, who had just enough height not to be considered a stunted man, was obviously quite young. He appeared to be the self-assured and flirtatious type. He was now turning on the charm rather thickly with the pretty PD desk clerk. He had reddish blonde hair and a stocky build. The two constables innocently reminded Ruby of Laurel and Hardy, two American comedians she remembered from the late 1930s and the 1940s. Laurel and Hardy were two funny men most famous for their slapstick comedy shows. A smile crossed her age-speckled face as she remembered her father Horace and her Uncle Reggie roaring with laughter while watching Laurel and Hardy reruns on BBC television.

Those were good times, before the Nazi's and smog filled layer of fog bloody first ruined, then destroyed everything McEwen, she recalled.

Filled with the memory of both light-hearted and tragic times gone by; Ruby impulsively turned her antiquated charm on. From the visitor's bench, she attempted to ask one of the constables if they could save her seat while she went to the loo.

"Excuse me officers," she said, waving her arm above her head.

Apparently, they couldn't hear her over an excessive amount of loud noises and human babbling echoing off the precinct's walls.

Ruby called out again, a bit louder, "Excuse me officers!"

Still no reaction, aside from more flirting and blushed giggles from the younger clerk. The three of them were having such a fine time of it over there that they were oblivious to the old lady with seriously sore butt bones and an about to burst bladder who needed their goddamn assistance! As Ruby looked up at the clock and realized only twenty-three minutes had passed, her tolerance shattered and scattered like broken pieces of patience across the precinct floor. Then, in a dangerously blind-siding way, the leash on her temper snapped in two!

Going off half-cocked, she stood up, turned herself in the direction of the officers and clerk, and shrieked at the very top of her very strong lungs, "Help me!" For a second time, waving both arms, she cried out again, "Heeeelp meeee!"

"What the bloody fucking hell!" the startled prostitute, who was sitting next to an elderly white-haired broad, screamed back.

The half-naked hooker held her hands up, turned her palms upward, looked towards the constables, and shrugged her shoulders. Apparently, this was a commonly used, guilt free sign of being an innocent and non-threatening bystander. An alcohol sloshed, redheaded man, who stunk like onions boiled in vodka, instantly repeated through boisterous, drunken slurs, "Here comes the fuzz, the fuzz is gunna get'cha. Here comes the fuzz, the fuzz is gunna get'cha. Here comes the fuzz, the fuzz is gunna get'cha."

The officers and the PD clerk had reacted even faster than the drunk did, and the hooker had. The cute clerk with a scared look on her face swiftly ducked down and disappeared behind the front desk. The stocky built MP put his hand on his baton, dashed over to the massive wooden entry doors, and within seconds directly locked them. He then removed his baton and used a sentry stance to block and guard Precinct 616. The taller, older PD officer had also withdrawn his baton and was sprinting towards Ruby. She was still standing upright but was now tottering and hysterically shaking. Disregarding her age, the tall constable bore down and got right in her face.

With an authority packed voice filled with a dominate volume, he blared, "Sit back down and raise your hands above your head right now!"

The prostitute, who obviously knew the drill, lowered her arms and robotically plopped herself back down onto the bench. Then she leaned into Ruby and laughingly murmured, "Old lady, you are so fucked."

The armed officer jarred at the whore with his baton and screeched, "Shut up!" The skimpy dressed, paid for sex woman did as told, stared down at the floor and kept her mouth shut. Even the plastered, rancid smelling drunk fella knew enough to zip his intoxicated lips, sit up straight, and stop his wobbling about on the bench.

As the officer locked eyes with the person who had both of her crooked hands raised high above her head, it took every single ounce of bodily control that Ruby Adeline McEwen had left in her not to piss on the floor.

Chapter 58

Since the London Bridge attack, when three terrorists wearing fake suicide bombs drove a van into pedestrians crossing the city's historic landmark, the entire police force of Great Britain was on high alert. Anyone, regardless of sex, creed, colour, or age, who triggered a community scare, was considered a danger. Until proven otherwise the elderly woman who had just caused a scene and threatened Precinct 616 was no exception.

The instigator, a white-haired female suspect, who had sat back down on the visitor's bench as ordered, continued to tremble with her frail arms held as high up as she could hold them. It looked as though she'd stopped breathing. As she stared into the intense face of the Metropolitan Police Constable who had bent down on one knee in front of her, tears dangled off her eyelids and dripped onto the rims of her round, black spectacles. As he leaned in, his objective was to make eye contact with her and to sum the unexpected state of affairs up. He still held his wooden side-handle baton firmly between himself and the person who had screamed for help, caused a ruckus, and posed a potential security threat to his precinct and everyone in the building. "Madam, what is wrong?" he asked.

She didn't answer.

"Madam, what is wrong?" he repeated.

Again, he got no answer.

Ruby knew she'd gone too far, but she was too bowled over to react. Her rigid body was mildly jolting as if she was having some kind of seizure. Given that she appeared to have slipped into a state of shock, the Officer fixed his sharp gaze deeper into her now paranoid looking, alert green eyes, to determine if there was pupil activity. Befitting of the situation, he flashed his pen light across her eyes. He got no physical reaction from her. Not even a blink. For a very brief moment, he doubted himself, thinking he'd been too extreme with his brutal reaction to her screeching throughout the precinct like she was being attacked. She appeared to be traumatised into a shell-shocked state. The pupils of her stunned and scared, jade green eyes were so enlarged that the constable could see his badge reflecting in them. The bold, white letters of his surname, O'Bannon, embossed on his uniform, were just as visible in the black inner circle of her eyes.

This old woman has the biggest, most prominent eyes I've ever seen, he thought as he continued observing her.

Ruby shifted the direction of her stare onto his face and scrutinized him for a few moments. It was obvious to the officer him that she was studying him as raptly as he was studying her. His observation was beyond correct. As Ruby's eyes searched, her mind raced and she uncontrollably trembled. Then out of nowhere it came to her. The PD officer who was scrutinizing her looked very much like the older version someone she used to know. When she heard his intermingled American and British accents, her mind began filling with extreme curiosity. The officer intentionally remained calm and allowed her gaze to move up and down, and from left to right, across his face. Officer O'Bannon had yet to determine if her lapse in blinking, her contracted pupils and her fixed stare, were indications of domination, or the use of some sort of mental power he'd yet to witness in a person of her age.

"Madam, do you know where you are?" he asked, breaking the silence that had blanketed the precinct since she'd screamed for help.

He got no response.

"Madam, do you know who I am?" he asked Ruby, expecting her to reply by saying, a constable, or a police officer.

Again, he got no response from her.

With the precinct still on high alert, he reached out to lower her arms in an effort to instil a response from her. He could see that she was blinking again, which told him that he was making progress. Unexpectedly, she spoke.

"How old are you?" she replied, answering his question with a question.

This was the last thing he expected her to say. Despite that he was grateful she was responding, he refused to sway from police protocol.

Officer O'Bannon sternly spat, "I will be asking the questions today madam."

Slightly relieved that she appeared to be lucid again, he toned his voice down and said, "I asked you what was wrong? And, if you know where you are? And who I am?"

She looked once more at his nametag and boldly hissed, "Of course I know who you are. Even without your name on your uniform, I'd know who you were. You look exactly like your father did when he was a young man. If ever there was a spitting image of a father and son, you are it!"

This elderly, white-haired spitfire is taking over my interrogation, the constable determined, not quite sure how to react.

Ruby was coherent again. Her fears had been replaced with a probable recognition, her self-confidence, and a degree of enthusiasm.

Before the officer could respond, she point-blank asked, "Is your father an American man named Otis?"

Officer Griffin O'Bannon was totally caught off guard, which Ruby and others could easily see. Although nothing had been confirmed, he was trapped between the code of behaviour as a policeman and his demur to this complete stranger who seemed to know that he was son of an American named Otis O'Bannon. The bewildered and slack-jawed constable didn't precisely know how to conduct himself. He'd just heard his father's name being spoken for the first time since he was a teenage boy. Griffin O'Bannon was not prepared for this; not at all. The experienced Metropolitan Police constable couldn't switch between law enforcement protocols and her questions with the required and necessary speed. He immediately needed to get his head back in the game, do his job, and ignore this stranger on the bench's inquiries. Hence, he regained his equanimity, reeled her in, reclaimed his authority, and continued his questioning.

"Madam, is anything wrong with you? Did someone accost you? Why did you cry out for help?" he asked her with self-control that was more professional and less antagonistic.

Officer O'Bannon attempted to execute additional police procedure and hide the question marks on his forehead; question marks that were a result of what this very old British lady had snappishly just jammed into his brain. Virtually everyone in the station house was watching their offbeat interaction taking place. A hush hush of whispering and rumouring had already begun.

"Yes, there is indeed something not right with me," Ruby answered. "I need to take a wizz very badly and I need somebody to tell me if Nico Rossario is in the building."

Officer O'Bannon stood up, signalled his colleague's that the situation was contained and then he escorted the overcome woman to the restrooms. As they passed by the front desk, Ruby could see that the precinct's perky clerk was no longer taking shelter behind the counter. The stocky built MP Constable, guarding the entryway, was unlocking the double doors. Precinct 616 had reopened for business. Constable O'Bannon was standing outside the loo waiting for Ruby to exit, which given the fullness of her bladder and her desire to freshen up again, was taking a considerable amount of time. Truth be told, she didn't need to freshen anything up. She was positive that she was about to spend time with the son of her daughter Eliza's Yankee admirer, Otis, from the late 1960s. She was certain Griffin and Otis were related. The elderly woman was notoriously bad with numbers, but she never forgot a face. Neither never, nor ever. If the constable indeed was the son of Otis O'Bannon, perhaps he could be playing a role in helping her finding Nico, The Seaside's nowhere to be found dishwasher. Her devious side was wide awake and more than ready to roam.

After all, Otis O'Bannon's last words to Ruby, in 1968, before he was deported back to America, were, "I owe you a huge debt Mrs. Ruby. If you ever need a favour, no matter how much time goes by, just let me know."

Neither Eliza nor Ruby ever heard from Otis again. The huge debt and favour had been long since forgotten, until a few minutes ago when the diner owner crossed paths with a man she was confident was Otis's son.

"That was more than thirty-five years ago." Ruby said aloud as she flushed the toilet and washed her hands.

She hoped this time fate would be on her side. If the constable was not Otis O'Bannon's son, then he was a dead ringer for the young draft dodger she'd taken in during the height of the Vietnam War. Her spine pain was gruelling as she exited the Loo. Limping towards Constable O'Bannon, who'd been waiting for her, she crossed two crooked fingers on one hand for luck and tightly clasped her purse with the other hand.

"It just has to be him," she muttered under her breath.

Chapter 59

The enclosed constricting cubicle reminded her of a pigeon-hole. It was a plain and basic space with substandard government issued furniture. The insignificant padded room had only three chairs in it. She assumed two were for detectives and the one bolted to the floor was for suspects. Sitting on the bolted chair made her feel bloody guilty as all hell, even though she hadn't broken any laws.

There was a steel table between the chairs and a desk. Each of the four walls were bare. She presumed that this was deliberately done to create a prickly sense of exposure. The space generated a deliberate type of emotional nakedness and isolation that was intended to increase the suspect's hunger to end the cross-examination and be released. A voice recorder was mounted on one of the cubicles concrete, soundproofed walls. She wasn't planning to scream out again. After Ruby was officially identified and a background check had been done, it had been determined that she wasn't a risk to anyone. Therefore, muffling their conversation in a sealed off room was, as far as the she was concerned, 'a bloody goddam, stupid exaggeration'!

At least the soundproof walls will stop all of the other annoying noises from getting into this room, she gratefully thought. Ruby loathed trivial background sounds.

Now that the chaotic pandemonium of the precinct had been muted behind the cross-examination room's isolated walls, the elderly woman was feeling a touch more relaxed. The customary interview room that she now waited in was much better maintained than the one she'd been detained in sixty something years ago. It was an experience easily remembered, given that it happened because her publicly anti-war protesting daughter, Eliza, and her wild unrefined mouth had both been arrested. In Ruby's eight plus decade opinion, coppers tolerated much more from teenagers nowadays than they did back when her daughter was a member of the younger generation.

Now, all these years later she could see that there were definite similarities between the two different interrogation rooms she'd been in. Nothing much had changed within the precincts of the City of London Police Department since the '60s and '70s. Both interview rooms she'd been questioned in were disorderly, small, and musty. Even the holes in the fabricated soundproof wall panels, which were still being picked apart by detainees, had withstood the test of time. The room had a clock and a camera mounted high on its wall just under the ceiling. Obviously, the modern, state-of-the art camera was used for taping suspect's behaviours and recording conversations during interviews. Ruby felt herself filling with anticipation as she balanced on the edge of her chair while thinking about the countless and different conversations that must have taken place in this room. The constable would be returning soon. She hoped he'd bring something for her to eat and drink.

She had, on the spot, changed the course of Officer O'Bannon's morning, and likewise stolen the concentration the man needed to properly do his job. Especially on a day like today, when London's streets and airports were so dangerously fogged in. Statistically, crime rates increased across the country during low visibility. Griffin knew he should have escorted the old Brit out of the precinct and carried on with his patrolling responsibilities, however, he anticipated that if this woman knew the name of his father and where his father was from, then she must also know 'the girl from England'. The girl that his, then married father, had fallen in love with. The girl Griffin had seen in a series of black and white Polaroid's his father had cleverly hidden, deep in his toolbox in the garage. The girl who his father Otis most definitely wasn't married to, and who was undeniably not his mother.

He'd always wanted to know who the British girl was that his father and mother had bitterly argued over when he was just a boy. They'd fought about so many war-related issues as he grew up, recalling the reasons for their fights wasn't possible anymore. Regardless, in this moment, the officer was both dumbstruck and conflicted that an old Londoner, with a British link to the father that he'd once passionately searched for, had just come out of nowhere, and entered his life. He wasn't sure if this was luck or fate, or the beginning of something he either didn't want to know about or couldn't handle. Griffin had lived his life with so many conflicting questions and unproven scenario's revolving around Otis; the ability to forgive his father still hadn't arrived.

Who knows, he thought, *perhaps forgiveness had just shown up in the shape of an eighty-eight-year-old answer*. He thought.

On the other hand, his mind countered, *what she reveals could spark the start an entirely new type of disgust for my father*.

Either way, he felt wedged in the middle of a quandary that had yet to be defined and understood. The Chief Constable had followed protocol and locked the interrogation room door after she'd entered it. He intentionally left her alone long enough to revaluate the situation. He needed time to think. His head was spinning. Griffin O'Bannon wanted to be certain that he could trust her before he asked her to fill in the emptiness that his father's life had left him with. Over time, these voids became life gaps, which were partly the reason why he'd transferred police precincts and moved from Indiana to Great Britain just a year ago. The O'Bannon family's past and his ancestral roots were extremely important to him. Years back, he'd earned his degree in American History after tales of his father's bravery during the Vietnam War strongly influenced him as a pubescent boy. Having inherited Otis's gallant valour, when he was a thirty-two-year-old man, an unexplainable craving to change his life came knocking. Like a nagging visitor who'd overstayed a hospitable welcome, he couldn't get rid of his deep desire to transform himself and his life. He was ready to serve more than just students and a faculty at the high school he'd been employed at for almost eleven years. For this reason, the educator shocked his entire American family and their friends, the neighbours and his colleagues, by resigning from his job and choosing a completely different and new career path.

After deciding to become a police officer, rather than a second-generation soldier, or a tenured history teacher, Griffin O'Bannon enlisted at the Indiana Law Enforcement Academy. After completing his training with honours, just over a year ago he applied for a transfer to an English-speaking country in Europe. Relocating to, and working in England, wouldn't require him, or his young family to learn a foreign language. Like his father before him, he sold his possessions and bought six one-way tickets to a new life. The major difference between him and his father was that Griffin didn't leave children and a wife behind. He took all of them and each of their passports with him as they boarded their British Airways flight. None of them had ever flown before, which made the experience even more adventurous. Despite that his young son and one of his three daughters had experienced airsickness throughout most of the turbulent flight, changing his life had begun.

Ten minutes ago, when Constable O'Bannon escorted the elderly woman through the precinct's double maroon doors and into one of its interview rooms, his partner was waiting for him outside in front of the station house. Griffin was seriously in a hurry when he pointed to the chair that he told her to sit in. They hadn't been formally introduced yet and he had no time for introductions or senescent pleasantries. Ruby immediately tried to tell him who she was and start a balanced conversation, but the telephone in the room kept ringing and interrupting him. Through his clenched jaw and exasperated lips, he irately expelled stress filled air each time he picked up the receiver.

"It's the fog. We are swamped out there," he said, impatiently glancing over at the door. "I need to get back to work madam."

He explained that his break was coming up soon and invited her to have a cupper with him when he returned for lunch.

"I can then give you forty-five minutes, max, of my uninterrupted time," he suggested, still not knowing her background. All he had was her name to go on.

She agreed and asked if it was possible to have tall glass of ice-water and maybe a newspaper, or a gossip tabloid brought to her while she waited? Ruby adored a scandalous story. Knowing the in's and out of Britain's rich and famous entertained her and connected her to a kind of glitter and glamour that The Seaside, nor her income, ever offered her. Keeping up with whatever the world's celebrities and the Royal Family were doing had always been a hobby of hers. Despite that she didn't believe squat of what was written, Ruby had a grand time of it while reading the gossip and stepping out of her routine world and into their posh aristocratic worlds. Not many people knew about this weekly guilty pleasure of hers. Coca Cola, Harlequin Romance novels, and a fine bottle of cabernet wine were her second, third, and fourth guilty pleasures.

To each his own, she wryly thought.

The Deputy Chief Constable answered her. "Sorry, this isn't the waiting room at a doctor's office or a cafeteria madam. Water or tea I can arrange for you, but there are no magazines that I know of in the precinct."

Despite her pouty reaction, he went on to confirm that he'd have the desk clerk bring her something to drink. He then asked her if she was hungry. She told him she was indeed craving food and thanked him. She didn't want to push it. Ruby was confident that she was 'his connection' to Otis, and he was 'her connection' to Nico.

"The door needs to be locked while you are alone in here madam. This is for your own security," he dutifully declared.

"Be safe out their Constable O'Bannon," she said as he opened the door and stepped into the hallway.

"Sit tight. I will be back in thirty minutes, or so, when my lunchbreak begins."

He still hadn't confirmed if she'd correctly predicted who he was.

Sensing her stubborn interest in him, he paused, turned to face her, and said, "I really don't know if I can help you madam."

Then he pulled the steel door shut and left her alone in the room. For some unsettling reason, she felt like a piece of decrepit and grizzled garbage that had been chucked away. For a reason she didn't rightly understand, she liked it when he called her madam. For a reason he was afraid of, he was drawn to her. For her, he felt like someone she could trust, and this made her feel rather safe. For him, she felt like family, and this made him feel extremely vulnerable.

Hearing the door being locked, she realized that this senior officer had a fogged in city to tend to and she was nowhere near the top of his priority list. She also knew that she needed him. Likewise, she was going ask him a favour. She hoped to redeem the 1960s promise his father Otis had made to her. Consequently, she would be on her best behaviour before and after he returned.

It took only a few minutes for her to feel at ease and calm in the soundproof room. The shambolic and frantic goings on of the precinct had been completely muffled. Although she was grateful for the stillness, the silence was making her drowsy. To avoid falling asleep, she leaned forward, rested her elbows on the interview table, and began observing the room she'd just been dumped in. Although she could use an overdue nap, Ruby McEwen didn't want to miss out on one of life's unexpected and golden opportunities.

Within five seconds she'd kick started her determined psyche and both of her curiously sharp eyes began scanning the room.

Chapter 60

A fully dressed, Chief of Police Constable, locked the door to the Loo, took off his helmet and hung it on a hook. Then he sat on a toilet seat and rested his elbows on his thighs. Running his fingers through his hair, he put his head in his hands and let out a heavy, passionate sigh. He wasn't ready resume walking his beat. Not just yet. His partner would need to wait for him while he shook off the mental murkiness, he was trapped in. The wrought-up American man needed to regain his concentration before finishing his morning shift on the foggy streets of London.

Officer Griffin O'Bannon was a fast thinker. He had IQ scores that classified him as having a superior, nearly genius level of intelligence. Learning and retaining information came easily to him. It always had. He was a person with a brain that could store so much memory and recall facts so quickly that as a student he'd been nicknamed 'circuit board'. Without awareness or consideration of his abilities, an hour ago a meddlesome and charming old lady had yanked him out of his comfort zone. This was why he was hiding out and sitting fully dressed on the top of a stupid, slightly crooked toilet seat. Officer O'Bannon needed a few moments to rehash his past and collect his thoughts. The woman, who had put his precinct into a mandatory lockdown, had also set fire to his memories, which now threatened his deeply hidden secrets. Secrets and threats he needed to douse before he emotionally combusted. He'd taken an oath, To Serve and To Protect. It was an oath he could rightly uphold and execute if he maintained an organized and concentrated state of mind. Just five or six minutes alone were all he needed. Chief Constable Griffin O'Bannon closed his eyes and summoned up thoughts of the Vietnam War and Otis O'Bannon.

Otis was a man, a husband, and a father, who had served his country, died a hero, and cheated on his wife. He was a man Griffin barely knew and seldom saw, yet he'd modelled himself after. The Chief Constable's higher education had taught him that young American men and woman, like his father, who fought in Vietnam, were equals in one way; they took part in what was globally reported and labelled as "the most unpopular war in America's history." Whether they'd enlisted voluntarily or were drafted into service, they were equals. The Vietnam War was a twenty-year long conflict that conjured up more anti-war protests than pro-war enthusiasms.

Griffin O'Bannon was a baby born out of wedlock. Otis was sixteen, and his mother just fifteen years old, when they became parents. Despite the never-ending gossip, ridicule, and stares, together they both committed to keeping their child and graduating high school. This was something Griffin naturally valued more and more as he grew up to become older and wiser. The day after his mother graduated, she and Otis were married in a civil ceremony at the town hall. The parishes that each of their parent's attended had denied them a church wedding. In early 1963, Griffin's parents saw to it that Otis avoided the governmental draft in every possible way. By this time, the war had escalated, and the draft was a very ominous threat for his young father. As a result, Otis sold his motorcycle and his cherry-red Cadillac convertible, bought a plane ticket, and fled to Canada. He responsibly left the rest of his money behind with his wife and their then toddler son.

Later that same year, when Griffin was just four, President John F. Kennedy was assassinated. The boy was watching his favourite cartoon after dinner when his mother asked him *to tell her if any special broadcasts interrupted his TV time.* She was she vacuuming the living room at the time and the Hoover was too loud for her to hear the radio in the kitchen. Therefore, she needed him to be her little reporter. A then pint-sized Griffin felt needed and proudly accepted the assignment. Even in this stressful moment, decades later, he still could remember pulling on his mommy's apron that evening and how she looked down at him while she was attacking the dirty carpets with her Hoover. He was able to tell her that a man in a car was shot and a pretty lady wearing a pink hat was lying on top of the man, or the car. He wasn't exactly sure where the blood was coming from, but he thought he saw red goo. Being so young, he didn't really know who the man was, or why a pretty lady with a bright pink hat on was interrupting his cartoons?

He would grow up to never forget the sounds of his momma screaming, "Oh Dear God. No!"

Then, she fell to the floor on her knees and prayed. Her cries were louder than the Hoover that was still whooshing and swooshing upside down on the carpet. The boy pulled out the vacuum cleaners plug at the same time a plug of a different kind was being pulled out on an entire world.

At the time, JFK's assassination changed everything. The President's death didn't mean much to Griffin, until 1975, when his father came home in a body bag. In that same week, his high school history teacher instructed his entire class to stand up and sing the National Anthem in honour of the town's most recently deceased soldier, Sergeant Otis O'Bannon. It was the first time and the last time Griffin O'Bannon had cried. Likewise, it was day he knew he would become a student of American History at the University of Indiana and not a young soldier buried six feet under in a family plot next to a dead guy who was more of a stranger to him than a father.

Years later, as an educated adult man, Griffin had grown to believe that the young populations of Americans today were no less patriotic than they were during the time when his own outspoken parents were young anti-war protesters. The 60's and 70s hippy demonstrators, rebelling against a war they didn't agree with, chose flower power and peace over weapons and death. After following Otis's military career, Griffin learned to respect his father's moral convictions and confidences. Over time, he grew to rely on and trust historical facts in ways he never could rely on or trust the man he'd grown up calling sir.

Otis O'Bannon was but one of some fifty-thousand others, who at the time fled the draft because of their utter distrust in the cause for which the USA was fighting for in Vietnam. Their suspicions and doubts in the American government had motivated an entire generation to become activists rather than conformists. Otis, like so many other freshly called up draftees, had objections to being recruited into military service. They were likewise, powerfully resentful. Thousands of them were opposed to being sent off to die for a war they didn't believe in. Griffin's mother once told him that, Otis didn't know the reason why U.S. citizens were being sent into the jungles and swamps of a country that was as far away as Vietnam was. Consequently, the war efforts were too surreal for countless soldiers and medics to fathom dying for. She went on to tell him that his father alleged that his vanishing in a foreign bog or being killed in a tropical forest, for a cause he didn't support, would eventually make his mother an instant widow with a very young child to fend for.

Because of his studies and the world he grew up in between 1959 and 1975, the chief constable, deeply absorbed in his rapid thoughts and still sitting on a toilet seat, was familiar with various illegal methods that were used to assist the draft dodgers. Griffin discovered numerous forged documents in the same toolbox that had hidden his father's secret Polaroid's of the time he'd spent in Canada and England. He suspected that they were illegal documents Otis had purchased as phony registration papers he needed to enable him to flee the country. Regardless of what was presumed at the time, or despite what he'd discovered in an old and rusty toolbox, his father wasn't a draft card burner. Nor was he the type of protester who was more occupied with demonstrating his own political opposition to the war in an effort to stimulate the anti-war causes globally.

Otis O'Bannon was a draft dodger, whose sole purpose was to evade the draft and not die on Vietnamese soil, only to leave a widow and fatherless son behind. His father didn't try to deceive the Draft Medical Board into classifying him as unfit for service. Nor did he humiliate or imitate homosexual men, with a sexuality unlike his own, by wearing lace panties and pretending to be 'a queer' when he was given his pre-enlistment health physical. On top of all of this, he was not a phony drug addict who pricked his arm with a sewing needle, so he'd be medically disqualified for service. He was just one of the millions of young men, who were faced with the vexing dilemma of *what to do about the draft?*

Just before his father Otis's four years status as a deferred college student was about to expire, he fled to Canada and then later that same year to England. The events of living abroad were something his father had kept extremely private. When he was home on leave, the details of his draft evasion and military service were not spoken about. The secrets from the time he'd spent in Canada, Great Britain, overseas in Saigon's battlegrounds, and especially in combat, were never discussed.

Up until the year 1968, Griffin was able to piece together some detailed facts about his father. In that year, it was gossiped that Otis had been arrested during Britain's largest anti-Vietnam War demonstration. He knew that Otis had been detained at a British police station and within a week his student visa was withdrawn. Two days later, he was deported back to the States. Upon his escorted arrival to the Indianapolis International Airport, the threat of his ensuing detainment was presented to him. Unless he reported for duty immediately, he'd face charges as a draft dodger, go to prison, and be labelled, for life, as an American coward. Failing to register was considered a felony, punishable by a fine of up to $250,000, and/or five years imprisonment.

Years later, as a student, Griffin learned that his father was only one of millions of men who had violated a draft law that required them to register for military service and deployment to Vietnam. It was a law which the government and recruiters professed would offer enlisted young men and women the chance become heroes. There was, nonetheless, a consequential drawback to the law. Before they would actually be recognized as heroes, like his father Otis, they had to die on foreign soil first.

Letting out another long relieving sigh, the constable remembered how people residing in the Indiana town where they lived at the time had made his mother cry by publicly calling her husband everything from a skiver, to a delinquent, to a cowardly shirker. Nevertheless, his mother knew differently. She taught the young Griffin that Otis had undeniably dodged nothing. *He was an evader, not a dodger*. Nor was his father a coward. After his arrest, Otis enlisted of his own free will. Or at least with as much free will as American men and women between the ages of eighteen and twenty-six were allowed to have in the year 1968. Otis registered because he didn't want to shame his wife, his son, and the parents on both sides of their family. The same four parents he had already shamed by birthing a baby out of wedlock. On top of it all, Otis's parents had bid both of his brother's separate farewells at their military deployment ceremonies. Otis had missed both of these U.S. Armed Service formalities because he was overseas evading the draft and secretly falling in love with a girl who was nearly five years his younger.

Despite the events leading up to his own deployment, Otis O'Bannon was on active duty for seven full years. During each of those seven years his only son grew up without a father. Otis began his military service as a Private in the United Sates Army. He then fought his way, bullet by bullet, and hand grenade by hand grenade, in the wastelands and marshes. Simultaneously, he climbed out of the bogs and up the military ladder to the rank of Sergeant. His younger brother was killed in Vietcong the year before Otis himself passed away. His older brother was listed as a POW in 1970. To this day, he'd never been heard from or seen again. Griffin O'Bannon's father made it out of Vietnam alive, during the height of the Liberation of Saigon. In spite of everything that had been done and said, or avoided and kept secret, Otis died a week later as the result of a tetanus bacterial blood infection he'd sustained from enemy barbed wire that had deeply wounded him during the liberation.

Sergeant Otis O'Bannon played a major role in the capture of Saigon, the rescue of countless innocent Vietnamese children, and the crucial events that marked the end of the Vietnam War. Very few people knew this, because in 1975, after a twenty-year long war finally ended, on the 30th of April, very few Americans cared anymore.

Years later at a Vietnam War Veteran's ceremony, his son Griffin accepted a Medal of Honour on his father's behalf. The teenage boy, wearing a camouflage print tuxedo, stood on the stage behind a lectern and next to his mother. Griffin stood rigidly and stared out over the podium, at hundreds of military officers and veterans who were applauding his father's service to the Army of the United States of America. In the auditorium, standing alongside many physically unscathed veterans, were countless disfigured faces and deformed bodies. Filled with military pride, they all clapped, cheered, and gave his father a standing ovation. The veterans who had lost limbs and couldn't stand up occupied the first three rows. They sat in wheelchairs that had been positioned closest to the stage. Vivid images of these maimed men and women haunted Griffin's sleep until he was in his early thirties.

These imageries, and the nightmares they caused, were the reason why Griffin had made a lifelong pledge to himself. On that night, as he stood on that celebratory stage and held Otis's Medal of Honour up high for all to see, the boy swore that he would never become a soldier. During the ceremony, while two hundred and twenty-five veterans and active military men honoured his deceased father, Sergeant Otis O'Bannon's composed and dignified fifteen-year-old son became a man.

During the award tribute, Griffin O'Bannon clutched his father's Medal of honour so tightly that the sharp tips of Otis's five-pointed star made his son's fingers bleed. The tight grip Griffin had on his dead father's Medal of Honour had nothing to do with nerves, military pride, or honour. In that moment, on that ceremonious night, the young, fatherless O'Bannon adolescent just needed to feel pain. And he needed to bleed.

Sergeant Otis O'Bannon's government issued draft card
and his love letters from the British girl, were never found.

Chapter 61

The elderly, white-haired key to the pre-military life of Sergeant Otis O'Bannon was doing her best not to fall asleep.

The interview room was so quiet. Much quieter than the droning, humming, and peeping sounds in Jazz's ICU room had been in the past two days. Ruby knew she needed sleep, but she also knew a dapper constable would be spending his lunchbreak with her. He'd promised her forty-five minutes of his time, which was something she needed to be wide-awake for. Griffin may actually be the answer to an unanswered question she'd been harbouring in the recesses of her mind since the year 1969. Not at any point, especially under the current circumstances, could she have ever anticipated that, while searching for Nico, her path would collide with Otis O'Bannon's adult son.

With thoughts of both Otis and her daughter Eliza in her lacklustre mind, visions of the 1968 anti-Vietnam War rally held at London's Trafalgar Square, began to spiral through her brain. She remembered Eliza's rendition of the rally extremely well and recollected vividly how her then, barely 15-year-old daughter, had been forever altered during and after the historic events of that day. For years following the rally, it was rumoured that everyone who'd been there, was in one way or another changed.

Back then, Great Britain was experiencing a new wave of worldwide press coverage concerning radical events during the time of the Vietnam War. The world's attention was again focused on the series of global protests that had taken place back in the late 1960s. From mass media to political forums, the importance, consequences, and legacy of that volatile year were on many fronts still being challenged and openly debated. The opinions on the incidents of 1968 remained divided. As divided as the stride between pro-war protesters and anti-war protesters had been. People, born in the 1920s, experienced first-hand a number of world events and lived long enough to read about them afterwards. Ruby McEwen was one of these people. The elderly woman knew that there had been a cosmic amount literature written on the Vietnam War. Likewise, she rightly thought that much too much had been publicized about the anti-war movement and the impact it had on American policymaking. In her vastly shared opinion, the political affairs of the United States had taken front page across the world for much too long. She'd often wondered why practically no attention was given to the other Americans; those citizens who actually supported the war. Probably because they were outnumbered, she'd concluded, knowing personally how being outnumbered typically made underdogs out of people and societies.

Thinking about this reminded her of being outnumbered just a few hours ago in the child's room at the ICU. If she hadn't been forced to stand firmly, on her very solid and stubborn ground, against an equally obstinate police detective, she wouldn't be sitting where she now sat. Moreover, she wouldn't have coincidentally met Chief Constable O'Bannon.

"Focus old girl, just focus." She heard herself saying aloud, as she steered her mind back to where it had just been.

Ruby had her own, typically opinionated way of viewing that chronological time in the world. As she summed up the current media coverage about that period, she believed that a handful of the pro-civic and pro-political groups still regarded the demonstrations as 'the personification of everything that was reckless, senseless, dangerous, and risky about the Sixties'. Anti-war groups were on the flipside of their assertive attitudes. Despite their convictions and origins, they regarded the events of that year as 'the last and the greatest, deep-seated revolutionary movement of the times'. It was a movement filled with oppositional opportunity that was based on a glorified prospect, which people by the masses seized and marched towards their futures with. At the time, her young daughter and the American bloke Eliza was too infatuated and influenced by, were just a few among the thousands who shared anger-filled views against the violent war.

Even back then, Ruby suspected that 'the truth probably could be found somewhere in between the pro and anti-war theories and rallies. One thing she was sure of was that during that time, something unique and potentially ground-breaking was happening around the world. What those who'd been there could not deny or doubt, was that the rallies continue to shape present day life, in ways people involved in the protests couldn't foresee in 1968. Eliza, Otis O'Bannon, and Ruby's mother, Sadie, were no exception. The old woman was certain, beyond the shadow of any political doubt, that the majority of today's digitally and globally connected younger generations were utterly unaware of what they gained from a war that took place decades before their births. Not to mention, how the generations from the Sixties and Seventies had paved new political and social paths for them.

"Lest they forget the price millions of dead civilians and soldiers had paid for the sake of the current generation's ability to have a voice and speak their minds while demanding and declaring their freedom," Ruby heard herself patriotically proclaiming. She was looking up at the ceiling, as though she was speaking for all the dead war souls fluttering above the earth.

All of the thinking she'd just done, the ruckus she'd just created, and the boomerang type of morning she'd just caused, had caught up with the elderly British woman waiting in the interview room. Telling herself that, she'd *just rest her eyes for a few minutes*, she laid her head on the table. Straightaway, the old emotive woman slithered into a dreamlike state. Her brain was taking her back to 1968, which was no surprise to her, given what she'd just heard herself boisterously declare. She had a brain that was terrifically good at recalling the past, even incidents that had taken place fifty or more years ago. Closing her eyes and inhaling deeply, the 88-year-old let out a long surrendering sigh. She knew that memories of Eliza and Otis were about to take her mind on another interesting ride through the hang loose, far out and groovy decade of peace, love, and harmony.

As her mental journey started, she couldn't help wondering where her jaunt would begin and where it would end. The old Brit's curious mind was drifting again.

For those living in Great Britain at the time, it often seemed as though the whole world was observing and scrutinizing the Vietnam War. By the time 1968 was born, the conflict in Asia had escalated and already claimed the lives of nearly 16,000 young Americans. When the Tet Offensive broke out, Viet Cong guerrillas carried out suicide attacks on the American Embassy in Saigon. Images of a fierce and hysterical battle were broadcasted almost instantaneously. Nations across the globe, especially the United States, were not used to seeing soldiers looking and being terrified, ravaged, and confused during war. Their 'boys' looked especially disorientated, in shock and scared stiff, as the media publicized footage of a military conflict that the majority of US citizens were reluctantly, yet rapidly, starting to believe America could not win.

The Vietnam War became the first combat to be transmitted live and straight into the living rooms of The United States through televisions. The unedited raw war images that hundreds of thousands of soldier's families viewed were as foreign to them as they were primitive. An entire horrified and grieving nation watched while its young fighters died on the battlefields as the wounded were being carried off by medics on bloodied stretchers. Too many of them were recognized by their own families, who were glued to their televisions. Relatives of the soldiers and citizens of countries involved could do nothing but watch their kin and friends being injured, maimed, mutilated, and slaughtered. Television in the Sixties increased, three-fold, the intensity of what was going on in the world. People had seen war footage before, but this was the first time they'd seen it as it unfolded in Cambodian villages and on combat lines. Because of the media coverage and live reports on radios and televisions across the world, a war zone knew and had no boundaries. For this reason, people started to develop an intense sense of the sheer lop-sidedness of what the Vietnamese were calling, The Resistance War against America.

On March 17, 1968, Eliza and Otis were serving tables and washing dishes during what began as a relatively normal workday at The Seaside diner. Ruby's mother Sadie, who was visiting from Essex, had persuaded her only daughter to take the day off and go shopping. The plan was that they'd finish their work and then close up the diner after the lunch crowd had left. Afterwards, Sadie would meticulously watch Eliza, who was at a very rebellious age during a globally rebellious time.

"Watch her like you have binoculars for eyes," Ruby had specifically told her mother before leaving.

Sadie committed to her worried daughter Ruby that Eliza, and the older American boy that her smitten granddaughter had a colossal crush on, would get away with nothing. Ruby seldom took a day off, but she'd had quite enough of Sadie's grandma meddling and hypochondriac personality. So, distancing herself from it was appealing. She realized that Sadie meant well, nonetheless, while being together with her complex mother for nearly two weeks, in such cramped quarters as the diner, she was reminded too often and too much of being stuck in the confining childhood Sadie had devised for her. Despite that her mother had mended most of the damaged fences between them, she still could be the suffocating and smothering type. All in all, until now, they'd managed to get on in a decent way during her most recent stay. In an effort to keep the last day and night of Sadie's visit incident free, Ruby left her rambunctious and besotted adolescent daughter with her grandmother and went shopping on Oxford Street for the afternoon.

Furthermore, Ruby thought, as she drove off in the taxi that had picked her up, *let my mother see for herself that I was a very easy teenage girl compared to the one I am bloody raising!*

This was why the diner owner Ruby wasn't at The Seaside diner when a group of peaceful looking, anti-Vietnam war hippies entered the packed to the brim restaurant. The activists were carrying protest signs and enticing customers of all ages to get involved and demonstrate with them, a few eager people jumped up in support of their cause, but not enough of them rallied around their campaign to satisfy the hippy's desires. When they announced that Vanessa Redgrave, the popular stunning performer and political activist was planning to deliver a letter of protest to the US Embassy, more customers sprung off their seats to join forces with them. One geezer, smoking a fat joint, yelled out that Mick Jagger had been seen in the crowd and that he was one of the protesters at Grosvenor Square where the embassy was located. Given the Rolling Stones popularity in Britain, this was all the remaining customers needed to hear. When the group of overexcited people left, filled with hopes of seeing the sexy Vanessa Redgrave and the lead singer of the Rolling Stones, The Seaside was nearly emptied. The entire shabam took less than ten minutes. Little did they know that thousands of protesters were already marching towards the embassy and the demonstration would soon escalate to an unforeseen hazardous level?

Because Sadie was so preoccupied with trying to process what was happening in the city centre and getting customers to pay for their orders before they took off, she never saw Eliza and Otis slip out the back door until it was too late. When she realized they were gone, she was overcome by the extreme situation and her inability to keep her watchful eye on Ruby's sneaky daughter. Knowing that the 'wrath of Ruby' would be harsh and merciless, she quickly scribbled on a napkin:

Gone To Grosvenor Square at The US Embassy.

Come quick. Need help!

Her hands were shaking so much that she could barely hold the pen. She then told the remaining customers that their meals were free if they left immediately. A few tips and numerous plates filled with uneaten food were left behind on now vacant tables. Sadie then dismissed the only remaining employee, The Seaside's short-order cook. He wasn't the least bit interested in the Vietnam War, so he closed the kitchen down and went home early to play with his kids and dog. On her way out the door, Sadie reached on top of the menu rack that was next to the booths overlooking the English Channel. She grabbed a pair of the binoculars that Ruby stored up there and offered customers with coastal view seats. Then she double-checked that all of the appliances and gas stoves were shut off. The last thing she needed on top of this ridiculous situation was to burn her daughter's life to the ground.

Sadie locked the diner doors and jumped into the back seat of a psychedelically painted Volkswagen van just as the driver started its sputtering engine. She was pretending to be an excited protester whose grandson was fighting in the war. As the van drove too fast and furiously along the winding coastline road, within two minutes Ruby's neurotic mother was an emotional wreck on the edge of a panic attack. A young girl sitting across from her in the overcrowded van could see that the group's oldest protester was struggling. The girl, wearing a glassy-eyed, stoned appearance, had gorgeous, long and thick hair that was decoratively beaded and blonde. It flowed freely under her stylish beatnik headband and encircled her cheeks, which were bedecked by two boldly painted peace symbols. Living in the countryside, in the rather tame village of Essex, Sadie had never been this close to hippies before. The girl could see that Sadie was nearing a nervous collapse, so she inhaled deeply on the freshly rolled joint she was smoking and made eye contact with the out of place grandmother. Once she knew that Sadie had seen how it was done, with one swift movement she propped the joint in Ruby's 65-year-old mother's mouth and told her to *take a long and deep hit off it*. Too afraid to refuse, Sadie did as she was told. Not just once, but three times in a row. About two minutes later, Eliza's grandmother couldn't feel her hands or her head, but her nerves were rock steady. She remained numb and tranquil until the VW bus stopped, and its sliding doors opened. Less than a foot away from the open van was a crowd of people bigger than any crowd she'd ever seen in her life. The blaring of the protesters repetitive chanting, and the bullhorns that the mounted police officers were using as they tried to disperse the crowd, was deafening. Likewise, it was all extremely intimidating. Sadie Dutton McEwen was frightened and utterly alone to fend for herself and find Otis O'Bannon and her naïve granddaughter Eliza. To make matters worse than they already were, she was stoned out of her bloody mind.

The elderly woman, waiting for Griffin O'Bannon in an interview room at Precinct 616, shifted in her seat. She was hungry. Mind travel tended to increase her appetite. It was a wonder she wasn't obese. She looked up at the clock and saw that she'd only been waiting ten minutes, so she decided to stay calm, lean back in her chair and reflect some more about life in the 50s and '60s. After all, she was properly enjoying herself.

Like Griffin O'Bannon, Ruby had also taken pride in studying American History. She was eager to reminisce more about two decades that simultaneously changed the United States, Great Britain, and other countries across the world.

Chapter 62

Universally, throughout the 1950s, young people were the new energy and power. By the time, the 1960s arrived, for the first time, a fresh generation was choosing to join forces for the sake of their peers and their futures.

In America, Britain and Europe, the progression of education and prosperity had the younger generation of the times, more so than any generation before them, defining themselves as 'distinct'. They allied to form a powerful force that contradicted the political beliefs and religious values of their parents, who were the embodiment of a conforming generation that preceded them. The anti-Vietnam war movement literally began on the college and university campuses in America. Students of the 1960s quickly began using doctrines of the civil rights campaign being professed by Martin Luther King Jr. His creeds and dogmas became anew foundation for them to stand on. In record time, Doctor King likewise became their African American mentor and popular role model.

Many of the Civil Rights leading protestors, Negros and causations alike, came of age while either disputing or supporting the discrimination of African Americans and segregation in the southern states. Activists on both sides were taught that 'fear was the enemy and overcoming fear was the spirit of the fight'. This Civil Rights mentality filtered over and into the protests against the Vietnam War. The draft had a way of capturing the free and educated minds of young people who were building their futures while standing up against the government for their civilian rights and their right to live as they chose to. Consequently, the anti-draft movement began. In no time, thousands of young men deferred from the draft by utilizing their status and rights as students, or by fleeing America to avoid being recruited against their will.

It was during this time, when a young, particularly good-looking American exchange student, with no other reason than to eat, walked into The Seaside. He ordered a burger, fries, a Coca Cola, and extra ketchup. Eliza waited on him at the counter. She was bitten by 'the bug of love' the moment he looked up at her with his coquettish, flirty grin, and impressionably large brown eyes. Ruby was used to seeing her fourteen-year-old daughter turn on the charm with boys, so she ignored the lovesick expression she'd been wearing daily on her face since the witty and magnetic bloke had arrived. She rightly expected that her daughter's newest crush was 'as normal as normal could be', for an overemotional juvenescent girl her age. Later that day the overseas student named, Otis O'Bannon, asked for a job and a place to live. Eliza was standing behind him, as he faced Ruby and confidently promoted himself. She mockingly made the sign of the cross and mouthed, *please, please, please,* while begging her mother to say yes to his requests. The fetching foreigner, with a distinct accent, pledged an oath to The Seaside's owner. He would work hard, study harder, and not get in her way. Ruby suspected he was running from something, but she liked him just the same.

He was a real enchanter; therefore, she gave him a chance. Otis had a mature coolness about him that made Ruby feel safe and at ease. After three days of working wage free to prove himself worthy of the chance he'd been given, he moved his things into the attic and started working for pay the next morning at 5.30 am.

On his first day of work, Eliza sauntered into the kitchen, fully uniformed and all dolled up at 6:00am, which took her mother by surprise. Ruby's daughter hadn't been on time for work, not even once over the past two years, and she lived a mere twenty-five feet away from the kitchen in their diner apartment. For the next fourteen months life with her teenager and Otis was upbeat, rather fun, refreshing, and incident free. Then, arbitrarily, it all took a drastic turn, in a direction that Ruby and the majority of Londoner's never in their wildest of dreams saw coming.

On March 17, 1968, an extremely large anti-Vietnam war rally was taking place Trafalgar Square, in the Westminster area of Central London. At the time the protest escalated, Ruby was having a grand time of it popping in and out of infamous Piccadilly Circus shops.

As time passed, what began as a relatively small group of protesters quickly grew in numbers and intensity. She was aware that there was quite a buzz outside on the streets, but this was England in the late 1960s, so a buzz on the city streets was expected, accepted, and rightly normal. While she shopped, some eight thousand, mostly young protesters who were attending a rally at Grosvenor Square, started marching towards the American Embassy. Ruby had no idea Eliza and Otis were in the crowd. Nor did she know that her mother Sadie, whose marijuana high had vanished, was on perched atop the concrete base of a statue just outside the embassy gates. Two protesters looking down at the massive crowd below had seen her being nearly trampled, so they'd pulled her up and out of harm's way.

For this reason, and this reason only, there Sadie stood, next to two strange and angry men holding picket signs that read, Hell NO, Don't GO! Johnson is a WAR CRIMINAL! For about twenty minutes, Sadie aimlessly searched, through binoculars, for her granddaughter and Otis. Then, she unexpectedly lost her footing on the statue's slippery, rain-soaked foundation and fell brutally hard onto the street below. The two protesters on the statue didn't even see her fall or notice that she wasn't there. The noise from the crowd was so loud that they never heard her cry out before she hit the ground. Sadie laid exposed, unconscious, and bleeding on the pavement. The angry crowd refused to scatter and disband. An aggressive clash broke out between the demonstrators and riot police.

Hundreds of protesters hurled mud, rocks, firecrackers, and smoke bombs as retribution. The mounted police responded by charging at the crowd on horseback. Grosvenor Square protesters were seen throwing ball bearings under the hooves of police horses, overturning cars, destroying stores, and breaking a sea of windows in the streets surrounding the clash. In no time, word spread like wildfire that Mick Jagger had disappeared into the crowd, while Vanessa Redgrave, the popular performer, was allowed to enter and deliver a letter of War Protest to the US embassy. Redgrave's security team and small group of friends were permitted entry through the police barricades outside the embassy.

But the crowds were held back. This caused plunderers and protestors to become even angrier. Then, they became violently aggressive and refused to back off. It was the first time the city of London, or the world for that matter, had seen the magnitude of such a protest before.

Less than one month after the uprising as Brits were cooling off, American protesters began ranting again. On April 4, 1968, Martin Luther King, Jr, a Baptist minister and social rights activist since the 1950s, was planning to give the speech of his life as the leader of the American civil rights movement. At the very same time, an American draft dodger, who had been arrested three weeks earlier at a US Embassy protest, was in federal custody. Earlier that morning, handcuffed and under police escort, he'd boarded a plane that would return him to his motherland, where he would remain in custody pending a military hearing. His student visa and work permit had both been revoked. The draft dodger had been expelled from the UK and was being sent back to his country of birth to enlist for military duty or face certain legal charges. If he was tried and convicted of failing to comply with terms of recruitment as defined by The Draft, he would be guilty of a felony offense.

Draft dodgers, like the man who'd been forcefully seated on the plane, in a row between two federal marshals, risked a fine of up to a quarter of a million dollars, a prison term of up to five years, or in some cases, both. The skiver in custody knew he had a choice to make after the airplane landed. Regardless, the handcuffed, anti-Vietnam war activist fell asleep soon after his police escorted flight took off; acting as though he didn't give a shit what happened to him.

As the draft dodger flew and slept through the night, Doctor Martin Luther King Jr. was scheduled to lead a protest rally, in Memphis, Tennessee, to support local striking garbage workers. At 6:01pm, on the same day, King was fatally shot by James Earl Ray, a fugitive from the Missouri State Penitentiary. The bullet entered King's body through his right cheek, then it moved downwards and pierced the major vein and arteries in his neck before stopping in his shoulder. He was shot while standing on a balcony outside his second-floor hotel room. His murder shocked an already fearful and traumatized Land of Liberty. Post King assassination riots, which would come to be known as the 'Holy Week Uprising', turned into a wave of civil disturbances that swept the United States following his murder. Millions of people worldwide believed the retaliation to his death to be "the greatest wave of social unrest the United States had experienced since the Civil War."

An hour and ten minutes after the implacable mortal shot was fired, Martin Luther King Jr. was already dead when the handcuffed arrestee woke up as his flight landed. It was reported that the shot that killed Dr. King had been fired from the bathroom window of a Memphis rooming house on South Main Street. The shooter had fled on foot. The identity of the draft dodger being returned to his country, at the very same time shock waves over the death of an 'apostle of non-violence' spread across the United States, was Otis O'Bannon.

Twenty-three days before Otis's flight from the Oceanic building at Heathrow Airport in London, the British Mounted Police Force was seen charging the crowds of protestors outside Trafalgar Square. In an attempt to escape being stampeded to death, people of all ages, races, and genders, scattered like trapped mice. Nonetheless, the hordes of protestor's were too large. Demonstrators were crushed under, and by, each other. Many of them were seriously wounded underneath the hoofs of police horses.

Protesters, peaceful or not, were being dragged through shrubs and beaten up by riot police. By the end of the afternoon, the anti-war march crowds had dispersed. Eighty-six people were injured, and two hundred demonstrators had been arrested. The chaos of the demonstration crisis was nearly over by the time the diner owner's shopping spree had ended.

When Ruby returned to The Seaside, she immediately could see the how upside-down her favourite place on the planet was. Then she found Sadie's note. She'd barely had a chance to start reading the message on a napkin when the telephone rang, and the second crisis of the day began.

A panic-stricken, hysterically sobbing Eliza, was on the other end of the line, telling her mother that she and Otis had been arrested and Grandma Sadie had been trampled by a police horse.

"Help us, Mummy."

Chapter 63

When the Precinct 616's front desk clerk came into the room she saw that the guest detainee had made a makeshift pillow from her crossed arms. Her head was comfortably burrowed in the padding her folded arms provided. Although her eyeglasses were in a rather warped position, they were still on the tip of her nose. Seeing her sleeping in this way had the considerate, dimple faced clerk wishing she had a blanket to cover the elderly woman with.

What a beautiful head of white hair she has, the clerk thought, observing the lady she had been asked to keep an eye on and tend to.

Snoring lightly and being at the tail end of an erratic and dreamlike journey, Ruby didn't hear the clerk enter or leave the room. Just a few minutes later, she was awoken by the sweet aromas of a warm honey coated, walnut sprinkled scone, and a large cupper of steaming hot coffee. A tumbler of water, a napkin, and cream and sugar were also on the tray someone in the precinct had left behind for her. When she lifted the tray to bring it closer to the side of the table she was sitting at, she saw a brand-new copy of Celebrity News, Britain's most popular, high-glossy gossip magazine. It had a yellow post-it note attached to it. She let out a gleeful gasp and seized the magazine with a speed people her age typically didn't use.

Before she'd dozed off, she had reminisced, in reverse, back to 50s and 60s. Now she was thirsty, hungry, slightly dazed, and very eager to flip through the tabloid and munch on her third scone of the day. She looked at the clock again. She'd been waiting for the constable for about thirty-five minutes, which meant he'd be returning soon. Ruby peeled the yellow post-it off the cover of the magazine and adjusted her round spectacles to a proper reading position on the bridge of her nose. The she peered down to read what was on the note.

I will bring lunch ASAP. Wait for me. I have questions.
DCC, O'Bannon.

The issue of Celebrity News that she now held in her enthusiastic hands was the exact copy she'd planned to thumb through a few days ago, but never had gotten the chance to do because of the accident. On the afternoon Jazz and Nico were on their first date, she had planned to finish another chapter of her Harlequin Romance novel and then catch up on the latest celebrity gossip. Her plan had abruptly ended the moment the police made an appearance at The Seaside and informed her about the boating incident. She assumed that the tabloid and her Harlequin were probably still laying in the sand next to her chaise lounge. No doubt by now, they'd been washed away by the tide.

It felt like weeks had passed since the officers shocked her with the news of the child and Nico. It was now hard for her to believe that the accident had happened just two days ago. There was still so much she hadn't been told and needed to know. Being prepared for Jazz's family's arrival was crucial. She understood that they would want, need, and deserved answers. Trying to ignore the worrisome thoughts that were creeping into her mind, Ruby opened the tabloid's front cover and took a hefty bite out of the honey-covered scone. The sugar went straight into her blood like a carb filled injection of needed energy.

"Perhaps you should skip lunch today Ruby girl," she distinctly told her rational self.

"Scrumptious," she heard her sugar addicted self, muttering back.

The way she could eat, it was a wonder she didn't weigh fourteen stones. With a scone filled mouth, she began reading about The Ten Most Beautiful British Women. She hadn't been this relaxed since the day before an 18-year-old, rebel-devil with purple hair and a nose piercing crashed into her life. Ruby was reading about another Royal Wedding and the decorative carriage procession through Windsor when the steel door of the interview room finally opened. She acted all distracted and casual like, not wanting to give her impatience away with as a first impression. As Officer O'Bannon walked in and put two white paper bags down on the table in front of her, she was looking at a photo reportage of the bride and groom, which in her experienced opinion, had been tastefully done with elegance and style.

"How is the fog out there?" Ruby asked, as she closed the tabloid and slyly stuffed it inside her open handbag on the floor next to her feet.

"It seems to be lifting slightly, but it's taking its time. The BBC reports that by tomorrow evening the moon will be shining again over the city. Perhaps the day after tomorrow we' will all wake up to see sunlight," the Detective Chief Constable answered.

She noticed that his guarded tone was slightly melting.

"How are you feeling?" he amiably asked her, even though he could see she was doing just fine.

A bit of colour had returned to her cheeks. The empty coffee mug and leftover walnut sprinkles on her table napkin were signs that she'd enjoyed his small gesture. Ruby thanked him straightaway for his thoughtfulness and brushed the crumbs of the scone off the table and onto the tray. She almost propped the leftover morsels into her mouth and nibbled on them but opted for acting more refined in front of the man she was certain to be Otis's son. After all, he was an Officer of the Law, whom she'd not yet been introduced to. DCC, O'Bannon had felt uncertain and guilty after he finished being consumed by his thoughts while he'd hidden out in the men's loo atop a toilet seat. By the time he was back out on the streets, he was considering that he'd perhaps been too tough with her. He didn't doubt, for even a split second, his use of police protocol, however, afterwards he could have eased his power over her in a timelier manner. Truth be told, Officer Griffin O'Bannon wasn't a man who doubted himself. Despite her age, with her unwarranted outburst and cries for help, she'd crossed a code of behaviour line. Nevertheless, there was something about this woman that made him interested in her. Just as well, he wanted to be courteous, pleasing, and use his manners, the same as he'd had always done with his own grandparents before they'd passed on.

"We haven't yet been formally introduced, madam," he said extending his hand across the table. "My name is Griffin O'Bannon. Who might you be?"

This time, Ruby didn't need to fight her thirst for reacting arrogantly. She already was cocksure of who he was, therefore, a formal introduction wasn't necessary. Purposely, she pulled herself up and onto her feet. Wanting to greet him properly, she amicably shook his hand.

"I am Ruby McEwen. It is a pleasure to meet you Mr. Griffin O'Bannon."

"Likewise, madam," he replied.

"I need to bloody pee again," she boldly stated. "Is there a toilet nearby?"

Wondering why women over the age of sixty talked so openly and so freely about their need to urinate, Griffin said, "I will escort you to the restroom madam. It is just outside the door, only a few steps away."

"I can manage on my own," she independently retorted.

"An escort is required madam. Let's go as quickly as we can," he said holding the door open for her, "my lunchbreak will be over soon."

So be it, Ruby thought, but didn't say.

Her visit to the powder room didn't take but a few minutes and Griffin was indeed waiting for her in the hallway when she'd finished her business. Back in the interview room, Ruby poked at a few holes in the soundproof panelling and then sat back down while the constable unpacked two identical lunches. Today they'd be dining on a ham and cheese sandwiches on dark rye bread, a bottle of orange juice, and Macintosh apples.

"I hope you like ham on rye madam?" he asked her, using his very refined American manners.

"I do" she politely fibbed. Then she said, "Constable, let's skip the formalities shall we. Call me Ruby, being called madam makes me feel old and extinct."

He looked up at her not sure whether to laugh or be in awe at how she couldn't possibly 'feel old' given her age, and how she managed to take over and lead a conversation before he was even aware she'd done so.

"We have no time for dilly dallying young man."

Young man, he smirked hearing this, I'll be fifty in a few years, and she's calling me young man. She saw his grins but ignored them.

The constable stood up, extended his hand to her, and repeated his politeness by saying, "Madam, please call me Griffin."

She remained seated, took his hand, and impishly granted him permission in return. "Sir, please call me Ruby."

The old woman had a lot to accomplish today. If the man she was eating lunch with was who she was certain he was, she needed to call in his father's favour without wasting time on American small talk or British pleasantries. Ruby hated small talk and was never very good at fake banter. For these reasons, she got straight to it.

"Was your father Otis O'Bannon? Did he come from Indiana, and did he study in England during the late 1960s at the time of the Vietnam War?"

Despite, that his slightly astonished, yet confirming look was answer enough for Ruby, she waited for his reply.

"Yes, yes, and yes," he answered.

"Now I have questions," he said. "Between 1967 and 1968 did my married father work for you somewhere here in London? Did he hire living space in an attic above a diner while having a love affair with some girl named Eliza?"

Ruby's pure joy for being right and her shock at hearing the word 'married' was all Griffin needed to see. He now realized that even though she once knew his father, when Otis as a young man, she didn't really know who he 'actually' was, and what he'd left behind when he fled America in 1967.

She reacted honestly, "Yes, yes, and I certainly hope not."

"Seems we have a lot to talk about Ruby," Griffin said, as he took a bite out of his sandwich.

His stomach was in knots and bile was rising into his throat. He could see that she was distracted when she started waving her arms above her head and stared at their reflection waving back at her from the mirror on the wall.

Griffin then asked, "Is the two-way mirror a problem for you Ruby?"

In her typical, sly style, she responded by answering his question with her own question, "Can other constables, or detainees, in the hall outside this room, see us sitting in here?"

Griffin said, "Yes, they can. Does this make you nervous?"

Still not wanting to be recognized by the precinct detectives who were banned from the ICU by the child's neurologist, Dr. Zamier, she stealthily said, "Actually, truth be told, it makes me feel like I am suspect who is being cross-examined."

Being a follower of the truth, Griffin stood up and walked over to the video camera system mounted high on the wall. His 6'4" height enabled him to easily reach a remote control stowed atop the monitor. He proceeded to point the remote at the mirror and press button so that the electrical metal blinds could descend from the top frame of the two-way. About eight seconds later, the blinds clicked into the frame below, concealing the window and the people inside the room.

The elderly woman who didn't own a television or remote control exclaimed, "Aces!"

Griffin O'Bannon had lived in England long enough to know that when a Brit cries out *Aces* they were impressed and considered something to be brilliant. He was glad that something as simple as the privacy the electrical blinds offered had made this interesting and avant-garde type of woman happy. Although he'd known her for only twenty minutes or so, something about her told him she was spirited and easily pleased. Therefore, he decided that she was a sanguine and sensitive person who was most likely swathed in historical memories. Or so he earnestly hoped. In his line of work, the Deputy Chief had met all sorts of people from all backgrounds and lifestyles; people who he'd determined to be normal, boring, odd, strange, dangerous, and even bizarre. Rarely, and on an odd occasion, as he went about his daily business, he would meet someone he thought to be extraordinary. Then, there was today. Today, he was sitting, rather covertly, in an interview room with a person he now knew to be directly connected to a suspect in his custody. He still wasn't sure if she was odd, strange, bizarre, or amazing? Not knowing was distracting him. Then again, she still didn't know what Griffin knew about her employee Nico, his incarcerated suspect just down the hall. She still wasn't sure if he was to be trusted in the way she had once trusted his father. Not knowing was making her bloody bonkers all over again!

Why don't I feel the least bit threatened that she knows more about my father's time in England than I do? He asked himself, as she chewed her last bit of ham on rye.

Perhaps, he concluded, it was because she had lived to survive and witness much more of life than he had. He must need her in some way, otherwise she wouldn't have so randomly stumbled into him. Unbeknownst to her, he wanted to both probe her for information and pamper her with kindness. Griffin also believed in destiny and fate, therefore, he decided that she must be authentic and extraordinary; why else would he risk what he was risking? Up until today, Griffin O'Bannon had met only a few astonishing people in his lifetime, nonetheless, he knew that being phenomenal wasn't reserved for the intelligent, the innovators, and the rich and famous, or even for the powerful and privileged. In his opinion, she was both an unconventional and ordinary person, who was content and satisfied to lead an interesting, yet simple life.

Even though this woman sitting across from him now was doing something as normal as wiping the mayo off her cheek with the back of her age-spotted hand, he sensed that there was nothing commonplace, or unassuming about her. When it came to people, he would guess that she was most likely someone with a knack for thinking eccentrically and living openly and candidly. Glancing up at the old lady drinking her orange juice, he was more than certain that she could be a shifty and nifty kind of troublemaker. The rascally snazzy dressed old lady finishing her lunch looked up, zoomed in on him through her round, black spectacles, and coyly winked. *It was as though she can read my mind*, he predicted.

Griffin O'Bannon suspected that this elderly person was one of those rare and impacting people that someone meets once, maybe twice in their lifetime. Little did he know, his assumption was everything but farfetched.

Chapter 64

While Ruby and the constable finished eating, they took turns exchanging their stories about Otis and Eliza. Both of them were attentive listeners. Their conversation was essentially a repetition of Ruby's earliest memoirs of his father. He shared with her the thoughts, heartaches, and memories that had consumed him while he was in the loo. Their exchange of stories and recollections was done openly and effortlessly.

Griffin was a historian who had studied the Vietnam War in depth. Ruby was a woman who had lived through nearly eight decades of history. This made her fascinating for him. In his refined opinion, this made her even more astute and educated than he was. He was classroom and library educated. She was an authentic, educated student of life. They were strangers to each other, yet the two of them agreed that when it came to his father and her daughter, they shared two distinct things. The first was that Ruby knew Otis for eighteen months before he enlisted and was sent into combat. At the time, a rather young Griffin had seen his father for only two days when he returned to the States after his arrest and deportation from England. As time passed, he saw him over the next seven years, only occasionally, when Otis was home on leave. Back then, Ruby knew the effect Otis had on her daughter, and Griffin knew the effects Otis's affair with her daughter had on his mother. The second thing they mutually shared was that they both had letters and Polaroid's that had been exchanged between Eliza and Otis. Between 1967 and 1969, pictures of his father's time abroad had been taken and letters were swapped between a 19-year-old draft evader and a 15-year-old lovesick girl. It seemed all of their time together had been recorded and saved.

"I have eleven letters she wrote to my father. Some of your daughter's letters had pictures taped to them. There may be more of her love letters to my father hidden somewhere that I am not aware of. Either way, I never read any of Eliza's letters until years after Otis died."

"Sweet Jesus," was her emotional two-word reply. "That was a rightly a loyal and noble gesture for an anger filled suspicious son. Perhaps a gesture your father didn't deserve," she added.

"Perhaps not," he replied. "My mother worked until 5pm during the week, so I was the one who emptied our mailbox each day after school." Griffin told her. "Fortunately for my parents, back in those days, mail wasn't delivered on the weekends"

Ruby could see that thinking about this part of the past was troubling him, even after all these years.

"Whenever any mail came from England, I hid it from my mother," he said with a hint of boyish pride. "Sons are protective of mothers in this way. Privacy and discretion were two building blocks of the foundation I was raised on. Therefore, I made sure my father received your daughter's letters when he was home on furlough. He never said a word to me as I passed his secrets on to him. He'd just tip his head, then firmly shake my hand, as if I was the mail boy in Vietnam handing him a letter from home. Despite the backbone he was instilling in my character, I was too afraid of the thrashing I'd receive if he ever, even once, knew that I'd read his mail, given it to my mother, or thrown it away," Griffin confessed.

"Military fathers are known to be tough men, domestically and on the battlefield," Ruby said, trying to lighten his load. "Being the keeper of your father's secrets must have been so tough for the boy you were at the time?" she asked him, realizing this was the third thing that they had in common. It wasn't often in her life that she met another 'Keeper of Secrets'. Having witnessed her ability to take over a conversation, he ignored her question and continued telling her a few of his memories of the events that defined him when he was a child.

"In the beginning I never opened his mail. In all probability this was because I was just a boy, too young to suspect anything. In hindsight, this was probably a good thing given that it is difficult for young children to read cursive writing and understand complicated words. A few years later as time passed us both by, something changed. On one particular day, when he was home on military leave, I handed him two of your daughter Eliza's letters. After he banally tipped his head and took my hand, I realized my hand had outgrown his hand and my grip was firmer than his was. In that instant, he looked up at me, his now 6' 2", and still growing son. I felt empowered for the first time in my life."

Ruby could only imagine what a turning point that moment must have been for the man sitting across from her.

"He had a daunting expression in his eyes that confirmed to me that he knew his boy was now a man," Griffin told her.

"Did he say anything to you?" Ruby sceptically asked.

Truth be told, she was feeling rather culpable for her daughter's role in making the constables youth so difficult and unfair. There was still too much she didn't know. So many blanks needed to be filled in before she could form any solid opinions or beliefs. Yet, in lieu of this, her instincts had always told her that there was much more to Eliza's peculiar and unhinged behaviour in the late 1960s than she revealed. Much more, she'd suspected back then, than just her daughter being sad and angry because Otis was arrested and deported.

"No madam, he didn't say much of anything to me." Griffin answered, "I was the one who broke the secret letter silence between us. On that day, of what I called a father son recognition, I told him that this was the last time I would retrieve the mail, keep his secrets, and deceive his wife." Griffin's poignant eyes stared vacantly, high above Ruby's head as he spoke.

"I told him that if this Eliza girl wanted to write to him, her letters needed to be sent straight to Vietnam. Let the Vietnamese Postal Department have its turn at protecting him. I was done with being his top-secret messenger boy!"

Griffin paused for a moment and then made a confession.

"This was the first time in my life I tasted real freedom."

Nagging questions on the tip of her tongue were demanding Ruby's attention. Similar to her father, Horace, it had always been hard for her to ignore rash, impending thoughts. Tactlessly, she blurted her questions out.

"Do you think that keeping your father's secrets from your mother, made you feel worse than you would have, if you had given her Eliza's letters?"

He lowered his gaze and stared directly at her. She then took a quick breath and continued.

"I mean, well at least I can imagine, the most stressful part of keeping Otis's secrets was hiding them. Despite your honourable, even protective reasoning behind you choosing to be the keeper of his secrets, hiding his secret life abroad must have weighed heavily on your conscience as you grew up?"

She could see that she had the constable's full attention now, which stimulated her to go on.

"I mean, is it possible that Otis's secrets were not worth the heartache of keeping them? That they were trivial in comparison?"

"Trivial!" Griffin cried out. "Apparently you madam, were not aware of what was happening between your young teenage daughter and my father! A man who was nearly five years older than she was might I add!"

He barked across small interrogation table that separated them. He was rightly startling the elderly woman, who despite his outburst, remained neutral and calm.

"Perhaps I was not entirely aware constable? Considering that it was a very long time ago and when your father stayed with us it was an exceptionally turbulent time in both America and Great Britain. Regardless sir, even at my age, I know heartache when I see it. And what I undoubtedly can very clearly see, is that forty something years later, your heart is still aching."

Griffin O'Bannon briefly locked eyes with Ruby. They both were contemplating their accusations, questions, and impressions of each other. Officer O'Bannon didn't mind, for one reason and one reason only, that she'd interrupted him and had turned his mind into a spinning mess of challenging and muddled memories. This extraordinary, elderly, astute, female sitting across from him, with rye breadcrumbs stuck to her brightly coloured striped scarf, was 'spot on the British button' correct. Griffin O'Bannon was a rational man with crumbs of a different kind stuck to who he was. Accordingly, he knew that her questions were valid ones.

He then said, "I never really thought about it in the way you just described it madam. You see, it actually wasn't difficult for me to be 'a Keeper of Secrets' as you called me, which in hindsight, I really was. Mrs. McEwen, I..."

"Call me Ruby," she interrupted with two blinks followed by a wink.

Dammit, he silently thought, *I really like this old British dame.*

"Ruby, you need to realize something very important. I was, as you defined me, a juvenile Keeper of Secrets living up to a Code of Honor. Do your best to grasp this fact and never to let go of it!" He was with good reason riled up again.

Her aroused, feisty personality countered with, "Depends on what it is you are asking me to grasp young man?"

"Don't be cute with me madam. You know I am a middle-aged man, not a young one."

"My dear man, anyone half my age is still young in my eyes!" she amusingly exclaimed.

"Let's not get too distracted with humour madam, I need to get back to my job." The Deputy Chief Constable had gone all serious on her again. Griffin did his best to hide his reaction and fondness of her. Then he continued talking in a more demur manner. She then mimicked zipping her mouth shut, locking it, then throwing the key over her shoulder. In an effort to regain some semblance of a normal conversation, he ignored his urge to smile.

"Madam, I was only one of some twenty-thousand American boys and girls who lost a parent in Vietnam. Each and every one of the innumerable mothers and fathers who died for the sake of that incomprehensible war were our heroes. They may not have been heroes to the majority of the American people, but they were family heroes. To children like me, having a hero for a father was like having our own personal Superman. The secrets our Supermen had and kept in Asia, or in America, were trivial in comparison to the barbarity they witnessed before their deaths."

The more Ruby listened, the more she admired Griffin's strength, domestic integrity, and righteousness. What he was saying reminded her of a conversation she had with her father, Horace, after his bother Reginald died during the Great Smog Fog 1952. Reggie, like Otis, was a War Hero. He was someone's brother, someone's uncle, and someone's son. Different wars with the same Code of honour.

Stay focused old girl, she reminded herself. *There's no need to tell the Griffin what you're thinking. This is his story, not yours.*

"Constable," Ruby grippingly asked, "I am curious to know if you ever recovered from the loss of your father to a war that so many people worldwide didn't support. A war a plethora of people globally, then and later, concluded to be a complete waste of life on both sides of the battle lines. How did you manage to carry on with life, especially as a child, without your superman in it?"

Griffin was very quiet. The traumas of his childhood were written all over his dark, etched and chiselled face. She wondered, but didn't ask, if he knew how much he physically looked like and took after his father?

"Please go on," she encouraged the tall, slightly greying, broad shouldered man sitting a meter away from her. He was still wearing his uniform cap, so she couldn't see if she was bald-headed or not. Which wouldn't matter one iota, she decided. With his beautifully masculine face, the man could unquestionably get away with baldness. He resembled Otis so much that it practically spooked her. Which was something bewildering, given that the elderly woman, who still talked to dead people and saw their spirits, had never spooked easily.

"Back in 1990, I joined an American organization called Sons and Daughters in Touch. They are a group that unites and supports Gold Star children. Have you ever heard of a Gold Star child?" he asked her.

"No, I have not, but then again, seeing the stars on your uniform, I can imagine it has something to do with the uniform the Vietnam soldiers wore?" she guessed.

"Not a bad prediction." Griffin complimented.

"A gold star is a symbol of honour that commemorates a soldier's honourable service. Members of this organization have lost their fathers and mothers that were in service during the Vietnam War. Sons and Daughters in Touch is an all-volunteer, national support organization committed to uniting the Gold Star sons and daughters of American service members who were killed, or who remain missing, as a result of the Vietnam War. The Gold Stars are a group of family members and numerous military veterans who served with our fathers and mothers. We all gather in the Washington once a year to honour our fallen parents, to reflect upon our mutual grief, to ask questions, and to support one another in ways that no one else can."

He paused and took a deep breath.

"Ruby, can I now ask you a personal question?"

"Ask away," she flippantly said, reaching for her apple.

"Okay. Would you consider yourself a person with an all-embracing, perhaps extensive knowledge of the Second World War?"

Before she could open her mouth to answer, the constable went on.

"I am assuming you went through it and naturally survived it, given that you are still alive? Of course, I have already known how old you are, even though you probably act and think in a much younger way than the date on your national identity card."

Ruby busted out with a loud, unexpected, snorting type of laugh that expelled chewed apple pieces onto the napkin her sandwich had been laid out on. With no time for embarrassments, she wiped her chin and reacted with the speed of sound.

"What kind of a bloody American bullshit line is that? You are your father's true son, through and through, Deputy Chief Constable O'Bannon! Otis was always spewing out charming one-liners. No wonder my Eliza was so infatuated with him."

She was a hell of a lot more than smitten with my father, Griffin knew but didn't say. He was raised to respect his elders and uphold his allegiances, regardless of the circumstances. Besides, time had actually had its own way of softening him and easing his anger at a young girl he'd never met. If this old woman's daughter had even half of her now very elderly mother's appeal, he was starting to realize that they must have had the kind of female magnetism. After all, despite this Eliza's young age at the time, his nearly twenty year old father couldn't ignore his attraction to her. Ruby then responded to his question about the Second World War.

"Mr. O'Bannon," she firmly said attempting to reel him back in and carry on.

How, did I go, from being Chief Constable to Mr. O'Bannon, he thought, wondering which nerve he'd struck in her.

"Mr. O'Bannon," she repeated, regaining his attention, "I was a very young Nurse's Aide during World War II. Later, in the years that followed, I was a volunteer at various soup kitchens, triage clinics, and veteran shelters across Essex County. Many dreadful things happened all around me, and to me, in the 1940s and early 1950s. Horrific things that I buried, a very long time ago, deep in a plot of ground I call *what was*. Wartime events and experiences that were not forgotten, or covered up, but buried, nonetheless. Given that I am not fond of digging up past trauma's and deceased people, let's leave my World War Two memories where they belong; in the past and in the coffins of everything and everyone Hitler and his Nazi regime took from the world and from me."

She wiped tears from her eyes. "Allow the war stay behind me."

Wordlessly, the gentleman in Griffin handed her a fresh napkin from his lunch bag and continued listening.

"Despite my stubbornness and steadfast war related philosophies, I will share this with you. It is something I memorized and still remember word for word. Even sixty-four years after I first read it, in 1944, I recall it. I must have read it more fifty times in that year, as German bombs continued to rain down upon Great Britain. I can remember it word for word because it was, and still is, is exactly how I felt between 1944 and 1946."

Filled with respect and interest, Griffin leaned forward in his chair to give her his utmost attention. For a few seconds, seeing him so close-up, she felt as though she was about to recite, The War Nurses passage, to Sergeant Otis O'Bannon. If the father and son had been brothers, they could have been identical twins. Their likenesses were daunting her all over again.

Ruby positioned her elbows on the edge of the table, intertwined her fingers, leaned forward, and rested her chin on top of her interlocked hands. Then she closed her eyes, inhaled deeply, and found her concentration.

Chapter 65

"There is no glamour about a wounded boy. He is dirty, with foxhole grime, and he is in pain. His clothes are matted with mud and blood, and he has a week's beard. He is often more dead than alive, and he is tired, so tired. There is no glamour about him. But I've seen his strained old face relax in peace and go young again at the touch of our hands. His gratitude for a bath and shave, our clean sheets and a chance to sleep, for our anxiety and for our care, is so stupendous that it makes us humble. He is so grateful for so little."

Ruby was rather delighted with herself for memorizing the passage, still recalling it, and pronouncing every word faultlessly. Her cheerfulness reminded the constable of a young girl who'd just won a spelling bee. She wore a cocky expression as she leaned back in her chair and spoke.

"Your turn Mr. Griffin the Historian," she announced.

"Give me your rundown of the war that turned your absentee father into your Superhero. No mockery intended dear boy," she said, obviously feeling very comfortable with this police officer.

"Okay madam, my pleasure."

Griffin O'Bannon liked this elderly woman. In the short time that he'd known her, she'd proven herself to be moral, honest, and ethical with him. She hadn't criticized his views, doubted his memories, or challenged his beliefs. Two hours ago, this old and intuitive Brit was a virtual stranger who had taken an insightful interest in who he was and how he felt. In his opinion, this counted for, and deserved, much more than an ordinary superficial chitchat. The circumstances that had led up to their coincidental meeting were unique enough for Griffin to want to do whatever it took to preserve her attention. She was one of the eldest and least mundane people he had ever encountered. She was the quintessence of a historical book; something and someone he absolutely couldn't get enough, was curious about, and anxious to get to know better.

Otis O'Bannon's son had never given many people access to the private corners of himself. Then again, truth be told, this very old and very spirited woman, with an intricate personality, had very nearly instantly won him over. He even liked her eccentric fashion taste and the three opal earring studs she wore in each of her irrefutably large ears. He gathered his thoughts, also inhaled deeply, and then took his turn. She leaned forward, rested her elbows on the table's edge, cupped her chin in her hands, and gave him all of her attention.

"Ruby, I have strong opinions about the Vietnam War. Although some of them are bias, most of them are based on facts. Historical facts and truths that came straight from war evidence and the veterans I know and befriended. Other, perhaps even stronger opinions, are those of a boy who lost his father to a war that took him away from him years before he enlisted or died. I wholeheartedly believe that the Vietnam War was perhaps the most traumatic event for the American society since the Second World War. In my slightly biased opinion, it was a war with nothing but the word *no* in it. It had *no* official beginning and *no* glorious ending. It had *no* celebrations in the streets and *no* actual publicly recognized heroes. Instead, there was guilt, misperception, and shock. It was difficult for me, and millions of my fellow Americans, to understand how we'd lost the war. Nearly two billion dollars had been invested in a battle that, at its peak, had more than a half a million American recruits, in all types of workforces imaginable, stationed in Vietnam."

Ruby could tell, by Griffin's passionate and composed tone that Otis's son had strong appetite for learning about the war that had robbed him of a reliable male role model. His appetite to accept the circumstances of his childhood surpassed his need to know about her daughter, Eliza's, relationship with his father. It was very apparent that Griffin O'Bannon had a deep seeded need to talk about his pre-war issues with the woman who knew his father in a way he didn't know him. DCC, O'Bannon continued.

"The unfriendliness that veterans received when returning to their motherland highlighted the confused bewilderment of the American civilization they returned to. In my very bias opinion, America's ego, which had been inflated after the success of World War II, was crushed by an apparently dreadful defeat at the hands of an insurgent Asian army. Our soldiers fought in the bayous and bushes with little, often no, noteworthy military hardware. For those that did fight, it was a revolutionary experience. When they came back home, they were emotionally and physically disfigured. Most of them had to reclaim leftovers of the lives they'd ruined and left behind when they deployed. As for the South Vietnamese troops, again, in my opinion as a Historian, they were reluctant, often unwillingly, to engage in combat with their guerrilla counterparts. The Vietcong were more interested in surviving the war than they were in winning it."

Griffin stood up and stretched his long body. He then reached in his pocket and took out his wallet. He removed a folded-up piece of paper that was being neatly protected in a clear, see through, credit card sized pouch.

"Ruby," he said, "this is the one and only thing I carry of my fathers. I am quite certain he wrote this at some time during one of his many tours of duty. He may have copied it from something he'd heard or read. I am actually not sure of this. A few days after we buried him, I found it hidden in his tool chest, together with your daughter's pictures and letters."

He handed it to Ruby, who held it as he continued talking.

"Given that he was promoted to the rank of Sergeant and received a Medal of Honour for his military service, I think he was wise to keep his emotional state, and his opinions about the war, secret and hidden in a box full of corroded tools."

As Griffin paced the room, Ruby silently read the handwritten note she'd been handed.

I am a soldier. Just one of thousands being drafted into agony, through this Godforsaken Vietnam fiasco in this Godforsaken land. I am just one of many, drafted resentfully into the Army and kept in this war's clutches against my will. I am not a killer. I am a man being forced to kill. I am a man partaking in this illegal, immoral, and unjust war. If I die here, in this Vietnamese Hell, know this. My voice is my forte. Alone I may perish, but united with my brothers on the battlefields, and in the jungle's, we all will triumph. O.B.

Both the American constable and the elderly British woman knew that they'd barely scratched the surface of who Otis O'Bannon was. The man who had altered two different women's lives on two different continents. All of a sudden and out of the bloody blue, Griffin converted himself back into Deputy Chief Constable O'Bannon. She handed his father's verse back, thanked him for trusting her with it and then waited while he carefully refolded it and returned it to its proper, protected place.

"I was supposed to be back on duty ten minutes ago madam," he hurriedly admitted.

As she saw it happening, she effortlessly accepted the drastic change in him. After all, she rightly knew that he'd reached an emotional limit for the day. Likewise, he'd already spent more time with her than police protocol allowed, especially on a dangerously fogged in day as this day was. His complete role transition happened so quickly, Ruby wasn't actually fully aware it was over of it until she heard the London City's Deputy Chief's deep, commander-like voice replacing the curious, searching voice of Otis O'Bannon's son.

"Thank you kindly, Madam Ruby, for your time and information. Is there anything I can do to repay your generosity?" he asked her.

"Actually, there are two things," she answered.

She saw him roll his eyes and smirk in a way that told her he already knew she needed something from him.

"I would like to meet with you again tomorrow to continue our important and enlightening conversation. You know the contents of my daughter Eliza's letters written to your father. This gives you an advantage and an edge that I don't have. You refer to her in a way that makes me suspect you know things that I don't know about my then 15-year-old child. I too am a strong and stringent advocate of privacy. Which is why I have not read any of Eliza's letters from your father. They are all stored safely in one of her suitcases in the annex attached to my diner, together with a collection her other prized possessions," the very elderly and now somewhat emotional woman concluded.

"Yes, I agree we should meet again tomorrow. Now that I have found an overseas direct link to my father, I am hesitant to let that link go."

He flashed her broad, satisfied smile.

Bloody hell, he's a dashing man, she thought but didn't say.

391

After her cafeteria experience earlier that morning, and then meeting Jazz's neurologist, it seemed today was destined to be the day she'd chance upon fine looking, interesting and decent men.

"I have an early morning funeral to attend, however afterwards we could have brunch at my home. Would you like to meet my family madam?" Griffin asked in an organized manner.

"Yes, sir I most certainly would!" she eagerly answered.

After nearly an hour of engaging and conversing with him, Ruby already liked this American fellow. Perhaps she even liked him as much as she and Eliza had once liked his dodgy and appealing father.

"Okay then," he said, "I will send my clerk to escort you back to the front desk. There you can call a taxi to take you to your next destination."

The constable had already pushed his chair back from under the table and was stepping towards the door.

Then, Ruby almost too confidently said, "That won't be necessary constable, I am not ready to leave the building yet."

Taken aback by her brash response, he bruskly turned and faced her. Wearing a proper bamboozled police expression, he said, "Explain yourself madam?"

She countered with, "There is a second thing you can do for me to repay my generosity."

"And what would that be?" Griffin said, biting at her bait. He already anticipated what she wanted but couldn't resist toying with her a bit longer.

"I want to see Nico Rossario. He is one of my employees and he is being held at this precinct."

The DC constable remained professional and responded within questionable procedure. He asked for no details from her about Nico. What she had just done for him deserved an uncomplicated favour in return. Therefore, an uncomplicated favour she would receive. He was an educated, righteous, and decisive man, who never wasted time contemplating over choices or decisions regardless of their magnitude.

"Acceptable," he said. "If Mr. Rossario is indeed being held at this precinct, I will arrange to have him brought here to you. I can allow you only ten minutes with him, otherwise, I will be putting my job in serious jeopardy. I will first need to do a criminal offense background check on him to determine if you are at risk by seeing 'this Nico'. If you are at risk, my clerk will come directly and escort you out of this room. If she does so, ask no questions. Any attempts from you, to try to change the decision that I make, will not be accepted, or even remotely considered. If you are not at risk, I will have one of my men assist you. A detective will be waiting outside the door with strict orders. Be warned madam, after ten minutes, not one moment longer, your visiting time with Mr. Rossario will be over. The two-way blind will be opened, and remain opened, the entire time. If the visit ends without a hitch, you may visit your employee tomorrow during scheduled precinct visiting hours. I will leave approval for this, and visitors pass for you with my personal front desk assistant. Agreed?"

Constable O'Bannon raised the electric blind back up with the remote and then turned to face Ruby.

"This is a courtesy I am granting you in the name of my deceased father. It is my way of thanking you madam. Do not abuse my generosity," the Deputy Chief clearly requested of her.

"Your instructions are completely understood," Ruby replied. "Thank you, kind sir."

Then she kiddingly saluted him, in a dismissive, yet appreciative way. Just as DCC, O'Bannon was unlocking the interview room door he turned about and openly asked Ruby something that had been hankering at him for the past hour.

"Would it be at all possible for me to meet the girl who stole my father's heart in 1968?"

Not one single, negative sentiment entered Ruby's mind after hearing Griffin's question. The emotional pain, shock, and rage she'd once felt when reminiscing over her daughter no longer threatened her. Time had generously taken care of this. Placidly, she answered his question.

"No you can't. Eliza committed suicide in 1975."

Chapter 66

Feeling the need to continue being cautious not to be seen by the constable detective that she'd tangled with earlier at Saint Matthew's Hospital, Ruby boldly disobeyed the Deputy Chief's orders and shut the electrical blinds. Griffin had absentmindedly left the remote control behind on the table.

The elderly woman was famous for her ability to bend the rules, just enough as not to break them entirely and get herself into needless trouble. This skill had enabled her to weave in and out of precarious situations since she was a little girl. Her father Horace had been a superior role model for her in this way. He'd once had the same rascally character and clever personality as she still did. A wily voice inside her head was telling her that Otis's son had intentionally left the remote on the table she was still sitting at. She was certain that there was nothing in the least absentminded about DC, Griffin O'Bannon. Otherwise, he'd have put the remote back atop the camera monitor, up high and out of a cunning woman's trammelling reach. Regardless, she was grateful to be shrouded in privacy again.

Ruby had been sitting for too long. Her lengthy, fragile body had stiffened up something awful and it was now aching the way a rotted molar embedded in a jawbone did. She was certain that one day all her joints would rust together, just like the engine of a vintage, century old automobile left outside and overly exposed to the elements did.

"Sweet Jesus," she heard herself saying, as she painstakingly stood up.

She stretched her crooked limbs upwards and outwards, as a tree extended its branches. Stretching like this had provided her relief from her arthritis since she was in her early sixties. Arthritis had undeniably put the brakes on her body, nonetheless, she was still able to shift her mind between first and fifth gear with the ease of a skilled race car driver. She grinned, thinking of how often she compared herself to a motor vehicle.

With her stretching almost completed, she was feeling more limber, yet somewhat fretful because she still was anticipating who would be stepping into the interview room when the door next opened. By nature, Ruby wasn't an impatient person. Not in the least. Yet, despite this character trait, the unknown was making her antsy again. Impatience was foreign to her, whereas being on the edge of any event, at any given time, was second nature to her. For that reason, there she stood, balancing on her tiptoes reaching for the ceiling while stretching a gratifying type of relief into her age crippled body. All of the sudden, the old Indonesian looking woman, whose life had been a very long series of never-ending events and experiences, lost her equilibrium. After grasping the rim of the table to avoid a nasty fall, she steadied herself, found her balance, and began pacing around the interview room while counting the holes in the soundproof panelling. She felt the need move about a bit longer. With Nico now engraved in her worried mind, she admitted to herself that she was slightly apprehensive about seeing him because she feared what the truth of the accident would reveal. And, more so, because she realized that she cared about the young Italian man who, about two years ago, had stepped into her diner with great urgency and changed her life in a trice.

What if revealed facts or uncovered evidence revolving around the boating accident were more difficult to handle than what she was already handling? What if Jazz's being in a coma proved to be easier than what lay ahead for her great granddaughter? Her mind was taking her to a dark and frightening place, so, she flicked her mental switch and changed directions.

"One, two, three, four," she continued pacing and counting holes as her thoughts drifted.

It was her birthday. He had been in her employ for six weeks since she'd hired him and rented him a spacious room and bath. One late afternoon, after they'd closed the diner together, Nico spontaneously began opening up to Ruby about himself. They were sitting in the counter drinking thick, frothy milkshakes when he struck up a conversation with his boss and landlady. He was learning to use the diner's electrical appliances and he'd insisted on making her a celebratory milkshake. He was attentive in this way, and a nimble-fingered crackerjack who was more than capable in the kitchen. These were character traits about him that Ruby later learned were because of his Italian mother's influence. The diner owner savoured her milkshake and listened intently while he talked. He'd made the shake from whole milk, vanilla extract, and fresh fruit. Nico had added a sprinkle of nutmeg to add a subtle, spicy hint to the shake, giving it an extra rich taste. His employer leaned back in her Barcalounger and adjusted the footrest to a comfortable position with the new handle he'd just hand-made for her from solid mahogany wood. Having little money to spend, he handcrafted her a birthday gift rather than purchase it. The old woman sucked through her straw and tried not to slurp too loudly, while listening to the fine looking, twenty-two-year-old, athletic, sun tinted man from Milan tell her about himself and his Italian roots. Nico Romeo Rossario was the oldest child in a family of seven. He had two younger sisters and two younger brothers, which made for a chaotic, noisy, and blisteringly expressive Italian household. Under one chestnut-coloured, clay-tiled roof, in the centre of the city of Milan, his family shared oodles of dark haired and dark-skinned affection, hot-temperedness, and laughter. Nico, being the oldest, was by birth right the protector of his sisters and the righteous role model for his little bothers. He was a brother who was always on guard and looking out for the younger lads, as well as the safety of his exasperatingly mischievous sisters. He'd laughed, telling Ruby that *if he saw a prowling boy showing the slightest sign of 'more than an appropriate amount of interest' in either of his sisters, he'd assume the worst of the fella, step in and run him off.* His sisters would regularly show their tempers, even in public, as they raged and threw tantrums because of Nico's overprotectiveness. They'd call him a hypocrite, then would whine and complain to their mother that they'd never find husbands if Nico kept following them around.

Nico went on to admit that he was himself a master male flirt. Women flocked at his feet, just like pigeons clustering around the tourists visiting the

Duomo di Milano, their city's most famous Cathedral. His father, who always sided with the much too coddled female side of his gene pool, would demand that his oldest son back off and leave his sisters alone. They were old enough to fend for themselves when they left the house. His father avowed that no sex hungry Italian boy in his right mind would attempt to cross a dating line and mess with either one of his then, fourteen or fifteen year old daughters. The girls followed a five-generation long pedigree of gorgeous Rossario females who knew how to slap hard and scream loud. They were young Italian Mademoiselles who would aim with precision and squarely kick a bloke in his love spot, long before he saw their stilettos leave the ground.

Eventually, tired of his daughters constant whining, his father demanded that Nico spend his free time teaching his eight and ten old brothers to play soccer. They were the ones, not his daughter's, who needed to learn how to kick a ball hard and squarely, past a goalkeeper, to score points for their teams. Both of his brothers, like hundreds of other young Milan lads, were planning to play for the Italian National Soccer Team when they grew up. Nico had told Ruby that he'd found it ironic that in the same conversation, his father was attempting to educate him about the concept of scoring points by comparing little boys scoring goals at a soccer match, to teenage boys trying to score with his sisters. *Italian fathers were infamous for having double standards when it came to their male and female offspring*, he'd said. Eventually, Nico succumbed and left his sisters alone. Given that he was as talented and adept with a soccer ball, as he was with high-strung stunning Italian women, he made the transition with ease.

"Eleven, twelve, thirteen," she continued to count holes in the padded walls and wait for the steel, maroon door to open.

Nico went on to share with Ruby that his choice to leave Italy had nothing to do with being pushed out by his parent's because he'd reached an age of being too old to live at home. This was typically what many of his Italian friends, and Italian males in general, experienced. Many of them, too many of them, were monstrously pampered by their overindulgent mamma's. It was presumed that an Italian mother's love for her sons was bigger than the entire country of Italy was. This was why so many Italian men were still living with their parents until they were in their late twenties, sometimes their mid-thirties. Nico assured Ruby he was not like most Italian men, who have longstanding love affairs with their mamma's that date back to the womb.

While his devotion to his mother was strong, she'd taught him to have great respect for women. This way she'd be certain he would be able to one day pledge his love to someone aside from her. Then together, Nico and his wife would make her five, or six, beautiful Italian grandbabies that she could cook for and spoil. His mother was certain that she'd always be his number one. This was why she helped him paint and decorate his first apartment, rather than tie him to her kitchen table, forcing him to stay at home. Ruby remembered how much she'd laughed when he told her that for twelve days in a row, after he moved away, he'd come home from his job to find groceries that his mother had left behind on his doorstep. He was amazed that the food never, not even once, was stolen. Groceries on the threshold of his ground floor studio became a weekly ritual that she continued to enjoy, despite his pleas for her to stop. Eventually, after his father intervened the food ritual of theirs did end.

In 2007, the economic crisis hit Italy hard. Continuously, for months throughout the financial disaster, the country continued to perform badly. By 2008, both Nico and his father were unemployed, which put a huge financial strain on the family. When he realized that his handsome face and charming personality couldn't pay the rent or fill his belly, he was forced to sell all of his possessions. In search of a better future, Nico left his family and his country behind. He promised his mother he'd write and swore to his father to find a way to wire and deposit money he earned into the Rossario family bank account. The family needed money, therefore, Nico's desperate and pride-wounded father had no other choice but to accept his son's righteous offer.

"Twenty-three, twenty-four," the elderly woman kept counting out loud.

"Bloody hell what's taking so goddam long?" Ruby pleaded, while looking at a door that still hadn't opened.

She was getting impatient and had to pee again. Knowing she was at the mercy of Precinct 616, she swallowed her irritability, continued looking for holes in the walls, and reminisced more about Nico's life story.

Italy was a political and economic mess when he left. Nico was just one of thousands fleeing the country at the time. A few of the advantages Papa Rossario's son had was his intuition, foxiness, striking face, and adept clever mind. For these reasons, Mr. Rossario made a deal with his son. If Nico vowed to his father that he would find his way, stay safe, and come back to them one day, then his father would agree to accept his money. Mr. Rossario was a sensitive, proud, and realistic Italian man. He had three honourable character traits that he'd passed onto his oldest son. He was certain the Nico's beauteous face and convincing charms would enable him to cross every border he needed to cross on his way to London. His son had an uncle named Giovanni, and two cousins already legally living in England, which were three optimistic family ties that Mr. Rossario could lean on for confidence that his son would be safe.

Throughout the city of Milan and all around the country, people were very disheartened by the slow-paced change in Italy. The rising rate of unemployment and homelessness added to the difficulty Italians had with finding employment that would offer them earnest wages and full-time work. A deep anger and a lack of faith in their homeland existed among Italians who were leaving the country and illegally or legally moving abroad. At the time Nico was planning his departure, Italy witnessed an incalculable number of its citizens fleeing the country. They were not departing voluntarily or happily, but out of pure necessity. Almost all of them had one thing in common; they were rebelling against a system that offered its people virtually no hope.

After they finished their milkshakes, Nico told her about his travels to England while he cleaned up their glasses, straws, and napkins. He'd gone into the kitchen to set the water kettle on and make them a pot of tea. He kept on talking, loud enough for Ruby to hear him. From her Barcalounger, his elderly employer was enjoying her birthday, another sugar high, and his company

"Bloody hell! Thirty, thirty-one, thirty-two..." Despite her impatience and nearly ruptured bladder, Ruby kept counting and reminiscing about the reason she'd come to Precinct 616.

All of a sudden, mid-memory, she grew tired of counting holes. Her mind was overflowing with a serious type of concern for Nico. She was on the edge of mental exhaustion and boredom. Nevertheless, she reminded herself that 'she didn't do boredom', so she kept her eyes wide open. Then she sat back down and deliberately decided to shift her attention towards the door and away from the pressure in her bladder and the holes in the soundproof walls. Ruby was a master at visualizing and reminiscing. Whenever necessary, in an effort to not sit idly and allow her thoughts to drift into the past, she'd intentionally give herself menial tasks to pass the time. Her desire to mind travel was strong, but her need to have her wits about her when the door opened, was even stronger.

Without drifting, and in complete control, she let her memories take her back to the day she met Nico.

Even from an interview room in a police station, she could still see and hear him on that particular day at The Seaside, as he shouted his story out from the diner's kitchen. He had told her about hitchhiking from Italy to Paris. She knew he was leaving out any harrowing details, like sticking his thumb out to get a lift from one destination to another. This was something she'd prefer not to hear about, given that she'd grown surprisingly fond of him since his arrival. He told her that he'd considered stopping in Germany or France and trying to find work there, but he spoke not even one word of German or French. He was however fluent in English, so England was logically his country of choice. Nico had travelled with a tourist visa and a roundtrip Ferry ticket from Calais, France to Dover, England. He then spent four days and nights on the streets searching for any means of shelter, food, and money. Italian men were well-known for their desire for food and sex. He assured her that the sex part of his urges he could easily ignore, however, an empty and rumbling stomach was another matter entirely. Ruby recalled having an innocent, old lady laugh, when he so openly told her this about himself.

At the time of his arrival, England was having a long and unusual period of dryness and warm temperatures, which made sleeping under the stars rather enjoyable. To avoid risky confrontations with immigration enforcement officers, who were actively doing random searches for illegals along the motorways and back roads, he deceitfully dyed his hair blonde in a gas station restroom. Then he stripped down to his boxers and a tee shirt. The hair dye was apparently an idea of his oldest sister and a going away gift from her. Now that he appeared to be less of a Mediterranean immigrant and more of a Caucasian UK citizen, he nonchalantly walked barefoot along the English Channel coastline. His strategy was to blend in with the hundreds of Brits who were getting sunburned whilst delighting in an unusually exceptional heatwave over the British Isles. Although his Italian olive toned skin didn't sunburn, he acted like a local and applied generous amounts sunscreen. To appear to be a home-grown Londoner at the coastline, he avoided taking pictures with his smart phone, searched for seashells, laid on the beach every thirty minutes or so, and swam in the North Sea. He avoided conversations with people because, despite that his English was fluent, his Italian accent was too strong to hide behind.

Still eyeing the interrogation room door while tightly clenching her bladder muscles, she remembered that particular heatwave and what had happened on that day, as if it had happened just yesterday.

She was just getting ready to lock up The Seaside and call a taxicab so she could go to a dentist's appointment, when she heard someone hysterically knocking on the diner's back door. She thought a customer must have left something behind. Looking out one of the side windows, she saw a darkly tanned, very distressed, blonde headed man frantically banging on the door. Fair-haired or not, she presumed that he was either Italian, or Greek, given his dark features and striking face. Ruby had treated Italian soldiers during WWII, so she expected that the young man with the classic good looks, who was banging on her door, was not British bred. Every now and then, as a wartime nurses' aide, one of the wounded Italian men she'd patch up, or cover up after they'd died, revealed a head of blonde hair under their military helmets. It was quite uncommon in the 1940s, but not unheard of.

On that particular day, British beaches were overcrowded with sunbathers, boaters, and people of all ages who were playing hooky from school and work because of the UK's uncommon weather. She had just served a record number of customers for her third day in a row, thanks to Mother Nature's gracious summertime surprise. The rest of the week promised to be just as sunny and hot, which meant that after her appointment she'd need to order extra burgers, crisps, and soft drinks for the upcoming crowds she anticipated.

"Focus Ruby, your minds skipping beats again," the old woman with bladder cramps instructed herself to do.

Hearing the banging on the diner door getting louder and louder, she was suddenly aware and reminded of the threats of accidental coastal drownings, which happened at least once or twice a year in the proximity of The Seaside. Given the amazing weather, the odds of unintentional drownings were a real threat. Filled with apprehension, she quickly went to the door and opened it. There he stood, barefoot, wearing nothing but tropically dark skin and black boxers. He was covered with sand, so she assumed there had been a misfortune on the beach, or another serious emergency somewhere nearby her diner. Before she could open her mouth to speak, he frenziedly told her, through a very heavy, southern European accent, that, he needed to use her toilet. His stomach was very sick! Not wanting him to dump any unforeseen messes on her diner's freshly mopped checkered tile floor, she pointed to the men's toilet. He dropped his knapsack, loafers, and beach towel where he stood, then sprinted past her, leaving at least ten of his size forty-four, sand soiled footprints behind.

"Grazie, grazie signora!" he enthusiastically called out as he entered the restroom.

It was in that very moment when she was certain he was from Italy. Actually, even for a person of her age, his nationality was a no-brainer.

That was two years ago, and like today, when she was confident that she knew who Griffin O'Bannon was, she had basked in being right. Ruby was chuckling now. She'd grown dithery and was playing with the remote control. Having just pictured the moment she met Nico, and then his mad dash to the loo, had lightened up her mood. Her memories of how they'd chanced upon each other and then getting to know him, had helped her pass the time while she waited, obediently, as DC Constable O'Bannon had told her to. Feeling her bladder swelling had her impatience waking up again. In an effort to snub her annoyance, she steered her mind returned back to that gorgeous sunny day at The Seaside.

She remembered how Nico came out of the loo about six minutes later. He was all apologetic, and obliging. The Seaside's owner was waiting for him, in the same spot where he'd dropped his sparse possessions onto her floor. She was holding his damp, sand-filled towel in one hand and a mop in the other hand. She told him to get dressed and put his shoes on. Then she handed him the mop and insisted that he clean up the mess he'd made on the floor. Spit spot young man! He cleaned in record speed. She was rapt, especially after he went outside and rinsed the sand out of the mop using an outdoor water spigot. When he came back, he asked her for toilet cleaning supplies, which she gave him straightway. He showed a natural sense of consideration and resourcefulness.

When he returned from the loo, she asked him if he was Italian and if he was hungry. As expected, he was greenhorn Italian man who'd just bravely thumbed his way across three countries and was ravished with hunger pangs. She told him to go into the kitchen and make himself some food. Later she realized that it wasn't necessary, but nonetheless, out of habit she'd told him that he was to clean up after himself before he came out to sit with her while he ate. She went on to introduce herself to him and make it clear that she prided herself on running a tidy establishment. He politely introduced himself in return. His hands were still a bit wet, so she knew he'd properly washed them before leaving the loo. This pleased her because she was resolute about hygiene.

Then, Nico Rossario went into the kitchen, as instructed, to make whatever he wanted to eat. As long as it was something straight from the fridge, she demanded, because she had just cleaned all of grill pits. He went on to tell her he'd be eating lightly because his stomach was not right, but at least now it was completely empty. He hadn't eaten since yesterday morning and was quite certain that it was the egg salad he'd eaten from a vending machine that had caused his stomach to explode in her loo. He laughed loudly, spun on his now dry, sandaled feet, and went into the kitchen.

Ruby was impressed when the young Italian, who had just stormed into her diner and sprinted to use her toilet, offered to make her a cup of tea. After he returned, Nico ate a turkey sandwich while she sipped on her Earl Grey. Then she cleverly asked him what time he needed to be at work? Perhaps they could share a taxi fare into the city considering that she had a dental appointment. He confessed that he didn't have a job. His answer was something she had quite anticipated even before she'd asked him about his work. She then shuffled herself into the kitchen to pour another cup of tea and saw that it was as tidy as she had ever seen it to be. The Italian who'd without doubt had just dyed his hair, had charmed Ruby within fifteen short minutes. He obviously knew his way around a kitchen and could precisely follow instructions. In addition to this, he was well-mannered and fetching enough to have her female patrons drooling over him and then returning for more. Despite her delicious food, she knew that his presence at The Seaside would add a flare to the diner that her establishment could take advantage of. With this in mind, she offered him a job. Within an hour after meeting her, he had employment and she'd hired a 'charmer' worth keeping.

Truth be told, the old lady waiting in the interrogation room, despite her age, liked attractive and charismatic men. They had a way of making her feel young, energetic, and alive.

Ruby was, and had always been, coy and flirtatious. Working side by side with this young man from Italy was going to be pleasurable. Less than a month later, Nico Rossario, the humble, vivacious, and homeless immigrant, gradually became a real-life memorable version of the son Ruby had miscarried in the early 1950s. The son she'd never forgotten and occasionally still yearned for, even at her very old age. As she grew to know him better, she learned that Nico was a dependable and hardworking young man who refused to accept handouts. His eclectic, tantalizing qualities had intrigued her from the moment he'd run to the toilet and then heard him crying out, Grazie signora, grazie!

For these reasons, twenty-seven months ago tomorrow, Ruby missed her dentist's appointment and offered the unemployed, so-called traveling tourist, a job as a dishwasher and handyman. He'd been living in the attic above her diner ever since. For reasons she still was clueless about, her now comatose great granddaughter, Jazz Durant, was lying in the ICU at Saint Matthew's Hospital. For reasons that were now making her fume and cringe, her fear for Nico cruelly swarmed through her brain while she angrily waited for someone to open the bloody goddam door!

It was simple. The elderly woman, who still needed to pee something terrible had completely run out of patience. She felt caged and on a risky edge of losing her temper, pissing all over the floor, and not giving a bloody rat's ass about doing so!

Chapter 67

She was pacing again. The clock on the wall, handing above the two-way mirror told Ruby that it was already 2:44pm. She had stopped counting holes in the soundproof walls a long while ago. Her bright green eyes needed an overdue rest. They were almost as tired as her entire body was.

She was fighting her urge to start banging on the interview room door, just as hysterically as Nico had once banged on her diner door the day she'd first met him. Nonetheless, she ignored her impetuosity and wisely, essentially more so out of necessity, sat back down on her bony bum to suppress her intense need to use the toilet. Sitting firmly on her bladder because a loo was out of reach, had been helping her conquer her urinary requirements since she was about 70 years old. Feeling all keyed up, her brain started skipping beats.

"I do believe I have aged better than my mother did or would have. Poor Sadie, with her neurotic tendencies, had just gotten a semblance of her life back when she met her unexpected demise." Ruby heard herself empathetically saying. Apparently, monotony had set in, given that she was talking to herself again.

"Get a grip old girl," she scolded herself aloud. "It's just a worn-out old bladder, not the end of the bloody world! It serves you right for drinking so much caffeine and eating so much sugar. You get what you deserve, you dumbass!"

Ruby had been scolding and talking to herself since she could remember. When she was younger, chatting to herself was shunned upon. The global stigma at the time was that doing so could be a serious sign a mental disorder. As the decades passed, a growing amount of research indicated that self-talk could help a person's memory recall, boost their confidence, and increase focus. By the time she had heard of the studies, she was already completely at ease with who she was, so she dismissed it all to being nothing more than 'good old fashioned British hodgepodge'. As for her lifelong cussing habit, she had no one to blame for this but herself.

She was now past being tired out. The eventful morning had been too exciting and hectic for the likes of someone pushing ninety. The absence of sunshine wasn't making it any easier for her to stay wake. Just as she was about to make a pillow from her folded arms again, so she could rest her head on the table, she overheard a muffled commotion in the hallway outside the interrogation room. Having a strong sensation that someone was about to open the door, she quickly grabbed the remote and closed the two-way's electrical blind. She was old but still swift. When she heard its metallic hinges clicking into the frame at the base of the mirrored window, her claustrophobia came out of nowhere and swooped in. She felt a heaviness bearing down on her and panicky sense of being entombed. Her angst was yanking on her courage, and she sensed an anxiety attack just around the bend. The last thing she wanted to do was loose control in front of Otis's son Griffin.

In that moment she realized that she should have told Officer O'Bannon about her claustrophobia. Even so, they'd been knee deep in conversation during his lunchbreak that she hadn't thought of doing so. To calm herself, she closed her eyes, inhaled deeply, and slid into the quiet of the soundproof room. The sheer sound of nothing was strong, and likewise the reason why she didn't hear the door being unlocked. When it swung open, without forethought, her startled eyes popped open, and she impulsively sprang to her feet. Her leap was much too youthful and reckless for her stiffened body to handle. The pain in her arthritis ridden and curved spine shot down through her crooked hips and into her long legs. As she tried to steady again herself on the edge of the table, Ruby's knees buckled out from under her. The broad shouldered, body-builder type of a uniformed constable, who'd entered the room, sprung forward and caught her in his arms before she crashed into the table.

He gently eased her back into the chair and said, "Madam, be careful. Are you alright?"

Ruby's temper, being fuelled by pain, was on fire!

"Don't call me madam!" she screamed at the officer.

The Deputy Chief told me she was a gutsy one, DCC, O'Bannon's assistant thought as he sat her down and let go of her as quickly as he'd caught her.

Don't be fooled by her age. She's as mischievous as mischievous gets, was the second warning the officer who'd just prevented her from smacking the concrete floor had been told. Although by nature, Griffin's assistant was vocally impetuous, he sensibly kept what he was thinking to himself. He was trained not to be opinionated. However, for the love of Saint Peter, his gut told him that this old woman was a going to be a bloody handful!

Ruby screamed at the assistant officer, "I need to goddam friggen pee!"

He replied, forgetting that he was not to call her madam.

"Yes madam. Right this way madam."

Bollocks! He thought.

Her 'don't call me madam crap' was something he was having difficulty wrapping his well-mannered head around. Leaning against the wall next to the restroom door, Griffin's frustrated assistant waited for her and her battle-ax personality to finish their business in the loo. He estimated her to be old enough to be his great granny. He had a message from the Deputy Chief that he was told to deliver to the, in his opinion, 'crabby old timer taking a whiz'. The assistant officer was under strict orders to take extremely good care of the important person waiting in Interview Room 4; the same important person who had just nearly fallen and urinated in her pantyhose while she was in his care. He stood there feeling defeated, as he shook his head and schemed a way to pass her off to another officer before it was too late and he was stuck with 'she-devil duty'.

Fortunately, for him, she was more unruffled and reasonable when she came back out into the corridor. Ruby knew that shouting at people generally got her nowhere. Even so, her cantankerous side, the side she'd inherited from her father, Horace, often prevented her from being courteous. She knew that she'd gone too far with the constable, so she apologized to him for her rude and brash mouth, using a type of borderline counterfeit sincerity. Ignoring his suspicions of her quick change in attitude, the man with an assignment extended a hand and introduced himself as, Officer Raleigh, an assistant to DCC, O'Bannon.

The elderly woman skipped over his introduction like he was as insignificant as piece of dog shit on the sidewalk. Then, with an authoritarian tone, she immediately asked, "Where is Nico Rossario?"

Obviously, Officer Raleigh knew he'd been stepped over like dog shit on the sidewalk, nonetheless, he ignored her chutzpah-like style, because he'd been explicitly told to. What Officer Raleigh didn't know was that she and Otis's son had a firm agreement. After Griffin had done his background check on Nico, if he posed no risk to Ruby, he would have one of his men bring Nico to the interview room. His man would then wait outside the door with strict orders that after ten minutes, not one moment longer, their visitation would end. So, where was Nico? She wondered. He must be here. For whatever other reason would I have written 616 on my hand? Did I read the coppers badge number wrong back at the ICU? She was now rightly confused and not sure if she should be disappointed yet. Nico wasn't standing in the hallway, but Griffin's uniformed assistant was. She'd taken this as an encouraging sign that she'd have her ten minutes with Nico as she'd been promised.

"I don't know anything about a Nico Rossario madam. I have been instructed to give you this note and then to escort you to the front desk. Our precinct's desk clerk will help you further," O'Bannon's assistant Raleigh told her.

Feeling a mite sceptical of the man, whom she construed as being a burly constable with an abnormally thick neck, she took a step backwards. Sensing her wariness in him, he held out his arm and offered to assist her while they walked together to the front desk. His tone was intentionally serene, genuine, and inviting.

She instantly slapped his arm away and bit his head off by screeching, "Don't touch me! As long as I have two legs and a heart that's beating, I can walk on my own!"

Ruby wasn't intentionally trying to be so insolent. It was her shattered hope of seeing Nico that was making her act so crudely.

What a piss ass mood this old harridan is in! The assistant constable rightfully thought. His not knowing what she was going through, or what she'd been through since last week, had prompted his ignorant reaction to her obvious nastiness.

"As you wish madam," he affably said, lowering his arm.

After letting her step ahead of him they went through the double maroon swinging doors and walked across the precinct's open and spacious work floor.

"Be careful not to trip over any of the floor cables madam," he warned her, lingering just long enough to fall a step behind her and out of slapping range.

Despite that she'd already seen the cables and should have nonetheless appreciated his warning her, Ruby turned and glared at him with wrath-filled expression. She wasn't mad at Officer Raleigh. She was bloody boiling over and goddam angry at the situation! Truth be told, she was still concerned about being seen by the evidence seeking coppers from the hospital. Keeping her head down low, while cautiously stepping over the cables was a piece of advice she graciously accepted.

"Hello love," the pretty, dimple faced, brunette clerk behind the information desk gleefully said when she saw Ruby again. "Did you enjoy your magazine?"

Ruby quickly reached inside her handbag and pulled the tabloid out. Then she held up the copy of Celebrity News she'd intended to steal from the interview room. She had no need to force a grateful smile this time because she had absolutely relished in reading the latest Celeb gossip. In addition, she hadn't stolen anything from the police, so she'd be leaving the building with a clear conscience.

"The cappuccino and scone were delicious," she told the perky breasted precinct clerk. "Thank you kindly dear."

"I thought you'd enjoy them. You can take the tabloid home with you if you'd like mam. DCC, O'Bannon crossed the street earlier and bought it at the newsstand for you, so it is yours to keep," the clerk told her.

Again, Griffin's kindness reminded Ruby of his father, Otis, and his knack for doing generous things for her back in the 1960s.

"She's all yours Darby," the clerk's colleague said.

Officer Raleigh then bid Ruby a courteous, British farewell by saying, "Cheerio," as he exited the building. He was beyond ready to distance himself from such an elderly handful of geriatric female mood swings and cheekiness.

Ruby, who had just been passed off like a prehistoric football, knew she needed to change her attitude and be exceedingly polite to the PD desk clerk because she needed her help.

Comparable to her 'meet and greet' with Griffin, Ruby performed her second intentionally well-mannered deed of the day by asking the clerk, "May I call you Darby?"

She went on to tell her that she liked her name. Which wasn't a ploy. She'd never heard the name before. Nevertheless, she considered it to be a rather badass name and rightly fitting for a woman overseeing a police precinct.

"Please do madam," was the reply she received. "I have something for you from Deputy Chief O'Bannon."

The PD clerk handed Ruby an envelope with her name on it and then said, "I also have a visitor's pass for you for tomorrow."

She gave Ruby the pass that Griffin had arranged for her.

"I hope you don't find it rude of me, but I assumed that you most likely don't have access to a computer. Therefore, I took the liberty to register your visitation request digitally. I then printed the pass for you and DCC, O'Bannon signed it before he left," she explained, as she handed Ruby her visitor's pass.

Ruby opened her handbag and put the tabloid, the envelope from Griffin, and the visitor's pass into it. After she buckled her bag, she asked the clerk, "Would you be a dear and Google two addresses for me while I go to the restroom?"

The clerk, like the assistant constable, was under strict instructions from her superior, Chief O'Bannon, to take exceptionally good care of this old woman. This was an order that neither of them quite understood, but nonetheless, they'd do as they'd been ordered to do. The clerk was amused at how the word Google awkwardly trickled out of her mouth as if she was speaking a foreign language. She had no idea that Google was as abstract to Ruby as a mobile telephone, Wi-Fi, or anything digital was. Until now, this was an unknown fact that had everything to do with one of the two addresses Ruby needed. She would need an address of a store where she could buy her first, and her last, prepaid telephone. The second address she'd asked the desk clerk to look up for her was the home of a Mr. Giovanni Rossario, Nico's uncle who lived somewhere in London. Nico had once told Ruby that his last name, Rossario, was a very common Italian surname. However, his family name was rather distinguishing because it was spelled with two S's instead of one. How many Italian's living in the city of spelled their last name the exact way Nico did? One, maybe two, was what she was hoping for.

For the second time in one exhausting afternoon, Ruby McEwen, who was rarely wrong, was wrong again.

Darby informed her that, "There are nine Rossario's with the same spelling you gave me, residing in the city. If you give me about three or four minutes, I can narrow the search for you madam by doing some creative cross referencing."

"Do you know the man's first name?

"Giovanni," Ruby said, extremely grateful for her young, sharp mind.

She looked across the entryway at the long metal bench she had been sitting on a few hours earlier. The hooker and the drunk were long gone, but the bench was still overfilled with too many strange, dangerous, and peculiar looking people for the likes of a woman her age. As Ruby limped off towards the restroom, she decided to take a different route than the one nearby the visitor's area. She was tired and feeling vulnerable, so she opted for distancing herself from the amount of intimidating menace that still occupied the visitor's bench. Likewise, she wanted to open Griffin's envelope in private and redo her makeup. It was important to her that she looked her best when she met Nico's family.

As she opened the door to the loo, for the first time since she'd woken up earlier in Jazz's hospital room, Ruby realized she didn't need to pee.

Chapter 68

A flashy dressed old lady, wearing spectacles and a glitzy, floral printed jacket, stood nearby the concrete curb outside the entrance of Precinct 616. Her snow-white hair, radiant striped scarf, yellow coloured stockings, and cognac leather boots, made it very easy for the cabbie to spot his pick-up through the thick fog.

As he parked in front of the precinct and stepped onto the sidewalk to assist her, Ruby was relieved to see that her 2nd cabbie of the day wasn't chewing gum or blowing spit filled bubbles. In fact, the middle-aged bloke driving the cab was being as cordial as Deniz with a Z had been to her. The fog was still dense and blinding, so she'd willingly leaned on the driver's professional and strong arm for assistance. She gave the cabbie Giovanni's address in the Clerkenwell area of the city. The city's Clerkenwell region was globally known as Little Italy, so she wasn't the least bit surprised that Nico's uncle and cousins lived there. She also knew that this was where Italians had created their own large community within the heart of the London. Little Italy was a collective, distinct area with a long, rich history and monastic traditions. Trying to get a better view of the streets, she rubbed the condensation off the inside of the passenger window with the end of her scarf.

"Roll it down madam," the full-bodied, deep voiced driver suggested, seeing her in his review. "I can turn the cab heater up. Then we will be warm enough and you can enjoy your ride."

His considerate idea reminded her once more of riding in Deniz's cab. Deniz had also adjusted his taxi's heater to its highest setting to keep her warm. As the cab slowly crept its way onto a city roundabout, through a dismal and nebulous foggy haze, Ruby caught glimpse of one of London's largest illuminated, bronze, WWII memorials that commemorated The Blitz. Because she'd personally experienced the Blitz, her mind easily evoked memories of when Hitler's German bombs rained down on London in 1940 and 1941. Back then, whenever she and her parents were forced to spend hours on end in a bomb shelter, she was gripped by an indescribable, oppressive fusion of her fear of both confinement and death. Those bomb repellent, steel framed spaces deep under the ground had choked the bravery out of her an incalculable number of times throughout the 1940s. There were times when she literally hated that such a nasty reminder of the war could still pump fear back into a historical time she'd already outlived by nearly seventy-five years. Nonetheless, whatever the reason, it was happening again.

Ce la bloody vie, she thought with a surrendering sigh, as she abdicated herself to another time gone by.

Her entire body shuddered as she gazed out the window through the mist, at what her psyche was perceiving as a mid-20th century city under attack; a city that had withstood intense bombarding, initially for fifty-seven consecutive days, and then almost daily. With her mind again in the bygone, it recapped her memory of how she'd repeatedly heard Winston Churchill's messages to the nation on the radio. The now very old WWII survivor could still recall, verbatim, one of Winston's broadcasts. As the missiles dropped over England, Churchill told a traumatized and grief-stricken Monarchy that, *Hitler hopes, by killing large numbers of civilians and women and children, that he will terrorize and cow the people of this mighty imperial city and make them a burden and anxiety to the government. Little does he know the spirit of the British Nation?*

She was trembling again, filled with too many tragic memories echoing through her war besieged brain. *It is true*, she thought, *certain trauma's never die.* Even at her superannuated age, wartime memories could still be much too daunting. Therefore, she quickly took control of her thoughts and put her WWII recollections behind her, back where they belonged. She flicked her mental switch and began to focus her attentions on finding Nico's family. It was that simple. She was in control again.

"Let the past lie Ruby-girl," she heard herself saying. "Let it lie."

"Pardon madam," the cabbie in the front seat inquired.

"Nothing," she dryly replied.

She was too wrapped up in reclaiming her focus her to explain to a stranger how, or why, she was chatting it up with herself again.

Ignoring the cabdriver, she made mental note to *retire early tonight after she'd read to Jazz from Minnie's journal.*

The elderly woman knew all too well that she had a knack for obsessing over situations that posed no obvious or genuine danger to her. Furthermore, if she didn't regain control over them, her gripping memories would have her senses dangling on the danger line again. In the late 1970s, after her daughter Eliza's abrupt and unexplainable death, she'd learned to rein her brain in and cope with having an overactive and overwhelmed mind. Even after experiencing so much death and loss throughout her lifetime, she still didn't believe in grief counselling. She believed in healing her own mind and soul. For this reason, she sought out console through tapping into inner strength rather than swallowing antidepressants or signing up for therapy. However, since Jazz's arrival, she had paid virtually no attention to this side of who she was. Truth be told, she'd been too preoccupied and side-tracked to think of it, let alone miss it. Aside from a quick dose of mind drifting she'd done back at the precinct, she knew she was entirely disconnected from herself. Her first mistake was ignoring her necessity to find a daily dose of serenity in the midst of the bedlam of her tremendously eventful life. She didn't make this mistake often, but when she did, she paid a personal price.

Maybe my disconnection is why I've been doing an unusual amount of mental drifting recently, she silently questioned.

Then, without warning, she received an unexpected and rather alarming mental message. *Sweet Jesus*, she anxiously thought, *the child's family would be arriving in a little more than 24 hours from now.*

Knowing how extreme and irrational the child's mother Zofia was, Ruby anticipated that an unbridled female force was encroaching upon her world. It was a storm of a different kind and it would be making landfall tomorrow evening. This was something she knew that she needed to be extremely well prepared for. The clock was ticking down. Unfortunately, for the now slightly panicked great grandmother riding in the back seat of yet another London taxicab, rewinding time wasn't an option.

She was rightly looking forward to greeting her great grandson, Thatcher, after so long.

She selfishly hoped that being with him again would be much less intense and affecting than it was when she and Jazz were reunited after more than a decade. For Ruby, seeing the child again felt like two strangers, separated by two generations, were meeting each other for the first time. Since she'd spoken with him on the phone a few days ago, she predicted that Thatcher wouldn't be bringing as many complex issues with him as his sister had. In Ruby's opinion, too many of the Durant's from America had seriously derailed; starting with Tucker, the man who once had professed himself as being the leader of the family. She knew that she needed the child's brother's intelligence to help her with legal matters she'd yet to confront. This meant that she needed him to have himself and his life on the right track. She realized it was unfair of her to need and hope for so much from a relative she hadn't seen in so many years. Nevertheless, like most incidences that crossed her path, it was what it was, and it was out of her hands. Even at her old age, she was attempting to accept that *there were times when she just needed to ask for help.*

With the cab's floor heater now on, Ruby's feet and legs were warm and comfortable. Looking out her open window, she easily noticed that visibility was to some extent improving. She could now see a bit farther down the street; farther than she could when an overweight, sloppy, bubble-blowing driver had picked her up at earlier at Saint Matthew's Hospital. The fogged in city was still a major hindrance, so the cabbie in the front seat was driving at a much slower speed than normal. He had just announced that they'd entered London's Italian District.

In Ruby's boldly, strong opinion, Little Italy was one area of the city that people didn't hear enough about. This area of London hadn't been a regular topic of conversation at The Seaside. Despite this, she was mindful enough to realize that since a hypnotic Italian named Nico began working for her, Little Italy was being cast into the spotlight more and more. Similar to other Italians, Nico's distinct Mediterranean features and his strong passionate accent were as unmistakably evident, and as appealing, as the Little Italy district was. As a rule, China Town, Oxford Street, Westminster Abby, and Piccadilly Circus received most of the attention from sightseers. These traveller hotspots were located in areas of the city that also offered a wide selection of boutiques, galleries, shops, ethnic restaurants, and famed attractions. Just thinking about it all made her realize how much she actually adored London and being a Brit.

While riding to the home of G. Rossario, a heavy weariness was reminding her that it had already been a long and action-packed day. Despite that the fog was attempting to lift outside, it was doing so at a much too sluggish and stubborn pace. As she stared out of the cab's window, into nothing but a grey and dreary haze, Ruby had a hunch. Her notion was that the fog had a misty mind of its own and it was determined to allow people to revel in one more, slower paced day. It was a meteorological fact that when the sun shone, especially during early morning hours, people woke to a vigorous and spirited type of energy. It was as if a new kind of vitality had been delivered to them while they'd been cossetted in the darkness of sleep. Then again, when it was fogged in, the city and its people became more obscure and dismal. The colour of the sky indisputably controlled the moods of populations worldwide. Great Britain's residents and its tourists included. More than six hours of fog was all it took to render people downright miserable. Her mind silently rambled on.

Anticipating meeting Nico's uncle had her questioning what had enticed so many Italians to immigrate to England. After she'd given the cabdriver Giovanni's address, he'd excitedly told her that he was a fourth-generation Italian man. The pride in his voice was as notable as it was annoying. She, for no definable reason, wasn't in the mood for an enthusiastic Italian. Once he got started, she feared that she wouldn't be able to shut him up. He'd already declared to her that *whenever he had the pleasure of taking customers to the Little Italy's Clerkenwell area, he would often share his knowledge and opinions about Little Italy with the person riding in his cab.* Given that cabbies were known to be even chattier than hairdressers and bartenders, she didn't doubt for a second that he was at ease with incessant blabbering and doling out facts and strong opinions.

Of this, she was certain, and this time Ruby McEwen got it right.

The first five minutes of his ceaseless jibber jabber went in and straight out both of her rather large, opal studded ears. She was too preoccupied with her own thoughts to listen to him. Besides, the onset of headache was tapping on her forehead. The last thing she needed was more clamour in her head.

The cabdriver's voluminous, white noise *blah, blah, blah* began with, "London is basically an Italian city! Don't you agree madam? I believe that very few normal people, like you and I, can afford to live in the city centre anymore."

Normal, Ruby brazenly thought, *there is absolutely bloody nothing normal about me! Bollocks! Where does this opinionated, Italian idiot bloody get off clumping me in with the normal people!*

Within six short minutes, he'd put her in a proper shitty mood! The naïve and gullible cabdriver had made his first serious *snafu.* The headache tapping on her forehead was advising her to avoid a confrontation by not reacting to the man.

The cabbie went on to say, "I mean, given that working-class people like us cannot afford to live anywhere near the city's centre, we are partially to blame for the huge influx of foreigners. Don't you agree madam?" he asked.

Eyeing his customer again in his review, he saw an old, white-haired woman staring out the window oblivious to the conversation he was trying to have with her. Oddly enough, her gazing out at the streets passing them by wasn't enough to stop his need to run off at the mouth. So, the now 'feeling ignored' driver went on, and on, and on. And then he went on, and on, and on some more.

"The invasion of foreigners to this city is somewhat scandalous and disturbing, nonetheless. I don't mean to speak ill of the Russian criminal organizations, with their corruption and self-governing ways, mind you madam. I am a practical man who believes that even the Middle Eastern billionaires may be fleeing difficulties at home. Perhaps these tycoons buy up city property in order to give their families and their ill-gotten gains, a safe and profitable refuge," he stated, filled with obstinacy.

Tap, tap, and tap. Ignore, ignore, and ignore, her brain reminded her. Blah, blah, blah, and more verbal blazing was all she heard.

"Nor do I mean the Poles, or other East Europeans who come there to find work as builders and domestic servants to meet their needs. I'm referring to the well-educated, young alumni from Western European countries who are pouring in and looking for employment. I ask myself this, as a man who drives the streets from sunup to sundown, and as a hardworking, middle class man who talks with up to a hundred people a day in my cab. I ask myself, where will everyone be able to afford to live, once the city is overpopulated? Then I ask myself what jobs they expect to find once there are no more jobs to be found?"

It was obvious that the cabbie was on an unrelenting oral roll. Ruby was very tempted to ask him, *if he bloody had diarrhea of the mouth?* However, wisely, but definitely not effortlessly, she said nothing and showed him some respect. For the life of her, she didn't know why she wasn't attacking him with verbal backlash from the rear seat of a cab he'd so politely warmed up to an extra high temperature?

"Don't you agree madam?" he asked, locking his curious, dark Italian eyes with hers in his rearview mirror. Her lack of chatting it up with him had him teetering and tottering between professional patience and the fiery Italian temperament he'd been born with.

Sensing that her cab ride would be ending soon, she answered the man's last question without hesitation. She'd already forgotten what his other questions were. Her forgetfulness had nothing to do with her age. It was a natural consequence of his nonstop blah, blah, blah, babbling.

Then Ruby spoke to him while he was still, in her opinion, creepily staring at her for too long from his mirror.

Her first attempt at communicating with him was a slight mixture of proper British etiquette and a rather strict demand, "Sir, please keep your goddamn eyes on the bloody road!"

Then, hearing her tone, she instantly and intentionally dropped her nasty, old-bitch attitude and switched gears. After all, she wasn't a stupid person, she knew he could pull his cab over to dump her arse off curbside anytime if he wanted to. Since the 1960s, she was a pro at switching gears and saving her without warning crotchety personality from trouble she'd caused, or hadn't been able to handle. So, with this in mind, she switched gears and started over using an artificial and nicer attitude.

"My apologies sir, that was rude of me. May I ask you, what your name is?" she said, with a faked admission of guilty interest.

The driver, who'd already told her that he was a fourth generation Italian, thickened his already thick accent and began to talk with more passion and flare in his voice.

"My name is Renzo Bianchi madam and I know this city like the back of my hand!" he told her. "I could drive through Little Italy blindfolded. This is why I never need to use my little helper," he said, smugly pointing at a TomTom attached to his windshield.

Whether Renzo knew it or not, he was treating her as if she was an ignorant dumb, airheaded woman. Or one that was blind and unaware that he had a stupid navigation device.

Jesus Christ, she furiously thought, *I wasn't flipping born yesterday, you bloody, arrogant fool! What a brimming self-esteem this one has!*

His involuntary arrogance had instantly filled her with a perilously high amount of oversensitive exasperation. *So much for effing gear switching*, she silently thought.

"What is your name dear madam and where are you from?" he cordially asked.

"Vivian," the elderly woman impulsively lied.

Since she was a girl, she'd wanted to change her name to Vivian, after Vivian Leigh, the famous Gone with the Wind actress. She knew if she were going to survive riding in this pompous man's cab and avoid a migraine, she needed to adjust her critical attitude and have a bit of fun teasing him. Therefore, fun she would have. Her kenspeckled deceitfulness was wide awake and Vivian was ready to engage in a slaphappy conversation.

"I am originally from..." she tried to answer, but he interrupted her.

"What a delightfully elegant name. May I call you Vivian?" Renzo replied.

His customer, Vivian, shut her eyes and convinced herself to disregard how much she absolutely detested being interrupted! Then, with every ounce of self-control she could muster up, she tried not to laugh and replied, "Yes, you may, kind sir."

Ruby instantly knew that she had him exactly where she wanted him. Taunting this overconfident and egotistical Italian jackass was going to be entertaining for Vivian.

Chapter 69

Within three minutes after exchanging names, oral diarrhea began squirting out of the driver's flapping trap again. Words poured out of him so fast, Ruby's head was spinning. The overconfident Italian side of his personality was undeniably on the verge of smothering his passenger, who was trying to act sophisticatedly and remain true to her new, dignified name. The man was clearly was a flirt who adored talking and was in need of a never-ending supply of attention.

Staring at the back of Renzo's blackish-grey, wavy hair, she defined him as a chap who was possibly lonely, with a small, limited circle of friends that replaced the family he didn't have. She would have felt a bit sorry for him, but his Italian egotism had convinced her that regardless of random, unavoidable hindrances, he had a rightly fine relationship with life. Despite her assumptions of a man she knew nothing about, she was reputed to be an above adequate judge of character. Therefore, to prove herself right, she allowed her alter self, Vivian, to take the conversation over.

"I am originally from Essex. Since 1960, long before you were born, or immigrated, I have spent ninety-five percent of my time at The Seaside, my coastline diner. For this reason, I don't visit the Clerkenwell area very often."

In Vivian's opinion, before she'd had enough time to inhale and start another sentence, he'd interrupted her again.

"My dear Vivian," he began. "You have never seen a real coastline until you see the Amalfi coast of Italy. I visit Costiera Amalfitana often. With my love for Italy nestled deep in my patriotic heart, I have often walked the magnificent Amalfi coastline, with her twisting streets, magical contoured cliffs, and deep gorges. I have witnessed many Italian beaches and inhaled limitless breath-taking views. Amore a prima vista!" the cabbie exclaimed as threw his arm passionately up into the air.

Bloody hell, Ruby thought, *would he ever stop his goddamn bragging?*

"England, my dear white-haired, spectacled woman, is nothing in comparison to the coast of Italy!" he zealously cried out.

The very unaware cab driver had just made *snafu* number two.

Vivian was staring out the window at the fog whilst doing her very best to ignore her driver's huge ego and his Italian 'blahh, blahh, and more blahh'. Despite his persistent need to blab about Italy and about himself, he seemed to be an honourable and educated immigrant. Nonetheless, she believed that he needed to be careful with his outspoken candour. His pride and attitude could get him into trouble in these openly aggressive modern times. The man had just negatively compared the Italian coast to the English Channel's shoreline. The bloody idiot had no idea that his pride-filled customer in the backseat owned a small section of British coastline. How could he? The man only goddam talked about himself and his own motherland! Vivian found it to be comical that despite his now knowing that she lived in London, he still treated her like a tourist visiting the city for the first time.

What an utter dimwit. She thought but wisely didn't express aloud.

The tapping she'd felt inside her forehead was now a painful clopping. He'd officially given her a splitting headache, which had officially slammed her into a foul mood within three blinks of her drooping eyes. She removed her spectacles and cleaned them off on her dazzlingly striped, silk scarf. She then let her spectacles dangle from their suede-looped cord around her neck while she gently rubbed exhaustion out of her eyes. A few moments later, she perched them back on her delicately tinted, age-spot speckled face, and gazed again out the cabs window. Either her spectacles were exceptionally clean, or the fog was visibly lifting?

Naively assuming that the cab driver's gift of gab had gone on a short sabbatical, Vivian drifted off into the haze outside her window. Her plan was to treat herself to another mini mind traveling moment. Her brain desperately needed to distance itself from the blabbermouth Italian in the front seat and ignore him until she arrived at Giovanni's residence. Then, randomly, as if the cabdriver could read her mind, he started ranting up again for the umpteenth time in one short drive. The next thing she remembered hearing was his comparing the United Kingdom to Italy all over again. The stupidly unaware cab driver was still completely ignorant to what he was doing. He'd just, much too quickly made *snafu* number three.

"Many of this city's magnificent buildings were inspired by Italian architecture," he explained. "The dome of St. Paul's Cathedral is the second largest dome in the world. St. Peter's Basilica is located in the Italian capital of Rome. It is the biggest dome in the world. Did you know this madam?" Renzo quizzed her while he pulled off the road and parked his cab curbside.

For the love of Jesus, shut your bloody mouth man! Vivian exasperatedly thought but didn't blurt out.

This time around, her opinions of this man were ablaze on her lips, but for the love of a God she still didn't believe in, she managed to keep her composure. Even so, again, this time around, it was a narrow escape. Keeping a lid on her emotions, especially the radical ones, had always gifted her with brutal headaches. She took another familiar, and this time a slightly longer, deep breath.

"No, I didn't know that Italians had such an architectural influence on this great city," Vivian replied and lied. She'd chosen to put an end to his relentless babbling by answering the man.

Maybe replying to him would shut him the hell up! She simultaneously hoped and doubted.

Renzo's customer, fidgeting in the back seat, had all together run out of both energy and patience. This was a double pitfall that left her extremely edgy and irritable. She was geared up to speak with Nico's Uncle Giovanni, but she had nothing left to give anyone. More so, she very much needed to take a catnap. Vivian was seconds away from turning into a proper raving British woman. A bad mood swing was coming at her with a speed she was too wacked to be able to control. She had tried to manage her temper for the past ten minutes, however, she was now more than little doubtful that she'd succeeded in doing so in time?

As luck would have it, they'd arrived at her destination. Just in time for the unsuspecting blabbermouth in the front seat to avoid being properly raked over the coals by his elderly customer. A massive, teal blue front door, of the apartment building where she hoped Nico's uncle and two cousins still lived, was just across the sidewalk from where the cabdriver had stopped. The buildings door had a vibrancy to it that was no match for the fogged in streets surrounding it. The headache that elderly proprietor of The Seaside had tried to avoid, had arrived. Straightaway, her head pain crashed into her crabby mood. She spastically hoisted her arthritic, tender body out of the cab; this time around refusing to accept any help from the likes of him.

Then, she proceeded to instruct the overtalkative, glib driver named Renzo, to wait for her. Her business inside would take ten minutes to fifteen minutes. She was feeling a strong desire to get back to Jazz, who she'd left alone for too long at St. Matthew's Hospital. She hadn't been away from the ICU for this long since the day of the boating accident. Induced coma or not, she was worried about the child. She anticipated holding her hand again, checking the temperature of her feet, reading to her, and chatting more with her.

With a worried mind, she curtly told the cabbie to "Beep your horn three or four times when fifteen minutes has passed. I don't have a watch on."

Renzo rolled his dark brown eyes upwards and around in a circle. She'd lit his mood on fire with her demanding tone. He was clearly exasperated and perturbed with this dominant female customer trying to dictate to him how HE would conduct HIS taxi business!

Vivian should have known better than to piss of an Italian! He firmly told himself.

Little did she know, he too was on his own dangerous edge of having a testosterone driven temper tantrum! To avoid this, and at the same time not relinquish the upper hand, he offhandedly groaned his reply, using his supreme male authoritarian tone.

"Tooting my horn at full volume in a residential area is something that I DO NOT DO and is something that I WILL NOT DO madam! It is rude behaviour! On top of this, it is disruptive for the people living here. Many of the residents in this neighbourhood work night shifts in factories, hospitals, hotels, and shelters. A number of them are night-time emergency service employees and are trying to sleep!"

Then he lowered his voice after finding his calmer side again. Glibly, he spoke again and added fuel to a fire that was already burning through an invisible leash his cattish customer had put on her temper.

"Can Madam Vivian not just set the alarm on her mobile telephone? Wouldn't this be the logical thing for the demanding Madam Bossy to do?"

The look she shot him from the sidewalk had Renzo seriously considering taking refuge under his taxi. Or, better yet, leaving her rude, elderly booty on the sidewalk and driving off. *Shit, shit and triple shit,* he regrettably thought. He was too late. In a flash, Vivian's leash and temper both completely snapped in two and she exploded!

415

"NO, Vivian cannot!" she furiously snapped back at him. "Vivian does NOT have a godamned mobile phone and madam friggen bossy is in a bloody hurry!"

Like a pistol aimed to hit its mark, her long, bony finger was pointing at him the entire time. The pissed off, shocked cabbie's jaw dropped, which was exactly her intention. Renzo, in his entire adult life, had never allowed a woman, of any age, to speak to him in this way! For the first time in his forty-three yearlong Italian existence, a woman had rendered the ox of a man gob struck and flabbergasted. By the time is wits had returned Vivian was already limping over the rutted cobblestone footpath towards the front entrance of a titanic-sized apartment building.

Strangely, and rather uncharacteristically, Renzo knew that enough was enough. Therefore, he surrendered himself to the mercy of her petulant and venerable age. The old woman had already turned her back on the rather red-faced Italian cabdriver who was attempting to find his docile side again. His jaw had landed on the floor of his cab, on top of his overpriced leather Berluti shoes. Above the teal blue double doors of Georgian styled building, hung a brass street sign. It read 100 Farrington Street. The fictitious and mischievous Vivian McEwen had arrived. Just as he was feeling calmer, she turned around. Her big, fat sassy mouth started in again.

Locking eyes with the cabbie, she bellowed, "F.Y.I. dumbass, your cabs meter is bloody friggen ticking away, costing Madam Vivian more and more bloody money as we bloody speak!"

Her head was pounding, she was ablaze with anger and unable to control her sharp tongue. Pain had its way of turning her into a real cantankerous bitch!

This old battle-ax has to have hot Italian blood running through her gutsy veins. She has one of the shortest fuses I have ever seen in my life! He thought, while keeping his justifiably ticked off mouth shut and succumbing to her foul mood like professional cabbies were trained to do.

Little did Renzo know, fifteen second after her outburst, the old lady across the street had already appeased herself with ease and switched mental gears like the mastermind that she was? A few moments later, she knocked on the lofty wooden door. The entrance door was street side and roughly two meters away from the parked taxicab.

"Chi troppo vuole nulla stringe!" the Italian cabbie muttered under his breath. His comment penetrated the dense fog with ease.

"I heard that!" his customer, with two conveniently oversized ears, yelled over her shoulder. She was still waiting for someone to answer the door.

"Che palle, madam!" he snapped back, flapping his hands in the air to add some flare to his now sizzling opinion of her bad manners.

So much for my docile side, he thought again.

Very much in the same way as it was for the elderly woman, tameness and obedience did not come naturally to Renzo. Italians were generally zealous people who were regarded as being hasty and argumentative. This was something the crooked and cranky wench leaning against the apartment building door frame had apparently forgotten about. Again, Ruby, who was pretending to be someone named Vivian, knew she'd gone too far. She realized that it was rightly possible that her disinterest in the cabdriver and his Italian culture was because she'd never travelled to Italy. Not even once as a tourist, or for a vacation. Her experience with Italians went no farther than Nico and a handful of wounded Second World War soldiers; all of whom were very different than this Renzo bloke was. The Italian soldiers she had treated throughout WWII were much more predictable and respectable compared to this temperamental cabbie. Simply said, and wisely known, they were wounded and traumatized men, too beholden to their survival to be erratic and volatile.

The angry cabdriver, who hadn't been paid yet, and who was strictly instructed to wait for his fare, got back in his taxi. After slamming his door as hard as he could, he lit up a fat, extra-long Cuban cigar with his prized titanium Zippo lighter. After biting off the cigar's cap and spitting it out and onto the sidewalk, he ignited the tobacco filled tip, blew out the flame, flicked the Zippo's cover shut, and rolled his window all the way back up. He intended to seal off his cab's interior in an effectively airtight manner, which he did. Being a London cabdriver for twenty-two years, he would act ethically and gave his customer the fifteen minutes she'd requested. After all, she was a client, and he was a certified cabdriver with his own taxicab and his own route. Nonetheless, he would be paying back 'rude with rude' by taking a long, drawn out puffs off his Havana and blowing the stink from it into the backseat, where the old bitchy broad would be returning to.

The cigar in the car was a retaliation tactic he used, once or twice a year, when a female customer had angered him much as this old biddy had just done. He knew how nearly every woman, of any age, hated the stench of a man's cigar. Therefore, as he deflated his mouth and puffed heavy Havana fumes out for a fourth time, a sly grin appeared on his face as his cab clouded up.

"Let Madame Crotchety smell how much I don't like being spoken to so disrespectfully," he said, after he exhaled another greyish plume of tobacco smoke, for the fifth time, and blew it directly into the backseat.

"That British witch's snippy attitude and brashness wouldn't get her far in Italy!" he loudly said.

The mischievous, slightly revenging Italian was coughing on his own smoke while laughing at his prank, which made him cough even harder. Seeing the double teal coloured doors shut behind his infuriating customer, he welcomed the next fifteen uneventful minutes; fifteen minutes that he, without question, believed he had justly earned. As he saw her enter the stone building, through circular lips the cabbie blew a flawless twisting smoke ring. It propelled and hovered in front of his face, like a circle of sweet revenge. It was as perfect a ring as he'd ever seen. He was truly pleased with himself and his cigar smoke ring blowing skill. Renzo predicted that despite her age, Vivian's behaviour would absolutely not be as tolerated in Italy as it was in Great Britain. Not for a day, an hour, or even a minute.

"Anyone, especially a woman of advanced age, using the words bloody, goddamn, or friggen so often, when speaking with a true Italian man, would be locking horns with his angry and erratic reaction that demanded an apology and respect!"

Just thinking about her bad attitude had his blood boiling. This was precisely the reason why he'd boisterously just shown her his own true Italian hot-blooded colours. The cab driver was blabbing again. Apparently, he couldn't get enough of the sound of his own voice. He stared at his riled-up image in his review and started up a chat with himself.

"We Italians are considered to be impulsive and argumentative because we can't hold our tongues. We raise our voices, and we protect our opinions with forcefulness, no matter what!" His proclamation was filled with the pride and passion he'd been born.

Renzo, the London cabbie, was a true advocate for any cause that he came across. This was a transparent part of his dissident character. He'd been born with a rebellious genetic factor that he couldn't get rid of even if he wanted to. Similar to the flashy dressed customer who he'd just seen entering the building, he too had a habit of chin wagging and yackety yakking, which were two more likenesses he and Vivian shared that he'd yet to realize.

"Dear God," he said, passionately looking out the front windshield and up at the misty sky, in search of a glimpse of heaven. "You certainly gave this Holy child of yours a big, fat female mouth!"

The cabbie believed wholeheartedly that the Divine Being residing 'above the earth' would agree with him. Then again, Renzo believed that most people residing 'on the earth' agreed with him. Especially women. *Until today*, he thought. Given that his male ego had just been ridiculously challenged by a wrinkle-ridden vixen named Vivian!

"We Italian's are like this because we're incapable of thinking before we speak," he said, still talking to himself in the mirror. We are born with no filters between our brains and our mouths. This is regarded as a liability, especially by the millions of tourists who visit our great country yearly. It is a damn pity that they don't see us from another point of view. You see, from a born and raised Italian person's viewpoint, being part of a class of passionate and spontaneous people is a virtuous thing. Therefore it is our strength, not our weakness!" he proudly professed. The man couldn't get enough of the sound of his own voice.

Unexpectedly, an unfamiliar type of rare insight overcame him. Because of it, he felt as though he'd been emotionally smacked about and woken up from something he couldn't quite lay his finger on. Whatever it was that had so unexpectedly just pummelled his integrity, it did so with the same speed that his Italian mamma used when swatting him upside his bullish and cocky head in an effort to wise him up. Despite his forty-three years of age, his purebred Italian mamma remained the iron-fisted matriarch of their large family. Although he was utterly clueless as to what was happening to him, he was experiencing an unfamiliar snippet of needing to clear his conscience and act scrupulously. Fortunately, for his female customer who was still inside the apartment building, in that very impacting moment, the cabdriver grew his first pair of empathetic male balls. As his virgin-like, sympathetic side spoke to him, he shamefully thought about how he'd just treated the oldest person who had ever ridden in his taxicab. Now, feeling a sincere type of shame, he hung his head slightly and began whispering to himself.

"Renzo," he said, "that old, white-haired, tough lady, who you just tangled up so nastily with, was just being herself." *Maybe it was his Roman Catholic mamma's voice he heard speaking to him and setting him straight?*

He understood now that the way Vivian had stood her ground and rebounded against his comments had properly caught him off guard. He likewise realized that he'd most likely reacted harshly to her disrespect because she'd been acting like a blistering Italian woman, and not a properly upright or uptight British woman. He reminded himself that, because he'd been born and raised in Rome, he should have been more Christian-like and handled her impolite, defiant personality, in a kindlier way.

After all, he thought, *how could he spite her for being her genuine self? He had no idea what kind of life she had lived through up until today. Dammit, she's just another hot-headed woman. Not so unlike the Italian females he knew, with their flashy styles and sharp, pointed tongues.*

So there he sat, in his smelly, cigar smoke-filled cab, giving it his 'Italian all' to change his ways and act more like the respectable and tender-hearted man his mamma had raised.

"Gesù Cristo era una vecchia Donna calda!" he yelled out, clenching his hands into fists.

His pondering over his behaviour continued. Vivian had only been openly reacting what she was thinking and feeling in the very second, she thought it and felt it. Like half of the population he was born into and raised alongside in Italy, she too lacked a verbal filter.

"Who am I to judge her for being exactly who she is with me? He asked himself aloud. "I am just like Vivian is. I am a proud person being exactly who I am. What an arrogant bastard I've been," he dishonourably and openly admitted to himself.

This perceptive way of thinking was as foreign to Renzo as he was to England. The man had been acting like a patronizing, ego-driven scoundrel. For this reason he was now rebuking himself for being a real shithead and pulling such a revengeful cigar prank on a woman who was easily twice his age. His Italian mother would be disgraced at his lack of manners and his disrespectful ploy to get even with such an elderly person. Through his cab's smoky haze, he reminded himself that his mamma had raised him to be a kind man, not a petty scoundrel. With the threat of his rigorous mamma's disappointment in him now hanging over his head, the Italian man puffing on a big, fat, stinky stogie, quickly rolled down his window, opened his cab door and jumped out onto the street. Even at his age, his mamma still held the reins attached to his conscience and behaviour. Even from Italy, she'd expect him to treat people in England in the same courteous way she'd raised him to treat her and their fellow Italians. With this in his now crestfallen mind, he threw the burning revenge of his cigar stub into the cobblestone streets rain filled gutter. Then, he quickly went about opening all of the cab's bright yellow doors to air the smoky stench out of it. Just last week, he'd painted his taxi bright yellow, hoping to increase its visibility on the competitive and crowded streets of London. Looking now, at his steel livelihood, he was taken back by how much it resembled a lemon with wheels. Especially on a dark, dismal British day like this one was.

After driving a black cab for nearly twenty-two years, this colour would indeed take some getting used to, he decided.

Observing his citrus coloured source of revenue from the sidewalk, the shame-faced Italian stood on the curb and watched as the remainder of his Havana's smoulder billowed out of his taxi. As it blended in with the fogged in neighbourhood, his cigar smoke became completely undetectable to the human eye.

In that moment, Renzo sincerely regretted not respecting his elderly female customer's lively spirit and sassiness, rather than punishing her for it by filling his cab with the smell of Cuba.

Chapter 70

Exactly fifteen minutes later, as instructed, a very contrite and punctual cabdriver swallowed the remains of a peppermint candy he'd been sucking on since he'd thrown his stogie into the sewer. With the leftover smoke gone from his taxicab and the cigar taste gone from his mouth, he knocked firmly on the apartment buildings massive, blue wooden door. No one answered.

It wasn't that Renzo didn't enjoy the rich, organic, full-bodied flavour his cigars gifted him with. It was that he suspected that Vivian, despite her age, had a keen mind that could spot a bad deed a mile away. To top this off, he wasn't in the mood for round two with an elderly Brit, who he planned to immediately start respecting rather than verbally jabbing at. A moment or two later, the massive doors sluggishly began to move. He could see Vivian's old hands and crooked fingers attempting to grip the doors and push them open. As a true gentleman would, he took over and held the heavy teal blue doors open for her to pass by.

"After you Bella Signora," he cordially said

He motioned her to take his arm and let him escort her to the cab. He was, after all, raised to be a polished and kind Italian man. She batted his arm away and ignored his suddenly strange attempt at friendly behaviour. Just as she was about to step through the doorway, a young woman came running towards the exit. She was frantically waving a piece of paper in the air above her head.

"Mrs. McEwen, you forgot this!" she called out as she swiftly approached the elderly woman. Handing her the sheet of paper, she said, "When you see Nico tell him *Sii forte* from us. Stay strong and we will visit him as soon as we can. Help is on its way. It was nice to meet you Madam Ruby," she said, shaking her hand before going back inside.

Standing on opposite sides of the buildings egress, Renzo and Vivian watched as the tall lofty wooden doors closed behind Giovanni Rossario's daughter. Nico's uncle wasn't at home, nonetheless she felt relieved that she was able to pass on information to him about Nico's situation through his cousin. The old woman was beyond confident that Nico's family in Italy would be contacted, which meant a solution to his predicament was imminent. She'd do her part once she had a chance to speak with Thatcher and Griffin about legal matters concerning her employee's arrest. As for the repercussions stemming from his illegal status, she was out of her league. She'd need help resolving this part of the serious mess Nico had landed himself in since he'd arrived in England and met Jazz. This was one of those rare times in her life when she'd ask for help rather than try to solve matters on her own.

"After you Bella Signora," he repeated, offering her his strong, escorting arm again.

She batted him even harder this time! He took a deep, exasperated breath before stepping aside and gesturing, with the swooping swipe of his arm, for her to pass by. He started to sweat from his atypically kind gesture.

As Vivian sceptically followed his lead, she sarcastically glared at him. A very obvious smug-like grin had returned to his face. His smugness instantly triggered something lingering under the surface of her patience.

What an arrogant ass! She thought but didn't say.

With a somewhat jaunty and overconfident tone, he asked her, "Why doesn't Madam Vivian like being assisted by a strappingly handsome Italian man?"

What a personality this one has! Vivian knew a flirt with an inflated ego when she met one.

Bloody idiot has no idea who his opponent is! She silently declared with an equal amount of smugness. Unexpectedly, she stopped directly in front of him and turned around. Seeing a world renowned, silver foil wrapper sticking out of his jacket pocket, she teasingly said, "This lovely madam will take your arm if you give her one of her favourite chocolate mint candies?"

Waiting for him to appease her, she held out her right hand, with its four crooked fingers and even more crooked thumb. Grateful that he could calm her down, he took the only Peppermint Paddy's he had left out of his pocket and placed it in her hand. Giving his last shot of sugar away was not something the chubby, sweet-toothed Italian did very often.

Desperate times eh Renzo, he optimistically determined.

Then he extended his arm, for a third time, to assist her safely across the uneven cobblestones sidewalk, to where his solid steel lemon was waiting for them.

"Where to madam?" he asked, helping her sit and position her rather crippled and frail body into the back seat.

"Saint Matthew's Hospital," she mumbled as her eyes closed.

Within less than five hundred meters away from Giovanni's residence, Vivian, who attentively licked at the chocolate layer of her candy, was deep in thought. What her chauffeur didn't know, but nonetheless was beginning to comprehend, was that silence and relaxation were exactly what she needed. The plump cabbie could see her deep concentration from his rear view. Accordingly, he drove her to her next destination in complete silence. What very few people knew, and even less people could fathom, was that Italians could also be very passive and mummed. This was something he planned on allowing his passenger to experience while he drove in complete stillness, whilst reminiscing more about Italy, the parents he'd left behind years ago, and his six children who were scattered around London going about their different lives. Aside from, the slurping sound of an old lady's tongue lapping at mint flavoured chocolate and some random lip smacking from the backseat, nothing but a blue wall of silence filled Renzo's taxi.

In the back seat, the elderly lady was recalling the decision she had made while she'd been at Precinct 616. She'd return to Saint Matthew's Hospital early and set her preparation for Jazz's family to arrive in motion. She had a plan. After doting on herself and having a chat with the child, she'd retire on time. She'd likewise read an entry or two from one of Minnie or Bessie's journals. Given all of this, plus the events of the past few days, in addition to what was yet to come, Ruby rightly knew she'd need a proper eight hours of solid slumber. Moreover, given that she still had an entire day ahead of her before the Durant's flight landed at Heathrow tomorrow early evening, she'd need more energy. Keeping the child's recently divorced parents from 'offing each other' while they were in London was not her responsibility. Nor did it interest her. Not even in the slightest of ways. As long as they didn't disrupt the insensate serenity of the sphere their daughter was now confined in, she would not interfere in their personal or marital affairs. She would, however, fight to protect the child's wellbeing with every bit of stamina she had left in her. Even, if this meant pitting them against her, or they ended up hating her more than they most likely already did given the dire circumstances.

"Ce la goddam vie," she said articulately, breaking the taxi's silence.

"Pardon signora," the plump cheeked cabdriver replied, looking at her from his front seat vantage point.

"Nothing, kind sir," she answered with a forced smile.

Vivian was trying to change her disposition and give the man at least half a chance. After all, she did realize that while she'd ridden in his taxicab earlier, her fears for Jazz and lingering memories of her daughter Eliza, plus fatigue and a biased headache, had affected her normally unsullied British manners. It was true, she could be hot-headed, but being an 'insensitive despot' she was not.

Get a grip old girl, she silently told herself.

She was still enjoying a sugar rush that Renzo's candy had given her. He returned her smile with a sociable, gentlemanly nod. Their silence sustained as her mental preparation continued.

Both Tucker and Zofia Durant had sent, to their oldest living relative from Great Britain, much more than a juvenile handful for the summer. They'd sent her a teenage anarchist who had style and ambition, combined with a desperate a need to seek out a revolution at every turn. Jazz was a lost, angry, rebellious, and defiant young woman with an impressive and quite possibly secretive photographic talent. Whether they knew it or not, their daughter had natural and intimate abilities. She could express the diverse sides of herself, by communicating thought-provoking stories via the images she captured with two observant eyes and a one camera lens. The collaged wall in Eliza's old bedroom that Jazz had created was a strong indication that Zofia's daughter viewed the world contrarily to how others viewed it. Licking the last sweet pecks of peppermint candy off her sticky fingers, the teen's photographs swirled through the elderly woman's curious mind.

It had been an eventful day. Despite what she'd discovered about Griffin O'Bannon's and Giovanni Rossario, only Jazz and The Seaside's dishwasher and handyman, Nico, knew the actual facts surrounding the boating accident. The old Brit was still rightly confident that the teen from California didn't intentionally choose to be wilful or malicious. Wisely she'd already deduced that Jazz Durant knew from a very young age that she'd been born different and that she didn't want to be caged or confined by anyone or anything. What other choice did her parent's give their eccentric and bolshie daughter than to search for herself beyond the borders of their own wacky lives, declare her independence, and demand her freedom? Zofia and Tucker Durant had screwed the pooch one too many times. They were about to learn the true and harsh meaning of the classic and timeless cliché, 'what goes around comes around'.

For the old woman, thinking in this way was like looking in a cracked mirror filled with nostalgic images of herself and her long since deceased parent's Horace and Sadie. Her past life was coming full circle and had landed directly in her lap.

Chapter 71

Living and breathing on the other side of the elderly woman's gutsy, headstrong, and ornery personality, was a very hospitable and intuitive person. Pondering over this impressive description of herself, she closed her eyes and relaxed.

A few minutes later, with her renowned Cheetah-like speed, in three flickers of her fatigued mind, Ruby summoned up her alternative self. It was the version of herself that Renzo the cabbie hadn't yet met. Having beckoned her alter-self hundreds of times throughout her lifetime, she knew this wouldn't take long. The other, gentler version the old woman, who also wore two keys around her neck, six opal earring studs, and her departed parent's gold wedding rings, was returning. Aside from a keepsake hankie she'd preserved inside her bra for forty-five years, she had shed her cantankerous skin and was now feeling at home and secure inside her second, more charismatic skin.

If Ruby McEwen had been born an animal of a different kind, she would have been born a Chameleon. She possessed the distinctive core of one of the most changeable and highly specialized 'clade of Old-World lizards'. She had an unwilling and subliminal way of adapting to situations she encountered and to the ambiances of life. She also had a virtuoso ability to tailor her behaviour in ways that enabled her to cope with a slew of contrasting demeanours of the seemingly jillions of people and events she'd encountered since the 1920s. She was someone who set out, with the precise intention, to mold and re-invent herself in an effort to surmise and withstand any situation at any given time.

She could effortlessly change the course she was on as circumstances deemed necessary, and in a similar manner, she could easily switch from being outgoing, involved, and social, to being the silent type. Ruby's adaptability made her highly skilled at bending truths and soothing the windswept feathers of others when situations, or people, went awry. She was a fiercely adaptable person. She knew exactly when to defend and when to embrace, and she was a pro at combining patience with intuition. She could read people without them uttering a word. She did realize that having a chameleon character also made her susceptible to the energy and the behaviours of others. Nonetheless, this was a trait she'd frequently use to her advantage. She didn't do this in a manipulative way, but rather, in an adaptable way. She knew a 'great bluffer and bull-shitter' when she saw one. Of course, having the phenomenal storyteller, Horace McEwen, as her father, played a role in her refined ability to distinguish between fabrication and truth. Horace had taught her to twist the truth just enough, and to her advantage, without being altogether dishonest. The only real disadvantage to having the character of the chameleon was that she tended to focus too much on the past, particularly when her thoughts drifted or her mind travelled. This was a tendency she was aware of and even more so wary of. The older she got the more she wished that almost everything in life didn't have to be past tense.

Sitting behind the Italian cabbie, with her eyes still closed, she reminded herself of her ability to steer and control her mind.

Throughout her lifetime, she'd often wondered where this skill came from. Whenever she drifted into a mental void or an abyss, she'd transmute into a person she referred to as her *clandestine self*. A covert type of person whom she concealed from others in an effort to protect the secrets that made her who she was. As wee lassie, she'd learned to mentally travel in and out of the past while simultaneously guiding her mind and its flow of energy. This was something very powerful, especially for a growing and persuasive child. By the time she was ten or eleven years old, she'd nearly mastered her intimate brain control skill. Her ability to steer her brain became a mental device that she referred to as an 'abstract brain switch'. It was a switch only she controlled and only she could turn off and on at will. Something she'd endlessly done throughout the past eight decades.

Cocooned in the stillness that still filled the taxicab, she was reminded of how clever and practiced she was at paranormally drifting. Guiding her mind is what made her unique. Her ability to steer and control her awareness connected her to the people and events that came before her. She had a strong inclination and hoped beyond hope that Jazz possessed similar abilities. Until now, her optimisms for this were not much more than wishful inklings. More time was needed before the similarities they shared could surface. If Ruby was fortunate enough, she'd still be alive when they did. Despite her endless hopes, she knew that she needed to get her grizzled head out of the past and focus on the future. She anticipated that she and Jazz were on the cusp of one of those rare times; a time when, simultaneously, the future was demanding her attention and her intuition was strongly advising her *not to ignore what was coming*.

Straightforwardly, the only future that interested Ruby right now was the most immediate one, which was tonight's preparation for the Durant family's arrival tomorrow evening. It was a preparation that she'd set in motion about fifteen minutes ago after deciding to return early to Saint Matthew's Hospital. Taking a notepad and pen out of her handbag, she began to write her strategies down. On the top of the list of things she'd need to do, was asking her great grandson, Thatcher, to venture out and buy her a prepaid mobile phone. This would give her an opportunity to see how proficient the young man was. She quite anticipated that he was a tolerant chap with a far-reaching understanding of people. She'd need him be able to follow directions without her having to repeat them back to him. Otherwise he'd feel the fury of a mentally intact, old British woman, who detested reiteration. Thatcher would learn soon enough that she considered repetitious behaviour a proper waste of time, breath, and energy. Likewise, that she was extremely and rightly inflexible in this way.

Once she was back at the ICU, she'd have a meal followed by a warm shower. The turmoil of the past few days had attached itself to her flabby armpits and the undersides of her sagging, yet still abnormally full breasts. Support bra or not, a limp and wilting bosom was a definite female haven for perspiration and body odours. Once she'd cleansed herself, she planned to retire early after chatting it up a bit with the child and reading an entry or two from one of Minnie or Bessie's journals. Ruby was very aware of the child's mum's emotional instabilities. Moreover, she was, in her opinion, too befittingly acquainted and knowledgeable with aspects of her granddaughter weaker sides. Ruby's five-year long history with her daughter Eliza's own Borderline Personality Disorder in the 1970s, in addition to a lifetime filled with her own mother Sadie's imbalances and phobia's, had made her, again in her opinion, something of a mental illness expert.

"We have arrived madam," her Italian cabdriver unexpectedly, yet graciously said. Little did the man realize, he'd interrupted her flow of thoughts at the perfect time? Like an act of wizardry, Sadie and Eliza both disappeared from her mind.

Thank you Renzo! She thought but didn't say.

"Did you enjoy your ride, Vivian?" he timidly asked her while he checked the meter's total.

Still being in a rightfully jovial mood, the chameleon residing in her easily remained in its role as an agreeable, alive, and empirical version of a human British antique. Ruby answered by showing a touch of spirited gratitude to the man in the front seat.

"Grazie kind sir, for the glorious smell you left behind for me in your taxicab while I was inside the apartment building," she vivaciously said.

The humiliated and guilty as sin expressions on Renzo's face she saw from his rearview was a pure and priceless kind of payback. She'd hoped to get a surprised reaction out of him, and she did. She went on to tell the cabbie that one of her favourite smells was the smell of an imported cigar. That the cigar he'd smoked smelled like a freshly sown field. She blabbed on and on about his prank. As his baffled look intensified, she exaggeratedly carried on like a Cuban cigar connoisseur.

"The aroma reminds me of rich and spicy soil after a squall has drenched the earth in rain. A cigar smells like a pasture under the noonday sun and like a barn loft that's filled with bails of dry, meadow-fresh hay," she badgered.

Still eyeing Renzo from the back seat, she was thoroughly delighting in picking on this Italian man, whom she'd rightly taken quite an unexplainable fancy to since he'd fetched her from Precinct 616. What she was doing was obvious, yet he didn't have a clue that his unpredictable customer was, in effect, just teasing him.

"Men can be so daft," she said a titch too loudly.

"What did you say?"

"Nothing important kind sir," the cordial chameleon in the back seat replied.

Without missing a verbal beat, she went on to tell him that her grandfather was an avid cigar smoker. That even today, after she got a good strong whiff of a cigar, it was as if she was, in a wonderfully pungent and smelly way, returning to her childhood. When he opened her door and offered her his supportive hand, she was still thanking him profusely for the smell of Cuba, his services, and her memories. She was enjoying herself so much, she hadn't noticed that they'd already arrived at the hospital's main entrance and that he'd parked his cab.

He knew he'd been cheated out of a prank by this very cheeky customer, so he surrendered to her by sombrely saying, "Grazie my dear Vivian."

Forgetting that she'd told him her name was Vivian, she snorted out another one of her reputed unexpected hoots of laughter.

"What is so funny my lady?" he charmingly asked.

Although she'd earlier, without a doubt wounded his ego, knowing that he was now being consciously considerate and polite was enough to put an end to his self-inflicted humiliation for the sake of her getting even. After all, tit for tat wasn't really her style.

"Nothing kind sir," was her artificially charming reply.

Renzo then helped the long legged yet frail Vivian hoist herself out of the backseat. He then steadied her feet securely on the pavement in front of Saint Matthew's Hospital. He could see that she was in pain, worn out and struggling. For these reasons, he insisted that she allow him to escort her to the final step of her destination. He would NOT take no for an answer. Being too tired for a debate and knowing that characteristically Italians were even more stubborn than Brits were, she surrendered and accepted his offer. His cab was parked in the same fogged in location where Deniz had also parked his taxi the night before. Ruby felt an incoming 'Deja vu' moment as she watched him locking his cab's doors and setting the car alarm with his digital key. Renzo held out his arm in the same way the classy and chivalrous Deniz had done the night before.

Her driver then said, using an intentionally hefty Italian accent, "At your service signora."

Treating her like a well-deserving sophisticated woman, he escorted her to her final destination. They half walked and half hobbled, arm in arm, the entire way. Then they rode the elevator together and exited after it had reached the top floor. When the cabbie pushed elevator button number seven, he noticed the engraved metallic ICU sign next to it. This undoubtedly told him where her last stop of the day was. Because of this, he was thankful to himself for deciding not to yammer or blab nonstop during her return trip from Little Italy. His curious mind questioned what she was doing at the intensive care unit of one of Britain's finest medical facilities. Most people her age were already living in a retirement home or an assisted care facility. Many more of them had long since passed away. Renzo was starting to believe that perhaps his most elderly customer to date had needed and rightly deserved the sound of silence. He now regretted not showing her more respect and using better manners with her than he had. As he accompanied her to the end of the line of her day, he was still deeply ashamed that he and his cigar had selfishly and thoughtlessly bullied a woman, who he now rightly hoped, would one day live long enough to become one of the United Kingdom's centenarians.

Standing in front of the nurse's station, the old lady turned and asked the cabdriver, "How much fare do I owe you sir?"

In reply, he put a soft, courteous kiss on top of her thin-skinned, vein-lined hand and replied, "Non mi Devi niente Signora. You own me nothing madam."

Before she could react, he revealed a glimmer of victory by saying, "Ciao Bella Madame Ruby."

The stunned look on her age splotched face was reward enough for his being forced to tolerate her quirkiness, sharp-tongue, and mood swings in the past ninety minutes. The now elated cabbie knew he'd gotten the last word in. He was thrilled. Before she could reply with even a simple thank you, he had turned around and was walking back down the long corridor towards the elevator. The last thing she noticed about was his expensive Italian designer shoes.

The plump, talkative, and irresistibly charming cabdriver didn't need money or appreciation from her. Despite that she'd faked her identity and relished in the smell of Cuba, just knowing that the long-distance threat of his Italian mamma's disappointment in him wasn't hanging over his head anymore was worth his pro bono gesture.

Chapter 72

An elderly woman with tinted skin the shade of raw hazelnuts crawled into a spare bed that had been properly made up for her in the child's ICU room. Her snow-white hair was still damp and she smelled like a hint of lilac shower gel as she felt the mattress caress her long, drowsy body. Less than an hour ago, after entering Jazz's ICU room, she'd smoothly left her need to be Vivian behind, on the other side of the door. Ruby McEwen was back.

The spare bed, which she looked more than forward to sleeping in, was the electrically adjustable type. She'd contemplated for years about buying herself an electric bed, but never had done so. After playing with it like a little girl would, she raised the single-sized bed into a comfortable position and let out a deep, relieving sigh. Once her aching legs and lower back were elevated to the right angle, she felt weightless and pain free. Ruby was rather grateful that the last part of her eventful day had been spent with more Italian people. Given the events of the past ten days, the Italians she'd crossed paths recently, including Deniz with a Z, had made her feel young and alive again; the way she used to feel whenever she visited Zofia and Tucker Durant's American brood years ago.

"That was then, this is now," she heard herself saying as she reached for the duvet that covered her bed.

Her body was screaming out at her because she'd overused and abused all of its limbs today on the streets of London. She tended to overstep 'age-appropriate boundaries' whenever her mind tricked her into believing she was much younger than she was. Every time this happened, her body, consumed with pain, cried out and reminded her of how hard it had worked for her over the past nearly ninety years. Lately, this type of painful retaliation had been happening almost daily, which she silently loathed, tried to ignore, yet couldn't avoid. She never was one to offer her pain or challenges up to a God, or the good of a greater purpose. She was more the type to solve problems and ignore trials and tribulations. Or, to pretend and then push herself past whatever stood in her way, even if it was no one, or nothing, other than herself. When none of these methods worked, she'd mumble, grumble, and gripe, before swearing and using vulgarity to rid herself of inconveniences and annoyances.

Ruby sincerely couldn't remember the last time she was so eager to pull the bedcovers up under her neck, unwind, and read. She'd asked an orderly, who came into the room to clear her dinner tray, if he'd push her bed closer to the child's bed, which he naturally did. She wanted to sleep as close to Jazz tonight as she could. This would be their last night alone together and the last opportunity she'd have to help prepare the child for a journey the old woman knew Jazz needed to take. It was a journey, Ruby was convinced, could and would, eventually return her only great granddaughter to a conscious life among the living.

Tonight, she'd be taking Jazz backwards, to the beginning of each of their Ballinger Dutton-McEwen ancestries. As far back as the contents of an antique wooden trunk with its decorative handles and a bronze-hinged lock would enable them to roam. She believed that once the child went where she needed to go, and she'd learned from who and what came before her, returning to her current life would be something only Jazz could do. The experienced and wise mental drifter, abounding in conviction and intuition, nestled under a warm hospital blanket, believed this to be true. For this reason, the wooden trunk had crept into in her mind again. She glanced across the room at the closet where she'd stored it and smirked. The elderly woman felt relieved and safe, knowing that her vintage trunk, filled with a historical past, was so nearby. In that moment, she recognized that she was more connected to the trunk and its contents, since they'd been passed onto to her back in 1936, than she'd realized.

With this comforting recognition, she looked over at Jazz. Despite her current medical condition, Ruby had strong and innate predictions about her great granddaughter's future. The first prediction was that in order for her to regain consciousness and find her way back, the child needed use her unconscious mind to travel backwards. Then, she would need to encounter and connect with the ancestors and events of previous family generations that had come and gone before both of them. Ruby's second prediction was that the child's journey would become a rebirth of the past and an intertwining saga, to and through, their deceased kinfolks wounded minds and searching souls. Jazz would need to live through, and survive, a few generations of life that had preceded her. She also wondered how much of the past the child would recollect after she left her coma and began living consciously again in the here and now. Despite an expected degree of memory loss, Jazz's neurologist, Dr. Zamier, anticipated, Ruby was certain that what the teenager was now experiencing, and what she'd yet to encounter, would change her; as it challenged her stamina, offered her new choices, enlightened her fledging mind, and guided her back to a conscious life. The old woman suddenly realized that she'd begun staring intently at the child lying in the bed, now so very close to her. She wasn't scrutinizing her great granddaughter, she was compassionately observing the patient's young, petite, and wounded body. It was so bruised and broken. Then, she noticed that her respiration was much shallower than it had been when she'd last seen her. Despite that she knew this was a normal reaction to an induced coma, it was a trifle frightening.

Despite her incorrigible religious doubts Ruby instinctively pleaded, "Dear Lord, help her."

In the juncture of time, between when she'd left the ICU earlier and when she'd returned, the puffiness around the child's eyes had noticeably decreased. Even with their bruised discolouration, she could see the lass's long, dark eyelashes again. Inspecting her further, she saw that the patch of purple hair, which had been shaven off to create a sterile space for the cranial drainage tubes, had already begun to grow back in. Her fast hair growth was something Ruby's attributed to the vitamin and nutrient rich IV fluids she was being fed round the clock. As she'd anticipated, the colour of the child's hair was indeed auburn. The very same chestnut colour as her own hair used to be, before old age had turned it into the pure white colour it now was. As peculiar as it seemed, for the first time, she noticed that Jazz also had the same full, burgundy-coloured lips as she did. She wondered why she hadn't seen this before now. She secretly hoped that after the child woke up, she'd let her hair's natural colour grow out again. For as much as she cared about her, the teenager's purple hair dye, piercings, and punkish attitude were nothing more than bloody dreadful! Ruby knew that she herself was known for being someone with her own distinct style. Despite that she was from a very different, less outwardly expressive generation, she had easily accepted Jazz's peculiar flamboyance.

She was astute enough to know that her outlandish and scandalous appearances were all calculated and precisely her intention. Given the state of Zofia and Tucker's relationship, Ruby was cocksure, that Jazz was attempting to shock both of them into paying more attention to the serious mess they'd both made of their daughter's life, and less attention to the mess they'd made of their own lives. Tomorrow evening, her parents would be arriving at Saint Matthew's Hospital. When they did, they would need to make the dire situation solely about their daughter and not about what they feel when they see the terrible physical state she's in. Ruby was committed to making sure that this happened. It was the least she could do for Jazz, given what she was going through. Not to mention an unpredictable amount of *the unknown* that still lay ahead.

The very elderly granny, patting the coma patient's hand, wisely whispered, "Time will tell love, it always does."

There they both were. Two women separated by three generations, seventy years of age, and ten centimetres of space between their matrasses. Ruby reached over, just as she had done the day of the accident, and gently laid the palm of her time lined hand over Jazz's hand. The stiff, plastic intravenous tubes she felt reminded her that because of the modern-day digitized medical practices, Jazz's body was being nourished and kept alive. Despite her old age and the deplorable circumstances, her awareness and astuteness was still strong. For the third time since the accident, Ruby felt the warmth of their female energies exchanging.

"Can you feel it?" she whispered to the child.

The old woman knew that skin on skin contact was vital for physical, emotional, and mental health, because it joined one person's vitality to the other. However, she was realistic enough to know that a genuine bonding with Jazz, if it ever occurred, would take more time, and definitely much more than skin on skin contact. Nevertheless, in this moment, whether the accident victim was aware of it or not, a seasoned British woman was passing the difference between knowledge and wisdom onto a young American woman fighting for her life. Similar to the afternoon of the boat crash, the patient lying in the ICU bed still appeared to be in a peaceful sleep. Likewise, the various life support apparatuses surrounding her bed continued to emit their continuous humming, peeping, and droning sounds. Crisscrossing over her bantam body was network of different tubes. Because she was still unable to breathe on her own, a larger tracheal tube had been inserted into her mouth. It went down her oesophagus and into her now 'machine pumped' lungs. The six-centimetre deep laceration in her skull that had been stitched up was still uncovered. Although Ruby was curious as to why it had not yet been bandaged, she could see that the sutures were healing beautifully.

Must be the sterile air in the room, she thought.

The hole in Jazz's pierced nose, where the silver stud had once been, was a bit of an eyesore the elderly woman. After seeing so many bullet and M2 grenade holes in the mutilated bodies of wounded WWII soldiers, Ruby never understood why young people these days insisted on intentionally putting holes in their flawless bodies. Seeing the tiny, yet obvious hole in the child's nostril, reminded her to ask Olivia Davies, the child's staunch night nurse, where Jazz's silver nose stud was? She still intended to polish it up and keep it in a safe until the patient woke up, or the hole in her nose closed first.

Preferably the latter, she hoped.

"I wonder if Olivia is working tonight," Ruby asked Jazz out loud.

The whiteness of the plaster casts on the child's arm and leg, her sterile pillow and the hygienic bed linens, were continuously aglow because of the blueish radiance the digital lights emitted. Even though the sheen of the lights were still making Jazz appear to be angelic, as Ruby knew, beyond the shadow of any holy doubt, that there was a devious, dinky insurgent inside her motionless, ICU roommate for the night. She could already see, by the physical changes in one short day, that the child's damaged body was working very hard to heal. She hoped that Jazz's mind was also fighting hard to return from wherever it was. Throughout her diverse lifetime, the astute woman, touching the wounded patient, had been a spectator to how violence and tenderness, piety, and even crime, could unite the most terrified tangles of a person's crippled emotions.

Ruby McEwen wasn't conceited. Not by a long shot. She was a realist. Nothing more and nothing less. She hoped beyond hope that Tucker and Zofia would have just one single smidgeon of her strength, beliefs, and insight.

"Lord knows they're going to need it. What if Jazz chooses not to return to her life?" she asked herself, as she released the child's hand and began rubbing her own aching hands together.

She then leaned back against the head of her bed and continued to observe the puny, purple haired nonconformist lying in the bed next to her. An unexpected wave of compassion washed over her. It wasn't compassion for the child, but for the family who would be arriving in less than 24 hours. She knew that when they saw Jazz in the condition she was in, it would be rightly shocking for them. She also knew that their reactions would be even more appalling than the obviously radical style and methods of self-expression their daughter and Thatcher's only sister had chosen. Ruby had already accepted that the Durant's reactions, no matter what they were, would be raw and completely justified. Likewise, she anticipated, when Zofia and Tucker first laid eyes on the injured, coma patient, they'd project their fears and anger onto the person who'd been responsible for Jazz's well-being. Despite, that blaming someone else for what was wrong, was a normal human reaction during times of calamity, in this particular case, it would be extremely unfair.

Shifting about to find a more comfortable position in the bed, she took comfort in this credence. In the long run, what other comfort did she have to get her through the night? Even at her age, she was a resilient person with an overabundance amount of hellfire coursing through her veins. It was the pure fire and brimstone in her that enabled her to believe that she could handle anything that happened tomorrow. *Besides, old girl*, she reminded herself with a cheeky smile, *you have a plan for the Americans stranded in Amsterdam.*

Ruby then inwardly reiterated her nimble plan for the child's family, which actually was more of a scheme. She would do her best to politely instruct Zofia and Tucker to take turns in the room, reading to their daughter from the journals she'd select for them. While they were unaccompanied in Jazz's room, for obvious reasons, she would keep the journals locked inside the trunk. Zofia and Tucker, even Thatcher, would have to obey the twenty-minute visitation rule Dr. Zamier had ordered. The 'one person in the room at a time' part of the neurologist's visitation restriction would keep them all separated, which in turn, would keep the patient's room relatively stress-free and quiet. With the two of them taking turns by their daughter's bedside during the day, she planned to take Thatcher under her wing and pick his legal brain to see if he could, according to British law and immigration regulations, help her to help Nico. Tomorrow, she'd know more about what this entailed after she visited Nico in his jail cell and Griffin at his home. She was very much looking forward to brunch with the O'Bannon's.

Given that Ruby had seen such intimate and idyllic collaged photos of Thatcher and his sister on the bedroom wall yesterday at The Seaside, she surmised that the siblings shared a unique connection. She needed this to be 'an indisputable bond' that would have a brother doing anything he could for his sister, and likewise for Nico Rossario; their direct source and eyewitness evidence to the boating accident. By 7pm each night when visitation hours ended, the Durant's would have no choice but to troll the vibrant and culture rich the city of London or return to their hotel. Afterwards, she would resume her own nightly ritual of caring for the child and guiding her back to life again.

In that moment of deftness, the lilac smelling elderly woman, wearing a flowered flannel nightgown, made a definitive and reassuring decision. She would not be sleeping in her own bed again until Jazz left her coma, opened her eyes, and recognized her.

Chapter 73

Ruby strongly believed that once Jazz earned the right, history and fate would enable her to exist between life and death long enough to walk the paths of five generations that had lived and died before her time. With each step she took, alongside her courageous, amusing, tenacious, and wise ancestors, she'd learn about men, relationships, choice, survival, and life. A life linked to theirs and one not so unlike her own.

Despite her instinctiveness, the old British native was wise enough to know that while the child was on her journey, the threat of drawbacks was very real. By the same token, the snags Jazz would encounter were necessary parts of the subconscious trip she'd begun taking the second her brain and body were enfeebled. She knew, from first-hand experience, that a worthwhile passage between 'what was and what is' had dangers attached to it. For this reason, hazards, in her experience, were always unavoidable when rewards were involved. Ruby McEwen adored predictions. Her predictions were made up of signs, theories, intuition, and premonitions of what she expected would happen in the future. It didn't matter if the future was one minute, one year, or even one hundred years away. Her intuitions about time and life were typically based on facts and evidence laden with philosophies and scandal. Her instincts were never based on rumour, guesstimations, heresies, or gossip. They hinged on eyewitness accounts, experiences, and facts. Either way, in this very moment, in a fifty-fifty way, she was being inspired and persuaded by her most recent prediction.

Wherever Jazz's journey took her, no matter how far into the past she went, or how long she stayed, in due course she would step onto a different path and follow it towards another destination. Whether that destination was home or not, only the unconscious, nomadic traveling teenager would know. Then, a turning point would arrive and the petite troublemaker with a half shaven head, would need to choose which path she'd walk upon. Ruby trusted that once the journey began, her ancestors would cross her path and lead the way. Ultimately, this would be Jazz's own version of 'a saving grace'.

Despite the imperative circumstances and the crucial nature of the situation, after nearly nine decades of life, what the future held didn't interest her. Tonight, she would begin to guide the patient, confined in a coma towards her historical and ancestral past. Ruby would take her as far back as the contents of the ornate wooden trunk enabled her to, and do so for as long as she could stay awake. It had been an intense few days. When days like these were layered with chaos, she tended to unintentionally ignore her age. Despite that she was now feeling slightly weak and fragile, she was more than eager to take the child back to the early 1800s folktale and a now ancient tree.

Back then, as a five year old, although she could barely grasp the concept behind the legend, she didn't dismiss or forget the tree. *Probably*, she thought, *because I was born under a tree*. Recently, she'd come to learn that her lineage was directly connected to the events of two young black-skinned sisters who were kidnapped in 1860 by commissioned slave traders. Those two little, abducted African girls, who'd been flung onto a filthy slave ship and then hidden under the deck, in the ship's deep and dark belly. Alongside hundreds more illegally seized Africans, they were exported as tellurian captives to a foreign land. The African sisters, then only three and seven years old, had been stolen from their family, were never returned, and over time presumed dead by those who had vainly searched for them. The old woman knew that this was where her bloodline began and Jazz's bloodline continued.

Ruby's life was the sum of her choices, driblets of pure luck, her hard-earned achievements, and numerous rightly deserved failures. She'd done her best to shelter, encourage, evade, and rescue the lives of those in need. Those whose lives intersected with her own life. She sincerely had given life her very all, despite that life had a habit of handing it all back to her, time and time again, in unfair and perplexing ways. Truth being told, regardless of her reputation, wisdom, determination, and vast amount of proficiency, she didn't always get it right. She'd made an endless number of mistakes and been devilishly robbed of righteousness by people and circumstances over the course of her lifetime. From Hitler, who destroyed her motherland and stole her adolescence, to Peg a leg Pete, the Greek cook who'd destroyed her trust and stole her money.

Nevertheless, when she did get it right, she got it exactly right. Fortunately for the very elderly, very wacked, and very reputable owner of The Seaside, since the day the child arrived from America smelling like booze and looking like crime, she'd been getting it more right than wrong.

She planned to stay awake long enough tonight to read to the patient from one of her African slave relative's earliest journals. Her intention was to remind Jazz of how Minnie had sheltered her younger sister, Bessie, with her own life. The child would come to learn more about the elderly woman and the part she played in becoming the caretaker of an antique, wooden trunk, with forged iron handles, a decorative bevelled cover, and a shiny burnished lock. The memoirs in the trunk would teach the child how her once 11-year-old great grandmother had been cast into a lifelong role as the Keeper of the Past.

Ruby's impatient insights and intuitions were now demanding her attention and speaking to her. They were basically telling her that the patient needed to travel into the past and search for a way back. She believed, beyond the shadow of a single doubt, that Jazz needed to go backwards before she could go forwards again. She rightly suspected that her great granddaughter's solo journey had already begun. Only fate and Jazz could decide which choices she'd make, and which routes she'd take. In addition, while in the historical bygone, her existence would become the essence of a clock rotating in a counter clockwise direction. First, the child would need to travel in reverse, before she could turn herself around, and go clockwise again, in the direction of her future. Wherever and whatever her future was? With this being determined, for the third time within one day, Ruby made the wise choice to *start at the very beginning*.

About ten minutes ago, after showering, she'd taken three journals out of the brass-studded trunk. They were waiting for her on the nightstand next to her bed. Her fantasy rich, forever searching mind, wondered if the antedated journals had been preserved precisely for this moment in time. The remarkably wise, arthritis ridden woman was in good spirits, relaxed, and feeling properly satisfied with herself. Her shower had cleansed her and rinsed the events of the day off her mind. Events that began with waking up in the ICU next to the child and later discovering Starbucks one floor up, where she deviously played the 'geriatric card' to get her way, enjoy a free breakfast and a delicious coffee macchiato topped with a sweet, creamy froth. Not to mention events that took her mind back in time and dragged her thoughts through her tumultuous past; a past filled with everything from two world wars to a deadly smog. From fresh squeezed lemonade, to Winston Churchill. From meeting Grady Walsh, to giving into her sexual attraction for another woman. She'd listened to the advice that the child's neurologist, Dr. Zamier, had given her and taken time for herself and her personal affairs throughout the day. Today, similar to yesterday, had been an eye-opening and momentous twelve hours. A half a day filled with episodes of mind travel and drifting, which brought her new encounters and old recollections; such as her being directly related to a viciously, notorious bootlegger and rum-running man named Ezra.

Now that her hectic day was winding down, she was impressed with herself for almost staying out of trouble and returning early to the hospital at a decent hour. She planned on a full night's sleep, which her body now demanded. If she hadn't listened to Dr. Zamier, and taken care of a few private matters, she wouldn't have ventured out into the fog, met Deniz the cabbie, found Nico, and then located his uncle, Giovanni Rossario, living in the heart of London's Little Italy District. Nor would she have met Griffin O'Bannon, the adult son of Otis O'Bannon, a Vietnam War farce turned hero, whom she'd befriended in the 1960s. Thanks to Griffin, today Ruby had spoken freely about her daughter Eliza for the first time in decades. She was not a hard-hearted mother of a daughter who had committed suicide. Not in the least. She simply had a pure knack and suitably inbred ability to let bygones be bygones. For as long as she could recall, she'd been putting the past behind her and carrying on with living life in the moment. The events, during and after World War II, had engrained this mindset on her. It was a mindset that had remained consistent, despite how the world around her changed.

Truthfully, although she passionately adored the past and mentally drifted in and out of it while learning from it, she did not exist in it. She existed in the midst of the here and now, and she journeyed through life alongside the rhythm of her impulses and beating heart. Griffin O'Bannon and Ruby McEwen's fog-filled and unpredicted encounter with each other at Precinct 616, was one of the purest forms of destiny she'd ever experienced. She was eager and anxious to meet his family tomorrow for brunch, and then, together with him, take a few steps backwards, while they entered her daughter Eliza's short and tumultuous life. However, tonight, another daughter from another time needed her. In this moment, Zofia and Tucker Durant's daughter, lying in her ICU bed, needed Ruby more than Ruby's deceased daughter, lying in her grave needed her. When it came to her dead daughter, she was deservingly blameworthy and unemotional. She had buried the perplexity and lies surrounding Eliza's suicide in her coffin, together with her corpse.

Despite the decisions that tragedy had forced her to make between 1969 and 1975, she'd never felt remorseful about what she'd done. Or not done for that matter. Even meeting Otis's son today hadn't challenged her convictions. She didn't believe in do-overs, consequently her mind was only ever so often clogged with doubt or hearsay. She'd done what she needed to do at the time, given the seriousness of the predicament and the unforeseeable, ruinous circumstances that prevented her from mourning her dead daughter. In light of it all, back then, it was nothing more than *a sign of the times*. Besides, even forty-five years later, she rightly knew that what Eliza left behind had taken up all of her time and energy. For the better part of sixteen years following her daughter's suicide, beyond earning a dependable living, she had absolutely nothing left to give. At the time, Ruby McEwen's life was claimed by something much more important than The Seaside or she was.

"Focus old woman!" she heard herself again strictly demand.

She truly had become an expert at reeling herself in whenever her mind wandered too far off. Otis's son Griffin deserved to have his questions answered while she was still alive to answer them. As far as she knew, no one else could tell the man as much as she could about his father's time in England. Ruby had outlived every immediate O'Bannon family member, from the 1940s, who'd once known Otis. Therefore, she felt obligated to his only son. Regardless, it was an obligation that would have to wait until tomorrow to receive any more of her attention. With ease, she readily dismissed thoughts of her deceased daughter, and Eliza's draft dodger heartthrob saga, by switching gears in the quick and masterful way she had been switching gears her entire life. It was time to wrap this day up and leave a bit of herself behind.

"If not now, then when?" she bravely reminded herself of, with an unyielding and unflustered voice.

Then the elderly, white-haired woman snuggled deeper into her mattress and pulled the covers up high around her neck and under her chin. She was ready to begin a conversation with Jazz, who was now less than an arm's length away from her.

"You see child, people habitually bury their problems and their history. After they do this, ninety percent of the time an unanticipated need starts to boil in their gut. It's a simmering kind of need that often confuses their troubled minds. As a result, they start to search for answers to the questions they'd buried alongside their past. When this happens, if they want to learn more about their identities and their legacies, they have to start digging up their yesteryears and then take a hard, analysing look at them. If they aren't diggers, they need to be listeners. The past has a voice all its own. If people

438

would just turn their busy brains off long enough to listen, they'd learn a more than imaginable from what is out of sight, but not out of mind."

The rhythmic sounds of the life support machines accented the message Ruby was attempting to convey to the patient. With a dignified and conclusive tone, she continued to talk with the tenacious teen by using a bit more verbal conviction this time. Out of respect for her surroundings, she'd raise her voice slightly without yelling.

"Listen to me child. I know you are in there and can hear me."

She then reached over and laid her cold, crooked hand on the child's blanket covered thigh.

"You are buried inside and under a type of oblivion. I suspect that your coma has you trapped in a part of your own history and in a place that you have never been to before. It may feel like a type of virtual reality has disconnected you from others, and the parts of your life that are actually nothing more than fragments and wreckage. Don't be afraid. Every life, even mine, is filled with a certain amount of fragment and wreckage. When you enter the remains of a time that 'once was' it will feel like a thousand puzzle pieces are raining down from the sky and landing on top of you."

She began tapping on the child's thigh, keeping rhythm with the pulsing sounds of the machines keeping her great granddaughter alive.

"Listen carefully to me girl. It's crucial that you hear my words. Connect to the world you are now in, put the puzzle pieces together and follow the sound of my voice!" She sternly instructed, "Never lose track of the sound of my voice!"

Then she sagely declared, "You have embarked upon a prodigious voyage that very few people embark upon. From this moment on, I will only call you by your name, because you have earned your name. I will call you Jazz."

Ruby swiped at a tear before it rolled off her cheek.

"As it happens to be, your name means Voyager. You are now a brave and fearless voyager. You, Jazz Durant, despite our tense and turbulent reunion, have earned my respect."

The elderly woman gave her great granddaughter's thigh one final, somewhat hard, salute-like, farewell tap.

"Safe travels my devious little American doppelgänger. Dig up your history until you have no dig left in you. I'll be here when this part of your journey ends."

Cheekily she added a hint of humour to the seriousness, by saying, "Don't take too long love. I have too many bloody years behind me and not enough goddamn years ahead of me. I want to still be alive when you return. We have a mountain of things to talk about." Even at her ripe, old age, she still swore like a sailor.

With that being said and done, the oldest female in Jazz Durant's life wiped three more tears off her cheeks before they were able to roll off her chin, fall into her cleavage, and tickle her bosom. Ruby hardly ever cried. She wasn't an insensitive or compassionless person, she merely processed emotions differently than others did. Since she was a young girl, to avoid dilemmas and maintain her dignity, she'd weep on the inside, where her tears couldn't draw attention to her emotions. Hidden tears never betrayed her privacy. As a sign that she had switched gears again, she adjusted her spectacles, tucked the keys that hung from her neck in between her sagging breasts, and reached over to the nightstand where two journals waited for her. She was antsy to begin reading to Jazz again. Randomly, she picked one of the chronicled diaries up, then carefully untied a thin, faded, pea green hair ribbon from around the threadbare, water stained journal. With ten cautious, crooked, quivering fingers, she opened the brittle cover and looked at the first page.

The page broke free from its dried-out binding and fell into her hands like it an airborne, time traveling feather. Apparently, the 1800s desired some overdue attention.

Chapter 74

I think my little sister Bessie and I we be now slaves livin' in New Orleans for six months long. Maybe longer. Time is hard to keep up with in a hell like this place be. I will be writing about it all like my memory tells me to. I hope my mind says it right and I don't be choking on tears. These have been real hard times with what we went through. We are learnin' that it be not so bad cuz' we are together.

The big ship we came on made me all skin and bones. We got sick lots and puked 'til our guts slid off our tongues. Then we walked on land. We was sold to a big and tall man who dressed fancy like. We was told to call him our master. Not our mister but our master. Other slaves tell us this be important. Bessie was too little to be saying many words so I was saying things for her when I could. Master he likes Bessie cuz she got light skin and is sweet looking. I got dark skin and be not so pretty a girl as my little sister be. She made a big fuss when we was sold. She held me tight like I was her mammy and bawled and bawled. The man who buys us hated crying children. This be why Bessie and I be still sleeping together in this here small cabin. If our master or mistress takes Bessie from me then she cries and cries. The ship we was on for a long spell of time stopped in a big harbor. A man on that ship says then that we was in a place called New Orleans. It be nothing like Africa. I miss Africa. We were on the water a long time. Some slaves say it was near 50 days. I still am not so sure.

Bessie and I are in a land called America. Slavery is a great big oozing wound here. Like the cuts under my feet that hurt and bleed every day and night. Slavery is horrible and ugly. It hurts all the niggers I know. A slave girl name of Cecilia is teaching me not to say nigger no more. She says slaves be hating this word cuz it has no high opinion to it. Cecilia says the white folks be using this word cuz they own us. Niggers don't own niggers. They are equal so they call each other Negro or by their birth name or by their slave given name. Cecilia gave me this here book and a pencil so I can practice my writing and tell my story.

I am a learning more every day the sun be coming up in here in America. I am trying to write and read better. Little Bessie is starting to talk more now so I will be teaching her the right words just like Cecilia, she helps me. I still got lots to learn. Bessie she be now sleeping while I am writing in this book. Bessie is still sucking on her thumb just like a new baby sucks for milk. When I pull it out of her mouth it makes a popping sound. Her popping thumb makes me laugh. She puts it back in again like a she be a sucking on mama's titty. I think this be a sign Bessie she be missing our mammy Abada. Maybe more than I miss her. When her eyes are shut, my little sister she be scared all the time. She is making little friends and plays now more. She grew bigger and I still am not a woman yet. When I do became a woman, I will be more fearing of men wanting to do the dirty deed to me, so I keep my eyes open all the time. I have big eyes that see everything in the light and in the dark.

I cut the tips off Bessie her shoes. I made holes for her toes so they have room to keep growing. Then I polished them up real pretty with oil I found in a shed. Now they look all shined, even with holes in the tips. I made Bessie a doll from straw and wrapped cloth around it, so it looks like has a party dress on. I think every small girl needs a doll. I made Cecilia a heart pillow from cloth scraps my mistress threw away. I had to be careful not to be caught taking cloth from the garbage. Taking garbage from the big house is stealing and gets a slave child a bad beating. I wanted to thank Cecilia for teaching me writing so I picked like a hungry mouse in the garbage.

Tomorrow it be Christmas day. It is the day baby Jesus was born. It is the first Christmas for my sister and me since we got off that dirty ship. I am too excited for Christmas so I can't find me any sleep here in this cold and lonely one room cabin. This cabin be what Bessie and I call our sister house. I am now writing in this here journal book by the light of a candle. Since I was sold, I am learnin' to read and write better. I keep my learnin' a secret cause slaves with good smarts who speak with no stutters are hit with a bullwhip. Bullwhips are evil on this here plantation. Some slaves call them the devil's toy. When we first gots off that ship, I pleaded with God that Bessie be soon freed from

442

this hell even if she went away to be with the dead ones. I don't want my little sister dead, so I stopped pleading and praying months back.

~ Now that I can write better, I will tell my tales about being a slave girl. I love writing cuz it frees my sad soul and makes me a better kind of slave from Africa. Tonight I covered up a broken window. Cold wind was a blowing in our sister house. I used my blanket. I hope our master can't be seeing the light from my candle or I will get a whipping. I am so cold, but it matters not cuz in here we be safe from the whip and the wind. I rather be cold than gets me a beating the night before Christmas. Now I am tired. I think I will be sleeping with Bessie this night so I can keep her warm and safe like mama used to. I am blowing out my candle now. I do not want to be burnin this here cabin with me and Bessie and her new straw dolly down to the earth on the night before Jesus has his birthday.

~ It be now a bit later cuz' I can see the sun coming up. Today is gunna to be fun. I wonder what Negro slave people do with Christmas. I wonder what white people do with this holy day. I wonder what holy is.

~ Minnie ~

The elderly woman put the journal on her lap and removed her spectacles. She wasn't sure exactly when what she'd just read had been written, nonetheless, she was impressed with Minnie's aptitude and rapid learning abilities for such a young age. *Hmmm*, she thought, *she was most likely about seven or eight years old when she wrote this.* Within a year, after being sold into slavery, Minnie had learned to express herself almost fluently. Her writing was that of a child who hadn't learned cursive penmanship yet, despite this, she had a way natural with words. She wanted to pay homage to what she'd just read to Jazz. Minnie was from Africa and she was Ruby's great aunt. Minnie was her family and she knew practically nothing about her. Ruby didn't even know Minnie and Bessie's last name. What she did know was that Minnie was the person who had rescued and protected Bessie, her little sister and Ruby's grandmother.

"Why didn't my grandma ever speak about her sister when I visited the Dutton ranch in Montana?" She heard a whispering, childlike voice asking as she glanced up at Jazz.

If Bessie had ever talked about her life as a slave girl, Ruby couldn't recall her doing so. This made the old woman with a journal laying on her lap wonder what eventually happened to Minnie after the Emancipation Proclamation was signed. As a little girl and a student, she did remember a man named Mister Jackson who worked on the Dutton Ranch with her grandma. When Bessie died, Jackson told Ruby and her father Horace many riveting stories about the past. Nevertheless, whenever she visited her Montana ranch during school summer holidays, her grandma never mentioned slavery, the American Civil War, or even a dumb, smelly old donkey with the runs. With her mind moving onwards, she carried on with her one-sided conversation.

"That was a very long time ago. Even so, Jackson didn't say much either about being a Negro. I think slaves have been too damaged by life to talk about themselves with any kind of decency. I was probably blessed that I was too young to remember," she told Jazz with a pacifying tone.

Despite that she was unaware of it, talking as openly with Jazz as she was doing was giving Ruby a new sense of purpose.

Perhaps some memories are too agonizing to pass down to the next generation? I too have kept my share of pain filled memories and secrets for more than eighty years. She silently confessed.

She then reached inside her brassiere, pulled the red polka dotted handkerchief out, hastily leaned over her side of the bed and dabbed at the drool leaking from the side of Jazz's breathing tube. Then she realized, from a sterile standpoint, that she shouldn't have done this with a fifty-nine-year-old hankie; so she made a sanitized decision not to dab at the moisture around the patient's closed and lubricated eyes.

Remnants of Minnie and Bessie spun through her weary, yet intuitive mind. She was intrigued to read about how two of her earliest ancestor's had celebrated the holiday of Christmas. She was steadfast in her belief that globally, in these modern and commercially materialistic times, Christmas was being taken for granted. Despite the popular worldly belief that *Christmas is a time of love and happiness for everyone*, many countries have no understanding of this westernized Christian holiday.

Ruby was an opinionated and decisive old lady, so for this reason, her mind continued to explore, and it took her thoughts with it.

In her opinion, the extreme number of presents given, and money spent during this holiday was inconceivable for poverty-stricken areas of the world. Her slave sister relatives had both once been impoverished people. The holes in Bessie's polished shoes and the straw, hand-sewn doll she'd received from Minnie as a Christmas gift, reminded Ruby how the girls had come from less than nothing. Likewise, she believed that even slaves living within the scarcity of the bare necessities were not focusing on what they didn't have, they were grateful for what they did have. Because of this, Ruby viewed her African relatives as the epitome of the modern-day cliché, *less is more*. Recalling the past while coupling it with her intellect had always helped her feel closer to those who had lived and died before her. This included more people than she could count on both of her age-flecked hands and all of her hammer clawed toes. She questioned if *the fact that she'd outlived every relative born before her birth was a feat to be proud of, or a risky fact that could, in due course, lead to a lonely life?* For however much life she still had.

Unexpectedly, her nomadic mind decided that it desired wandering back to the 1940s and '50s. Because she was curious as to which facts and memories craved being conjured up, she let the probing nomad in her have its way.

The younger version of Ruby had studied slavery while attending school in Essex County. As an exchange student of journalism, she expanded her education in history at the University of Dublin. Journalism majors, like she was, who were studying towards a career in writing, reporting, commentary, or broadcasting, were required to know a substantial amount about the histories of different countries, eras, and ethnic groups. The Dean of Students, Mr. O'Sullivan, had seen potential in Ruby when she was just a freshman. He had considered her one of his most intelligent and dedicated pupils; therefore he'd pushed her slightly harder than he'd pushed other students. Dean O'Sullivan taught Ruby to *tap into her potential and to focus on who she was by distinguishing herself as an intelligent and promising young person, rather than overly concerning herself with what others thought she should be doing in life.* At the time, she wasn't aware that he was instilling such a convicting mindset in her, however in hindsight, the man deserved a lot of credit for the person she eventually became. Dean O'Sullivan had assisted her with flying to England in 1952 during the aftermath of the Great Smog, and he'd also taken her on her first ride in a German-made, Volkswagen Beetle. Likewise, he'd seen to it that as a shunned and unmarried, 4.0 GPA graduate, she received her diploma after giving birth to a baby girl. During these years, a time when her parents were out of her sight and even more out of her mind, the dean stimulated and challenged her to become an intellect and a gifted writer.

Thinking about him now made her realize that he was the reason why, as a young woman in the male world of journalistic publishing, she'd become so passionate about people, life, and the histories of both. It had been many decades since she'd researched or thought about what the holidays had been like for slaves living on American plantations. She was taken back at, how nowadays, current world events and the events of people's personal lives rapidly overshadowed and replaced the events that preceded them. Reminiscing about Minnie and Bessie had confirmed to her that she herself was no exception to this very common and rather ignorant behaviour. She realized that being the sole proprietor of a popular vintage diner, which served more than 150 people a day, caused her to *occasionally be in the wrong for not keeping the past alive.* She vowed to change this about herself by making a personal pact to carry on with mentally visiting what came before her. Then she'd talk about it and record her thoughts, apparitions, and memories in her journals while she was still alive to do so. In great part she was already doing this with Jazz. Tomorrow she would continue doing this with Griffin and Thatcher.

Since Jazz was admitted to the ICU, Ruby had read from a few different journals of Minnie's. The improvements in Minnie's spelling and grammar revealed to her just how much her slave relative's reading and writing skills had advanced over four short years. The quick advances the captive girl made back then were nothing shy of extraordinary. It was evident that between 1860 and 1868, Minnie's listening, and learning, had taken her ability to communicate to a much higher level. Spontaneously, she began to speak to Jazz again, telling her what she knew about their earliest ancestors.

"Minnie began writing about her life about six short months after she and her very young sister were abducted from their African village and transported, like livestock, on an overcrowded slave ship to a foreign country. The girls were sold into slavery and brought to live and work at a New Orleans plantation. It was a southern plantation with a large estate that looked spectacular to visitors viewing it from the outside. However, it was an exceptionally dangerous place for its black inhabitants. More so than not, slaves worked under horrifying conditions with the threat of harsh and coldblooded punishments lurking around every corner of every mistake they made. Nearly everything was threatening and unknown for the two, then, very young slave sisters."

Suddenly feeling an intense lack of energy, Ruby inhaled deeply before continuing. As she began to speak, she felt torn between sleeping and reminiscing. Before she had time to choose an action, she'd begun talking with Jazz again.

"How a seven-year-old and her three-year-old sister, plus tens of thousands of other slave children learned to adapt and survive slavery, surpasses the realm of anything I can begin to comprehend."

Clearly, her brain wasn't in the mood to sleep. She inhaled again to slow her racing heart.

"Minnie and Bessie's abilities to learn to speak and write, using fluent English, in addition to their astute capacities for survival, were by all rights fine and deserving testaments to their astuteness and perseverance.

Ruby believed beyond any doubt that Minnie would have become a recognized scholar had she only lived long enough to see her talent with the written word come to life.

Chapter 75

Long before she knew that she had a direct heredity to them, Ruby had been both fascinated and confounded by the dire straits of slaves. She proceeded with her best attempt at storytelling by using the same passion and flair that her deceased, historian-like father, Horace McEwen, used when he told his tales.

"Jazz," she began, "the African American blood running through my veins and rooted in my DNA explains my tinted skin. My skin doesn't pale with age, it fades with fear and exhaustion. Which is why I try to avoid both," she declared with a slight hint of vanity in her voice. "Since my birth, with each birthday I've celebrated, I have kept my smooth, hazelnut coloured complexion," she smugly concluded, giggling at her foolish and now openly vain comments.

Ruby reached out to touch the patient's hand again. Just having read from one of Minnie's earliest journal reminded her of what she'd recited to Jazz a few days ago. It was the day the police had come to The Seaside to tell her about the boating accident. Just two days and two nights ago, an elderly woman with red wine-coloured lips, very few wrinkles, and attentive eyes, had stepped off an elevator on the seventh floor of Saint Matthew's Hospital. Her arthritis-crippled hands were tightly gripping an antique wooden trunks forged iron handles. It had taken her nearly eighteen painfully awkward minutes to bring the bulky antique trunk from the hospital's main entrance, up an elevator, and then down the ICU's long, 7th floor corridor. Because the trunk was filled with the history of her ancestral lineage and the elements of time, despite her aged and frail body, it had been worth all of her physical effort to bring it to Jazz.

Burrowing her head comfortably into the pillow, she closed her eyes and turned the switch in her brain on. With the flick of her mental button she was recalling what she'd learned back in the 1950's, as a university student, about slaves during the holidays. Since she'd just shared Minnie's earliest journal entries about Christmas in New Orleans with Jazz, she was now desiring connecting herself to her most distant relative by using the only sharp and functional tools she had left, her brain and her great love of a true story.

"Now my girl, let's see how much your great granny can remember from she was a very young undergraduate with very young and pliable mind."

"Listen up Jazz!" she loudly demanded. "Pay attention. I have a flamboyant story to tell you about your ancestors."

Before she began with her tale, she explained to Jazz that many times throughout her lifetime she'd felt the plight of slaves deep in her soul and heard their cries in her dreams. Despite, that her blood relation to Negros' was never legally documented, verified, or even spoken of; she was a part of them, and they were a part of her. She'd known that she was connected to unfamiliar people from the time she was a very young girl, laying on her back in the grass between tombstones, while staring up at the clouds. She remembered how she'd been so careful not to step on coffins because stepping on coffins was known to be 'disgraceful to the dead'. She'd been a child herself once. A different kind of child who liked dead people and talked to dead people, whether they had white skin or black skin. With her pa Horace, the eminent and great storyteller still on her mind, Ruby began her rendition. The old lady, who still wasn't sure she believed in God, looked up at the ceiling and pretended it was heaven. Paying tribute to her dead father, she began telling Jazz a factual slave story. Later on, after tomorrow arrived, she'd come to realize that she was doing this more for herself than for Jazz.

With slavery and Christmas still occupying her brain, as she opened her mouth to speak, she was certain she knew where her mind was headed.

"African American slaves, like Minnie and Bessie, experienced the Christmas holiday in different ways while living on plantations. For many slaves, merriment, religion, faith, and festivity each played their roles during the holiday season. This was however not the way it was for all slaves. For some, the holidays conjured up visions of freedom, and a cleverness to seek out and attempt to find this liberation. Still others saw the holidays as just another burden to be endured while in captivity. The enslaved Negro owners of southern plantations were also known for their efforts to give kinder, more sympathetic treatments to slaves during the Christmas holiday. Christmas brought with it a prosperity and relaxed discipline that enabled slaves to relate to each other in ways that they couldn't during other months throughout the year. Slaves often received material goods from their masters, like a yearly allotment of clothing, or an edible treat, or a gift that wasn't necessarily related to what they needed to survive or do their work with. Because of the festive and decorative ambiances on the plantation, slaves frequently married during the Christmas season."

Ruby reached for a glass of water and took a long drink before continuing. The night nurse was right, ICU air was indeed very dry. She swallowed meticulously and continued with her reminiscent story.

"Okay, that's better. Now' let's see, where was I?" She took a deep breath and carried on. She was rather enjoying testing her old memory and even older mental capacities.

"During the holidays, some slaves were given a day or two off to celebrate and rest up, while others were made to continue working. In some parts of America they were given a yule log to burn in the plantation house. Did you know that yule logs can be traced back to medieval times? Now isn't that just an amazing fact."

The mellow, great grandmother, in the bed next to Jazz was on a smooth mental roll and relishing in every twist and turn her mind was taking.

"The large yule log was traditionally burned in the hearth of the plantation parlour on Christmas Eve. As long as the log burned, slaves and other domestic workers were granted time off during the holiday season. Occasionally, they were fortunate, and the log would burn until the New Year. During the days of respite, slaves would use their downtime to gather

448

together and hold quilting bees for both men and women. The quilting tradition provided a social space for them to come together and to gossip while showing off their artistic capabilities. Some of the plantation masters and mistresses customarily allowed their slaves to keep the money they earned from the sale of goods at public markets during the holidays. This depended, for the most part, on their work reputation and the amount of trust the slave's owner had in their living property. While the holidays were meant to be a jubilant time, slaves that worked inside the house were obliged to work even harder and longer during Christmas and the celebration of the New Year. This was because many plantation owners and their families hosted parties for their friends and relatives."

Ruby stopped talking and continued thinking about her female kith and kin in silence. Fatigue had arrived. She was waning fast, and her jaws ached.

She knew that both Minnie and Bessie were domestic slaves whose duties were performed in the main house. Because of her position, it was fated that Minnie, as a house cleaner, was required to toil up to sixteen hours a day before Christmas Eve whilst preparing for the festivities. Bessie was a young slave being trained to prepare the food in the main kitchen after she'd picked fresh vegetables from the garden. This meant that her training was equally intense during the holidays because of the number of extra mouths to feed on the plantation. For as gruelling as the long holiday workdays were, their duties brought the African sisters together, in a side-by-side way, more often at Christmastime than throughout the rest of the year.

During her studies at Essex County High School and at University of Dublin, Ruby had learned that on plantations, holiday seasons were also a time when some masters and mistresses gave wine, cider, and alcoholic beverages to their slaves. The effects of alcohol were something quite unknown to many of them. Most slaves, being overcome by the jovial season and the festivities, would overindulge. Slave masters, scheming in their own right, knew that liquor, extra time off and increased inactivity would decrease the number of runaways during the festivities. Despite, their ingenuity, occasionally more trustworthy slaves were given visitation passes, which enabled them to see nearby relatives. Although this was rare, some slaves were even allowed to receive visitors from different neighbouring plantations.

Feeling an emotive urge, Ruby looked over at a motionless Jazz and started talking out loud with her again.

"Along with the traditions of the Christmas holiday in the westernized American culture, slaves partook in dancing and singing in their own cabins and rooms. Sometimes the white masters would come to the slave quarters to watch them celebrating. Slave parents would give children small, homemade tokens as gifts."

She took a yawning breath and scrabbled deeper beneath her blanket before continuing. She was enjoying using her brain for something other than mental drifting. She was likewise, as the younger generation of today would say, 'blown away' by how much she still could recall from her studies between the 1930s and the 1950s. Ruby liked challenging her intellect. Doing so kept her senses sharp and free of dementia. She went on to tell Jazz that another celebration, known as Jonkonnu, or the Christmas masquerade, also was a common holiday event on many plantations. The Jonkonnu was an uncomplicated traveling show. During the show, slaves would put on makeshift costumes and go from house to house to perform short musical or theatrical acts for gifts, and sometimes for money. For Negroes being held captive during the time of slavery, despite the inhumane and unforgiving work and living conditions they were subjected to yearly, the traditions of Christmas and Jonkonnu were a means of celebration. Many of the white folks living in plantation houses, who celebrated the holidays, shared a portion of their gifts and delicious food with their captives. Despite these rare acts of decency, kindness, and honour, at the same time plantation owners shrewdly used festivities as an opportunity to convince the slaves that captivity was their best option for living peacefully and safely alongside their masters and mistresses."

Hearing herself speaking about the imbalance between kind gestures and the legendary inhumane plight of her slave relatives, was pumping life back into her lifelong disbelief in God.

"In other words," Ruby told Jazz, "Slaves were coerced and deceived for the sake of a baby named Jesus."

In that very moment, the elderly woman realized that, like her father Horace once had been, she too would have made an exceptional storyteller and historian.

Thoughts of Minnie and Bessie being overworked, drunken slaves passing out next to scraggily, nearly lifeless Christmas trees, plus a female tornado arriving from Amsterdam tomorrow evening spun mercilessly through her mind. Her brain was ready to relent and effortlessly give into its exhaustion. She was chilled and dwindling fast.

For the second time since she'd showered, Ruby laid her open palm over Jazz's still warm hand. Within a few minutes, the subtle wheezing sounds coming from her half-open mouth merged with the pulsating hums, peeps, and drones of the room's life-support machines. Together, lying across from each other in their hospital beds, one hundred and six combined years of life continued to breathe and sustain. Ruby's last conscious thought, before sleep claimed her, was that she'd taken Jazz back to the beginning and foundation of her ancestral life. Where her cataleptic journey went from this moment on was utterly out of her hands.

Less than an hour after Ruby had crawled into the spare bed next to Jazz, the door slowly opened. Olivia Davies quietly entered the room and found the worn-out woman fast asleep and snoring heavily. It was 10:15pm and her shift had just started. She was overcome by admiration with how loyal to and protective of her patient the sleeping woman was. Suspecting that Ruby would decide to spend each night in the ICU's youngest patient's room was a comforting thought for the night nurse. Tending to young people trapped in the confines of comas had always deeply affected her. An important thing she'd learned from working in an intensive care unit was that 'life was undefined'. What she'd witnessed, since caring for patients with low brain activity, had taught her that ultimately a divine decree of destiny was in control, and every living being was susceptible to the uncertainties of life and death circumstances beyond their control.

As the night nurse tiptoed over to Ruby's bedside to remove her spectacles that dangled from a cord around her neck, her foot slipped on something. She bent down and retrieved a handkerchief and folded sheet of paper stuck to the underside of one of her white hospital Crocs. She recognized the hankie at once, having seen it sticking out of Ruby's blouse a few times since she'd met her. She carefully tucked the thin piece of cloth in between the blanket pleats nearby the sleeping woman's hand. She wanted Mrs. McEwen to be able to grasp it easily whenever she woke up. Then, she gradually removed Ruby's hand that was resting over her patient's hand with an IV line in it. She placed the elderly hand gently on her blanket covered stomach. Just like the night before, Ruby was lying on her back and wheezing like a British buzz saw. The considerate nurse was pleased that the exhausted old caregiver's sleep was deep, and that she wouldn't be easily disturbed by her tending to Jazz's needs. Olivia then closed the journal that she'd taken off the slumbering great grandmother's stomach and set it on the nightstand on top of a few other journals. Then, something on the open piece of paper she'd just plucked from under her shoe caught her attention.

Looking closer at it, she could see that it was a rather detailed bullet list. The nurse was certain Ruby's stiff fingers had written the list, given the jagged shape of the letters and words. A vertical row of large, dark blue circles had been drawn on the paper. Next to each of the circular marks were short, choppy sentences. Olivia looked at the piece of paper and immediately recognized it as an old-fashioned 'to do list'. She knew that what was on this list was private, nonetheless, she felt reasonably responsible for this very old person, therefore she was likewise interested to know if she could help her with anything she'd written down. Actually, despite that this was indeed true, Olivia had a streak of curiosity in her which often got the best of her and lead her straight to trouble. Unable to fight off her nosiness, she went into the small bathroom, turned on the ceiling light, and locked the door. Leaning against the bathroom sink, she looked again at the list and tried to read the scribbles. Shaking her head from side to side from disbelief, the night nurse was taken back that Ruby had listed six things she needed to accomplish tomorrow. Six tasks in one day that had everything 'to do' with helping others and absolutely nothing 'to do' with reminding herself that she was nearly nine bloody decades old!

This old woman sets the bar very high for herself. Much too high for someone her age, she silently decided.

Olivia felt the urge to laugh when she read the last bulleted item. Not wanting to make any noise, she instinctively covered her mouth and muted an impetuous reaction that was trying to escape her. Even though 'lunatic' was a very strong way for Ruby to be defining her patient's mother, the night nurse was herself to blame for often using this word, given that she had a sister, who was, to say the least, 'hair brained'. Olivia's sister had made the ICU employee's life everything but uncomplicated in the past eight years. Therefore, she understood why Mrs. McEwen needed to protect Jazz from 'a lunatic', especially one that the patient was forced to, by birth, call mother.

Mrs. McEwen has a busy day planned for tomorrow, Olivia thought as she left the visitor's bathroom.

"Much too busy a day for a woman of your age if you ask me," she hinted with a soft voice, glancing over at perhaps the most driven and eldest utilitarian she'd ever met.

After reading Ruby's list, she realized that the strongminded, feisty, wheezing, and snoring lady, lying in a spare ICU bed, needed a long and uninterrupted night's sleep. For this reason, the night nurse neatly refolded the bullet list and placed it, along with Ruby's spectacles, on the nightstand. She wasn't feeling guilty for breaking any privacy codes. Doing so had given her a deeper insight into who this very interesting woman was. For this reason, she decided to compliment her snooping habit rather than punish herself for it. She rightly knew that this sweet lady had a nutty madcap in her family and handful of different men in her life. The nurse already had a few brilliant ideas as to what she could do to make Ruby's stay at the ICU more accommodating. She would do this graciously, despite her patient's apparently whacky mother and absentee father, whom, for reasons Olivia didn't rightly understand, Ruby felt the need to appease.

"Starting tonight, I have your back madam," she whispered, looking down at the overambitious, sleeping woman.

As she checked her patient's vitals, the great grandmother's snoring not only persisted, it became even louder. She was satisfied with the results of Miss Durant's vital signs, knowing that her brain's lesion accounted for Jazz's cerebral impairment and lack of consciousness. Given the extent of her injuries and the effects that the induced coma was having on her cerebrum, her systolic and diastolic blood pressures were within acceptable ranges. The ICU employee with intense blue eyes that looked like two dazzling sapphires, had developed a new fondness for the elderly woman and her youngest patient on the ward. Olivia was feeling medically confident because of the monitor's encouraging statistics and her patient's progress in two short days. Knowing that both the systolic and diastolic pulse pressures were imperative, she'd been rather concerned since the induced coma treatment had been administered. If the readings had been too high, hypertension most likely would be present. This could result in Jazz having a stroke. If the blood pressure readings were too low, this would indicate a dangerously insufficient blood flow to the patient's critical organs, including her brain. Her pulse rate and body temperature were both slightly on the low side, which was nothing alarming or noteworthy. The night nurse could see that the neurologist, Dr. Zamier, had ordered another electroencephalography for 7:45am tomorrow. The EEG results would indicate if Jazz's brain had reached the prescribed level of catalepsy. It was a level that he'd deemed necessary for his patient's optimal recovery over the next five to seven days.

Because Jazz Durant's oblivion was the result of a head trauma, her medical case was determined to be a crisis which required 24-hour, round the clock supervision. This meant that Olivia Davies would be returning, every hour on the hour, throughout the night, to recheck her patient's vitals and to look in on Ruby.

452

Chapter 76

Life is the most unstable, fragile, and unpredictable thing that exists.

Beams of soft, hazy, golden sunlight were shining through the small window in the farthest corner of the room. The fog had lifted and the sun had risen with a type of hell-bent, energetic pride. Sunbeams were dancing across the room's pastel yellow linoleum floor tiles and across the entire metropolis of London.

A wide-eyed, nearly ninety-year-old woman had slept soundly and straight through the night. She didn't hear the night nurse or the orderly's coming in and out of the room. Ruby sat up and gazed blurrily over at the patient in the bed next to her. She thought she saw a healthier colour returning to Jazz's cheeks, but she wasn't sure. Perhaps this was just wishful thinking on her part, she concluded. She'd need to put her spectacles on before she could know for certain.

The elderly woman knew it was early morning because she'd been awakened by the smell of bacon, eggs, coffee, and a sweet scone. Her mouth was watering with the anticipation of a hearty breakfast. While she'd slept, her belly had rumbled the night away with hunger. Due to morning rounds breakfast was served early on the 7th floor of the Intensive care unit. Seeing steam escaping from the ventilation hole in the top the dish cover, she presumed it was now about 7am. It didn't matter one iota that the owner of a popular diner hated the smell of bacon and loathed the taste of eggs; she was bloody famished and eager to dig into her protein and carbs. She hadn't eaten dinner last night and although she'd sept like a newborn baby, hunger made her grouchy and gave her obnoxious headaches. As she reached over to the tray table to grasp her spectacles, her brain woke up and reminded her of something that the smell of another free meal had caused her to forget.

"Blimey!" she cried out, remembering that she had made brunch plans with Griffin. She'd also forgotten to leave a 'no breakfast request' with the ICU's receptionist yesterday after returning to the hospital under the escort of Renzo, the magnetic, pain in the ass Italian cabdriver.

"Where is my goddamn bullet list?" she questioned, impatiently groping at the inside of her bra. All she felt was the outsides of limp breasts. It wasn't in there.

"Dammit!" she scorned.

Her feeble search was interrupted by something that unexpectedly caught her eye. There was a folded post-it note taped to the top of her breakfast dish cover. When she saw the note, a strong sensation of dread began to mingle with the sulphurous and fatty odours of eggs and greasy, burnt bacon. Her hunger pangs croaked straightaway as nausea and queasiness crept relentlessly upwards and entered her throat. She wished she could just belch it all away and carry on with her day, but she knew it wasn't this easy. She swallowed back her nervous stomach and reached for the yellow post-it note. Given the events of the past few days, her nerves were more fragile than she'd realized. She needed to be brave. She put her spectacles on, adjusted them, and carried on with the task at hand.

The message read:

Fog lifted. Took earlier flight. Arrival time 5:30am. Thatcher Durant

"Bollocks!" she swore before rightly panicking.

The clock hanging above the room's closet, told her that it was 7:03am. The frayed Briton knew she needed to hurry.

"Bloody freaking hell!" she swore even louder.

She was still half-asleep, infuriated, and swearing like a deranged woman. She was justly shaken up because a lunatic, a womanizer, and a young lawyer, each of whom she hadn't seen in nearly eleven years, were already in London! After reading the message from Thatcher, she realized that Jazz's family had arrived at Heathrow some two hours ago, meaning that she'd lost an entire day. A day she thought she had to prepare for this very moment. She was absolutely, not ready for this. Not ready for this at all!

"Bollocks! Where is Mia's handkerchief?" she screamed out with a primal need for security.

"They were supposed to arrive tonight! I am not even dressed yet! Goddammit, where's my bullet list?" she questioned herself again, scanning the room. Fanatically she rechecked the inside of her brassiere.

Maybe I missed it in there the first time I looked, she thought, trying to no avail to calm herself.

After a repeated search, the only thing she found inside her bra was a lingering scent of lilac shower gel and two large wilted female body parts that she'd inherited from her once overly endowed mother Sadie.

Blimey, she alleged, *if there was ever a time for me to switch emotional and mental gears it is now.*

Then, tapping into her calmer side, she promptly changed her mindset, found her self-confidence, and began thinking more insightfully.

She turned, looked over at Jazz and said, "The reason I have lived this long is because I never let myself get maniacal over the unexpected side of life. And I loudly and properly cuss my anger out. There is no need for me to be dropping dead right here and now just because your parents arrived early."

Ruby rightly knew that if she hurried, she'd have time to call Griffin and change their brunch plans before his wife went to too much trouble. The thought of this made her even madder and hotter under her snow-white hair. She didn't want to miss seeing DCC O'Bannon again and meeting his family. Her temper started to flare up for a second time.

454

"So much for not getting all friggen worked up!" she mockingly told herself.

Then, acting like a real female whacko, she threw a proper British fit. As her emotions exploded, she furiously shoved at the tray table to get it the hell out of her way! Her annoyance resulted in a huge culinary mess. The coffee cup bounced off its saucer and hit the floor. Black caffeine splashed and spattered all over the heart monitor and the sterile wall next to Jazz's bed. A tall glass of orange juice and a plate landed next to the coffee cup, littering the linoleum floor with even more broken glass. A sweet English breakfast scone landed smack dab in the middle of a puddle of hot coffee on the other side of the shattered cup, the juice glass, and the plate. The food table that she'd heatedly bulldozed at had rolled itself away from the edge of her bed and stopped trundling just in front of the room's door. She was furious with herself for her outburst and the mess she'd made. She felt like a casualty of another unforeseeable situation. A situation that she had absolutely no control over. Dismissing her self-pity party, she hastily stood up and stiffly staggered over to the foot of the patient's bed. Dizzy and in pain, she gently embraced Jazz's feet and said a proper good morning to her. Her feet were still warm, and her heart monitor still hummed and peeped, rhythmically, in reassuringly tranquil way. Realizing that her outburst hadn't affected Jazz was comforting for Ruby, who knew she was dangling on the edge of an intensely difficult situation.

Given the unexpected turn of events, she knew that she needed to devise a new plan. Therefore, she did. Despite her age, she still was a fast thinker and an organized planner. Now that her brain was churning in the right direction again, she felt her fears being replaced by a solid kind of determination. As soon as the Durant's arrived, she would remain courteous and composed. Then, she would ask Olivia to come into the room and inform her patient's family of the grim condition Jazz had been in on the afternoon she was admitted. Ruby was wise enough to know that Zofia and Tucker would accept what they were told about their daughter's condition from a member of the ICU's professional staff, in ways they wouldn't be ready or willing to hear it from her. She rightly anticipated that they would become decidedly very mistrusting of her once they'd laid their eyes and hands upon their broken, bruised, and unconscious daughter.

Understandably, she admitted with a twinge of the compassion she knew they'd be needing from her, and she'd be needing from herself. After they arrived, she genuinely wanted to be able to express empathy towards them. Nonetheless, best intentions aside, the born and raised Brit was sceptical and predicted that doing so would be much easier said than done. She would need Olivia Davies to tell each of them how Jazz had been pronounced clinically dead, not once, but twice, on the shoreline of an isolated island where the boating accident had occurred. How medics at the scene had resuscitated her, two times, before transporting her by helicopter to the mainland. How, while in transit to St. Matthew's Hospital, a tracheal tube was inserted through her mouth to enable her lungs to receive oxygen.

The night nurse would need to go on to explain to them how saline solution, oxygen, anaesthetics, and vaporous medications were being given to her through various other tubes and lines. How the conduits, wires, and lines would only be removed after she regained consciousness and could eat and breathe on her own. All of this would be overwhelming for each of them, nonetheless, it was unavoidable. The apprehensive old woman also planned to ask Dr. Zamier to explain, in detail, what an induced coma was, and what the scheduled treatment plan for their daughter would be. Logically, the Durant's would have much more confidence in his neurological expertise than they would in the opinions of an eighty-eight-year-old, incompetent diner owner who, without doubt, knew they would blame for the accident.

Again, understandably so, she silently concluded once more.

It seemed that compassion had indeed come to the surface of her stalwart character and brought a touch of empathy with it. She didn't want to be the messenger between an ICU staff, Dr. Zamier, and the medically uniformed and distraught family from the States. Despite her emerging sympathy and indulgence, for as long as she needed to, she would protect Jazz from her parents. The wise woman knew that her great granddaughter was trying to find her way home again. Likewise, her intuition told her whether Jazz chose to return or not, only time and the future knew for certain.

The orange, yellow, and bluish-green lights from the life support machines continued to flicker and pirouette around the patient's petite, motionless body. In unison, the monitors and machines vibrated and pulsated. By now, the she had come to rely on the different sounds and lights in the ICU room. They'd become a perpetual reminder for her that the teenager was still thriving. She knew that, despite what may or may not happen today, in this very moment Jazz was alive. Given her vast experience with death, she believed this was a fact worth celebrating. Out of the corner of one of her jade coloured eyes she saw Mia's hankie sticking out from between the bedsheets. She snatched it up and tucked in back inside her brassiere where it belonged.

Then the arthritis crippled woman woefully limped to the side of the patient's bed and took Jazz's hand in hers. Her intravenous tube still felt cool beneath her thin-skinned palm.

By definition, the paternalistic version of Ruby was a mortal and earthly essence of a living history book. She was a rare type who was filled with bravery, hidden secrets, and a lifetime of proficient memories. She wanted Jazz to know that she wasn't alone, and there was nothing for her to fear. As she bent over the bed a sly grin appeared across her delicate, hazel tinted face. The Keeper of Secrets crouched down a tad more, moved in closer to Jazz, and softly whispered in her ear.

"Today is..."

Then, midsentence and without warning, before she'd even had time to wink or blink, the great grandmother was robbed of divulging her latest secret by extremely loud, hysterical shrieks coming from ICU's corridor. The screeching immediately split the room's tranquillity and her nerves in half! While vigilantly holding, skin-tight, onto Jazz's vulnerable hand, it felt as though a razor's sharp blade had sliced and diced what was left of her stamina in two. Never before had she been so cruelly dissected by the sound of a person's squeals and squawks. Not when treating injured WWII soldiers and civilians, or even when she found Eliza hanging by her neck from an attic beam at The Seaside.

"Jazz-baby where are you? Jazzzzzzz!" the thunder-packed, approaching voice in the corridor bellowed out.

Even if she were dead and buried six feet underground, Ruby would recognize the sound of Zofia Durant's hysteria.

"The American train wreck has arrived," she heard herself announcing.

Then, instantaneously, in a bizarre and unforeseen way, Jazz's hand suddenly twitched.

"What the bloody hell," the shocked woman surprisingly slurred, unsure if she really felt movement. Before she had time to reach over and push the nurse's call button on the bed's rail, she felt a second twitch under the palm of her now trembling hand.

"Sweet Jesus Jazz, you can hear sounds!"

Not wanting to alarm Jazz any more than the lunatic in the lobby's screams obviously had, she immediately found her focus and told herself to remain steady and composed. She didn't know whether to be grateful to Zofia for prompting a physical reaction from Jazz, or if she should wring her bloody, psychotic neck for having the audacity to screech out in an ICU ward like she had! Regardless, she refused to let a fanatic female like Zofia endanger the patient in any way. Spontaneously, and ever so slightly, she tightened her grip on Jazz's hand and wrist.

"Madam, visiting hours don't begin until ten o'clock!" the ICU receptionist sternly shouted out from the corridor.

"Goddammit, shut up you stupid little skank! I am her fucking mother!" Zofia's frenzied and encroaching voice yelled back.

This time Jazz's hand jolted. The sudden, strong hand movement was beyond belief. She'd forgotten what a lewd and obscene mouth Eliza's daughter, Zofia, had been born with. Intuitively, despite her arthritic spine, she leaned deeper over the bed. Ignoring the sciatic nerve pain shooting down her buttocks, through her shins and into her ankles, she used stable composure and spoke directly to Jazz. What she was about to tell her great granddaughter was crucial to her survival and chances of being released from a coma that had imprisoned her three days ago. For this vital exchange, she leaned in, as close as being nose to nose and cheek on cheek would allow. Then she spoke in an instructive manner.

"Pay attention and remember what I tell you. This is important. Travel in a counterclockwise direction, through time, from right to left. Witness life and learn. When you are ready, turn yourself around and come back," she instructed her. "Follow the sound of my voice."

Knowing what was waiting for her out in the hallway, the wise woman doubted whether Jazz would choose to come back or stay wherever she now was. She then shifted her attention to the warm energy she felt pulsating between the matronly hand of an eighty-nine-year-old and the sporadic fluttering hand of an eighteen year old. Hot tears welling up in her eyes blurred her vision as she shunned her emotions and blocked out the commotion in the hallway.

"Madam, STOP! You can't go in there!" a familiar and capable voice demanded. "Madam, stop. STOP NOW!" Olivia Davies irately screeched out.

Then, in a heartbeat, all bloody hell broke loose outside the patient's room. Ruby instinctively bent back down and whispered more explicit instructions into the ear of the youngest living member of the Ballinger Dutton-McEwen clan.

"Go Jazz," she instructed her. "Go to them. Time doesn't move in a straight line. It moves in circles. As time passes you will witness what life does to people and what people do to life. Follow the sound of my voice. Let what you hear and witness to guide you home. Go now. Hurry, before it's too late."

Jazz's hand faintly jerked again. This time, it was a feeble, nearly undetectable spasm. She had crossed over and left the elderly woman behind.

Of this, she was certain. And Ruby McEwen was rarely wrong.

Chapter 77

Tears wrapped up in every possible type of emotion rolled off Ruby's chin and dripped one by one onto the patient's face and neck. Drip after drip, after drip. Drop after drop, after drop. Unstoppable tear, after tear, after tear.

Within seconds a middle aged, fuming, jet-lagged woman from California thrust past the night nurse and like a raging bull burst into the room! The automatic swinging door smashed into the food trolley and instantly knocked it over. The slamming thuds that the metal tray and trolley made as they smacked the floor was staggering. The sound of metal battering into crashing glass was doubly ear-splitting. As the remains of an uneaten breakfast were strewn across the room, more dishes broke and the alarm on the ICU patient's heart monitor went berserk! Like bolts of lightning, the life support machine's high-pitched warning sounds ricocheted off the walls and ceiling. Echoes of the alarm warnings were easily heard at the nurse's station, down the long corridor, and between the elevators opening doors. Beep, beeep, beeeep, beeeeep, beeeeeep!!!

A sobbing white-haired woman lowered her crooked body protectively over the comatose patient. Her little round, black spectacles grazed the time honoured scar on her forehead, fell to the floor, and shattered. Although Jazz's face was still swollen and distorted, the panic-stricken bull recognized her teenage daughter immediately. The scared and immobilized mother, who was now being physically restrained by Olivia Davies, let out a penetrating animal-like shrill and screamed, "Jaaazzzzie!!!!!"

At the far end of the ICU's long corridor outside the patient's room, an emergency team equipped with a crash cart sprinted past the nurse's station towards room 07.11. The night nurse, who actually did believe in God, prayed that the Code Blue team would arrive on time.

Haphazardly, a stunned and barefoot elderly woman stood upright too quickly, lost her balance, and stepped with one foot in broken glass that littered the floor. Like a dart hitting a bullseye, her other foot landed directly on top of her crushed spectacles. Dark red blood oozed outwards over the floor from beneath her feet and between her toes. Unaware that she had jagged pieces of thick splintered glass embedded in her, she continued to caress the patient's lifeless hand while stroking her bruised and lacerated cheek. Jazz's tracheal tube, forehead, face, and neck were soaked in the old woman's warm, fear-filled tears. Ruby no longer felt a pulse. Instinct told her that they were all standing on the edge of another harrowing dilemma.

When Zofia Durant saw her daughter's half shaven head and the tubes and wires running in and out of her injured body she let out another thunderous, piercing shriek. Olivia Davies automatically tightened the grip she had on the violent woman's flaying arms. The ICU night nurse knew first-hand the signs of a thrashing person on the brink of a fierce emotional breakdown.

The bleeding and daring Brit, wearing nothing but two cast-iron keys around her neck and a flowered flannel nightgown, stood tall and poised, like a warrior who was equipped to defend and conquer. Resembling a symbolic badge of heroism, a timeworn polka dotted hankie hung over her partially exposed cleavage.

A nearly nine-decade old heart racing with dread-filled rage beat at a dangerously fast pace for its age. A petrified mother from America, with vicious, hate-filled eyes, escaped the physical stronghold the dog-tired night nurse had on her and lunged at her archenemy. A fearless and wise old woman, brimming with ironclad strength and passion, wasn't the least bit threatened or impressed. With nerves of steel, standing on deeply gashed and hemorrhaging feet, the barefoot Londoner firmly stood her ground. Using a skilled type of swiftness, she plucked an invisible mask out of thin air. The mask was a lifelong disguise she used to protect herself and conceal her reaction to being threatened. The invisible disguise would enable her to take control, display bravery, and hide behind her blistering fears.

Within two rapid blinks the blank faced mask was securely in place. Camouflaged behind a composed and confident shield of courage, Ruby Adeline McEwen was ageless and ready for anything. With the speed of a Cheetah, the guardian of the antique wooden trunk and human gateway to the past leashed her temper and raised her arms just in time to intercept the raging maternal tornado charging towards Jazz. With a blazing fire in her eyes and a remarkable type of calmness in her voice, she spoke.

"Lose your shit tomorrow Zofia. Today is not the day to fall part."

A split second later, the elderly masked woman's world went black. She staggered, slumped over, fell to the floor, and landed in a pool of her own blood. Everything had gone wrong.

It had all gone terribly wrong.

The end.
To be continued.

COUNTER CLOCKWISE
Book Two of the Ancestry Series

Prologue

Some people hear their inner voice with natural clarity, while others don't hear the sounds stirring within until it is too late. For some people, intuition is a gift. For Jazz Durant, it was a curse. Voices were calling to her again, from a place she'd been taught as a child not to explore. Echoes of memories that were not ready to die, had reappeared. No matter how hard she tried to kill them, they kept haunting her. Ignoring them was no longer an option. They had found her.

~1871~

Seven is a significant spiritual number for the Cherokee Indian tribe. Their society consists of seven clans that exist along seven universal planes. Seven ancient ceremonies form the Cherokee tribe's yearly religious rotation. Six out of the seven takes place each year. The last ceremony of their cycle is celebrated every seventh year.

The Cherokee people follow the moon's phases and rely on the gods while raising their offspring and burying their dead. When a new life enters the clan, a ritual is held within seven days after the birth. In the days leading up to the event, priests, and the wisest tribal women watch over the newborn. During the ceremony, the eldest, most prominent female member of the clan names the infant. The name she selects is a reflection of the newborn's appearance, a birthing sign, and its resemblance to an object or an animal. As the baby grows into an adult, the birth name is often changed, according to the child's perceived destiny, performance, and life experiences.

On the seventh night of the seventh ceremonial year, a red-skinned, white-haired baby boy was born by the light of a full, harvest moon. By virtue of the timing of his birth and his bizarre appearance, he was considered an extraordinary gift from the gods. To honour the tribe's birthing ritual, the clan's leader held the naked newborn over a ceremonial fire. The tranquil infant made no noise and showed no fear. While viewing the ceremonious act the tribe's wisest female, who possessed mystical intuition and insight, saw two translucent, outstretched wings attached to the baby's broad back. The glowing, black-tipped wings, symbolizing endurance, were larger than he was. For this reason, the newest member of the Cherokee tribe was named, Onacona (oh-nah-koh-nah), after the Great White Owl.

It would take many cycles of the moon before baby Onacona grew to realize that he was an intelligent human symbol of wisdom, who could see what was not visible to others. Onacona soon discovered he was born with the power of shapeshifting. At will, he could change from human form to animal form. His insightful spirit, closely related to the moon and the darkness, gifted him with night vision. Onacona could see the unseen. This rare human ability was fortunate for the white man's child, who was now vividly passing through his dream.

Her small, broken body laid wounded, unconscious, and exposed to the harsh night time elements of the open tundra. Bright pink and yellow ribbons were entangled in her windblown hair. She had straight bangs, cut just above her dark eyebrows. Reddish-brown, curly ringlets were sprawled out over the dusty ground beneath her bleeding head.

She wore a flowing dress with puffy sleeves and knee-length, pastel-coloured bloomers. He could see that her tiny, beige gloves, had protected her little hands from the nasty tumble she'd just taken. The gloves were torn and bloodstained. The Indian was quite certain she'd broken her left arm. It laid crooked, in an oddly angled position above her head. Her laced clothing, now grass stained, had been delicately trimmed. Even though the soles of her buttoned-up leather boots were scuffed with prairie dust, they were otherwise shiny and polished. Her clothes looked nothing like the beaded deerskin attire Cherokee children wore. Onacona could see that the small girl was groomed and well cared for. She had a round face with cherub cheeks and full, burgundy-coloured lips.

Never before had the Indian warrior seen an image of a white-faced child who looked and dressed the way she did. His intelligent wisdom told him that she came from another time and another place. Despite that she was a vision passing through his dream, the girl-child had charmed him and captured his curiosity. A saddle-less, Palomino pony, with a straggly rope dangling from its neck, stood protectively by her side. Vulture's encircling the child's battered body told him that a pending death was on the horizon.

With spear in hand, he tightened the strap of his fur-lined breechcloth, opened the flap of his wigwam, and stepped outside into the stony cold murkiness. The pupils of his onyx eyes instantly widened, enabling him to see clearly through the blindness of the night. Onacona took a deep, inhaling breath and then exhaled with a long, shrilling howl of the wild coyote.

The Cherokee Indian warrior spread his long, black-tipped wings, leapt high in the air, and flew across the Great Plains in search of the injured child. The colour of her skin didn't matter. Before sunrise she would be dead.

COUNTER CLOCKWISE
Book Two of the Ancestry Series

Sneak Peek

Everything that exists in your life does so because of two things.
Something you did or something you didn't do.
Albert Einstein

Ruby McEwen's WWII medical training told her immediately what the intensive care unit's crash cart team was about to do. Her great granddaughter, Jazz Durant, still trapped in a coma, had flat lined and they were losing her. To make space for an emergency cardioversion recovery procedure, Olivia Davies, the ICU night nurse on duty, had cleared her patient's room of everyone in it. A barefoot, wide-eyed, white-haired woman, kneeling in her own blood, held tightly onto the nurse's ankle. The elderly woman was the only person allowed to remain in the room.

Olivia bent down and picked up a crushed pair of blood spattered spectacles from the floor. The last remnants of splintered glass trickled out of them. Using her shoe, she swept countless shards of broken glassware away from the old woman's knees and feet. Then she gently took Ruby's frail arm, carefully pulled her upright, and turned her around. After scooping her up, the nurse carried her to an empty recliner just a few steps away. As the emergency team attached two round, adhesive conductors to Jazz's exposed chest, the badly injured great grandmother dabbed at leftover tears. The electrodes would serve as a curative channel delivering an electrical shock to the patient's heart in an attempt to restore its natural rhythm. Seeing the defibrillator's paddles correctly positioned just above the teenager's bare breasts, Olivia slowly lifted Ruby's feet to examine the damage the snippets of glass and broken dishes had caused. The amount of blood on the floor was worrying the night nurse.

"You will need a pair of new spectacles and a slew of stitches, mam," she said, reaching into her uniform pocket for a roll of sterile gauze. "And you will need a round of antibiotics and a wheelchair."

The age-spotted old Brit, wearing nothing but a floral flannel nightgown and two iron skeleton keys around her neck, was oblivious to what the night nurse had just said. Her blurred and fear-filled gaze was intently fixed upon the youngest female member of her family.

As the first jolt of life was administered, Ruby wondered where Jazz would end up after she was no longer dislocated in time.

The ANTIQUE WOODEN TRUNK
Book One of the Ancestry Series

Cast of Characters

Abraham Lincoln ~ Abe was the 16th American president who was famous for the Gettysburg Address, abolishing slavery and being one of four U.S. presidents to have been assassinated. Despite that Lincoln's wife came from a wealthy slave-owning family, he politically fought to end slavery on New Year's Day 1863. His main purpose during the Civil War was to preserve the Union. On April 14, 1865, John Wilkes Booth became the first person to assassinate an American president, when he shot and killed Abraham in Washington. A supporter of slavery, Booth believed that Lincoln was determined to overthrow the Constitution and destroy Booth's beloved south. Honest Abe died at 56 years old.

Adolf Hitler ~ Hitler was an Austrian-born German politician and dictator who advanced to power as the leader of the Nazi Party. During his dictatorship, he initiated World War II in Europe by invading Poland on September 1, 1939. He was meticulously involved in military operations throughout the war and was the kingpin in the perpetration of the Holocaust, the genocide of approximately 6 million Jews and millions of other victims. In Hitler's controversial view, the greatest enemy of Nazism was Marxism. He believed the second greatest enemy of all to be the Jew, who was for Hitler, the incarnation of evil.

Al Jolson ~ Al was an American singer, comedian, and actor. Jolson was dubbed "The World's Greatest Entertainer" at the peak of his career and has been referred to by modern critics as "The King of Blackface Performers." In the 1920s, Jolson was America's most famous and highest-paid entertainer. Ruby's mother, Sadie, listened to his music to drown out the sounds of her unhappy domestic life.

Amos McEwen ~ Amos was the youngest of four brothers, whose notorious father was the dreaded and powerful rumrunner, Ezra McEwen. Amos was Liza's happy boozer husband, father of Horace and grandfather of Ruby. Amos was believed to be Ezra's illegal bastard child, who for the sake of his young family, fled to England to avoid a predestined and rigorous life as bootlegger. He died during the Great Smog of 1952.

Bessie ~ Bessie is the younger sister of Minnie. As a three-year-old she was abducted by slave traders, taken from her African village, shipped overseas, and sold into captivity. The child slave grew up alongside her sister on a New Orleans plantation owned by General Master Ballinger Dutton. At a mere 15 years old, together with one of her master's sons, the dauntless and driven African slave girl escaped plantation life and the discrimination of being a Negro. Bessie outlived her sister Minnie by decades and received her freedom by means of a determined will and a multi-racial relationship. To her master and mistress she was nothing more than a plump penniless, black-skinned slave who'd deviously run off with their blood-rich, white-skinned Yankee son. Together with Samuel, she denounced the Ballinger name and went on to become a pioneer whilst birthing five Dutton offspring. Her daughter Sadie McEwen-Durant was Ruby's mother and Eliza's grandmother. Bessie and Samuel lived as a secret, interracial homesteading couple on a private ranch hidden by the vastness of the Great Plains in Montana. Bessie never knew her surname. She was the original guardian of the antique wooden trunk and a wisely shrewd woman. Being a true humanitarian, she lived a hard, diverse, and often dangerous life. Bessie Dutton died in 1959, at the age of 102.

Cicely McEwen ~ Amos and Liza's only daughter, Cicely, was known for her secret relationship with an American tycoon, her slutty erotic behaviour, and her family abandonment. After fleeing her homeland to live a scandalous, yet lavish mistress's life abroad, she was presumed dead in the 1940's. It was a death that was never verified or registered in either Great Britain or America.

Coach Driver ~ The heavyset, bearded man who was hired by Ma and Pa Doherty to secretly transport their immoral and pregnant, unwed daughter, Emilia, to Dublin. When the driver stopped to take a proper crapper in the woods Mia was too scared to run away, so she had to endure his disgust while he hunkered down behind a large pine tree, a mere meter away from her, and pushed Irish poo out of his hairy and fat, pimple-covered bum.

Darby ~ London Police Precinct 616's perky breasted, dimple faced front desk clerk who adores flirting with men and loathes mumbling old people. Nonetheless, she assists, tolerates, and respects the dodgy elderly woman.

Darius McEwen ~ Darius was Horace's great-great grandfather and an adventurous and ambitious young man, who at only nineteen years old travelled all the way to North America by passing himself off as a U.S. Citizen. Many years later, as grown man, he came to be a daredevil and a respected entrepreneur. In 1761, together with sixty-five brave and determined visionaries, he chartered a new region of the American Northeast Territory.

Dean O'Sullivan ~ Throughout the 1950s, he was the University of Dublin's undersized, sharply dressed, balding Dean of Students. Seeing a raw type of potential in his exchange student from England, he assisted Ruby through numerous challenging private matters. He became instrumental in her ability to receive her diploma and academic accolades in Journalism, as a pregnant, unwed student and mother. The dean was a WWII survivor and the proud owner of one of Germany's first exported Volkswagen Beetles.

Deniz with a Z ~ The gentle mannered, fetching, and patient cabdriver who takes a keen interest in his elderly customer's wit, resilience, and the historical tales of Ruby's grandmother, an African slave named Bessie.

Dr. Vijay Zamier ~ Jazz Durant's neurologist from India. Vijay takes Ruby under his wing and shields her against intrusive police officers and the stress of patient care in an ICU. He informatively guides her through Jazz's comatose medical state with kindness and respect for the great grandmother's dedication, stamina, and age.

Dutton Brothers ~ The first born sons of Bessie and Samuel Dutton, they were Sadie's oldest brothers, whom she last saw as a wee three-year-old lass. In an effort to save the family's nearly poverty-stricken property, the two Dutton brothers left the homestead to work for the Union Pacific Railroad. They returned together in pine coffins.

Dutton Twins ~ Sadie's brothers, born three years before her birth. The twins died in a tool shed during the Schoolchildren's Blizzard of 1888. The boys were wearing only their nightshirts, underwear, and little matching cowboy boots when they were found unconscious and huddled together after searching for the family cat. Being exposed for too long to the -50°F weather, they perished simultaneously of hypothermia at the Dutton's Montana ranch.

Eli & Isaac Ballinger Dutton ~ Samuel and Jacob's lazy, twin brothers who avoided active duty in the Civil War thanks to the Twenty-Slave Law. Similar to their father, General Ballinger, Eli and Isaac were routine sexual abusers of girls on their family's slave plantation. The brothers perished on the same day, in the Tunica Hills area of New Orleans. It was presumed that they'd tempted fate, by trying to manoeuvre a canoe over one of the many waterfalls in the region, where their lifeless bodies were found.

Eliza McEwen ~ The elderly woman's only child, Eliza was born in Ireland in the 1950s. She grew up in London throughout the 60s and 70s as the daughter of a popular, progressive, and outgoing diner owner. The beginning of the end of Eliza life began the day she fell head over heels, and smack on her smitten teenage ass, for a cheeky American draft dodger named, Otis O'Bannon. After leaving a part of herself behind, she committed suicide in 1975.

Emilia 'Mia' Doherty ~ After tarnishing the Doherty name and reputation, camouflaged by the darkness of the night, Emilia was forced to leave her family's farm with nothing but the clothes on her back. Mia was the headstrong Irish girl from Belfast, who Ruby befriended at a home for unwed mothers. Pregnant at 15 years old, she is disowned by her family and sent away to avoid a scandal. After returning to the family farm in Belfast, she endures abusive parents and an imbecilic, jealous brother. Mia plays a large role in Ruby's life as her best friend and trusting confidant, through whatever happens to, or with, them. Between them, their sexual and undeclared secrets are safe.

Ezra McEwen ~ Ezra was Horace McEwen's grandfather and Ruby's great grandfather. He was a second-generation bootlegging drunk who beat his wife and children during the day and pissed his bed at night. He was a bully with a stone-cold heart and a twisted mind. Ezra was born out of hate, stunk like a pig, and lived like a coward. His father was the owner of a bootlegging and rum running cartel that roamed the English and Irish Seas in the 1800's. The McEwen cartel played a major role in monopolizing the trade of alcohol and spices from India.

Emmet 'Mac' McEwen Doherty ~ Mac is the son of Emilia, Ruby's female sidekick from Ireland. Emmet was born at an unwed mother's home in Dublin. He was a child pawn, who was used by his Doherty grandparents and a Catholic priest, to swindle parishioners out of a record amount of money. Mac later becomes the owner of a popular pub in downtown Belfast and the father of triplets. Together with his mum Mia, and his wee ones, he endures and survives the IRA's terroristic deeds throughout the 1970s.

Finn McGee ~ Finn is the elderly woman's neighbour boy, kitchen helper, and the youngest employee at The Seaside. Finn is beyond afraid of Jazz's wild-child appearance and her unpredictable foreign temper.

Grady Walsh ~ Grady is the young Ruby's love crush who works as the assistant to Dean O'Sullivan. The cat hating, blonde haired, cleft chinned university student is infatuated by Ruby and the spell she casts on him from the moment he meets her. Grady goes on to play an important, yet anonymous part in Ruby's life during the 1950s.

Griffin O'Bannon ~ The American son of Otis O'Bannon, Griffin is a degreed historian and Chief of Police, at London's Precinct 616. As a boy, who grew up in the shadows of his draft dodging father's deeds, he is heavily burdened by his parent's sordid past and his father's secrets. Officer O'Bannon is a fast thinker with an IQ score that classified him as having a superior, nearly genius level of intelligence. As a student, he'd been nicknamed 'circuit board'. After unexpectedly coming face to face with an elderly woman who posed a security threat to his precinct, he realizes that he holds the key to crucial parts of Ruby's past. Parts she has yet to uncover. What he doesn't know is that Ruby holds similar life-altering keys to his past.

Horace McEwen ~ Horace McEwen is a man with many roles. He is Eliza's grandpa, Shep's British comrade, and Ruby's one-eyed father. He is a renowned storyteller, World War One survivor, and a proud bearer of the Tibet Medal. He is also an avid whiskey lover, womanizer, husband to Sadie Dutton, son of Amos and Liza McEwen, brother to Cicely and Reggie, and grandson of Ezra, the notorious bootlegger. From the moment he and Sadie hand deliver their wee newborn lass, outdoors under an oak tree, Horace plays a charismatic and important role in his only daughter's life. The more Ruby pushes him away, the closer he moves in her direction.

Ida ~ The New Orleans domestic slave girl who works and lives on the Ballinger Plantation. Ida is one of a handful of Master Ballinger's weekly sexual abuse victims. She is badly beaten and forced to starve by her mistress when she is found on the floor 'doing the dirty deed' with Mistress Annabel's husband, the General, inside their plantation home.

Jackson Boy Shepherd (younger version) ~ Boy was forcefully taken from his mother as a baby and bought at a slave auction. Sold into slavery, Boy grew up on the Jackson Plantation and was known his entire slave life as, The Sheep Keeper.

Jackson Boy 'Shep' Shepherd (older version) ~ With the enactment of the Emancipation Proclamation, Shep's sharpshooter master, General Jackson, bid farewell to the most profitable sheep keeper he'd ever owned by using his infantry rifle. Like an evil-crazed man, he shot at him like he was a wild turkey trying to run free. Later Shep becomes the caregiver to a 'lost and found' roaming donkey with diarrhea. He goes on to meet Miss Bessie and become a foreman at her Dutton Ranch. Jackson is Bessie's right hand man and Horace's brother of another colour. He plays a large role in Sadie McEwen's early life and later in Ruby's young life, as Bessie's granddaughter from England, who visits the ranch during school holidays. Together with Horace and Ruby, he buries Bessie and reconnects a father and daughter by means of sharing his wisdom and stories from the past.

Jacob Ballinger Dutton ~ Jacob is the African slave girl, Minnie's, secret beau. He is the son of General Ballinger and an American Civil War soldier who, on the sly, teaches Minnie to read and write before his untimely and tragic death.

James Earl Ray ~ James was the 'accused' assassin of Martin Luther King, Jr. He pleaded guilty and was sentenced to 99 years in the Tennessee State Penitentiary. He later made many attempts to withdraw his guilty plea and to be tried by a jury, but was unsuccessful. Ray died in prison in 1998. The King family believed he was a political scapegoat and that the assassination was part of a conspiracy involving the U.S. government, the mafia, and Memphis police. In 1999, the King family filed a wrongful death lawsuit for the sum of $10 million. During closing arguments, their attorney asked the jury to award damages of $100, to make the point that 'it was not about the money'.

Jazz Durant ~ Jazz is exceedingly complicated. She's Ruby McEwen's great granddaughter from the States, who arrives in London smelling like booze and looking like crime. She is a purple-haired, tattooed, and pierced younger version of the elderly woman. She's a sister with four older brothers and a wild child from California working at The Seaside diner for the summer. Jazz is smitten by an Italian named Nico and is a boating accident victim, fighting to awaken from the coma she's trapped in. She is a casualty of the stride between her divorced parents, an 18-year-old pack of trouble, and the doormat of her father's abandonment and her neurotic mother's narcistic personality. Jazz is also an unknown, talented photographer, hiding behind a rebellious façade. She is given the opportunity to unconsciously travel, in a counterclockwise direction, in an effort to find her way back to her current life. Alongside Ruby, and the written legends in the journals, she journeys in reverse, to the early 1800s, where the tales of her deceased ancestors chaperon her and attempt to guide her home. Wherever home is.

Liza McEwen ~ Liza is the wife of Amos McEwen and mother to Horace, Cicely, and Reginald. She is a survivor of three major wars and life with an alcoholic husband, who is related to a bootlegging family with a sordid past. She's dominate and brave, because she has to be. Liza helped Amos and Horace escape a horrendous, dangerous, illegal moonshine legacy that was fated to claim them all. After World War One, she began mending clothes for others out of pure necessity and kindness. Later, during the post WWII years, Liza became a well-known and respected seamstress by trade, before she died during the Great Smog of 1952.

Ma Doherty ~ Mother to Emilia and grandmother to Emmet, she is a rigid, scheming, and domineering Catholic farm wife and mother. Taking on the role of surrogate matriarch to baby Emmet, she subjugated his upbringing whilst controlling Mia's contact with her son. Ma Doherty cleverly swindled her parish's congregation out of their donations to the church for the sake of keeping a family secret and making money off the sins of her 'whorish daughter'.

Martin Luther King, Jr. ~ Dr. King was famous Baptist minister and social rights activist in the United States during the 1950s and '60s. He was the father of four and a prominent leader of the American civil rights movement. King's, I Have a Dream speech went on to become one of the things he remains globally remembered for. At the age of thirty-five, Martin Luther King, Jr. was the youngest man to have received the Nobel Peace Prize. He was assassinated on the evening of April 4, 1968, while standing on the balcony of his motel room in Memphis, Tennessee. Dr. King was in Memphis to lead a protest march to show his support and sympathy for striking garbage workers of that city.

Master General Albert Jackson ~ Albert was a general and military sharpshooter in the US Army. The General owned and oversaw the Appalachian Jackson Plantation and the slave child he named Boy. As a master of slaves, he sporadically left his estate to go hunting, or to attend a slave auction in an effort to increase his human stock of niggers and his yearly profits. Weekly, he'd leave his plantation-home to seek out relief for the uncomfortable, erotic bulge that his hunger for women grew in his britches. The General nearly killed Boy, his prized sheep keeper slave, by shooting at him when the Negro ran off his property towards Abraham Lincoln's promise of freedom.

Master General Ballinger Dutton ~ Owner of and master to Minnie and Bessie, he was an active member of the Democratic Party who publically supported slavery prior to, and during, the Civil War. Master Ballinger buried three sons at the height of the conflict between the Confederate and Union Armies. He was a dominant slave owner who, after the war ended, disowned his only remaining heir Samuel, after his son renounced the family estate for the sake of a Negro girl. The General was married to Annabel, a viciously jealous and bitter woman, who was forced to tolerate his sexual indiscretions for the sake of living a posh life as the wife of a prominent Louisiana plantation owner and a decorated American military man.

Mick Jagger ~ A renowned musician and band member of The Rolling Stones, Mick was a presumed participant at the anti-Vietnam peace march in London. A march that began in Trafalgar Square then moved on to the American Embassy in Grosvenor Square, where it turned violent and made headlines worldwide.

Minnie ~ The African girl, with skin the colour of mud, who was kidnapped by slave traders as a seven year old child. She was the protector and older sister of the elderly woman's grandmother, Bessie. On the slave ship that carried the sisters to a new world, she endured the groans and crying of sick and dying slave's by covering her ears and singing. When the ship made landfall, she considered herself nothing but an ugly skeleton girl wearing black skin. Minnie's secret love was Jacob Ballinger Dutton, the son of her owner and master. Jacob taught her to read become an outspoken writer, who wrote about what she witnessed as a 'captive to slavery' in the 1800's. The elderly woman believed that Minnie could have become a recognized scholar, had she only lived long enough to see her 'talent with the written word' come to life.

Mildred ~ Mildred was the last female member of a once massive cattle herd. She a lonely cow, still residing at the Dutton Ranch in 1959, the year Bessie died.

Mistress Annabel ~ Annabel is the wife of General Ballinger Dutton, and the victim of her husband's roaming eyes and the carnal swelling in his britches. She is known for carrying out unjust and brutal punishments to slaves who have sexual relations with her husband. Young Ida, a domestic worker at their New Orleans plantation, was one of her most cruelly treated victims. Annabel would spite her husband's frequent marital indiscretions by spending as much of his money on expensive and unnecessary luxuries.

Nico Rossario ~ The strikingly handsome and humble Italian bloke with two younger sisters and two younger brothers, whom Jazz fancied. Soon after his chance meeting with the elderly woman at The Seaside, he proved himself to be the polite, hardworking type who refused to accept handouts. This impressed Ruby, so she offered him a job and living space in the garret above the diner. Nico knew that his employer was an independent authoritarian, therefore he knew his place as an illegal immigrant. He fled his homeland, during the 2007 economic crisis, after promising his mother he'd write and vowing to his unemployed, ashamed pa that he'd send money back home. Nico is The Seaside's dishwasher and the elderly woman's arrested 'clue in a jail cell' who was in the boating accident with Jazz.

Olivia Davies ~ Olivia is an ICU night nurse at Saint Mathew's Hospital in London with a gentle touch and sapphire blue-eyes. She takes an extra interest in tending to, and protecting, her comatose patient, Jazz, and an elderly woman named Ruby McEwen. Olivia is instrumental in coming to the rescue when Jazz's panicked and phobic mother, Zofia Durant, becomes hostile and aggressive.

Orphan Girl in London ~ Like hundreds of other London children, she lost both parents during the Great Smog of 1952. The croaky and grizzly looking youngster is in shock when she meets Ruby on a city sidewalk, where she's vigilantly sitting between the bodies of her dead parents. She tells Jazz that, for almost three full days, fragments of soot as big as snowflakes fell to the ground. It was as though black snow was falling over the city. The orphan can't afford to bury her parents. Without hesitation, Ruby gives her all the money Dean O'Sullivan had given her to travel to London with.

Otis O'Bannon ~ as an unwed, 15-year-old teenager, Otis stood firm on his convictions to stand by his pregnant American girlfriend, birth his child, and graduate high school. In the late 1960's, he was a Vietnam War draft dodger and the father of Griffin O'Bannon. As a student, deferring the draft, he was employed by Ruby and loved by her daughter Eliza. After being arrested at a protest in London, Otis was deported back to America to serve his country. As the draft skiver flew through the night, Doctor Martin Luther King Jr. was scheduled to lead a protest rally, in Memphis, Tennessee. During the flight, Dr. King was assassinated, and already dead when Otis's plane landed. Otis himself died shortly after the liberation of Saigon in 1975, from a tetanus infection that spread to his blood while he helped airlift hundreds of Vietnamese men, women, and children out of the forsaken city, to safety and a life of freedom.

Pa Doherty ~ Slapping and a symbolic soap cleansing, after behaviour violations that his children were guilty of making, were very common occurrences under Pa Doherty's Irish farmhouse roof. These were only a few types of juvenile punishments that Ma and Pa Doherty relied on to send clear disciplinary messages to their offspring. Physical pain was resorted to and used whenever needed. When their hard reprimands didn't impress their misbehaving children enough, off came their father's belt. Depending how many lashes one or both of their children received, they'd sit sorely and act accordingly for the next week to ten days. Pa Doherty was an abusive father to Emilia and a devious grandpa to her illegitimate son. In the 1950s, alongside his wife and an equally devious priest, he conned the Catholic Church out of hundreds of pounds in donations a month, in the name of his bastard grandson, Emmet Mac McEwen Doherty.

Peg-a-leg Petro ~ Greek thief and grill man at The Seaside Diner who tickled Ruby's fancy, then charmed his way into her cashbox before his arrest and deportation.

Precise Old Man ~ In the late 1940s, a post WWII, nit-picking monger, wielded his 91-year-old financial power and habitual sweet tooth to barter out the use of his telephone to his young neighbour Ruby. In exchange for her baking skills, twice a month, she was allowed to use the finicky old man's phone to make precisely one ten-minute phone call. Back then, as England recovered from the devastation that Nazi's left behind, a freshly baked fruit pie never smelled or tasted so good, and a ten-second or ten-minute phone, call truly was a 'gift from God'.

Raven the Cabbie ~ Raven is the sloppy, gum chewing, cheap looking, and rude cabdriver who infuriated the 'elderly hater of chewing gum' sitting in the back seat of her cab. In fairness to Raven, she did deliver Ruby safely to Precinct 616, despite the dangerously fogged in city streets and her slap dashed ways.

Reginald 'Reggie' McEwen ~ The last born of the 1920's McEwen clan, Reginald played a vital role in WWII, as an advocate for the constitutional Monarchy. In the name of Her Majesty the Queen, he'd perform any duty asked of him, He was an underage RAF fighter pilot, who was instrumental in the Battle of Iwo Jima in early 1945. Born just shy of two years before his niece Ruby, he was more of a brother to her than an uncle. After WWII ended, Reggie was burdened and scarred by the kind of mental and emotional impairments that couldn't be seen or grasped. Therefore, he moved back into his parents Friar Court's flat, where he died at home during the Great Smog of 1952, alongside his parents, Amos and Liza.

Registry Clerk US Army ~ He was an extremely impatient, Negro hating man, who was responsible for identifying and registering ex-slaves, including Jackson Boy Shephard. He openly detested all of the Negro's who had been freed by the decree of the Emancipation Proclamation. The clerk, out of impatient anger, legally named Jackson, just to be rid of his ignorant black ass.

Renzo ~ Renzo is a feisty, talkative, Cuban cigar smoking Italian cabbie with a huge ego. He is excessively patriotic to Italy and adores blabbering as much as he adores a fine pair of designer leather shoes. Even at his age, the middle-aged cabdriver and father of six still wants to please his Italian mother. He locks horns with his elderly, cantankerous customer named, Vivian, before mending his ways and airing the smell of Cuba out of his yellow taxi.

Ruby Adeline Dutton McEwen ~ Ruby is an eccentric elderly woman with full, burgundy-coloured lips, abnormally few wrinkles, dark prominent eyebrows, and wide observant jade green eyes. She is a 'keeper of secrets', who was born under an oak tree in 1925. She has an acute awareness and an energetically persuasive character that sees everything and misses nothing. Despite her tolerant disposition and open-mindedness, she's outspoken and easily irritated. She swears a lot, is somewhat critical, is very unpredictable, and effortlessly accepts what is beyond her control. Ruby has experienced a vast number of challenges and historical events. She takes on many different roles throughout her lifetime as a people-pleaser, and a hardworking, claustrophobic, spirited person. She's a WWII survivor, a former nurse's aide and journalism major, a published writer, a funky dresser, and an innovative businesswoman who is keenly opposed to the modern, digital Wi-Fi world. Ruby is Horace and Sadie's daughter, mother to Eliza, the grandma to Zofia, and the beneficiary guardian of an antique wooden trunk. She grew up as an only child, who went on to become a woman who meets and greets, up to a hundred people a week, at her iconic London diner. Since childhood, she's been a 'mind traveller' with an intimate brain switch, who drifts in and out of the past, talks to the dead, and visits graveyards. As an elderly owner of The Seaside, she becomes the caretaker of Jazz Durant, her great granddaughter from America. People who meet her for the first time are unexpectedly drawn to her in ways they don't understand. She is a highly regarded, wise, intuitive, and resourceful person, who wears little round, black spectacles and absorbs life in a natural and obscure way. This is something she is known for and something she is utterly unaware of. Likewise, this is what she will be remembered for long after she is dead and gone. Ruby is forever in awe of what people do to life and what life does to people. Despite her very old age, she believes that her journey is far from over.

Sadie Dutton McEwen ~ The youngest and only surviving child of Bessie and Samuel Dutton, she grew up on her parent's homestead, which later became a thriving American, Great Plains cattle ranch. When the deadly blizzard of 1887 killed her twin brothers, because she was newborn too young for even a memory, she was spared the tragedy. Three years later, she endured her older brother's simultaneous deaths. From the time she was a little girl she wrote and drew in journals. Jackson Shepard, the ex-slave and Dutton Ranch foreman, met her when she was a precocious toddler. He went on to watch her grow into Bessie's defiant and headstrong daughter, who fled the plains to start a surreptitious life abroad in England. Sadie was the spawn that pierced her mother's heart, Horace McEwen's wife, and Ruby's psychotic, overprotective mother. She grew to become the lifelong thorn in the elderly woman's side. Before Sadie's death, she experienced the loss of her own two sons and getting stoned in a van filled with Hippies, for the sake of protecting her Vietnam War protesting granddaughter, Eliza.

Samuel Ballinger Dutton ~ Civil War soldier turned coal miner, Samuel, brother to Jacob, Eli, and Isaac, was the only surviving post-war son of U.S. Army General Ballinger Dutton. Despite being born and raised on one of New Orleans's most prominent plantations, he is an underground slavery abolitionist. Refusing to live to the life his domineering father has mapped out for him, Samuel relinquishes his prominent southern status. He later flees his New Orleans inheritance for the sake of a black slave girl, whom he later weds. Together they become a homesteading family of seven, living on the Great Plains, in Montana. In the end, after a fatal mining explosion, nothing was left of Bessie's husband and Sadie's father, but his mangled miner's helmet and boots buried deep in the earth, atop a hill, at the Dutton family graveyard.

Temple ~ He is the university student, Ruby's, tomcat. The cat was named after Shirley Temple, Ruby's favourite childhood writer. Temple is the 'cat hater' Grady Walsh's feline enemy.

Tucker Durant ~ Married for 28 years to Zofia, Ruby's granddaughter, Tucker is the father of five, including Jazz and Thatcher. Unable to control his lust for women half his age, he cheated on his wife, divorced her, and then abandoned his family. Regardless of his volatile relationship with Zofia, he travels to England to be with Jazz after her accident. Loathing all adulterous men, the elderly woman is convinced that Jazz's life derailed the second Tucker started listening to his penis rather than his brain.

Thatcher Durant ~ Jazz's older brother. Thatcher is a socially, articulate, scholarly brother with a scallywag younger sister. He is Ruby's great-grandson and a recently degreed California lawyer. Thatcher Durant is every speck of the elderly woman's 'legal hopes and prayers' for her incarcerated and illicit Italian employee, Nico Rossario.

Vanessa Redgrave ~ Vanessa is currently an 84-year-old legendary British actress of stage and screen, and a long-time political activist. Vanessa hand delivered a letter of protest to the American embassy in 1968, when eight thousand predominantly youthful protesters, marched against the Vietnam War at Grosvenor Square in London.

Winston Churchill ~ As the smog of 1952 increased over the city if London, Churchill insisted that 'it was just fog and that it would lift'. In the aftermath of the tragedy, Mr. Churchill had been seen out in public, studying the damage on the streets and consoling the victims of the devastating debacle. On her way to her grandparent's apartment building, Ruby caught a quick glimpse of him in the distance. Churchill is best remembered for successfully leading Britain through World War Two. He was famous for his inspiring speeches and for his refusal to give in, even when things were going seriously wrong at home and across the globe. Many people consider Winston to be the greatest Briton of all time, and almost certainly the most famous British prime minister.

Zofia McEwen Durant ~ In a nutshell, Zofia is a train wreck waiting to happen. She is Jazz's mother, Eliza's daughter, and Ruby's granddaughter. She was born in England in 1972, is the mother of five, and currently lives in California. Zofia is a desperately byzantine woman with different complex personalities that make communicating with her dreadfully infuriating. The injured, coma patient's complex mum enjoys contradicting and arguing about nothing and everything under the sun and behind the moon. After conversations with her, the elderly woman is left feeling drained, exasperated, tangled up, and lost. Zofia is the divorced wife of Tucker Durant and a neurotic, psychotic, threatening human tornado, who has a mysterious vendetta against her archenemy and grandmother Ruby.

THE ANTIQUE WOODEN TRUNK
Book One of the Ancestry Series

Locations • Milestones • Events

Twenty Slave Law ~ A piece of legislation enacted by the Confederate Congress during the American Civil War, also known as the Twenty Negro Law. The law explicitly exempted, from Confederate military service, one white man for every twenty slaves owned on a Confederate plantation. Two or more plantations, within five miles of each other that collectively had twenty or more slaves, were likewise exempt under the terms of the Twenty Slave Law.

Friar Court Flats, London ~ Friar Courts is the five-story high London residence of Amos and Liza McEwen. This is where Ruby grew up while visiting her grandparents and where Horace's entire family perished during the Great Smog of 1952. At the end of WWII, it was considered to be a phenomenon that the Friar Court Flats building was still standing, given that two million houses, sixty percent them in London, were destroyed during the German Blitz. The original hand-carved wooden and forged iron Friar Courts sign, from the early 1800's, hangs as a decorative piece of nostalgia in the elderly woman's seaside diner.

American Civil War (cause) ~ In the mid-19th century, while the United States was experiencing an era of tremendous growth, a fundamental economic difference existed between its Northern and Southern regions. In the North, manufacturing and industry were well established, with agriculture mostly limited to small-scale farms. While the South's economy was based on a system of large-scale farming that depended on the labour of Black enslaved people to grow certain crops, especially cotton and tobacco. Growing abolitionist sentiment in the North, after the 1830s, and northern opposition to slavery's extension into the new western territories, led many southerners to fear that the existence of slavery in America, and thus the backbone of their economy, was in danger. Therefore, war broke out between the opposing civil parties.

American Civil War (consequences) ~ In 1861, after decades of festering tensions between northern and southern territories over slavery, the rights states, and westward expansion, a civil war started. The election of Abraham Lincoln, in 1860, caused seven southern states to withdraw and form the Confederate States of America. Four additional states joined them soon thereafter. The War Between the States, as the Civil War was also known, ended in Confederate surrender in 1865. The conflict was the costliest and deadliest war ever fought on American soil, with an estimated 624,000 deaths including 50,000 civilians. Millions more were injured, and an abundant amount of the South was left in ruin.

Emancipation Proclamation ~ On September the 22nd, in the year 1862, Abraham Lincoln issued his preliminary Emancipation Proclamation, which declared that as of January 1st, 1863, all enslaved people in the states, currently engaged in rebellion against the Union, "shall be then, thenceforward, and forever free." President Lincoln didn't actually free any of the approximately 4 million men, women, and children held in slavery in the United States when he signed the formal Emancipation Proclamation. The document applied only to enslaved people in the Confederacy, and not to those in the Border States that remained loyal to the Union. Even though it was presented chiefly as a military measure, the proclamation marked a crucial shift in Lincoln's views on slavery. Emancipation would redefine the Civil War, turning it from a struggle to preserve the Union to one focused on ending slavery.

Assassination of Martin Luther King, Jr. ~ Martin Luther King Jr. was an African-American clergyman and civil rights leader, who was fatally shot in Memphis, Tennessee, on April 4, 1968. He was a father of four and a prominent leader of the civil rights movement and a Nobel Peace Prize laureate. Dr. King was well-known for his use of nonviolence and civil disobedience. Post-King assassination riots, decreed as the 'Holy Week Uprising', turned into a wave of civil disturbances that swept the United States following his murder. Millions of people universally believed 'the retaliation to his death to be the greatest wave of social unrest the United States had experienced since the Civil War.

Unwed Mother's Homes, Ireland ~ Currently, Ireland still confronts its past regarding the treatment of unmarried mothers. Thousands of babies were adopted over the decades from the network of mother-and-baby homes operated by the Catholic religious orders. A much smaller number of Protestant-run homes may also come under the focus of the inquiry. From the Catholic homes, hundreds of babies were sent to America, with allegations of children being trafficked to wealthy Catholic families seeking white children. The Republic of Ireland is to investigate the homes for children born outside marriage and their mothers, run by religious institutions for most of the last century. The investigation follows concerns over the deaths of almost 800 children at a convent-run mother and baby home in Galway, spanning over several decades. A dispute over whether they were given proper burials or not is still active today.

British Expedition into Tibet 1903-1904 ~ Also known as the British invasion of Tibet, the expedition was a praiseworthy, temporary invasion by British Indian forces. The purported mission was to establish diplomatic relations and resolve the border disputes between Tibet and Sikkim. Tibet, ruled by the Dalai Lama, was the only Himalayan state under Chinese rule that was not subjected to British influence. The Dalai Lama fled to safety, first to Outer Mongolia and then to China. The poorly trained and equipped Tibetans proved no match for the modern equipment and training of the British Indian forces. The mission was recognized as a military expedition by the British Indian government, which issued a campaign medal, the Tibet Medal, to all those who took part in the expedition.

Draft Dodging & Evasion ~ U.S. law dictated that 'all male citizens of the United States and male immigrants have to register for the Selective Service System, or The Draft, within 30 days of their 18th birthday'. America first started drafting civilians during the Civil War. During the Vietnam War, draft evasion and draft resistance reached a historic level, nearly crippling the Selective Service System. Soldiers went AWOL. Alongside Draft Evader's, they fled to Canada through the Underground Railroad's network of anti-war supporters. Draft Dodgers, like The Antique Wooden Trunk's, Otis O'Bannon, and well-known U.S. politicians, used student deferments as a way of beating the draft.

Liberation of Saigon ~ On April 30, 1975, Communist North Vietnamese and Viet Cong forces captured the South Vietnamese capital of Saigon, forcing South Vietnam to surrender and bringing an end to the Vietnam War. For Americans, that day forever will be remembered for its images of overcrowded U.S. helicopters fleeing in a badly timed, but nearly flawless evacuation. Their flight to safety drew attention to the terror that gripped thousands of loyal South Vietnamese people left behind to their uncertain and grim fates. The media presented hundreds of gut-wrenching scenes of small boats overcrowded with soldiers and family members, people trying to force their way onto the US Embassy grounds, and Vietnamese babies being passed over barbed wire to waiting hands and unknown futures. To date, the evacuation remains the largest helicopter evacuation in history.

Declaration of Independence ~ Written by Thomas Jefferson and adopted by the Second Continental Congress, the declaration states specific reasons why the British colonies of North America sought independence in July of 1776. The Declaration of Independence cites three basic ideas: God made all men equal and gave them the rights of life, liberty, and the pursuit of happiness. The main business of government is to protect these rights. And, if a government tries to withhold these rights, the people are free to revolt and to set up a new government. All men are created equal and there are certain unalienable rights that governments should never violate. These rights include the right to life, liberty and the pursuit of happiness. When a government fails to protect those rights, it is not only the right, but also the duty of the people to overthrow that government.

Bootlegging 1800s ~ It is believed that the term 'bootlegging' originated during the American Civil War, when soldiers would sneak liquor into army camps by concealing pint bottles inside their boots or underneath their trouser legs. Later, throughout the prohibition period, bootlegging was popularized when thousands of dwellers all across major cities and rural areas sold liquor from flasks, they kept in their boot legs. Prohibition is the act or practice of forbidding something by law. It refers to the banning of the manufacture and storage of liquor, whether in barrels or in bottles; and the transportation, sale, possession, and consumption of alcoholic beverages.

Irish Republican Army ~ The IRA is a republican paramilitary organization, seeking the establishment of a republic, the end of British rule in Northern Ireland, and the reunification of Ireland. The IRA was created in 1919 as a successor to the Irish Volunteers, a militant nationalist organization founded in 1913. The IRA's purpose was to use armed force to render British rule in Ireland ineffective, thus to assist in achieving the broader objective of an independent republic. Beginning in 1970, members of the extremist faction of the Irish Republican Army carried out bombings, assassinations, and ambushes in a campaign they called the 'Long War'. In 1973, they expanded their attacks to create terror in mainland Britain and eventually even in continental Europe. It was estimated that, between 1969 and 1994, the IRA killed about 1,800 people, including approximately 600 civilians.

Bloody Friday ~ Bloody Friday is the name given to the events that occurred in Belfast on Friday 21 July 1972. During the afternoon of Bloody Friday the Irish Republican Army (IRA) planted and then detonated 22 bombs which, in over the course of 75 minutes, killed 9 people and seriously injured approximately 130 others. In addition to the bombs, there were many fake bomb threats, or hoax warnings, about other explosive devices planted throughout the city. This added to the chaos in the streets on that afternoon. Many people believe these prank bomb warnings were calculatingly used to reduce the effectiveness of the security force's ability to deal with the real bombs. Over the following twenty years, the IRA set upon a campaign of terror in mainland Britain and in Northern Ireland. Despite claiming to only attack military and financial targets, civilians were frequently caught up in their actions.

Homesteading ~ President Abraham Lincoln signed the Homestead Act in May of 1862. Six months later in January of 1863, the first claim under the Act, which gave citizens or future citizens up to 160 acres of public land provided they live on it, improve it, and pay a small registration fee was made. The US government granted more than 270 million acres of land. A homestead was a plot of land, typically 160 acres in size, that was awarded to any US citizen who pledged to settle and farm the land for at least five years. The only requirements were that the applicant must be at least 21 years of age (or be the head of a household) and the applicant must 'never have borne arms against the United States Government or given aid and comfort to its enemies'. After the Civil War, this meant that ex-Confederate soldiers were ineligible to apply for a homestead.

World War One ~ World War I, or the First World War, was a four yearlong global war originating in Europe that lasted from 1914 to 1918. WWI was likewise known as the Great War or 'the war to end all wars'. It led to the mobilization of more than 70 million military personnel, including 60 million Europeans, making it one of the largest wars in history. Much of the war along the western front was fought using trench warfare. Both sides dug long lines of trenches that helped to protect the soldiers from gunfire and artillery. The area between enemy trenches was called No Man's Land. The loss of life was greater than in any previous war in history, in part because militaries were using new technologies, including tanks, airplanes, submarines, machine guns, modern artillery, flamethrowers, and poisonous gas. It also was one of the deadliest conflicts in history, with an estimated 8.5 million combatant deaths and 13 million civilian deaths as a direct result of the war.

World War Two ~ On September 1, 1939, Hitler invaded Poland from the west and two days later, France and Britain declared war on Germany. This marked the beginning of the deadliest conflict in human history. WWII was a global war that lasted from 1939 to 1945. At the height of the war, 100 million recruits from more than thirty countries were directly involved. World War II resulted in 70 to 85 million fatalities, with more civilians than military personnel killed. Tens of millions of people died due to Holocaust genocides, premeditated death from starvation, massacres, and disease. Larger historical forces eventually brought the United States to the brink of World War II, but the direct and immediate cause of America's officially entering the war was the Japanese attack on Pearl Harbor. Despite what was globally believed, Hitler did not invent the hatred of Jews. Often for religious reasons, Jews in Europe had been victims of discrimination and persecution since the middle-ages. During WWII, approximately six million Jews were murdered methodically and with horrifying cruelty.

University of Dublin 1950s ~ The University of Dublin is an institution of higher education located in Dublin, Ireland. It is the degree-awarding embodiment of Trinity College Dublin. It was founded in 1592 when Queen Elizabeth I issued a charter for Trinity College as 'the mother of a university', thereby making it Ireland's oldest operating university. The University of Dublin is one of the seven ancient universities of Britain and Ireland. It was modelled after the collegiate universities of Oxford and Cambridge.

Trans-Atlantic Slave Trade ~ At least 10 million Africans were enslaved and transported to Europe and the Americas, between the 15th and 19th centuries, as part of the Atlantic slave trade. The brutal trade was spurred by a strong demand for labour on plantations in the Americas. Eventually, it became an integral part of an international trading system, in which

Europeans and North Americans exchanged merchandise for human cargo along Africa's western and west central Atlantic coasts.

Ireland's Homes for Unwed Mother's 1950s ~ The National Archives of Ireland contain just a few snippets, but they are enough to make clear that Irish State officials, in 1950s, knew that the country was a centre for illegal international baby trafficking. The number of children involved can't even be guessed at, but they most certainly were all illegitimate. Ireland was regarded as 'a hunting ground', in the words of an Irish senior civil servant. A country where foreigners in search of babies could easily obtain illegitimate children from mother-and-baby homes and private nursing homes, then remove them from the State without any formalities. There were both legal and illegal adoptions. During the 1950s up to 15% of all illegitimate Irish children born in mother-and-baby homes each year were taken to the United States with the full knowledge of the Irish State. In total more than 2,000 illegitimate children were removed from the country in this way. Most were adopted by wealthy American Catholics.

Schoolhouse Blizzard of 1888 ~ The Schoolhouse Blizzard, also known as the School Children's Blizzard, hit the U.S. plains states on January 12, 1888. The blizzard came unexpectedly on a relatively warm day, and many people were caught unaware, including children in one-room schoolhouses. The prairie states always get their share of blizzards, but the blizzard of 1888 was like no other. With hurricane force winds and icy temperatures this brutal storm raged for 18 hours and resulted in the deaths of approximately 230 people. The majority of these victims had been trying to seek shelter when the blinding wind and snow hit, only to become lost, and disoriented, in the swirling snow. Sadly, several people were found dead within a few yards of indoor safety and shelter.

Vietnam War ~ The Vietnam War was a long, costly, and divisive conflict that pitted the communist government of North Vietnam against South Vietnam and its principal ally, the United States. The conflict was intensified by the ongoing Cold War between the United States and the Soviet Union. More than 3 million people, including over 58,000 Americans, were killed in the Vietnam War and more than half of the dead were Vietnamese civilians. Opposition to the war in the United States bitterly divided Americans, even after President Richard Nixon ordered the withdrawal of U.S. forces in 1973. Communist forces ended the war by seizing control of South Vietnam in 1975. The country was unified as the Socialist Republic of Vietnam the following year.

Grosvenor Square Protest London ~ In 1968, an Anti-Vietnam demonstration turned violent during a big rally at London's Trafalgar Square. An estimated 10,000 people demonstrated against American action in Vietnam and British support for the United States. Initially, the mood at the rally was described as lighthearted. Violence soon broke out when protesters marched to the U.S. Embassy at Grosvenor Square. Hundreds of police officers, standing shoulder to shoulder, cordoned off the part of the square closest to the embassy. Tensions rose as the massive crowd refused to disperse and horse mounted officers charged demonstrators. During a long, drawn-out battle, stones, firecrackers, and smoke bombs were thrown. More than 200 people were arrested after thousands of demonstrators clashed with police. Eighty-six people were treated for injuries. Fifty of them were taken to hospitals, including up to 25 police officers.

Battle of Iwo Jima ~ Feb 19, 1945 to Mar 26, 1945. The Battle of Iwo Jima was a major battle in which the United States Marine Corps and Navy landed on and eventually captured the island of Iwo Jima from the Imperial Japanese Army during World War II. It had been one of the bloodiest battles in Marine Corps history. After the battle, Iwo Jima served as an emergency landing site for more than 2,200 B-29 bombers, saving the lives of 24,000 American airmen. Securing Iwo Jima prepared the way for the Invasion of Okinawa, the last and the largest battle in the Pacific. Some 75 years later, The Iwo Jima battle still holds untold secrets, in the midst of thousands of the Marines buried near its black sand beaches. The few surviving veterans of the 1945 island battle still talk of vicious fighting that left nearly 7,000 U.S. soldiers. Half of the six men, depicted in an iconic Marine Corp Flag-raising Monument, died during the battle.

The Great Smog London ~ The Great Smog of 1952 was a deadly and severe air pollution event that effected the British capital. Between, Dec 5th to the Dec 9th, a wintry cold snap gripped the British capital. As Londoners awoke, coal fireplaces were stoked in homes and at businesses across the city in an attempt to take the chill off the early morning air. Within a few hours the fog began to turn a nauseating shade of yellowish brown as it mixed with thousands of tons of soot being pumped into the air by the city's factory smokestacks, chimneys, and automobiles. The smog was so dense that many residents were unable to see their feet as they walked. For five days, the Great Smog paralyzed London as it seeped inside buildings, covering exposed surfaces with a greasy grime. It wasn't until undertakers began to run out of coffins that the deadly impact of the Great Smog was realized. After five days of living in a sulphurous hell, the smog finally lifted when a brisk wind from the west swept the toxic cloud away from the city and out to the North Sea. Experts believe the Great Smog claimed between 8,000 and 12,000 lives.

Thank you for purchasing and reading
The Antique Wooden Trunk, Book One of my Ancestry Series.

Book Two, Counterclockwise, and Book Three,
Black Snow, will be released in 2023.

Kindly,
The Author